BLESSOP'S WIFE

HISTORICAL MYSTERIES COLLECTION

BARBARA GASKELL DENVIL

ALSO BY BARBARA GASKELL DENVIL

For Emma

CHAPTER ONE

He reached out from the shadows and grabbed her. His torn fingernails splayed across her nose and cheeks as his thumb pinched up beneath her chin, dragging her towards him. Her eyes watered, blurring his snarl. His hand was scabby and smelled of shit where he'd scratched his arse, and of sour lard where he'd wiped his platter, of bile where he'd spat, and of snot where he'd snuffled onto his cuff.

She allowed his grip without struggle, obedient to her husband's demands. Then he shoved, sending her back against the wall. She huddled and waited, watching him, silent as he undid his belt. He gripped the long leather tongue, flexing it across his knee. Quickly he spun it out. The buckled end slashed across her mouth. Then she ran.

It was raining, a fine mist of drizzle that wove soft through the twilight. The last words, drunken slurred, faded as the door slammed back in his face, 'You whore. Come—'

Knowing he would follow, she gathered up her skirts and ran towards the river, keeping to the side lanes and across the shadowed churchyards. She made for the bridge, which he would not expect for she was frightened of the high tide; had good reason, and he knew it. Borin would try every other direction before he guessed right, and by then he would have snorted, cursed and trudged back into the warm.

1

Beneath the overhang down by the river's edge, the old stone dripped condensation and the bridge's first soaring pillar was wet against her back, drenching the shoulders of her gown. The usual bustle and traffic was quiet, London's gates long locked and the houses along the bridge's length were quiet. A cold night, a wet night; London's citizens slept. The rain was swollen with ice and the long grey angle of uninterrupted sleet now closed in the sky. Although the Thames ran turgid, a muffled silence rested patiently behind the insistent sounds of the weather. She hoped her own frantic breathing and the pound of her heartbeat would be heard only by herself. Crouching down, she became part of the gloom.

For a long time the rain fell and the river waters rose, the sky darkened and the night crept into the spaces the evening had left behind.

She was almost asleep when a voice said, 'You are in my way, little one.'

Tyballis felt a wave of nausea followed by fear. But it was not Borin's voice. She peered up and tried to answer. Her knees, squeezed into the little crannies where she had pushed them hours before, were now stiff and would not unfold. She dug her fingers into the cracks between the stones and hauled herself upwards. Her voice, when she discovered it, was only a whisper. 'Your way, sir?' She looked back at the heaving riverbank to her left. 'My apologies. Are you a boatman, sir?'

Seemingly part of the starless night, he was huge and shapeless as though he carried something so large it rearranged his silhouette. She thought she heard him chuckle but it might have been the gurgle of the tide. 'Neither a sir nor a gentleman. And not a wherryman, no, child. But stay where you are. I'll find another way and another place.'

'I – I'm sorry.' Dizzy and chilled, Tyballis stumbled, steadying herself against the great pillar. 'I shall leave at once, if you'll give me a moment, sir.'

The hand came out of the darkness. Accustomed to the dangers of an unexpected fist, she backed until the stone blocked her retreat. But it wasn't Borin's hand any more than it had been his voice, and she was not knocked down but held up. 'Steady, steady.' The hand was long-fingered, unclean and surprisingly strong. 'You've a face more tear-streaked and bruised than any child should be wearing. You're hiding, then.'

'I was. I am.' She still couldn't see the man who spoke, although it seemed he could see her. She mumbled, 'But I can't hide from him forever.'

The dark voice said, 'Do you dream, child?' though gave her no time to answer. 'Better not,' he continued. 'It's a grand gallantry of the human soul to dream, and believe in hope. But experience is a grim teacher. Go home, little one, and deal with your bastard father. Or is he your husband? A father's hand is said to be any child's destiny, but a husband is more easily avoided. He could be left. Or something – perhaps – more permanent.'

She was shivering and could barely stand. It was too wet and too cold and too late. 'I'd like to leave him. I'd run away, but I don't know where to run to.'

Something bumped down by her feet, long, narrow and rolled in oilcloth; the parcel as indistinct as its bearer. It was so heavy that in falling, it shook the ground. Tyballis again lurched backwards. Now more clearly recognisable as a man, without his burden his breath became gentler and the voice lighter. 'Never run. Keep your pride and walk,' he said, leaning towards her. 'It's your husband is the danger, then? And sons?'

'No children yet,' she whispered. It was an odd intimacy with a stranger she could not see and would never recognise again. The river was shrinking as the tide slunk low, but Tyballis knew her small cracked shoes and the hem of her gown were already sodden. Then she felt the blissful warmth of something wrapped around her shoulders. The smell of sweat and grime was momentarily pungent, then fading into the general riverside stench. 'I can't take this,' she said.

'Don't be a fool, girl. You'll freeze otherwise. I can get another. Go home and light a fire if your miserable wretch of a husband hasn't one waiting for you.' The man's shadow was receding. 'Kick the bastard in the balls if he tries to hit you. If he does it again, leave him. But don't expect happiness, child. That's not an option in this life. Nor, I doubt, in the next. Forget hope. Just fight to live, as long as living's what you prize. And if you don't want to risk being seen in a man's cloak, then sell it or leave it in a gutter for some other pauper to find. But it'll help keep you alive till you choose to throw it off.' He bent, his shadow flaring suddenly as he hauled up the great parcel he had dropped. He swung it across his shoulder and balanced it carelessly with both hands. The thing bent at its middle, quivered, then settled, hanging large over both sides. The man nodded, gruff-voiced again. 'Goodnight to you, child.' He was gone at once.

Tyballis trudged the long cold streets back home. It was well past curfew and the streets were almost empty but she kept to the back lanes, avoiding the Watch. The front door of her house was locked against her but from the doorstep she could hear Borin's snores. She hurried around to the back, where the latch was broken and the door wedged only with old threshing. She pushed her way in. As cold inside as out, the ashes scattered across the hearth were drifting black whispers. Tyballis cuddled the stranger's cape tightly around her and lay down on the floor to sleep.

CHAPTER TWO

Margery Blessop kicked her daughter-in-law awake.

The bells of St Martin's had rung for the opening of the gates, the calls to prayers at Prime pealing their echoes through the frost, and London was stirring. It was the year of our Lord 1482 during the reign of his grace the blessed King Edward, the fourth of that name. Under his rule peace and prosperity had spread across the land. The cold autumn morning now promised improvements as the sky lightened with a hint of lilac. A scurry of sheep brought in from their open grazing was shepherded into the Shambles and the usual queue pushed through the Bishopsgate, marketers with laden barrows trundling over the cobbles and on towards the foreigners' market past Crosby's Place; fresh orchard perfumes and smells of fennel, leeks and parsnips to wake the king's brother, the Duke of Gloucester, from his peaceful slumber and send him off to Mass with a good appetite.

The first chamber pots were emptied from the upper storeys, the first dip of the oars rippled the Thames, the first clatter as a thousand wooden shutters were lowered from a thousand windows, and the first spread of raven wings flung black shadows as glimpses of the rising sun curled over the coal-striped rooftops.

Mother Blessop kicked again and Tyballis groaned. Although her feet were still damp and she was muscle weary, the stranger's cloak had kept her warm. Scrambling upright, she readied, straight-backed for the challenge of another day. She lifted her apron and hung the cloak on the same peg, shrugged it on and tied the ribbons, then knelt, laying twigs for the fire. Borin continued to snore. His mother topped up the cauldron from the rain keg outside and Tyballis hung the pot on the hook over the fire, pulled up the stool and sat, scrubbing and cutting turnips to add to yesterday's remaining pottage.

The slap came unexpectedly and Tyballis dropped the knife. She looked up in surprise and her mother-in-law slapped her again.

'What's that? Come sneaking back in the small hours, clutching some filthy bugger's cape about you? Announcing yourself to all the world as the trollop you are? I'll have Borin flay the flesh from your back.'

Tyballis lowered her head. She tipped her lap load of vegetables into the simmering broth and said, 'It's not what you're thinking. I found it.'

Margery slapped her again. 'Liar. It's only whoring buys a man's cape in the rain, not the luck of the saints.'

Outside, the night's puddles sparkled with the sun's rise and the wet streets gleamed gold. The sparrows were bathing in a splutter and flurry as the waking householders let their pigs and chickens out for an early drink.

Three lanes down between Bread Street and the Corn Hill, Thomas, Baron Throckmorton, lay motionless in the central gutter. Half-naked and no sword left in its scabbard, his fine coat and doublet stolen, his bootless feet pointing cloudwards in their muddy stockings, Sir Thomas displayed a bloodstained rip across his fine Holland shirt. He reclined face-up but his hat had at least been left to him and it now obscured his open-eyed gape with its two partridge feathers.

The corpse was discovered first by the ravens and wandering dogs, but soon after by the shopkeepers ready for business. The constable was informed immediately. He sent his assistant, who bent and lifted the limp and bedraggled hat, dripping rain and gutter sludge.

Assistant Constable Webb recognised the man's thick red hair and beard at once. He drew in his breath with a whistle and set off to report the murder of one of the peers of the realm.

Just over an hour later, he stood between two armed guards on the Blessop doorstep and knocked loudly. He yelled, 'Open up, in the name of the law,' which could be heard in every adjacent household and right along the alley.

Borin Blessop had been about to piss through the broken upstairs window, but stopped abruptly. Downstairs his mother and Tyballis stared at each other. The pause lengthened as every one of the neighbours stopped work to listen. Then Tyballis cautiously approached the door and peered outside. The two armed guards stepped forwards and Assistant Constable Webb said, 'It's official, girl. Get your husband,' and pushed past her into the smoke-filled room. The guards followed, slamming the door shut behind them. The neighbours, tumbling over each other to listen from their doorways, now shook their heads, bustling further out onto the muddy lane to discover some part of what was happening.

Upstairs Borin cursed and tugged on his boots, thumped down the little rickety staircase and stood facing the three men filling his downstairs chamber. The fire was smoking as usual, distorting faces. Borin coughed and spat. The guards grabbed hold of both his arms. 'You'll come with us, Borin Blessop,' said the assistant constable, 'and come quietly, if you don't mind. It'll be questioning first and arrest right after.'

'You've lost your senses, man, and not for the first time, neither.' Borin stood solid. He was twice the size of both guards put together and they couldn't budge him. 'I'm a placid man, I am, and done nothing more than sleep through the night like any good Christian should. So, what nonsense is it you claim against me now?'

'Leave my boy alone,' squealed his mother. 'You can't drag a God-fearing man out in this weather in nothing but his shirt.'

'It's a God-fearing man lying in little else but his shirt not far from here,' said Webb. 'Dead as pie crust with a hole in his belly the size of my fist. And it's you what did it, Borin Blessop, so don't you pretend to fear the good Lord, as turned His righteous back on you many a long year past.'

'Bloody murder?' roared Borin. 'I've never killed no one, no not even on the battlefield. What's this to do with me, then?'

'Because,' announced the assistant constable, 'the body now messing up the sheriff's nice scrubbed floorboards is a body well known to you, try and deny it if you will. It's his lordship Baron Throckmorton lying dead and we all know it's your hand as did it. Own up, Blessop, and it'll go easier for you.'

'Oh Lord have mercy,' wailed Margery.

Borin swallowed hard. 'His lordship being deceased is bad news for me as it happens, Mister Webb, as you should rightly guess. And me knowing the man surely don't mean I done him in. Half of London were acquainted with the baron. You knew him yourself.'

'But how many villains knew him as intimate as you, eh, Blessop? Answer me that.'

'I don't rightly know,' Borin glared. 'I only know I ain't one of them.'

'My boy's no villain,' his mother objected loudly. 'He's a good boy.'

Mister Webb looked over to the younger woman standing silently in the far corner. 'Can you swear your husband spent the whole night beside you in his bed? Or was he out doing his cursed wickedness in the dark hours?'

Tyballis paused and took a deep breath. 'I have no idea,' she said.

After Borin was hauled away, her mother-in-law slapped Tyballis for the fourth time. 'You've the nerve to say that, slut, just to get a good honest man into a trouble he surely don't deserve.'

'It was the truth. You know it was. I wasn't here, so I don't know what Borin was up to.'

'And what has the truth to do with the law?' demanded Margery. 'I shall go straight down to the sheriff's chambers and inform him you were lying, spiteful wretch that you are. And you'd best back me up if they come asking, or you'll answer for it to me and Borin both. As for now, you stay here and get on with dinner.'

8

Outside, Mother Blessop could be heard arguing with the neighbours and relating the scandals of an unjust world. Tyballis wiped her hands on her apron, retrieved the stranger's cloak from the shadows and hugged it around her. Then she sat again on the stool by the hearth and gazed into the crackle of the flames. The cloak was felted wool, matted with age and waxed against the inclemency of English weather. Thickly impermeable, it now kept out the draughts while the fire scorched her face. The cloak still smelled of its owner. Once, she thought, it had been a deep forest green but now it was mostly black and stained with the residue of long-forgotten stories. Tyballis sighed, picked up her knife and bowl, and went back to peeling turnips.

The fresh tang of peelings tickled her nose. Her arms ached. But reared to a woman's work, an insistence on cleanliness and the simple safety of familiar routine, the only semblance of control she might claim was the maintenance of a respectable home. Working – pondering – and as she worked, she wondered if it was finally time to run away for good. Borin, however, remained both as motive and impediment, for since she was quite sure he had never murdered anyone, let alone his poppy-headed beetle-brained idiot of an employer, her loving husband might soon be set free. He would then search for her, having convinced the sheriff that her recent denials were wicked lies and that he could no more slay a nobleman than be elected Lord Mayor of London. It was true, after all, that Borin could not even bring himself to wring the neck of a chicken for their supper and instead left his mother to do it. But he had knocked his wife down the stairs on their wedding night and often beat her until she sobbed for mercy. Murder can take many forms.

The pottage was still simmering, and the house had warmed when Margery Blessop returned. Outside, the alleys steamed as the puddles dried. 'He'll be in Newgate by suppertime,' she said, briskly folding her cape and reaching for her apron. 'And it won't just be a day in the stocks this time, not being no simple theft nor the loading of dice. In all this filthy mire of a city, it's Newgate is the very worst. Hellfire makes a better bed, they say, and the devil a better bedfellow. But my boy'll be there till his trial, and it's there you'll visit the poor mite tomorrow morning. You'll take him a pie for his dinner and beg his forgiveness.'

'We've no money for pies,' Tyballis said. 'You can't buy a pie for less than four pence these days, and that's if you're lucky. Last wage Borin brought home was two shillings and tuppence, and that to feed three of us. We live on nothing but pottage and turnips as it is.'

'And there'll be less of that from now on,' nodded her mother-in-law. 'Borin'll not be working, not now nor when he gets out, what with Throckmorton dead and gone and his worthless brother waiting to snatch the title. That bully Harold won't keep my Borin on, not after this, innocent proved nor otherwise.'

Tyballis smiled. 'Borin hates him.'

'And don't you go repeating that to the sheriff, neither,' muttered Margery. 'You're a troublemaker, Tyballis Blessop, as I've said for nigh on five years now, and you've never shown the respect you ought. Go sell that cape you say you found last night and buy your man a decent dinner. Keep his poor guts full while he rots in the Limboes.'

Newgate spilled its debris and its stink for some distance beyond its confines. Borin was accustomed to spending a night or two in the Marshalsea or The Fleet and had once seen out a week in The Clink before being chained in the stocks with his feet in the rain and rotten eggs in his hair. Newgate, however, had as yet been unknown to him, so Tyballis had not passed there, either to visit the prison or to leave London through its western gate. But she knew before she reached the walls that she was close.

A small crowd, unaffronted by the smell, bustled and milled beneath the barred window slits calling to those held within. A thin-faced child, kicking at the remains of a dead kitten in the gutter, turned, saw Tyballis, thrust back her long uncombed hair and stuck out her hand. Two of her fingers were missing above the lower knuckle. She wore only a man's shirt, torn, dirty and frayed around her ankles.

Tyballis said, 'I've no money, child, and nothing to give you.'

The child sidled close and sniffed. 'You got pies. I can smell 'em.'

A pippin pie, four pence ha'penny and still hot. 'Only one pie. I can smell it, too, but it's for my husband.' Tyballis sighed. 'Not for you and not for me either, much as I'd like it.'

'Forget the bugger in there. Half for you, missus? An' half for me?'

Tyballis looked down at the top of the child's bright yellow curls and the lice crawling there. 'Sorry. I mustn't.'

The child sniffed again. 'Mustn't? I reckon growed-ups can do what they likes. No point to all that effort growing old if you still can't get no 'vantages.'

Tyballis hesitated. She stood for a moment beneath the raised iron portcullis and felt the sudden chill of utter hopelessness which gathered there. One of the gaolers was cursing a woman who, basket carefully covered, had come to see her son.

'Only dinner your boy'll be getting, missus,' yelled the warden, 'is likely the pains o' purgatory. Gone to the gibbet this morning two hours past, he did.'

'I brought my Bertram his favourite dinner,' wailed the old woman. 'A man needs a hearty meal afore facing the swing.'

'What you want me to do then, missus?' demanded the gaoler. 'Call him back? You'd do best to leave that basket with me, what'll appreciate it, while you get yourself up to Tyburn.'

'I'd not give you the snot from my nose for your dinner, Jimmy Hale,' the woman shouted and turned, trudging off. Tyballis stared across the short stretch of cobbles, and the small girl stared back. Hanging loose around her, the man's shirt, streaked in dirt, had worn thin and the girl's bones showed through. Tyballis said suddenly, 'When did you last eat, child?'

The girl shook her head. Her curls bobbed but the lice clung on. 'Dunno. Two days pr'haps. Drew give me cheat and bacon scraps for supper night before last.'

Tyballis exhaled on a sigh. She said, 'Come with me.'

They sat together on the old church wall and licked the meat juices from their lips. Tyballis pointed to the drip of gravy on her companion's chin. The little girl nodded, wiped it off and licked it from her hand. Tyballis licked her own fingers, increasingly aware that a few bites of pastry had divided her past from her future and that a decision had somehow been made without her own conscious intention. She said, 'You'd better go home now, child. I have – quite a lot to think about.'

'My pa says thinking's the scourge of a decent man's proper rest,' the child informed her.

'But I'm not a decent man,' Tyballis smiled to her shadow, hovering small and dark below her swinging toes. A sharp wind was sweeping up from the river. She pulled her cape tighter and said, 'I don't think I'm a decent anything. But at least I'm not as hungry as I was.'

'Nor me, thanks to you, missus.' The child paused. 'So, I'll be going now, then?' She looked up hopefully, but when nothing more was offered, she slipped off the wall, bare feet to the mud, and began trotting east along Distaff Street. Tyballis watched her go and then turned in the opposite direction. After a moment she paused and looked back over her shoulder. The child, tiny now in the distance, had stopped at the same moment and was also looking back.

'Where do you live?' Tyballis called.

'It's a real long way,' answered the child. 'T'other side of the city.'

'No matter,' Tyballis said. 'I need to walk, and I need to think. I'll see you home. You can tell me your name and something about yourself on the way.'

CHAPTER THREE

Having sold the recently acquired cloak, Tyballis was once again reduced to the threadbare inadequacy of her knitted and unlined cape, but the child's lack of any warm covering shamed her shivers. The intermittent sun shone pallid.

They walked briskly through the back streets, sheltered from the river chill by the wharves and warehouses along the bank. The scuttle of shoppers had thinned, few women clutching their headdresses and men clutching their feathers remained, for the bustling barter of shopkeepers was over, stalls were closing, and shutters were hoisted fast. The sun had dipped into its afternoon slide towards grey, and as they passed through the huge shadows of The Tower, it seemed that night was already come. Then, once beyond the turreted walls, an open sweep of grassy rises claimed the horizon. They skirted Tower Hill and headed for the Aldgate, crossing the bridged ditch into the first streets outside London.

'Ellen, then. Well, Ellen,' Tyballis said as they walked, 'can your parents not feed you? Now we've crossed the whole city gate to gate. It seems you walked a very long way to search for food.'

'No point begging round my way,' said the child. 'Folks is poor as us and twice as stingy. My ma tries, but there's all the little ones to feed.'

Tyballis nodded. 'I see, though I should call you quite little yourself. Doesn't your father have employment?'

'My pa can do anything,' Ellen insisted, 'but there ain't decent work to be had no more. We'll be rich one day, when Pa gets the job he proper deserves.'

Between London's wall and the distant pastures, the weavers, dyers and their tenters crammed into the Portsoken Ward. Tyballis and the child walked between the long dark of the tenements, skies hidden behind rooftops, streets dipping down towards the river and the docks. Then, one corner more and up a hidden lane, and a sudden explosion of greenery danced in the brief unleashed sunbeams. An unguarded entrance lay open with iron gates slumped on their broken hinges. A swaying tumult of leaf and bough filled the stretch of gardens within. Beyond the trees, echoes of reflected light glistened along two rows of windows, and tall brick chimneys striped the sky.

'Here,' said Ellen.

'You live here?' Tyballis gazed, disbelieving.

Ellen was disappointed. 'Don't you like it, missus? I reckon it's a grand house. I'll show you. Come in and meet my ma.'

Tyballis shook her head. 'Who owns this place? Not your family, surely?'

Ellen giggled. 'No, silly. Not likely. 'Tis Drew's house. Mister Cobham. He lets us stay, like all the others. There ain't none of us has money, though nor does Drew, far as I can see. But he won't likely be in. Never is past midday. Come on. Come meet my folks.'

The pocket of sunshine persisted, but the insidious smell of the tanneries blew in from the east as the wind announced encroaching cloud and rain to come. Within two hours or three, ice would lid the puddles with moonshine and traceries of frost would clamber along the window ledges.

'I might come in, for a moment,' Tyballis said. It was a long walk back to her Bishopsgate house, with nothing there but unpleasantness. She would, of course, keep her silence regarding her theft of Borin's pie, but Margery would certainly discover it the following day when she visited her son at Newgate. A month of

14

misery would then bridge the slide from autumn into winter. It was not something to rush home for.

The wide avenue inside the gates was trampled mud beneath wet leaf from the overhanging trees. At its end, a house of long windows gazed back. The upper storey jutted out precariously over the lower, its supports cracked and sagging. The old plaster flaked like oats ready for porridge, while the unpainted beams had lost their nails. There were thorn bushes around the doorway where the little hedges of a once-trim garden had now grown wild, but the doors were brass-handled and the tiled roof, peaked over the attic's dormer windows, appeared in good repair. Huge chimney pots smoked, and a weather vane swung hard, a ship in full sail riding the breezes. So, the old sad house had been beautiful once.

Ellen pushed the door wide. Inside was blackness. Ellen called, 'Come on. Upstairs.' Without lamp or candle, Tyballis followed the blonde bounce of curls. Ten careful steps into the darkness, and she felt the curve of a balustrade and held to it, then the touch of the first stair against her toe. She stepped up, moved forwards – and found her way blocked.

The sudden shadow had a voice. A bright voice, a young voice, and welcoming words. 'Well now, darling. Nice to see a new face. And a pretty young face it is, too.'

He stood on the stairs directly in front of her, a thin man with a large smile emerging from the darkness. Tyballis frowned. 'I've come – with the child.'

Ellen sniffed. 'No need to answer him. He's nobody. Lodges free here, like the rest of us.'

From behind and below, a sudden shaft of light, cerise and gold, slanted through a ground-floor window. The sun was setting. Tyballis clung to cape and balustrade as the child and the nobody were lit with unexpected brilliance. The nobody wore black-and-gold striped hose and a peacock-blue doublet beneath a draped coat so fiercely scarlet it challenged the sinking sun. He bowed, grinned and stood his ground. 'Davey Lyttle at your service, ma'am, long as that service earns the proper reward it deserves.'

'I need no service and have nothing to offer as reward, sir.' Tyballis followed as the child pushed past.

The staircase was handsome and wide, but many steps were broken where splintered holes gaped through the tread. 'Best not touch much,' advised Ellen. 'There's summit or other breaks most days.' Doors opened either side along the lightless upstairs passageway, but Ellen marched past them all. Someone was singing, a woman's voice, high and thin, and Ellen flung open the door to her left. Light once again dazzled as Tyballis walked into a chamber of immediate warmth. She heard the snoring and the singing before she saw either of them. The man was sprawled asleep across the cushioned settle. The woman on her knees by the hearth, turned, a broken stool, part singed, still in her hand. Ellen said, "Look, Ma. It's my new friend, what gived me half her pie. Look, this is my ma. Mistress Felicia Spiers they calls her. Being as that's her name."

Ellen's mother wiped her hands on her apron. 'How kind of you, my dear,' she said. 'But I've nought to give in return. Only a good, warm fire and my thanks.' A scramble of small legs, skinny pink arms and little grasping fingers entangled her skirts. The woman lifted one wailing bundle and nodded earnestly at the other two. She wiped three pairs of eyes with the corner of her apron. 'Poor little mites are hungry, too,' she said. 'But my Jon can't get work this whole year past, so we must wait for Mister Cobham to return, and hope he has a crust or more to share with us.'

'Them's my little brothers,' Ellen announced. 'The Spiers, we are. And there's Pa Spiers by the window.'

The sleeping man did not stir as the chatter and scramble increased around him. 'The poor soul's exhausted with the worry,' explained his wife. 'Dejection can tire a man more than anything else.'

Ellen nodded cheerfully, skipping to the fireside. 'Drew's off working at summit or other all the time and he's never tired. But my pa's always wore out. So's it's not work as does it.'

Tyballis smiled vaguely and introduced herself. 'It's so nice to meet you all. But the day's sinking, I must be off before curfew.' No candles were lit but the unshuttered window welcomed the sky through its small square panes and the fire blazed brightly. Barely furnished, the room glowed into its empty corners, and cobwebs hung like chandeliers from the beams. Cockroaches and mice paws had pressed a pattern of sooty exploration across the fire-bright rafters.

Turning to leave, Tyballis opened the door as the departing daylight tinged the tumbling clouds crimson. Abruptly a clash of metal, scuffling feet and a shout echoed from the stairs. Someone thundered down the passage, someone else followed close behind. The shouting increased. A body crashed into Tyballis, thrust her aside and hurtled into the tranquil chamber, sudden steel catching the light. Small children scattered in all directions, Mister Spiers awoke and sat up with a mangled curse and Mistress Spiers began to wail.

The man, narrow-shouldered and urgent, tumbled headlong into Felicia Spiers' outstretched arms and collapsed. He was bleeding from a shallow sword cut in his thigh and his breathing was laboured, his face flushed. Dropping his own sword, he sank to the ground, dragging Ellen's mother down with him.

Tyballis saw no advantage in delaying her return home. In fact, home seemed suddenly attractive. But Davey Lyttle once again stood in her way. His scarlet doublet pressed hard against her chin, his moth-eaten badger trimming to her nose. His sword, bloodstained, was already raised. Tyballis stepped quickly back.

Davey's grin was still in place. 'You again? Well, girl, how are you at binding wounds?'

Mister Spiers was on his knees peering with some concern at the injured newcomer in his wife's arms. He mumbled, 'Ralph, is it? Is that you, Ralph? Or Nat? Never can tell you two apart. You sick, Ralph? What you doing on my floor?'

'Bleeding,' said the man. 'And I'm Ralph's brother, Nathaniel, you drunken old fool.'

'Wouldn't do no more bleeding if I was you,' decided Ellen's father. 'Spoil Mister Cobham's Turkey rug, it will. He won't like it.'

'This bugger's heavy,' interrupted his wife. 'Get him off me.'

'Allow me,' said Davey, stepping around Tyballis and approaching the heap on the floor. He hoisted up the wounded man and dragged him to the fireside, where he let him fall. The boards vibrated. 'Nat's been nicking again,' Davey continued, 'and had his nasty little paws in my coffers. I caught him at it.'

'Whatever I stole from you, you stole from someone else in the first place,' objected Nat from his seat amongst the ashes. 'Just that I'm good at picking locks, and you ain't.'

'You pick my locks again and I'll pick your nose, but use my sword to do it, you little toad,' said Davey, seating himself on the settle which Mister Spiers had reluctantly vacated. 'I may only have scratched your scrawny leg this time but take it as a warning. Next time I'll decorate your face.'

Felicia Spiers interrupted. 'Ellen, run and find bandages. But I've no needle or thread for stitches and I'll not cauterise the wound. I tried that with Mister Cobham's arm once. Told me to, he did, but the smell was shocking. I near fainted.'

Davey sniggered. 'It's the victim supposed to faint, not the surgeon, my dear. But this silly bugger's got no more than a tiny hole in his leg, which he proper deserves.'

Ellen ran off as directed while her three little brothers sat facing the bleeding man, their legs outstretched, knees bare beneath their damp and trailing nether cloths, thumbs in their mouths while regarding the growing red stain with silent interest. Their father remained on his knees, evidently lacking the strength or determination to rise. His wife came to crouch beside him, poking at Nat's wound. Davey Lyttle watched with an amused lack of sympathy.

Tyballis left the chamber and hurried quietly down the stairs. The shadowed hallway below was empty. She slipped from the great house, lowering her head against the sudden cold outside. The first stars hesitated as a fitful wind blew sharply in from the sea. A strange day's ending threatened a bleak wet night and she was far from home, wondering why she had risked so much for so little. Barely more than a mouthful of meat and gravy had tempted her, the pleading blue eyes of an unknown child, and the wearisome weight of a life always too dreary, too demanding and too much the same.

She was home in less than an hour. A thin crescent of moon-gleam quickened the deepening night, but she was not stopped by the Watch. She was, however, stopped on her own doorstep by Margery Blessop who was waiting for her – and furious.

CHAPTER FOUR

A heaving rumble of continuous sound smothered the smaller noises. Moaning drowned out the incessant coughing and spitting of blood, while the bursting grumble of argument was louder than anything else. But there was little space for more strenuous quarrel, since the prisoners seemed woven one amongst the other, their legs entwined as they searched for comfort on the hard, damp ground. Borin, his ankles shackled and chained, spread himself amongst the huddled misery of Newgate's Limboes. His size gained respect and no other prisoner challenged the space he took, but the irons rubbed his skin raw and dried blood matted his body. Although the filth further increased the darkness, Tyballis found him at once. Borin had always been easily distinguishable. She knelt beside him and presented the basket.

His heaving sullens were barely cowed by his surroundings, and he glowered beneath his jutting eyebrows. 'Ma says,' Borin began, eyeing her with aggrieved displeasure, 'yesterday she got me a hot pie. She says you ate it. She says you was supposed to bring it to me. I says you never did. You never even come to see me. I got a chunk of black bread and half a mug of ale watered down straight from the river muck far as taste could tell, and that nigh thrown in my face by the bloody warden. I was hungry. All night I was hungry. Ma says as how you stole my pie. You know you got a beating soon as I'm out of here.'

'I'm sorry.' She was, too, not because of the pie, which she had enjoyed, but because of the trouble that would come of it. She unpacked her basket and spread its contents on her husband's lap. There was fresh bread, an apple and a small hunk of cheese. She avoided his eyes. 'I'm – very sorry.'

Borin pulled the bread into three pieces and shoved one of them into his mouth with the cheese. 'Should be, too,' he said, spitting crumbs. 'Costs a shilling a week for proper food in here. That's what I deserves, and that's what I wants. So, you bring me dinner every day, or you gets me the shilling.'

Tyballis hoped her scowl was hidden in the gloom, though she could now see Borin's eyes clearly. They were bloodshot. She raised her voice to be heard over the shifting shove of misery around her. 'I don't see how I can. I've nothing left to sell. And it wasn't your mother who bought the pie yesterday, it was me. I sold a cloak – something I found – but it only brought enough for one pie and this bread and cheese. I meant the pie for you, but I was starving, so I ate it. Now I've no money left unless you want me to sell the bed.'

Borin glared. 'Sell yourself, stupid trollop. Ma says you do anyway, soon as my back's turned.'

Tyballis saw the fist coming and stood abruptly. Borin's swipe went wild as Tyballis staggered, stabilising herself against another prisoner's shoulder. The stranger yelped and wriggled quickly away. Borin sighed and went on eating his apple. Tyballis risked coming close again and said, 'You know that's a lie. You know it is.'

'Humph.' Borin stuffed the apple core in his mouth. 'Best get over to Throckmorton's, then. Ask for a loan against future business.'

She had never much credited her husband's intelligence, but this surprised her. 'Borin, you must remember – him being dead, that is. Throckmorton was murdered. That's why you're in here.'

'Stupid trollop. It's the bloody bastard brother, Harold, I'm talking about. The bugger what surely walloped his own brother to get the title. Well, I can't expect him to fucking confess, can I? But the least he can do is pay my way.' Borin prodded his wife's concave midriff. 'Get

20

down there and see the bastard. Threaten him. Tell him I'll squeal 'less he pays up. We might as well get a fair purse out of him – and then I'll squeal on him anyway.'

'Do you know he did it?' demanded Tyballis.

'Course I do.' Borin paused, thinking a moment. 'Stands to reason. But I can't prove it,' he admitted, 'or I'd be out of here already.'

'Throckmorton will realise that. He won't pay up.'

'Threaten the bugger,' Borin scowled. 'Or hitch up your skirts. Squeeze his cods and kiss his arse. Do something. Bad enough being in here without starving too.' He scratched his groin. The lice and fleas wove their own trails through the damp and into the prisoners' clothes and hair. 'And after that,' Borin continued, 'you'll start working on that bloody Constable Webb. Reckon the blind bugger fancies you.'

'You expect me to seduce half of London?'

'You're no fucking use in bed anyways,' Borin muttered with sullen resignation. 'Just lie there puling like some stray dog got kicked. You can't swive your way past the bedposts. Might as well do something worth all the whimpering.'

The neighbours were becoming interested. Several, hoisting themselves up onto their elbows and waggling the teeth they had left, became alert. Tyballis picked up her empty basket. 'I'm going. I won't be doing any of that, but I'll try and find a shilling from somewhere. I suppose I could ask to see the new baron, but I doubt he'd agree to speak to me. But you've got a nasty mind, Borin Blessop, and while you're in here at least, you could try being more friendly.' Borin appeared startled by this suggestion. 'I'm your bloody husband, not your bloody friend,' he reminded her.

Through the centre of the reeking dungeon, an open trench bubbled with urine and excrement. Rats waded from one side to the other, nibbling at the prisoners' bare toes and the frayed hems of their shirts. There were no windows but two high arrow slits allowed both a pale semblance of gloomy light and a bitter biting draught. Slime trickled a different stream down the walls and the damp oozed between the great stones. Thirty or more prisoners packed the stone floor. Some slept, grunting and snoring. The weakest, hungry and injured, moaned as they lay in their own piss. In a far corner two men were fighting, using their chains as weapons. Fleas searched for blood and found it everywhere. Borin, again absorbed with his crotch, caught something small, fat and pale, and squashed it between his fingers. The stench was making Tyballis nauseous. She began to move away, searching for a place to tread between bodies. 'People who have to live together,' she murmured, more to herself than to Borin, 'especially while one is particularly dependent on the other, could still try and be nice to each other.' Accustomed to the noise around him, Borin heard her, and sighed. 'Brainless trollop,' he mumbled as he closed his eyes.

Throckmorton Hall stood in considerable contrast to Newgate's dungeons. Although not as grand as the great palaces that lined The Strand, it was a neat house, set back from the bustle of Bradstrete in the vicinity of the Austin Friary. Only a short walk from her own alley, it was a building Tyballis knew well. Borin had worked for the first baron in many capacities for some years, so she had been summoned there frequently for a variety of reasons, including that of coaxing her drunken husband home after he had finished whatever was required of him. But this was a new baron. She had never met him.

Although not such a grand house as that she had visited outside London's walls only two days before, this was in far better repair. Tyballis pulled her cape over her headdress, found her way around to the back and entered under the archway leading to the stables, slipping through the familiar open door of the pantries. The perfumes of cooking seemed even less welcome than the stinks of Newgate, for she had eaten nothing since the pie shared with the beggar girl. Now Throckmorton's midday dinner announced itself in clouds of aromatic steam.

The evaporating billows almost hid her, but she knew that a female daring entrance into John Knody's kitchens would never pass unnoticed. A damp, large-knuckled hand grasped the back of her collar as Tyballis scuttled through. 'You,' exclaimed the head cook.

Tyballis spoke as quickly as she might while being hoisted back towards the doors through which she had come. 'The new steward doesn't know me. He'd never let me in.'

'Of course not. You're the wife of the man what slaughtered the last baron and now rots in gaol for the doing of it. So, you expect to be welcome here, girl?'

Tyballis shook her head. 'He didn't do it. And I have to see the baron.'

'And I'm busy, with a dozen dishes to prepare afore the hour is up.' John Knody wiped condensation from his forehead and sighed. 'Go on then, girl. Get in there. And if you says as I was the one as gave you entrance, then I'll swear different and get you the thrashing you no doubt deserve. Understood?'

She did. 'Thank you, Johnny. You're a nice man, though I suppose you'd deny it if I told anyone else.'

She dodged through the far doors and into the winding passageway to the main hall. A large fire was evenly spread across the hearth. Set in brick, the fire belched, and the flames lurched from their shelter, veneering the great chamber in shimmering light. A man stood alone in front of the hearth, his hands behind his back, standing close enough to singe his hair. Tyballis approached carefully but the man heard her at once and turned.

He was unusually tall, and beneath the dark sobriety of his clothes he was clearly well muscled. His hair was black and thick, and his face was strong-jawed with a large crooked nose between heavy cheekbones. The eyes, deep-lidded, were glazed scarlet in the firelight. He was not a handsome man.

Tyballis was surprised. Sir Thomas had been red-haired, small, bandy-legged and wiry. This man did not in any way resemble the brother. She curtsied low, stayed down and mumbled, 'I apologise, my lord, for the interruption. I would not have come, except for it being so important. Perhaps, my lord, a matter of life or death.'

The man looked her over. It was some time before he spoke. He stood quite motionless, his hands still clasped behind his back, and eventually said, 'I doubt it is me you've come to see, child.'

There was something strangely familiar about the voice. Tyballis looked up. 'But it must be, sir. I must speak with the new Baron Throckmorton. Is that not you, my lord?'

Then she saw that his boots were scuffed and his coat, though of mahogany velvet and fur-trimmed, was old. The hem was worn and one long sleeve, the cuff drifting loose to his side, was partially torn. The man read her eyes. 'As you see, child, I am not the man you want,' he said softly. 'His lordship Baron Throckmorton is now standing behind you, and not, I am afraid, much amused.' The man smiled, and his face softened. 'Not that dear Harold is a man much given to amusement,' he said. 'I believe he will attempt to throw you out. You had better speak quickly.'

Tyballis whirled around and tripped over her toes. She sank directly into another curtsey and kept her head down. 'My lord forgive me. It's about my husband, my lord. He is in terrible circumstances, my lord, and not of his own making.'

The baron resembled his brother, after all. 'What the devil are you talking about, drab? Who are you? How did you get in?'

'Tyballis Blessop, my lord. My husband worked some years for his lordship your brother. And he is innocent, sir, I swear it.'

Throckmorton flicked one long white finger. 'Whoever my brother employed is of no interest to me. You should never have been allowed in. Now, get out.'

'My lord—' Tyballis stuttered, but she was interrupted.

The tall man remained motionless. When he spoke it seemed even his mouth did not move, and his voice stayed steady, low and soft. The bursting fury of the fire spoke louder. 'Listen to the child, Harold,' he murmured. 'She will take up very little of our time.'

To her astonishment, the baron hesitated, biting his lip. 'Oh, very well. Speak up then, trollop. Quick, quick. What is it you want of me?'

Tyballis found herself gabbling. 'My husband was loyal to your brother, my lord. He would never have killed him. Yet he's shackled in Newgate's Limboes without food or medicines and can afford no attorney to plead his case.' Bent almost to one knee, Tyballis saw only the baron's blue silk ankles and the high shine on his pointed shoes. She continued hurriedly, 'In your great mercy, my lord, and your brother's memory, and in consideration of my husband's long service, would you give something – anything at all – for his rations in prison, sir, and for the safekeeping of his wife and mother?'

She did not dare look up. She could hear only the busy crackle of the fire. The pause stretched. Finally, it was not the baron, but the other voice that said, 'I believe you might offer some charity, might you not, Harold? From your – renowned generosity, let us say, and the – great kindness for which you are so unconscionably famed.'

After a moment, Tyballis heard metal chink against metal and a small purse was flung at her feet. Its ties were well knotted, but the leather seemed full and heavy. She leaned out and clasped it before his lordship changed his mind, then scrambled up and for the first time looked at both the men who faced her. The unnamed stranger, his back to the blazing flames and his legs solid to the rug, had not moved. His heavy-boned face appeared expressionless. The baron, in height only to the other man's shoulder, was animated and clearly angry. 'Now get out,' spat the baron. 'And don't ever dare come back, or I'll have you thrown into Newgate yourself.' His hair, as red as the fire, was thick-curled and carefully arranged, but his face sweated and his mouth clamped thin. Tyballis straightened, turning quickly to leave. She was stopped.

The soft voice softened further, and she could barely hear it. 'And did you keep my cloak, little one?' said the stranger. 'Or did you sell it, since you now wear only a thin cape? And I see you have not run – or walked – away from your wretched husband. A mistake, I imagine. No matter. I wish you better fortune to come.'

Tyballis stood a moment. She could find no words for reply. But the baron had already begun talking to his visitor, and so she turned again, and ran.

CHAPTER FIVE

'Whoring. No doubt at all,' spat Mother Blessop.

'If you don't want it, give it back,' said Tyballis. But her mother-in-law kept a tight hold. It was a fine leather purse, marked with the Throckmorton arms, and held the unexpected weight of three marks. Tyballis had never seen such a fortune together at one time, forty shillings and almost equal to a year of Borin's salary. 'I'd be a fine whore,' Tyballis said, 'if I could make as much as this just for raising my skirts.'

'Then Throckmorton's miserable brother is a better man than ever expected,' muttered Margery. Tyballis shook her head. 'It was someone else shamed him into giving the purse or he wouldn't have given a penny. He told me never to come back.' She thought a moment, as if preferring not to speak. Then she said it anyway. 'You know the Throckmorton household better than I do. There's a man, a very large man, who talks like a lord but wears shabby grandeur. His hair's out of style and his boots have holes. But he seems to have influence, despite his appearance. Do you have any idea who he might be?'

Margery Blessop tied the heavy purse tightly to her belt and snorted. 'Could be anyone. How should I know?' She hung up her apron and wrapped her cape around her shoulders. 'Six shillings of this is going straight to Borin for his keep, and then I'm off down the market. You keep that fire going till I get back.'

'The fire doesn't need tending,' Tyballis said. 'I could come with you. Or go to market alone while you visit Newgate. I'm tired of sitting here doubled up like an old crone. I got the money for us. Don't I have any say on how it's spent?'

Her mother-in-law turned on Tyballis in fury. 'There's times when I regret ever having taken pity on you in the first place, let alone allowing you to marry my son. Been like a mother to you for years, I have, miserable orphaned waif that you were, and never any good for anything. And what respect do I get? A pert trollop, you are, and no better than the whore Borin suspects you of being.'

Tyballis accepted the slap. She did not move aside, though her face stung. First, she controlled her breathing. Then, keeping her voice low, she said, 'An orphan I was, but not such a waif. Ten years old, and the only heir to my father's house and furniture. It's his house you live in now, and his bed your son sleeps in. You and Borin were only tenants next door, and when my parents drowned you took me in just to lay claim to the house and chattels. You won't admit it, but you know it, and I know it, too. And you made me marry Borin soon as I turned fourteen, only so the house became his and I couldn't claim it back. Maybe I can't do anything about it, but at least don't think me a fool. I know your mind and I know Borin's.'

'And I know yours, whoring bitch,' Margery shouted, slamming down her shopping basket and aiming another slap. 'I'll get no thanks for all my sacrifice and kindness, that's clear. But I won't take your impudence, and I won't take your insults. I'll have Borin tip you out in the gutter if you talk like this when he comes back.'

'If he comes back.'

'Oh, he will, dirty little harlot, and will beat you black and blue soon as he walks back in.'

Tyballis sighed. 'Borin only calls me whore because you've filled his simple head with lies,' she said. 'There's never been an instant, not one, when you had reason to believe it of me. Why are you so ready with the word? Was that what you once were yourself, to think of the accusation so readily?'

Never before had she dared say as much. She expected retaliation but had not expected the broom, swung full force. The bundled reeds cut across her cheeks and mouth and Tyballis tasted blood. She stumbled to her knees, head down. Through warm red trickles, the old splintered floorboards heaved up towards her. She staggered, her ears buzzing, as the room rocked around her like a cradle in the wind. When she shook her head to clear her sight, it hurt her more. Then the broom's handle crashed against the back of her head and she fell again. Her chin hit the floor and she bit her lip. More blood filled her mouth, dribbling in bright spots onto the floor she had scrubbed that morning. She thought vaguely of how she would now have to scrub it again.

Both feet flat in the bloody smears, Margery Blessop stood over her daughter-in-law. Looking up, Tyballis watched one shoe lift, ready for the kick. She rolled over, reached out and grabbed the hovering leg. Between her fingers the ankle bones protruded from the thin grey woollen stocking. Tyballis wrenched and the woman thundered down in a heap, skirts up around her garters, feet in the air. Tyballis scrambled out of the way, but a sharp and flailing heel caught her nose. She yelped. Margery bounced upright, looking for a quick attack. Tyballis read her eyes and dodged. Margery gave chase.

Caught against the wall, Tyballis was slammed back as the plaster cracked, feeling both Margery's hands around her neck, the scratch of broken nails and fingertips like little cold pebbles. Tyballis hesitated, pulled Margery's hands from her neck and flung her bodily. The older woman staggered, slipped in blood and fell. Tyballis snorted and turned away. The cauldron, heavy with pottage, hit her hard from behind. The slime of broth and cold turnips slipped over her little cap, into her eyes and down her back. The iron rim sent her reeling back on the floor, on her hands and knees with her face to the wasted dinner and her nose and mouth covered in blood.

'Clean it up, whore,' hissed the voice from behind her. 'I've money now, plenty to buy a better supper. Turnips is only for horses and I'll eat no more of your rancid stews. I'll get me a pie and one for Borin, but I'll not be bringing one home for you. If you're hungry, lick it up from the floor like the dogs do. When I get back, I'll expect your apology, or there'll be more of the same kind to come.'

Tyballis heard the door slam and sighed with relief. She sank back, sitting in pottage. Strings of cooked leeks clung to her skirts. She put her hands to her head and unpinned her ruined cap. Her head was pounding, and her fingers shook, but she smiled at herself. Such a nonsense squabble, and of her own making for once.

Bringing water in a shallow bowl from the rain keg outside, she gazed at her reflection. As she started to laugh, her lower lip split and bled again. Cleaning herself was a slow job. With resolute concentration, she washed the blood from her face, dug out a splinter lodged in her chin and wiped the muck from her clothes. Her headdress was beyond salvage, so she combed her hair and left it loose. Checking the ripples in the water bowl once more, she grimaced. Only a sloven stared back, lacking even the respectability of a covering for her hair.

Tyballis did not attempt to clean the floor. The trail of blood continued to spread through the desultory pools of stew. She tipped the bowl of water over the hearth's last hot ashes and watched the eager flames splutter and sink. Then she took down her cape, draped it over her head and tucked the ends across her shoulders. Taking nothing, she opened the door of her own house and walked out into the patter of autumn drizzle. Standing a moment, she breathed deep. Sunshine was lurking behind the clouds.

She said no silent goodbyes as she closed the door and started to walk briskly down the street. She knew already; this time there would be no going back. Cutting across the churchyard from Whistle Alley into Fynkes Lane, Tyballis hurried through the unpaved back streets, puddle-pocked where ravens washed their outstretched wings like a group of gossiping widows over the communal tub. She had not yet admitted to herself where she intended to go, but she headed east and did not falter.

CHAPTER SIX

The stench from the busy tanneries was carried in from the east, the stinks of the great dung vats and the filth and gore of the soaking skins, the tubs of scraped fat and the decomposition of the residue boiled for glue. Not far off, a thousand hides were stretched on their tenters, their careful preparation already foul on the wind.

When Tyballis arrived at the high wall, she stopped at last by the swinging gate, catching her breath as she tucked her near-frozen fingers inside the ends of her cape. The drizzle had turned to a bitter sleet and her toes were numb. From where she stood, the house seemed only toppling brick chimneys climbing out from the surrounding trees. Autumn leaves, dripping russet and copper, poured filtered rain onto the slush of the pathway. Tyballis stood a moment, resting against the musty bark. The moment stretched and the shadows grew long.

She contemplated her decision. There was neither purpose nor future in her life. Just the temptation of warmth and comfort ahead, and the longing of a welcome, since none lay behind her. But even having come this far, she hesitated.

The whisper came from the damp dark silence. 'Well darling,' so close it tickled her ear. 'Don't I know you? Coming to visit me, was you?' Tyballis kicked backwards, and the man chuckled. 'What a vixen. And there was me thinking you a proper lady.'

He let her go suddenly and she whirled around. Knowing the stains on her clothes, the swollen lip and bruised face would make her into the slattern she knew herself but hated to seem, Tyballis lifted her chin and changed the glare to disdain. 'I don't care to be mauled, sir,' she said.

Davey Lyttle grinned. 'That's better, mistress. Remember your pride. And wait to cut my bollocks off until you get to know me better.'

'I won't be getting to know you at all, neither for better nor worse,' Tyballis said. 'I was simply passing by. I've not come to visit.'

The man shook his head. 'Lying is a sin, my girl. There's no one passes by here, lest they're looking for Drew or one of the rest of us. Even the bloody tanners don't dare come too close, since it's known we bite.'

'Whatever you care to think, I intend leaving now,' Tyballis said. 'If you'll please stand aside, it's getting late and I should be on my way home.'

'Back to the city?' Davey laughed. 'Well, Beautiful, it's later than you think. The gates will be closed before you could reach them. Forget those cold streets. Come on in. No doubt someone will have a little supper to spare, though it won't be me. I'll be looking for a handout myself.'

Since her cuts and bruises would certainly look as bad as they felt, being called beautiful annoyed her. But it was, originally, food and company she had hoped for and still craved. 'The gates are shut?' she said, already knowing it must be true. He took her hand. 'Just look at the sky, my dear. Trust me, though there's few who do. But you'll be welcome indoors, that I can promise.'

Tyballis allowed herself to be drawn towards the house. The looping shadows parted, and inside the warmth and light reasserted. No expensive wax candles, but a huge hearth bursting flame and the soft aromatic smells of burning wood lit the main hall. Tyballis moved tentatively towards the fire, but Davey called her back. 'Not down here, darling,' he waved a casual hand. 'There's the kitchens behind, but for the rest it's Drew's place and he keeps downstairs for himself. His hall, his fire. Come on up with me.'

Tyballis climbed, wary for gaping holes. 'But,' she said, 'surely it's this landlord I should speak to first. Though,' she added in a rush, 'I've no intention of staying.'

Davey sniggered. 'State of your face, girl, you'll stay. You're on the run from someone. Husband, father, or the law. Besides, it's usual for travellers to take shelter where they can, and few who'd refuse to offer it. Not that respectable females on their own is common. But there's rooms enough upstairs, empty for the taking and Drew don't care and turns no one away.'

'Empty rooms?' Tyballis had been hoping to reacquaint herself with the Spiers, and perhaps be taken in by Felicia to help care for the children.

Davey's grin was visible even in the darkness. 'Stay with me, darling, if you don't fancy the draughts to yourself. You'll not be lonely and it surely seems you need looking after.'

Tyballis stiffened. 'I'm a married woman and can look after myself.'

A shriek interrupted, a door slamming, and the sudden black head of a poker emerged from the dark passageway. Davey turned and grabbed a flailing wrist. A woman's voice squealing. 'Let me go, bastard.' The woman, all dark hair and fury, lashed out. Davey forced her arm back until she dropped the poker.

'I'll let you go when I know whose skull you're planning on cracking.'

'Not yours, thief. You've a head thicker than quarried stone, with neither sense nor a decent idea in there worth the stealing.' The woman stood rubbing her wrist and glaring. 'It's Drew I'm after, and none of your bloody business.'

Davey grinned. 'I doubt Drew's even here. Never is past curfew. And if he's in, then leave him be, before he throws us all out. Come to my room later, then I'll teach you better habits. In my arms, you'll forget the poor bugger downstairs.'

'Why choose the rat, when I can have the lion?' She panted, leaning back against the passage wall.

'But if the lion's so willing, why the poker?'

She glared over his shoulder. 'And who's she? Yours? Or his?'

'Drew's?' Davey laughed. 'They've never even met each other. No, not his, nor mine neither. A newcomer. And a right fine welcome she's getting. So, get out of my way, Lizzie, and take your foul temper elsewhere.'

In the lightless passageway the woman was only a shadow. Her loose hair hid her face but her eyes were hugely black. She bent quickly and retrieved her poker, then ran down the stairs.

Tyballis moved aside. 'She lives here, too?'

The shadows melted back into place and the footsteps from below muffled into silence. 'Elizabeth,' Davey said simply. 'Sleeps with Drew when he'll have her, or me, when he won't. I reckon she'd take old widower Switt if he asked. But it needn't concern you, sweetheart. I'll take you instead.'

Tyballis turned, recognising the Spiers' doorway. 'I told you, I'm not interested. I'm married and won't take another man. If I stay, which I haven't said I will, then I'll talk to Felicia first.'

'No good talking to her.' Davey shook his head, moving in so close she smelled the sweet musk of Spanish soap on his hair. 'Poor old drudge don't get neither coin nor bread from her useless husband, not enough to feed her brats let alone visitors. Jon don't even move himself to go out on the cadge nor the pilfer and cutting a purse would take more energy than he's prepared to spend on anything more than getting out of bed and then back into it. You'd do better with me, darling.'

Tyballis sighed. 'I told you—'

'I know, I know, Mistress Proper and Prim,' Davey grinned. 'You told me to get lost. But I can be patient. There's enough of us here, but you'll find no one else capable as me. Apart from Lizzie the whore and the Spiers, there's widower Switt as only fancies the little ones, and will grope the children when Felicia's not looking. Nat and Ralph, well, a useless pair they are, though Ralph has some small claim to sense. But they look so alike, you could climb into Ralph's arms and find yourself with Nat's hands on your arse. Luke Parris, now he's a dirty little heathen, he is, what was put to be a monk, seduced his abbot, I reckon, or stole the charity box, and ran from his monastery years back. I doubt he has a prick, and if he has then he don't know what to do with it. Then there's those that come and go, since Drew lets in all and sundry, mostly the tanners when they're too pissed to find their way home, and some of the local whores and their pimps when there's no business and the streets too cold to sleep in. So, which of them will you choose, Lady Prude? Or will you come to Davey Lyttle, and keep his pallet warm through the long winter nights?'

'Or maybe I'll take one of those empty chambers you spoke of and find that girl's poker and keep it to protect myself.' Tyballis was leaning hard up against the Spiers' door. When the door opened suddenly behind her, she almost fell backwards. Hearing voices, someone had come, but no vivid light of fire or warmth of welcome lit the chamber. Tyballis turned, facing only shadow and chill. 'It's me, Tyballis Blessop. I visited with Ellen yesterday,' she whispered. 'Is that Felicia?'

The answer, another whisper, came from lower down. 'It's not me ma, it's me,' said the child. 'Me little brother Gyles is sick and we've no firewood, nor supper.'

Tyballis bent towards the hovering shadow. 'Perhaps I might come in, Ellen, and help look after him.'

Ellen shook her curls. 'Might be the pox. Drew says as how we must keep shut up till we knows. Whenever there's sickness, Drew shuts us in. Won't risk pestilence through the house. But I'll show you where to go, if you wants a place to yourself.'

Tyballis sighed, reaching for the child's hand. 'Another room? Yes, thank you. Davey Lyttle is here, but I would sooner not – that is, I would prefer—'

'That's Davey nobody, that is. Come with me,' announced Ellen, emerging from her doorway.

Davey chuckled. 'Since I am clearly no more than a nuisance, I must allow the child to lead the child. But remember, Mistress Blessop, I can be relied upon, whatever appearances to the contrary, and will protect you if you need it.' He stepped back as Ellen danced forwards, clearly pleased to escape the silent misery of the sickbed.

It was a small chamber where Tyballis finally took refuge, the larger rooms already taken. Across the stone hearth a smattering of cold ashes smelled of loneliness. The window was cracked and the shutters missing. The solitary pallet had lost much of its straw, now a small pile of refuse accumulated in a corner. Otherwise the chamber was empty.

There was furniture to spare downstairs, Ellen said, but Drew would not distribute this to the rooms until they were inhabited, or others would steal it. And a fire? Well, kindling and faggots could be collected from the copses nearby, mixed with twigs from the garden. Drew sometimes gave his own firewood to the Spiers, being a family much in need of warming. 'We've two rooms,' Ellen gossiped. 'Right big and pretty. The other folk here, well, they've only one chamber each, or share one like Ralph and Nat. Luke's quarters is the biggest with an annexe for his scribing, but that's right up under the roof and he don't much bother with the rest of us.'

'This little chamber is cosy enough,' Tyballis told her. 'In any case, I may leave tomorrow. If I do, I shall come and say goodbye first.'

Once alone, Tyballis took off her wet shoes and sat them neatly before the empty hearth. Outside, pelting and persistent, the rain obscured the moon and no light intruded through the unshuttered windowpanes. With no blanket to warm her, Tyballis curled herself fully dressed deep into the pallet's straw. She closed her eyes but remained awake, her thoughts turning more melancholy as the silent hours lengthened. The dispossessed filth of the city had rustled through her nights since birth, and she had no cause to be afraid of something long accustomed, but she had not felt so dispossessed since her parents had died, when she was rescued, half-drowned, from the flooded Thames and its rising tide. She would, she thought, if she permitted such pitiful nonsense to swallow her thoughts, soon begin to cry. If not careful, she might trick herself into missing a house and a family she loathed though had never before found the courage to leave.

She sat up. Through the cold remained the vivid memory of a fire blazing futile and unwatched down in the great empty hall, where the flames cheered no one, gave no miserable pauper welcome and served no purpose. The man Drew, they said, solitary misanthropist, was absent during the evenings and the nights, leaving before curfew and sometimes not returning for days. The fire he had lit would now be begging for company.

Tyballis found her shoes but did not put them on. She carried them and carefully slipped downstairs.

CHAPTER SEVEN

At the bottom of the stairs she stopped a moment. Straight ahead was the main entrance, shielded by a narrow screen. To her left stretched the great hall, billowing with crimson light. The swelter absorbed the draughts, and the wooden panelling sighed and cracked like a careened ship's boards shrinking in the dry. Huge and sweating, the hall murmured complacent.

Between herself and the soaring hearth drifted dust, ashes from old fires and soot from those even older. A Turkey rug was worn to the weft where a hundred boots had crossed. A table leaned its shadows against the far wall, a clutter of stools pulled to the side. The beamed ceiling was unpainted, and an ancient iron chandelier hung high, still clinging to its solidified wax. There were no candles in any place, but the fire lit everything in dancing glory and the dazzle of the flames reflected back from a wall of windows. Tapestries glinted, shelves of painted earthenware, a long bench and all the paraphernalia of a well-furnished Hall. Two large chairs, high-backed, deep-armed and cushioned, were drawn before the fire.

Outside, black night had closed in the land, but no chill bluster found its path down the chimney nor past the crackle of the burning logs. Tyballis crept forwards, still clutching her shoes. Already her face was bright in the heat's soothing embrace.

She curled tightly to the grate, tucking her toes beneath her skirts as she squatted down. Breathing deeply brought the warmth into her lungs and through her bones. The tension in her shoulders melted. She cuddled her knees, gazing in peaceful contemplation as a hundred fantasies flared and faded within the light and shadow, faeries flying and imps hiding in their caves, dragons and monsters and sea creatures spouting fountains, and all the adventure of ancient history and pagan myth dancing before her face. The light, the heat and the busy crackle enveloped her.

Not risking sleep by lying down, although the thought was unutterably tempting, Tyballis closed her eyes and leaned back just a little, supporting herself against the chair legs behind her. She did not want to think, and she did not want to dream, but it would be safe, she thought, to doze a moment and to relinquish the misery of memory. She knew that, once thoroughly warmed, she must return to her cold waiting pallet.

She was almost asleep when the chair legs moved imperceptibly, as if conveniently adjusting themselves to her weight. She snuggled down and settled again, resting her head against the yielding curves at her back.

When she finally awoke, she was somewhere else entirely.

Tyballis sat up in utter confusion. Then, since dreaming was the only possible explanation, she looked around with curiosity. Through the darkness she could see very little. No longer was there a huge scarlet fire and a row of reflecting glass, but she could study the shadows sufficiently to make out the room around her and the bed beneath her. The palliasse creaked as she moved and long curtains whispered. The smells were of dust, tired sweat and fresh herbs. She patted her coverings, discovering velvet and fine linen, soft cushions and a deep filled bolster. Puzzled and increasingly wary, she no longer believed she was dreaming. Touch, texture and smells were too real, and her body was too aware of its aches and its warmth. She was definitely not in her own home, but lay, well wrapped and snug, in a bed of some luxury. Even more perplexing, she had been disrobed, and now wore only her chemise.

Reaching up, Tyballis fingered the bed posts behind her, carved and hung with silks. Against her hand she could feel the polished patterns of the wood, the sheen of the curtains and the small rips that told of age and abandon. Carried in her sleep and taken to some unknown bed, she had been undressed, tucked in and covered up. It was a concept that, in spite of the considerable comfort, she found increasingly uncomfortable.

From the bewildering darkness, the sudden voice was as soft as the contradictory perfumes. 'Well, little one,' it said. 'You are quite safe here. Did you come to find me for reasons of your own? Or is it what men choose to call coincidence?'

Tyballis turned in a hurry. The figure sat, large and at ease in the darkest corner of the chamber. But this time, she knew his voice. 'You? Is it you? I didn't expect, didn't know, still don't know. Who are you? Where am I?'

'You are in my bed,' replied the imperceptible voice.

'You undressed me!'

A pause. Then, 'How many gowns do you own, child?'

She sighed. There seemed little point in refusing to answer. 'One, of course.'

'Then,' smiled the voice, 'it is presumably best not slept in. I have hung it on one of the pegs.' The smile audibly widened. 'You are hardly naked, child, and will notice you are still wearing your shift.'

'Who are you?' Tyballis again demanded into the shadows.

He said, 'I am Andrew Cobham, though a name means very little, and mine less than most. I am usually called Drew.'

'Drew. The landlord. You own this house, then.'

'I do.' He still sounded amused.

It occurred to Tyballis that to discover a truth did not help when that truth was more perplexing than previous ignorance. 'I didn't realise. It being yours, I mean.' Blanket to her chin, she stared into invisibility. 'I'd met the child, Ellen, and some of the others. Ellen's mother was kind. Then I had to leave my own home, and so I came back here because I didn't know where else to go. How strange – since it was you who told me to run away, and that's what I did.' Unable to see his reaction, she foundered, but remembered her manners. 'So, I have to thank you.' Though embarrassed, she mumbled, 'But to undress me. Instead of waking me ...'

'Why did you have to leave your home, child?' he said. 'Your husband has been released from Newgate?'

'No. Borin's still there.'

He murmured, 'Yet once more you bear the marks of attack.'

She was embarrassed again, remembering the broom, the years of Margery Blessop's temper and how much she didn't ever want to go home again. 'His mother beat me. I called her a whore. I shouldn't have said it. I was upset.'

Andrew Cobham materialised as he unwound from his chair, seeming very large as he stood before the bed. 'There are whores who come here,' he said, 'and are welcome. They are as welcome as any woman, or any man who does what he must to keep food in his belly and the wolf from the door. I do not judge a woman's choice of endeavour, but I will not treat any woman as a whore if she chooses to behave otherwise. You are quite safe in my bed, Mistress Blessop, and in my house if you decide to remain here.'

She was surprised he remembered her name. 'But to find myself unclothed ... I – I only meant to doze a little by the fire.'

He chuckled suddenly, as if releasing something long held back. 'You did doze, child, and I left you to dream a little. But my legs were becoming stiff, and I had a great desire to move them. Removing you to a more comfortable place seemed the best way to please us both.'

'You were already there when I came down into the hall?' she said in surprise. 'I thought I was leaning back against the chair legs.'

'I have been mistaken for many things in my life,' the man nodded, 'but usually more interesting, and more active than a chair. No matter. I am clearly getting old.' Even in the dark, she saw the sudden crinkle of his eyes and knew he smiled. 'Stay where you are,' he said. 'I'm going out and will be gone for many hours. Tomorrow, if you wish to stay, I'll have an upstairs chamber furnished for you. In the meanwhile, sleep. Decisions of the night are false friends. Sleep alters priorities and waking opens new horizons. I shall see you, perhaps, when I return.'

Tyballis sat staring as the door quietly closed and the emptiness shuffled back around her. But it was a long time before she once again fell asleep.

⸺❖⸺

She was woken by sunbeams. As with so much else within the house, the window shutters of Andrew Cobham's bedchamber were broken with two slats missing. It had rained in the small hours and a sparkle of wet glass caught the rainbows in soft rosy streaks. Tyballis sat up in a flurry but she was quite alone. So she scrambled out of bed, found her old gown hanging forlorn and stained on a far peg, hurried into it and pulled the ties tight under her arm, discovered her shoes and stepped into them, had nothing to tidy her hair with and so simply pushed it from her eyes before finally rushing from the room. She looked back only briefly.

Grand once, and still retaining its shabby luxury, the chamber was huge. The fire tools by the empty grate were brass-handled and expensive. The one window was set behind a padded seat covered in faded tapestry. There were no candles in the chandelier nor the sconces, but the ceiling was vaulted, and its beams were carved. Fresh herbs had been strewn and perfumes of camomile and mint danced with the sunbeams. The bed rose from its central place like a gigantic throne, swathed in purples and golds, though the threads had fallen loose and hung in frayed scraps and dangling curls, the tassels unravelled. But the linen was clean, and the pillows fat with feather. Tyballis sighed. She had never slept in so wondrous a chamber before and doubted she would ever do so again.

Following the passage outside, she hurried upstairs to the tiny room where her pallet of the previous evening lay scattered. She was wondering what to do next when Felicia Spiers found her. 'Mister Cobham has asked me specially to look after you, my dear,' said the woman. 'To make you welcome and find you a better lodging. I hadn't realised you already knew our kind Mister Cobham.'

'Oh, I don't,' Tyballis said quickly. 'That is, I met him twice, but I never knew his name. And kind certainly seems an appropriate description. But perhaps mysterious as well.'

41

Felicia Spiers shook her starched headdress and a few wisps of greying hair struggled out to curl around her ears. 'I would hardly call Mister Cobham mysterious, my dear. He is our benefactor and allows all of us – let us say, those in need – to stay in his home free of any rental charge, which is remarkably charitable of him, as I'm sure you'll agree. I don't question his motives, but he's well respected and well liked here. I hope you're not saying you don't trust him, my dear?'

Tyballis certainly wasn't going to mention finding herself undressed in his bed. 'I simply meant he doesn't appear to be a wealthy man, yet this house is a palace. Or it was once, though it's gone to rack and ruin. I expect he has no money for repairs, but if he charged his tenants a reasonable rent, I imagine the building could be restored.'

'Please don't suggest any such thing to him, my dear,' Mistress Spiers became quite agitated and twisted her hands in her apron. 'My dearest Jon, my husband you know, has been incapacitated for some considerable time and we barely manage to feed the little ones as it is. If we had to pay for our board, I doubt we could stay.'

The same applied to herself. 'But you must admit, it's extraordinary for any common man to allow numerous folk to stay quite freely in his home.'

'Most kind. Most charitable,' bobbed Felicia. 'He even brings us food sometimes, and medicines and kindling. He allows us to collect berries and herbs and salad greens from his gardens, and there is a little lake at the back where fish breed, so we have water as well, which is very nearly clean.'

'So, the man is a paragon though not a handsome gentleman, you must admit, and wears a face marked by violence. They say our appearance never belies our virtue, so perhaps Mister Cobham is atoning for past sins.'

'Hardly appreciative, my dear.' Felicia pursed her lips. 'Kindness is kindness, and a good man should be respected. There are few enough in the world, such as the Lord Mayor for instance, and all the Archbishops, his holiness the Pope naturally, and his noble grace our king, who is so beautiful I had to avert my eyes on the one occasion I saw his magnificence riding by.'

'Our good King Edward,' sniffed Tyballis, 'is by all accounts a glutton and a whoremonger and they say half our bishops and monks are avaricious lechers. Every man has his faults. And every woman, too.'

Mistress Spiers stiffened. 'I shall ask Ralph and Nat to carry out Mister Cobham's instructions,' she said and turned her back. 'No doubt once you've moved into a nicer chamber, you'll feel better disposed towards the man who gave it to you.'

'I'm sorry – I didn't mean to antagonise. And Gyles, your little boy?' Tyballis asked in a hurry. 'Is he well?'

'Much better,' Felicia said, determinedly sullen. 'So, you need not fear for infection as well as fearing our landlord's character.'

Guilt displaced all other discomforts. 'I'd be pleased to help you with the children, if I may. I have no experience, but I hope to make myself useful.'

'Useful is as useful does,' said Felicia Spiers.

CHAPTER EIGHT

To have glass in the windows of the hall downstairs was grand enough; to have glass upstairs in the bedchambers was a ludicrous luxury. Now, washing windows, sweeping and scrubbing took her mind off other things. Tyballis permitted only fleeting thoughts of her husband wallowing in Newgate's freezing filth, reassured to remember he now had money enough, which she had procured. She herself, of course, had no money at all and although it appeared she would be welcomed rent-free, there was still the consideration of food, soap, darning wool and other small expenses. Having been accused often enough of prostitution, and considering Andrew Cobham's refusal to condemn the practice, she pondered briefly whether she might sell the only thing she now had to offer. She was fairly sure, however, that her body would be unlikely to fetch more than a penny farthing, and since Borin's physical attentions had always left her sore and faintly disgusted, she could hardly hope that a stranger would prove any more appealing.

Bricks, well heated from the hall's perpetual fire, lay over her new bed like the pustules of the pox, steaming cheerfully in an attempt to dry out the musty damp. The blanket and bedraggled eiderdown in patched cambric, lay on the newly swept floor. As yet her hearth was empty, but she could collect wood whenever she wished, Ralph Tame said, for when the evening chills bore down. A single stool was drawn towards the place where she dreamed of solitary cosiness to come. Ralph had set her up with the bedding and the furniture donated by their landlord, and his brother Nat had helped carry up the bed. Nat she had seen before, running from Davey Lyttle. Indeed she felt she had met them both, since their appearance seemed identical.

'But it's simply annoying,' Ralph said, dumping down his end of the mattress. 'And as far as I'm concerned, we look nothing alike. Yet people persist in pretending they can't tell us apart.'

Nat snorted. 'As if they can't see the difference. It's clear as the moon in the Thames. Look at him. At least a finger's-width shorter. Ankles like spindles and a great lump on his nose.'

'And look at him,' Ralph objected. 'Skin blotched like a half-ripe blackberry and eyes far too close together.'

'His eyebrows are straggly,' Nat pointed out, busy hoisting the mattress onto the strings. 'Mine are neat and tidy. It makes all the difference in the world.'

'I expect,' Tyballis said carefully, 'I shall recognise those differences in time. For the moment, since I don't know either of you very well, perhaps you'd forgive me if I use the wrong name from time to time. And you are both excessively kind.'

'Call if you want me,' Ralph nodded, edging towards the door. 'Though not too late, you understand. I shall be out working most of the night. Nat, too.'

Tyballis sighed. 'Do all of you work nights, then?'

'Jon Spiers don't,' Nat said. 'He don't leave the house at all. Don't ever work at anything.'

Tyballis sat on her bed, which was when she discovered it was exceedingly damp. 'Doesn't the curfew bother you? Or the Watch?'

'Don't be daft, mistress,' said Nat. 'Only a fool gets seen by the Watch.'

'And only a fool discusses his business with a stranger,' Ralph said. 'See! We're not the same at all. He's stupid. I'm not.'

'But you are twins, after all,' said Tyballis. 'And that means you are very similar.'

'We aren't twins,' Nat said, looking sullen. 'Twins means born at

45

the same time, and we weren't. Our ma said as how we was born half of an hour apart. So, that's not the same time, is it? We're not twins at all.'

There was no dinner although it was dinnertime. Tyballis had not eaten for two days and saw no reason to expect any supper. Although she was long accustomed, the pain and heaving disappointment of hunger seemed no less bearable in her new surroundings. In the past Borin had always earned money eventually, enabling a hurried trip to the market stalls. At least one day in three she had eaten, and a pottage could be made to last four days with a sensibly regular addition of water, turnips and cabbage. Tyballis had never starved. It was different now. She would have to manage for herself.

When she could find nothing else in her chamber to scrub, she wiped her hands and went outside. Crossing from the bottom of the stairs to the outer doors, she once again passed the sudden crimson and scarlet reflections of Andrew Cobham's fire. The stairs led directly past the archway into the great hall, and there the heat billowed as always. Tyballis slipped out into the gardens and shut the warmth away with a bang.

Fallen wood was easily found, cracked branches tumbling from each ivy-covered tree, while twig and bark lay sodden in leafy heaps. Everything was wet. Tyballis could light her own fire that evening though it would smoke and make her chamber filthy again. But better dirty than cold. She used her knotted wrap to collect what she could. It had started to rain once more, just a sloppy patter sparkling in the spiders' webs and decorating her hair with pearl drops. It was a large garden, ruined and overgrown, and the fish pond was green with algae. Bubbles popped along the surface from the falling rain above and the fish gulping below. A tangle of blackberry bushes had long been cleared of their fruit, but she found a twist of vine hidden behind dripping foliage and collected a handful of overripe grapes.

It was too soaked to light but Tyballis stacked the firewood beside her hearth and mopped up the oozing puddles. Now wet and cold, she sat a long time and wondered what her future should become. Loneliness threatened but she was her own mistress. No one could order her behaviour, nor criticise or beat her. She was in debt to no

46

one except the owner of this house, but as yet he had demanded nothing of her. He was, said the others, a good man. That might even be true, for a night in his bed had brought no molestation. There was Felicia and the children to visit along the corridor, and friendship might follow.

Instead, she imagined returning contrite to her own little semblance of family, to the house which was truly hers, and to the life which was, if nothing else, familiar. Hugging herself warm and resting her chin on her knees, she contemplated both the courage of such a return, and the cowardice of it. The unknown threatened, but only a fool goes back to the prison he has escaped.

She had made up her mind when she finally went downstairs again. The shadows slanted through the struts of the balustrade and across the broken boards, but at the base of the stairs the fire's golden reflections stained the steps with light. Tyballis crept into the hall and towards the hearth, but this time she was prepared and turned, facing the large chair set there. Andrew Cobham's deep-set eyes were closed, his arms resting on the chair arms and his hands hanging loose. His long legs were stretched towards the blaze, ankles crossed.

He did not open his eyes. 'Can I help you, child?' his voice no louder than the murmur of the flames.

'How did you know it was me?' Tyballis objected.

He opened his eyes. In the firelight they were crimson. 'Is that all you wish to know?' he said.

She hovered, glad of the heat at her back. 'I came to get warm, but I hoped you'd be here. I wanted to thank you. But I know the downstairs rooms are your private quarters. If you tell me to go away, I won't be offended.'

'You are clearly accustomed to men of few manners, child.' The man straightened a little and a slow half-smile softened his eyes. Not a handsome man, and heavy boned, his face was marred by a large and once broken nose. Yet his smile was gentle, lifting his expression and lightening the strength of his jaw. 'You need not go away,' he said, 'but I have little use for your thanks. Has no one given you kindling to warm your chamber?'

She nodded. 'But it's wet. And I wanted to say more than just thank you. I wanted to suggest – to ask – if I might work for you. Cooking and cleaning. I could work while you're out, so as not to be in your way.' Tyballis drew a deep breath and stood looking earnestly down at the figure lounging before her. 'I could make life – nicer for you. Polishing, and dusting, and washing. I could make this hall glorious again. It would repay your kindness in letting me stay here. And perhaps, just perhaps, if you liked what I did, sometimes you could pay me, too. Just a few pennies for food.'

She stood between him and the fire and now he sat in her shadow, his eyes changing from red to black. His hair, thicker and longer than was fashionable, was a deeper shadow. He lifted one dark eyebrow, the lazy smile remaining. 'You look for payment? Are you wanting back in my bed, little one?'

Flustered, Tyballis took a step backwards and the heat blasted her shoulders. She recoiled, blushing. 'That wasn't my intention at all, sir. I'm good at cleaning and scrubbing. I'm not good at … other things. You wouldn't want me.'

Andrew Cobham's smile deepened, and his eyebrow raised a little further. 'An intriguing confession,' he said softly. 'But I will try not to tease you, Mistress Blessop. I appreciate your attempt to compensate for your board, but I have no interest in your talents or your cleaning. Or perhaps you simply wish to remind me how unkempt my living quarters have become?'

'No, sir. I wouldn't be so rude.' She shook her head wildly. 'Of course, there is some dust, and the soot from the fire, and the window glass – such beautiful windows – but long unpolished. I could improve both their appearance and your comfort if you'd allow me. And then – there is the difficulty of food.'

His expression settled into amused contentment. 'I cook for myself,' he said.

'It was more my own food I was thinking of, sir. And a little money, just a penny or two, you understand, to enable me to buy some necessities. I would do anything you require, should my cleaning not interest you, sir.'

'Ah,' he murmured, 'we are once again back to the bedchamber.'

'You aren't taking me seriously,' Tyballis said with an affronted sniff. 'So, I apologise for having interrupted you.' She turned abruptly, tossed her head and marched back towards the stairs.

She was stopped by a firm hand on her shoulder. He had overtaken her in two steps and now stood, looking down into her eyes. 'Join me,' he said. 'Being a man of few pretentions, as you have seen, I usually eat in the kitchens. There is enough already prepared for a hot supper, and far more than I can use myself.'

'You want me to share your – meal?' hiccupped Tyballis.

'Certainly. And while we eat, we can discuss exactly what you may do for me, Mistress Blessop, to earn the payment you require. It will involve neither cleaning nor the other services we have been carefully not discussing. I could have brought servants in at any time had I cared about the appearance of an ordered household. I do not care and want no woman on her knees scrubbing for me. Nor will I suggest that other common use a man finds for a woman, at which you claim to be – unskilled. There are other possibilities which interest me far more. Now, come and eat.'

She dared not answer. She simply followed him. As they left the hall, the warmth shrank back, but then they turned a narrow corner beyond the stairwell and stood in the polished sparkle of clean tiles and the burnished copper utensils of the kitchens. Another fire roared up the wide chimney, smothering the bubble and crackle of the food cooking there. Leaping reflections lit brighter than candles and the smell of roasting meat burst like gunpowder from a cannon. Tyballis sank down on the bench beside the kitchen table and gazed in awe at the chicken carcass on the spit, dripping its juices into the flames below.

'Hungry, little one?'

'Oh, very much,' breathed Tyballis.

Andrew Cobham took up a long carving knife and began to sharpen it, flicking water from the bowl to dampen the whetting stone by the grate. He indicated the long shelves and the crockery piled there. 'Then, help me plate what is needed for us both,' he said. 'First we eat. And then we talk.'

CHAPTER NINE

Gliding high over the rooftops, the kestrel caught the first soft warmth of the sun on her primary feathers. She peered down over the meandering fields towards the riverbanks and back again to the hedges and lanes. Hunger did not spoil her patience. She was searching for rats, mice or voles, and looked for any sudden movement amongst the damp grasses.

In a small chamber within the house standing directly below, Tyballis struggled into her new clothes. She had never worn so much or anything so grand, and the fastenings puzzled her. He had said he would help her dress if she needed it, and when, embarrassed, she had refused, he had offered to send Elizabeth or Felicia. But a woman, she thought, must surely be able to put her gown over her own head, however unaccustomed. Now she was finding it far more difficult than she had supposed. Eventually, wrapping the great fur lined cloak around her ineptitude, Tyballis went back down into the hall.

He was standing in front of the fire, his hands clasped behind his back, staring down into the flames as he so often did. He turned as she approached and regarded her. 'Let me see,' he said. She presented herself, feeling foolish.

He had been her landlord for a little more than a week, though she had seen little of him. That first evening in his company she had eaten well, she had warmed herself within and without, she had drunk good Burgundy wine for the first time in her life and she had listened at length. Finally, understanding some and agreeing to all, she had climbed back upstairs to her cold and solitary chamber, had gone to bed and had slept deeply.

The next days had passed, sweet and fast. Andrew Cobham did not contact her directly, but he sent food to the Spiers and asked that they include Tyballis in their rations. Although their youngest child was no longer ill, the family had eaten little for some time. Now each day there came fresh bread from the Portsoken bakers, once a full leg of salted bacon and then two fine pullets for broiling. Tyballis collected herbs from the garden to add to the pot, and firewood stacked to dry in the grate. She and her new friends ate well. Felicia quickly discovered that Tyballis was useful to have around, after all.

Felicia watched with interest as Tyballis washed Ellen's tangled curls in a bowl of warmed lavender water, then with Ellen at her feet, cleaned the child's hair of lice, combing out the eggs onto a kerchief spread on her lap. At the same time, she told the children stories – four bright little faces raised to hers, mouths open and eyes wide at the tales of the magical King Arthur, the amazing travels of Marco Polo, and Mister Chaucer's House of Fame. During the long evenings Jon Spiers' gentle snores echoed from the other chamber, but he always woke in time for meals. The perfumes of cooking preceded his hurried arrival.

Tyballis was in her own chamber when Ralph Tame delivered four shiny silver pennies. An advance payment, he said, by order of their landlord, for the business to come. Ralph looked with curiosity and a little suspicion, but Tyballis simply thanked him and walked down to the riverside and the wharves. The lighters were gathering for business at the base of the old steps. Tyballis found one carrying eels from Marlowe's quay just the other side of The Tower. She bought enough for the entire household and spent the next day cooking alone in the huge hot kitchens. She made a pottage with onions, barley and herbs. As it bubbled, she made a custard flavoured with syrup from Andrew Cobham's pantry. She stewed eels, made a broth from the juices, a tart from a little of the residue, and finished with a galantine of eels to bake in pastry.

Already she had begun to receive visitors. Felicia Spiers and her children visited often. Davey Lyttle came to offer unnamed and unspecified services, and to offer them again each time she refused. Both Ralph and Nat Tame brought dry kindling and warm hens' eggs collected from the garden. Now Tyballis invited the household to a great dinner of her own making. Acting the hostess, and making her own choices, had rarely been possible before. She sent a message by Ellen, asking if Mister Cobham would care to eat with them all, and if she might use the great table in the hall. She received no reply for Andrew Cobham was not at home, and Luke the runaway monk had not answered the knock on his door. But few ever turned down an opportunity to eat for free, so it was a little squashed, but no one complained. The dinner was a success. Davey made up rhymes rich in double meanings, the elderly Mister Swift said little but smiled incessantly, Ralph and Nat sat together and sang out of tune, Felicia Spiers helped serve, and her husband Jon managed to stay awake while the children rolled and played beneath the little overcrowded table. They called it a feast and Tyballis felt fully accepted amongst them.

On her eighth evening in the house, her landlord came. He explained briefly what he wanted, offered her the choice to comply or refuse, and then handed her a great armful of clothes. Tyballis nodded in amazement. At dawn the next morning, she rose and began to dress.

Now she stood very straight for her landlord's inspection and waited. After a moment Andrew lifted her face to his, one finger beneath her chin. 'The marks are fading,' he said.

She had forgotten the marks, since she had no mirror in which to look. She had almost forgotten Margery Blessop's attack, and she had barely spared Borin a thought this past glorious week. 'Oh,' she said. 'Was it so bad?'

'Let us say it was – noticeable. Now it is less so.' He leaned down, turned back the edges of her cloak and shook his head. 'Stand still,' he said, and briskly began to tidy her appearance. He commanded her to lift her left arm, tightened the laces of her gown, rehooked her stomacher so that it lay neatly folded beneath her breasts down to her waist, and flicked her skirts straight. He shook his head again at the creased fichu of starched chiffon over her breasts. Frightened he might put his fingers into her cleavage, Tyballis closed her eyes, but instead he began to rearrange her headdress, reapplying the pins and tucking in the curls of hair above her ears. 'My dear child,' he said eventually, 'short of undressing you and starting again, this will suffice. No one will have particular cause to notice you today and we're unlikely to meet anyone who would know your true identity on this occasion.'

Tyballis looked at her toes. 'There's no one in the world who'd remember me anyhow.'

'You are presumably unaware of how memorable you are, my dear,' Andrew Cobham said. 'But dressed like this, you are somewhat disguised.' He shrugged into his great coat, and looked down at her, smiling suddenly. 'Frightened, little one?'

She shook her head. 'No.'

'You are a poor liar, like most women,' he said. 'But you are quite safe with me as long as you follow instructions.'

The kestrel sighted prey and dropped. Between the mossy flagstones of an open courtyard, the mouse sensed danger but froze too late. With the struggling rodent in its claws, the kestrel flew up and was gone instantly behind the clouds.

Sitting beside the adjacent window, Margery Blessop saw nothing but the sudden flurry of feathers. She was concentrating on the man who sat opposite and was listening carefully. When he stopped talking, she took a deep breath and began again. 'I have no wish,' she said, clasping her fingers a little tighter in her lap, 'to repeat myself to the sheriff, Mister Webb. But if you won't take my word for it, I shall have to go to a higher authority.'

'I'm the highest authority you're likely to get within bowshot of today, mistress,' the assistant constable informed her with a sniff. 'And

I've not got all day, neither. We all know you want your son out of gaol. Tell the truth, you being his mother and him the only child, I might sympathise. Not that the streets aren't a good deal safer with him locked away. But trying to tell me as how that poor little wife of his has been and gone and slaughtered his Lordship of Throckmorton in the middle of the night with a bloody great sword in his guts, well, it don't make sense. I've known young Tyballis for years and I won't believe it. Go tell it to them wriggly tadpole things in the water barrel outside. They might listen. I won't.'

'I shall go directly to the sheriff,' warned Mistress Blessop.

'Try it,' grinned Assistant Constable Webb. 'Sheriff Wharton is busier than me and more. He'll throw you out, like as not. In fact, since it's been more than a week since your great lump of a son got put away, I reckon you've already tried all the bailiffs and the sheriff's chambers too and been promptly escorted from the premises. Which is why you've come crawling back to me. Well, I'm not interested.'

'I shall find someone who is,' insisted Margery. 'There are those in this city with more brains and power than you, Mister Webb.'

The assistant constable sniggered. 'Have a word with our good king, will you, mistress? No doubt he'll be mighty sympathetic. His grace King Edward will open his great doors, I'm sure, and call you in for a nice cosy chat beside the throne.'

Margery Blessop stood with dignity. 'You speak like a fool, Rob Webb, just like your father before you,' she said. 'Just because you've made a little money and got a trade and some property, don't make you as important as you like to think. Constable indeed. Assistant Constables don't impress me none. Now, that miserable trollop was out on the streets all that night when his lordship was knifed. Useless she might be at anything worth the while, and can't even clean a hearth without direction. But has a violent streak against men, she has, and if poor Throckmorton saw her and gave her insult – as who wouldn't – then she'd as soon stick a sword in his belly as wish him a warm goodnight.'

'Beats up her husband regular, does she, your daughter-in-law?' smiled Webb. 'Strange it's her little face I see covered in bruises day after day.'

'Nevertheless,' said Mistress Blessop, 'the wench has run off and it's a whole week she's been gone. Hooked up with some man, I guess, whore that she is. But it's proof of guilt to run away soon as her crime is under question.'

Assistant Constable Webb sniggered again. 'Run away from you, no doubt, mistress. And I'm thinking you'd best be careful what words you choose. Remembering my father knew you well when I was a little lad, you should be wary as to who you go calling whore.' He stood too, and came to stand before her. 'Now off with you, mistress, and go visit your wretched son afore we drag him off to Tyburn.'

'You can't do that,' squeaked Margery. 'His trial's not been held yet.'

'Will be, soon as the courts get to his name on the list. And since the result's an easy one, there'll be no time for dinner nor the washing of his hands afore he swings on the rope. And good riddance it will be. He'll be lucky to get a free mug of ale from the tavern on his last ride, for no one likes a murdering bugger.'

'I know where to go,' Margery Blessop said, marching from the room. 'I shall go where my information will be taken a sight more seriously. And then you'll be sorry, Rob Webb. And so will that wicked Tyballis, slut and murderess that she is.'

The kestrel was roosting high above the city. She had finished her meal and was satisfied, settling high on The Tower's white keep overlooking the Thames, the great stone sheltering her back. The sun had gained strength. The kestrel felt the warmth and ruffled her feathers.

Beyond The Tower's far eastern wall within the kestrel's sight but entirely outside her interest, Andrew Cobham tucked his small companion's hand through the crook of his arm, clasping it firmly against the soft velvet sleeve at his elbow. He felt her shiver. 'Cold, little one?'

Tyballis shook her head. 'I've never worn such a well-lined cloak.' Her voice trembled.

'Still frightened then?' Her fingers clutched a little at his coat.

Andrew Cobham patted them gently. 'If you forget my instructions, or are not sure what to say,' he told her, 'it would be better to say nothing. I can explain away a timid child who dares not speak openly to her elders.'

'Then I'll seem like some silly country bumpkin of a maidservant.'

He chuckled. 'Not dressed like that, you won't. But if you wish to play the lady, then remember what I've told you.' He smiled down at her upturned face. 'I would not have planned this meeting, nor arranged to take you with me, had I not trusted you to act the part. You are young but you are not stupid, Mistress Blessop.'

'And the bruises?'

'It is better if you keep the tippet over your headdress,' he told her, 'and your cloak tightly around you. But I have an excuse for the bruises, if they are noted. Now, are you brave enough to start, child?'

She frowned. 'Of course, I am. And I'm not a child. I'm not so little either, only that you're so very large. I'm nearly nineteen and I've been married for five years.'

'Impressive,' smiled the man. 'Now, we shall go down to the wharf and hire a boat upriver.'

Tyballis stopped at once. She felt a peculiar black stone form in her stomach. 'Not the river,' she whispered. 'Please. Can we not travel by boat?'

He looked at her for a moment, eyebrows raised. He began to speak, then paused. Finally, he asked no questions and made no complaint, but clasped her hand tightly to the inside of his elbow. 'Very well,' he said. 'It is a long way. But we shall walk.'

They walked through the cheaps, heading west. It was mid-November, the third official day of winter, but the breeze was mild and the sky clear. The crowds squeezed through the narrow streets, pushing and gossiping, and the market stalls were busy with arguments over quality and price. Some of the younger women, seeing how Tyballis and Andrew Cobham were dressed, curtsied before hurrying on. Tyballis smiled for the first time that morning.

Tucked close to the tall pillars of St Paul's and within a few steps of the Ludgate, Warwyke Lane basked in wintry sunshine. Halfway along was a tall house, four proud storeys high. The dark beams and white plaster were newly painted, the gutter outside was clean and the street was affluent. Andrew Cobham paused before the shining windows and once again patted his small companion's hand. 'Not too tired?'

Tyballis shook her head. 'I enjoyed it. The weather is lovely, and I feel so well dressed. A merchant I've never met in my life swept off his hat and bowed. It's been quite an experience.'

Andrew chuckled. 'Then presumably you are prepared for what we need to do?'

Tyballis hesitated. 'We're going to the front entrance?'

'Did you think such an important couple should creep in through the stables?' Tyballis believed him, for not only were his clothes impressive, but Andrew Cobham's normal expression could appear positively fearsome. He kept her close as he knocked, and she thought him imperious; standing straight and tall as the echoes resounded within. The door opened. Tyballis tried to hold her head up, though she wore her hood pulled low and shrank a little into its shadows. Andrew Cobham stared down at the steward and said, 'You will immediately inform Mister Perryvall that I have come as expected.'

The steward bowed at once, and as Andrew and Tyballis followed him into the dark interior, he said, 'I will inform Mister Perryvall of your arrival, sir. May I bring your lady some refreshment? A little light beer, or some hippocras?'

'No,' said Mister Cobham. 'I have no intention of wasting time. You will tell Mister Perryvall that I am waiting.'

CHAPTER TEN

On the way home he bought her a hot pie. It had all started with a pie. This was pigeon thick with buttered gravy from the cookshop, but he did not let her eat it in the street. 'You are not wearing the clothes of a beggar or a stew-keeper's brat. You will behave as you are dressed. And I will not permit food spilled on that cloak.'

She looked up at him. 'It's a very nice cloak. And a very nice pie. It smells delicious. But it'll be cold by the time we get home.'

'No doubt,' he said absently. 'But since you have less appetite for river travel than for your dinner, you will have to accept the wait.'

Tyballis tucked her parcel – two warm pies neatly wrapped in linen – within the furred swathes of her cloak. 'Is this cloak yours?' she ventured. 'And is this ermine?'

'Don't be absurd,' said Mister Cobham, not pausing in his stride. 'I do not wear women's clothing, and we are not kings. The fur is miniver. But you may keep it.' He smiled suddenly, looking down at her. 'It seems I make a habit of presenting you with capes of various designs, however inappropriate.'

'I can keep it?' disbelieved Tyballis.

'No doubt a little more attractive than the first,' he nodded. 'But equally unsuitable. No matter. Use it as a bedcover. But don't eat in it.'

'But if it doesn't belong to you,' Tyballis suggested, 'should you not give it back?'

Andrew once again appeared to be laughing. 'Quite impractical under the circumstances, my dear. You may now count it your own, and, within certain limitations, do with it what you will. But as you may need it again one day, I advise against gravy.'

It was late in the afternoon when they eventually arrived back at the house. Tyballis scurried up the stairs, quickly changed out of her grand new clothes and packed them with care into her empty coffer. She then flopped onto her bed, which creaked and swung a little, and ate her pie in a great hurry, not caring that it was cold. She licked her fingers and stared up at the beamed ceiling, reliving the excitement. But her thoughts were interrupted. Someone banged on her door and Davey Lyttle's voice reverberated. Tyballis let him in.

'I smell pies. My darling girl, you have raided Paradise, yet not invited me.' He was wearing a doublet embroidered in white roses on tawny duffel, loosely belted and so short it presented his legs in full graceful evidence; fashion's vanity. His hose were striped, his shirt was good bleached linen, and his hat was in his hand. 'I believe I've barely eaten since the great feast of eels five days back,' he said. 'Now, Mistress Tyballis, you cannot deny you have pies in your possession.'

She grinned. 'I don't. Not anymore.'

Davey shook his head sadly. 'I had hoped – but you have been out all day with our inestimable Mister Cobham, and come home many hours later with the aroma of food so strong, it tempts us from our doleful chambers. Only to find you have eaten every crumb?'

'One pie only.' She had not yet lit the fire, and the room was chilly. She crossed over to the hearth and bent, collecting a handful of twigs. 'Besides,' she said, looking back up at him, 'I thought you a gentleman of resource and ambition, Mister Lyttle. How is it you never seem to have a farthing to feed yourself?'

Davey came across to her and went down on one knee, pulling out his tinderbox and taking over the laying of the fire. 'A man's job, my dear girl, leave it to me,' he said. 'And as for ambition, I consider it a sad reflection on the human race and London's population in particular, that they are learning to lock their doors, keep their purses well tied and in their hands, and have even begun to hold their fellow man in suspicion. How am I meant to earn my fortune when the city's respectable multitude has developed sufficient intelligence to avoid me?'

Tyballis allowed him to build and light her fire, and stood back watching and warming her hands. 'You don't include me amongst the respectable multitudes, I assume?'

'My dear girl, you are above us all.' He bowed, smiling. 'Even our delightfully unrespectable Mister Cobham has taken you to his bosom.' As the flames gained strength, the gloom unravelled. 'And what, though perhaps I should not ask,' Davey said, coming to sit on the little window seat, 'have you been up to all day, Mistress Blessop? Don't tell me you and our admirable landlord have simply been taking the air together?'

'I shan't tell you anything of the sort, Mister Lyttle,' Tyballis told him. 'But nor shall I tell you anything else. My business is my own, and Mister Cobham's is his.'

Andrew Cobham had already discussed the possibility of her confiding in her new friends. 'I would greatly prefer,' he had said as they crossed through his gardens and approached the house, 'that you do not entertain my other tenants with the story of how we have spent this day. I must admit to being a man of secrets. And I am, let us say, jealous of my secrets. There are dangers involved, and I consider it wise to mitigate those dangers.'

She had shaken her head vehemently. 'I wouldn't say a word. All the people here are thoroughly dishonest. I don't trust any of them. They don't even trust each other.'

'I have no great pretence to being entirely honest myself,' he said with a sigh. 'I do not aspire to the humility of common trust. Although I have no intention of explaining the precise purpose of our expedition today, or the need for our subterfuge, you must have gathered that, falsehoods apart, I considered the occasion and its success particularly important. Naturally I have reasons, but my reasons are my own. One day I may tell you more. But I know my tenants well, and I know their levels of dishonesty. I ask you not to share my secrets with anyone else, either here or elsewhere.'

'I won't. I promise. Do you trust me?'

They had reached the doorway. He pushed open the doors and stood back smiling. 'No,' he said. 'But you may earn my trust, if you wish.'

Tyballis now took the chair beside the fire and smiled at Davey. 'Perhaps you'd prefer to tell me what you know about our landlord, Mister Lyttle. It seems most odd for a man with no wealth to own such a grand house, and then to open it freely to a parcel of beggars and thieves who pay him no rent at all. Mister Cobham is clearly a man of secrets. I don't wish to interfere with his secrets, but it is all rather intriguing. How long have you known him?'

Davey grinned. 'Long enough. Doesn't mean I know much about the man. He comes and goes, but goes more than he comes and he's certainly out most nights. Once I saw him burying something in the garden, but I never asked and never looked. I've a feeling our Mister Cobham might not be such a generous host should he ever consider his privacy threatened.'

Felicia Spiers peered around the open door. 'Tyballis, dear, such a nice fire. And the enticing smell of cooking.'

Both Tyballis and Davey shook their heads. 'Drew bought her a pie from the Ordinary,' Davey told Felicia. 'Eaten an hour back. We must content ourselves with the aroma alone.'

Tyballis stood and took Felicia's arm. 'But come in by the fire. I've no wish to be alone with Davey, I assure you.'

Felicia took the chair Tyballis had left. 'I shan't stay long. Poor dearest Jon, you know, is tired and quite unwell. He has been most helpful to me today, speaking to me most sympathetically about the baby's health, and has promised to assist me if little Gyles is sick again. But now my dear husband's quite exhausted and must rest. Naturally he's hoping I will return with supper, since we've had nothing at all for dinner. If dear Mister Cobham is at home now, perhaps I should go down and have a quiet word.'

'Well, he's in,' said Davey. 'But Mistress Blessop refuses to divulge what he and she have been up to for the best part of the day.'

'You should not be prying, Davey Lyttle,' said Felicia with a sniff. 'And since dear Tyballis is not anything at all like that good-for-nothing Elizabeth, I can only be sure they have been indulging in some entirely innocent pastime. Isn't that so, my dear?'

Tyballis nodded. 'And I'm exceedingly sorry Mister Spiers isn't feeling well. The children are fine, I hope?'

'They will be, if I find them something to eat,' Felicia said.

Margery Blessop had spent the past four days furiously attempting admittance into Throckmorton House and had finally achieved entrance through the kitchens. 'You're a tiresome woman, Mistress Blessop,' John Knody told her. 'And if you dare inform his lordship how you managed to set foot in his private quarters, I shall skewer you on the spit and roast you with onions for his dinner.'

Taking immediate advantage of the chief cook's benevolence before he changed his mind, Margery scuttled through the pantries and found the main hall unlit and empty. It was the steward, Bodge, who discovered her. Since she was closely examining a tall silver candlestick at that precise moment, her presence was not warmly received. The steward recognised the woman he had managed to get rid of several times already over previous days. Bodge had therefore taken hold of her arm and began to drag her towards the main doors. Margery Blessop wedged both heels into the Turkey rug and wrestled desperately.

His lordship the new Baron Throckmorton, hearing an unexpected commotion, entered his hall to find his steward in an unseemly struggle with an elderly and unknown woman. Her headdress had become unattached in the struggle, and she was red-faced from the exertion. On seeing the baron, she quickly flung herself at his feet.

'Oh my lord,' spluttered Mistress Blessop from the floorboards, 'I've come to explain the terrible death of your late noble brother. But this heartless man will not listen. I beg your lordship to hear my story. It is a matter of life and death, sir.'

Throckmorton regarded the dishevelled creature at his feet. Her hair was grizzled, her eyes were teary and her nose was large and damp. He resisted the urge to kick her. 'Get up, woman,' he objected. 'What are you blubbering about? Bodge, this female will first explain herself and then you will throw her out.'

Margery got up as far as her knees. 'I am Borin Blessop's mother, my lord. He was a loyal servant to your brother the baron, and never did him harm, I swear it.' Throckmorton made impatient gestures to his steward, and Margery gabbled on in a hurry. 'It's my daughter-in-law did it, my lord. That is, she murdered your brother, wicked harlot that she is. I can prove it, my lord. You can avenge your brother's death and exonerate my boy Borin at the same time. And,' she added quickly, 'overcome any possible accusation to your own noble self that might possibly arise when my dear son is proved innocent at his trial.'

Throckmorton sniffed. 'What are you blathering about, woman? You stink of garlic.' But he waved Bodge back.

'My Borin's wife,' Margery said. 'She's a hussy and a whore, and has murdered your brother, my lord. She had an assignation with him that night, a sordid business as you can guess, sir. I cannot know what went wrong, but perhaps he refused to pay her, since her services were no doubt of – inferior quality. So, she stabbed him. I can prove it.'

'You saw this?' demanded the baron in amazement. 'Or she confessed?'

'Not exactly,' Margery Blessop admitted. 'But what's the word of a whore against that of a respectable mother? Besides, I could force her to confess if I ever got my hands on her scrawny neck. She's been a blight on my house ever since she married my boy. And she was out all that night, out on her own in the rain and the dark. No decent woman tramps the cold streets of London on her own at night. Then she came sneaking back in the small hours, drenched to the skin and wearing a cape she'd stolen from some customer. A man's cape. Perhaps his lordship's.'

Throckmorton shook his head, hiding a small malicious smile. 'A vile creature indeed. And to think it was her I gave money to, just a few days afterwards. That was thanks to – well, enough of that. But I shall not forget – not him, interfering bastard. Nor the trollop.' The baron scratched his nose, imagining the pleasures of multiple retributions. 'What was it like, this cloak?' he asked. 'And where is it now?'

'A fine cloak, my lord, such as your brother might have worn. Crimson velvet, I seem to remember, and fur-trimmed.' Margery bit her lip. 'I noticed a bloodstain on it myself, where the poor sainted body was stabbed through, though being red on red as it were, was not immediately noticeable. But unfortunately, my lord, the cape is gone. The wench sold it. Got a tidy sum, and then ran away. And if you gave her some money from the kindness of your heart, my lord, then she took that, too. I've not seen her since. Left her own home, and abandoned her poor innocent husband starving in Newgate. Now that's proof of her vile guilt, if ever proof was needed.'

Harold, Baron Throckmorton pursed his lips and glared. 'Then you've neither bloodstained cape nor culprit to hand me,' he said. 'This is a useless story.'

'My lord,' Margery persisted. 'I shall stand up in court and swear this doxy admitted to me in the morning what she'd done in the night. I saw the blood on the cloak myself – as I said, a thick red velvet cloak with dark fur, it was – I'm sure you could corroborate that your good brother owned just such a one, my lord. I seem to remember his fine figure wearing exactly that in the past. And if we can arrange for my poor boy's release, I will get him to find the wretched trollop, and beat the truth out of her. She can't be gone far.'

'I shall hunt her down,' said Throckmorton with quiet satisfaction. 'I will not allow my brother's murder to go unpunished.'

CHAPTER ELEVEN

The straw smelled musty with rat urine and poultry droppings, but it was dry and had blown thick where it banked at the back wall of the stables and into the corners. There had been no horses for a very long time though the straw had once been theirs. Tyballis was searching for fresh laid eggs.

Outside it had begun to rain and the chickens were seeking shelter as she was. The slosh and pound pelted over the wooden roofs of the outbuildings and cascaded outside the open doorways. The stables had all lost their doors where broken hinges had never been repaired. Some stalls had kept their divisions. Others had tumbled altogether, straw, splinters and planks hiding the horse manure so old it had turned to straw itself.

The hens were fussing and pecking through the upturned bales. Tyballis waved off the squawking of wet feathers in her face. Careful not to kneel or stand where eggs might have been laid, she had no wish to break her last chance of supper. Digging deep, she was almost upside down when she heard the noises. First the heavy footsteps, running in from the rain. Laughing. A woman. Then the crash as someone hurtled down onto the straw, and a smaller thump as someone else landed on top.

Two people laughing. 'You're sodden, girl. Get your clothes off.'

'Such a naughty suggestion, Mister Cobham, considering what a good girl I am, as you ought to remember. And what if I catch a cold?'

'Don't be foolish, my dear.'

'How ungallant, Drew. But – if you promise to keep me warm,' said the woman's voice, 'then perhaps – if you help me undress.'

'What I have in mind should keep you warm enough.'

Tyballis dared not move. With straw in her hair, dust up her nose, her skirts around her thighs and stalks scratching her legs, she sat as still as she could and hardly dared breathe in case she sneezed. The hens were squabbling. Their noise, she hoped, would disguise any of her own. The sounds of energetic movement and laughter from the adjacent stall were also increasing. She clutched her basket to her lap, two small white eggs nestled within it.

The girl giggled. 'Drew, you're tearing the hooks of my gown. Wait. Will you promise me something first?'

There was a pause. 'Unlikely, my dear,' said Andrew Cobham. 'I never make promises.'

'I believe you're going to be unpleasant again, Drew. If you are,' said the girl, 'I shall leave you here and go back into the house.'

'A terrible threat indeed.' The man chuckled softly. 'So tell me what you're after, Elizabeth, that's so different from the usual. I already give you enough for food and anything else you need. My means are hardly unlimited.'

The rustling straw was stilled, the two bodies had settled and they spoke quietly. 'I don't want paying, Drew dearest. That makes me – well, you know what it makes me. I want – well, let us say – presents.' The woman's voice was plaintive. 'I heard you gave – that other female – presents. Clothes. Beautiful things.' Receiving no immediate answer, she continued, 'That skinny trollop's too young to be properly experienced. She can't be any better at it than me.'

Andrew Cobham sighed. 'You're a whore, my dear, why be shy of the word? I've no objections. Never have had.' He lay back, hands clasped behind his head. 'My own profession is one of the world's oldest, as yours is, and quite as disreputable. Must we argue niceties?'

'You never talk about your work, Drew.'

'No and won't now. I don't make promises, I don't discuss my private life and I don't answer questions. You know that.'

The sounds of upheaval again, and the female voice was muffled. 'Don't be horrid, Drew dearest. Can't I expect nice gifts too? And don't I have the right to be jealous?'

'No, my sweet, you don't,' Andrew said softly. 'Now follow through on your threat if you wish, and go back to the house. I shan't restrain or chase you.'

The girl had begun to sniff. 'Don't say that, it isn't fair. Make love to me Drew. That's all I want.'

'Then don't cry, Lizzie.' There was still laughter in his voice. 'False tears don't mix with passion, my dear, and too much playacting will have me losing inclination altogether, which will do neither of us any good.'

She continued to sniff. 'Drew, you never lose all inclination.'

'Then come here,' he answered, 'and I shall keep one promise at least.'

'You will? Which promise, my love?' She was suddenly excited.

'To keep you warm,' he said. 'Your skin is puckered blue in the cold. Come here.'

The sounds that followed made Tyballis increasingly uncomfortable. She wondered whether she might make some sort of careful retreat. She began to edge forwards.

'Oh, Mister Cobham,' crowed the woman's voice. 'You are – you are—'

But Tyballis had underestimated the depth of the straw. She had crawled only a short distance when the debris beneath her collapsed and she tumbled through, feet in the air. When she scrambled up, she first had to put down her basket in order to push back her hair from her face and tug her skirts back over her legs. She managed both, took a deep breath and looked up.

A very tall man, entirely naked, was standing on the other side of two rickety planks, once the division between the stalls. He was gazing down at her with uncontrolled amusement, the shadows emphasising the deep cut of his cheekbones and the slant of his broken nose. Beside and slightly behind him, a naked woman was trying to hide. Tyballis gulped. Andrew Cobham appeared completely unconcerned regarding both his nakedness and her embarrassment. He said, 'I believe you have a hen on your head.'

Tyballis escaped. Outside the rain was a freezing torrent. She had forgotten the eggs.

She was sitting on the floor in front of her own little hearth and drying herself at the small fire she had lit, when her landlord made a personal visit to her chamber. He had brought her basket back to her. It was almost full of eggs. After knocking, he walked straight in, put the basket on her table, and said, 'On reflection, I decided you'd be more comfortable if I apologised.'

'Oh.' Tyballis stayed where she was.

His shirt, open necked and unbelted over his hose, was soaked. 'As it happens,' he continued, 'I'm not entirely clear regarding the precise nature of my apology. However, apologies may be considered appropriate. I don't normally choose to dance naked in front of respectable young women, especially those barely known to me.' He indicated the eggs. 'Bribery,' he said, 'to fog the inconvenient memory.'

'It's your house. I probably shouldn't have been there,' mumbled Tyballis.

'You shouldn't, as it happens,' he smiled. 'But stealing my eggs is a common enough practice around here, and I doubt I ever bothered to expressly forbid it. Every man, woman and child living in this house is a practised thief and I expect no different from you. Indeed, I hereby offer the free use of both eggs and outhouses at any time you wish. But perhaps you should make sure the place is empty of – all other activity first.'

Tyballis stared into the fire. 'That's kind, and thank you. Though since I was told I might freely collect herbs and salad greens and firewood from your garden, I assumed eggs would be free for the taking too.'

'And no doubt my pullets to pluck and boil whenever you feel inclined?'

'No, that's different,' blushed Tyballis, staring into her lap.

He came and sat on the small stool beside her, looking down at her discomfort. 'Don't let me tease you, little one,' he said softly. 'You are welcome to the eggs, and the fault was mine for not first checking the stables for any unexpected presence.' He waited until she looked back up at him, and smiled into her eyes. 'You did very well during our excursion the other day. I shall be pleased if you'll accompany me again tomorrow, though to a different house and with a different message. Naturally I'll explain the plan first. Will you do it, little one?'

She managed to smile. 'I'd like to. And I apologise as well. If you aren't embarrassed, then I shouldn't be either.'

'You made a point the other day of informing me you'd been married five years,' Andrew smiled widely. 'So you're not a child, for all that you look like one. I'm certainly not the first naked man you've ever seen.'

Tyballis stared back down at her toes. She had no intention of telling him how Borin had never undressed in his life, and had simply unfastened his codpiece and braies after he jumped into bed. 'Do I need to wear the grand clothes again?' she asked.

'Certainly. The marks on your face are finally gone, so there's no need to hide beneath a hood this time. Get Felicia to help you dress, since I doubt you'd allow me to touch you now. But this time your headdress and clothes must be exact and you will need to look the part.'

'Felicia,' Tyballis pointed out, 'will want to know what I'm doing and where the clothes came from.'

Andrew shook his head. 'She will ask no questions. Her family eats – most of the time – simply because she is discreet. Otherwise she'd be working for the tanners by now, or her family would starve.'

'Or Mister Spiers would have to get a job for once.'

'Highly unlikely.' He grinned, moving back towards the door. 'Tomorrow morning then, little one. Soon after dawn if you can be ready so early.'

'I promise,' Tyballis said. 'And I'm happy to keep my promises.'

CHAPTER TWELVE

I t was shortly after dawn the following morning, and Andrew Cobham was already waiting in the hall by the hearth as she had expected. He turned and looked at her searchingly in the glow of the firelight. Tyballis was impressed, though it seemed he was not. 'Do you comb your hair with your fingers, child? Come here, and stand still.' She did as she was told.

The early sun had not reached the western windows but Andrew Cobham's finery seemed even richer in the fire's dancing lights. He was dressed not in the shabby and worn velvets of their previous outing, but in black and persimmon silks, the neck and sweeping sleeves trimmed in sleek dark marten. The doublet was very short, pleated and laced in gold thread. Tyballis carefully did not look at his hose and kept her gaze studiously fixed across his right ear as he bent over her, adjusting the folds of her headdress.

'I tried very hard to dress properly,' she insisted. 'Felicia helped and it was her who combed my hair.' Then Tyballis hesitated, adding in a half-whisper, 'Felicia thought – she said – I looked – pretty.'

Andrew Cobham entirely ignored this timid plea for approval. He continued to re-pin her headdress and straighten the gauze veil across it. 'We have roles to fulfil today, child, and they are imperative. I will explain the details as we walk, but the most important thing to remember is that for today, I am Lord Feayton.'

Tyballis decided no one would dare doubt him. She took a deep breath. 'I'll remember,' she said. 'And who am I?'

'Lady Feayton,' he replied, pressing the last pin through the beaded wings of her headdress, and began to arrange the flow of her sleeves. 'You are my wife. A little young, and probably somewhat cowed, since I am no doubt an arrogant and insensitive husband. I doubt we share more than some fleeting affection, but you are presumably a dutiful companion. Now, hold out your hand.' She did so, puzzled and more cowed than he supposed. He turned her hand over and took her fingers in his. Then, onto her finger he slipped a ring, huge with amethysts. Tyballis stared at it in amazement. The jewels clustered in four squares along a thick gold band. She clutched her newly glowing hand with the other, staring down at the unaccustomed beauty. Andrew interrupted. 'It is not to keep, I'm afraid. But I think, for today, my wife should do me justice.'

'I don't see why,' Tyballis said as they walked, 'we have to be quite so grand, if we're only going to a horrid little house in Southwark.'

'We are dressed to impress, not to emulate the standards of our host,' replied her suddenly appointed husband. 'We will be meeting a man already well acquainted with the behaviour of his betters, who perfectly understands power and wealth even if he holds neither himself. Those who deal in corruption and treason themselves are always more inclined to be suspicious of the motives of others, but a title tends, absurdly, to reassure. We must convince this creature of our authority. Hence the subterfuge.'

'I don't think I could convince anyone of my authority,' admitted Tyballis.

Andrew Cobham smiled faintly. 'The authority will be mine. You are simply my ornament, and need only behave as such. You are also my protection.'

'Protection?' Tyballis wondered if he had gone quite mad. 'I don't think – I mean, I've never hit anyone in my life. Except Borin, of course, sometimes in defence, and he wouldn't feel anything anyway, not even if you hit him with a brick.'

'A different type of protection, child.' Andrew's mouth twitched. 'I doubt I shall require you to physically defend my honour. But first we need to cross the river for Southwark. Would you prefer to cross by wherry or by bridge?'

London Bridge was busy and the shops had opened. Crammed side by side, they had let down their shutters into counters and opened their doors to the first crowds an hour back. Now business was raucous and squashed, though edging a path between the shoppers was easier for a tall man wearing the clothes of a prince and the expression of a bishop.

Beneath the bridge, the tide ran low. The muddy banks slunk to their shingles and exposed the stark rising foundations of the planks holding back the waters. The wooden quays and their clambering ramshackle steps stood stark in the sludge but the noise below the bridge was as clamorous as that above. The wherrymen were touting for customers. Small boats barged and banged, oars poised and splashed, goods were piled high and travellers balanced in a hurry. A woman, toppled by the next boat's wake, dropped the half bread roll she was clutching and with a sudden flurry beneath the water's surface, the floating crumbs were taken by avid invisible mouths.

Despite the multitude of diverting fascinations to either side of her or the sudden wind blowing in from the estuary, Tyballis attempted to keep her head up. Never having previously worn anything grander than a linen cap or a hood, she worried that the sharp breezes would catch her veil. She would have liked to hold her hat on. Andrew forbade it. 'You will act the lady,' he reminded her, 'even here, where we are not known. London breathes gossip, and gossip, not money, oils its cogs. A young woman dressed as fine as a countess but behaving like a seamstress will attract notice whether she is aware of it or not. Her entrance into Southwark's slums would subsequently be noted, particularly since we have no accompanying retinue. I wish us to be noted for quite different reasons. So, straighten your back, hold your head up and raise your nose in the air to avoid the foul miasma of the river's stench. Do not scuttle, shuffle or hunch. I refuse to be married to a slouch, or a slattern. Hold gracefully to the crook of my elbow with only your fingertips and do not pinch at my sleeve or mark the silk as if afraid I might abandon you at any moment. With your other hand, you will gently lift the front of your skirts with two fingers at your waist, to avoid dragging your hems in the filth. Do not raise your feet too high at each step. You should appear to be gliding, not trudging, and you should not look as though you are more used to carrying bales of hay or buckets of water on your shoulders. You will not stare at those passing by but will regard them with utter contempt, and you will not gasp at the jewellers' or haberdashers' windows. You are neither credulous nor ingenuous. You are a lady, and will remember your dignity.'

Tyballis giggled. 'That's an awful lot of do and don't. Too many for my very small and obviously deficient faculties to digest. But I shall try my best.'

Once beyond the bridge's southern gate and into the tavern-lined streets of Southwark, Andrew Cobham increased his pace. The sky, already sullen with unshed rain, now glowered, barely seen between tall buildings. Each dark and slanted house frontage supported its neighbours, shedding old plaster and broken beams. The tiny windows held no glass and although some were paned in polished horn, most were only closed with oiled parchment. The dank shadows enclosed the stink of destitution and the central gutters were open sewers. Now Tyballis kept her head down.

Andrew turned abruptly and marched over the beaten earth and occasional cobbles of a tavern's stable courtyard. He waved the scurrying ostler aside and crossed to the far entrance, leading into an even darker corridor with narrow steps at the far end. He climbed the steps and at the top he turned right, facing another door, this time closed. He kicked it open and marched in. Tyballis followed close.

'Mister Colyngbourne,' Andrew Cobham announced. 'You have never previously enjoyed the pleasure of my company. You are about to get to know me rather better.'

In the middle of the chamber a stocky man sat at a small table, spooning pottage. He looked up, spluttering broth. 'What the—?' Seeing the style of his unwanted visitors, he jumped up and wiped his mouth. 'My apologies, my lord. My lady.' He bowed, stiff-kneed and nervous. 'But, with further apologies to the lady, may I point out that I am armed, sir, and my sword is at hand.'

'I've not come to kill you,' Andrew said pleasantly. 'At least, not yet.' He stepped forwards and took hold of the stool on which the man had been sitting. He swung it from the table and set it for Tyballis, nodding with a slight bow. 'Sit, my dear. We will not stay long. Mister Colyngbourne, I present my wife, Lady Feayton.'

'I'm honoured, your ladyship.' The man looked quite otherwise. 'But I must request an explanation, sir. I know nothing of your title or your mission.'

Andrew remained standing, looking down at the shivering man clutching the edge of the table. 'Neither my title nor my identity are any of your business,' he said, 'but my – mission – is of a far more serious nature. I am, let us say, personally acquainted with his lordship, Geoffrey Marrott, and also with her grace the queen's close relatives; her son the Marquess of Dorset, and his inestimable uncle, the worthy Earl Rivers. I have less personal knowledge of one Henry Tudor, but I know sufficient – once again, let us generalise – to be interested in what interests him.'

William Colyngbourne shook his head. 'I have no idea what you are talking about, my lord. You refer to four different noblemen of some considerable importance. I am not – to use your word – acquainted with these mighty lords. On the contrary, sir, I am, as you see, without means. I cannot at all understand why you are here.'

'Perhaps I should point out,' said Andrew Cobham very softly, 'that already you betray yourself. You refer to four noblemen. Yet I have spoken of only three – since Henry Tudor lives in exile, and his previous title is no longer recognised by the king. It is interesting that you refer to him otherwise.'

Tyballis sat straight and unmoving. Her bodice was tighter than she was used to, the small room was cold, she had walked a long way and she was a little frightened. She was also intrigued. Much shorter than Andrew but respectably dressed, the other man was clearly more nervous than she was. 'My lord,' he said, 'a slip of the tongue. I know nothing of such grand persons. Knowing nothing, I do not remember, or perhaps never knew, the many titles of the realm, nor of attaintings and politics since such matters hardly concern me. I am a humble man, my lord.'

'Humility,' said Andrew quietly, 'is the prerequisite of honest men. That does not describe you. Being ostensibly in service to the Duchess of York, your opposing affiliations seem particularly suspect. I know a good deal of your business, and am here to warn you that you are watched.'

William Colyngbourne once again shook his head. 'I am a tailor by trade, sir. Only that. Clearly you are mistaking me for another man entirely.'

'I doubt that, Mister Colyngbourne, I doubt it very much.' Andrew smiled. His hands were now on the back of the chair where Tyballis sat, and he was leaning over her shoulder. She could feel the warmth of his breath against her cheek. 'Let me make myself a little clearer, Mister Colyngbourne. I know the tentative aims and present plans of one Lord Marrott. Believe me, I know very well. And you have been seen – I have witnesses – frequently entering his court chambers. Strange, is it not, for such an honest, humble and common man? Even stranger, when I know full well that you carry messages from Henry Tudor in Brittany, and frequently take ship over the Narrow Sea. Yet Tudor and the Woodvilles are not natural allies. The servant of one should not by rights be the friend of the other, and the servant of her grace, the Duchess of York, should have no dealings with either.'

'My lord—'

Drew smiled a little wider. 'Remember that my lady wife is present, my good man, and she is witness to this conversation. Remember also that in killing me, you would also have to kill her. Both Lord and Lady Feayton done to death might seem a little – hard to hide, perhaps? And what, may I ask, will you explain to our retinue, which waits for us outside? Now, let us return to the conversation in hand.' Both men stood straighter now and neither smiled. Andrew continued, choosing his words with care. 'It does not take the cunning of a lawyer to realise that your master Henry Tudor is attempting, while keeping his own involvement entirely secret, to encourage Lord Marrott, close friend of the Woodville lords, in a certain course of action. I know exactly what that course of action is, my friend. Perhaps those grand lords, being close to his highness, know nothing of your aims. Perhaps they know, and do not approve. But remember, you are watched. You see, a recent shipment of certain noxious powders smuggled in from Venice was brought into London just a sennight gone. It was carried by a Flanders carvel into London's docks, having been imported by an Italian gentleman known to me. This interesting shipment of the powder known as arsenic never passed through English customs and its importation was accompanied by monies paid surreptitiously. It was secretly collected by one Thomas Yate, and then delivered personally to a Mister Perryvall. This final transaction was witnessed by a certain young female known to me. I spoke to Mister Perryvall some days ago, and produced my witness. Since it is perfectly clear that Perryvall is neither medic nor apothecary, such a quantity of a substance known to be highly poisonous if administered other than by a doctor, arouses suspicion and in particular when illegally imported into the country. Under the circumstances, he had no choice but to confess. I believe he has now left London for the north. He left in rather a hurry, but before he went he gave me your name, Mister Colyngbourne. Mister Perryvall did not, he claimed, know the eventual purpose of the smuggled arsenic. But I do. An interesting quandary, don't you think?'

'He lied,' spluttered the other man.

'Oh, I don't believe so,' said Andrew Cobham softly. 'You see, not only was my witness brought before him, occasioning a confrontation he could not deny, but I threatened Perryvall with certain disembowelment. Hung, drawn and quartered is the term I think, is it not?'

'You have no proof, sir.' Colyngbourne was shaking from both fear and fury. 'You presented Perryvall with a witness you say, but there is none to my so-called crime. I refute everything you have said of me. I have been engaged by Lord Marrott on occasion, but simply for the business of tailoring. His lordship, becoming rather more stout in recent months, has simply required an easing of the seams. I do not know the Earl of Richmond – Henry Tudor, as you say he is called now. But since I have some family in Brittany, I have indeed travelled there for personal reasons. Your threats do not frighten me, my lord. I am innocent of everything.'

'Then no doubt you will sleep very well tonight, my friend,' smiled Andrew Cobham with a slight bow. 'A clear conscience is, after all, the best armour a man can wear.' He reached out to Tyballis, his palm beneath her elbow as she stood again and moved to his side. He turned back once. Colyngbourne glared. 'But remember, and think on what I have said,' murmured Andrew as he opened the door. 'You will be watched, and you will be followed. Arsenic, as I am sure you know full well, can kill. It is even more dangerous than – high treason.'

He was smiling broadly as they went back down the stairs and out into the courtyard. It was raining again. Tyballis said nothing. Her feelings were too confused for words and she was not sure she yet understood them herself. Finally Andrew said, 'I hope you have enjoyed yourself, little one.'

'Oh, enormously,' retorted Tyballis. 'Acting a part I have absolutely no talent for, trying to look perfectly confident while quaking in my very tight new shoes, and finally being threatened with death! What more delightfully peaceful morning could I ever wish for?'

Andrew chuckled. 'The morning's entertainment isn't over yet, little one.'

'Of course, I should have guessed,' said Tyballis, ducking under the sleet. 'So, before I freeze, what new charms do you have in mind?'

'Frozen?' grinned Andrew. 'I've dressed you warmer than you've been since the womb.'

'But,' Tyballis nodded, 'my beautiful cloak will soon be sodden. I shall be wrapped in ice.'

'You are unaccustomed to luxury, my child,' Andrew laughed. 'The outer velvet will soak but the fur lining will stay dry and warm. Now, come here and stop complaining.'

Quite suddenly he pulled her into his arms and Tyballis was so startled, her headdress nearly fell off. But she had simply been drawn into the porch of an inn, its bustle, noise and heat billowing out beyond its doors. Although the squash was of standing customers, there were benches and two small tables at the back near the hearth, and it was here that Andrew led her, where the fire sizzled and spat.

They sat together, and at once, seeing their clothes and bearing, the landlord hurried over. Tyballis rubbed her hands together, careful not to lose her amethyst ring, now reflecting the flames. Andrew Cobham addressed the landlord. 'My good man, you will bring whatever you recommend as your very best,' he told him. 'Both food and wine for myself and my wife. I expect quality, and I expect speed. It is already past dinnertime.'

'Eating,' breathed Tyballis when the landlord had hurried off, 'in an inn. I have never – ever – done that before. Is this what you meant by the morning not being over yet?'

Andrew grinned. 'Should I let my poor wife starve? Especially after she has been so particularly dutiful, and played her part so well!'

'Did I do well?' She was pleased. 'But I just sat there.'

'You stared at the wretch with contempt, you acted with disdain and you looked both extremely superior and remarkably beautiful.'

Tyballis was astounded. 'I did?'

'You did indeed,' said Andrew. 'Now, ladies do not customarily frequent common taverns, but this inn is renowned for its dining and caters for those on pilgrimage to Canterbury. Your reputation will therefore remain intact. So, eat and drink, my dear. Though not to the extent of inebriation. If impelled to carry you across the bridge, I might just be tempted to throw you over.'

Her animation faded. A sudden rush of dark waves engulfed her memory, and she shut her mouth with a snap. 'I promise,' she muttered. 'I'm not used to good wine, so I'll drink very little.' He noted her change of expression but said nothing. The food arrived – cold meats, cheese and manchet, boiled tripe with cinnamon and radishes, and hot gingered rabbit in pastry – and while they ate, they spoke very little. Tyballis was, as usual, extremely hungry. Finally she said, 'I couldn't eat any more. Thank you.'

'Unusually polite,' he answered. 'Clearly you have not drunk enough wine. It's a good Burgundy, so must not be wasted. I retract my threat, and promise not to deposit you in the river.' She obediently drained her cup but shook her head when he offered the rest of the flagon. He drank it himself.

They had once more crossed the bridge and were approaching

home, now with less chance of being overheard, when Tyballis said, 'Will you tell me, who is to be poisoned, sir?'

Andrew Cobham looked down at her. 'I am no sir, my name is Drew, and clearly you are more cupshotten than I had supposed. I imagined you had understood the rules of this game already. No questions. No assumptions.'

'Is it a game?'

'A dangerous game. You are better off not knowing who, nor what, nor when, and never why.' He continued walking and was silent for some time. They had passed through the Aldgate, crossed London's wide defensive ditch, and the Portsoken Ward with its suffocating stench was before them when suddenly he said, 'You are a courageous child, Mistress Blessop, and deserve a better husband. One day perhaps you'll find your own Lord Feayton.'

Tyballis was startled. She wondered if he was cupshotten himself. 'I don't think I'm courageous,' she said. 'Or I'd have run away from Borin and Margery years ago.' She paused, before continuing. 'But it is my house, you see. I didn't want to lose it. Now I don't own anything at all.'

'I imagine,' Andrew murmured, 'you did not before. I presume your husband took over ownership of anything you had. You were not married with dower rights, I imagine, nor any arranged jointure?'

The rain had turned to a muddy drizzle and was ruining her new shoes. She sighed. 'No. You're right. My parents both died suddenly. Borin's mother took me in. Or rather – she moved in with me. But the house still felt like mine.'

There was a further pause, then Andrew said, 'I must warn you that this sudden desire to unburden your past will not be reciprocated. You are better off not knowing my secrets, little one. But if you wish to talk, we may do so at home, where it is warm and dry.'

CHAPTER THIRTEEN

He poured her wine and when she refused it, he pressed the cup into her hand. It was a grand cup, fluted and scrolled, and Tyballis suspected it was silver. 'Don't be foolish,' Andrew said. 'Drink and relax. I am not going to rape you. Talk to me if you wish. If not, then dream your own dreams into the firelight, as I do.'

'Do you do that?' She was interested. 'I do that too. Is that why you like such big fires, and have such a huge one burning all the time, even when you aren't at home?'

'We are here to talk about you, little one. Not me.' He leaned back in the deep chair, elbows resting on the high curved arms. 'Tell me how your parents died, and of your life, and your wretched husband and his wretched mother. Tell me your hopes, if you are young enough to have any left. And tell me if you would like me to get your house back for you.'

She sat up straight and stared at him. 'You could do that?'

'Talk to me,' Andrew said very softly. 'Close your eyes and lose your fears in the heat and the darkness. Drink your wine, forget me and talk to the flames in your head.'

The great hall felt more like home than ever, and the loss of her own had become somehow less tragic. The shadows flared, shot with foaming scarlet as the fire leapt and roared up the huge chimney.

Andrew Cobham lit no candles. They were not needed. Although it was only late afternoon, it was already winter dark beyond the unshuttered windows and the steady rain thrummed loudly against the glass. The fire lit the hall in its accustomed swelter. Tyballis sat, knees together, on a small stool as close to the flames as she dared. She drank and the wine also warmed her. 'My father was a corvisor,' she murmured. 'He made shoes and belts and supported the guild. He was well respected and twice he was taken as a bailiff's assistant. He even volunteered for the Watch. He never beat me and he used to tell me stories. I loved him.' She had taken off her shoes and stretched her stockinged feet to the blaze, her toes steaming as she wriggled them inside the wet woollen knit. 'Most days my mother worked in the brewers by Cripplegate,' she continued, half-dreaming. 'So, there was a good income and I was an only child. We were comfortably off and owned our own house. It wasn't a grand street, but we had the grandest house in it.'

'How old were you, child, when they drowned?' Andrew said.

The dream evaporated. 'How did you know they drowned?' Tyballis demanded. 'You don't even know their names.'

'Names are invariably unimportant,' he said. 'I use several myself, and none means a jot. But understanding lives is my business. You were ten? Eleven? You were with them in the boat, I presume, when it happened?'

She muttered, 'I don't want to talk about it, after all.'

'Remember your courage, child,' he told her softly. 'Misery is always better faced and pain admitted, before being safely hidden again. The pretence of forgetting festers like an untended wound. Every one of us has something we would sooner wash clean yet cannot, but no man lives long unless he owns his own shadows.'

A flagon stood on the stool at his side, and he had again filled both their cups. Tyballis lowered her eyes, watching without seeming to watch. Her heartbeat had quickened, an uncomfortable feeling which she both understood and repudiated. Now she drank without caring. 'All right. You're right about everything. I was eleven and they were drowned and I was in the boat with them. We were only going upriver a little way, but there was a jam by the bridge and it was high tide. The waves were big and smelly and one of the wherrymen was angry because he couldn't get through and he had an important fare. I can still remember his face.' She disappeared a moment, her nose in her cup. Then she spoke to the fire as she had been told. 'His eyes were mean and his nose was red-blotched and he shouted and swore at our boatman. I stared into his face and the next thing I remember, we were all underwater. Two boats went down. There was ours, and another one full of pigs. It was a pig I hung onto. It was frantic but it could swim and I couldn't, and it pulled me up to the surface. I saw my mother. Her skirts dragged her down, billowing out like barrels. Her cap had come off and the river filth was in her hair. I felt my father's hands. He was struggling to push me up onto a boat. Then he went back down for my mother. I never saw them again.'

Her voice trailed off, lost behind the crackle of burning logs. Once again her feelings confused her. She wondered if she was half-asleep, and for a moment seemed to be flying. Then the soft voice in her ear said, 'Don't cry, little one. Misery rarely repeats, and once related, always diminishes. Lean back and close your eyes. You have no need to continue. I can guess what happened next.'

She sniffed, vaguely aware of a velvet shoulder and the soothing softness of thick black hair against her forehead, the heat at her back and careful hands around her. She curled a little and closed her eyes as commanded. 'I don't remember it very well,' she whispered. 'But I remember the taste of river filth and I kept being sick. Someone ran to get the sheriff and Constable Webb came and collected me and took me home. That was when Margery and Borin moved in. They used to rent the top floor in the old lodging house next door, but my mother never spoke to them because they weren't respectable. I was too little to look after myself properly, but they didn't look after me properly either. I was an awful mess for a long, long time.'

'I assume you were forced to marry this charitable neighbour?' The voice was a soft tickle in her ear. 'Your father's guild did not claim you as ward?'

'The Blessops took me over first. They wanted the house, not me. Borin never liked me. I didn't like him either.'

'Brutality is the defence of the stupid.' Tyballis found her cup

82

refilled yet again, and then it was held enticingly to her lips. The soft voice continued. 'Drink, little one. It's time to forget again. Perhaps time to sleep.'

She nodded. 'But I don't want to go upstairs in the cold. I like the fire. It's so nice being warm and cosy. When I'm cold, I remember the water over my head pushing me down. And I did do the right thing, didn't I? Running away, I mean, even if I've lost my house.'

'You don't need my approval, child.'

'But it was you who told me to run away. No one ever told me to leave him before. People sympathised but they said, Be strong. Put up with it. A wife must obey her husband, and if he beats her, she must try harder. But you said, Leave him. And I did.' As she looked up it occurred to her that she was now curled on his lap, though she had no clear memory of how she got there. It didn't seem to matter. There was something else far more interesting that nagged at the back of her mind. 'It's the king, isn't it?' she said suddenly.

There was a short but noticeable pause. Then Andrew Cobham said, 'Perhaps you are not as drunk as I thought you.'

Tyballis, immediately pleased, said, 'Do you think that was clever of me?' Her voice, she decided, sounded quite distinct, and not at all like Borin's slurred mumbles when he was cupshotten. Indeed, she felt deliciously comforted and delightfully comfortable. Her head, however, had begun to spin. 'I worked it out,' she hurried on, 'about the poison, I mean. You keep saying you're not a lord or a sir, but it's the king you work for, isn't it? So, you are important.'

He chuckled and his arms loosened, allowing her to sit a little straighter. 'The people I work for are important, it is true. I am not. And at present I answer not to the king, but to his brother. But I can tell you nothing else, child, and hopefully you will have forgotten all this entirely once you are sober.'

Tyballis frowned. 'I do understand. Borin used to work for a real baron, but Borin certainly wasn't important. People owed the baron money and if they didn't pay up, Borin would go and hit them until they did.' She tried to focus on her host's eyes but found that, inexplicably, this was increasingly difficult to achieve. 'But I'm not tipsy,' she insisted. 'Borin used to get drunk all the time, so I know what it sounds like and I don't sound like that at all. Listen. I can talk perfectly well and I know exactly what's happening. Though I'm not sure I should be sitting on your lap and I'm not sure how I got here.'

'You were crying,' he explained gently, though she thought she heard him laughing. 'And your voice is neither perfectly clear nor at all sensible. On the other hand, your guess about the king was inspired. Now, shall I put you to bed?'

'That would be even more improper,' she said, voice muffled as she leaned back, accepting the comfortable security of his embrace. 'Even though,' she added politely, 'you do look very nice in those clothes.'

Now he was certainly laughing. 'Most kind,' he murmured. 'Drink a little more and I might become almost attractive.'

'Um,' said Tyballis, and fell asleep against his shoulder.

CHAPTER FOURTEEN

Someone was banging on the door. It seemed as though the banging was on the back of her head. Opening her eyes hurt, but she struggled up and put her mind back together. It was cold, dawn was oozing in pink streamers through her window and she was in bed, tucked under new woollen blankets she had never seen before, but safely back in her own chamber. She seemed to be wearing nothing at all and her beautiful clothes of the previous day were neatly folded on top of her coffer across the room. She had a splitting headache and someone appeared to be trying to break through her door. She shouted, 'Go away,' which made her head hurt even more, but the banging stopped abruptly so she turned over, curled once again into the feathered warmth and went back to sleep.

It was late when she got up and her head was still hurting. Of yesterday's interesting daytime, she remembered it all but she had only a clouded and contradictory recollection of the evening. Where memory transposed, certain small instances and the doubts they awakened bothered her extremely. Finding herself quite naked beneath her bedcovers also troubled her, since getting to bed at all seemed to have happened without her conscious co-operation. She decided she needed both food and answers, and wanted very much to speak to Andrew Cobham. So she dressed in her old gown and tiptoed downstairs.

Daylight, though dull and cloud swept, had brightened each long window and Tyballis immediately saw someone standing in the half shadows at the bottom of the steps. He was watching her and waiting. It was not Andrew Cobham and she had never seen him before in her life.

The young man did not speak until she came down beside him. Then he said quietly, 'Mistress Blessop? If it is you, since you so entirely fit the description I was given, I carry a message from Mister Cobham. Will you come into the hall, mistress, where we can speak in warmth and privacy?'

The suggestion of warmth was always pleasant but Tyballis shook her head. 'I don't know you, sir. Where is Mister Cobham?'

'That is part of the message,' said the young man. The fire in the hall blazed unwatched and unheeded, and here Tyballis eventually followed the unknown messenger. He stood while she sat by the hearth, and cleared his throat. 'I am Luke Parris,' he said, 'and we have not met before, but I also live here and lodge in the attic chambers. I do not – socialise much – with the other tenants, but Mister Cobham knows me well. I must apologise, mistress, both for waking you earlier this morning, and for refusing your invitation to dinner in the past.'

'Oh,' said Tyballis. 'You're him.'

The young man smiled suddenly. 'The mad monk. Yes. That's me,' Luke said. 'Andrew – Mister Cobham – left London at dawn and will be gone for some days. He has taken a carrier to Wales, and particularly wished me to tell you he must travel to Ludlow, as if it might mean something to you. He told me nothing else, except that he thanks you for your help and your company and will return when he can. And,' Luke reached to the small purse hanging at his belt, 'he asked me to give you this.'

Tyballis received the full leather weight in her palm. She was surprised, and guessed the sum contained was a large one. Then something occurred to her, and her fragments of disconnected memory suggested another kind of payment for another kind of service entirely. She blushed, and tied the purse strings to her belt in a hurry. She asked, 'He explained nothing else?'

'Nothing, mistress.'

'And did he,' she continued, 'ask that this information – this message – be kept secret from the others?'

Luke smiled. 'Mister Cobham said only that you would know his wishes.'

'Mister Parris, you said you recognised me from his description.' Tyballis kept her face down. 'What exactly was – if you don't mind – that description?'

Luke frowned. 'The very words, mistress? Small and slim with large blue eyes, a pointed chin, and the expression of a startled and much bullied child.'

'Oh.' She thanked him and scurried back to her room, relieved to see no one else on the way. Then she lit her own little fire and sank down beside the hearth to untie the purse strings. Ten coins rolled across the boards and settled with a rattle and clank amongst the rushes. There was considerably more than she had guessed, for each coin was a florin. Only once had she ever seen a florin before, and now she owned ten of them. A sense of absolute unreality overwhelmed her and she sat quite still for sometime, finally heaping the gold into two identical little piles on the floor in front of her. When someone again banged on her door, she threw her money back into the purse in such a rush that she felt quite guilty, as if it was stolen. It then occurred to her that it probably was. She tumbled the purse into her coffer, snapped shut the lid on money and clothes, and hurried to her door.

'You, mistress,' said Davey Lyttle, 'have been talking to that Godless pederast from upstairs. I warn you, he's the worst of us. Trust no one and none of us in particular, darling, but that heathen least of all.'

'I suppose you'd better come in,' Tyballis said. 'And Luke only gave me a message from Drew. That's all. He says Drew's gone away for a few days.'

'Happens regularly,' nodded Davey. 'Nothing new in that. In the meantime, I was wondering if you had any food on the boil. I've a hunger big enough to use as a dye tub, and a gut as empty as Jon Spiers' ambitions.'

'I have eggs,' remembered Tyballis. 'And I was thinking of exploring Drew's kitchen for stale bread or cheese. And there is – at least there was – a haunch of salted bacon hanging from the beams in the pantry.'

'That's it then,' grinned Davey, reaching for her hand. 'Bring your eggs, girl, and we shall raid Drew's domain. But quietly now. I've no wish to alert the others.'

Tyballis hesitated. 'But if the others are hungry—'

'My dear child, they are all permanently hungry,' Davey told her. 'But if we share, there will not be enough for us. It's a feast I need, not a damp morsel.'

'I shall cook enough for us and the children too,' Tyballis objected, 'and the others can help themselves after we've finished.'

'What you set out for the children will instead be eaten by their father,' Davey pointed out. 'And whatever is left over, might feed a lucky mouse if it hurries. Now,' he led the way downstairs, 'where did our lord and master say he was going? And why, in particular, did he send his message to you? I see I shall have to watch you more closely from now on.'

His teasing was too close to her own discomforting doubts. 'If you want my eggs and my cooking skills,' she told him, 'you can mind your own business.' It was later when they sat together on either side of the benched kitchen table that Tyballis asked, with apparently casual disinterest, 'By the way, Davey. You're a man of experience and must know the lie of the land. Ludlow, I believe, is in the Welsh Marches. I've heard of a grand castle there. Does the king visit?'

'Ignorant wench,' Davey said, gulping crumbs. 'I cannot imagine why you dream of Ludlow, since it's a windy wet place with more crags than valleys, and overlooks the damned Welsh hordes who never cut their hair and don't know how to say their prayers. They eat babies for breakfast in Wales, you know, and light their fires with dragons' breath.'

'It sounds even worse than Scotland,' agreed Tyballis, awed. 'So why would anyone want to go there?'

88

Davey mopped up the egg yolk with his crusts. 'For the king's boy, idiot girl, who was made Prince of Wales. Our blessed monarch's eldest son lives there and his household inhabit the castle, though I pity them. The draughts must whistle under every door and blow out every candle.'

'So the king does live there sometimes?'

'Certainly not. He has more sense. Our glorious King Edward lives at Westminster with the occasional hop to Windsor and back when he's bored staring at the same old thrones and golden chalices and wants a change. It's his son, as I told you, being the next little Edward, who is stuck there in the west. I guess a Woodville or two looks after the brat since the queen's brother is the prince's tutor, and you can find a Woodville lurking wherever there's money and power to be had.' He regarded Tyballis with curiosity. 'Now, just why should you need to know all this, miss? Not planning on saddling your fine palfrey and leaving us, are you?'

'Don't be silly,' Tyballis sniffed. 'If I ever had a palfrey, which I never did, I'd have sold it by now. I've never even sat on a horse, as I'm sure you know. It was just – well – it was Luke who said he was thinking of going to Ludlow. Perhaps he wants to be a priest after all, and convert those Welsh heathens you were talking about. I was interested.' She paused, wondering how many lies she might get away with. 'So,' she added, collecting the two wooden trenchers for washing, 'who exactly is this little prince's tutor?'

'Earl Rivers, the queen's brother,' Davey told her, screwing up his very fine nose. 'Who is said to be a nobleman of great chivalry and book learning, a master of the joust and a mighty statesman of culture and skill. He is also well known as a paragon of virtue and of strict religious adherence. And you will certainly never meet him in your life, my dear.'

'Is he,' wondered Tyballis, choosing her words with continued care, 'the king's brother?'

'Are you deaf?' demanded Davey. 'Earl Rivers is a member of the Woodville family, the queen's brother. The king's only remaining brother is Richard of Gloucester, the hero of the recent Scottish wars, another paragon of courage and virtue – indeed, there are far too many of them – and someone else you will most certainly never meet. But these are strange questions. I'm beginning to suspect you of ulterior motives, Mistress Blessop.'

'Nonsense.' Tyballis hoisted up the larger platter from the table. 'Now I'm going to take the rest of the food up to the Spiers. I shall no doubt see you later, though I suppose now you won't bother to visit until you're hungry again.'

The weather worsened as a gale blew in from the east. By December the sixth, the Christmas season officially began, though only one person at the ragtaggle Portsoken palace had the means to celebrate St. Nicholas' Day and she was keeping her money secret and safe. A flurry of seasonal black storms followed the gale, a slime green sky persistently threatened snow, and lightning tweaked the clouds into sudden displays of white firecrackers. By mid-December, Andrew Cobham had still not returned from Wales and Tyballis wondered many things.

Without the distraction of their landlord's presence and without the swelling ferment of his constant fires, the chilly household rattled and rummaged its best, more whine than whim and more desperation than daring. Sometimes, early and unseen, Tyballis hurried out to the markets and bought what produce she thought might feed the most without causing suspicion, then ate what she wanted herself and took the rest to the Spiers. The children thrived. They bounced down the stairs on their damp padded bottoms, climbed the balustrade and tumbled howling, slid the polished tiles in the hitherto forbidden kitchens, and crawled the boards before getting splinters in their knees and collapsing in wails of contrition. One day Tyballis discovered Gyles in her chamber attempting to pick the lock of her coffer. Since he was only two years old, she thought him unnecessarily precocious, stifled his yells with her hand as he tried to bite her finger, tucked him up under her arm and called for Ellen. Calling for Felicia would only have caused offence for any hinted criticism of her offspring, while calling for

Jon would have brought no answer whatsoever. Ellen, however, always came running. Davey Lyttle also made sure he was not forgotten, while Ralph and Nat were a bustling breeze in and out. Tenant unity was gradually strengthening but she saw Elizabeth rarely and she saw widower Switt only when passing on the stairs. When not wishing to be alone, she invariably sought the company of the Spiers, but it was Davey who sought hers. The next time Luke Parris found her, she was in the garden, on her knees and almost under a bush, and was not, in her own opinion at least, presenting her best side.

From behind her, Luke said suddenly, 'The hens are no longer laying, Mistress Blessop. In deep winter they take to the sheds and we find barely an egg for all their squawking. Andrew usually shuts them in, for there's a danger from wandering foxes.'

Tyballis scrambled to her feet. 'Thank you, Mister Parris. In truth I was searching for winter herbs and salads.' Her basket was already full of nettles and dandelion leaves for soup, a small handful of acorns previously overlooked, some twigs of wild thyme and the bulbous root of an onion.

'I learned about the distillation of medicinal herbs in the monastery,' nodded Luke. 'The monks prized valerian. But I learned about the herbs that kill as well, and you, mistress, were under a thorn apple bush, which is far better avoided.'

'So you were a monk?' said Tyballis, intrigued. 'I thought that was just one of Davey's silly stories.'

'I was never ordained. A novice only, and that was against my will.' He frowned. 'I left. Mister Cobham found me.'

'Drew has a habit of finding people in need,' smiled Tyballis. 'But now I can't find him. Has he still not come back from the Welsh Marches?'

'Not as far as I'm aware,' Luke said. 'Though he's not a man who usually chooses to discuss his business with others. His message to you was unique, mistress. I've never known him to tell anyone else here where he's going, or why, and only rarely discusses small matters with myself.'

Walking back together to the house, Luke carried the basket. As they took the stairs, Tyballis indicated the hall and its darkened chill. 'See. No fire! He cannot be back, and it's almost Christmas.'

Keeping her hoard of gold a secret made buying supplies difficult. There was not a soul in the house who would not leap to the challenge of the intrigue if they suspected her of hidden wealth, but Tyballis bought and cooked sparingly, adding grains and roots to make each dish feed more for longer. That she had some money from time to time was obvious, but it seemed, she thought sadly, that a woman's coin was generally presumed to have come from the solitary source that everyone expected.

And so buying, planning and cooking became the distractions that Tyballis used to escape from her own thoughts. Thinking of him was, after all, another road to hopelessness. What she was beginning to want beyond all else, was what she knew could never happen.

CHAPTER FIFTEEN

In spite of arousing probable suspicion concerning the source of her wealth, Tyballis decided on a Christmas feast. At first, as the one person already aware of the money she had received from Andrew Cobham, it was only Luke with whom Tyballis discussed her plans. Evidently the household had never before celebrated together, but Tyballis remembered when she was little, and her father had been sufficiently affluent to obtain at least some belly of salt pork, onions and spiced suet dumplings each Christmas, and often a good deal more. She now planned something even grander. 'I shall spend tomorrow at Cheapside,' she told Luke. 'It will be the first time in my life I've bought so much food all at one time, so I shall enjoy every moment.'

'You will need help with the baskets.' Luke said at once.

Tyballis shook her head. 'You and I? Away for the whole day together? It would arouse the anger and suspicion of every single person in the house. Thank you, but I've long practice at coping alone, Mister Parris.'

She then searched out Mistress Spiers, and between them they decided upon the requisite type and number of ingredients to feed the inhabitants of the house. 'There are nine of us altogether, and the children of course,' said Felicia. 'Unless Elizabeth brings her brother, in which case there'll be ten. But I hope she doesn't, since I prefer not to speak to the horrid man. Not that I usually speak to her either, but I shall make an exception for Christmas.'

'You see, I have a little – very little – money saved,' admitted Tyballis, 'for precisely such occasions. But please don't tell anyone or I shall have Davey and Nat sneaking into my chamber and poking under the mattress.'

Felicia smiled with superior sympathy. 'Your secrets are safe with me, I assure you. Not one of us would dream of condemning your – ingenuity, or your methods, my dear. Especially while you are so delightfully generous with your, let us call them – profits. I should never compare you to that horrid Elizabeth, not for a minute.'

Tyballis hiccupped. 'It's not like that, Felicia. But I'm determined we shall all have a wonderful Christmas and eat and eat and eat. I'm going to buy ale, and maybe wine too for making my own hippocras.'

'I shall accompany you to market,' Felicia said at once. 'You will certainly need my advice.'

Imagining the difficulty of hiding her gold florins, Tyballis promptly shook her head. 'Please don't take offence,' she said. 'But for me this is an adventure, and I should really prefer to savour it alone.'

Two days before Christmas Eve, the city was jostling. The cheaps were busier than they had been for months and all along the Shambles the butchers displayed sheeps' heads, stuffed intestines, hams, plucked geese, smoked bacon and haunches of pork, far more than was usual at any other time during winter. A thin sleet iced the streets, and from the Poultry up into Cheapside where the stalls narrowed the road to a bare trickle of passageway, the cobbles shone and feet slipped. But the mood remained cheerful and Tyballis clasped her basket, pulled her cape over her head and squeezed between the clamouring crowds. Having decided to steal her landlord's pullets, she avoided the Poultry, made for the clustered counters from Old Jewry to Honey Lane by the conduit, and began to choose many interesting ingredients for the coming feast.

A troop of jugglers paraded and the spectators were tightly packed. Tyballis used her elbows and squeezed through, wondering if she would spy Davey or Nat nearby, for it seemed an ideal spot for a cutpurse. Keeping a wary hand on her own purse, she headed up towards Ironmonger Lane.

Shops were bright with novelties, painted puppets, tin whistles and wooden hoops, ideal Epiphany gifts. A barrow from the Ordinary was selling hot pastries and a stall keeper was sluicing down the blood where it had collected around his boards. Tyballis was avoiding both blood and water when a group of horsemen thundered by, sending every shopper scrambling to the walls.

The cantering horses splashed up muck and wet debris from the gutters; the leader, glorious in embroidered brocade and more fur than a baited bear, laughed with his companions riding hard at his side. One was an unusually tall man, wide-shouldered and dressed in mahogany velvet with a swirl of coat-tails lined in persimmon silk and trimmed in marten. He sat at ease in the saddle with only one hand to the reins, the other resting on the heavy silver of his belt buckle. His huge sleeves draped almost to the ground, sweeping the horse's flanks. Both men's hats sparkled with raindrops, but a greater brilliance shone from the golden collars across their chests, the signature of the royal House of York.

In just a few moments they were gone, disappearing up the Cheapside into Goldsmith's Row. There were flecks of filth on her nose and cheeks but Tyballis made no attempt to wipe her face. She simply stood in churned mud and stared in silence at the place the horses had been. She had not recognised the elegant gentleman leading the party, but she knew one of his companions very well. How Andrew Cobham had acquired a great bay hunter saddled in fine soft leather and decorated with ribbons and silver buckles, she had no idea. The Portsoken stables housed only chickens and old straw, and Mister Cobham was supposed to be in Wales. She could not assume that the gold collar across his breast was worth any less than the ten florins he had inexplicably given her, and she had no idea where he could have found anything so incredibly precious, nor how he had the courage to openly wear it.

Feeling somehow very small, Tyballis turned away. It had been a shock. She had wanted, so very much, to see him again. Now the thrill died, like cold ashes after the fire. But immediately she found herself facing someone else she knew very well, and had equally not expected to see. Margery Blessop squealed and grabbed.

'Whore. Where've you been hiding? I've got you now.'

Tyballis gasped, turned and turned again. The crowd pushed forwards. One stall holder, belligerent but eager, yelled, 'Stop, thief.'

Arms reached for her. Although five years married to a petty criminal, and now the companion of thieves living in what seemed little more than a den of dishonesty, Tyballis had never in her life expected to be the centre of a hue and cry. She made no attempt to run, though this appeared to disappoint the crowd, which shouted repeatedly for her to stop. Instead she was held firm by both her mother-in-law and the firm officialdom of Assistant Constable Webb.

Robert Webb looked apologetic. 'I'm sorry to have to inform you, Mistress Blessop,' he said with slow deliberation, 'but 'tis my duty, not being neither by choice nor pleasure, to arrest you in the name of the law.'

Tyballis gulped. 'What have I done?' she whispered.

'Murder and mayhem,' nodded the assistant constable. 'I'm taking you in, Tyballis Blessop, for the wicked slaughter of his lordship, Baron Throckmorton, God rest his soul, though no doubt He won't, since I'd wager the wretch will wander many a long year lost in Purgatory. Reckon there'll be few honest citizens saying prayers in his memory. But being a miserable miserly bastard up to his scrawny neck in nasty deeds with a whole mire of sins to repent don't make nobody worthy of being done in, nor left to bleed out in the gutter while the ravens peck his eyes out. So, along you comes with me, mistress, and we'll see what the courts make of it.'

Throughout this speech Tyballis stared in confusion. Finally she mumbled, 'You've already got Borin for it. You think it was me, too?'

'Once you go in,' Mister Webb nodded, 'Borin comes out. Not of my doing, but it's not me as decides the law. So, let's get it over with and come quiet, which will be the easiest for all of us.'

Tyballis made no attempt to escape, but she quickly loosened the leather strings at her belt. She had brought a full florin to market in addition to the several pennies' change from her previous purchases, and this hoard was still untouched. Should it be found on her, how she came into such wealth would arouse serious suspicion. Its ties surreptitiously released, the heavy purse fell to the cobbles. Someone else might profit at least, which certainly was preferable to adding accusations of theft to her supposed list of crimes.

But she was too late. The money jangled as it hit the street. 'What's that?' yelled a stall keeper. 'The wench has throwed something.'

Amid a scrabble of other fingers, Robert Webb bent and retrieved it. 'A fine full purse this is, mistress, for the likes of you.'

Tyballis sighed. 'It's not mine. It was given to me. I was – shopping for someone else.'

'And who'd that be, then, since you don't know nobody?' demanded Margery Blessop, pushing forwards. 'Lest it's whoring has brought in a sight more than you're worth. It's more likely stolen.'

'Tell us who give it to you, my girl,' nodded Webb. 'Don't be frightened, now.'

Tyballis shook her head. She hesitated, remembering the small cavalcade of mounted men, their sumptuous clothes and their golden collars. Then she said, 'No one. I can't and won't give his name. Accuse me of stealing, if you like. Since it seems I've been accused of murder, a little larceny is hardly going to make much difference.'

CHAPTER SIXTEEN

She sat very straight, feet together, hands clasped in her lap, and stared meekly down at her toes. Assistant Constable Webb stood solid behind her, and facing her across the table was Sheriff Wharton. The sheriff said, 'Oh, for pity's sake, girl. There's no rhyme nor reason in denying it anymore. I've my dinner waiting and getting cold, with my wife expecting me an hour back. Own up to it and let's be done.'

'I'm hungry, too,' muttered Tyballis.

Assistant Constable Webb cleared his throat and looked with caution at his superior. 'I could go get us all a bite to eat from the Ordinary, if you'd allow it, Mister Sheriff.'

'Certainly not,' sniffed the sheriff. 'This is no charity hospice. The girl must confess, it's as simple as that. Then we can all get back to our own homes.'

'Except me, of course,' said Tyballis, looking up. 'Where are you planning on throwing me? Newgate?'

Robert Webb leaned over her shoulder and spoke with some sympathy. 'It's his lordship himself has laid charges, mistress. There's no way it can be ignored, you know. But maybe, if you'd admit to some part at least, with mitigating circumstances perhaps, then maybe we could keep you here for a while rather than Newgate and the shackles. At least until the trial.'

'Mister Webb,' the sheriff interrupted with severity, 'has been pleading your case with me all morning, ungrateful girl. I've agreed, if you're cooperative, to keep you out of Newgate for the time being.'

'We all knows what goes on in Newgate,' mumbled the assistant constable. ''Specially to young women. It's a lot easier here in Bread Street, and I could keep an eye out for you whenever I can. You know what it's like since you've visited your wretched husband here often enough in the past.'

'I would appreciate it.' Her back ached and she could no longer sit straight. 'But how can I confess to something I didn't do? It would mean – I think it would mean – hanging within the fortnight. Do you expect me to sign my own death warrant?'

The sheriff frowned. 'With the Constable of the Ward absent, you have the advantage of the assistant constable's existing acquaintance. But don't force my patience, foolish girl. I have other business to attend to today, so tell us the truth, and be done with it.'

'I have already, sir.' Tyballis shook her head. 'I've admitted I was out very late that night. I ran away, you see – from my husband. He was beating me. But I never saw his lordship, neither alive nor dead. I was acquainted with the baron, of course, since my husband worked for him. But that night I saw nobody. I got home very late and I slept downstairs by the hearth. Then Constable Webb came for Borin in the morning.'

'So, why implicate your poor husband, then?' demanded Sheriff Wharton. 'Since you knew quite well he was innocent? It's a small wonder the poor man beats you. A vindictive trollop it seems you are, my girl.'

The shaking of her head became a little wild. 'I didn't implicate him. I only said I couldn't swear to where he was all night, which was true because I never went to his bed. But I thought he was innocent, too. Borin never liked blood. He used to faint away at the sight of it, both his own and other people's, too.'

The sheriff leaned across the battered table. 'But there's more to this business than you're letting on, isn't there? It's your own mother-in-law has given information as to your usual habits, and nasty sordid habits they are too, mistress. And what about this cloak you came home with, then? His lordship's own velvet cloak, identified by the new baron himself. How did you get that, then? Are you trying to say it was pure coincidence you being out the same night his lordship was murdered almost on your doorstep? And you wearing his bloodstained cloak about your miserable shoulders!'

Tyballis stared at him. 'I don't understand. There isn't a coincidence because one thing has nothing to do with the other. And I've never seen his lordship's bloodstained cloak. I wasn't wearing any such thing.'

'More lies,' sighed the sheriff. 'Seems there's no point talking to this trollop, Webb. It's simply a waste of time and my dinner's ruined already. Throw the wench into Newgate.'

'By your leave, sir,' said the assistant constable, one hand heavy on her shoulder, 'you let me keep her here and I'll watch her close and get the answers we need over time. Begging your pardon, sir, but I've knowed her a long time and she's a good girl. We both knows what'll happen if we chucks her in Newgate's Limboes. Savage buggers they are in there, and they'll have her soon as the key turns.'

The sheriff rubbed his nose. 'Maybe. I'll think about it. In the meantime, Webb, you must convince the girl to confess.'

'And,' the assistant constable saw his advantage, 'she has the coin on her and can easy pay for the Female Ward upstairs. We could make a right good profit.'

But the sheriff was also conscious of his superiors, and the officious nobleman who had demanded the arrest. 'Can't do that, Webb,' he said regretfully. 'That money's surely stolen, and already claimed as rights by his lordship the new baron as says it's his, and Margery Blessop in the husband's name both. I might allow the wench to stay here in the Bread Street Gaol, but it'll be the communal Tuppenny downstairs, and no special privileges.'

Feet moved for her, a shuffle of bodies and space made. Someone was moaning faintly, someone else crying. She was led slowly from the steps into the small squash and the rank stench of sweat. 'Sit here,' Assistant Constable Webb said in her ear, then turned to the space through which she had stumbled. 'You'll leave her alone, all you buggers, d'you hear?'

An incoherent mumbling answered, but someone said, 'It's a pretty lass. Is that our supper you've brung us then, constable?'

'You touch her, and I'll have your hide for my new hat,' barked Robert Webb. 'She'll not be here long, and when I comes to get her, I wants to see her look the same as she does now, and no worse. She tells me anyone of you bastards has had his grubby hands up her skirts, there'll be beatings all round, mark my words.' Robert Webb patted her shoulder and left.

One window let in a glum light and, having no closure apart from thick iron bars, also let in the bitter cold. A hole at the base of one wall supplied a drain but was also the entrance for rats, mice and cockroaches that wandered the perimeters, sniffing for food. Several straw pallets lined the walls but they were not sufficient for the number of inmates enclosed there, and although the ground was damp stone, and although her clothes were already soaked from the rain, Tyballis was offered no other bed. Those who occupied the pallets and who fiercely claimed the only blankets would neither move nor share. It was a small room, and the excess prisoners, a few men and two women, lay sprawled or squatted morose across the floor. Tyballis sighed and sank down, sitting curled where she found space. She had been here before to visit Borin, and knew the rules, though his size and reputation had always found him a bed. Tuppence a week bought black bread and beer each midday. After a few days most felons were hauled out to pass time in the stocks or pillory at Cornhill and then released. She, however, would not leave until her trial, a week or two away perhaps, and with her purse taken from her, she had no money for an attorney. She presumed neither Borin nor Margery would come to see her. No one else knew where she was.

The whisper in her ear at first seemed simply a draught. Then she sat up, hearing words. 'Rob Webb's little darling, are you, dearie? His special little whore? So, what do you do for him, then? And what would you do for me, if I was to do something special for you?'

Tyballis swallowed hard. 'You heard what Constable Webb said. Leave me alone, or I'll scream.'

'I can look after you better than he can, my pretty doxy. But I'll want something worthwhile in return. Give me what I wants, when I wants it, and we'll call it a fair exchange. There'll be no one else dares touch you with my hand clamped safe on your arse.'

The man who spoke squatted in front of her, peering through the gloom. Small and hunch-shouldered, wide-mouthed but toothless, he possessed only one eye, with a black hole where the other should be. His solitary eye winked slowly, evidently to entice. Tyballis cringed back. 'Please. Please don't touch me.'

'I'll not force you, darling. That's not the way I like it. But I can look after you, if you wants me for a friend. I makes a good friend, I do, and I keeps my word once a bargain's made.' The half-blind man paused, hopeful. 'What's your name, pretty?'

Tyballis whispered her name. 'And I'm innocent. Constable Webb knows I am.'

'Ah.' The frog mouth snapped shut. 'Blessop, is it? Would that be – Borin Blessop's – sister, perhaps?'

Tyballis shook her head. 'His wife.'

There was no silence, for the noise sank and rose in waves of restless humanity, the coughing, spitting, choking and the muttering of eternal argument. Finally, only a little louder than the background discomfort, the one-eyed man said, 'Well, mistress. It's a shame, for you're the prettiest I've seen in here for many a long day, and I reckon we'd have made a good pair. But Borin Blessop was my friend once, and he walloped the bugger what tried to stick his dagger in my balls. I'll not harm you, Borin's wife, nor let no one else. Casper's my name, and when you next see your man, you tell him I looked out for you in here. Tell him I've not forgot him.'

Casper patted her cheek with a hand so thick with filth, her voice wavered. But she said with enormous relief. 'Oh, sweet Jesus, thank you. Borin will be – grateful, of course.'

The man wobbled his bald head. 'No matter gratitude, darling. Three days more, and I'm for the drop. Maybe Borin can put in a good word for me with the Almighty afterwards, but I doubt it'd do much good. Hellfire is nice and warm, they says, and that's the best I can hope for. I'd thought my last days might be warmed with a little plump flesh instead, and a memory of them times when I had a woman at home. But no matter. You get to sleep now, Mistress

Blessop. I'll just sit here and keep the rats from your nose whilst you snores.'

When she woke, she did not at first realise she had been crying. Her face was quite wet, but she thought it the oozing damp and the rain from her hair. Then the unutterable melancholy impinged, and as the misery swept in, she cried again. The man Casper was sleeping with his back hard up against her feet. She wondered how she had managed to sleep herself, and thought it the inevitable exhaustion of hopelessness. Other sleepers stretched out one against the other, snuffling and dribbling away their hunger and desperation, grumbling through their slumber. Rats prowled. They worked in teams, sniffing into lolling mouths and groins, disappearing suddenly inside shirt collars, thin bare tails flicking from torn cuffs. Sharp teeth sank suddenly into toes poking from frayed hose or fingers twitching in sleep. No one woke. They were accustomed. Tyballis tucked her skirts tightly around her legs, crossing her arms over her breasts and pulling her damp cape once more over her head. She did not sleep again.

When Casper woke, others made room for him. He turned a toothless grin to Tyballis and winked his one eye. 'Slept well, darling? No one dared molest nor even speak to you, I'll be sure. One word from Casper Wallop, and folks knows their place.'

Tyballis nodded bleakly. 'I'm grateful. Is it a new day?'

'And for me, one day closer to the rope.'

The guards brought ale, thick with the dying scum of the yard – beetles, fleas and larvae. Two men, each carrying a great jug, ladled out the brew in tin cups. Tyballis held her breath and drank. The gaoler regarded her before snatching back the cup for the next man. 'Constable Webb's girl, aren't you? Said he'd be down this afternoon after dinner. Wants a word with you.'

'There you are, pretty,' Casper said. 'He'll see you all right, Rob Webb will.' He winked again with conspiratorial cheer. 'And what was it then, darling, what you didn't do?'

Tyballis smiled faintly. 'They think I killed the Baron Throckmorton. First they thought it was Borin. He didn't do it either.'

'Ah,' sighed Casper, 'then it'll be the drop for you, too. I'm sorry for it. Not that they likes hanging females. Maybe they'll send you to the press instead.'

'Oh, please don't say that,' Tyballis gulped. 'Borin told me about a woman who wouldn't plead to her crime, so they pressed her until she died. They piled huge rocks, he said, until the poor thing was squashed and broken.'

Casper nodded with relish. 'It's a wicked thing, it is. The woman lies flat on her back between two wooden boards. They piles up the rocks on top till she's proper flattened. They says as how they'll keep on till she pleads, but I reckons they'd not hear her voice after the first half-dozen stones, and after that her chest is all crushed up and she'd have no voice to plead with anyways.'

'Heaven help me,' whispered Tyballis.

'Heaven?' Casper shook his head. 'Maybe will, maybe won't. Ain't never helped me. But that pressing's a bad business, though they don't see the poor mashed face while they heap up them rocks, so perhaps it seems cleaner. But them boards is left right mucky, a proper inconvenience, I reckon, since they usually comes off the sheriff's table top, being part of his trestle for dinner. Just imagine all them nasty stains beneath his platter.'

'I'd rather be hanged,' whispered Tyballis.

Casper shook his head. 'Now, that's a nasty business, too, is hanging. Can take a right long time, with you kicking around for an hour or more, feeling your breath all squeezed out. And your innards fall down between your legs, you know, soon as your feet leaves the ladder. That's why they don't like swinging the females.'

Tyballis gazed in horror at her new friend. 'How can you talk like that,' she demanded, 'when you know it's what you'll be facing yourself?'

Casper grinned. 'I done what they says I done, sure enough, so it ain't worth repining. I've had a good life as it happens, and did pretty much as I wanted. My time is up, simple as that. Comes to us all one day.'

'But not by – hanging.'

'One way may be as good as any other when it comes to it,' said Casper, leaning back comfortably against the wall and taking a long breath to prepare for his speech. 'Least I never caught the pestilence,' he continued. 'They say that's a nasty way to go. Never liked the sound of them big black bulges under the arms, and I seen folks go mad with the pain. And your man Borin, he saved me from a bit of bother when that bugger had his knife in my bollocks. Having your cods cut off would be a right shame, I reckon, and spoil a man's hope for a few good turns before the end. I'll not be expecting you to oblige with that, mistress, being the wife of a man I respect, but there's a few others fair willing in here, though nowhere as pretty. But I still got my capabilities, and that's a blessing and thanks to your Borin.' He sighed before beginning again. 'Then there's the yellow pox, too, with all them mucky pustules. Now, that's no way for a decent man to pass over, though once you got it then it's better to go than stay. You're mucked up both ways.'

'Please,' begged Tyballis, 'you're not going to list every single vile manner of meeting a violent death, are you? Don't tell me anymore. I can't bear it.'

Casper seemed a little disappointed. 'As you say, mistress, as you say. I'll have a nice little snooze, then, till they brings the bread round for dinner.' He tipped his head back against the wall, grunted once and was asleep.

Tyballis gazed at him with envy. She had drunk very little of the revolting beer delivered that morning, and now she was thirsty. She did not dare cry again, afraid Casper would hear her, wake and take pity, and put his arm around her shoulders to comfort her. So, she stifled the tears, and the thirst, and the bleak misery welling up in her chest. She could not stifle the fear. It filled her stomach like the stones of the pressing. She felt sticky and hot. Despite the open window, the squash of humanity leeched the air and the room stank of sweat, rat urine, mouse droppings and old vomit.

She thought of Felicia, who had doubtless waited all afternoon and most of the evening for her to return with mountains of shopping. She thought of Luke, quietly scribing by the attic window, not knowing what had happened to her. She thought of Andrew Cobham galloping past the gaol, the fine feathers of his hat catching the breeze and his huge fur-trimmed sleeves flying as the horse gained speed. For some moments she remembered him as she had last seen him: the golden collar of York dazzling across his doublet, and his open surcoat turned back to show the persimmon silk lining, brilliant in the sun. His boots were polished, his spurs were silver, and he had cut his hair, neat and clean to just below his ears.

Tyballis shivered as her own sweat cooled and her thoughts turned to ice. Where she had dared to dream of strong arms around her; holding her and protecting her, now she imagined the stretching years of loneliness which, even if free, would be the best she might expect.

She opened her eyes slowly when the smell of burning oil invaded and the flare of sudden light turned the inside of her eyelids orange. She blinked, seeing a huge shadowed figure loom above her, his grip to the lantern, face lost behind the brilliance, and the sweep of his grand clothes disguising his shape.

'This nightmare is now over, little one,' said a soft voice. 'Come with me, and I will take you home.'

CHAPTER SEVENTEEN

Andrew Cobham took her up before him on his horse, and he rode with her along the bustling London rise of the Cornhill. Tyballis had never before sat on a horse, but she felt only the strength of the arms around her and the silky sheen of velvet firm at her back. She was sheltered from the wind and the rain and her misery had faded into sunbeams.

They rode slowly, avoiding the Cornhill stocks and the tired body slumped there amongst the debris. Tyballis did not see him, or the shoppers she passed, their faces upturned to the highness of the man and the simple stained clothes of the girl. Nor did she glimpse the shining windows of the grand houses to either side, glimmering through the drizzle. She gazed only at Andrew's gloved hands clasping the reins before her, and the sweeping fur cuffs of his surcoat. The horse quickened pace up Bishopsgate. Now to their right, four storeys high and set well back from the smells and noise, Crosby's slanted its shadows across their path. Arched high over Crosby's chimneys and half-lost in the thickening cloud, a partial rainbow caught the sun into shimmering stripes of unexpected pastel beauty. Here beneath the hesitant colours, before reaching the green spread of St Helen's Priory and between Crosby's Place and the street, a frontage of several smaller buildings faced the public gaze. Andrew abruptly reined in and turned up a narrow lane towards the courtyard that held the stables and the back doorways of the houses.

Andrew dismounted. He held up his arms and took Tyballis down from the saddle. She mumbled, 'I can walk, really, I can,' but he took no notice, and as the ostler led away the steaming hunter, strode with her to an open back door at the far end of the courtyard.

It was dark inside but the staircase was wide, the balustrade smooth and the spindles of the banister carved. Andrew carried her easily, taking her quickly upstairs. He kicked open the door beyond, and the world suddenly came alive.

Two windows were smeared by raindrops but a faint tinge of pink rainbow reflected in every rosy drop. The hearth, deep and wide, was huge with fire and the heat sweltered into every corner and crackled up the chimney. It was a small room but richly comfortable with polished furniture, cushions and rugs. A padded settle stood to one side of the fireplace and here Andrew bent and sat her carefully, so she faced the flames and began to steam like washed sheets drying on a hedge in the sun. He stood, one foot to the grate and his elbow to the stone lintel, and looked down thoughtfully at her. 'Do you wish to talk?' he said softly. 'If not, there is a bedchamber, the mattress is warmed, and you can sleep. I have ordered dinner to be served within the hour, since I imagine you're hungry. And I've no need to go out, unless you prefer to be alone.'

'You make me feel like an invalid.' She gazed up at him. 'I'm not hurt. And I don't want to be alone. Not at all.'

He smiled faintly. 'I'm pleased to hear it, child, since it is perfectly objectionable outside and I have a singular dislike of the cold.'

A small burning log tumbled from its place and Andrew kicked it back. She wanted his caring embrace and she wanted his breath against her cheek, but instead she simply smiled too, keeping a hopeful but tenuous grip on her pride. 'I'd noticed.'

'Does my scrutiny make you uncomfortable?' He had been watching Tyballis with such care, she had blushed. 'Being well accustomed to this city's gaols, I risk holding them in little account. I am therefore attempting, though sadly unpractised, to understand how shocking it must have seemed to you.' He was still watching her intently. 'Will you trust me sufficiently,' he continued, 'to admit if you have been injured? I have the means to help a little – whatever the injury.'

'I wouldn't ever have guessed,' Tyballis sat up, surprised, 'that you'd spent time in prison.'

He chuckled. 'No doubt I've deserved no less, but indeed, I've had occasion to visit almost every one of the city's shackle-haunts, yet never before Bread Street's gaol. A delightful new experience.'

'I'm glad to oblige,' sniffed Tyballis. 'But I really can't see why you want to visit gaols so often, especially in those clothes. Unless you had – a father, or a brother perhaps ...'

'Luckily, no.' Andrew crossed to the small table, lifted the jug and poured two cups of wine. He brought one to Tyballis and drank from the other. 'And for your information,' he said, 'I simply wear whatever clothes seem suitable for whichever errand I happen to be on. Now, drink up, child. It will do you good.' She obeyed, drinking in both wine and warmth. 'Now,' he continued, 'we've not yet discussed either your present needs or the particular difficulties that led to your incarceration. I'm afraid you will have to be honest with me. A troublesome necessity, but imperative. First, will you tell me truthfully if you were hurt?'

She shook her head. 'I wasn't.'

His smile did not reach his eyes. 'Having some experience with prison conditions,' he said softly, 'I have rarely known of a woman – of even passable appearance – who was not molested upon entering an unsegregated cell. I cannot undo what is done, but I can help in other ways.'

Tyballis blushed again. 'No one touched me. The constable was someone I used to know, and he told the other prisoners to leave me alone. Then there was Casper Wallop.' Andrew raised one eyebrow. 'He frightened me at first,' she admitted, 'and he looks like an ogre. But then he was kind and kept the rats and everyone else away. He knew Borin, you see. I didn't tell him I'd run off from home and didn't talk to my husband anymore. And I don't know what crime he committed, but he's going to be hanged in two days. I expect he did something horrible but I'm awfully glad he was still in there because he was exceedingly kind to me.'

'Then I'm very much obliged to Mister Wallop,' Andrew said, his smile a little more relaxed. 'Now, drink your wine. Food will arrive in due course, but since I have no manservant of my own, I'm at present served by a clutch of dawdling northerners who feel both overawed and misunderstood. They work at a speed that reminds me of monks at prayer.' He waited until she had sipped her wine, then said, 'Are you hungry, little one?'

'Starving.'

'We shall eat first and you can sleep afterwards,' he said. 'But while we wait, I wish to understand how you came to be in gaol. Naturally I've spoken at some length to the sheriff, but the information he gave seemed singularly unlikely.'

'It was Margery,' said Tyballis simply. 'She's Borin's mother and she hates me. Of course, she wanted any excuse to get Borin out of Newgate, so she made up a story about it being me who killed the baron. I think she told the sheriff that I came home that night in Throckmorton's cloak, which of course I didn't, because it was your cloak, and it wasn't velvet at all, and I didn't see any bloodstains either.'

'Though always possible it had some,' said Andrew. 'You told me you sold it. I imagine it was worth a penny, no more.'

'I got nearly a shilling,' smiled Tyballis. 'And I bought some bread and cheese and a pie for Borin. But that's a long story. Anyway, Margery told the sheriff I'd stabbed the baron, and she told the new baron the same thing. I don't think it was very fair of the sheriff just to take their word for it, though I suppose Throckmorton intimidated him.'

'No doubt. I believe I shall do him the honour of visiting dear Harold tomorrow morning.'

'And I don't see why he thought I did it either,' objected Tyballis. 'After all, I'm not really a convincing murderess, am I? And what possible motive would I have?'

'I've a fairly good idea of Throckmorton's motives,' Andrew said.

'But I shall discuss that with you another time, child. I hear our dinner approaching.'

It was over a pleasant meal of salted beef, capon in pastry and pork broiled in vinegar sauce, and after Andrew had waved away the two men hovering with their ladles in hand, that Tyballis said, 'I've answered all your questions, Mister Cobham, which of course I'm happy to do, and I am intensely grateful for what you've done and will do anything – I mean anything you like – to show my thanks, but would you be so kind as to answer some questions yourself? I am dying of curiosity.'

'Having rescued you from the pit,' he said, cutting her a thick slice of salted beef and depositing it on her platter, 'it would now seem a shame were you to expire of curiosity.' He looked up and smiled at her. 'However, you should really not speak with your mouth full. Nor, may I remind you, should you call me Mister Cobham again, or I shall take it as an insult.'

'Well, Drew, then.' She swallowed her mouthful of beef with a gulp and frowned. 'If you stop calling me child. You make me feel like a little girl, and I'm not. None of it makes sense to me, but how did you manage to walk into the gaol and just get me out like that without anyone stopping us? And how did you know I was there, anyway? And where are we, and is this your house? How can it be? And what were you doing yesterday, riding with those people? I was amazed to see you. One of them looked so grand he was positively terrifying. You looked really grand as well, and you still do, though at least you're not still wearing that gold collar or I should be scared to talk to you.'

'And how sadly disappointing that would be,' smiled her companion, 'since your conversation is so riveting.' He refilled her wine cup and smiled. 'The terrifying man was the Duke of Gloucester, who owns the horse I was riding and the house in which we are now sitting, although naturally it is not ever inhabited by dukes. These rooms are part of the annexes attached to Crosby's Place, being Gloucester's London home. He has rented it for some years now, and the additional buildings of the annexe are used by those to whom his grace gives his permission for reasons of temporary convenience. I am in his service, hence the collar of York. Gloucester is a prince who believes in justice, and it was by his authority that you were released today.'

'He doesn't know me.'

'But he knows me,' said Andrew, 'which was sufficient. Now, finish your wine. You have not had an easy night, I'm sure, and should rest now. I'll show you the bedchamber.'

Tyballis quickly drained her cup and blushed the colour of the wine. 'Yes, of course. I see,' she said in a small voice. She had not expected it, but then, remembering the men in her past, she thought she should have expected it after all. 'I understand. I'm ready.'

Andrew regarded her for a moment and then snorted loudly. 'As usual, my dear, you understand nothing at all. Unfortunately there is only one bedchamber here, but I intend you to occupy it alone. For one thing, you must be exhausted, and for another, you smell of the gutter and the latrine. Once you have removed your gown, I intend to have it burned.'

'It's the only one I have,' she objected.

'You will find others in the garderobe,' he said.

Tyballis shook her head with sudden determination. 'Certainly not. I won't wear things left by your – other women. And I don't care what I smell like. It isn't my fault and it's not at all nice of you to mention it.'

'Tiresome girl.' Andrew stood and took a firm hold of her arm. 'I have no intention of discussing my bedchamber arrangements with you now or ever, but in fact the clothes have never belonged to anyone else known to me. You may have a bath when you wake, and I'll arrange a tub set up here in front of the fire. In the meantime, you'll remove those disgusting threads, or I shall do it myself. I imagine you're perfectly well aware that I don't object to undressing young women when necessary.'

She remembered. 'And that's another thing,' she said, dropping her napkin and reluctantly allowing herself to be tugged to her feet. 'I was – I was just a little the worse for wine that evening – which you kept making me drink, so it wasn't my fault, anyway – and you took advantage of me.'

Andrew chuckled as he marched her into the adjoining room.

'Think whatever you like, my dear,' he said. 'But now you are going to rest. You are going to take off every single item of clothing, and put it all on the floor where I can collect it later and arrange for its immediate destruction. You will then climb, quite alone, into the bed that has been specifically aired and warmed for you, and you will sleep until I give permission for you to wake.'

She managed a smile. 'I suppose you think me lying between your nice clean sheets will ruin them forever.'

'Indubitably. But they can be washed later, as you can. Now,' he pointed, 'there is the bed. I shall come back in about half an hour, and expect to find you within it. A fact that,' he added with a slow grin, 'will not, I assure you, tempt me into – how did you put it? – taking advantage of you. Strangely enough I prefer my women sober and conscious.'

He closed the bedchamber door behind him and Tyballis stood in the semi dark and gazed in wonder. She had greatly admired the dishevelled beauty of Andrew Cobham's bedchamber at the Portsoken Ward, but this was not only grander, it was also remarkably clean. The bed rose beneath a tapestried tester, swathes of scarlet velvet disguising each post with swirls and tassels. The mattress was high, the linen sweet-smelling and the pillows soft. The small hearth had been laid with a blaze that neither coughed smoke nor spat sparks into the draught. The lumps of charcoal sat smugly in their crimson ashes and the chamber was positively cosy.

Within a few minutes Tyballis had scrambled out of her clothes and heaped them in the middle of the floor as ordered. She crawled quickly between the sheets and discovered that hot bricks had indeed warmed the bed. Collapsing beneath the plumped quilt was like being swallowed by feathers. In less than a blink, she was asleep.

CHAPTER EIGHTEEN

She woke alone, as promised. Having no idea what time it might be after a thoroughly confusing day, she saw only that the little pile of the clothes she had worn in prison was no longer on her floor, and the fire had been built up considerably higher. She had heard none of this. Now she lay in the satisfying warmth, and wondered whether she should make an attempt to get up, or whether it might be the middle of the night. The one long window was heavily shuttered, with no boards missing or gaps showing light between the slats. There was therefore no indication of either daylight, or stars. If it was night indeed, then Andrew Cobham had not slept in his own bedchamber. No pallet or truckle was in evidence, and clearly no one had climbed into bed with her.

A small table was tucked beside the bed and on it stood a jug of light ale and a small cup. Tyballis drank, took a deep breath, hopped out of bed and scurried to the garderobe. There she gazed carefully around.

The garderobe held its usual row of pegs either side of the privy, and beneath the pegs were large wooden trunks, their lids open. Tyballis stared. Each peg held gowns, cloaks, hoods and cotes. The trunks were packed. There were shifts as transparent as gauze veils and as prettily trimmed as a kerchief. There were stiffened stomachers in every colour, narrow leather belts, a variety of folded headdresses, stockings in fine knitted silk and frilled satin garters. On the ground were shoes in many fabrics as dainty as flowers, and on a shelf was a tiny unlocked casket of jewellery, the amethyst ring she had worn before amongst a tangle of glitter.

Retreating to the bed, she sat for some time in puzzled indecision before finally choosing the plainest clothes she could find. She was at first frightened of ruining the stockings, but, since her nails were all worn to the quick, she was able to pull the thin silky wool up to her thighs and tie them in place with satin garters, all without snagging the delicate knit. She then chose a bleached linen undergown which fitted her body so closely above the waist that she wondered if she might have trouble breathing. The over-gown made this danger more likely, since it was just as tight. She pulled it carefully over her head and attempted to attach the little hooks beneath her arm. By twisting and turning, she managed to hook two into place but the rest she had to leave open. The over-gown was pale summer green, soft and flowing below the hips. The neckline, however, was cut so low in front that it formed a deep V almost to her waist, and the chemise beneath covered this intimate space in the merest suggestion of white gossamer. Nor could she attach the stomacher, though she thought she had chosen the widest, so she slipped her feet into a pair of pretty white leather shoes, sat on the bed, stared at her little pointed toes and sighed.

Andrew Cobham had an awkward habit of entering the rooms of his own quarters without knocking. He laughed at her from the doorway. 'Stand up, child,' he said, 'and I will help.'

Tyballis whirled around. 'What if I'd been naked?' she complained.

'Then I should have been even more delighted to see you than I am,' he replied. 'Now, do as you're told and breathe in while I lace you up.'

His closeness and the efficiency of his hands against her body made her uncomfortable. Within the bleak stench of gaol, she had craved the comfort of his embrace. But now herself again, his fingers within the folds of her gown seemed intrusive. She stared resolutely at the ceiling and said faintly, 'I may never breathe again.'

He shook his head. 'The silk will stretch very quickly to your body warmth,' he told her, 'and mould to your shape, as it should. Now – the stomacher.' He looked her over with approval. 'You've chosen well,' he said, 'and once your hair is tidied, you'll look as you should for the part.'

Tyballis squinted down at her uncovered cleavage. 'I'm half-undressed,' she decided.

Drew led her to the silvered mirror beside the garderobe door. 'Fashion demands it. I personally have no objections.'

Tyballis gazed at her reflection in the mirror with only a vague glimmer of recognition. 'Gracious,' she gasped.

'Graceful might be a better description,' Andrew said. 'But your hair is appallingly tousled and I have no particular skills at combing or braiding. You will find the necessary tools in the garderobe, and I suggest you choose the easiest hairpiece you can find. A simple mesh would do. I can at least help you pin it.' He had turned to go and was striding back to the doorway, when he turned once, smiling. 'By the way,' he said. 'I have just employed a new manservant. You'll see him directly. Come into the adjoining chamber when you're ready.'

'Is it still day, then?' she asked.

'Day? It's already late morning,' he replied, 'and we're about to eat an early dinner. I've been up since five this morning, and am hungry. You, on the other hand, have managed to sleep undisturbed for nearly eighteen hours.'

Tyballis screwed up her nose. 'I couldn't have.'

He smiled. 'As you please, I won't argue. But don't take too long, since we are going visiting this afternoon, and I believe it's an appointment you may enjoy.'

She thought it unlikely. 'You don't think I still smell, then?'

'Ah. That. The bath will come this evening, I think, and I hope you will enjoy that, too. I certainly shall.' He left with a grin, and she hurried into the garderobe to find a comb.

Once again the parlour was lit by the force of a huge fire roaring up the chimney. Tyballis sat obediently at the little table, put her napkin over her shoulder and smiled at her host. She was bubbling with a hundred questions, but when Casper Wallop, smartly dressed in a brown livery that did not entirely fit him, began to spread the dinner platters across the tablecloth, she stared in speechless amazement. Casper offered her a roll of manchet and blinked his one eye. 'Washed my hands, I have,' he pointed out, 'and a few other bits, too. Now dinner's coming, and plenty good stuff it is. Be sure you leave enough, mistress, for I'm looking forward to what's leftover.'

Tyballis stared at him, quite speechless. Andrew leaned back in his chair and watched her with amusement. 'I told you I'd been busy,' he said once the eager Mister Wallop had left the room. 'It seems your saviour of yesterday is a man after my own heart. He has a fair understanding of the matters that interest me, and will no doubt be of considerable use in the weeks to come.'

'But he was condemned to hang tomorrow,' stuttered Tyballis.

'Certainly he was,' Andrew nodded. 'For multiple theft. Does that trouble you?'

'It doesn't make him sound altogether – trustworthy,' she admitted.

'Trust,' said Mister Cobham, 'is rarely something I associate with those of my acquaintance. It is an unfamiliar – and unnecessary – commendation, bringing few benefits for the giver, and with the subsequent disadvantage of leaving oneself open to permanent disillusion. I do not trust this world, my dear, nor do I need to. But I like your Mister Wallop. I intend to find him useful.'

Tyballis finished her lobster broth and chose a small apple coddling from the platter in front of her. 'I'm sure I've never chosen to trust anybody,' she said. 'It just happens. Either I do or I don't. Usually I do.'

'A particularly feminine viewpoint, no doubt,' he smiled. 'I cannot afford blind misconceptions in my line of work. Do you always accept life with such a total lack of discernment?'

'Well, you certainly don't have a very high opinion of women,' sniffed Tyballis. 'Nor anyone else, it seems. You probably only put up with me because you're clearly convinced I'm no more than a small, useless child. And what exactly is your line of work, anyway?'

'As it happens, and speaking of trust,' he informed her, 'I've already told you a good deal more than I usually tell anybody. And that is certainly sufficient. The rest does not concern you.'

'Oh well,' she said, 'I suppose, since I have no judgement and probably no intelligence either, that's just as well. And I won't attempt to earn your trust, since that would be impossible, especially for me, being a small and lowly female. I shall simply do as I'm told.'

'I'm glad to hear it,' said Andrew. 'Now you will wipe your mouth and go and fetch your cloak. We are going out.'

The cold bit but it was no longer raining. Tyballis, snug beneath sumptuous billows of fur and velvet, took Andrew's arm as he commanded. She adored her transformation. The great hoop of her hood enveloped her face, tickling her cheeks as the fur snuggled around her ears. She watched her well-clad leather toes patter from beneath her skirts, and tried to avoid any puddles that might spoil them. She was also quietly impressed by her companion. He wore the mahogany velvet and persimmon silk with which she was now familiar, but his hat was in the Italian style, and his hose were knitted grey silk so close-fitting that his calves seemed carved from dark marble.

They did not walk far. From Bishopsgate, Mister Cobham led his charge down the slope to Cornhill, around the corner, and stopped at the tall house Tyballis recognised. But this time she did not have to creep through the kitchens. Bodge answered the door. He no longer gazed down his nose or looked disdainfully aloof, but bowed very low and stood back for them to enter. Clearly he had no idea he had ever seen this grand lady before, and Tyballis had to stop herself smiling smugly at him and skipping over the threshold with too much obvious satisfaction.

Baron Throckmorton was waiting for them in the main hall, and stood immediately they entered. He appeared nervous, and his curled red hair was dishevelled, as if he had been running his fingers through it. There was no blazing fire, but hot ashes smouldered low across the hearth. Two candles were already lit in their wall sconces, for the murk of heavy cloud had closed in the day and only a little greyish light entered through the mullioned windows. Andrew Cobham did not bow, but nodded briefly and walked to the hearthside, taking

Tyballis with him. He showed her to a chair, where she sat, and he stood next to her, gazing at the baron. 'Well, Harold,' he said softly, 'it seems you have been behaving unwisely – once again.'

Tyballis kept her head down but saw Throckmorton stride forwards. 'Certainly not, my lord,' he said at once. 'I've had no contact whatsoever with any of them, neither here nor in Wales. I haven't even been anywhere near the docks. Indeed, I've been extremely busy with – more personal matters. My brother, you know. He left a mountain of debts and I've had damnable trouble getting credit.'

'You'll get none from me, in case you were thinking of asking,' Andrew smiled faintly. 'Contact the Medici banks or try the money-lenders, Harold. There are still some in town, and I'm quite sure you know where to look. But don't pretend you can't pay me this month, my friend. I do not accept excuses.'

Tyballis looked up with sudden interest. The baron had clearly not recognised her, and was standing staring at Andrew, twisting his fingers in obvious alarm. 'Just a little more time, my lord, I beg you. Your demands are a great burden to me, sir. You already understand my situation well. I have no other resources – only those you are aware of. You know almost all our family property was confiscated after Tewkesbury.'

Andrew nodded. 'But the king was good enough to pardon your late father, and restore his title.'

'His title but not his lands,' mumbled Throckmorton, an aggrieved eye to the unwanted female sitting as witness to his stammering discomfort. 'We've had virtually no reliable income for years. Which is why all this started – but you know that. What you don't know is – well, now I'm working on another – possible source. I can't explain what it is but I expect the first payment by next week or shortly after. If you'd just wait a little longer, my lord.'

'But you see, I do know, Harold,' smiled Mister Cobham softly. His eyes narrowed slightly. 'I know exactly what you're up to. Let me summarise the situation for you. A few years past, your brother Thomas, a man I despised just as much as I despise you, decided to augment the meagre family income by assisting with the purchase, import, collection, accumulation and subsequent sale of certain substances not normally associated with, let us say, any respectable transaction beyond that of apothecary or physician. In other words, he became a merchant of death and a dabbler in poisons. The deals he made for selling at the greatest profit were invariably both secret and dangerous. Some months back he sold small quantities of arsenic to a certain person of my acquaintance. The young Lord Marrott – Geoffrey by name, and friend of the highest. Although your brother was not privy to its final intended use, the buyer in question was taking no risks. He decided that Thomas, Baron Throckmorton, should be silenced. I imagine Thomas had been wise enough to make some intelligent guesses, and foolish enough to speak aloud and let those guesses be known. Your brother was murdered.'

Throckmorton was growing explosively pink. 'My lord,' he interrupted, 'remember my position, sir, and say no more. I have no idea why you have brought your – companion – here this afternoon, but what you say should not be overheard by anyone. It places me – perhaps us both – in a most perilous situation.'

Andrew continued to smile. 'On the contrary, Harold. The young woman has every right to be present and I hope she finds my story of interest. Now, where was I? Ah, yes. Your brother's death. I am not entirely sure who killed him, but I know exactly on whose orders it was done. The good sheriff, however, having no idea of the true circumstances of your family's business, promptly arrested the easiest target. This, of course, was Borin Blessop, a heavy-handed henchman your brother occasionally employed to frighten his debtors and enemies.' At this point Tyballis gulped, and Mister Cobham rested one hand firmly on her shoulder. 'There was a problem, however,' Andrew went on. 'Mister Blessop not only loudly proclaimed his innocence and chose to point the finger at your good self as the more likely perpetrator, but he also appeared to have someone secretly working in the background to prove he could not have committed the crime. Myself, in fact.' Tyballis stirred again, and Andrew placed his other hand on her other shoulder with the gentle pressure of reassurance. 'At this point,' he continued, 'both you and the gentleman who ordered your brother's death became uneasy. He decided a new culprit, more easily cowed, should be named. He sent men to speak both with the innocent prisoner in Newgate, and that prisoner's mother. It was decided between them to implicate this fool's estranged wife instead. You, of course, my friend, had already taken over both the noble title and the less noble family business. You immediately saw the advantages of accusing this new suspect – and perhaps someone quietly suggested, with additional threats, that you go along with the story. Therefore Mistress Blessop, helpless beneath a canopy of lies, was taken by the law and promptly incarcerated without possibility of legal assistance or any other form of exoneration. At the same time Borin Blessop was released from Newgate, and was warned to keep his mouth shut and ensure his freedom by keeping to the lies regarding his wife.'

The baron was stuttering wildly. 'You assume too much, my lord. Some of this – well, you know it to be true. But this other business – it is all guesses, sir, and I swear I have no idea.'

'Don't make me angry, Harold,' Andrew answered. 'You should know I never speak without conviction. Nor do I make – guesses. Perhaps it is now the relevant moment for you to make the acquaintance of my companion. Let me introduce Mistress Tyballis Blessop.'

The baron's expression turned so violent that Tyballis clung to the edge of her seat. Andrew Cobham kept his hands hard on her shoulders. 'This – this trollop?' Throckmorton spat. 'And you've disguised the wench in finery to trick me. Had I known, sir, I would not have allowed her to enter, nor to sit in my presence, and never to overhear the details of my private life.'

'Your bluster is quite unnecessary, Harold,' replied Andrew, 'since you would have done as I instructed, as usual. Mistress Blessop is my companion, and as such demands your civility and respect. Having become the victim of your self-serving manipulations, she is perfectly entitled to hear the truth regarding her situation, and will therefore be in a better position to protect herself should you have any further unpleasant intentions. In the meantime, I have something more to say.'

Throckmorton retreated behind the long dining table. 'I won't listen. I've no more interest, sir,' he mumbled. 'I've told you I should have your money by next month. Perhaps next week. And I swear I'll do no more business with – the gentlemen you refer to. I see no reason to prolong this interview.'

'But I do, Harold,' Andrew said calmly. 'So you will come back over here, and take your hand away from the knife you're now trying to extricate from its hiding place beneath the table. I know perfectly well why and where you keep some defence at hand. Now, come here.'

Once again coming to face his unwanted visitors, the baron refused to look at Tyballis, but raised his palms. 'No sword, no knife,' he said plaintively. 'You misjudge me, my lord, as so often.'

'I rarely misjudge anyone, Harold, and certainly no one as manifestly inconsequential as yourself.' Andrew still spoke softly, barely changing position, while the baron fidgeted and twitched, moving uncomfortably from one foot to the other. 'In the meantime,' Andrew continued, 'you will do nothing – I repeat, nothing – to further the accusation against Mistress Blessop regarding your brother's death. Do I make myself absolutely clear? Instead, you will visit the good sheriff, and admit you were mistaken concerning the theft of poor Thomas's cloak. You will say it has been found amongst your brother's possessions, safe, dry and without stains of blood or anything else. You will shake your head sadly, and express the opinion that Mistress Blessop's incarceration was clearly a mistake.'

'And if the authorities decide to investigate me for the murder instead?'

'It would be unfortunate for you, of course,' said Andrew patiently. 'But unlikely, under the circumstances. Having arrested both the Blessops, then released them and subsequently been made to look foolish, the sheriff will be wary of making further blunders, especially against a peer of the realm, whatever the reputation of that peer may be. I fear you will be safe to continue with your – delightful business, Harold.'

'I trust so.' Throckmorton bowed low with a sarcastic smile. 'Until next month then, sir.'

Andrew Cobham raised a finger. 'Just one thing more, Harold. As for the money, I will agree to accept the next instalment rather later than usual, for reasons we now both understand. So I will return next month. However, I have reason to believe you expect considerable sums from the gentleman to whom your brother sold the poison before his death. You are wrong. This man's promises were to ensure your silence. But now that Mistress Blessop is free and no longer a useful scapegoat, he will not be pleased. I think you should watch your back, Harold. And my advice is to contact the Medici bank as soon as possible. A lengthy visit to Florence might even be wise, don't you think?'

'I can't pay you from Italy.' His lordship looked sullen. 'Aren't you afraid to lose your own income, my lord?'

'Have you ever watched the effects of arsenic?' Andrew said. 'The pain, and the gradual degeneration of the system, is excruciating. Have you ever truly considered the business you are in, sir? Arsenic is a slow agony. It eats away the tongue and the mouth, leading to convulsions and the collapse of the lungs, the stomach and the bowels. There is no way back once taken, and for many terrible hours in constant terror and pain, wallowing in a bed fouled with shit and vomit, the victim faces his inevitable death. How many have known such an ending because of you?'

Throckmorton shuddered, looking away. 'Yet you take a slice of my profits, my lord, and kindly permit me to stay in the business you so dislike.'

'The miserable penance you pay,' Andrew said softly, 'is little enough in the cause of justice, I think. As for leaving you in business: better the man I know and can control than a new merchant unknown to me. After all, there is always someone to fill a space left open in the popular commerce of our times.'

'Control? You don't control me, sir.'

'You had better make sure that I do,' Andrew said. 'Your life is already at risk. I can increase those risks if I wish. But I am not your principal threat, as you should already be aware. It is Lord Marrott who now holds your life in his hands.' He bowed slightly and began walking towards the door, leading Tyballis with him. 'Remember my words, Throckmorton. I shall come again next month, and I shall expect full payment of the money you owe – or news that you have sailed for Italy.'

Tyballis kept her nose in the air until they had left the house but once outside, she grabbed her companion's hand and hopped enthusiastically around to face him. 'That was – amazing,' she said, breathless. 'You are the most incredible man. And he – that miserable wretch – told lies and got me arrested? I would have liked to kill him myself.'

'A conversation better kept for when we are back indoors,' Andrew suggested gently. 'But at least let me remind you of what you've just heard. Harold is hardly innocent, but it was principally your dear husband, your mother-in-law and the actual killer of Thomas Throckmorton who are to blame. And they will all be dealt with – in time.'

'They will?' Tyballis was skipping again, forgetting ladylike dignity.

Andrew nodded. 'But this is a complicated story, little one, and you do not know all the facts. Nor do I have the remotest intention of telling you. I simply wished you to understand a little about your recent misfortunes, and to be in a position to refute anything your mother-in-law may try to bring against you in the future. I also wished to humiliate the baron.'

'Well, you certainly did that.' It was not raining but a chill mist indicated the probable night's downpour. Tyballis pulled her hood tight. 'And anyway,' she said, 'how did Margery and Robert Webb know to find me at Cheapside? Was it just my bad luck they happened to be there? And how on earth did you know what had happened? And who told you I was in gaol, and which gaol it was? Surely you didn't rush away from the duke just to come and find me?'

'Hardly, my dear.' Andrew smiled faintly. 'I'd already left his grace of Gloucester. I had returned home, expecting to find you there. Our friend Davey Lyttle told me he'd seen you arrested. That was coincidence indeed, but he often mingles, surreptitiously I imagine, at Cheapside, since crowds are naturally of benefit in his particular choice of occupation. I immediately questioned the sheriff. He told me where you were being kept.'

'And then you had to go and ask the duke for permission to get me out? And what about Casper Wallop? Because he's guilty. He told me so himself.'

'No, his grace did not specifically authorise your freedom, and certainly not that of your dubious friend.' Andrew chuckled. 'Let us say I have a permanent authorisation, specifically with regard to the city's dungeons and other places of confinement. It is the nature of my work. Gloucester trusts me, you see. I've already had occasion to speak to his grace on this subject. Trust should never be so easily bestowed. But sadly the duke has a great passion for the merits of trust and loyalty. I am simply the beneficiary.'

They had returned to Crosby's Place and sat again by the roaring fire in the comfortable parlour, where Tyballis kicked off her shoes and wriggled her toes. It was Casper Wallop who promptly brought the wine, and it seemed he had already tried it out himself.

Andrew appeared quite unconcerned by his new servant's unsteady state, as the man rummaged with the tray and jug, finally serving an overfilled cup to each. 'Nice stuff this, yer honour,' Casper muttered. 'Needed a drink. Cold outside.'

'But rather warm in here,' Andrew pointed out. 'Leave the jug on the table. Order me a light supper from the kitchens, and then arrange for the bathtub to be set up in front of the fire. Once it is well filled, you may retire to bed. I return to my own home early in the morning and I intend that you accompany me.'

Mister Wallop grinned toothless satisfaction. 'Pleased to hear it, mister. You can count on me.'

'How disappointing,' smiled Andrew. 'I was quite sure I could not.'

'Is the bath for me?' inquired Tyballis after Casper had left the room.

'Certainly,' Andrew said. 'It will be far easier and more private here rather than waiting until tomorrow at home. Unfortunately I have no female staff in attendance, so there's no one, except myself, of course, to scrub your back. But at least there are several able-bodied northerners quite capable of humping hot water up and down stairs, and an extra cauldron can be hung over the flames in here.'

She didn't question his smiles, and, a little intimidated by the circumstances, hardly spoke over supper. They ate cold salted beef served with plentiful Burgundy wine but Tyballis drank very little, keeping her thoughts and her emotional confusion to herself... She did not ask her host if he also had the duke's authorisation to blackmail Baron Throckmorton, but she did wonder if her own hoard of florins had come from that source. Though her purse had been taken from her by the sheriff after her arrest, eight untouched florins remained locked in her coffer at Cobham Hall.

Andrew watched her as he ate. He spoke only once, saying quite suddenly after refilling her cup, 'We've spoken several times recently regarding trust.' He drained his own wine as he spoke. 'You do know, I hope little one, that you must not trust me.'

Tyballis spluttered and hurriedly put the cup back on the table. 'But you've been enormously kind to me,' she said. 'I know I have to look ladylike working for you, so the beautiful clothes just serve a purpose ... But getting me out of gaol and bringing me here – then taking me to the baron's and explaining everything. That was kind. I should very much like to trust you.'

He was still looking at her searchingly when they were interrupted. The platters were cleared away and the tub set up. Tyballis watched as her bath was prepared. The barrel, held tight within copper bands, was caulked like a ship and lined in soft bleached linen. The hurrying servants, their shirt sleeves rolled up and their foreheads dripping sweat, continued to haul up their buckets, checking the temperature until it was correct. Finally one bowed to Mister Cobham. 'It is ready, my lord.' It had taken some time, but the hot water now puffed curls of steam high to the ceiling beams, condensing there into drops like rain.

Andrew did not at first seem inclined to move, chin sunk into the soft fur of his collar and eyes half-closed. 'I do hope,' Tyballis said eventually, clearing her throat in slight embarrassment, 'you're not planning on watching me?'

He looked up suddenly as if he had forgotten she was there, and laughed. 'Since I believe it was only yesterday that you very particularly offered yourself to me?'

'You know why I did that,' complained Tyballis. 'I was so terribly grateful – and I didn't have anything else to offer. I thought – I thought I ought to.'

'How sad,' he grinned. 'Obligation, rather than inclination. But since you seem convinced I took wicked advantage of you some weeks back when you were cupshotten and virtually unconscious, there would seem very little you still have to hide. So, why should you need to be alone now?'

'That was different,' she objected. 'I don't remember much about that night, and if you did anything – and you certainly seemed to have undressed me – at least I wasn't aware of it. This time if you absolutely refuse to go away, I shall have to sit and watch you watching me.'

'Perhaps I should have had the bath set up in the bedchamber instead,' he said. 'The fire isn't as high in there, nor the room as hot, but you might have felt more comfortable.' Tyballis looked down, avoiding his scrutiny. His eyes had suddenly intensified, as if leading somewhere she did not understand. 'But I had other things on my mind,' he continued softly. 'Distractions are invariably – distracting.' He smiled and nodded. 'Nor am I used to considerations of privacy, especially with the women in my life. I simply arranged what seemed to fulfil the requirements. Now we have the difficulty of your bath taking up the space where my sleeping pallet should be laid out. Instead, if I retire to the other chamber, you will lose your bed.'

'Oh.' She hung her head. 'But it's your bed anyway. I can sleep on the pallet.'

'But it isn't my bed at all,' he answered her. 'Everything here, including the building itself, belongs to Richard, his grace of Gloucester. That includes the clothes and jewellery that are stacked in the garderobe. Everything has a purpose, and I am part of that purpose. Indeed, only four days ago a friend of mine, Robert Brackenbury, slept here. So, while I have, let us say, other matters I need to consider, my own need for solitude is as great as yours. I shall therefore retire to the bedchamber while you bathe. Once finished, knock on the door and I shall come out and arrange for the tub to be taken down and emptied. Then you can go to bed.' His gaze was still attentive. 'First, perhaps,' he said, 'you should go to the garderobe and find yourself some wash sponges, a keg of soap and a bedrobe for afterwards. Then I'll help you with those bothersome hooks and fasteners.'

She was greatly relieved and looked up at him. 'I realise I'm in the way. But what is it, anyway, that's so important? What are you thinking about?'

The pause lengthened. She expected him to avoid her question, but his expression had made her hope he might say something entirely different. Instead, quite quietly he said, 'As it happens, I am thinking of my king's life. Or indeed, of his imminent death.'

CHAPTER NINETEEN

They were met at the doorway. The wind was hurtling the garden's last greenery around in blasts of sleet and bluster. Not a leaf remained, but twigs whirled in flurries while branches lashed a colourless sky. Ralph opened the door and both rubbish and draught rushed inside. 'You're back,' he said.

'Both of you, thank the Lord,' Felicia squeaked from behind his shoulder. 'I wondered if I should ever see either of you again. The tales we have heard!'

'Lies, no doubt,' nodded Ralph. 'Davey's tales usually are a touch on the exaggerated side, and that's me being kind.'

'But it's all true,' insisted Tyballis. 'And Drew took me to market, too. Now we have piles and piles of wonderful things for the Christmas feast, and only one day left to prepare.'

'Told you,' Sniggered Davey from somewhere invisible beyond the crush. 'Our Tybbs was taken by the law in full view of the crowd, manhandled, hauled off and slung into gaol. Unfortunately, I was, under the particular circumstances, you understand, quite unable to assist. And if it weren't for our mighty Sir Galahad, she'd still be mouldering there.'

'So,' Ralph gazed in wonder at his scuffed and shabby landlord, 'Davey was right, then? You marched into the sheriff's chambers and told the bugger what to do with his rotten injustice, or else. Got the lass freed without even a penny in bribes!'

Andrew Cobham strode into his great hall and smiled in faint approval at the massive fire set to blaze in preparation for his return. He tugged off his gloves and threw them to the chair by the hearth. He had not yet spoken. Instead Felicia said, 'Had I known prayers could work so quickly, and without even a priest or a candle, I'd have taken up my prayers again some years ago.'

Tyballis did not look as fine as she had the day before during her visit to Baron Throckmorton, but she looked a good deal grander than she had in Bread Street Gaol. On Andrew's orders she had appropriated a dark green gown of worsted with olive velvet trimmings, wide sleeves lined in crimson and edged in beaver, and a hooded cape. In contrast, Andrew Cobham had changed out of his previous magnificence and once again wore his dark grey and dusty velvets, a little torn, a little threadbare and significantly old.

He turned now and faced his lodgers. 'Stories are for long evenings,' he said, 'and mornings for aspiration and preparation. First, you must meet my new tenant. This is Casper Wallop, a recent acquaintance of Tyballis. He will now, I hope, discover the very decent Burgundy that I hid in the cellar, if no one has yet stolen it. I need a drink. Then there are pullets to throttle and pluck, raisins to soak in honey, pie fillings and forcemeat to mix, wine to be spiced and the wassail cup to be brewed. This Christmas feast must serve until Epiphany.'

The conditions of Casper's most recent accommodation needed no explanation, for he smelled of the gaol. He stank of the particular filth that accumulates amongst those living in close confinement and without either hope or purposeful activity. Everyone present knew that smell. Casper was therefore immediately accepted, and had already been talking to anyone who would listen to him. Disappointed to discover that Felicia was married to a still living husband and burdened with a brood of rollicking brats, he was now reconciled to a lack of female companionship. Hearing his name called, he hurried off, after requesting directions, to discover wine for his eccentric new master, and afterwards to be settled into an upstairs chamber of his own.

Without access to the expensive diversions of the rich and noble, the mystery plays or mummings, jugglers or musicians, the inhabitants of Cobham Hall quickly made their own seasonal entertainments. Felicia, helped by Ellen, her small fingers unhampered by the lack of two on her left hand, wove garlands of ivy sprigged with holly, and spread these around the hall, looping them down from the ceiling beams and over the lintel. Branches of holly still nursing bright berries were stuffed into the empty candle sconces. Ralph nailed cut branches into a square, which Felicia and Tyballis then decorated with mistletoe, the fat white berries contrasting with the red. 'A kissing bough, indeed. The priest would probably threaten to excommunicate us as pagan sinners if he knew,' crowed Davey. 'But where are the women to ravish beneath it? We have only three females, and will need to share them between eight men. What justice is that?'

'Mamma won't let you kiss her,' Ellen pointed out. 'But I will.'

'That makes four of you, my dearest,' said Davey, swirling the child up onto his shoulders.

Casper, a man much interested in the art of intoxication, was in charge of the brewing, and kept himself happily busy, working and tasting.

Slipping into the house late in the day, Elizabeth Ingwood was soaked by storm and marked by three new scratches across her face. Tyballis looked at her in surprise, remembering her own disfiguring scars of not too long ago. Tyballis said, 'It's Elizabeth, isn't it? We've seen so little of each other but I'm glad you're here now. We're about to have a Christmas to remember.'

'I'm not staying,' the girl muttered, turning away. 'I only came to see Drew. Or Davey, if Drew's not around.'

'They are both around,' Tyballis told her. 'But please do stay. We're all preparing for a great feast and it starts tomorrow. Even Drew has promised to celebrate with us, and I'm sure he'd like you to be here.'

Elizabeth raised her eyebrows. It accentuated the ragged nail marks over her cheek. 'Stupid slut,' she said. 'It's not me he'll want.

And besides, I've a family of my own, so why should I stay here? I'm no beggar to scrounge my rations or sing for my supper.'

Tyballis paused, then said, 'My husband used to beat me, too, you know.'

Elizabeth shrugged. 'I've no husband, since no one would have me. It's my brother with a ready hand.'

'Brother?' Tyballis stopped stirring the cauldron. 'We're classed as wicked women if we leave our husbands, and the church would send us back to the brutes if they could. But there's no creed says we must stay with a bully of a brother. Why go back to him? Is he so huge?'

'Weasely little bugger, he is.' Elizabeth shrugged again, slumping onto the stool by the fireside, and stretching her legs to the warmth. She was barefoot, and thick mud coated her toes. 'Two years younger than me, too. But at least the bastard keeps me in work. I'd starve without him. And he protects me from the customers, them that's drunk or turns nasty. He hits me when he's pissed, but won't let no one else.'

'It sounds like a bad deal to me. You should leave him to work for himself, and then it's him who would starve.' Tyballis handed her the wooden spoon. 'Will you stir? It's forcemeat for stuffing the hens, and I made it with rather too much cider, so it has to boil up and condense or it will be horribly sloppy. But I still have the suet codlings to make, and it's getting late.'

'What hens?' demanded Elizabeth, dutifully stirring.

'The ones Drew and Ralph are out catching in the shed right now,' Tyballis said. 'I'd planned on two or three, you know. But Drew says four. He said if we didn't kill four, none of us would get more than a wing and a burnt feather. But that means a lot of forcemeat, or the birds will never hold to the spit.' She eyed the bedraggled woman now bent over the cauldron. 'Elizabeth, do you – know anything about cooking?'

'Not much.' Elizabeth peered into the pot and sniffed, then smiled reluctantly. 'Smells good, I'll say that for you. All I ever done was porridge and barley soup. There weren't much to cook in my house when I was little. But I reckon I can stir, if you do the mixing.'

A few hours later, Davey appeared with a gittern, and announced to the household's surprise that he could play it with moderate competence. 'Has one string broken, but that won't put me off,' Davey said, gleefully rubbing the old veneer with his thumb. 'There's no cracks and the other seven strings are good. I'll fiddle while we dance, and Jon has a fine voice if he stays awake long enough to remember the words.'

'We have fine voices, too,' Ralph and Nat said together.

'You both sound like frogs on a wet night,' said Davey. 'What about you, Tybbs, my dear? Do you sing like an angel?'

'No, I don't,' she said quickly. 'But with an upturned bucket, I can play the drums.'

'Two buckets, then, to make a knackerer,' grinned Davey, 'though will be strange from a female, with no knackers in sight.'

'I can rattle spoons to the rhythm, and I shall make sure Jon sings all our favourite songs,' said Felicia. 'The poor dear is tired out, you know, and needs his nap. But tomorrow he'll certainly be awake for the feast, and will lead us all in the carolling.'

'I can sing a little,' murmured Elizabeth cautiously from the shadows. She had been plucking chickens and there were still feathers in her hair. The scratches on her face looked like deep scarlet welts in the firelight.

'And I got a wooden whistle,' Ellen said, tugging at her mother's skirt. 'Drew whittled it ages ago, and give it me when I were littler. I kept it special. But I don't know how to play it.'

'Now that's something I can do, my dear,' announced George Switt from the corner. The elderly widower had hovered for some time in the hope of catching Ellen for a quick cuddle. 'I have an ear for a tune, and used to pipe with a small band of minstrels in my youth. I played for nobility, you know, and all the city aldermen.'

'But where is Drew?' demanded Davey. 'Not planning on sneaking away, is he, like he's always done before?'

Tyballis shook her head. 'He and Luke are out in the big shed chopping that old fallen pine in half for the Yule log. He said it fell in the gales last March, so it might still be rather green, but it's huge and dry, and it wouldn't be Christmas without a great big fire and a Yule log.'

'Would be a better Christmas without Luke Parris,' muttered Davey.

'But Drew will surely have the biggest fire,' grinned Ralph. 'And not one of us will complain about that.'

'Father Horace will complain, all right,' Nat said. 'If there's not one of us at midnight Mass tonight, and he hears of mistletoe and us buggers feasting without giving a penny to the poor nor lighting a candle to Our Lady.'

'Drew don't buy candles,' muttered George Switt.

'Wax is too expensive, and Drew don't like the tallow ones. Says they stink,' Nat nodded. 'Firelight is all we need. But I were talking of Mother Church and that little bald priest at St Mary's. Isn't there none of us going to remember what the day is, and do the proper thing?'

'Drew don't buy candles and he don't go to church.' Ellen sat with her brothers, who were aggrieved at the blissful smells coming from the kitchen yet with nothing put in front of them to eat. Ellen hugged them all and said, 'I'd be proper happy to go to church.'

Her mother shook her head. 'I have nothing decent to wear,' she said, 'and nor do you, my dear. But we could put on our own nativity play. We all know our Bible stories, I hope.'

'Prefer mummings myself,' objected Davey. 'I could play the dragon and Ralph can be St George.'

'I believe that part should rightly be mine,' said George Switt, looking up.

'But mystery plays are more the proper thing, you know,' said Nat, 'and them mummings is nearly as shocking as the mistletoe. Ralph and Davey and I can be the Magi. Well, we're wise and we live in the east, don't we! We got three choices for Our Virgin Lady, and perhaps Luke can play Joseph, having been a monk once. Then there's Gyles for the holy babe Himself, and it'll be shepherds and sheep for the rest of you.'

The rain finally stopped as, with a thumping and thudding, Andrew and Luke dragged in the massive pine trunk, still sticky with straw and chicken droppings from its summer bedding. Casper heard and hurried in with a tray of mulled wine he had prepared, and platters of honeyed bread rolls stuck on little twigs and stuffed with raisins. The children all started to squeal and crawled to Casper's feet, which unbalanced him somewhat but he and the wine made it to their destination unspoiled.

Andrew hauled the log onto the hearth, kicking it far back into place as Luke and Ralph pushed from the front. Without even being doused in alcohol, the bark took flame with a burst of sparks and small scraps of straw flew in cartwheels up the chimney. The smoke made them all cough but the mulled wine helped exceedingly with all problems and everyone raised their cups to the glorious birth of Christianity, to Tyballis, her lucky release from gaol and the miraculous fact that none of the rest of them had yet been arrested that year. Finally, they drank to the generosity and unaccountable wisdom of their enigmatic host, who was enabling them all to celebrate the best Christmas of their lives.

CHAPTER TWENTY

J ust a few miles upriver, the royal court at Westminster was much
involved with a similar although considerably more lavish
celebration.

His gracious highness King Edward IV had momentarily slipped
behind the tapestry screen in order to piss, fart and heave out a small
space in his belly sufficient to fill anew, while still complying with the
etiquette of the occasion. The king enjoyed his food and, thankfully,
the strictly prescribed diet of milk sops and gruel had been long
abandoned. However, even though the sudden and terrifying bout of
dysentery that had inspired the diet, the enforced sickbed and the
frequent rebalancing of the humours by regular bleeding was three
months in the past, the tyranny of memory remained. Certainly the
Christmas season might now pass in the accepted style.

The king returned to his seat on the high dais beneath the golden
canopy, sat heavily and folded his hands over his paunch. He gazed
out at his courtiers with benign approval. During his disastrous illness
an excess of vomiting had left him almost concave; he had felt
strangely slim for the first time since his buoyant youth, but he had
been far too ill to enjoy it. Now the satisfaction of a middle-aged
rotundity had returned, and his grace had every intention of
spreading himself even wider.

Although the feast was confined to three courses, each course consisted of eighteen separate dishes, and King Edward intended to sample them all. His brother, Richard Duke of Gloucester, and his friend William, Lord Hastings might fuss about their monarch's health, but that, the king held, was the business of the physicians. Her grace his queen had been even more frightened about his illness than he had himself, and now, invigorated by relief, encouraged all his appetites once again. Not that he particularly cared for those more strenuous desires these days, but he found it pleasant to have his wife refrain from the complaints and criticisms with which she had previously endowed him. Her son, his stepson, the Marquess of Dorset encouraged him too, as long as he and Hastings were kept safely apart, of course. Meanwhile the king's own two sons were far too young to raise objections about anything except when being told to practise their archery in the rain.

The thickly draped greenery smelled sweet and an aromatic dusting of dried lavender and sprinkled spice tickled his highness's nose and reminded him to call for his cup to be quickly refilled. Nearby he noticed Dorset already boss-eyed and raucous. On the other side, the queen looked prim. No doubt something had touched Elizabeth's sense of her own importance. He would hear about it later but had no intention of thinking about it now. Meanwhile, Richard was deep in conversation with Hastings, also something he'd hear about later no doubt, but they were old friends who saw little of each other during these days of wearisome politics and Richard's endless obligations in the north. His illustrious highness let them talk, and reached for his knife. The roast boar was particularly succulent. He cut a wedge from the huge slice on his platter. The pork skin crackled as he bit and the soft fatty juices rolled over his tongue. He stretched his legs, leaned back in his vast chair and smiled.

Brother Richard, Duke of Gloucester was also enjoying the roast pig. William, Lord Hastings, regarded him with a frown. 'You say this man has proof?' he said quietly.

Richard shook his head, an imperceptible movement that attracted no attention from others at the table. 'I said there is sufficient proof to convince me. Not to present to the king. Nor would I ever consider taking such a matter to trial. It must be dealt with quietly.'

'I have a trusted retainer,' Hastings said. 'Will Catesby, a good lawyer. He can take what is little more than a suggestion and draw up a document that transforms it neatly into proof.'

Gloucester lowered his eyes to his platter. 'Edward would never permit that, nor forgive us for suggesting it. It would shame him, humiliate him. His own family? His most trusted liegemen? His friends? I am somewhat fond of enforcing justice myself, but even an open investigation would be unthinkable. No, I won't make it public, nor even open it to the rumour mill.'

'So, we'll sit back and just watch?'

'This is a conversation for another place. Another time. Not now, my friend. Not here.'

'Tonight, then.'

Richard sighed. 'Christmas night at court? What time will we have for secrets and shadows?'

'I shall come to your chambers directly after Mass tomorrow morning,' nodded Hastings. 'Just tell me one thing first. This man of yours – this secret "war hammer" as you call him – Richard, are you sure he is entirely trustworthy? You think you can go back to Yorkshire and leave this dangerous creature unsupervised? At least give me his name. Then I can set one of my own people to watch him.'

'And must I then set another to watch the man you set to watch mine?' Richard smiled briefly and shook his head again. 'No, William. I trust my friend completely, though he doesn't hold trust as a virtue, calling it a trap for the gullible. But he is the best spy I have ever employed, and has the intelligence to act on his own initiative. I won't have him watched, for he'd know it at once, and I won't risk his identity by giving anyone his name, even you, Will.'

'This matter is far too serious for mistakes, Richard. Your brother—'

'Is enjoying the return to his customary good health. That's enough for the moment. If we are overheard now, it would become more serious still.'

The jugglers had danced the full width of the great hall of

Westminster Palace, and then the full length of the courtiers' table. The Marquess of Dorset, tipsy as a baker's forcemeat pudding, reached out and caught the next whirling baton, crimson streamers fanning a breeze. Dorset's companions dutifully laughed.

'The fool is already cupshotten,' hissed Hastings. 'Yet Edward smiles on him as he would his own son.'

'Never been pissed, Will?' Richard of Gloucester regarded his friend with a slight twitch of a smile.

'– Not that it has any relevance now, but you know perfectly well I dislike the boy, and he makes my skin crawl. Conniving. Grasping. Arrogant. And now this!' Hastings leaned toward Richard, lowering his voice even further. 'And what of our ambitious queen? Could she possibly be involved?'

'I don't believe so,' said the duke at once. 'My man thinks her innocent – in this, at least. As for greed and ambition, why not? Don't we all have a duty to increase our family wealth, barter our loyalty in exchange for property and leave a fair inheritance for our sons? I'll build up my power in the north whenever I can, as you do here at court. This other matter is entirely different. This isn't simply ambition, it's high treason and bloody murder.'

'If we only had proof, Richard.'

'I need no more than I have. That's enough for now, William.' Richard laid his knife down with a snap. 'And I repeat, this conversation is too dangerous. However drunk they are, we might still be overheard. I'll expect you tomorrow morning and we can talk then. But remember, Will, no more hints to my brother.'

'Tell the king his life is in danger from his own wife's family? Not again, I won't. When I hinted before, he was virtually on his deathbed and you'd have expected him to take the story seriously. He didn't. He threw me out. Still thinks I'm jealous of that little slug Dorset. Thinks I'm making absurd accusations just to get the bastard stepson into trouble.'

The final dishes were carried in to the sound of trumpets and fanfare by a flurry of liveried servants all as proud as the royal chef who led the procession. Great platters of silver were heaped with tarts, pies and jellies, but the principal glory was the huge carved subtlety, a great standing sunburst in glimmering sugar, surrounded by winged angels all overlooking the scene of the sugared nativity. Each feather on the angels wings was perfectly formed, each scrap of straw in the manger was finely etched and the Holy Infant's face was as pretty as the queen's. From around the many tables a heaving, mounting murmur rose like the river waters at high tide. Even those too drunk to stand sat up straight, awed and sighing. The king smiled into both his chins.

The royal minstrels had piped in the last course, and now played the most rousing of all the Christmas carols, those known to be the favourites of the king. The king had dressed with some care that morning, choosing the new style of shorter doublet and the long silk knitted hose in disparate stripes so beloved of the Italians. The doublet unfortunately accentuated his girth and hinted at a glimpse of very plump buttocks, but Edward knew a king must show off his power in every sense, and a surfeit of food and drink was a sign of powerful good living. It was true he had trouble getting into his saddle, but he was still a young man of forty years, no more, although his energy was no longer prodigious. Once the most handsome, the king was still, after all, the tallest man at court.

His highness raised a spilling cup. 'To my beloved little brother, famed military leader and hero of the Scottish wars, whom I see all too rarely, and hope to see more often this coming year.'

Richard smiled back and drank deeply. 'To your good health, your grace. And long may you reign in peace.'

The winds had increased considerably overnight. A sleet-bearing gale had toppled chimneys and whistled down every flue, flung open locked doors, broken windows and created draughts where there had been none before. It sent thatches whirling, uprooted fences and snapped whole branches from leafless trees. The river was a raging grey sludge, hurling its waves against the docks and piers and slopping over into the streets. Even the gutters were swept clean by the wind, and along London Bridge the two crammed rows of houses swung and creaked, groaning louder than the chapel choir.

A little downriver, outside London's great eastern wall and past the long shadows of The Tower, Cobham Hall in the Portsoken Ward was as cosy as a nest in spring. Andrew was also raising his cup. 'To the Lord of Misrule,' he called. 'Mister Lyttle, your jester's hat is askew. Are you in charge of this celebration, or not? My cup has been empty this half hour.'

Davey swept off the offending hat, bowing low. 'My lord, this is surely a hanging offence. I shall have all the servants whipped and cast off.' He turned to his neighbour. 'Mister Wallop, where is the master's wine? Keep him waiting any longer, and he'll turn sober on us.'

Casper snorted and set off for the kitchens, an empty jug in each hand. Ralph thumped the table as he left. 'No jugglers, no mumming, and now no wine? The gittern player is pissed and can't keep his hat on, the whistler is in a sulk for having been sat at the opposite end of the table from the children, and the children are all about to be sick from eating more food than they've ever seen in their lives. I say,' he thumped the table again, 'we get up a game of blind-hoodman's buff, and it's Nat we should blind first off.'

Tyballis, the glow of the firelight illuminating her glow of contentment, sighed, nodded, and drank her wine. 'You should enjoy chasing others, Nat,' she smiled, 'instead of being chased yourself for once.'

Nat sniffed. 'Not me. Not being that steady on my feet just at the moment. Set up Casper Wallop. He's half-blind already.'

'Blind one of the women,' grinned Davey. 'With a hood over their heads, they'll be ripe for a grope.' He pointed up at the mistletoe bough above their heads. 'Or we'll play a different game and I'm first in the queue to stand under that.'

'Then get in the queue quick,' advised Elizabeth Ingwood with a toss of her curls, 'and pucker up your lips, my love. Then surely widower Switt will give you a kiss, sweet as you like.'

'Who's got a cape with a hood?' yelled Ralph. 'I got one upstairs. Do I go get it?'

Luke had been sitting quietly, but now said, 'I have a suitable cape,

I believe. It is long and deep-hooded. I left it over the banister rail this morning.' He got up, and in a few moments returned with a long cloak of coarse red dyed buckram, oiled but unlined. He handed it to Ralph, who immediately threw it over his brother's head.

Andrew was drinking deep. 'So – entertain us.' He raised his cup again as Nat stumbled up. 'You cannot catch me, since I've not the slightest intention of climbing to my feet. But catch as catch can – and since everyone here has escaped a hue and cry at some time in their lives, we're all practised runners. Hopefully no one will fall into the fire.'

Nat stretched out both arms, turning his head from side to side. He wore the cape backwards, and the hood entirely covered his face. His voice was muffled, speaking through buckram. 'Felicia must watch the children or I shall stand on them.'

'Everybody up, my beloveds,' yelled Davey.

'Except Drew – and Jon,' chortled Ralph. 'Mister Spiers has once again fallen asleep. His head's in the codlings.'

'How did that man ever find the energy to produce children?' Davey demanded. 'Yet Gyles is only one year old, and looks sufficiently like him.'

'Enough of that,' sniffed Felicia. 'You're a loathsome creature, Davey Lyttle, and Jon is worth a baker's dozen of you. It's true he hasn't found employment recently, but at least he doesn't steal.'

Davey continued to grin. 'Sadly, nor do I, my dear,' he said. 'Not recently, anyway. I try – certainly I try, but opportunity is increasingly hard to come by. But this is Christmas, and with gracious thanks to our sainted Mister Cobham, it seems we eat whether we work or not.'

'Is anyone playing?' objected Nat. 'Or just going to stand arguing?' He turned, arms out, reaching for unseen contact.

'Here,' called Elizabeth.

'Here,' shouted Ralph, dancing out of his brother's reach.

'No, here,' Davey sprang forwards, touching, hopping back and hissing suddenly into Nat's ear. The group skipped around as Nat stumbled from side to side. Felicia darted in to tickle the back of his neck. He heard the swish of her skirts and grabbed, found something and hung on, encircling the small figure with both arms. Delighted, he began to guess the name of his prisoner. 'George Switt,' he decided. 'No, too small even for him. Too skinny for Casper. It's a woman. Elizabeth, I reckon. What luck. Ripe for kissing under the mistletoe.'

Tyballis found herself hugged so tightly she gasped for breath, her complaints smothered. Nat groped her body, rummaging happily across her breasts and discovering the scoop of her neckline. His fingers, greasy with chicken fat and honeyed codlings, were tempted deeper. Tyballis struggled away but was held too tightly, and felt her feet leave the ground. One large hand pushed into her cleavage. She squeaked, but was not heeded. 'Come on, Elizabeth, never known you to be shy,' Nat chuckled. 'Give us a kiss and a squeeze.'

Andrew Cobham rose lazily to his feet. 'I believe,' he said softly, 'I must stop you, my friend. It seems the game has run its course. It is now over.'

CHAPTER TWENTY-ONE

He stood afterwards, tall and still in front of the fire, his hands behind his back. His shadow flared across the floorboards before him and at his back the Yule log blazed and crackled. The wind howled outside, barely muffled by the shutters as twigs and debris were flung against the glass. Gusts blew down the chimney and the flames leapt. It was very late. The party had finished in the small hours. Luke, somewhat glazed, left first, and then the Spiers staggered off just before midnight, their sleeping children tucked beneath their arms; Jon had revived sufficiently in time for bed. The others had stayed, rollicking and joyous, until they could no longer stand.

Fallen holly berries lay half-submerged in pie filling, the pastry case shattered in pieces to either side, and a trickle of spilled wine reflected the fire's waning sparks. The platters had been stacked, spoons heaped, and all of it left for a more industrious morning. Tyballis sat on the little cushioned tuffet, her arms tightly encircling her knees, feet tucked together beneath her skirts, head raised and eyes wide, silently watching Andrew Cobham. She was waiting for him to speak, for he had asked her to stay behind when the others left.

He spoke quite suddenly into the quiet. 'I leave at first light. I will be gone for some time. I thought you should know.'

She swallowed back the disappointment. She had hoped he

144

intended to say something quite different. 'Why should I know? Why are you leaving?' She wished to sound confident but her voice came out in a whisper.

His own voice was so soft that it merged with the rhythmic murmur of the burning logs. 'I should have left before,' he said. 'I stayed only to celebrate – with you. Because I knew it was what you wanted.'

She looked up at him for some time before deciding on her words. 'It is reasonable, of course,' she said at last, 'to want to enjoy a pleasant Christmas with your friends. But if you should have left before, I suppose you are now in a hurry. I ought not to be keeping you from your bed.'

'I've not the slightest interest in the company of the others,' Andrew replied. 'I stayed, as I said, for you. When I returned here some days ago, I came simply to pack for my journey. But I then heard of your arrest. Arranging your release delayed my departure, and I then chose to delay it further. But no excuses remain, and I have no intention of inventing any. I leave tomorrow. You know why.'

She nodded. 'It's about your work. It's about poison. It's about the king.'

'Do you need money?' he said.

She raised her chin. 'Throckmorton's money? Profit from death and poison? I don't want it.'

He laughed softly. 'What a charmingly moral child you are, my dear. Why I choose to defend myself I have no idea, but let me tell you the considerable sums of money I earn come directly from Richard of Gloucester. It is the duke who paid for the Christmas dinner you have eaten, and the florins I gave you previously. I blackmail, bribe and otherwise offend against your standards in order to continue my work while the duke is absent, as he is for long periods, but principally to create fear and caution amongst those I wish to threaten. Throckmorton's money, should he provide me with the next instalment, will certainly be spent in Gloucester's service. However, if dear Harold takes heed of the warning I gave him, he will leave the country at once. If he stays here, he'll be dead by Epiphany or soon after.'

145

'Oh.' Tyballis stared at her toes. 'I see. I have eight florins left and that will probably last me until next Christmas. It's not as if I do anything except buy food. I'll feed the Spiers family, too, like I did before, and sometimes help the others. I expect you want me to do that.'

'You may do exactly as you wish, my dear.'

Although she thought him tired, Andrew made no move towards his own chambers, but there seemed nothing more to say. The silence dragged, broken only by the sounds of the wind outside and the flames in the hearth. Tyballis stood slowly. She hoped he would stop her, but he did not. She paused a moment, preparing only to wish him a good night and a safe journey. He smiled, just a tuck at the corner of his mouth as if he had no energy for more. There were tiny points of flames reflected in the black depths of his eyes. She sighed and then took a deep breath, clenching her hands at her sides, her arms stiff to stop them trembling, and said quietly, 'I wish you wouldn't go, though I understand you have to. I worked for you before and you said I did well. If I could come with you this time, I would do anything, play any part just as you tell me. But more, too, if it interests you and if you … want me.' She stopped and held her breath. He said nothing, but frowned at her, as if no longer sure who she was. So, she took another breath and continued in a rush. 'I mean inclination, not obligation – as you once told me. You see, everything's altered. You altered it. When you come into the room, it's as if someone has lit all the candles. You don't ever buy candles, but it's almost as if you are one. And when you go away, the light goes, too, as if someone blew out the candles. So, if you go away for a very long time, I shall truly be left in the dark.'

Into the huge echoing silence that followed, Andrew took one quick stride towards her, his arm around her and his palm pressing firmly at the back of her waist. She was drawn close and held tight. Then he leaned down and kissed her hard on the mouth. She saw his eyes open, and closed her own, tasting the heat of his breath as it rushed into her throat.

He released her suddenly. His hands had not roamed, and his retreat was abrupt. As he stood there, watching her again in silence, she thought his expression not avid but thoughtful, while in contrast she was breathless and excited. Eventually he said, very softly, 'I would bring you no happiness, little one. This is a dalliance I will not begin. You must neither trust me nor care for me.'

The shock hurt. She thought she might cry, turning instead to anger. 'Dalliance? I see. Then I don't trust you, nor care for you. Go to Elizabeth Ingwood if you want a woman.'

He smiled very slightly. 'I'm sorry, child. Which is, strangely enough, the truth. I am sorry, though more for myself than for you. In losing me, you lose nothing. But I shall return in a month or two, and will see you then perhaps, if you choose to stay.'

Tyballis sighed and looked away, took one more deep breath and whispered, 'But you kissed me.'

'It is something I shall remember,' he said, unsmiling, 'when the nights are cold and the bed in some wayside tavern is unaired and unwarmed.' He turned away and faced the fire, his back to her as he looked down into the flames. His voice and the flames sounded the same, one merging into the other. 'Goodnight, little one.'

She fled, running up the stairs, stumbling and half tripping. She pushed her own chamber door shut and leaned against it, gasping and sobbing. Then she fell into bed fully dressed and cried herself to sleep.

In the morning Andrew Cobham had gone.

CHAPTER TWENTY-TWO

The winter worsened yet again. It was a bleak Epiphany and the following day it snowed. Since the weather matched her mood, Tyballis did not complain. She lit her own fires high and piled up old twigs and fallen branches collected from the gardens. When the damp wood smoked too much or became hard to find, she bought bundled faggots from the tanner's little roofed market, where the stench of the urine kegs seeped into the taste of the bacon hanging from the rafters. But it was not so far to walk home with the weight of wood overflowing her basket, kindling cost less than the London Cheaps, and the people were friendlier. Tyballis shared her firewood and her food with the Spiers, and frequently with the others. She came to be known as a woman of means, though what fuelled her generosity puzzled them all. Questions were never openly asked but everyone enjoyed guessing. The guesses were always quite wrong.

The hearth in the great hall downstairs stayed dark, empty and unused, while the shadows took up permanent residence and the cold shivered through the old timbers, but Tyballis continued to use the kitchens and she rarely ate alone. Sometimes only Ellen joined her, sometimes the Tame twins came, sometimes Davey, often Casper, or all of them together, with stories to tell and plenty of laughter. Tyballis twice invited Luke Parris but he blushed and refused her, and she rarely cared to ask widower Switt. Elizabeth Ingwood had left the house soon after Andrew's departure, and was not seen for weeks. When she returned, her face was bruised again and she hid away either in her own room, or in Davey's.

With little to do except purchase, prepare and eat meals, Tyballis searched for any activity to keep her mind blank and her body tired. She darned stockings, helped wash and delouse the children, scoured pots in the kitchen and pulled weeds from the wreckage of the old herb plot in the garden. But her room was too small to scrub every day, and even the ashes from her busy fires took only minutes to clear. After too many desperate days she decided to clean downstairs. There was no one to stop her anymore.

Andrew Cobham's quarters fascinated at once. Knowing she should not investigate without the owner's permission, Tyballis was immediately attracted. Exploring hesitantly, she carried bucket, brush, broom and a fearsome expression of guilt.

Leading from the familiarity of the great hall was an unlit passage opening directly into the large bedchamber with garderobe, and through that a tiny staircase leading up to what had originally been a minstrel's gallery, now enclosed and divided into two chambers. The smaller appeared to be a study and library, the other a place of storage heaped with dusty furniture, piled trunks, rolled tapestries, chairs, trestles, splintered coffers and bed stands with missing strings. These rooms were not locked, so Tyballis decided she might clean and tidy at will.

She had barely known the man when she first woke in his bed. She knew him little better now. His chamber introduced him further. Rising from its own shadows like an exhausted peacock, the bed filled half the space, its curtains dust-thick and heavy in unravelling embroidery over velvets of imperial purple. Tyballis sat. The covers had not been straightened since Andrew Cobham's last night and she could almost smell him, seeing the shape of his body beneath the coverlet, the indention of his head still clear on the bolster.

Finding clean linen inside the window seat, Tyballis remade the bed, smoothed her hands across the fine sheets, remembering, wondering, imagining as she tucked in their frayed edges. She did not have the strength to turn the mattress or fluff up its filling, though she thought it had not been turned for years and would benefit greatly from some care. Instead she lifted her broom and began to beat the curtains. The dust hurtled out in clouds and made her sneeze as threads of embroidery snagged on the broom's rushes.

The smaller room taking up the other half of the enclosed minstrel's gallery interested her. Shelves festooned with spiders' webs held books and parchments. She did not know her letters well enough to read what was in them, but she recognised the recent printing of Arthur's Tales. A great cushioned chair, as comfortable as a bed, stood beside the little empty hearth. This was a place, she supposed, for a serious man to enjoy his studies. There were also three small carved coffers, each latched and locked. It was true that Andrew Cobham did not trust his fellow man.

Everywhere downstairs the style was heavy and gilded with gothic archways, high inlet windows and carved beams. Beyond this private domain, the outhouses and pantries clustering around the tiled kitchens were also clearly old, for they were poorly thatched and tumbledown. Yet the main staircase and the rooms upstairs were plastered and lime-washed, wide-windowed and plain-beamed, as if they had been added later in accordance with necessity and modern fashions. At the same time perhaps, the minstrel's gallery had been divided with thin-planked boards. It was a house, she decided, first built long ago in the grand style, but in accordance with a growing family's needs it had been extended to include more bedchambers upstairs and within the attic. It was, above all else, a house that did not in the least suit its current owner, a man holding neither wealth nor family, nor any need for such a mansion. So, he opened his many rooms to those who could not easily pay for their own. Yet the house would, Tyballis decided, be worth a fair sum. She had no idea how Mister Cobham had originally got to know his motley lodgers, or why a man who trusted no one would choose to live amongst thieves. Possible answers, to a hundred possible questions, rose like dust from the corners of her mind.

Over several days she cleaned without prying. On the fourth day she pried. Taking a deep breath, she explored under the bed and within the window seats, climbing the shelves and looking behind the books. She searched the stuffy pegs of hanging clothes in the garderobe, discovering there such diversity she thought a whole troop of play actors might find costumes sufficient for a dozen mystery plays. She crawled beneath stacked trestles and old chairs, she peeped under cushions. She tried the lids of trunks and coffers and she swung back the bed curtains. Everywhere she found secrets, and could decipher none of them. A wooden chest as small as a child's toy sat right on top of the bed's canopied tester, nearly as high as the ceiling beams and completely hidden. But it was locked. There was no key. Behind the books on the shelves she saw only dead spiders, but beneath the bed and right at the back was a rolled parchment tied in string and sealed in rich red wax. Many boxes in oak and mahogany were casually strewn, others concealed. All were impossible to open. Tucked beneath the folded linen in the window seat were two books bound in plain leather, the parchment pages either thick with listed numbers, or blank, awaiting the scribe. The huge chair in the study held its own special secret, for the cushion lifted and inside a shallow space lay other scrolls. One carried a grand coat of arms and all were crammed with writing she did not understand. In the toe of a pair of bright new shoes casually set amongst others in the garderobe, a small iron key was hidden. She then discovered others, yet since a hundred trunks, boxes and coffers were locked and locked again, she did not know which one any key fitted.

Tyballis left Andrew Cobham's quarters, carefully closing each door behind her. She continued to cook for the other occupants of the house, but she did not inquire into anyone's personal relationship to their landlord. Questions were avoided in a house where each man's habits were better undisclosed.

However, it was not at home that she received the first small answers, but at St Katherine's docks. Snow had smothered the city again that night, and the port was quiet. Few of the great trading ships braved the winter oceans and few merchants would chance losing their entire cargo in a January storm. But Tyballis was shopping for eels and the little eel boats often rowed down from Marlowe's Quay to sell off the last of their fish cheaply to the impoverished and less fussy buyers of the Portsoken Ward. One small crier had braved the gales and now rode at anchor, waiting mid port for the custom's men to board her. Someone else was waiting on land. Striding the quay, Harold, fifth Baron Throckmorton, kicked at the fresh snow banking the idle cranes. He was impatient and not expecting to be seen, for there were few sailors, few customers and few officials working during the stultifying freeze.

He saw Tyballis at the same moment she saw him. Their reaction was similar. Both started, glared and took two quick steps, Throckmorton forwards, Tyballis back. The baron was quicker. His grip fastened on her shoulder. 'You, you slut. Dared to face the world without your protector, have you? So, where's Feayton?'

Tyballis tried to twist loose. 'I've no idea. And you've no right to touch me. Let me go.'

'Not dressed so fine now, are you, slut?' Throckmorton held her tighter. 'So, you're not Feayton's mistress anymore, perhaps. But you've not returned to your husband either, as I know full well, so a whore now maybe, or if Feayton's thrown you out, a slattern working the tanneries.'

Neat in green worsted, Tyballis was well aware she fitted none of Throckmorton's accusations. She scowled into the baron's pale eyes. He was not much taller than she was, and his red curls, damp and snow-speckled beneath his felt cap, tickled her nose as he pulled her closer. She wrenched back. 'How dare you? You laid false witness against me before. There's not a sheriff nor a constable will believe you again.'

'It's not the law will deal with you this time,' Throckmorton spat. 'I'm taking you into custody myself. I've a nice little wine cellar beneath my kitchens, damp and dark and just the perfect dungeon for trollops who won't talk. Feayton's threatened me for the very last time. Let's see if he still demands his damned money once he learns his doxy's locked up in my cellars.'

Throckmorton's two companions stepped forwards and gripped Tyballis between them. 'You can't drag me all through London,' she said, struggling. 'And don't think I'll come quietly, for I'll be shouting all the way, and shouting everything I know. That will alert the law, I promise.'

'Dirty whore,' snarled the baron. 'You've just made my choice a damned sight easier.' He turned to one of his companions. 'Hire a horse and cart from the tavern stables, and get it back here quickly.'

As the man hurried away, the other turned to Throckmorton. 'But we've not collected the goods from the ship yet, my lord. Will you leave what we came to get, just for some skinny wench who double-crossed you?'

'Idiot.' His lordship was losing patience. 'Double-crossing me is something no one gets away with, and you remember that. This is a different matter, and well nigh as important as the cargo. But it'll be you and Hammon will take the trollop back to the house and lock her in the cellars. Avoid the servants, especially Bodge. Meanwhile I stay here to meet Francesco and collect whatever he's smuggled in as soon as he comes ashore.'

The baron's companion sniffed. 'Drive a cart all the way to Bradstrete with some female shrieking and struggling in the back? Look – we've already got a few folk watching and wondering. When her people find she's gone and start asking questions, there'll be those here that remember. Hanged for kidnap's not my choice of payment.'

'Keep your voice down and watch what you say.' Throckmorton turned quickly to Tyballis, fisting one hand heavy with jewelled rings. Then he struck her full force to the jaw. She collapsed in his arms.

Several times she opened her eyes as the cart rolled and tumbled her across its boards. At each bump of the road and rattle of the wheels, she bounced and discovered new bruises. Each time she heaved and spluttered against the hands holding her down and gagging her. Twice again she was knocked unconscious.

When eventually Tyballis woke quite alone, the darkness was utterly silent and bitterly cold.

CHAPTER TWENTY-THREE

Tyballis smelled sour wine and oozing damp, mould on old stone and mouse droppings. Sitting up hurt as her head pounded like thunder, but eventually she stood, reaching out to discover the walls. It was not as foul as Bread Street prison but it was far more frightening.

She was neither bound nor chained, but the freedom to explore her cage gave little benefit. The space was small, four steps in one direction, ten in the other. There were no windows, and the only door, thick oak and heavy-hinged, was locked. The walls were wet stone. The floor was beaten earth, and also wet. In a corner stood two large wooden butts, each empty but smelling of old wine. Several long shelves banked one wall, also empty. There was nothing else.

Soft woollen and fur-lined, her cloak – Drew's gift – was her greatest comfort. Her jaw throbbed and she remained disorientated. Several hours passed as she slumped, trying not to cry. She forced herself to think how she might approach whatever happened next, and how she might extricate herself from the worst disaster since escaping her husband. Being sure this time that none of her new friends had been at the port to watch her abduction, she expected no rescue. Drew was gone. She would have to help herself.

It seemed a very long time later when the door was unlocked and creaked open, allowing light to flood in. She was immediately blinded. Throckmorton's voice said, 'Well, slut? Ready to talk?'

Tyballis squinted at the dark shape looming in the doorway. She croaked, 'I'll tell you anything you want if you let me out of here.' Then she remembered her courage. 'But first I need something to drink. You've probably broken my jaw, and if I die, Lord Feayton will kill you.'

'He won't have the faintest idea where you are, stupid bitch.' Throckmorton stepped within the cellar's gloom and peered down into her face. 'But I'll take you upstairs if you're obedient. I have questions and I want answers.'

'And then you'll let me go?'

He sniggered. 'We'll see about that.'

It was someone else who grabbed her arm and hauled her from the cellar and up the stone steps. A narrow corridor led from the stairs directly into the hall, but she was marched away from this into a small parlour to the side. It was unheated, and one window, paned in thick green glass, let in a trickle of sallow light. The thickset man who had brought Tyballis upstairs now dragged her to face her captor. She stared into the baron's angry eyes and tried to stand proud.

'Now,' he said. 'Tell me about Feayton. Where is he? And exactly what else do you know about him?'

She had been thinking fast for some minutes. 'Lord Feayton's left London, my lord. He travelled west immediately after Christmas,' she said. 'He went to Wales. I believe he was invited to spend Epiphany at Ludlow Castle. He didn't tell me why, or with whom. I am, after all, just a woman.'

Throckmorton seemed to find nothing wrong with this assertion, but he blanched at the news, and bit his lip. 'Ludlow? By invitation?'

Tyballis gained confidence. 'Yes, my lord. He left on the morning of St Stephen's, taking a great deal of luggage with him and his squire and servants. He told me to expect his return within the month. You expect him yourself before the end of January, I believe. When we last met, I remember Lord Feayton saying he would be back to collect the monies that were due.'

'None of your business, trollop.' The baron glowered. 'Let's see what else you remember. When Feayton left you, did he mention whom he meant to meet? Did he mention Lord Rivers? Or any other name?'

Tyballis hid her smile. 'No, my lord. Lord Feayton mentioned no one. He would not tell me such intimate details.'

'Damnation, girl, do you ask nothing of the man?' Throckmorton sat rigid, tapping his foot, hands gripping his knees. 'Very well. Now tell me, and in detail, exactly what you do know. I'm not interested in rumour, nor bedroom fumbles, but tell me exactly how you met him, and what you know of his lineage, his family and his title. Who else have you met in his company? And where does he live while in London?'

Thinking fast, she frowned and said, 'I don't know much, my lord. I met his lordship after being arrested, when he got me out. Then he took me to a tavern. That's all I know of him.'

Throckmorton scowled. He nodded at the other man who immediately boxed her ears. She winced, almost falling. The baron said, 'Each time she lies to me, John, you will punish her.' He turned again to Tyballis. 'If you continue to annoy me,' he told her coldly, 'I shall have you stripped and thrashed. How dare you think me so easily deceived? Now, if you want to avoid punishment, answer my questions, and this time make sure it's the truth.'

She believed his threats. She knew very well what Borin used to do for this man's brother. 'I've never met any of Lord Feayton's friends,' she said at once. 'And I know nothing at all about his family. He never discusses his private business with a – common woman.'

'Yet he got you out of prison. A woman he'd never met? Why?'

'He's interested in justice. Lord Feayton is a wealthy man, and friend of dukes. I don't know any more.'

Throckmorton stood suddenly, gripping her chin between his fingers and forcing her to look into his face. The pain made her eyes water. 'Feayton may be wealthy now, Mistress Blessop, from the money I pay him and whatever he steals from others like myself. But he was no friend of dukes when I first knew him. His clothes were old and ragged, his boots worn out. I don't believe he's a man of property. There are impoverished noblemen as I happen to know very well, and

Feayton was one.' He released her, stepping back again. 'Now, tell me where this creature lives.'

Tyballis shook her head. 'He doesn't take me to his home, my lord. I've never seen it. He takes me to the tavern, when he wishes to – be with me. I told you, my lord. The White Rose, down by the river.'

The baron stared searchingly at her. 'You've no home of your own since you ran from Blessop. Don't tell me Feayton puts you up permanently at a respectable inn.'

Tyballis murmured, 'Usually I stay with a friend near the tanneries.'

Throckmorton began to pace. Hands behind his back, he strode the boards. His legs, curved like those of a child still in nether-cloths, were thin and his hose wrinkled in crimson folds around knees and ankles. 'Very well,' he said, looking up at last. 'Perhaps it's the truth. I'll accept your word for now.' He beckoned to his henchman. 'Take her back below, John. When Feayton turns up, he'll get a damn sight more than the money he thinks to steal from me. He'll find six armed men ready to pounce, and his slut of a mistress dragged up naked from the cellar. Then, instead of listening to his demands for coin, I'll have him on his knees begging for both your lives.'

Tyballis kicked out at the man holding her. John Hammon, heavily muscled and permanently bad-tempered, smashed the back of his hand across her face. She bit her lip on a whimper. 'Bastards,' she yelled. 'You said you'd let me go if I answered your questions.'

'You've answered little enough,' sneered the baron. 'And I never said as much, since I had no intention of letting you go. What, let you free to run straight off to your friend the constable? You're going nowhere, Mistress Blessop. First I think I'll send for your fool of a husband and give him the satisfaction of thrashing you. Will that seem fair enough to your justice-loving master, I wonder, before I finish him off as well?'

'Borin won't – he doesn't—' Tyballis felt herself go white. 'Besides, Lord Feayton won't care! He doesn't even know Borin and he'll never fall into your horrid trap. He's much too careful.'

'Feayton not know your charming husband?' Throckmorton grinned. 'There's not much you understand about either of your bedfellows, is there, stupid slut! Borin's been working for Feayton as long as he did for my dear brother. Perhaps the one of us can beat you while the other watches, though who, I wonder, will enjoy it most? Myself, or Blessop?' The baron turned again to his henchman. Tyballis was now trembling. John Hammon had her hands forced so high up behind her back that the strain on her shoulders and elbows was becoming unbearable. She no longer had the strength to kick. 'In the meantime,' Throckmorton continued, 'I want her alive so give the slut ale and gruel, but make sure none of the servants see what's going on.'

Hauled once again down the little steps, Tyballis was thrown to the damp dark ground and heard the door lock. This time she cried.

She thought it was probably the next morning when she awoke, finding herself curled and stiff, wretchedly sore and utterly miserable. She rubbed her jaw carefully and decided it was neither broken nor dislocated, although the bruising would be ugly. Edging her way around the perimeter of her dungeon, she discovered a scattering of stones that had dislodged from the base of the old wall. She scrabbled in the dirt and found two pebbles of a reasonable size. One was sharp cornered, the other smaller but pointed. She stuffed both into her purse. The purse given her by Andrew Cobham had been taken by the sheriff, but this was her own, coarse unbleached hessian. It held only pennies but together with the weight of the pebbles it would, she thought, make a weapon of sorts, as would the heels of her boots which had come from the Duke of Gloucester's annexe garderobe and were well soled.

Time dragged, but Tyballis sat, nursing her determination. She honed her plans as she honed the stones she had found, chipping away to sharpen the edges. When finally someone came to bring her food, she was ready. She held her breath, hearing the clank and then the squeak of iron against iron as the door was unlocked.

John Hammon, holding a candle in one hand, a mug of ale and a wedge of black bread balancing on a wooden trencher in the other, found himself gazing into an empty chamber. He gulped, wondering what in pity's name he had done to allow her escape, and how he would certainly be punished for it. He set the trencher down to one side, pulled the door almost closed behind him and, candle held high, began to poke around the corners of the room. He was passing the two large wine butts when he was hit extremely hard over the head. Then from nowhere something very sharp dug deep into his face.

John staggered back, his hand to his forehead as warm sticky blood began to drip into his eyes. Trying to wipe his face, he dropped the candle and the flame went out at once. He heard a bang as one of the wine barrels toppled, then something hit him again. At almost the same time a small well-shod foot kicked him hard between his legs. John Hammon groaned. The pain struck him from groin to belly and he doubled over, nursing his middle. The foot came once more between his legs, this time from the back. John squealed. He was still gasping for breath when the heavy wooden trencher he had been carrying struck between his shoulder blades, and as he turned, struck his nose full on. Blood poured from nostrils to mouth, and made him wail. He had not yet managed to rise, was still on his knees and groping blindly, when he heard the patter of small feet running fast up the stone steps outside.

Tyballis raced through the empty and shadowed hall, quickly found the great double doors through which she had sometimes entered, and flung them open. The discreet cough behind her, sounding almost apologetic, made her jump. The steward's large hand slapped down on her shoulder and she whirled round. 'Explain yourself at once, my girl,' Bodge said. 'And then you'll wait here while I summon his lordship.'

Tyballis shrugged off the startled hand. 'Your vile master is a criminal and a – a poisoner.' She ran past him, out through the doors and down into the street. It was snowing. The world had been muffled by freeze. Shrinking into the long shadows as she crept through the back streets towards London's eastern wall and the gate into the Portsoken Ward, she stopped three times, leaning over into the whitened gutters to vomit. Before she was home again, something occurred to her and she wondered if the beer she'd been given had been poisoned, since keeping a healthy and furious prisoner secret from a household of servants would be remarkably difficult.

Through the Aldgate, avoiding the scrutiny of the gatekeeper and just a few minutes from home, she stopped, crouched down and stuck her fingers as far as she could down her throat. Her throat was already sore. She vomited until sure there was nothing left of whatever she had drunk in Throckmorton's cellar.

The Cobham Hall garden was white. Snow dripped from branches, banked against bushes, and hid both weed and path. The hush was soft and gentle and etched with tiny paw and claw prints and the little spots of melt where icicles had snapped and fallen. Tyballis barely recognised her way to the house.

Davey Lyttle found her on the doorstep.

He knelt, the glories of his turquoise silk hose spoiling in the snow, clasped her tightly and began to lift her.

She shut her eyes, smiled weakly and said, 'Hello Davey. There's someone I want you to help me murder.'

CHAPTER TWENTY-FOUR

They put her to bed, crowding around and watching her earnestly, trying to make out some meaning in her small croaks and whispers. They were too concerned about both her disappearance and her reappearance to remark on the fact that she smelled remarkably strongly of very sour wine. Indeed, her skirt hems seemed to be stained with it.

Sometime later it was Andrew's wine – leftover from Christmas, now newly heated, spiced and sweetened with honey – which they gave her. Casper, increasingly interested in the state of his new host's secret supplies, had recently mastered the addition of spices. 'A nice cup o' clarry, mistress,' cooed Casper. 'Will do you good, and bring back the colour to your little cheeks.'

'Damn well coloured already, if you ask me,' muttered Nat. 'Face is as purple as Davey's new doublet.'

'No one is asking you,' Davey pointed out. 'Our Tybbs has been brutally attacked, and once I find out who did it, I'll demand a reckoning.'

'Did she really tell you she wanted someone killed?' whispered Felicia.

Davey nodded. 'Not exactly in my line,' he said, keeping his own voice low. 'But I shall do my best.'

'If you don't – I will,' decided Casper. 'Never been put off by a nice bit of blood-letting myself. Now, I've always said the best way – and too often overlooked by them as ought to know better – is right through the lug-hole. You gets a sudden rush of muck, of course, and needs step back right quick, but it does the job.'

'Might be her husband did it,' pondered Nat with a grumble. 'I happen to know she has one. Wears her hair loose most of the time, but I've heard her mention a Mister Blessop. Maybe she went back to him, or maybe he ran into her by chance. Can't blame a man for beating his wife, specially if she's run away. Can't go killing the poor bastard just for what he does to his own wife.'

'I can if I want,' scowled Davey. 'I can do whatever I wish, and no need to ask you, you light-fingered bugger. Husband or no husband, bully nor coward, I've no friendship for a man I've never met and already don't like. Tybbs wants the bastard dead? Well, I'll see what I can do.'

'Besides – weren't her husband,' added Casper. 'I knows him.'

'Oh hush, both of you,' said Felicia. 'This is silly talk. First we must find out what really happened and nurse the poor dear back to health.'

'Specially since it's her has the money,' sniffed Nat, 'and her that buys most of your food. You'll be looking after your own best interests, no doubt.'

'You're turning into a right miserable bugger, Nat Tame,' objected his brother. 'The lass has given you plenty of free meals, too. You're just sour since Drew stopped you groping her at Christmas. Cheer up, now, and let's see what we can do to help and not hinder.'

The discussion had drowned out her attempts to explain herself, but now Tyballis struggled up a little and glared at them. 'You all keep arguing over my head,' she croaked. 'But you're not listening. I was kidnapped. Kept in a cellar and maybe even poisoned.'

Several faces stared down at her in evident disbelief. 'Shock and too much wine,' suggested Nat. 'Lost her wits.'

Tyballis shook her head a little wildly and then wished she hadn't. 'I was at the docks. I was grabbed by three men including Baron Throckmorton. He's a skinny little pig with bandy legs and red hair. He has – well, I suppose you could say – a reason to hate me as much

162

as I hate him. They dragged me off in a cart and locked me up in the cellar.'

'There was a full moon last night,' remembered Nat gloomily.

'I am not a lunatic,' said Tyballis, taking a long and furious breath. 'Look at my bruises. The bastards punched me and the baron wore big rings. Those hurt.'

'You do look a touch – the worse for something,' admitted Davey. 'Don't worry, it's not too bad. The marks will fade soon enough.'

'Don't tell fibs, Davey Lyttle,' said Felicia. 'The poor dear is very badly bruised and looks terrible. Now, Tybbs dearest, tell us the rest.'

Half way through her story Elizabeth peeped past the open door of the chamber and, intrigued, joined the crowd around the bed. The noise also attracted Mister Switt who hovered in the background. Only Luke and Jon, the latter fast asleep in bed, remained absent.

Tyballis explained the previous baron's sudden death and Borin's arrest for the murder, his eventual release and her own resulting incarceration. Some of this was already known to the household, though not the full details, and she offered only a vague description of Andrew's interactions with both barons Throckmorton.

'Andrew Cobham is a money lender?' gulped Felicia. Tyballis denied this quickly, then finished her story.

After a few moments, Davey broke the silence. 'The story's a little hard to follow, my lovely, but it's clear something must be done.'

Casper, torn between old loyalties to Borin and new loyalties to everyone else, got the hiccups. Nat was simply confused. Widower Swirt shook his head and sat down in a hurry. Ralph said, 'But you're here. And where's Drew?'

'I escaped,' Tyballis said. 'And I don't know where Drew is.'

'You were locked in a cellar? By a baron? Kidnapped by a load of armed men? And you escaped?' objected Nat.

Elizabeth quickly pushed to the front of the crowd and scowled at everyone. 'And why shouldn't she escape?' she demanded. 'You think a woman too weak? Well, let me tell you, women are smarter and quicker – and any woman could escape a bunch of stupid men if she wanted.'

Tyballis smiled. It made her face hurt. 'Thank you, Lizzie,' she said.

'I hid in an empty wine barrel and the man who came in was stupid. When his candle blew out, he started stumbling around like a drunken bear. I was accustomed to the dark already and I could see quite well so I kicked him and got away while he was still doubled over.'

'Kicked him in his cods, I hope,' said Elizabeth.

'But unfortunately Throckmorton isn't as stupid as his henchmen.' Tyballis nodded to no one in particular. 'All I know is, he owes Drew money and doesn't want to pay. He was going to use me as bait to lure Drew in because he wants to kill him. Now he's lost his bait, but he won't drop his plans that easily. He will still try, I'm sure.' Tyballis paused and took a deep breath. 'So, we have to kill Throckmorton first.'

'Ah,' said Ralph. 'Murder a baron? Might be a problem.'

'Get Borin,' Casper advised. 'Not a bad man. Saved my life.'

'Borin couldn't kill a mouse,' snorted Tyballis. 'And it was him got me chucked in prison in the first place. Him and his vile mother and the revolting baron.'

'Well,' said Elizabeth, sitting heavily on the edge of the bed, 'I'll stab the bastard if you want. I'll do all three.'

Which was when Mister Switt pushed forwards and, clasping his hands earnestly before him, looked down at Tyballis and said, 'My dear young woman, may I make a suggestion? This appears to be a grave and sinister matter. You have clearly been put in great danger, and subjected to shocking violence. That you got away is certainly a credit to your own ingenuity, but ingenuity may not be enough. It seems we must all work together and devise a plan to keep our esteemed Mister Cobham free from harm. Amongst us there are many diverse talents, and I hesitate to speak for myself, but I venture to suggest that not one of us is entirely without wit. Personally, I shall do whatever is required of me. We owe Mister Cobham our allegiance. We must devise a plan.'

Everyone turned their head in surprise. It was Elizabeth who, after a brief pause, said, 'Right as nine pence, George. So, ain't no bugger of a baron will get the better of me. Less Drew comes back in the meantime, it's down to us.'

The following morning they took over the grand table in the hall. Widower Switt declined the honour of sitting at the head, so Davey cheerfully claimed the place. Tyballis sat in the middle where they could all hear her explanations, since her voice was still hoarse. The children quickly gathered beneath the table and squabbled as to who should sit on their mother's feet. It was, however, a faint shock to everyone when, at the moment of scraping of chairs, rustling of skirts and pouring of ale, Jon Spiers trotted down the stairs and abruptly sat at the table's vacant end. A startled silence continued until Felicia cleared her throat and said mildly, 'Dear Jon is feeling a little better today. And we would sorely miss his suggestions if he did not attend. I see no reason for everyone's surprise.'

Everyone quickly denied either surprise or objection, and began instead to discuss what was needed. 'I have a little money,' Tyballis told them. 'I'll be happy to use every penny on this – this – whatever we decide.'

'And none of us will ask where you got it, my dear,' Felicia assured her.

Tyballis glowered and Casper cackled. 'Reckon I knows more, and no harm in telling,' he said. He looked, one eye blinking hard, to Tyballis for direction. She blushed and looked down meekly, so Casper continued. 'What you lot don't know, is this Mister Cobham is a man what leads two different lives and Mistress Tyballis be a fair part o' both. Well, he didn't make me swear no oaths to keep me mouth shut, so I can tell you he surely ain't no beggar, this gent o' yorn. Took me to his quarters in Bishopsgate, he did, right next to Crosby's. Now, I knows, and no doubt you lot does too, that's where the Duke o' Gloucester lives when in London, and I reckon there ain't no one stays there without his proper permission. So, what's our Mister Cobham doing with dukes and barons, then? Dressed up like a duke himself he was when I seen him there. And Mistress Blessop could have been a duchess, and no argument. Nobody told me what were going on, nor I weren't going to ask. But summit is. And I reckon that's where the money come from, and proper legal it is, too. Understood?'

Tyballis blushed again. 'It's true,' she said, though it was whether to tell the truth, or whether to lie, and which would help Andrew the most, that she was now struggling with. 'But I have no right at all to speak of Drew's private business, and to be honest, I know very little of it myself. Only that he is a man of honour, he works against wickedness, and he's loyal to the king.'

Nathaniel Tame had gone white. 'A duke's man? Working with the law?'

Davey shook his head at once. 'Drew's no informer. We'd all be in prison this twelvemonth if he were.'

Jon Spiers looked suddenly exceedingly awake. 'Clearly Mister Cobham knows exactly what you lot get up to,' he said. 'It's him we don't know about. But my Felicia helped young Tyballis dress up grand once before, and then she went off helping him with something secret. This Throckmorton gent owes Drew money, does he? And Drew sometimes goes off and lives in duke's houses, does he? Well, put it all together and it's clear as the ale in my cup. Our landlord works for the crown. It's not us little bastards he's interested in. Reckon he's capable of a bit of false dealing and sneak-thieving himself if needs be, not to mention a knife between someone's ribs if called for. But it's treason he's fighting, and those as threatens the peace of the land. Them bloody Lancastrians, for instance, the Tudor bastard over the water, and them filthy French sinners what would drown the whole of England if they got the chance. Indeed, I'd guess our Mister Cobham is a mighty important man.'

Davey nodded emphatically. 'A most intelligent summary. I agree with every word. Though anyone choosing to live here yet could do better, seems a touch loose-in-the-attic to me. To choose the smell of the tanneries when you could have the perfumes of palaces – well, it's a mighty strange choice.'

Elizabeth Ingwood poured everyone more beer. Casper had the hiccups again and drank heavily. Widower Switt tapped his fingertips on the table top and said, 'Well, my friends. It appears we are beginning to understand just what a serious situation we find ourselves in. We must save our benefactor from harm. It appears that the security of our king and country may even be at risk. Now, most humbly, I have a suggestion. In fact, I believe I have a plan.'

CHAPTER TWENTY-FIVE

Tyballis pushed the door open and marched in. Margery Blessop was kneeling at the fireplace, laying twigs. She gazed up at her daughter-in-law in astonishment, and stared with even more concern at the two men who entered beside her.

Mistress Blessop, being well used to her son, a man who frightened most other men, was not intimidated by the slender, sinuous and overdressed creature with passionate eyes and voluptuous mouth. His clothes of turquoise and lavender were impressive, however, and people of quality had never before entered her house. She was even more careful of the other man, sufficiently gnome-like to be either demon or outcast from Bedlam.

Tyballis said, 'If you lay one finger on me you'll answer not only to the sheriff, but to his lordship.'

Her mother-in-law winced. 'Lordship? Well, my Borin is – out. And he's every right to lay a good deal more than a finger on you, lazy trollop. You're his legal wife, and running away surely don't change that.'

Smart in her green worsted, the wine stains hidden beneath her fur-lined cloak, Tyballis wore a headdress borrowed from Felicia. A felt bonnet with a cobalt peak, this was adorned with a gauze veil pinned ear to ear, covering a good deal of the bruising on her face.

The low light in the house hid the rest. 'If Borin is out,' she said, 'I shall sit here and wait for his return. But since I know his habits very well, if he's not beating someone to smashed daub on Throckmorton's orders, I'd guess he's in bed. So, if he is, rather than put up with me and my companions all day, you'd better fetch him. It's important.'

Never having before spoken to her husband's mother with such imperious authority, Tyballis was enjoying herself. Margery Blessop, however, was both nervous and increasingly angry. 'You want him, you go up and get him yourself,' she glared.

But the commotion had woken Borin and his enormous bulk now protruded through the shadows at the top of the stairs. 'What's going on?' he demanded. 'And you, you whore! You got no right coming back here. No shame at all, you haven't, and with your fancy men bold as bollocks. Go on with you, back to your brothel.'

Davey had unsheathed his sword and was twirling it beautifully, being rather more practised at the twirl than the thrust. It was Casper who stepped forwards. He peered up the stairs and grinned in frog-like greeting. 'My old friend Borin,' he said. 'An' a right pleasure it is, seeing you again. Reckon you'll remember me, right enough?'

Borin grunted, now confused. 'Thought you was in clink.'

'I were,' Casper admitted, 'but held under a misunderstanding. Now released and pardoned, I am, thanks to our old friend.'

Borin plodded downstairs. 'Throckmorton?' he frowned, dubious.

'No, no, he don't know me. T'was someone o' far more influence than that silly bugger,' grinned Casper cheerfully. 'The Lord Feayton, in fact. An' he remembers you pretty good, too.'

'Ah.' Clearly, Borin also remembered.

'I believe you used to work for Feayton?' Tyballis said, nose in the air. 'Not that you ever told me about him. Well, now I work for him, too. And he requires a message taken to Throckmorton.'

'Take it yourself, then,' grumbled Borin, now looming over her. 'I never hardly knew the man. Running messages, here and there, and bossy as buggery. Nor never paid me much, neither.'

Tyballis lowered her voice, attempting a casual half-interest. 'So, you didn't thump people for him? Not like you do for Throckmorton?'

Borin shook his woolly head. Having just scrambled from bed, his hair was a knotty brown thatch. This now brushed the lower edges of the ceiling beams as he stood bare legged in the middle of the room. He wore only his shirt, frayed hem floating above grubby pink knees. His toenails were even grubbier and his feet were the size of a baker's shovel. He kicked one against his mother's rump. Margery was still crouched by the hearth, clearly deciding it safest to stay down. 'No fire, Ma?' Borin grumbled. 'Bloody cold, it is.' He turned back to Tyballis, frowning at her from his considerably superior height. 'Never did understand a decent man's honest toil, did you, then?' he objected with vague affection. 'But, no, I never done much for Feayton, as it happens. Messages. Watching folk. But it were him put me onto Throckmorton. And what I do for him is my own business.'

Davey Lyttle, having fully appreciated Borin Blessop's considerable size, had stopped dancing around but did not return his sword to its scabbard. Casper clasped Borin's hand and continued to nod and grin with as much reassurance as he could summon. Tyballis, however, in case of a sudden flying fist, kept close to Davey and said, 'Well, Lord Feayton has particularly asked me to entrust this message to you. No one else, he said. A message for the Baron Throckmorton, and to be taken by Mister Blessop and no other.' She smiled encouragingly. 'I can't take it. You know Throckmorton. He despises women.'

Borin glowered, still in evident confusion. He indicated Davey and Casper. 'But there's him – and him. They could do it. Why me? It don't smell right.'

'Since it is a – sensitive and private message,' Tyballis said, 'Lord Feayton believes it should be delivered by someone well trusted both by himself, and by the baron. However,' she waved a casual hand and yawned widely, 'if you can't be bothered, I'll inform Lord Feayton that you didn't want his money.'

'What money?' demanded Margery, standing up suddenly.

Tyballis turned to Davey. 'Mister Lyttle, if you wouldn't mind?' Davey immediately untied the purse strings at his belt, emptying the little bag into his palm and holding it beneath Borin's nose. The silver clinked. Tyballis said, 'Rather more than usual, considering the sensitivity of the message.'

Borin grinned. 'I'll do it,' he said. 'So, what do I say?'

Margery, keeping her eyes on the money, quickly stood between her son and her daughter-in-law. 'How do we know it's from Lord Feayton?' she demanded. 'What if it's a trick to get my Borin into trouble?'

'How would I know Borin used to work for Lord Feayton, if his lordship hadn't told me himself?' sniffed Tyballis. 'Borin certainly never told me. Who else knows? It could only be Lord Feayton. But if you prefer, I'll inform his lordship you refuse to go. I'm sure he'll be delighted to hear you don't trust him.'

'Little liar,' Margery hissed, 'causing trouble, just like always.'

'Shurrup, Ma,' said Borin, shoving her out of the way. 'It's good money and I'll take it. I got to go to Throckmorton's later on anyway. Easy earned, I reckon.'

'And you knows me,' Casper insisted. 'I don't forget favours. You saved my arse once, so I won't do you no wrong. This message come straight from Lord Feayton's estate, and so does your coin, true as our sainted knight George killed them dragons. So, take the money, my friend, and go get pissed down the tavern tonight.'

'There are certain important instructions, my good man,' Davey interrupted, his sword catching the first rising flickers of firelight. 'There is a sealed message to be delivered, and you will put this into the baron's hand personally, and show no one else. Do you understand?'

'Course I do,' objected Borin. 'I ain't stoopid.'

'And,' Davey continued, 'you will say nothing of how it came to you. You will simply say it was brought to your house by a messenger boy.'

'Why's that, then?' interrupted Margery. 'Mighty suspicious, I call it.'

'Call it what you will, madam,' said Davey with hauteur. 'If your son prefers to admit to the Baron Throckmorton that he takes orders from his own wife—'

'Shurrup, Ma,' said Borin again. 'I'll do what's asked. Just give me

171

the money.' He turned to Tyballis. 'And you, you come crawling back here again, I'll give you the walloping you deserve.'

'I wouldn't ever come back,' said Tyballis, going pink, 'not if you paid me. Not if you begged. I'm not even sure if we're legally married since you forced me into it right at the beginning.'

'If we're not married,' Borin sniggered, 'then it's a whore you've been this past five years.'

'But if you're not my husband,' glared Tyballis, 'then you're living in my house.' Davey quickly drew out the folded paper from the opening of his doublet and handed it to Borin. It was sealed with a huge and somewhat exaggerated smudge of red wax, though unmarked by any coat of arms. Borin received the paper between careful fingers. Davey then turned back to Tyballis and took her arm.

'We should now report back to his lordship. I trust you'll fulfil your obligations to the letter, Mister Blessop? Or his lordship will not be pleased.'

'To the letter?' muttered Borin. 'Don't know my letters and got no cause for reading stuff. But I'll take the message, never fear. You go tell his lordship he can trust me. He pays this much again, I'll do whatever he says.'

Ralph Tame was resplendent in a dark madder surcoat over an azurite silk doublet, belted tightly. His hose were rather too long for him and the sleek black wool wrinkled a little at the ankles, but he remembered not to keep hitching them up and simply hoped they would not fall down at some inappropriate moment. 'Drew won't mind,' Tyballis had assured him after they purloined the clothes from Drew's garderobe, despite having not the remotest idea whether this was true.

'Drew's a good deal taller and a fair bit wider,' Ralph had pointed out. 'His things don't fit.'

'You can hardly impersonate a lord in your own clothes, can you?' Tyballis pointed out. 'So, tighten your belt and just do your best.'

Ralph now smirked happily and called to his servant to keep up.

The elderly man, bent and obsequious, wore simple dark livery and kept his head down. Scurrying at his young master's heels, he was clearly finding it hard to keep up. Arriving at Throckmorton House and as his master was shown into the great hall, the panting servant grasped at the steward's sleeve. 'If it pleases you. I need a drink or am like to collapse on your nice clean tiles.'

The steward removed his sleeve from the skinny fingers. 'Very well, wait here. I'll send a boy with ale.'

'Ah, thank you kindly,' widower Switt grabbed the steward's coat sleeve again. 'Most thoughtful. A good man you are, and surprised I am to see how you stayed on.' He lowered his voice into a conspiratorial whisper. 'Would have thought – you know – what with the goings on here – you'd have left. When you realised, that is.'

The steward stared down his nose. 'I don't listen to gossip, my good man. Wait here. The ale will be sent directly.'

'Ah, well, most kind.' Mister Switt again took a good hold of the steward's sleeve. 'But it'll be ale from the kitchens, and used regular by the staff, I hope,' he said with a knowing wink. 'Not the other stuff his lordship keeps special – if you know what I mean. Not what he gave that girl he stuck in the cellar a few days gone, for instance. Well – she didn't last long, did she?'

Despite himself, Mister Bodge lingered. He certainly remembered the terrified and badly bruised girl who had rushed past him some time back, shouting accusations of wickedness and poisoning. 'What about it?' He now lowered his voice.

George Switt sighed. 'Aaah, yes, poor lass. Expired in agony, she did. Imprisoned in your master's cellar for his pleasure. Then when he'd done with her, she were poisoned. A nasty way to go. Escaped the cellar, she did, only to die in the gutter.'

'Nonsense,' said Bodge with a disdainful sniff. 'I have a good mind to inform his lordship of your ridiculous slanders. You continue spreading such rumours, and I shall call the constable.'

'You do that,' cackled Mister Switt. 'But I warn you, your master surely won't be pleased. What – call the constable, when his lordship's in there selling poisons to my master right now! Can just imagine his face, I can.'

'Selling poison?' Bodge repeated faintly.

'Have a look,' suggested widower Switt.

Throckmorton stood in the small chilly antechamber and regarded his visitor with some suspicion. 'Sir Ralph Tame? I don't believe I have the pleasure of your acquaintance, sir.'

'You don't,' Ralph said, removing his gloves and slapping them impatiently from one hand to the other. 'But I come from Lord Feayton. You won't deny knowing him, I hope?'

Harold Throckmorton winced. 'I know his lordship well, sir. He is a – particular – friend of mine.'

'Hardly the way he puts it,' smiled Ralph. 'Calls you a miserly liar and a murderer. But then, perhaps he knows you better than you think.'

'You are insulting, sir,' said Throckmorton, going red. 'Please state your business at once, or I must ask you to leave.'

'Ask away,' grinned Ralph. 'Won't do no good. And just to let you know, if I'm not seen by my men in half an hour, they'll call alarm. But I'm not here for trouble. Come on behalf of another of Lord Feayton's friends, a most important nobleman, him not wishing to be seen here himself. Perhaps you guess who I mean.'

The baron had several ideas. 'How could I, sir? Explain yourself.'

'A certain young lord, friend of a certain marquess, let's say,' smiled Ralph Tame. 'Growing impatient, too, waiting on a certain batch of merchandise, and knowing just what you picked up from St Katherine's Docks a few days past. Been expecting delivery for nearly a week now, and don't like being kept waiting.'

'I was not told – no one has informed me,' quavered the baron. 'If his lordship will send a personal messenger – an order carrying his seal? You understand I have to be extremely careful, sir. The dangers of my business—'

Ralph chuckled. 'Lest, having such a low opinion of you, my friend Feayton decided not to deliver Marrott's message.' He paused, winking. 'There now, I've gone and said the name I swore not to. But no doubt you guessed already, seeing as how you've done business with him before.'

Throckmorton nodded dumbly. 'I've certainly no wish to

antagonise his lordship,' he mumbled. 'But I have received no request, no order. And considering the nature of the merchandise you'll understand, sir I cannot entrust such a package to anyone but the servants I already recognise.'

'Oh, fair enough,' said Ralph cheerfully. 'I don't want your nasty little parcels in my hands, that's for sure. I'm just doing a favour. The order was supposed to be passed through Feayton, you know, though not risking his own seal to the wax, of course. But now Marrott's angry. If you care about losing business and making enemies – well, perhaps you'd best get off to court and deliver the stuff yourself.'

Throckmorton looked even glummer. 'I doubt I would be accepted at court, sir. And to think of the danger while carrying such a package.'

'A coward as well as a villain, eh?' Ralph nodded happily. 'But, I doubt the risk's as bad as you think. Tell me the day and time, and I'll warn Marrott you're coming with his secret supplies. He'll have someone ready and waiting. 'Tis in his own interests, and he won't want you falling into the wrong hands, that's for sure.'

'I suppose,' supposed the baron.

Ralph Tame collected his servant from the main doors, and left just as Borin Blessop, huge, ungainly and unmistakably himself, arrived, chugging through the growing blizzard. He was clutching a sealed message.

CHAPTER TWENTY-SIX

'That pompous fool will spread the news through the entire household within the hour,' said George SwITT, sitting down heavily. 'And from there it will be all over the city by tomorrow morning. Baron Throckmorton will be famed as a murderous poisoner throughout all England by the end of the week. Excellent. Went as well as could be expected, I believe. Though I really see no reason for you to have walked quite so fast, Ralph. My venerable age, you know.'

'Sorry,' muttered Ralph. 'Too much enthusiasm.'

'Or simple terror,' muttered his brother.

'Well,' smiled Felicia, 'our plans are well nigh complete, as long as Throckmorton takes the bait, of course. Dear Luke's beautiful scribing will convince him, I'm sure.'

'But since none of us can read, we can't check, can we?' Davey said, stabbing the air with sudden belligerence. 'Supposed to be an order from this Marrott fellow for the special powders as usual. So, what if the mad monk upstairs wrote something quite different – like what we're really planning?'

'Luke Parris is an educated man,' said Felicia firmly. 'You're a quarrelsome fool, Davey Lyttle. Luke is entirely trustworthy. He has as much to thank Drew for as the rest of us, and is surely just as determined to keep him safe.'

'And you definitely saw Borin arrive there with the message?' Tyballis demanded.

Ralph nodded. 'Had to be him. Big as a tree, proper daft-looking and dressed like a country yokel with too much hair to keep his hat on straight. Not the sort of man I'd expect as your husband, Tybbs.'

Davey, overcome with success, once again twirled his sword. 'Tybbs, my love,' he said, dancing forwards, feinting and turning swiftly to pierce his invisible adversary, 'why did you marry such a clod? And you the prettiest girl I've seen since my mother dumped me at the church door. Besides, you're bare old enough to take a man of any sort.'

Tyballis blushed and shook her head. 'Don't be silly, Davey. I'm nineteen and not pretty at all. As for Borin, well, he wanted the house after my parents died. The Blessops were due to be evicted because they didn't pay their rent next door. So, Borin dragged me up to the bedchamber while his mother stood at the bottom of the stairs with a poker in case I tried to get away. Then they said I was married, so that was that.'

Elizabeth scowled. 'Should have cut his knackers off soon as the bugger slept.'

'I was only fourteen,' Tyballis said. 'Anyway he would have killed me, or his mother would have.'

Ralph was still dressed in Andrew's silks, being loath to return to serge and buckram. He stretched an elegant ankle. 'Now we know when Throckmorton reckons on turning up at court,' he pointed out. 'And we need to get there first. No time to waste.'

'Got to warn the king,' nodded Nat.

'My dear boy,' sniffed George Switt, 'commoners do not trot unobstructed into court, nor directly warn his grace of anything. This part of the plan will be our moment of greatest risk. The king can only be approached through Baron Hastings. Finding that mighty gentleman and then convincing him without getting ourselves arrested will be the hardest challenge.'

'Women,' suggested Davey, nearly stabbing his own toes.

'Indeed,' agreed Mister Switt, looking with fond concern at Tyballis. 'Lord Hastings is particularly well known for his – predilection – for the female sex.'

Tyballis realised rather uncomfortably that everyone was looking at her. 'I ought – I suppose – I know it's for me to take the biggest risks,' she mumbled, 'but if you expect me to be blatantly seductive – well, I haven't the faintest idea how to do it.'

Mister Switt shook his head. 'I suggest something a little more – subtle,' he said. 'And now for the tools of our trade, courtesy of my good friend Mister Allard. I led a minstrel troop in my youth, but then, that was before I met my dearest Edalina. Now – this is what I suggest.'

The missing string on the gittern was repaired that evening, and the same elderly man, deep from the shadows of his little shop, unearthed a long slim flute of polished boxwood. It seemed that the genial Mister Allard was acquainted with widower Switt from the old days. 'Minstrels together,' George Switt explained. Reginald Allard was delighted to see his old friend.

'A shawm, perhaps? Or a sourdine? My dear George, ask whatever you will. The flute – well, I would never dream of charging. After all, this was once your own.'

Now George proudly clasped his flute to his chest, and explained his plan to Tyballis and the others. 'So Elizabeth will sing, since she has a fine voice, and you, my dear, will act the gypsy, and dance.'

It was once they were back home, the fire lit and the others crowding around, that Tyballis said, 'Please – no dancing! That's even worse than singing. I'd probably fall over. And how can I be a gypsy with fair hair?'

Mister Switt was imperturbable. 'I believe many easterners have blue eyes, and if they don't, well I doubt anyone else will be aware of it. Mister Lyttle could easily pass for a gypsy. Mister Spiers will also sing, and I will play the flute. Jon must use the tabor to keep the rhythm and Davey shall have the gittern. You, my dear Mistress Blessop, shall dance quite beautifully, I'm sure, and I promise not a man at court will object if your dancing is not exactly flawless. It is you who will ensure our admittance,' George Switt continued cheerfully. 'The dance, the temptress, the seduction of the aging baron, and then the whispering of the secret. To impart the knowledge of the traitorous plot – Baron Throckmorton meeting Lord Marrott; the exchange of coin for arsenic, with Hastings the unwitting witness – will be your most difficult task, and the magnificent climax to our plan. It will surely be the end of the wicked Throckmorton – and the saving of our magnanimous friend.'

Since no one knew what a gypsy dance might be like, Tyballis and Davey invented it between them while Felicia, wishing she were younger, sewed the costumes. Elizabeth then quietly confided to Tyballis something of her own past experiences in the rather less subtle arts, in case Tyballis should need to take a more active role in securing the attention of Baron Hastings, and some of Elizabeth's suggestions horrified Tyballis and sent her early to bed.

They dressed carefully the next day. Davey wore a turban he had designed, a complicated affair incorporating a ream of bandages and two of Felicia's best napkins. 'Gypsies don't wear turbans,' Ralph objected. 'That's them heathen Moors from Spain what winds things around their heads.'

'Not them, neither,' Nat shook his head. 'It's folk from the Spice Islands looks like that. Gypsies don't even wear hats.'

'So maybe I'm a Moorish gypsy from the Spice Islands,' decided Davey. 'I shall wear what I please. It's my gittern-playing is more the problem. The king's own players will be at court and you can guess they'll be the very best. Why should they let us in?'

'Attractive women,' said Nat. 'Tybbs in particular.'

It was Elizabeth who, taking the money offered by Tyballis, had previously bought the fabrics and helped Felicia sew their costumes. 'But there's not enough material here,' Tyballis had pointed out. 'If you think I'm going to court half naked – '

'Tits out and skirts up is the only way we'll get into court,' snorted Elizabeth. 'And it'll be a back door at that. But Hastings chooses the girls for the king's bed, so he's on the lookout. We have to be what he looks at.'

'I think,' Tyballis said faintly, 'I'd sooner not go.'

'All this is down to you,' Elizabeth told her, 'so go you will. We're saving Drew's miserable life, aren't we? Besides, there's no chance without you.'

'Never fear,' Mister Switt said, popping in from his own room, already dressed in his old minstrel's outfit. 'Shockingly shabby now, of course,' he said, 'but at least I can still fit the doublet. Now, what were we talking about? Ah, yes. Mistress Blessop, you need not suppose we will abandon you to the improper advances of any gentleman, not even his highness. But we must gain admittance, you see, and reach Lord Hastings' private ear. Without that, our whole plan is lost.'

They hired a cart. The last time Tyballis had sat in one was when she had been abducted. This occasion was only slightly less uncomfortable, but walking the entire breadth of London and over the Fleet to Westminster in the wind and sleet was hardly feasible. 'What, with every burgess and his wife staring, and then maybe arrive too late, soaked and bedraggled? I promise, no one would let us through the gardens, let alone past the gates,' said Davey.

'Wherry boat?' suggested Mister Switt.

Which was when Tyballis quickly suggested the cart and offered to pay for the hire.

Tyballis stood in the Palace of Westminster's long back corridor and shivered. Great burning torches flared from a hundred iron sconces and the blaze of light seemed bewildering. Behind her, the huge doors had shut fast and no draught threatened the torch flames. Above her head, carved and fluted, the ceiling caught the gold and scarlet, glowing with leaping flame-shadows. Tyballis felt wretched, but she was impressed. She had never in her life imagined entering the hallowed halls of the court. Admittance thus far had been accomplished only with greatest suspicion. 'Wait there,' sniffed the page, peering past Mister Switt's muddy shoes to the women's exposed ankles.

'So, we need a go-between to get to Hastings, who is himself a go-between to the king?' whispered Tyballis as the page retreated.

'It is no doubt a credit to your beautiful costume, my dear Mistress Blessop,' widower Switt whispered back, 'that we are not first shunted to the lower hierarchies. The steward's assistant, for instance. Or perhaps the steward's assistant's assistant. The steward's assistant's steward's page, or even the page's assistant.'

'Hush,' croaked Davey, adjusting his turban. 'Someone's coming.'

Many people came. Groups hurried through the great passages, talking, laughing and in general ignoring the small tattered group of minstrels waiting quietly in the shadows. Tyballis and Elizabeth attracted some notice, but disrobement at court was not sufficiently unusual to turn heads. Tyballis, on the other hand, remained embarrassed, and an hour passed ever more slowly. The pages were renewing the torches when finally someone came. 'Follow me,' and a curt nod. They followed, their footsteps echoing on the long polished boards. It was an interminable walk, but when a double door was flung open and they were shown into the vast colourful chamber beyond, they were overawed.

The sleet had chilled and turned to hail, hurtling against windows and collecting in crystal mounds in the gutters. The sky closed in behind the black clouds and the wind poured up the Thames. Nat, clutching tight to Ellen's small hand, made his way to Bradstrete as fast as he could, keeping where possible to the shelter of the overhanging houses. Once past the Austin priory's open gardens, Nat stopped, finger to his lips. Ellen sidled into the shade of the priory wall while Nat began to explore.

The weather was both sword and shield. Within Throckmorton Hall there was no one prepared to venture outside and anyone acting suspiciously on the perimeter was free to examine every entrance unseen. But Nat, even beneath the borrowed cover of Luke's hooded cape, was soaked. Ellen, wearing a brand new cape of waxed kersey bought by Tyballis and sewed by her mother, was up to her ankles in icy puddles. She sneezed and clamped her hand over her face to smother it, but there was no one to hear her. After a few moments Nat returned, looming through the storm, his sodden cape billowing in the wind. 'S'all right,' he muttered. Ellen trotted behind, kept close and kept small. She was as practised as he was.

Within the stable courtyard, two grooms, feet wedged up against the wall and cups in their hands, sat talking under cover. Nat, shadowed by Ellen, slipped past unnoticed.

A locked door, extremely narrow and almost unseen within the building's façade, stood two steps down. Nat already knew where it led, for Tyballis had described every entrance to him. He quickly pulled out his knife and a twist of steel wire, picked the lock and pushed through into the blackness inside. Again Ellen followed. Tyballis had warned of chief cook John Knody who would set up a cry to alarm the whole house. But another door led under the principal staircase directly into the main house. Since Baron Throckmorton would definitely be out, and his personal desire for secrecy meant few of his servants were permitted access to his private chambers, the security on his home was inevitably lax. Nathaniel Tame and his small companion would not be disturbed.

CHAPTER TWENTY-SEVEN

William, Baron Hastings, regarded the bunch of oddments standing trembling before him, and wondered why his steward had considered admitting them at all. Then he looked towards the smaller of the two women, and understood. His lordship waved an impatient hand. The two huge rings caught the firelight. 'Play, then,' he said wearily. 'Show me what you can do. But this palace teems with musicians, both resident and itinerant. I cannot promise payment.'

They had pushed her in front, and Tyballis curtsied, though not too deeply, uncomfortably aware of the depth of her neckline. Felicia had sewed this in gauzy linen, a bodice no more modest than that of a chemise and impossible to keep fastened either at her wrists or over her breasts. Equally improper, the gown's hemline purposefully exposed her ankles, and although she wore her own shift beneath, it was not long enough to compensate. Now the rain had plastered the thin material to her legs, outlining each curve. At least her head remained covered, the little headdress tied tightly beneath her chin also shading her face.

Davey, overawed and frightened of losing his turban with any sudden movement, looked to Jon. Jon Spiers looked to widower Switt. Mister Switt straightened his shoulders, bowed very low and brought his flute to his lips. Jon closed his eyes, rapped a slow, steady beat on the little drum hanging at his waist and began to sing. The flute, one note held high and long on a minor key, wavered only once. Davey moved beside Jon. He raised the bowl of the gittern against his shoulder, lowered his head and put the quill to the strings. Music, soft and plaintive, oozed into the great chamber, joining the thrum of the flames from the hearth and the sound of the rain outside.

Silently praying for courage, Tyballis stepped forwards. It was then that Elizabeth followed Davey's secret orders and, grabbing Tyballis, wrenched the neck of her bodice sharply downwards while pulling the covering from her hair. 'Now, dance,' hissed Elizabeth, and pushed.

Tyballis, long fair curls fluffed around her naked shoulders, knew her blushes must be vivid as the fire. With the unblinking gaze of Lord Hastings directly upon her, she tried to adjust her clothing. Hastings smiled slightly and shook his head. 'I would not do that, if I were you,' he murmured. 'Whatever you were hoping to achieve will surely be better served as you are.'

The music had not hesitated. Elizabeth, moving back to leave Tyballis standing alone, was now also singing, her thin soprano echoing Jon's rich baritone. Tyballis felt intoxicated, as she had once when Andrew had poured her too much good Burgundy. Lord Hastings' grandeur, his arrogance and his direct gaze discomforted her. She could not remember one step of the dance she had learned. Very softly she said, 'My lord, my companions make beautiful music, though I can neither sing nor dance and would spoil their melody if I tried. But there is something mightily important I have to say, if you will permit me to say it.'

'I believe I can imagine what that would be,' replied William Hastings.

Tyballis lowered her eyes, her voice meek. 'I am not – it isn't that, my lord. I fear for someone's life, and have come to ask – to beg for your help. Simply to permit me admittance, and to send guards – if it pleases you, my lord – to the apartments wherever Lord Geoffrey Marrott might be found.'

Hastings frowned and sat up. 'What trick is this? You come to me, but looking for that creature's bed?'

'No, my lord, I swear.' Her whisper almost faded. 'It concerns not only Lord Marrott, but the safety of the realm, my lord.'

'You make no sense, girl. What nonsense is this?'

'Danger, my lord. Poison, and treason.' She sank to her knees and clasped her hands. 'I come from Lord Feayton. But he is away with the duke, my lord, and cannot know the imminent threat to his own life. Someone is planning to kill him because he knows too much. He knows of plots – of treachery – and of poison brought to the court within the hour, ready for sale.'

Sitting abruptly forwards, Hastings, eyes narrowed, gripped Tyballis, his fingers biting into her naked shoulders. 'What duke? Who is Feayton? There's no Lord Feayton at court, nor ever has been. I know every peer of the land, and Feayton is not one of them. If you lie to me, girl, I'll have you whipped within an inch of your life.' He then relaxed suddenly, as if guessing at something, and released her. 'This Feayton,' he said more gently, 'who does he work for? Who are you?'

The music stopped. 'Tyballis Blessop, my lord. I work for Lord Feayton who works for the Duke of Gloucester. And what I can prove is of the utmost urgency.'

'Are you implying,' Hastings said, the quiet menace in his voice now silky, 'that Lord Geoffrey Marrott, close friend to his grace the Marquess of Dorset, is complicit in crimes against the state? I warn you again, if you lie I shall have you punished. But if you have proof, present it to me immediately.'

Tyballis cringed. She had forgotten her own near-nakedness and was now conscious only of the threat in Lord Hastings' eyes. 'If you will allow me access and set guards to watch, then there will be proof, my lord. Baron Throckmorton is coming in less than an hour, selling poison. The sale must be secretly witnessed. But the baron believes himself expected, and unless I see Lord Marrott first, he will not be, and the sale will not go ahead. '

'What foolishness is this?' His lordship was impatient. 'Throckmorton was found dead not four months past.'

One nervous squeak came from a plucked gittern string, and then was quiet. George Switt stepped forwards and bowed. 'If it pleases you, my lord, we speak of the new baron, Harold, the dead baron's brother.'

Hastings stared at Switt with contempt, then turned back to Tyballis. 'And you claim Throckmorton comes to see Lord Marrott for what purpose?'

There was a pause. 'To sell arsenic,' Tyballis whispered. 'Not as medicine, but for murder.'

She was allowed to adjust her clothing. Hastings watched her calmly, waiting as she fumbled with her bodice. Elizabeth helped her tighten the laces at her waist. At age fifty-three the baron had frequently felt some of his old strengths diminishing, but not yet in the area of libido. Now he was trying to remember when he had last seen such a delectable pair of breasts, high-set, firm, clear-skinned and just the right size for his hands. He sighed, looking to the slim pink wrists and then further down to the neat little ankles. The face above was remarkable, but it was not the face he would likely dream about later that night, for Hastings now knew the name of Gloucester's informer, whose identity the duke had refused to share. And the wench promised a more orgasmic climax still, for it seemed that vile little bastard friend of Dorset was close to proving his own guilt, and if Marrott could implicate Dorset too, so much the better. The deal would be witnessed, and Hastings would finally carry clear evidence to the king. He scratched the greying stubble on his chin, called for his page and smiled benignly at Tyballis. 'Tell Lord Marrott,' Hastings chuckled, 'you're a gift from Throckmorton. He's a fool and will suspect nothing. Meanwhile I shall set guards outside the doors. Immediately Throckmorton arrives they'll disperse, allowing sufficient time for the transaction to take place.' He looked Tyballis over again, and nodded, satisfied. 'Meanwhile I advise you keep to the bedchamber. Once Throckmorton leaves, I shall have him arrested. Then my men will push in and take Marrott into custody. I shall also send my page to bring you back to me.'

Huddled beneath a borrowed cape, Tyballis was led through torch-bright corridors. The group had been ordered to remain in Hastings' quarters. They would all be thrown in gaol should the story prove

186

untrue, but from the beginning they had known the risk and were not afraid. Tyballis, however, was terrified. She was relieved when Lord Geoffrey's steward informed them that his lordship was not at home.

Lord Hastings' page bowed. 'Sir Henry, I am instructed to present this gift from Harold, Baron Throckmorton to his lordship, Geoffrey Marrott. My master has substantiated the claimant's identity and authorised safe passage. May I assume you will accept responsibility for the package, my lord?'

The steward sniffed with faint distaste. 'Certainly, Roger. I shall take it from here.'

Tyballis was pushed into a low-beamed chamber busy with activity, pages chasing dogs and building up the fire, servants preparing wine and lifting the shutters for twilight closure. Before having time to gaze at the strewn luxury, she was quickly thrust into a second and finally into a third room. This last was empty of bustle and only the hangings shuffled and whispered. Tyballis peered through shadows at a bed larger than any she had seen before. 'Wait here,' the steward informed her, 'and touch nothing. Disrobe and leave your clothes by the garderobe door. His lordship will return presently. If he accepts you and after he has finished, you will make your departure through the private gallery to the rear of the bedchamber. If his lordship declines, you will immediately be removed the way you have come.'

He left her standing in the middle of the floor staring at the bed. She had never before, even on her wedding night, felt so humiliated. Her skin felt unclean, her eyes were blurred and moist, and she was bitterly cold. She swallowed hard, took a deep breath and began once again to loosen the top of her gown. She refused to remove all her clothes, but hoped that some bare flesh would at least be sufficient to start the conversation. Once alone with the man, she could give the message for which she had come. It must, she thought, be almost time for Throckmorton to turn up. His arrival would take Marrott away, and then she would be free to escape.

She clambered into the bed, tugging her bodice down to her hips and the downy covers up around her waist. Half-hidden by the bed curtains, she crossed her arms over her breasts and waited. The sheets smelled of sweet lavender, and perfumes of honeyed wax floated above her head. She felt increasingly sick. No one had offered wine, though she would have welcomed some additional courage. The bed was swelteringly comfortable, spread with furs, embroidered linens and silks, but she saw none of it. Although worried Throckmorton might arrive before Lord Marrott, she had no way of counting time, so she silently practised the words she planned to say. When she heard low voices in the outer chambers and finally the door opened, she jerked up, wondered what looking seductive might possibly entail, set her arms carefully at her sides and faced the distant and darkened doorway with rigid determination.

She was discomforted to realise that the first man who entered was shadowed by a second. These noblemen, she thought with annoyance, evidently went nowhere without their servants, not even to bed. She concentrated on the first to approach. He was at least smiling and, she could not help noticing, was extremely handsome. In fact, he was even more beautiful than Davey, and far better dressed. His furs were sumptuous sables, his velvets were vivid scarlet, his figure was tall, elegant and well muscled, and as his great coat swung back, his dark hose exposed a well-turned pair of legs. Tyballis forced herself to smile, and the man, standing just within the doorway with an expression of intense approval, smiled back. His plump mouth was perhaps a little loose and his eyes too avid, but Tyballis felt she was in no position to criticise. Quite naked to the waist, she leaned forwards a little and hoped the gloom would hide the depth of her blushes.

Lord Marrott came fully into the room. The long windows were still unshuttered but no light seeped through, for the day had disappeared behind the thrumming sleet. Nor had candles been lit, yet his lordship appeared so dazzling that Tyballis saw only him. He said softly, 'Well, I was told a gift from Throckmorton awaited me. For once the fool has shown some taste. What's your name, girl?'

Tyballis, shaking with nerves, stuttered, 'Tyballis, my lord. And if your lordship pleases, I have brought an important message.'

Marrott stepped closer. 'The message I see before me is undoubtedly sufficient, my dear. Nothing could surpass this proof of his generosity.'

She assumed this was a compliment. Receiving compliments from nobility was presumably something to be coveted, even if one was busy plotting his downfall. She tried not to cower. The man's gaze was now firmly attached to her breasts. 'My lord,' she said, 'forgive me, but the message is urgent. May I speak?'

He nodded, sitting suddenly on the edge of the bed beside her. 'Make it brief, my dear. Don't be frightened, I won't hurt you. But how cruel you are, to make me wait.'

The words she had silently practised now inexplicably rearranged themselves. 'The Baron Throckmorton is coming to see you, my lord, at exactly four of the clock. For important business. He'll be here directly. I beg you to see him first – before me. It must be four by now, my lord, isn't it? I've been a little delayed in giving the message, sir, and he believes you're expecting him.'

'Throckmorton coming here?' Lord Marrott laughed. 'I send my servants to him, girl. I'll not receive him here at court, whatever the quality of his gifts. He can go to hell for now, I'll deal with him later. First, let me see a little more of what he's sent.' Grasping her shoulders and thrusting her back with one hand, he threw off the covers with the other. His fingertips were like iron and he towered over her, filling her vision. The waiting servant had kept well back, hovering outside the doorway. There was, however, the faint sound of shifting feet and patient breathing. Marrott spoke over his shoulder. 'You still there, my friend? Wait for me in the outer solar, will you? I doubt I shall be long.'

The man had a very hard grip on her right breast and was leaning closer to kiss her, when Tyballis started to struggle. With his mouth half-clamped on hers, she mumbled, 'First the message, my lord. Please … no.'

Marrott, eyes steely, sat back. 'Don't be a fool, girl. What game are you playing now?'

'Throckmorton,' Tyballis said. 'Please – no.'

'If he dares turn up here, I shall have him thrown out,' Marrott said calmly. 'And if you think you can lead me on and then push me away, I shall have you thrown out too, Madam Whore. Has Throckmorton set you up to trick me?' Seeing nothing but the cold fury growing in his eyes, Tyballis stopped struggling. She cringed back as his hands grasped at her body and groped beneath the remaining bedcovers. Expecting rape, she closed her eyes.

It was then, although utterly impossible, that words began floating above her head, gentle and warm and strangely familiar. It was from the invisible shadows that a soft voice said, 'Leave the child alone, Geoffrey. You have frightened her enough.'

CHAPTER TWENTY-EIGHT

A ndrew Cobham walked over to the bed and stood looking down at the almost-naked woman staring back up at him in blushing amazement. He said softly, 'Well, little one. I believe it is high time I took you away from here.'

Lord Marrott stood abruptly. 'What is this?'

'Spare me your temper, Geoffrey,' Andrew said. 'It is simply a misunderstanding.'

'Misunderstanding be damned,' Marrott was breathing fast. 'If you think I'll stand back while you carry the trollop off from under my nose to your own bed—'

Andrew smiled. His eyes remained cold. 'It happens that I know this girl, although I had not expected to see her here,' he murmured. 'Throckmorton is no doubt to blame, and presumably the girl was simply obeying orders. She therefore deserves neither punishment nor your revenge.'

'A wench climbs bare-arsed into my bed, then tries to cry off? I'll have her thrashed. Don't stand in my way, Feayton.'

Tyballis was aware of approaching silver velvet, the delicate lace edge of a shirt collar, and the thick, soft warmth of grey fur. Large hands took hold of her, brushed over her breasts as he pulled away the covers she had tugged up, revealing the limp remainder of her skirts.

Andrew Cobham's smile was almost lazy, almost incidental. 'What a pity,' he said. 'You are not entirely naked after all.' He ignored the other man as he gathered Tyballis up in his arms. Then he turned. 'You really don't want my enmity, Geoffrey. Behaving in a manner you would very soon regret would not serve you in the least. And over such a small matter. What, I wonder, would your dear mother say?'

Marrott had turned quite red, an unfortunate match to his scarlet velvets. 'Don't pretend you have her ear, Feayton. And I don't believe you have the king's ear either. But if you think to make me look a fool—'

'We all do that for ourselves, my friend,' Andrew smiled. 'But I shall not mention this incident to anyone else, and will, if you wish it, approach Throckmorton on your behalf.'

'Throckmorton,' Tyballis stammered from the depths of his embrace. 'But he's coming – coming here – any minute – at four o'clock.'

Looking down at her nestled in his arms, it seemed he frowned a warning. 'No, child, he is not,' Andrew said softly. 'Throckmorton has not been welcome at court for some years, and will be less so now. He asked someone else to deliver the merchandise. This was a man who, somewhat ironically, asked that I come in his place, believing I should be more welcome due to my – friendship – with his lordship here. Our business is already settled. Now I shall take you home.'

'Business? Settled?' quavered Tyballis. 'But Lord Hastings – watching guards – outside—'

'Hush, little one. This is unwise. Trust me.' With Tyballis cradled against him, Andrew Cobham stood a moment. 'Forget this, Geoffrey. Throckmorton simply meant to secure his business with bribes, but is inept as always. Nothing more.'

Marrott stood solid in Andrew's path. 'Inept? More than that, I think. The damned man's never sent a trollop to me before, and this one is – well, never mind about that.' His eyes, furious and unblinking, remained fixed on Andrew. 'I never requested this last batch, you know Feayton. There's something dirty about the whole set up, and you seem too damned involved for my liking. Throckmorton may be a blackguard and a fool, but I warn you that I am not.'

Andrew Cobham still smiled. 'Fool is not one of the many things I've called you so far, Geoffrey. But your quarrel is with Harold, not with the girl. And if you wish to take it up with me, then I advise you to choose a better time. Certainly, if you wish to stay in his highness's good graces, then not here at court.' He bowed, an infinitesimal bend of the neck, stiff backed. 'But now I shall take your leave. Until the next time.' He lifted Tyballis a little higher, a little tighter, and strode quickly to the open doorway. She clung to him. He said nothing more until they had left Marrott's chambers.

They encountered no one. Some way down the corridor, Drew stopped and set Tyballis firmly back on her feet. He then swung off his great velvet coat and wrapped it around her shoulders. As he held it against her a moment, the fur-trimmed edges pulled together, the clasp of his fingers was hard knuckled against her. His voice and his expression remained cold. 'It seems you have left your shoes behind,' he said. 'It would be singularly futile to go back for them now, but just how do I carry a naked woman across the entire breadth of London in this storm?'

'I'm not naked,' Tyballis sniffed.

His gaze drifted slowly and almost contemptuously downwards from her face to her small bare toes. 'If you think that, then you are nearly as naive as dear Geoffrey.' Abruptly he tipped one finger beneath her chin, roughly forcing her face up to his. 'And just what the devil were you doing in his bed, anyway?' he demanded, his voice now harsh. 'I have had a damnable day, and you, my dear, are not at all what I expected at the end of it.'

'It's – complicated.' She shook him off and looked adamantly away.

'No doubt,' he said curtly. This time he took her hand and led her quickly along the corridor, several times turning to take narrower and darker passages.

His grip was firm. She made no attempt to wriggle free. 'The others,' she mumbled, panting a little. 'Lord Hastings' rooms. They're waiting.'

'They are not,' he said briefly. 'They have been sent home.'

Surprised, she said nothing else until suddenly he pushed open a small door and a blast of slanting rain hit them full square. A long wooden pier led directly from the door to the river and a turgid rush of sweeping grey waves lashed the sides, slopping over the boards. The Thames was in flood. She clung to Andrew. 'No,' she whispered, staring ahead at the angry water.

He shook his head. 'I have no choice,' and tossing her up again into his arms, strode with her along the rickety planks.

This was not the royal pier. No gilded barges fluttered their pennants and no liveried palace servants awaited their noble masters. This was the pier for the delivery of supplies and for the servants' use, so only small, battered wherries bobbed and danced, loosely roped. But it was late, and the wherrymen were no longer plying their trade, leaving the boats empty except for the stinking slop of the waves. This did not seem to concern Andrew Cobham, and with a sudden lurch that frightened her, he swung Tyballis over his shoulder and with one hand smacked hard against her rump, he began to climb down the steps into the water.

Taking the first covered tilt-boat, Andrew dumped his parcel onto the passenger bench under the awning, and with a small knife from inside his boot, loosened the locked bars holding down the oars. He rowed out immediately mid current, loose, easy strokes as the wherry cut through the storm. Tyballis crouched terrified in front of him, gripping white-fingered to the edges of the bench where she sat. Finally, she managed to gasp, 'You know how frightened I am of the river, and you know why. So, does it have to be this way? Are you so angry with me?'

His voice swept away on the wind. 'I cannot in all honestly say I am not angry. But travelling by river has nothing to do with that. Think, child. It is late evening, the city gates are locked against us. There is no other way home but by boat unless I wake up the Ludgate keeper. But offering bribes while carrying a naked woman might not be quickly forgotten. I've no wish to be arrested. And I cannot take you to an inn overnight, which I would infinitely prefer. Remember, the rest of your merry minstrels are waiting at home in agonised anticipation. We must at least put their fears to rest. But I shall not drown you. I am a fairly experienced oarsman.'

Tyballis squinted through dark bluster and freezing sleet. 'You keep telling me to trust you,' she muttered. 'But you used to tell me not to. And you haven't any right to be angry. I was just trying to save your life.'

Drew stared at her in sudden blank astonishment. 'Good God, child. You nearly got me killed.'

The waves reared, swamping the low gunwales, slapping against her face. At least she knew her tears would be disguised. Through the storm clouds, a full moon peeped, was hidden, then peeped again. Flashes of intermittent moonlight spangled silver flecks on wave crests, and slanted beneath the boat's cover, glowing on the damp sheen of her borrowed coat. Tyballis continued to clutch it desperately around her. Fur-trimmed, the sleek silvery velvet was sewn into padded folds, and although the lining was thin silk, the whole was as warm as a bed cover and even more impermeable. Her feet, however, were in water. The bottom of the small boat was a slurping dirty slush. She was trembling, eyes wide, teeth clenched, and only partly from the cold.

Andrew Cobham slowly relaxed the oars, looked at her with faint sympathy and smiled a little more gently. 'Come here,' he demanded over the wind.

There seemed nowhere to come. Already her knees touched his. She stared back, speechless, not daring to move as the boat rocked violently. So, he hitched both oars under his arms and reached for her, bringing her tight snuggled between his legs with her face buried against his chest. His velvet doublet was smooth and soft on her cheeks. 'Don't blow your nose on my coat,' he warned her. 'It's not mine. And don't look at the water. Keep tight against me and hang on. In a few minutes we'll be under the bridge and there'll be a drop of a few feet and a damned nasty surge. It's not dangerous, but you're better off not watching.'

'That's where—' she mumbled.

'I know,' he said. 'But this time you're with me.'

She clutched his coat around her and nestled against him, keeping her head obediently down, blind to the storm. The fear remained, but with each stroke of the oars she felt the sweeping control of his muscled arms and shoulders. His calm strength became her confidence. She simply hoped that, if they survived at all, he would not hate her.

It seemed to take forever but as the shadows of the bridge enclosed them in sudden blackness, the boat tilted and the current took them. Andrew stopped rowing but used one oar, flat-edged, to steer and to ward off the passing stone. They hurtled between the pillars, carried by the surge. Tipping forwards, the prow plunged into the whirling torrent, struck down, slammed the tidal swell and took on waves of white foaming spray. Paddling one handed, Andrew glanced frequently behind, keeping the course steady. His other hand held Tyballis crushed against him. She wriggled lower, hiding her face.

Then they had passed safely beneath the bridge. The overhanging shadows blinked out and the boat straightened at once. They floated free.

Andrew Cobham said, 'You may now remove your face from my groin. We are nearly home.' He pulled the wherry in to shore, looping a rope to the bottom step of the Portsoken pier and hauling it tight. The boat still danced on the waves, but the wind had calmed, and the rain had slunk to a misty drizzle. Balancing wide-legged against the keel's erratic roll, Andrew stood looking down at Tyballis.

'I can't stand,' she whispered.

He leaned down and again lifted her, propping her gently against his shoulder. She hung on. As he climbed the ladder up from the turbulent waters, she clung tighter. 'If you strangle me,' he said with faint amusement, 'I am more likely to drop you. Now, here we are. The ground is wet, but quite firm. Can you stand yet?'

Her knees shook. She said, 'I think I can.'

'But barefoot and soaked, you'll doubtless fall sick and delay my return to work yet again,' he said as he swung her once more into his arms and carried her into the dark alleys away from the Thames. 'However, if you've convinced yourself I can't see that you're crying, then you're quite mistaken.'

His stride was long, loose and rhythmic, and in minutes the frontage of Cobham Hall loomed, its dark struts and flaking plaster all suddenly lit by emerging moonshine. But Mister Cobham did not set her down. He kicked open the door and strode inside.

The cluster of people, forlorn, worried and grouped in the hall's dreary shadows, looked up expectantly and hurried forwards.

Drew said, 'No fire yet?' and marched past them towards his own quarters. Kicking open each door he passed, he entered his own bedchamber and dropped Tyballis unceremoniously onto the bed. Then he firmly removed his coat from around her, looked at her for a slow and thoughtful moment, then went to the window seat, lifted the lid and took out a wide linen towel, which he threw to the bed. 'Stand up,' he ordered, and she did.

She was shivering violently. Naked to the waist, all she now wore were the remains of her skirts barely held by torn ribbons to the belt around her hips. Both were soaked and clung to her. Tyballis, wrapping her arms around herself to hide the inevitable embarrassment, sniffed and wished she had a kerchief. She whispered, 'I can go upstairs to bed now. I don't need looking after. And there's Felicia –'

He was watching her intently but did not seem to be smiling. 'Nonsense,' he said. 'Since you appear quite willing to climb into other men's beds, you might as well climb into mine.'

The intensity of his gaze distressed her. She was more miserable, more embarrassed even than she had been struggling from Lord Marrott's embrace. Her arms crossed firmly over her breasts, she looked down at her wet toes and said very softly, 'I had a reason. It wasn't – not at all the way it must have looked.'

'Why apologise to me?' he said. 'I demand no explanations. I'm not your husband.'

His appraisal was undisguised, and she thought he looked haughty, angry, and even unkind. Clearly, he discounted her obvious discomfiture. She tried not to sniff. 'You – you rescued me. You keep rescuing me. So, I think perhaps you have a right to know why. And I want you to understand.'

'There will be a time for understanding,' he nodded. 'But not yet.' He pointed to the towel. 'Dry yourself. Then get into bed.'

Tyballis grabbed the towel and wrapped it quickly around her bare shoulders. The warmth was immediately reassuring and at last she was partially covered. She hesitated, hoping he would go. He did not.

She thought his eyes vaguely sinister as he slowly looked her over. She said, 'Do you mean to stay? I mean – you want me to —'

'Yes, I want you,' he interrupted her. 'Would that be unexpected? You have been almost naked in my arms for the past few hours.'

She hung her head again. 'You undressed me twice, so you ought to be ... used to me. You even kissed me and I – I said ... but then you went away. You didn't care.'

The smile started in the very corners of his mouth, tucking up tightly, lifting his cheekbones and gradually reaching his eyes. Yet his eyes remained cold. 'Are you, by any chance, offering to save my life a second time?' he said. 'How unwise. I am not in what you might call a gentle mood.'

'You haven't any right to be angry, or patronising,' Tyballis insisted, lifting her chin. 'And you don't know what I meant, or whether I was offering anything!'

'I know exactly what you meant.' He smiled, unblinking. 'But I do not accept bribes, nor do I recognise acts of shame or penance. I am moved neither by your guilt nor your gratitude. I can offer you nothing in comparison to Marrott's inducements and I have nothing to match his attractions. I warn you, my dear, you waste your time on me.'

There was only a candlestick to hand, and she threw it.

CHAPTER TWENTY-NINE

The candlestick hit him on the shoulder and rebounded, clattering to the floor. He did not flinch. This annoyed her even more.

'You've rescued me twice. Three times. A hundred times. I thought this time you were in terrible danger, and I wanted to save you, too. It meant all sorts of risks. Believe me, being married to Borin meant being humiliated over and over again, but never in my life have I been so humiliated as I was today. Sitting there almost naked in front of men I'd never met in my life before ... that popinjay's hands on me ... Lord Hastings leering down the front of my gown. It was all so disgusting.' She had started off raising her voice and now she was shouting. 'I had to pretend being eager, ready to do whatever – and I don't know how to pretend things like that. I know I was asking to be molested. You may not think being a whore is wrong, but I do. I've never, ever done anything – apart from my husband, and I would have avoided him too if he'd ever let me. And you may choose to be patronising and say whores have a right to do what they want, but you seem angry enough with me because you think I was. And all to try and save your miserable life, and to no avail since it seems you weren't in the slightest danger, after all. So, I've made a complete fool of myself – for nothing.'

He continued looking at her silently and without any change of expression she could discern, so she carried on. She was still shouting.

'The others, too. I know you didn't want them knowing anything about you, but everything changed – because of Throckmorton. He was planning to kill you. I had to tell them something, and they were all so kind and ready to help. They took terrible risks. Hastings could have had them whipped or even thrown into gaol. And all to rescue you. You said you were going away, and I thought you'd gone to Yorkshire after the duke. You lied. If I'd known you were in London, none of this need've happened.'

Andrew Cobham said nothing. To Tyballis his faint smirk of amusement seemed malevolent. It infuriated her. 'And now you dare to suggest,' she yelled, 'to hint that I was after that wretched Marrott because he's rich and handsome – or maybe you think I want to be some horrid lord's mistress. Me? And then you infer I'm after you, because of guilt and obligation! As if I would. You're –rude and – stupid. I wouldn't ever let you touch me. I hope Throckmorton kills you, after all.'

He stood so still and so silent that Tyballis felt an irresistible desire to shatter his immovability and looked around for something else to throw. She noticed the second candlestick, matching the first, and reached for it. 'I may be pathetic and get into muddles,' she glared at him. 'But at least I'm appreciative. You – you just don't think anyone else can do anything, only you.'

She threw the second candlestick. He had the nerve to catch it. Worse – he was now smiling with genuine pleasure, just as if all her fury was simply for his entertainment. She opened her mouth to object even more loudly but found herself inexplicably mute. Andrew Cobham was kissing her and she couldn't breathe.

'Now, I wonder,' he said softly, releasing her only an inch as he looked down into her startled expression, 'should I waste my time answering this absurd bombardment of accusations, or do I simply carry you to bed?'

'You can't —' she said, but managed no more. He had tossed away the towel from around her shoulders and was kissing her again. Peeping up at his face above hers, she thought his eyes glittered strangely. But his mouth was crushing hers, her lips felt bruised, his breath was burning her throat and the taste of him was on her tongue. She could think of nothing else. When he let her go, she staggered back against the bed post and stared at him, panting hard.

He looked her over for one slow moment, then leaned forwards and put both hands to the belt at her waist where her limp and bedraggled skirts remained attached. Just a brief twitch of his thumbs, and he watched as the last of her clothes tumbled to her feet. 'That's better,' he murmured, 'but not yet perfect. You are too cold.' And he picked up the towel from the floor and, stretching it between his hands, began to dry her.

He started with her hair, tousling it gently with the towel, absorbing the soaking ruin of the rain and returning her curls to a damp fluff of fair ringlets. His hands then followed down, rubbing around her ears, against the back of her neck and the curve of her spine. As he dried her, he spoke.

'So many complaints,' he smiled, 'and so many misunderstandings. I shall answer what I can. Firstly, I did not lie. Indeed, your guess was a good one. I went to Yorkshire and spent nearly three weeks at Middleham Castle. Finally, Gloucester gave new instructions, and ordered my return to London. I then stayed three days at the Crosby annexe, where you have stayed before. I was working, and therefore coming back here was not an option. You distract my purpose, little one, as you have again tonight. And my purpose is not an idle one. Would you have the king killed for the sake of seeing me?'

She would have objected to this, but was herself distracted. Andrew was drying her shoulders, then the pressure of his fingers within the warmth of the towel moved across her breasts, teasing. Still leaning against the bedpost, she sighed and forgot what she had intended to say.

Andrew Cobham's eyes were on her as he spoke. 'Seeing you in Marrott's bed was a shock,' he continued. 'I have no wish to be unappreciative, but I still cannot see why you sleeping with that creature was supposed to save my life. You mentioned Throckmorton. The man is a damnable nuisance and is no doubt plotting to slaughter me as he has before, but why you should have been involved with his plans is not at all clear. I am remarkably slow it seems, but these intrigues are beyond me. I was finishing a long day of tiresome negotiations and was looking forward to an undisturbed night's rest. Your sudden appearance, alarmingly naked and in the very last place I should have found you, did not, let us say, appeal to my sense of humour. Being then forced to subject you to a journey home by river, when in all truth I would gladly have thrown you into it, did not smooth my patience either.'

His hands were now beneath her breasts. 'Raise your arms,' he commanded and dried there, taking each arm, each hand and each finger separately. Tyballis was beginning to feel deliciously warm. 'For whatever attempts you made and risks you took to do what you thought would save me, I thank you, my dear. I do not understand what nor why, but no doubt you will explain tomorrow. But not now. I am in no condition to listen.'

He towelled the small of her back, bringing her hard against him, holding her gaze with his eyes as he continued to speak. 'As you have remarked, I undressed you before. But I took no advantage, although I confess the thought occurred to me. But ignoring temptation a third time appears to be beyond me. Now I fully intend taking advantage, and if you intend resisting, you may have to use considerably more force than a couple of candlesticks. I am not so easily dissuaded.'

The towel and his hands now kneaded her belly, rubbing over her hips. 'Marrott is no friend of mine, although I call him friend,' Andrew continued, his voice in her ear softer than his hands on her body. 'Taking you from him at the very moment of his arousal was hardly diplomatic. He already considers the world his for the taking, and with a beautiful woman flaunting her breasts in his bedchamber, he could be forgiven for thinking the right was his.'

Tyballis managed her first muffled objection. 'I wasn't flaunting.'

'You were most certainly flaunting,' said Andrew. 'Quite delectably, in fact. And young Geoffrey was on the point of fighting me for you.'

'But he didn't. And saying I'm beautiful is just silly.'

'Stand still and lift your left leg,' he ordered her. 'Indeed, after the fool decided not to fight me for you, he became far more dangerous.

He then wished to fight me purely from anger and hurt pride. Had he decided to do so, I would have been considerably disadvantaged.'

He dried the length of her left leg, took her left foot and rubbed between her toes. He then demanded she raise the other. She obeyed with a sniff. 'Don't you … I mean, does he fight so much better than you?'

Andrew paused momentarily in his work, smiled and bent to her right thigh. 'Do you suppose,' he murmured, 'that my killing the Marquess of Dorset's best friend, even in self-defence, would endear me to the king and his council? Especially within the confines of the palace itself! Even those who hate Marrott, and there are many, could not openly back me. I would also be at risk of personal detection, since I have no right at court, and my title is entirely false. I believe Gloucester would speak for me, but it would put him in a damned awkward position. No – I should have been obliged to let the fool wound me, and then extricate myself from any further damage if possible. Even on the point of death, I would have been obliged to defend myself with considerable care. And Marrott is no mean swordsman.'

He lifted and towelled her feet as she hopped one-legged, holding on to his shoulder to balance herself. His silvery velvet was still damp against her skin. She said softly, 'I'm sorry. I never meant it that way. I thought you were a long way away.'

'I don't need your apologies.' He put her foot back to the ground and brought her tightly to him again. 'My difficulties are of my own making. I work under a false name and a fraudulent title. This would mean certain arrest if I were discovered, since I am simply Andrew Cobham and no lord.' He looked at her suddenly and grinned. 'In truth, my name's not even Cobham.'

She realised he had dropped the towel. It was not soft linen that dried her now, but his bare hands, not so smooth and not so soft, but his palms stroked gently. She leaned against him, her hands, still shy, on his shoulders. Yet his breath was so hot in her face she felt scorched. 'Not?' she whispered. 'I mean – I wouldn't—'

'I was, I'm afraid, simply jealous.' His fingers explored. 'Seeing you like that, when I was already fractious and exhausted, angered me. At first, I meant to leave you there. I believed you'd chosen ambition and opportunity, that you intended making better use of your charms and Marrott's position. It was when I saw you struggle that I thought differently. By then it was almost too late. Geoffrey is not known for his humility or his patience.'

Tyballis clung to his neck as his hands wandered, and his voice, quiet and slow, tickled her ear. She half-grunted, 'Are you?'

Andrew grinned. 'No.' He hoisted her against him, then lifted her quickly backwards onto the bed. She lay uncovered, but curled immediately, wrapping her arms around herself. He shook his head, came to sit next to her on the mattress, and took her hands in his, again uncovering her. 'Don't hide, my love. Don't deny me. Let me look at you. It is the greatest pleasure I can imagine after a trying day.' His smile as he bent over her now shone deep in his eyes. He added softly, 'I intend making love to you. If you don't want me, then you'll have to fight me off, my dear.'

'That's not – chivalrous.' But she did not move.

'Not at all,' he said, and began to undress.

He had unlaced his doublet and shrugged it off, when she murmured, 'You're not angry with me anymore?'

'I never was.' He unhooked the fastening on his shirt cuffs, and loosened the neck. As he pulled the shirt off over his head, he said, 'I was angry with myself. For caring. For being jealous. For terrifying you on the river trip. For misjudging you. Finally for wanting you, while believing I must not take you.'

Tyballis whispered, 'Why – must not?'

Andrew had kicked off his boots and now stood only in fine knitted hose, the laces hanging in short loops around his waist, the grey silk clinging tightly to the long muscled curves of his legs. He watched her intently as he began to remove his hose, and the braies beneath. Now she also watched him. She said, 'I'm not a frightened virgin. And I'm not scared of hellfire. You don't even go to church so you can't be either. I already offered – and I said – twice over.'

He stood before her as naked as she was. 'You offered from duty, gratitude, and guilt. Not how I wanted you, little one.' Then he lay beside her, taking her swiftly into his arms. 'Now if it's still any of those things, I don't care. I want you too much to remember my manners.'

'It isn't those things.'

His hands roamed. 'You may be no virgin, my sweet, but you've hinted at your wretched husband's rough ineptitude. If you've learned to dislike a man's touch, then I've a lot of teaching to do.' She bit her lip and blushed. So, his hands wandered once more, and now when he spoke, it was little more than a whisper. 'This,' he murmured, 'is the place of learning. Breathe deep.

CHAPTER THIRTY

She woke with the warmth of him cupped behind her, and yet she was alone. He must have gone, she thought, only moments before. She lay, still feeling the recent warmth of his breath on the back of her neck. But he did not return, and she was disappointed. The tingling sensation of his strength slowly faded, and she felt cold again. If he had left and already gone back into the city, she thought she would never forgive him. Then she sighed. Whatever happened now, she knew she would not refuse him. Eventually she sat up, looked around, and clambered from the bed.

Searching for something to wrap around herself, she was tiptoeing across the chamber when he came at her from the garderobe shadows, slamming her against the wall with the ridge of a tapestry hem biting into the flesh of her back, and kissed her so hard she bit her tongue. He wore a bedrobe, heavy black brocade untied and swinging open, and his full weight pressed into her.

After a breathless gasp, she asked, 'Are you going away again?'

'I don't think so, not today.' He backed up a little to the edge of the bed, pulling her with him. 'Do you care?' he asked.

Various answers occurred to her, including some of the words she had heard Borin say in the past, which she had always been careful not to repeat. Instead, she said, 'Last night you told me some things I didn't really understand. And there are things you don't understand. I care so much, and if you don't know that, then you don't understand me at all.'

He laughed again. 'So, we take turns with a question?'

'You have to talk to the others, too. Of course, now they know I'm all right and they know you're all right. But they don't know how. They must be terribly confused.'

'I think we'll deal with your confusion first,' he said. 'Though I'd have thought what I did was fairly self-explanatory.'

'Not that,' she sniffed. 'Though actually it wasn't … I mean, I hadn't ever felt so … but that's not what I mean. I want to ask about Throckmorton and Lord Marrott and what you meant about settling the merchandise and knowing about Hastings and how it all happened. But most of all,' she said, looking down at her well-wrapped knees, 'I want to understand something quite different. Last night you said after you came back from Yorkshire you went to Crosby's because you couldn't come straight home here. You said it was because I was a distraction. Well, I know I asked to work with you again, and perhaps that was – annoying. And you keep having to rescue me from things. And you still call me a child, even though I asked you not to. So, do you think I'm just a – nuisance?'

He stared at her, momentarily uncomprehending. His smile faded as he reached forwards and clasped her hand. 'Beetle-brained brat,' he said fondly. 'Do I act as though I find you a nuisance? I'm not known as a man who accepts hindrances patiently – and never in my work. But the distractions you cause me are, in fact, entirely my own fault.'

She found it hard to believe. 'It's not your fault I got arrested, or locked in Throckmorton's horrid cellar.'

'I beg your pardon?' He looked at her in sudden blank amazement.

She had forgotten for a moment that he didn't know. 'It's complicated. Throckmorton recognised me at the docks. He was furious with me, from before. He just carried me off. That's when I found out he was plotting to kill you. But I rescued myself that time,' she said, with a touch of pride 'No one helped me, and I did it all alone. I wasn't even hurt. At least – only a little bit. And then I tried to rescue you, which wasn't successful at all. So, I'm sorry about that.'

Andrew had come much closer, and she felt his breath in her eyes as he spoke. 'Three times may seem somewhat insistent in just a few short hours, but it appears I have no choice.' He grasped her by the shoulders and pulled her towards him. Then he paused, as if something quite unaccustomed had occurred to him. 'Unless, that is,' he said rather more softly, 'you have any objections?'

'Object to what?' she said, startled.

'This,' he said, pushing her back to the bed.

It was sometime later when, once again dressed in her stained broadcloth, Tyballis sat meekly at the long table in the hall. It was raining heavily once more, beating against the windows and closing in the day. But the fire had been built to its usual massive proportions and the great chamber expanded, its frame heaving from the heat inside and the cold without. Every wooden beam creaked and sweated. The rich scent of burning wood mingled with the spices of mulled hippocras. Andrew sat at the head of his table, Tyballis to his side, and everyone else gathered tightly together on the long benches. The explanations became mellow as the wine jugs emptied.

'I ain't saying I don't understand,' muttered Casper, refilling his own cup, 'but I can't say it's right clear, neither. Here was me thinking you was a lord pretending to be an ordinary gent. But now you says you're just an ordinary gent pretending to be a lord.'

'And here was me thinking you were just an ordinary thief like the rest of us,' objected Ralph Tame. 'But looks like there's nothing ordinary about it.'

'A thief maybe, but a sight better at it than us,' nodded Nat, 'seeing as how this is your house and everything in it belongs to you. Stolen property maybe, but I'd an idea you won it cheating at dice.'

Andrew Cobham smiled faintly. 'The truth is far less interesting, I'm afraid.'

Tyballis turned crossly to Nat. 'That's a horrid suspicion,' she said. 'Of course Drew doesn't cheat at dice.'

'I most certainly do,' Andrew said. 'In fact, I see no conceivable reason to play at dice otherwise. What possible use would it be to risk losing? But when I play with loaded dice, I play for considerably more important wagers than simple greed. Indeed, this house is of very little service to me, which is why I fill it with a parcel of ne'er-do-wells and misbegotten beggars.'

The ne'er-do-wells and beggars sniggered cheerfully.

'I could not believe my eyes,' George Switt said in a voice of awe, 'when the young Mister Lyttle, Mister Spiers and myself cowered in Lord Hastings' apartments, expecting at any moment to be clapped in irons, and you, sir, marched in demanding to see his lordship.'

Davey interrupted. 'Not cowering, George, please. I never cower. But,' he turned to Andrew, 'we'd been waiting so long, you know, it seemed likely something had gone wrong. We were worried about Tybbs, of course, but tell the truth, we were a touch more worried about ourselves. Hastings had disappeared some time back and we were there in a huddle being watched over by six huge guards. And me without even a knife in my belt.'

'Coulda' defended yerself with the gittern,' suggested Casper. 'I reckon a splinter from that could be right nasty. Straight up a nostril, or into some bugger's eye. And the strings. Throttle nice and tight, I reckon. I seen some bastard garrotted once. Shit hisself as the wire cut right into his gullet. The blood were nothing compared to the other muck what came pouring out.'

Everyone pretended to ignore this insight. Jon Spiers, meanwhile, was unaccountably wide awake. 'We were remarkably pleased to see you, sir,' he told Andrew. 'But puzzled, I must admit, when you informed Lord Hastings that the Duke of Gloucester ordered our immediate release. Now, how would you know? And what did it have to do with him? Don't he like Throckmorton, neither?'

Andrew's lips twitched. 'I am sure he would not, had he ever met the man.'

Mistress Spiers was just as confused. 'I think,' Felicia said, 'it would be most helpful, Mister Cobham, if you would kindly explain what happened from the beginning. I'm sure we have no right whatsoever to question you, which we have never done in the past, as you know, but I admit we've often wondered about your situation.'

'True,' Ralph nodded. 'Can't help curiosity, you know. And you being the principal benefactor of our lives. But we knew when to keep our mouths shut before.'

'Until Tybbs got snatched by that miserable bastard,' grinned Davey, putting one booted foot up on the table, leaning back and draining his cup. 'And the poor girl came staggering home in such a sorry state, so she had to tell us what happened. Threw herself on my mercy, and of course I rose to the occasion, as always. That's when we started to put the clues together.'

They were all looking at Andrew when Ralph sat up very straight and said, 'You're a royal spy, aren't you, Mister Cobham?'

Andrew did not answer directly. He also leaned back in his chair and drained his cup. 'I notice that everyone is here,' he said softly, 'except our Mister Parris. Luke is, perhaps, too busy?'

Tyballis shook her head quickly before Davey could say anything rude. 'I think he's out. But he was just as helpful and involved as everyone else at the time, you know. He's the only one amongst us who could write, having been a monk of course. So he scribed the message we sent to Throckmorton, pretending it was from Lord Marrott ordering more arsenic. That's why I knew Throckmorton would come to see Marrott at four of the clock.'

'Luke Parris wrote the message?' Andrew's eyes narrowed. 'I see. A great deal becomes clear.'

'It was a good plan,' nodded Ralph. 'Mister Switt's plan mostly, with advice from the rest of us. And we all took a hand, even little Ellen. Went with Nat, she did. He's our best lockpick, and she's small enough to get into tight corners.'

'Picking whose locks?' demanded Andrew, turning to Nat.

'Ah, yes,' grinned Nat. 'That was something I was getting around to telling you. Thinking Throckmorton was plotting against you, we decided we'd take a look in his coffers. We grabbed whatever we found, mostly parchments. But the money – well, it went against the grain, but I only took a handful - not that there was too much of it, to tell the truth. Now you're here, sir, I shall simply hand the papers over.'

'How ... interesting,' decided Mister Cobham. 'But you need not address me as sir, you know. Andrew will do. I repeat, my use of the name Lord Feayton is simply for convenience. Mixing with the lords of this realm, befriending those at court and intimidating others would be considerably more tedious without some title to give me entrance. It denotes nothing, yet serves a purpose. My name is Cobham.'

'You told me it wasn't that either,' said Tyballis, but then looked quickly down at her lap. 'It's none of our business, of course.'

'No, it is not.' Andrew looked around at the cluster of eager faces. 'I have always had a great dislike of too many involvements, or of those who wish to know too much about me.' He turned to Ralph. 'You call me a spy. It is not a description I have ever used, but it is close enough to the truth. Therefore my trade is in secrecy, and my natural inclination is strictly private.' He looked back to Tyballis, and smiled gently. 'But it now seems I have acquired a parcel of interested allies who clearly deserve acknowledgement. I cannot and will not begin by unburdening my past, but it's true I have used many names. Indeed, I have always chosen to ignore my own, for reasons which are also my own. But as I say, Andrew is sufficient.'

'Fair enough. But I must say, I should be mighty curious to know how you came by this house,' Nat said.

'Which is another matter I consider utterly irrelevant to this discussion,' sighed Drew. 'What I can tell you is that when I returned to London just three days ago, I was approached by someone of my acquaintance, informing me Baron Throckmorton had been ordered by Lord Marrott to supply a quantity of arsenic, and bring it to him at Westminster. This acquaintance – being someone I have recently threatened with dire consequences should he ever again involve himself with poisons – begged me to deliver the package on his behalf. It happens that I know Marrott and have been endeavouring for some time to discover his motives with regard to – let us say – assassinations. However, that he should ever have ordered such a delivery at Westminster appeared absurd, even for someone of Marrott's arrogant stupidity, particularly since he certainly knows Throckmorton is not permitted entrance there. I therefore accepted the commission and approached Marrott, but without delivering the arsenic with which I had been supplied. Entering Westminster Palace armed with enough deadly poison to murder the entire court did not seem entirely wise. Indeed, I thought the whole business a trap. I was curious to know whose trap, either Throckmorton's, or Marrott's.' He nodded to Tyballis, still smiling. 'I admit it had not occurred to me that it might be yours, my dear.'

'My God, Drew. You really could have been killed.'

'Not for that reason. I am not so inexperienced, my dear. Indeed, I went to see Hastings first. Had the trap been intended to ensnare either Marrott or myself, undoubtedly the palace guards would have been warned to watch for my arrival. I therefore pre-empted my arrest, and disclosed the entire situation to Hastings. He already knew, you see, that Marrott was privately suspected of – certain transactions. Although I had never previously met Lord Hastings, I was aware that my own employer had spoken to him concerning me. I was therefore able to introduce myself and explain my mission. His lordship also explained the unexpected group of minstrels who had entertained him that afternoon. I was able to forestall their arrest, and having seen who they were, sent them home. Seeing them was a considerable surprise, I assure you.' Once again Andrew turned to Tyballis. 'Seeing you, my dear, was a far greater shock. Hastings had not prepared me for that.'

'But what did Marrott say?' insisted Jon.

'Apart from wanting to kill me?' Andrew laughed. 'He naturally denied ordering anything from Throckmorton. When I disclosed the business of the arsenic, he insisted that was purely a mistake. He claimed simply to have ordered digestive powders once before, and a minute quantity of arsenic is known to be useful for the treatment of many ailments. Lord Marrott is now equally furious both with myself, and with Throckmorton.'

'I'm sorry,' whispered Tyballis.

'There's no need for that,' Andrew said, holding out his cup for Casper's brimming jug. 'These have been useful days, after all. I have discovered a muster of highly talented musicians, evidently capable of many other varied and remarkable accomplishments. You call me a spy. If true, what better aid than an army of soldiers already experienced in crime and intrigue, and now prepared to adapt to the additional expertise of espionage. Indeed, wandering minstrels have excellent ears, and I often use them myself for uncovering, let us say, relevant facts.' He raised his newly filled cup to the many eager crowding faces, and drank deep. 'I thank all my willing apprentices.' Then he nodded to Nat, again holding his cup high. 'And I have also, it seems, acquired a package of Throckmorton's secret papers, which will no doubt prove invaluable once I get around to inspecting them.' He set his cup back on the table and turned instead to Tyballis. 'And what is more,' he said softly, so only she could hear, 'I have passed one of the most delightful nights of my entire life.'

CHAPTER THIRTY-ONE

'You won't go back to Crosby's?'

'Eventually I must, since I need the clothes from the garderobe, and many other matters are best dealt with there rather than here. But for the moment I stay.'

'Because of me?'

'Because of the others. When I do go, I may take you with me.'

She was curious. 'You trust the others at last, then?'

'I'm sure you know perfectly well that I do not. But they have proved themselves ready for the game. I ask for no commitment.'

'Nor from me?' She looked up at him. 'And should I not – from you?'

The gales rattled the windows and rushed down the chimneys, the rain pelted again and the night was black and bitter. But inside it was as warm and snug as a squirrel's nest. Across from the foot of the bed, the fire raged in swirls of bursting scarlet and as the wind gusted down the flue and caught up sparks and flying ash, so the flames fanned brighter as if from a bellows. Andrew Cobham lay spread across the tossed bedcovers, his head comfortable on the piled pillows and his eyes closed. He was unusually tired. Tyballis lay curled beside him, her head cushioned by his stomach. Her fingers ranged idly.

After a pause, he said, 'Your breath is the most tempting warm breeze, and your fingertips are tantalising.'

She moved her hand. 'You avoided my question.'

'Purposefully.' He squinted down at her and sighed. 'It is not an easy question, little one.' Andrew wedged himself up on one elbow, reached down and drew her up beside him, tucking her head into the curl of his neck.

She murmured, 'Once you spoke to me of dalliance. I demand nothing, but I have never been used to – dalliance.'

'Years ago, I committed myself to my work and my master,' Andrew told her, voice soft. 'Nothing else has mattered to me for a long time. Commitment to any other cause would be a hard habit to grasp. I could marry, if I wished, but I would make a poor husband. For one thing, my work is dangerous. If I were killed, as I could be almost every day, my death might be held secret for some months out of expediency or subterfuge. My salary is spasmodic, my habit is to spend it back on my work, my free time is limited, and this house is ill kept, as I prefer it to be. I could offer you neither security nor domestic comfort, my love. But in any case, how could I offer marriage, even if I wished and even under such meagre circumstances, when you are already married?'

'I never asked you for marriage,' she said at once.

'But you ask for commitment.'

'I hated being married. Commitment is different. You're committed to the Duke of Gloucester. You're not married to him.'

Andrew chuckled. 'I don't sleep with him either.'

'But you do sleep with Elizabeth,' Tyballis sighed. 'So, is this the same?'

'If you can't tell the difference, my sweet, then you're sorely inexperienced.' His hand moved to her breast, fingers gently wandering. 'I'll not criticise any woman I've known, at least not those I've known intimately. Some have come to me in affection, others simply for mercenary reasons, or begging sympathy and comfort. I'm fond of Lizzie. I don't deny using her. I know she uses me. Do you think I've used you?'

'Perhaps I don't mind if you do. But if you sleep with me one night, and then Elizabeth the next ...'

He sat up abruptly and stared down at her. 'I'd be too damned tired.' He frowned. 'So, do you want me to kill your wretched husband, and marry you instead?'

She was startled. 'Do you really think killing someone the easy solution?'

As finally the rain slowed and turned to freeze, the corners of the windowpanes outside began to frost. Tiny white crystals clung between glass and darkness, but inside, the bedchamber still glowed and gleamed in the firelight. Andrew leaned back against the pillows and stared up at the high drifts of dust on the ceiling beams. 'Why not?' he said softly. 'Life is only a temporary business, after all, and rarely fulfils its promises. I am no paid assassin, and have taken no one's life without reason, but in defence of my own life, in defence of my identity and in defence of my cause I have killed and may again. When I die, some higher authority will surely challenge me for my sins, but for now I do what I must when I must.'

Tyballis stared at him. 'You've – killed – people? The duke—'

'In his service, yes. Though not on his orders. Doubtless he would not approve, since he believes in the law rather more strongly than I do.'

'It's a dangerous world, but to choose ... if you mean'

'I mean I killed my first man when I was thirteen.' Andrew smiled back at her, gathering her to him again. 'But that's another story, and not one for tonight. I'm tired, my love. You have my commitment, if that's what you want. But one day when you change your mind and find me too difficult – or my immorality shocks you too much – then let me know and I shall adjust to your absence once again. In the meantime, iniquity can be exhausting. Does all that love-play not tire you, too?'

Tyballis mumbled, 'It wakes me up and I'm not tired at all.'

'Clearly I need to teach you how to share the load.' One arm clasped her firmly to him, his hand on her back. 'I have decisions to make in the morning, however. Sleep deep, little one.' And he kissed her lightly on the forehead, once again closing his eyes.

The fire had died down and the winter sun was bright through the rimed window glass as he brought her light beer the following morning, and sat beside her on the edge of the mattress. He was again wearing the black brocade bedrobe, and this time it was tied tight. He said, 'I intend seeing Throckmorton first. It would, of course, be most unwise for you to come. I will then attempt to see Lord Hastings. You cannot accompany me to court either, my love. Hastings would certainly recognise you and if we were to encounter Lord Marrott, it would be disastrous.'

He went straight from Portsoken to Crosby's annexe and there he changed his clothes. He slipped a thin Venetian dagger down the side of his riding boot, his penknife into the lining of his sweeping velvet sleeves and his long sword into its scabbard at his side. He then ordered the bay hunter saddled, strode out to the sun-dappled stables, mounted the waiting horse and rode quickly west. He did not, however, approach Bradstreet and it appeared that, despite what he had told Tyballis, he did not intend visiting Baron Throckmorton at all. Instead he rode directly to St Paul's.

Being too heavily armed to enter the cathedral proper, and having no wish to deposit his sword at the vestibule, Andrew strode into a small secluded office to one side, sat on the stool, put both legs up on the table and waited. After a moment a small boy poked his nose around the inner door. 'Tell your master Lord Feayton is come on the duke's orders,' Andrew said.

Andrew Cobham left London a little over an hour later, rode through the Ludgate, crossed the noisome chugging of The Fleet and continued through the gardened greenery of The Strand towards Westminster. At the Palace he once again left his horse at the stables and this time he also left his sword at the guards' offices. He was no longer alone. Mister William Catesby accompanied him, and together they strode the brightly lit corridors towards the great spread of apartments permanently occupied by the Baron Hastings. Here Mister Catesby and Mister Cobham accepted refreshment, refused an invitation to midday dinner in the High Hall, and settled down to lengthy discussion and negotiation.

'It is,' Lord Hastings said at last, 'of the greatest conceivable concern to this realm, and has been for some months. And yet we still have no proof? Nor could we prove the first attempt, though with thanks be to all the saints, the king survived. But if his grace were to succumb to such wickedness a second time, what then? And what of the subsequent intentions?'

'As far as I've been able to ascertain, the orders come directly from Ludlow,' Andrew said, his fingertip playing thoughtfully around the rim of his cup. 'Marrott complies, but the initiative is not his. Nor, it appears, does her highness know anything of the situation and would surely disapprove if she did.'

'The damned woman owes everything to Edward.' Hastings leaned forwards, frowning. 'Without the king where would she be? Back in poverty, scraping a meagre living for herself and her family as she did before. And to think it was me who introduced her to the king.'

Andrew acknowledged the irony. 'My lord, I state the circumstances without bias, but every situation is open to interpretation according to opinion. Some of these opinions are assumptions. Some are certainties. None are provable.'

Hastings leaned back again in his chair. 'Opinions and assumptions, my lord, yes indeed. And what, may I ask, am I to assume concerning a nobleman with a title I do not recognise? Do I trust the suspicions of a man, when I doubt the veracity of his identity?'

'My family is from the northeast, my lord,' Andrew replied, unperturbed. 'My father was related to the late Lord Leays. But I do not come to press any claim of my own, sir. Merely to present the facts.'

'Then tell me the facts as you see them, Feayton,' Hastings said. 'Give me something I can take to the king, provable or otherwise.'

'I cannot be sure, but I suspect Earl Rivers, and if I am right, his motives appear simple,' Andrew said softly. 'It is apparent that his highness is lately out of sympathy with her highness. You have confirmed this yourself, my lord. The king has made it known he intends removing the queen's name as principal executor of his will and testament. She will no longer officially be the prince's foremost guardian, nor the main recipient of the king's possessions should his highness die during his son's minority.'

Catesby smiled at Baron Hastings. 'These are legal matters. As a lawyer, and your loyal servant, my lord, I have been informing Lord Feayton for some weeks now. I can confirm that lawyers have been consulted and the intention is known at court.'

'The king has told me so himself,' Hastings snorted. 'I'm not on such an intimate footing with the queen to discuss these matters, but believe me, she knows. I'll wager the king's threat has her spitting venom.'

Andrew said, 'I spent some weeks at Ludlow before Christmas, my lord. The earl also knows, and is deeply concerned regarding his sister's fall in grace. If the queen loses influence, then so will her favourites and in particular her family. With his highness still young, there may be many years of continued disillusion to come. And the king's heir will mature, and even perhaps adopt his father's opinion, disassociating himself, in time, from Woodville influence.'

'Damned Dorset seems as popular as ever,' Hastings grumbled.

'As is Earl Rivers, I understand.' Andrew lowered his voice. 'But should her highness continue to lose favour, so, inevitably, will those she has championed. There is the risk that, in the future, they might lose everything. It has happened before to others.'

'Yes. Even to Warwick,' Hastings nodded. 'Long ago perhaps, but with a similar result, for such bias induced even Warwick to turn traitor. I consider Edward a great king and a good man. But under certain circumstances his admiration is known to grow suddenly cold, and can turn abruptly to contempt. He is remarkably stubborn – and he has a temper.'

'As your lordship says. At present Earl Rivers is one of the most powerful lords in the realm. More importantly, he holds the elder prince in his hand. As the heir's guardian and closest friend, his lordship is trusted as no other. Should his highness die soon, pray God keep him safe, so the new King Edward would immediately enrich and empower Rivers, Dorset and the others even beyond the favours they already hold.'

'The next king?' snorted Hastings. 'An insipid twelve-year-old, with more yellow curls on his head than brains inside it. The boy would be entirely ruled by his mother and his Uncle Rivers. A hundred bastard Woodvilles would crawl out of the woodwork to claim further rewards. Damnation! If Edward died now the country would soon be a Woodville trough for the picking. And Rivers would be king in all but name.'

Andrew bent his head again in acknowledgement. 'Precisely, my lord, it is how I see it. I believe it is how Earl Rivers sees it. So Rivers must move before the king amends his will. He must take advantage of a testament leaving the country open to himself and his sister the queen, and of a boy king, not a man capable of choosing to rule by his own hand.'

'And this wretch Marrott?'

'I have something approaching proof against Lord Marrott,' Andrew nodded. 'And by association perhaps the Marquess of Dorset, since they are particularly close friends. But against all but Marrott, there stands only suspicion.'

'If such disaster befell us – if such villainy were allowed to occur – then, perhaps ...' Hastings scratched his beard, his chin sunk into the high sable of his collar. 'The prince, our illustrious heir, may grow to be a fine man if his father reigns long enough for the son to mature. At present he knows only his Uncle Rivers' influence. If he were brought to the throne too soon, there are matters long hidden that I might bring to light. I believe I would do this, if I thought it just.'

Andrew's eyes narrowed. Catesby quickly interrupted. 'My lord, I have spoken to his highness's legal advisors, though naturally they have not confided the nature of the changes intended. The king will alter his testament as and when propitious, but as yet he sees no cause for haste. He enjoys good health and has no reason to expect otherwise. While his highness remains content to let matters lie, Earl Rivers has time to choose his moment and consider the risks most carefully.'

Hastings was watching Andrew with some interest. 'My lord

Feayton, you say you travelled to Ludlow before Christmas, and discovered something of Rivers' mind. How is this? Are you acquainted with him? The Duke of Gloucester spoke to me of you but always kept your identity private. Yet evidently this is known to others?'

'Indeed not, my lord.' Andrew smiled slightly. 'I prefer to operate with whatever secrecy is allowed me. It ensures my ability to travel incognito and to take on other names and personalities at will. I entered Ludlow Castle in another guise. Nor did I personally encounter Earl Rivers. But I was able to speak with some intimacy to those who have his trust. And as it happens, I have a certain ability – when needed – of encouraging others to break that trust.'

'One of the few things Richard said of you!' Hastings laughed suddenly, sitting forwards and clapping his hands to his knees. 'Told me you hold trust as a fool's illusion. Yet the duke says you've proved your mettle and he trusts you. How do you explain that then, my lord?'

'I should never attempt to explain his grace of Gloucester's motives, my lord, nor aspire to question them.' Andrew gazed directly into Hastings' bright, lascivious eyes. 'But however little respect I hold for trust as a virtue, my lord, I can swear to this. In all things now and forever, I will never betray the duke's trust in me. And perhaps alone in all the world, I trust his grace. Indeed, the work I do now and the dangers I risk are for him, and for the safety of this realm. I should not wish to live in an England ruled by Earl Rivers and a twelve-year-old puppet king.'

Hastings nodded, frowning. 'I have been assured of your discretion, Feayton.' His voice sunk. 'So, I will tell you this. The king's heir – this future puppet king you speak of, this insipid Woodville brat – should be no king of England. This is no treason. It is simple fact. The whelp is a bastard born of a bigamous marriage. While Edward lives I'll say nothing of this, but should his highness die under suspicion of Woodville malice – then, by God, I'll make the truth known.' He looked up suddenly and intently, eyes bright, regarding both his companions. 'And whether either of you choose to remember my words or not, remember this. What I say is truth, but if you think to gain something by repeating it, I'll deny every word and it will be you arrested for misprision of treason.'

Andrew raised an eyebrow. 'Being in the nature of my business, I had heard rumours, my lord, but am surprised to hear you speak of it. However, I believe it is another matter on which we have no proof. The lady in question is, I understand, deceased.'

Hastings grinned suddenly. 'Know about everything already, don't you, Feayton! Secrecy and discretion be damned. Richard has employed a good man.'

'My lord, secrecy and discretion are my trade,' Andrew said quietly. 'I repeat what I know only to his grace of Gloucester and no other. What I disclose to you, my lord, is on his grace's orders.'

Catesby interrupted again. 'But you assume there's no proof of his highness's earlier clandestine marriage, since the Lady Eleanor Butler is now deceased. But some of her family are aware, and indeed, there was a reliable witness, and he is still very much alive.'

'Enough, enough.' Hastings raised his hand. 'There are always rumours and the whole court knows of Edward's dalliances, past and present.' He turned again to Andrew. 'My lord, you're personally acquainted, I understood from our dealings the other day, with Lord Marrott, and through him, with Dorset. I hold Dorset in more contempt than I do Lord Rivers.'

Andrew sighed. 'The Marquess is – young, my lord.'

'Your own age, I imagine.'

'Truly. But his life in recent years has been – let us say – indulged. Easy living does not build maturity.' Andrew set his cup on the table before him. It was expensive, a standing cup of coloured Murano crystal, and he had seen a similar set long ago in another lord's house. He had broken one of them, purposefully snapping the heavy stem between his fingers. He still bore the scar. Brushing past uncomfortable memories, he continued speaking to the Lord Hastings. 'The situation is simple, my lord. The queen's family has benefited greatly from his highness's favour. Earl Rivers and the Marquess of Dorset in particular hold enormous power and great riches and have no intention of relinquishing them. But they risk ruin should the king turn his favour elsewhere. In recent months it appears this may indeed occur. Her highness the queen is losing her husband's ear. She has already lost his bed. If she loses his favour entirely, the house of Woodville will topple. Lord Rivers does not intend that to happen.'

'And Marrott? How does he benefit?'

Andrew shook his head slightly. 'As you know, sir, Lord Marrott comes from an old Lancastrian family, and his father was executed after Tewkesbury. Marrott, therefore, has no reason to love his highness. But principally I believe he hopes to gain by the king's death through his great friendship with the Marquess of Dorset. However, I beg you to remember, my lord, that against Earl Rivers and the Marquess of Dorset, there is only supposition, and although their behaviour seems to me suspicious, I have neither proof nor certainty. Yet Rivers holds the heir to the throne in the palm of his hand. Living together at Ludlow in some isolation from the court, the young prince looks to his uncle before anyone else. If Rivers is to benefit from this before the child grows to his majority, then the king must die, and before the royal testament is changed. The new king will then be his uncle's dupe, his mother's lap dog and the country's curse.'

Hastings said, 'It's clear enough. Unless I expose the brat as a bastard and no heir. But to do that while Edward lives? He would never forgive.'

'And there is another to benefit as much if not more from his highness's untimely passing,' Andrew said softly. 'And that, my lord, is France.'

Hastings let out a long slow breath, looking briefly to Catesby. 'You accept this as truth?' Catesby nodded.

Andrew said, 'It is irrefutable, my lord. I have spent some years building friendships in vital places, inspiring confidence, threatening and bribing. I have traced smuggled imports of arsenic from Venice, but it's not Italy that plots against us. I know the merchants, their servants and their masters, and have interrogated many. But there are none who dare testify openly to what they have seen or done. French spies roam our land. I also know the French to be in contact with Lord Rivers. He is a man of ingenuity and intelligence, and he makes few mistakes. The king trusts him utterly. The country trusts him. His nephew, the heir to the throne, trusts him absolutely. The earl is a nobleman of almost sainted reputation. His adherence to pilgrimage and the church is legendary.' Andrew smiled slightly. 'Whatever one's views on trust, my lord, it is always unwise to trust a man clearly working too hard to gain the trust of those in power. It is true we have no proof. But perhaps, if your lordship were to explain this situation to his highness? After all, I understand his highness also trusts you.'

CHAPTER THIRTY-TWO

Harold, Baron Throckmorton, sat and stared into his mirror. He had been shrieking at his servants for some hours, both individually and in groups, and the effort and strain showed in his eyes. They were red-rimmed. His golden red hair had fallen slack from its careful curls and now hung lank. His mouth looked drawn and white-lipped. Even his beautiful clothes now smelled inescapably of sour sweat.

The household at Throckmorton Hall was not privy to his lordship's private business, but that there were family secrets and dark deals aplenty, the staff had realised for some years. Now finance was in short supply but it seemed other even more important possessions had lately gone missing. His lordship blamed every one of his servants for the unaccountable thefts. He was also beginning to suspect a more probable culprit. Indeed, it seemed remarkably coincidental when all the dogs started barking and Bodge entered the baron's private solar to announce the arrival of visitors, one of whom was the suspicious personage himself.

Lord Feayton invariably conducted his business alone and rarely appeared in company with others. This time, however, he came accompanied by one William Catesby, lawyer to the great Lord Hastings; and although not personally known to the baron, he had certainly heard of him. These gentlemen were further flanked by a small armed guard, and for a moment Harold Throckmorton feared for his life and liberty. His pale and hollow face became hot and pink as he indicated to Bodge that the visitors must be kept waiting. He then hurriedly summoned John Hammon and cancelled the careful and secret orders previously applied to Lord Feayton's eventual reappearance.

'The damned man's not on his own,' Throckmorton hissed. 'Catesby indeed. One of Hastings' men. It would be disastrous to try and touch either of them now. You'd better watch from a distance and stay hidden.'

Lord Feayton and William Catesby were then admitted. Andrew strolled in with a wide smile, swept off his hat and gazed down at the baron standing quaking before him. 'Well, Harold,' he said, 'I've spoiled matters by bringing someone with me. You'll have to try to kill me off another day.'

Throckmorton blushed. 'Insult me as you wish, my lord,' he said, with a stiff and infinitesimal bow. 'It is true, of course, that I've been expecting you this week past. But I have nothing for you, sir, nothing at all.' He looked curiously at Catesby. 'I can only assume that business is no longer your purpose in coming here?'

'Now, why would you suppose that?' Andrew smiled. 'You assume I'd not demonstrate my habits of blackmailing my acquaintances in front of my friend William?' Without being invited, he dragged two small chairs from the shadows and sat on one, indicating the other for Catesby. 'I must inform you that Mister Catesby, being amongst other things my lawyer, knows a good deal of my business. No secrets, Harold, no secrets. However, I'm not at all surprised you can't pay me. I indicated as much the last time I was here. You expected to receive special monetary appreciation because of your part in putting Mistress Blessop in gaol, accused of your brother's murder. But Mistress Blessop was freed without charge. You then tried to please your masters and free yourself from my watchfulness by incriminating me at court with Geoffrey Marrott – or was it Baron Hastings – catching me peddling packages of suspicious powders. But you have failed yet again, Harold. Your hidden benefactor will not be pleased, and so you, my dear, must therefore continue to be sadly unappreciated, after all. My only surprise is to find you still alive.'

William Catesby also sat, although Throckmorton remained standing. Catesby said, 'I'm amazed you haven't dispatched him yourself, my lord.'

Andrew nodded. 'Dispatched – dispatches. Now, there's an interesting subject, Will. You see, in a quite remarkable manner, it so happens that some of dear Harold's dispatches have recently come into my possession. Merely by chance, you understand. And some of them are quite intriguing.' He turned to Throckmorton again. 'Do you know, my dear baron, the full consequences of high treason these days?'

Throckmorton felt his knees give way and quickly found another chair. 'Nonsense, my lord,' he managed to say. 'I would never indulge – that is to say, would never wish … I am a most loyal subject of our beloved king. Past family loyalties aside, it is a long time since those battles when my father fought against the Yorkist factions. And my family has suffered for this – suffered greatly as you know, my lord. The Throckmorton estates are almost all confiscated.'

'I've no time for this self pity, Lord Throckmorton,' Catesby said, tapping his heel. 'We are come about a certain letter once in your possession – and now safely in ours. Let me simply say, the letter is written in French.'

'Hardly an unusual circumstance,' Throckmorton said, growing rigid and nearly biting his tongue. 'Most court papers are still written principally in French, as you are obviously aware. And if this letter you refer to is no longer in my possession, then how can you be sure it ever was?' With a determined exhibition of confidence, he straightened his shoulders and clicked his fingers in Catesby's face. 'Proof, sirs, proof. Evidently you have none. You imply a libellous letter – a treasonous letter. In which case I assure you it was never mine.'

Andrew Cobham leaned forwards and spoke very softly and directly to Throckmorton's eyes. 'I've no need of proof, Harold. Mister Catesby may be a representative of the law, but I do not deal in the limitations of legal requirements. I deal in natural justice. Your

227

actual guilt is of great interest to me, and will be to others. So, I have come to tell you this: I know exactly what you are up to. You hoped to implicate me in smuggling poisonous powders into court, and you set a trap of ridiculous naivety. When you heard you had failed, you then returned to your previous plan and arranged to have me taken and slaughtered as soon as I set foot on your property. Naive again, Harold. You have been corresponding with one Dominico Mancini, a known French spy, with Venetian traders in poison, with Lancastrian traitors, and even been unwise enough to abduct Mistress Blessop, attempting to use her against me. But you fail constantly. Now let me warn you one last time. I am growing weary of your cruelty and your spite.'

'You are utterly mistaken in everything, my lord,' Throckmorton insisted. 'No such plan, no such plot—'

'Enough.' Andrew raised one finger. 'Listen to me. If you become further embroiled with the French, their spies and their schemes, you will die quickly. Either I shall kill you myself, or they will. The French leave no witnesses to their designs, for King Louis is both implacable and devious. There also remains another enemy still planning your destruction for the motives I explained earlier, as friends turn to enemies when you consistently fail them, Harold. You must know this. But there is one other likely fate, which you should consider most carefully. Under accusation of high treason, you may be arrested and thrown into the dungeons of The Tower. Since you deal with the French, you should know something of those masters in torture and persuasion. The use of torture is generally thought unacceptable in this country, but I assure you, once treason is suspected, the dungeons tell no tales.'

William Catesby stood, scraping back his chair so suddenly that Throckmorton quivered and shrank back. Catesby said, 'This is tedious, my lord. Why bother warning the fellow? Let's kill him and be done with it.'

Andrew's mouth twitched. 'Patience, patience, William,' he said. 'I have a use still for the wretch.' He turned back to the baron, who had once again turned quite white and was wondering how he might unobtrusively call for John Hammon, and whether one man would be of any use defending him against two. Andrew meanwhile sat forwards with a genial smile. 'Now, Harold,' he said. 'There is something I want you to do. Naturally you have no choice in the matter. This is not exactly complicated, but since your level of intelligence is clearly limited, you had better listen carefully while I explain.'

William Catesby and Andrew Cobham left Throckmorton Hall some two hours later and held their laughter in check until they were at a considerable distance from Bradstrete.

Catesby said, turning up his collar against the increasing cold, 'I'm not in the least surprised the duke trusts you so particularly, my lord. I imagine he finds you invaluable. I trust I may become as indispensable to my Lord Hastings, but I confess my own interests and career take a good deal of my time.'

Andrew smiled. 'Under the circumstances, Will, you should say no more. I am not perhaps the most suitable ear for confessions. I suggest Bishop Stillington?'

Catesby frowned, then laughed suddenly. 'Yes, Stillington indeed. I might have guessed you'd already know him as the witness to – well, enough said. A clandestine matter – be it marriage or otherwise – is best left unspoken. You're a master of diplomacy, and a man of many secrets. But do you respect the secrets of others, I wonder?'

Their horses trotted slowly, careful of slipping, for the streets were rimed between the cobbles. Andrew hunched a little in his saddle.

'My answer to that,' he murmured, 'would depend on who asked.'

'And if I asked?'

Drew looked abruptly across at the other man. 'An honest answer? How unwise to ask for honesty from a man who trades in subterfuge. But in all honesty, Will, if I knew that you cheated on your wife, which you do, I would respect your secret. If I knew you occasionally cheated in your profession, which I also know, then I would keep silent to all but his grace of Gloucester. But if I knew you traded in treason, which I am sure you do not, then our friendship would end and so would the secrecy.'

Catesby nodded, thoughtful. 'It's a fair answer. For some time now I've voluntarily aided you in uncovering the threats to his highness's life. So, you've reason to trust me, whatever your opinion of trust. And I have reason to trust you, whether you look for it or not. Keep me informed, if you will, my lord; I ask nothing more. My life and career may depend upon it.'

'I've no objection to your personal ambitions,' Andrew said. The wind had found the back of his neck, and he quickened his horse's pace a little. Catesby kept alongside. 'So, I shall keep you informed of eventualities,' Andrew continued, 'and I wish your career God speed. But remember ambition can also be used against you.'

'On the contrary,' grinned Catesby, 'it's a tool to use against others.'

'An opinion,' Andrew nodded, 'wiser not mentioned to Lord Hastings.'

As he saw Mister Catesby back to his lodgings, already the light was waning, and a thin silver-and-crimson lining had attached behind each blustering cloud. Mister Cobham then slowly turned his horse and rode back to Bishopsgate and the small annexes fronting Crosby's Place.

The winter evening settled sullen and chill, and the lingering sunset remained as listless as he felt. He was uncomfortably aware of an unaccountable melancholy and an unaccustomed tiredness. A sense of foreboding hung behind his more urgent thoughts, and irritated like a flea bite in the night. But the matters that had consumed him for so long, now seemed strangely less consequential, and a sudden desire to rest became paramount. He would have stayed where he was at Crosby's, where the troubles of the world could not enter, where the bed was deep, warm and aired, and the servants well trained. But he was expected at home. His freedom of choice had become suddenly limited, not only through his promise to return, but through the inescapable fact that he wished to. The interference of his own personal desires reminded him that he had, for the first time in his memory, something to look forward to. Which meant there was something he risked losing. The dangers of his life had become unexpectedly double-edged.

Andrew quickly entered the unlit inner chambers, shook the cobwebs of unwelcome introspection away, called for a servant to bring hippocras and began to change his clothes.

It was some considerable time later when he arrived at his own home, having passed through the Aldgate on foot only minutes before it closed for the night. The bright and frosty day had shed its ice over puddles and gutters, a brittle white gloss left for moonshine reflections to come. Hunching his shoulders beneath his shabby velvets, Andrew hoped someone had kept up the main fire in the hall, and pushed open his front door.

He was not fully inside when someone screamed.

The echoes settled, telling of direction. Swallowing exhaustion, Andrew Cobham took the stairs two at a time and ran to the room where the screaming had begun.

CHAPTER THIRTY-THREE

Although it was now some months that Tyballis had lived at Cobham Hall, she had never yet entered the attic lodgings. She was therefore pleased to be invited in. She had gone up there to inform Mister Parris regarding the complicated results of his kindly written message to Baron Throckmorton. The young man had smiled widely and asked if she would care for refreshment.

'I am not as casual in friendship as some of my neighbours,' Luke had said, 'and have always considered it highly improper to invite a solitary young woman into my chambers without chaperone. My upbringing, you know, Mistress Blessop, taught me a conventional attitude to feminine companionship. But we have, I believe, now become trusted friends. Forgive me, but perhaps you will therefore permit me to alter the habit of many years.'

'Many years, Mister Parris?' Tyballis had laughed. 'I can't believe you're much older than I am myself.'

He had bowed. 'But old in experience, mistress. Now please, won't you come in? All those stairs must be exhausting to a delicate female, and I had already prepared a little mulled wine, well spiced, which is still warm.'

Mindful of his timidity and sense of propriety, Tyballis sat on the edge of the stool, hands clasped in her lap. But within a short and amiable half-hour, she began to relax. 'It was particularly helpful of you to write the message to Throckmorton,' she said, 'especially considering your position. That is, everyone else here – well, it's no secret and you must know as well as I do – they are all petty thieves, or at least make some sort of living in a thoroughly illegal manner. Whereas you, Mister Parris, having been a man of the church, must disapprove of such matters. So, to falsify someone else's name and signature ...'

Luke nodded over his wine cup. 'I did not copy any signature, of course, mistress. I cannot know how Lord Marrott is apt to sign, and am quite incapable of convincing forgeries. However, I was content to write the letter since one small sin must be judged against the greater good. Mister Switt's plan was an excellent one, but if the baron had not trusted the order and refused to take the dreadful package to court, we should have been undone, I fear.'

'Well, nothing worked according to plan anyway,' Tyballis said. 'But Drew has been warned of Throckmorton's horrible plots, which is what really matters. I should have been exceedingly pleased to know the wretched baron was in gaol where he deserves to be, but at least he won't be kidnapping anyone else in the future. He must realise he's now in danger himself.'

Luke slowly sipped his wine. 'To be a trader in poisons – well, I cannot even imagine such horror. I would never sleep, never rest, were such a thing on my conscience. And Mister Cobham, of course, is just the same – searching out the evil in others while denying his own most appalling—' Tyballis looked up with a jerk, but Luke shook his head. 'I must say no more. Andrew Cobham has been a friend to me for many years and I owe him my loyalty.'

'You know him well, then?'

'Longer than the other tenants here.' Luke smiled. 'He rescued me – if rescue is not too grand a word – from the monastery where I was an unhappy novice – forced by my father, you see, and on deciding to leave I faced many difficulties I could not solve alone. Having nowhere to go – meeting Andrew was my salvation. So, I must not speak a word against him. I'm sure you will understand the necessity for my silence.'

Tyballis frowned. 'Well, to be honest I didn't have any idea there was anything to be silent about. You've intrigued me, Mister Parris.'

'Luke, please, mistress.'

'Then it will have to be Tyballis,' she insisted. 'And so, dear Luke, I should love to know anything you feel free to tell me about Andrew. He is, you see, becoming rather important to me.' She paused, blushing slightly. 'I suppose you'll think I have shockingly loose morals, but you see, I've grown exceedingly attached to him. He's remarkably kind, as you must know. And most protective. Like you, I can say Mister Cobham has, in effect, rescued me from my previous life. I owe him a great deal.'

Luke nodded politely. 'Then we both owe him the respect not to speak out of turn. Let us discuss other matters.'

Tyballis thought a moment. Finally she said, 'I wouldn't want to speak against Drew behind his back. But perhaps, in all innocence, if you could tell me a little about his background? I know nothing of him, except he did mention his name isn't even Cobham. I gather he likes to adopt secret identities. His work is so dangerous, of course, so he needs anonymity.'

Luke's room was sparsely furnished and spotlessly clean, and the door to his bedchamber beyond was firmly closed. Only his scriptoria beneath the slanted gable window appeared busily crowded, spread with books, parchments, papers and quills. The faint smell of gall ink was the solitary disturbance in the small, scrubbed chamber and Tyballis was reminded of a monk's cell. She tried not to look around with too much curiosity.

'I understand,' he said, 'and if you are on the threshold of becoming, let us say, more than a casual friend of his, then perhaps I am duty bound to mention a few matters. But I cannot say much. Please do not press me, mistress.'

'Tyballis. And I won't. But how did you meet him?'

'I hope you will not be shocked,' Luke said softly, 'if I admit it was during threat of excommunication. Mister Cobham came to the monastery to obtain help in overcoming – but no matter, the reasons are irrelevant now. We were much in each other's company for some weeks. Since during that time he confessed many things to me, I felt free to confess also to him, admitting my profound dissatisfaction with the life of absolute dedication to Holy Mother Church. I felt myself too worldly for monastic sacrifice.'

Tyballis clasped her hands a little tighter. 'Drew was threatened with excommunication? Whatever did he do?'

Luke shook his head. 'That I must not say. Although his talks with me were not strictly under the mantle of the confessional, doubtless he saw me in the guise of a man of the cloth and I consider myself bound to secrecy. I believe he has been equally circumspect as to my own difficulties.'

'I don't blame you for not wanting to be a monk,' Tyballis nodded, now a little abstracted. 'The really dedicated clergy must feel terribly stifled, poor souls, and perhaps quite lonely. I'm surprised you haven't married, Luke, now you're free.'

Luke Parris blushed. 'I do not have such desires, not at all. I despise man's lust for flesh. My nature is too serious, too modest.'

Tyballis remembered Davey Lyttle's rude remarks about pederasty and smiled. 'Well that's entirely your own business, Luke. But how did you escape from the monastery? Did Drew help you out of a window? Did you gallop off into the night?'

'No, no. Nothing of that sort.' Luke laughed. 'Indeed, it was all managed quite legally and with great propriety. Afterwards, Andrew kindly offered me unlimited hospitality without obligation, and I appreciated that. So, you see, despite what I know, I must not speak.'

'Despite what you know? And is what you know so terribly bad?'

'Some. But like all the Lord's creations, there is also much good. You have seen the better side of Mister Cobham, I think. Let that suffice.'

'And his name?' Tyballis insisted, feeling uncomfortably hot. 'If it isn't Cobham, or Feayton – do you know what it really is?'

'I do. But I cannot say.' Luke was looking equally uncomfortable.

'Oh dear.' Tyballis sighed and shook her head. 'Just tell me one thing, Luke,' she continued. 'To your knowledge, has Drew ever been married? Or perhaps, just perhaps, since he hides his real name – is he married now? That's not a terrible thing to divulge, and I think I have a right to know. Can you tell me that?'

But she received no answer. As Luke Parris prepared his reply, a shrill scream vibrated so loudly and from so close, that both Tyballis and Luke stopped and stared. Tyballis was up first and running to the door, out and down the winding attic stairs. Her feet slipped as the scream echoed as if rebounding. She was unutterably relieved when she realised the large shoulders she bumped into along the darkened corridor belonged to Andrew Cobham. They both then turned, watching the shadowed figure that approached them.

Tyballis saw his sword unsheathed in one hand, a knife in the other as he pushed her behind him and stood wide-legged, now blocking the stranger's approach. 'What,' he demanded, 'are you doing here? I've long forbidden you entrance to my home.'

The other man stopped. He also held a knife. It was bloodstained. 'The bitch crossed me,' he hissed. 'Then wanted me back. I won't stand for her games. Nor yours. You pretend to be mighty grand, mister, but you're shit, just like she is. You've gone and got another trollop for bedding now, I hear. So, what d'you care about Lizzie? Let me finish the ugly bitch, and be damned.'

Andrew took one step forward. 'While in my house Elizabeth is under my protection.' His voice sounded cold and distant and Tyballis shrank back. 'If you have injured her, step aside while I see to her. Your relationship gives you no rights that I recognise. If you do not stand aside, Oliver, I will kill you.'

'Kill me?' The other man sniggered. 'There's plenty tried, and ended floating in the Thames for their troubles. The most feared bastard on the streets, I am. D'you not know me, Andrew fucking Cobham? My sister's a simple whore, all right, but me, I swive with the devil.'

Andrew Cobham walked forwards, thrusting his sword back into its scabbard but kept hold of his knife. 'That doesn't surprise me,' he said. 'Lucifer is known for his execrable taste. But I've no interest in what filth you shove up your arse, Oliver. I give you one last chance to leave my house.'

Oliver raised his bloody knife. 'Come on, you bugger. Try me.'

It was too fast to follow. Tyballis had no weapon, but began, fumble-fingered, to unbuckle her belt. If Andrew needed help, as it seemed he would, she well knew the pain a whipping buckle could inflict on anyone unprepared. Then everything rushed past her and she lost both breath and belt.

Oliver Ingwood leapt forwards. Andrew stepped aside, one foot out for tripping. The other man stumbled but sprang around, tongue between his teeth and spitting phlegm. Andrew took him immediately around the neck, one hand forcing Oliver's arm up behind, the other bending his head forwards. The creature yelped and was pushed to his knees. It had taken no more than a blink.

'Remarkably simple,' Andrew said. He now stamped one booted foot hard to the back of Oliver's neck, so leaving one of his own hands free. Both Oliver's hands were gripped in an inescapable vice behind his back, with his nose now pressed to the dusty boards. Andrew smiled. 'Your famed fighting skills seem a touch exaggerated, Mister Ingwood. Now, before I break your neck, will you choose instead to leave? I would relish neither the stink of your blood on my floors, nor the reek of your carcass.' He looked back briefly over his shoulder to Tyballis and other figures running from their rooms. 'See to Lizzie,' he ordered curtly, then turned back to the body he had entrapped at his feet.

Doubled over, gurgling, spitting and heaving, Oliver had lost his voice. Andrew waited one moment, then dragged him face down to the top of the stairs and hauled him, struggling violently, over the edge of the first step. Opening his eyes to the drop immediately in front of him, Oliver managed a single word. 'Help.'

'The wrong word, I'm afraid,' Andrew said calmly. 'I would have preferred, forgive me, or perhaps, stop, I submit. There are various possibilities, but begging for help is not one of them. No one will help you, Oliver, nor would any right-minded person wish to. But I'll not clog my cesspits with you, excrement though you are. I have a simpler end in mind. If you do not agree to leave immediately and permanently, I doubt you'd survive a sudden fall down these stairs. Make your choice.'

'I'll leave, I'll leave,' stuttered Oliver Ingwood, his head now lower than his body and his feet just scraping the top step. Andrew held him tightly, half-strangled, elbows bent back close to breaking. He released him suddenly, flinging him to the boards. Elizabeth Ingwood's brother jerked backwards, just escaping the headlong hurtle to the lower floor.

Andrew shouted behind him, 'Is Lizzie alive?'

Felicia shouted back. 'She is. But badly hurt.'

Andrew gazed down on the cowering man clinging to the balustrade at his feet. 'Get out,' he said. 'The next time I see you, I will certainly kill you.'

Oliver Ingwood ran. Andrew waited until the front door slammed, then slumping his shoulders, trudged slowly back along the corridor to Elizabeth Ingwood's chamber.

CHAPTER THIRTY-FOUR

Elizabeth lay curled on the floor of her bedchamber. She was barefoot and her knees were drawn up to her chin, while her face was hidden by the loose strands of her hair. Her room was tiny, little larger than a spice cupboard, but did not smell as sweet. Old rags and debris clogged every corner, soot and dirt drifted across the litter, while one precious pane of glass in the window was broken and the wind whistled through like a shaft of ice. The puddled bloodstains splashed across the floorboards were the only bright colours in a place of drab despondency. Felicia and Tyballis bent over Elizabeth while Ralph held a torch, burning twigs that already scorched his fingers. Tyballis looked up as Andrew entered. 'He has cut her,' she said. 'I don't think she'll die if we can keep out infection, but it was a most vicious attack. Elizabeth has fainted. Her face is – ruined.'

Andrew came forwards and leaned over, one knee to the ground. He lifted Elizabeth's face carefully between both his hands and signalled to Ralph to bring the light closer. The torch flame danced, painting the cuts in vivid scarlet and black. Two gashes sliced the small pale face, one to the left and one to the right, each carved from the corner of her mouth across to the lobe of her ear. Andrew stared for a moment, speaking very softly and only to himself: 'These cannot be sutured, nor cauterised.' He stood again, his hands sticky with her blood, and this time spoke to Ralph. 'Get the others. We'll make up a bed for her in the hall beside the fire.'

They scurried, preparing, discussing. Ralph called for his brother, and between them they carried Elizabeth's heavy woollen mattress downstairs. It thumped, step by step, and was dragged to the hearth. 'It's rather damp,' Ralph said. 'I'd be pleased to give her mine instead. It's a better bed.'

'In this heat it will dry soon enough,' Andrew shook his head. 'Organise fresh sheeting and blankets. Her own are too badly soiled.' He turned to Tyballis, who carried an armful of pillows. 'There is clean linen in my bedchamber. No doubt you know where.'

She did and hurried off. Felicia said, 'Dear Jon – tired, you know, from so much exertion – is asleep in our chamber. But Ellen can tear up bandages, and I have an excellent salve that I've used many times on the children's cuts and grazes. It has always kept out infection.'

Tyballis and Felicia made up the bed on the floor. Andrew stood waiting, his back to the fire. He held Elizabeth cradled in his arms, her head curled against his chest. The blood still dripped from the open wounds and as his velvets turned black and sticky. Looking up from the floor as she tucked in the sheets, Tyballis swallowed hard. It had not been long ago that Andrew held her in just that way, and embraced her warm and safe and precious. She spoke to the floor, a half-whisper. 'The bed's ready. I think it will be quite comfortable and not too damp.'

Elizabeth wore only her shift and it was badly torn, outworn and thin, the linen almost transparent. As Andrew bent to lay her down, his fingers grasped her uncovered breasts. Tyballis sat on the ground beside the mattress and watched as, oblivious to where he touched, Andrew positioned and steadied the patient, making no effort to avoid intimacy, as if he accepted the familiarity of Elizabeth's body. Then his hands were straightening her legs, then pulled up the blankets, enclosing her in modesty again. Tyballis sighed.

Andrew looked up suddenly and regarded her. He said softly, 'She will need a great deal of looking after. Would you mind taking some share?'

'I want to help.' Tyballis smiled with studied sincerity. 'Do you have any idea – will she be all right?'

Elizabeth opened her eyes, the black stare first uncomprehending. Then the pain kicked hard, and she remembered the terror. Andrew once again knelt over her. 'You'll live, my sweet,' he said softly. 'And these are the last scars your brother will ever inflict on you. They'll fade in time. The pain must be borne for now, but that will also fade.'

'Scars?'

'He has cut your face. What do you feel?' She was crying. Frightened of stretching disfigured lips, Elizabeth turned her head away. Andrew turned her gently back to face him. 'No, my dear. Don't hide. I see only the woman I befriended long ago. There's no difference to me.' He looked up and spoke to Ralph. 'In my kitchens are potions of henbane water and poppy syrup, labelled tincture of hemp, another of willow bark. I also need salves, one of alum, another of goose grease. They are kept in a small trunk under the main window. The trunk is locked, and Tyballis will bring me the keys. I shall unlock it for you, since the method is particular. But be careful not to touch an unlabelled package of white powder you will find amongst the others.' He nodded to Tyballis. 'The key, my love. I believe you know them all.'

Tyballis gulped. 'How?'

He didn't smile. 'I know whatever changes occur in my rooms, what is touched, and what is moved. Fingerprints in dust tell stories and I know at once if someone explores the places I keep secret. You've cleaned away the dust, and that told me more. Quickly now, bring the key.'

She was not at all sure if she knew which was which, but bustled off to Andrew's chambers. Embarrassed and flustered, she hung to one comfort: although speaking with considerable affection to Elizabeth, he had not called her love. He had used that word only to Tyballis.

Felicia was already in the kitchen when Andrew entered with the keys to the medicine coffer. She was boiling a little wine and mixing the condensed syrup with egg white for ointments. Ellen sat wide-eyed on the cold tiles under the bench, tearing an old sheet into bandages. Andrew waited for Felicia to leave and then unlocked the chest.

'We could never stitch such wounds,' Felicia whispered to Ralph as they hurried back to the hall, 'so her face will be marked forever. Mister Cobham said her scars will fade but I'm quite sure they will not. So, what of her work? She'll never find clients again, even if she lowers her price. Or do such men not care about the woman's face? Hidden in some dark alley for a penny, perhaps. But who can live on that?'

'Then she won't work the streets anymore,' Ralph muttered. 'And will be the better for it.'

That night Tyballis returned to her own chamber and a solitary bed. She was cold and slept badly. She thought she heard Elizabeth crying. Then she realised she was crying herself.

When Davey came home the next morning, he found Andrew sitting beside Elizabeth's mattress in the hall, the great fire blazing bright behind them. Startled, he hurried over. But he could not look at the terrible wounds nor pretend them inconsequential, so he made a quick excuse and ran upstairs to find Tyballis.

Ralph and Nat came down early and offered to cook, should anyone want food; to slice cheese for breakfast, and then prepare a pottage dinner. Felicia shooed them off and said she would do the cooking. George Switt hurried outside to the Portsoken communal oven to buy the morning's fresh bread. 'Bring manchet, not cheat, if you can find any,' Ralph called after him. 'I'll pay the difference.'

Casper Wallop tumbled down the stairs to rub his cold hands in front of the fire. 'Cosy,' he remarked, gazing down with interest at the patient. 'These nice big flames will help close up them mucky flaps of skin quite quick, I reckon. Them folks living in hot countries, Italy and Spain and the like, they stab each other all the time, they do, and no one dies of it. Well, it stands to reason, for otherwise them crusaders would never have come home again, and them heathen Moors would all be long dead. Which they ain't. There's hundreds still wandering them hot desert sands, for it's the heat will stick the meat back on their bones. Now, talking of bones, seems there's a fair number of them in the head, being the skull, that is. And there's a fair number I can see right now, being as the skin is all rolled back just like a parchment under a raker's shovel.'

Andrew sat next to the hearth, his back against the wall, legs bent up and supporting his forehead. He still wore the clothes, now bloodstained, that he had worn the day before and it appeared he had passed the night where he now sat. He looked up briefly. 'Don't be a fool, Casper,' he said. 'Lizzie needs neither your medical advice nor exaggerated descriptions.'

'Well,' said Casper, affronted, 'if I ain't wanted, I'll go and fix up them wine tubs ready for the merchant coming this afternoon.'

'Bring some wine back here,' Andrew told him. 'Sufficient for myself and Lizzie too. And, Casper – a generous sufficiency.'

Elizabeth did not speak. She was awake but did not open her eyes.

Almost a week later, on the twelfth day of February 1483, his grace King Edward, being the fourth of that name, lost his temper with his best friend and trusted Chamberlain, William, Baron Hastings. Without troubling to call a meeting of his council, the king promptly called for his lawyer and his scribe, and made a rare proclamation depriving his Chamberlain of the highly profitable post of Master of the Mint, a position Hastings had been unofficially awarded for life. This unexpected and extraordinary ruling was pronounced as indefinite, and from that date Bartholomew Reed was startled but overjoyed to find himself promoted in Hastings' place.

The Mint's official engraver, Ralph Sharp, was informed within the hour and stopped work in amazement, his quill, feather quivering, hovering halfway between his table and his open mouth. Never before throughout their many years of enduring friendship had the monarch demoted Sir William in the slightest degree; on the contrary, he had always heaped him with honours. This sudden loss of a rich and important revenue was unique and therefore constituted a clear warning: no further tirades against the queen's close family would be permitted.

Baron Hastings stood glaring at his king, both fists quivering at his sides. 'Your grace,' he said between clenched teeth, 'I protest most strongly. I came here in good faith and with your grace's health foremost in my mind. It is only your grace's safety that forced me to speak, knowing you would disbelieve, but considering the warning imperative even without proof. The danger is too great to ignore. Your highness, I beg you to give this matter some credence.'

Edward looked down at him coldly from the royal dais. 'One more word, William, and you will lose Calais as well. I shall give it to Lord Rivers; we both know how long he's dreamed of that particular post. Or perhaps you would be delighted that Rivers prospers directly through your slanders?'

'Your grace.' Lord Hastings knelt. 'If you choose to reward the man who plots your murder, while you punish the true friend who seeks to save your life, then may history judge the outcome.'

The king narrowed his eyes. 'Get out, William,' he hissed, 'while you still keep your head and titles.'

Hastings bowed silently, stood and, walking slowly backwards, said only, 'If I have mistaken the truth, my king, then I beg you to forgive me. I will say no more of my fears, but as I love you with all my heart, so I swear these warnings are given in good faith, and not through spite towards those I believe plot against you. I shall pray for your continued health, your grace. Long may you reign.'

CHAPTER THIRTY-FIVE

Andrew leaned back in the chair, legs stretched out and up, ankles crossed and feet wedged high against the wall. The fire had burned gradually lower throughout the day, but the sparks still flared as the logs crumbled to soot and the last flames spluttered. Andrew looked absently into the waning blaze and his voice was soft, as if speaking to himself. 'I cannot stay here indefinitely, you know, my dear.'

Still in bed, Elizabeth was half-sitting, supported by pillows. She also faced the fire, her back solid to the rest of the world. She screwed up her nose, further distorting the dark ridges of healing scars. 'Go then. Bugger off. But if I can't have you, I'll have no other bastard tutting over me. Peering at me, wondering, muttering. Poor dear, how pathetic, how tragic but she was always ugly, after all, and what a shocking life she lived. She has certainly brought it all on herself. So, take your fancy sheets, and I'll get back to my own chamber. I don't need your help no more, and can sit myself on the pot to shit.'

'Self-pity?' Andrew turned towards her and smiled. 'You still need help with some things. It will do the others some good to concentrate on nursing instead of thieving. And it may do you good to practise humility.'

'Bastard!' Elizabeth declared. 'And what would you know of humility?'

'I know what it sounds like in others.'

'All right. Fuck off and send someone else to help me piss. But I don't want her. Or fucking Felicia, scarce hiding her bloody disapproval.' Elizabeth turned away again. 'Nor Ralph, too fucking timid to look me in the face. Nor pompous Luke-fucking-Parris, quivering at the wicked touch of me. Send me Davey. Then bugger off and leave me alone, if that's what you want.'

'Under the circumstances,' Andrew decided, 'both your self pity and your stupidity are entirely understandable. But I have spent more than five days at your bedside, and there is little more I can do for you. You still need liquid food but the cuts seem clean of infection. I've dosed you with every tonic and balm I can think of, and have kept down the worst of the pain. Once long, long ago you asked me to bring you new clothes. That I shall do, since you must soon face the world again. But then I must leave. My work suffers.'

'She does, you mean.'

'Does her misery diminish your own?'

Elizabeth nodded. 'Of course it does.'

Every lodger within the house had come daily, offering help. They had cooked for Elizabeth and Andrew, and for each other. Most had tried to sit close, to hold the patient's hands, to help her drink, comforted and comfortable. Some had avoided close contact but had helped from a distance, braving the sleet and the gales to bring back fresh food and medicines. Casper had offered to bleed her and was refused, but he stayed and told fireside stories, acting the clown. Davey brought sweetmeats, which Elizabeth could not eat. She had accepted everything except their company. She had, in particular, turned away from Tyballis.

So, Andrew had stayed. He had carried Elizabeth to his garderobe to piss, he had washed her face and hands, he had fed her, combed her hair, spooned her soups and medicines, and painted her face with unctions. He had assured her that her brother would die should he ever attack her again.

'Again?' sneered Elizabeth. 'Would be the death of me, too. How much of a face could the bastard leave me a second time?'

'No woman dies of disfigurement.'

'Call it plain don't you, you shit. No compliments, please!'

'I have compliments to offer, being the simple truth. That you're strong, and courageous, and you're as much my Lizzie as you always were.'

But he did not suggest removing Elizabeth to his own bed, nor sleeping the nights in her bed beside her. He slept very little at all. Each morning he was crouched, there relighting the fire as she woke, well before dawn touched the long windows or any other soul appeared to greet the day. He would say, 'Still alive, I see, Elizabeth. Welcome back to hope and health.'

Now he said, 'I won't pretend your disabilities are less than the truth, nor create a subterfuge. The welts and bruises on your body are incidental, even though they make it difficult for you to walk. It's your face that supports the greatest penalty. Now when you first look in the mirror you'll be already prepared, and not shocked by the unexpected. But the woman you are hasn't altered. Your brother didn't make you bitter, for you were that already. And he hasn't touched the heart of you, the strength of you, nor the loyalty and generosity of you. Nor has he altered my feelings for you. I care, as I've always cared. My affection was never influenced by your looks. You know that.'

'No. Since the bitch you do want is beautiful. And you'll be thinking her fucking beautiful inside, too, I reckon, since she's never had to work the streets. This makes the comparison complete. So, why bother with me now? Pity? Nothing more than fucking pity?'

'Would you think it kinder not to pity you?' Andrew smiled. 'What happened was not of your making. Injustice and misery, even of strangers, touches me. But you've long been a friend, Lizzie. Tyballis hasn't taken your place. The place she now occupies is a new one. An unexpected one. And as with you, so my feelings are not influenced by her looks.' He sighed, and slowly stood. 'Now I shall call Ralph to build up the fire. You chose David or Nat, but I choose Ralph to care for you in my absence, and my choice carries.'

'I want Davey.'

'You will have Ralph,' Drew said, and crossed slowly to the stairs.

He went first to the chamber Nat and Ralph shared. He then walked the rest of the dark corridor to the last room, which stood directly over his own. He pushed the door ajar and strode in.

'Busy, my love?'

He saw she was not. Tyballis was leaning on the windowsill, looking out across the last streams of daylight catching the tips of the shrubbery. She had been mending the rips in her one gown, so wore only her shift. She turned in a flurry, crossing her arms carefully over her breasts. 'What? Not bad news? How is she?'

Andrew shook his head. 'I came for you, child, not on Elizabeth's account. You believe I'd abandon you so easily?'

'I didn't think about it. I didn't care. You were busy,' she lied, looking away. 'I expect Elizabeth still needs you. It has nothing to do with me, does it? Perhaps – whether you want to or just because you ought to – you should stay with her now.'

'Jealous? You too, my love? Davey is the one who has women fighting over him. For me this is quite new. And not entirely welcome.' His smile widened. 'Come here, little one.'

'I'm not—' she said, but found herself pushed hard back against the window, the sill against her thighs. Her protective arms were forced aside and Andrew's hands were on her body, his face bent close to hers.

His voice was hot breath in her eyes. 'Only five days absent, my love, to give assurance and practical help. And during those five days I saw you each and every one, and watched you, and wanted you. Should I have explained, and asked if you minded? Should I have asked you to wait? Now I want you. Should I ask for that, too?'

She had lost her knees. 'What is wrong with asking?'

'Nothing. But I never learned the habit.'

He kissed her, then leaning down, he grasped her shift with both hands and pulled it up so it crumpled around her waist. Finding her voice, though unsteadily, she mumbled into his neck, 'I'm not – it isn't —' but her fingers curled around his shoulders.

'I can tell you're not ready, and it isn't – what? Courtly? I'm neither chivalrous nor courteous.' Andrew grinned, still delving, his lips brushing across her shoulder. 'I'm a common man, my love, and had no lordly father to teach me manners. But it's almost six days I've been dreaming about you, and desiring every part of you, and wanting your company most of all. Now I want you naked in my arms, but I've no time to undress myself. So, I'll ask, after all. Will you take me as I am?'

Her arms were already tight around him, fingers crawling his hair and inside the back of his collar. She murmured, 'You are courteous, and you act the lord so well, all the lords believe in you. And you are chivalrous. You have been – so kind – to Elizabeth – these five days and more.'

'Don't talk to me about Elizabeth. Just tell me if you want me.' He was kissing her again, his mouth so hard on hers she could not answer him. Instead, she kissed him back. Then his arm swept beneath her knees, and he lifted and carried her, half-tangled within her own chemise, and took her to her bed. He laid her there and tugged the linen from her body, then lay beside her, watching her. 'What, simple compliance? No objections, no protestations? Nor agreement, nor permission? Neither welcoming nor compliant? Are you so submissive? And am I free then, to bully and use, taking without thought for anything except my own urgency and greed?' He was laughing at her and the day's sinking scarlet lights, flooding into the chamber, lit his eyes.

'Isn't that what you want?' she said, breathless.

'No. Oh, sometimes perhaps. When wanting you hurts. Why suffer pain, when there's a chance of pleasure?'

She was able to say, while going pink with delight, 'You don't talk, I mean not usually. You're so reticent, and soft-spoken. Quiet-voiced. Almost menacing. But when it's like this – in bed – you talk and talk – and talk.'

He grinned, his hands gently tracing the lines of her ribs down to the soft curve of her belly. 'Would silence be more respectful? I like to talk love while making love. There's so much more to talk about. I adore seeing the blue veins up your arms. They snake and wind, so pale, almost luminous like the sky just after dawn. And your flesh is milky velvet, with a sheen like brushed sarsenet. Your wrists are tiny wingless birds, and your ankles as delicate as moths caught by moonlight.'

Tyballis gazed at him in wonder. 'I never expected you to say things like that,' she whispered. 'I never knew you thought things like that.'

He kissed her eyes, the tip of his tongue across her lashes. 'You know little of me yet, my love,' he said. 'I am not unselfish, but it is a very long time since I considered my own happiness as paramount. I can be as self-absorbed as any man, and often more. But until now, I held nothing worth the loss of it, nor objected to the uncomprehending sense of melancholy that for so long has permanently threaded my days to my nights.'

'You were sad?'

He shook his head and the thick black silk of his hair enclosed both their faces in a cave of shadows. 'The word has no meaning. Neither happiness, nor its lack concerned me. I did not question my choices, though was conscious of my freedom to make them. But now I glimpse something else, as if coming at my life anew and from a different direction never before travelled.'

She felt tipsy and full of bubbles. 'You must know I love you, Drew. Is that what you're saying? Might you – just a little – love me?'

'Love? Is that what it is? Perhaps.' He chuckled. 'You asked me for commitment. I was prepared to offer that. If you'd asked for love I would have denied it. I wanted nothing to weaken me, divert me from my chosen course, or cause distraction with the fear of loss. But this – if love it is – strengthens me. It wakens me. For those days caught up at Lizzie's side, with the smell of her vomit and her piss, and the whining and anger, I saw you as a passing shadow. Bringing bread and soup, and smiling at her as she turned away. Then leaving, with the kick of your skirts and the click of your heels up the stairs until silent again. Gone into shadows. Finding myself waiting then, for many hours, until you came once again.'

Once again his fingers travelled, wandering her face and the curve of her neck, down to the soft warm dip beneath. Tyballis sighed, leaning against him. 'I sat up here and cried until I had an excuse to come back down,' she murmured. 'Elizabeth doesn't like me. She wanted Davey but Davey couldn't look at her without cringing. Elizabeth must be angry. I understand. She has a right to whine.'

'Of course she does. It doesn't mean I have to find pleasure in it.'

'But you do – in me?' She smiled, tentative.

'In you, yes. With you.' He was half-cradling her. The dusty velvet of his doublet pressed against her. 'For six days you've been an endless but unobtainable temptation. Now I want your body against my body. No need to knock. Just let me in, my love.'

'I wouldn't know how to keep you out.'

'Just as well.' He grinned down at her. 'For many years I've taken whatever I wanted, but I wanted very little. That's no longer true.'

'Tell me what you want.'

'It seems I want you, my love.'

It was a long, long time before they collapsed together. Finally they lay entwined as their breathing gradually slowed, their grasp on each other mellowing to gentle. Tyballis, caressed his cheek with her fingertips. 'It was never so ... I've never known it like that,' she said softly. He grinned, too tired to talk. So she said, 'You must be hot, all dressed for winter. I know there's no fire in my room.'

'Your bed, my love,' he answered her, 'is as unyielding and lumpy as a hayloft. In future we sleep, and do everything else we decide to do, in my bed. There'll be a fire and there'll be soft pillows, and I'll even put on clean sheets if you want them. But never, if I value my health, will I bed you on this wretched paillasse again.' He turned, propped himself once more on his elbows, and regarded her. 'So, bring whatever you have that matters to you, and move yourself into my chambers downstairs.'

'Now? But Elizabeth ...'

'Not now, no. Later. I'll let Lizzie stay where she is for a day or two more. Watching you cross over her mattress as you carry your belongings into my domain would have her spitting. But I want you with me, little one, and there's another way of achieving that.'

251

'Climbing in the window?'

He chuckled. 'First I'm taking you to Crosby's,' he said. 'I have to go there, in any case. I need to change my clothes, since these are foul with Lizzie's blood. Then I intend getting back to work. I promised her I'd collect a gown for her, since she now owns nothing but a shift. And most important, I want a place to plot and rest in privacy without a parcel of cheats and cut-purses eager to watch each time I blow my nose.'

Her excitement lit her eyes as her smile grew wide. 'Those wonderful rooms? And wonderful clothes? And to live there? And work together?'

'We'll work together when it's possible and when I decide it's advisable. At court it would be too dangerous.' Andrew swung his legs from the bed and began to lace up his hose. 'It will mean you obeying me,' he said, 'for the danger is too great otherwise. No more beetle-brained ideas of your own, no hopping into other men's beds or deciding to follow me when I tell you to stay at home.'

'If home is Crosby's, I'll be delighted to stay there.'

'No woman is ever delighted to do as she's told,' Andrew said, looking down at her. 'But with me, it will be imperative. So – honour and obey, my love?'

'I promise.' She would have promised anything.

'Then get dressed,' he said. 'We leave immediately.'

CHAPTER THIRTY-SIX

'Earl Rivers,' Catesby said, 'has issued new instructions at Ludlow. His hold over the future king is tightening.'

'It could hardly be tighter than it is already.'

'It could, my lord. It could and now it is. From one week past there is no action allowed of any kind either for or by the prince, without the direct guidance and permission of the earl, or his two most trusted companions. It is official. Now the child cannot shit without their advice.' Catesby leaned back, stretching his legs to the fire. 'So, Feayton, tell me. What do they fear?'

'They fear nothing,' Andrew said. 'They prepare. When Edward dies as planned, the new king will be entirely under Woodville control. Thus the heir to the throne becomes Rivers' puppet.'

'So, has the order to poison the king been given a second time? Do you know already?'

Andrew Cobham shook his head. 'Rivers travels to London at the end of this month. Parliament sits, and he will therefore be present. The secret order will surely then be given. He cannot trust such words to paper, nor will he trust them to a messenger. And it is why Throckmorton has not yet been killed.'

'So, they have not yet taken a new supply of arsenic?'

'After the previous confusion in which I was involved? No.'

Andrew smiled. 'Hastings was alerted, Lord Marrott in particular is now watched, and the suspicion has spread to Dorset – now also under scrutiny. But I was too closely embroiled. They will not dare approach Throckmorton again until utterly necessary.'

Catesby nodded, sitting forwards. 'Surely they'll sidestep Throckmorton. Collect over time from different apothecaries, or order new supplies directly from Venice.'

'Too dangerous. They need a middle man to take the blame should the business be discovered.'

'Then they'll find another courier.'

'They have tried.' Andrew was standing, his elbow to the long marble lintel. He was drinking deep. 'I have been watching, Will, and following,' he nodded. 'Every sneaking wretch they employ – and I have spoken with most and threatened some – has been sent to search out another, more trustworthy dealer. But merchants in poison are not easily found on the open market and both barons Throckmorton long sweated over eradicating anyone fighting for a share of the death they dealt. Indeed, I have been busy in that direction myself.'

'You still hold the last package, I believe.'

'I do,' Andrew said. 'And intend keeping hold of it.'

Catesby frowned. 'And you have it here? At Crosby's? But if it should ever be discovered, and if his grace the duke were ever to be accused—'

'With respect, my friend, being neither fool nor traitor,' Andrew said, retaining his smile, 'I keep the package elsewhere.'

Catesby blushed and shook his head. 'I've no need to know where it is. Indeed, I prefer not to. But these new instructions at Ludlow will not be questioned either. Rivers may surprise some, and be suspected of seeking too much control. If so, he will simply claim a concern for security. Many will recognise his concern as principally for himself but, after all, the power-hungry are admired, not reviled, and he will not be condemned.'

'Nevertheless,' Andrew said, 'I shall inform his grace. This means their plans are near completion, and Rivers cannot risk failing this time. He must act before he finds himself recalled and a new favourite given charge of the prince. These tightening regulations are a proof to me, if not to others.'

'Not to the king.'

Andrew drained his cup. 'There is no clear proof against any of the Woodvilles. Nor will there be,' he said. 'They are not fools, and Rivers in particular is a man of culture and intelligence. Marrott is their willing dupe, but he is sufficiently close to Dorset to share the suspicion should proof against him be discovered. And although there remains nothing in writing, to the Duke of Gloucester,' he said, 'the proof will be clear.'

Catesby wrinkled his nose. 'And suppose – just suppose you are wrong. What if it is all this wretch Marrott, and the Woodvilles are not involved at all?'

'I am never wrong,' said Andrew Cobham.

The last days of February turned unexpectedly mild. The sun slipped through the windows of Crosby's small annexed buildings, finding the starched white linen of the hurrying servants, the spangle of sudden light on gold and glass, and the patina of grime on Casper Wallop's livery sleeves. Lord Feayton's personal manservant was both respected and disliked. Indeed the steward, a Yorkshire man owning to a natural dislike of southerners on principle, informed the household that Casper, one-eyed and toothless, nigh bald, bandy and as ugly as a toad, was without doubt a demonic sorcerer. The servants therefore regarded Lord Feayton with singular sympathy and hesitant suspicion. His habits being considered irregular and frequently eccentric, he was, they decided, either the trusted friend of the Duke of Gloucester and so requiring protection from the warlock in the nest, or the devil incarnate, subjugating demons to his service.

The sun shone on the fluttering sails of the little carvel from Flanders as she sailed into St Katherine's docks that afternoon, dipped her oars and dropped anchor, she rode the swell while she waited for the English customs. Her crew scurried to lower the sails, climbing the swaying mast and rigging as the choppy waters gradually calmed and the tide ebbed.

Many watched from the land, since ships trading in winter were rare and few braved seasonal storms at sea. The customs men were already rowing out to board. The swarming wharfside labourers, crane operators and itinerant workers watched closely from the bank, ready to unload as soon as the carvel docked. Several agents of London's merchant traders watched from the more pleasant shelter of the adjacent tavern. A cluster of less-important buyers gossiped, waiting by the old pier. And there were others. A thin man, dressed respectably and warm wrapped in a sheepskin cape stood in the tavern's shadows. He was well armed, and his fingers strayed often to the pommel of the sword at his side. Alone and wary, his eyes never left the splash of the custom's boat.

Then there were those who watched the fat carvel, and the thin man both. These did not stand together. One was small and squat. He sat half in the outlying gutter and he was, it seemed, exceedingly drunk. His hat, brimmed and feathered, hid his brow, though with close attention it was evident that the man was one-eyed. A black hole disarranged the symmetry of his face. But few noticed him. Small, pissed and seemingly unarmed, some lump in the gutter was of necessity disregarded.

Another man, although unusually tall, was equally unnoticeable. His clothes were dark and shabby. He lounged, back to the alley wall, brick dust on his shoulders. Too narrow for entering light, the shadowed alley led away from the docks and the river. The tall man did not appear to be watching anything or anyone in particular, and no one watched him. His cape hid whatever arms he carried, and equally disguised his station. He was, perhaps, someone used to remaining unseen.

Finally the carvel docked. Cleared by customs, it pulled to shore and was roped with the usual thud of straining timbers, the shouts of the sailors and the rattle of the gangplank slammed down between water and land. The merchants' agents hurried on board, the huge wooden crane rumbled alongside and the sailors began to haul up their crates. The thin man also moved forwards. He pulled up the collar of his sheepskin, straightened his scabbard and ambled, seemingly careless, to a place beside the ship's rising keel. The great curved sides streamed river water, rocking a little, faces peering down from along the gunwales. One face nodded a curt recognition. The thin man, looking up, nodded back.

The tall dark man from the alley had gone but the drunken lout had evidently recovered a little, and, hitching up his hose beneath a filthy torn shirt, now lumbered, swaying, across the cobbles. It seemed he had some interest in the ship after all for he kept a close watch on the unloading of its cargo as he edged closer.

It started to drizzle and the wan winter sunshine blinked out. An east wind gusted in from the sea. A small black kestrel rose keening into the damp mist and a pair of gulls balanced splay-footed on the ship's boom, noisy and squabbling.

The thin man, sidestepping the barrage of heavy-set sailors now hurrying in the opposite direction, sidled up the gangplank and quickly boarded the ship, immediately disappearing from view.

The old drunk was now clinging to the crane, in need, it seemed, of something to hold him up. As the crane swung, so he ducked. Not too drunk to mind his head but drunk enough to need support. Then with a squeal he fell. His feet slipped on the wet cobbles and he landed heavily, arse in the puddles and one hand protecting his groin. He began to roar, rolled over on the ground and roared again. Now wedged before the crane's huge wheels, he wheezed in pain. The crane driver paused. 'Here, mate, t'was none of my doing. Got no sense? You should stay clear.'

'Castrated me, you have, you bastard,' yelled the wounded drunk. He sat up and turned to the gawping sailors. 'Here look, mates. This slimy turd has sliced my cods, and left me prickless.'

There was a snorting of appreciative sniggers. 'Sure you had one in the first place?' one demanded. 'Reckon it's a fair few years since you used it.'

'Can't see it, can he?' another grinned. 'All slobber and lard, he is.'

'Muscle, all muscle,' cried the drunk. 'I've not a pinch o' fat on me, and will prove it if any of you lot wants a grapple. As for using it, I've a prick well prized, I'll have you know, and have helped many a fair maiden from her swoons. I piss when pissed, and swive better than most when sober.'

The crane driver was now boxed in. 'You stupid fuckers, get out my way,' he yelled. 'And take that dirty little bugger off with you. I've work to do.'

The drunk lay flat on his back before the crane's squeaking wheels, and waved two sodden arms above his head. 'Slaughter me now, would you, you heathen murderer? And me a decent God-fearing man. My father were a priest, he was, and my ma the best whore in Leicestershire, me uncle were the Pope and me brother a king. So, touch me if you dare.'

'Chuck him in the river, lying scum,' decided one of the sailors, dumping his load on the ground. 'We've a ship to unload. There's little enough work this time of year and I've sore need of a day's wages. Kick the little toad off the quay.'

A discussion followed and bets were taken as to whether the drunk, being already full to the bilges with liquid but possibly carrying sufficient ballast to compensate, would float if cast to the waves. The drunk began to sob again and wiped his one eye and his nose on his sleeve. One aggravated sailor kicked him in the ribs, the drunk grabbed the offending foot, and hauled. Both drunk and sailor sprawled together, flailing at each other's faces.

'Mind me eye, 'tis the only one I got,' whined the drunk. 'Attack a poor disabled soldier, would you, you vicious devil? Hero of Tewkesbury, I am, blinded by that bloodthirsty little bastard Edward of Lancaster himself.'

'Call the Watch,' complained the crane driver. 'Or it'll be nightfall before I get this bloody ship unloaded.'

'Send the swiving liar back to Tewkesbury,' someone snorted. 'Maybe he'll find his missing eyeball under a bush.'

'Then reckon it'll have a right few good tales to tell of all it's seen over the years,' chuckled the drunk.

It had begun to rain more heavily. A cold grey sleet closed in the sky and beat down across the river, water pelting on water, as the tall dark man from the alleyway inexplicably reappeared, unseen by the quarrelling rabble. He did not look around but lowered his hat a little and wandered up the deserted gangplank onto the swaying deck of the carvel.

Meanwhile a solitary woman had appeared in the alleyway. After a few moments peering from the shadows, she entered the main street portside, watching the furious bundle of arguing sailors and dock workers. Clearly, she was young and fashionably dressed, so evidently a lady of some substance, but being well wrapped against the weather there was little of her to recognise. Beneath the swirls of cape and skirts, her small feet, waterproofed by pattens, were leather shod and her fur-lined cloak enveloped her. Its hood covered her face in shadows and neither her hair nor headdress could be seen. Something of her stance, however, and her expression, could be glimpsed as she shook her head, dislodging the stream of rainwater that dripped from the brim of her hood.

But it was the air of frightened expectation that made the young woman particularly noticeable. She moved without confidence, darting from shelter to shelter while staring out intermittently at the river and its craft. Her hands, small and gloved, wrestled with each other, her fingers knotting as if in permanent indecision. She had come, it seemed, where there might be great danger. What she risked was in no way clear. But risk there evidently was.

Someone had come out from the tavern doorway. He stood just out of the rain as he watched the scene before him. He did not seem at all interested in the tumble and hassle around the inactive crane, where the Watch had at last been called and another argument had promptly broken out. Here the difficulty was aggravated by the sudden disappearance of the drunk who had started all the trouble, and now explanations between the sailors, the crane driver and the constable had grown increasingly complicated.

The newcomer from the tavern ignored this extraneous inconvenience. He had been concentrating only on the ship bobbing gently at the quayside, but he soon noticed the pacing woman, his attention inevitably attracted by her furtive behaviour. He immediately became curious.

Anticipating no motive for entering the freeze and soak of the open port, this man remained in the tavern's porch. Yet despite his shelter, the man was quite noticeable, not for his figure, which was small and unprepossessing, but for the grandeur of his clothes. A silken chaperon, expensive but quite unsuitable for the season, was clamped over carefully curled red hair, and his rings were worn outside the leather of his gloves, declaring status. Yet although clearly a personage of standing, he now seemingly preferred anonymity, choosing to watch while remaining unwatched. But now, his attention divided. It was the nervous woman who now interested him the most as he watched her, eyes narrowed, squinting through the rain. Yet she seemed oblivious of him as she flung off her hood, revealing her face, wiping the rain from her eyes before pulling back the hood's protection. Turning away at once, she did not see the man in the tavern doorway nor notice his sudden indrawn breath or how his fingers twitched towards the elaborate pummel of his sword.

Midst the wintry damp and dreary inactivity of the dock, the arrival of one small carvel appeared to have changed everything. The unloading finally began. The crane squeaked as it hauled and swung, the crates banged and streamed salt water, the men shouted from deck to shore, and from shore to ship. Men stomped wet boots on the cobbles, set back their shoulders and rolled up their sleeves, dragging the cargo crates from the dockside to stack the carts and from cart to warehouse. The sumpter ponies drooped their heads, dejected in the rain as the wind bit their ankles.

Yet beyond the noises of unloading, the dock was a place of unexplained patience. There were, it seemed, those who waited, noticed or unnoticed, and had business they preferred to keep secret. The woman, although she appeared unaware of all else, had been seen by the gentleman in the tavern. He, although perhaps originally in the company of the thin man in the sheepskin cape, also preferred to keep hidden. Sheepskin cape, having long since left the tavern, was now onboard the ship and had not reappeared. Meanwhile the drunk, presumably unconnected with all these silent and watchful shadows, had left before risking trouble from the law.

The carvel's captain briefly walked the poop deck, inspected his moorings, turned to discuss something with his two companions, shook his head, scratched his beard and strode once more below. The ship grew quiet. What happened below decks remained unseen. A handful of busy traders were no doubt still conducting their business and sheepskin cape was doing whatever he had come to do. Yet someone else, apparently unknown to all others, had boarded the carvel alone. There being no visible obstruction to his actions, the red-haired gentleman now made a quick decision. He left the tavern's porch and marched into the rain, crossed the open street to where the waiting woman still stood hesitant and fearful. He came up to her from behind, and put both his hands hard down on her shoulders. She turned with a gasp, and looked into the width of his exceedingly satisfied smile.

CHAPTER THIRTY-SEVEN

Harold, Baron Throckmorton, clamped his grip on the woman, each fingertip rigid, and hissed, 'How convenient, strumpet, to find you here. And all alone, too. No doubt you've been told to watch the results of my business. Feayton has put you up to this, hasn't he? So, you've every reason to be frightened and now I intend showing you exactly what fear is all about.'

Suddenly the baron became aware of something uncomfortably unexpected. The sharp point of a knife had entered through fur, velvet and linen, and was pricking deep into the delicate curve of his armpit. He spluttered a little and twisted back towards the danger, his hand firm on the hooded woman.

A voice just a little behind him said, 'Let her go, you silly bugger. There ain't no chance for abductions now. See, the lady ain't alone at all.'

'Lady?' squawked the baron. 'You're mistaken, sir. This is a trollop from the gutters and deserves no knight's protection.'

'And I ain't no knight,' cackled the invisible assailant. 'But my knife's as good as anyone's and sharper than most. It'll go deep, an' you tempt me to shove it right in, mister. Right under your dirty little arm and into your gizzards.'

The baron unhanded his captive. She took a quick step backwards and it appeared she was laughing. 'How very predictable you are, my lord,' Tyballis said, pushing back her hood a little. 'A female in distress evidently ignites very different emotions in you than most, and hardly chivalrous ones, it seems.'

Throckmorton ignored her and turned quickly, grappling with the assailant. But instead of disarming the man, he found himself bent over, one knee hard to the puddles and his arms wrenched high up behind his back. Now the knife pressed hard into his ear and a small one-eyed man was peering at him, grinning toothlessly. The man spat as he spoke, and the baron breathed in his attacker's saliva. 'I'd give in quick, were I you, me lord. Afore I break your scrawny little arms.'

Throckmorton spoke between gritted teeth, his nose almost to the cobbles. 'I'm not alone, you fool. Someone will come immediately. You will both be killed.'

Then there was another voice over his head, a soft and familiar voice of quiet menace. 'Oh, I don't think so,' said the voice. 'You gloat too soon. No one is coming to your aid. Perryvall is at this moment otherwise occupied swimming the Thames. A strange pastime, don't you think, at this time of year? I fear he will be quite chilled when he gets to the far bank.'

'Swimming?' spluttered Throckmorton.

'I must admit,' said the quiet voice, 'that I helped him a little, making his descent from ship to river somewhat easier, indeed rather peremptory. I did not approve of his business, you see, nor of the small packet he carried. I therefore removed the offending packet and threw it into the water. I'm afraid it will be quite ruined. It then seemed remarkably apt for Mister Perryvall to follow his parcel.'

Throckmorton looked furiously up into Andrew Cobham's black eyes. 'You've no right, my lord. You've always approved my business before – and profited from it.'

'I have decided,' Andrew said, 'to alter my habits. I decided – purely on a whim, that there was sufficient arsenic already in the world and therefore any further supply would work contrary to my designs. Your scattered powder now floats on the surface of our beloved Thames amongst the city's turds and piss. I can only hope it does not seriously disadvantage the fish.'

Tyballis screwed up her nose. 'But half of London gets their water supply—'

'A little arsenic may well prove less fatal than the filth already swelling the banks. A grain or two is said to be an excellent remedy for all sorts of ailments, I believe.' Mister Cobham briefly shook his head, turned back to Casper Wallop and smiled. 'Put away your knife, my friend. Bring the wretch and follow me.'

Casper gazed with distaste at the point of his knife. 'All waxy it is now,' he complained. 'That nasty little bugger's ear' ole must be clogged up with enuff tallow to make half a dozen candles.'

Andrew, his hand firm on Tyballis's back, was striding off to the back door of the tavern. The baron whimpered slightly as Casper kicked him to follow. Together the four entered the dark and quiet entrance and immediately climbed the lightless and rickety back staircase to a small room. Mister Wallop pushed the baron inside. Andrew locked the door behind them all and promptly seated himself on a low uncushioned settle, Tyballis beside him. Casper kept the baron standing. Andrew said, 'Now we have a little privacy, my dear Harold. I have a proposition to put to you.'

The baron shivered. 'What about Perryvall, my lord? I doubt he can swim.'

'Especially in that heavy sheepskin cape,' said Andrew with vague sympathy. 'A shame. But someone may find a ship's sail-hook to fish him from the sludge.'

'This is murder, Feayton.'

'Is it?' Andrew smiled gently. 'A word I imagine you well understand, Harold. So, it is fortunate, then, that no one saw me assist the poor man to his demise. But he may not die. I cannot claim to care either way. I warned Perryvall some months ago that he should not ever again become involved in the importation of dangerous substances. Occasionally it seems I need to remind my acquaintances and colleagues, lest they forget the wisdom of attending to my warnings. And that, my dear Harold, includes you.'

'I repeat, sir,' stuttered the baron, 'you already know my business, and in the past you encouraged it.'

'Let us not exaggerate,' sighed Mister Cobham. 'I have never encouraged any of your unsavoury dealings, Harold. I permitted your business to continue, it is true. But I now refer to something quite different. I refer to the matter of kidnapping and abduction. Was I wrong, perhaps, in thinking you were about to force Mistress Blessop into a compromising situation? No – I think not. You were planning an instant and unpleasant revenge. Had you not done so, you would instead have noticed my actions on board the carvel. You might even have drawn someone else's attention to what I was doing, which would have been unfortunate for me. Instead, I remained quite unnoticed and free to help Mister Perryvall to his soggy fate, while you were occupied with some very ungallant intentions elsewhere. Now you find yourself in an increasingly difficult situation, my friend.'

'I can only apologise,' gulped the baron. 'Let me go now, Feayton. I was tempted, I admit it. I was wrong. It will never happen again. Without taking delivery of the packet I expected, I must contact the buyer, and as soon as possible. Let me go, sir, and I will not bother you again. Indeed, I'll pay your share as soon as I'm able. I know I already stand in your debt, sir, and if you let me go now I shall be even more in your debt. A debt I swear I will pay. Otherwise, loath as I am to issue my own warnings – if you attempt to hold or kill me, I shall yell louder than you could possibly imagine. This whole tavern will come running.'

Andrew smiled. 'You underestimate me, my lord,' he said softly. 'As usual. The landlord, already well paid, would oblige me by hearing nothing. But there will be nothing to hear. I am not going to kill you, Harold. Someone else will do that soon enough.'

'Some beggar or cut-purse, hired by you?'

'Unnecessary,' Andrew shook his head. 'You will be dispatched by Lord Marrott's paid assassin or Rivers' agent as soon as you fail to deliver the arsenic this evening.'

The baron groaned. 'What do you want of me, sir?'

'Exactly what I asked once before,' Andrew said, 'and which I now insist upon receiving immediately. Your signed confession, Harold. Implicating both Marrott and Rivers and anyone else you know to be involved, explaining the amounts of arsenic you have been ordered to supply and when. You will include the names of every messenger you have met, how you have delivered the required packages, and whatever you know of the motive behind these orders.' He looked very closely into the baron's reddened eyes. 'Do you know, Harold, what was to be done with the poison you supplied?'

'No, no, not at all. Nothing,' trembled Throckmorton. 'Medicine, my lord, medicinal purposes only, I assure you. But I'll confess, and I'll write everything, if you help me get out of the country afterwards. Once the authorities know I've spoken, I'll be killed as poor Thomas was. If not by some thug of Marrott's, then executed by the crown. I must escape at once. Help me, and I'll help you, my lord.'

Andrew stood abruptly and crossed to a small scrivener beneath the window. He retrieved two sheets of Italian cut paper, a quill, ink pot and sander. He then turned to the baron and pointed to the scrivener, set a little chair before it, and nodded to Casper. 'Let him go,' he ordered briskly. 'Now, Harold. I shall watch as you write, so be very careful. Your confession must be comprehensive. I advise you to try and please me. It is, after all, your only chance now of leaving England alive.'

They sat together later that evening, Andrew, Tyballis and Casper, at the great trestle table at Cobham Hall. Several of the other lodgers had joined them. Felicia sat with Edmund and Walter both squashed upon her lap, and Ellen balanced on a high stool at her side. Widower Switt sat the other side of Ellen, as close as he dared while trying not to gaze into the child's wide blue eyes too often. Opposite them sat Elizabeth. She kept her head down, but in the firelight her scars were thick and black and impossible to hide. Ralph sat beside her, one hand warm and protective on her knee.

'You leave for the north, then?' Mister Switt asked.

'I will not ride to Middleham,' Andrew said. 'Yorkshire is too far, especially midwinter with the rivers flooded, bridges down and the fords impossible to cross. There'll be snow in the north, and too great a danger of arriving so late that action will be taken against the king before the Duke of Gloucester can prevent it. I therefore intend taking Throckmorton's confession directly to Lord Hastings.'

Ralph nodded. 'Then you trust Hastings entirely, sir?'

'I trust no one,' Andrew sighed. 'Many times not even myself. I trust no one at this table, nor any man at court, least of all the king himself.'

'But it's his highness we are working to save,' Felicia objected. 'What point then, if you think him such a poor monarch?'

'As a monarch, our king is as good as most, and better than many if we are to believe what history tells us.' Andrew drained his cup and signalled to Casper to refill it. 'Edward has made England prosperous. He's clever and cunning, he manipulates, keeps his secrets well hidden, and understands the propaganda of popularity. I'd choose no other king, save maybe his brother. But in his private life he's proved himself a fool more often than wise. Many before Edward have been governed by lust and temper, but foolish behaviour in private also leads to disastrous mistakes in public.'

Felicia sniffed. 'Even from you, Mister Cobham, that's a shocking thing to say. We aren't here to judge the Lord's own anointed sovereign. Criticism is treason.'

'Then don't listen,' Andrew said. 'Your opinion of my opinion is of as little consequence to me as mine is to the king. He'll not suffer from what I think of him, but will hopefully benefit from what I decide to do. Sadly the king has been unwise enough to disparage Hastings' warnings. Throckmorton's confession may at least force his grace to rethink.'

Tyballis said quietly, 'If you go to court, Marrott will be watching for you. It'll be dangerous.'

Elizabeth looked up quickly. 'I could go. With this fancy gown you brought me, I reckon I'd look the part.' Andrew did not answer and the pause lengthened. Each face turned to her in awkward silence. Finally Elizabeth hung her head. 'Ain't no need to say it. I know folks will stare. I ain't no lady, and now it's not the gown what'll matter, it's the face. But with a cloak and a hood ...'

Andrew said, 'A solitary woman may gain admittance to Hastings' chambers, but she'd simply find him between her legs, and he'd listen to nothing else. No, this time I play my part alone. Being late, I shall attend court tomorrow morning. In the meantime, I need to get Throckmorton out of the country.'

'It hardly seems,' widower Switt shook his head, 'that his lordship merits your efforts.'

'T'were up to me, I'd have had me knife up his arse and done him in before now,' snorted Casper, 'and watch him gurgle afore slinging him in the river.'

'I intend keeping my word,' Andrew said, 'since I may later require him as a witness.' He turned to Ralph. 'I know the ship and have spoken to the captain. Will you take it on?'

Ralph nodded. 'It's been settled between me and Davey. Davey's upstairs getting the cloaks. Had his own stolen, though won't admit it. Well, a thief's got his pride, after all. So, I've borrowed Luke's for him to wear, since he'd never ask Luke himself.'

Tyballis turned to Andrew. 'But about the arsenic you took off Perryvall. You told Throckmorton you'd dropped it all into the water. But Drew, to throw medicine – and you said it is poisonous – where people drink?'

Andrew smiled. 'Throckmorton had to believe the arsenic destroyed, my love. But in truth I have a far better use for it.'

Ralph and Davey had still not returned when Andrew set off the next morning for Westminster. Tyballis had spent the night in his arms, and now stood at the doorway to watch him go. Andrew stayed a moment on the worn threshold and kissed her lightly. 'Sadly you cannot come with me, my love, or risk meeting Marrott.'

'I know. And I promised to obey you.'

'Should I trust your promises, when I trust no other?'

She laughed. It was cold and her bare feet nearly froze to the step, but she wore Andrew's black damask bedrobe and was warmly snuggled inside. 'I helped yesterday at the docks,' she reminded him. 'There was some risk, wasn't there? It could have been dangerous. But I trusted you.'

'There was no risk at all, my own.' He kissed her again, this time gently on the cheek. His lips were sweet and moist and warm against her skin. 'When I fish,' he said, 'I protect my bait, or cannot fish again.'

CHAPTER THIRTY-EIGHT

Tyballis stood by the window in Elizabeth's chamber, washing what remained of the glass. 'There's a thick mist at ground level, and this house pops up like a little island. From Luke's attic it must look quite magical.'

'Tybbs, my dear,' Felicia sighed, looking up from her bucket and mop, 'you have such odd fancies. But there is still a great deal of work to be done if Elizabeth is to move back today.'

'I told you already,' Elizabeth insisted, 'it's of no account to me. If I want my room back, which I do, then I'll take it as it always was, and no need for all this scrubbing. It didn't do me no harm before, though I'd not object to a softer mattress.'

'Nat will bring you the promised new bed up from Drew's study as soon as Ralph and Davey are back home to help him,' Tyballis said. 'Nat can't carry it all on his own and Jon is presumably asleep.'

Felicia nodded, bending back to the bucket. 'Gyles, you know, has been fractious and a little unwell and kept us awake most of the night. Jon is exhausted, poor soul, and now he's watching over the babies while Ellen and I help here.'

'Humph,' muttered Ellen. 'Watching eyes shut. Just like Pa did when that mean piggy ate my fingers.'

With an armful of filthy sheets and accumulated mouse droppings,

Tyballis looked to Elizabeth. 'These could be washed, and I'm sure they would be serviceable again,' she said. 'But since you now have such nice new linen, perhaps you'd prefer me to rip these old things up for rags?'

'Do what you like,' said Elizabeth. 'I don't care, not one way nor the other. I never asked for no one to come poking and cleaning, and could have done it myself if I'd wanted. I'm not no invalid. Chuck the lot out, for all I care.'

'You shall have a nice clean chamber to go with your new bed,' Felicia insisted. 'Since Mister Cobham has brought you new sheets, bolster cases, blankets and pillows, not to mention that pretty shift and the blue gown, well – it is a wonder you aren't on your knees with gratitude.'

Elizabeth had helped very little with the cleaning and refurbishment of her chamber. Now she stood mid floor, glaring at Felicia. Her face was carved both left and right with long black puckered lines, turning every expression to a scowl. Her mouth, once full-lipped, now sneered even when she smiled. She was not smiling. 'Reckon there's only one thing I does on my knees, and it ain't praying. No whore knows gratitude, for every whore's a trollop? Is that it? A bitch on heat, not fit for nice clothes nor a decent bed. What am I, then? You'd have me stoned, perhaps?'

Felicia dropped her mop. 'I didn't mean …' she mumbled, eyes teary. 'But it is hard sometimes – to see others – and we struggle so, you see, when there is no wage and nothing for the little ones to eat. Were it not for Mister Cobham … but I do not complain about my dear husband. He does his best, you know. But the good Lord turned His back on us many years ago.' She sniffed, looking over at Ellen. 'My dear little girl,' she murmured, 'was my firstborn, eight years ago. But then, year after year five little babes were born to me, all dead either at birth or soon after from dysentery or other pestilence. Yet it was when I stopped attending church that finally I gave birth to dear little Edmund. So, you see—'

But Tyballis interrupted her. 'Look,' she whispered, 'something is terribly wrong.'

From the window she watched the fog curl up the walls, soupy

271

green tongues licking the sides of the building. Where it lay thickest, the mist covered the ground. But through it, rising like the fins of fish in water, two horses dragged, slow and tortuous as exhausted crusaders returning from war. The leading horse was ridden by a man so slumped that his face could not be seen. The second horse seemed to have no rider at all. Their hooves were muffled by fog, and no sound reached upwards, not even through the broken windowpanes.

Elizabeth and Felicia rushed to peer over Tyballis's shoulder. Then each woman turned and ran from the room and down the staircase. Tyballis flung the front doors open to see Ralph dismount, half-falling from his horse. As she reached him and took him into her arms, he croaked, 'Davey,' and collapsed. The second horse stood patiently. Across its back lay a man, face down. His legs dangled, their fine brightly striped hose ripped and bloodstained. His hat was gone and the back of his scalp was bloody.

Felicia and Elizabeth took Davey down from the horse, wrapping him with their arms, cradling and carrying him. 'Quick,' Elizabeth said urgently, 'onto my old bed in the hall where the fire's bright.'

Tyballis helped Ralph to his feet. 'Come by the fire, Ralph dear,' she said. 'Then we must call a doctor.'

Ralph winced. 'Where's Drew?'

'Not back from Westminster yet.' Tyballis called Ellen, who hovered, frightened, watching from the bottom of the stairs. 'Do you know where a local doctor lives? Good. Then run quickly and get him.'

They laid Davey gingerly on the mattress in front of the fire. The flaring scarlet flames lit his wounds. He was deeply unconscious. 'He's breathing,' Felicia said, stark-eyed. 'He's not – dead.'

Tyballis said, 'Cushions, quick. Make up a mattress for Ralph beside the other. They must both be kept warm.' She was already struggling with blankets and pillows, taking the excess from Elizabeth's old bed to use for Ralph.

Davey had not moved. His lips were white. Now beside him, Ralph closed his eyes. 'Just to … sleep,' he muttered. 'For pity's sake … to rest … just a moment.'

Elizabeth knelt, a bowl of water and clean rags on her lap. 'Tell me, my sweet love, where the hurt is. Then I'll nurse you as you sleep. Like you did for me, now I'll do for you.'

When Andrew returned, the doctor was still there. Ralph was conscious and talking but Davey was not. The rain once more drizzled, a silver mist splitting the thick sludge of fog into floating fingers. Ralph looked up as the great doors were flung open and Drew marched in, the rain spangled like stars across the swirling velvet of his surcoat. He stopped immediately, staring at the group by the fire.

Ralph groaned, 'We were betrayed.'

'What in damnation?' Andrew strode over and knelt at once by the straggling pillows and Ralph's bandaged face. The fire to his back, he threw off his coat. 'Tell me everything,' he said. 'Is this the doctor?'

With an eye to Mister Cobham's grand clothes and bearing, the doctor bowed. 'I am, my lord.'

Tyballis said quickly, 'I called him. And paid him.'

The doctor nodded. 'My lord, as you see, I have done what I can. This patient has been gravely wounded, but I believe he will recover. But the other gentleman … sadly that is another matter. I fear the worst, sir.'

'Fear is both unproductive and irrelevant. I expect a worthy result for a worthy fee, medic.' Andrew lifted Davey's head, gently turning it side to side. 'Is this the most serious injury, the damage to the skull?'

'It is, my lord. I have been debating whether to bleed the patient, but I fear that might kill as likely as cure him.'

'You'll take no unnecessary risk,' Andrew said. 'You will treat the wounds, attend both these men to the best of your ability, ask no questions and keep me informed.' He paused, then stood, went to the table and poured himself wine from the jug. He then sat heavily on the floor, his velvets in the soot and drifting ashes. 'Now,' he addressed Ralph, 'remembering the presence of the good doctor, you will tell me all you have the strength to explain.' Ralph had little voice and less energy but he spoke at some length. The others clustered around. Every one of Cobham Hall's lodgers was present, even Luke, who sat now at the far table looking grave. Casper kept Andrew's cup filled, and Andrew passed his cup to Ralph, holding it for him. 'Drink if you can,' he said. 'It may give you strength.'

273

Ralph sipped, shook his head and groaned. 'Not much to tell. We collected Throckmorton, borrowed his horses and took him to where the ship dropped anchor, just as you'd told us. There was no hitch. We saw the bugger sail off. But as soon as we turned for home, we were ambushed. Four well-armed bastards, they were, not thieves in the night nor passing braggarts taking advantage. I know thieves, and I know coincidence. These devils were prepared, with chain mail under their doublets. And they knew where to find us, and swore worse sacrilege than you'd hear in a brothel once they realised they'd missed Throckmorton. But they wanted us, too. And took us.'

'There was not a soul knew where you'd be but us, nor what ship Throckmorton was taking.'

'Throckmorton himself, then. A fool gabbles. Said goodbye to his mistress perhaps, or some other bugger who betrayed him.'

'He has neither friend nor mistress,' Andrew mused. 'Nor did he know which ship he'd be sailing, nor where it planned to drop anchor. That was known only to me. And then to you. And finally to those in this room.'

Nat had come to sit beside them, taking his brother's hand. 'This time of year there's no easy road out of England. The ship as brought the arsenic's not leaving St Katherine's till next week. So, what other? Only the one, I reckon. Rivers' spies must be well trained, and will know whatever you know. They'd find what ship's sailing, as you did. So, just luck, maybe – bad luck. Not betrayal.'

'It is certainly conceivable. Now, Ralph, finish your story.'

'We killed two,' Ralph muttered, staring up. 'Hard going it was, though we had an advantage being on horseback. But they were better fighters, trained soldiers I'd say, with experience. I thought they'd killed Davey. Then all of a sudden they whispered together, turned and ran off into the dark.'

'Ran? No horses? Yet you were miles from anywhere, out on the estuary.'

'So, some bugger was waiting, and whistled them off,' nodded Nat.

'That's what I thought, too,' Ralph said. 'I was on the ground, winded and sick and expecting a quick stab to the guts when they left.

I'm fair sure I heard what they said. Something like – Let them now, and they'll live to take back the warning.'

Tyballis whispered, 'Warn who?'

Ralph tried to wedge himself up. 'I heard, Feayton – or think I did. Let them live and take the warning back to Feayton. But the wind was howling and I was half-dead. Davey – well, he wasn't saying anything. The doctor reckons I'll live. But Davey?'

The doctor visited three times each day and remained for many hours. For both patients he undertook the stitching, and then the cauterising. 'To close a wound with heat is a painful business,' he admitted. 'But the injury to your thigh, Mister Tame, is deep. Either flame, sir, or amputate.'

Ralph nodded. 'Then cauterise. It's two legs I need, so hold me while I roar the house down.'

Elizabeth held his hand. 'Squeeze hard as you like, my love,' she said. 'Break my fingers if you want.'

Andrew was not always present. No one questioned his absences. On each return he came immediately to the low bedside, drawing up a chair or sitting on the boards beside the fire. He spoke often with the doctor, but there was little to tell and each change was itself apparent. Ralph continued to improve. Great gashes from thigh to calf made walking impossible, and Ralph stayed on the mattress in the hall, stumbling out only for chamber pot and when the bloody sheets were changed.

But beside him, Davey sweated and moaned, delirious and incoherent. He had not once opened his eyes beyond brief bloodshot confusion. He spoke only of things long past, beatings from his mother, his misery at the loss of his sister, then the black unnatural cold and the looming face of hell.

On the second day Andrew and Nat stripped Davey, bringing bowls of warm water to wash the sweat and blood from his body. His ruined clothes, the bright silks and fine Holland shirt of which he had been so proud, were thrown to the fire. At first it seemed Davey's wounds were minor and far less than Ralph's. Where the massive sword slashes had cut through Ralph's leg, pelvis and forearms, Davey carried only grazes across his ribs and shallow gashes through his knuckles, knees and back. But washing him, they found the depth of the wound to his head. His skull was crushed. Splinters of bone were caught in his curls. Drew said softly, 'Can a man live with an injury that touches even his brain?'

The doctor did not know. 'My lord, I am not experienced in battle wounds. But the gentleman still lives and breathes. I have done what I can. What more can I suggest, sir? If you would send for the priest?'

'I will find a surgeon,' Andrew said.

Tyballis went daily to the apothecary, returning with a basket full of remedies. Pounded willow bark in warm water was given a drop at a time between Davey's lips. Widower Switt stayed many hours grinding cloves and earth of alum, mixing this with egg white for ointments. On Ralph's wounds, the salves helped stop the bleeding. But for Davey the ointments did nothing. Finally able to walk once more, Ralph eventually limped upstairs to his own bed and the chamber he shared with his brother. Both Nat and Elizabeth continued to nurse him.

Then Andrew came back with the surgeon.

Davey's sheets were soaked again with sweat. His head and neck were drenched in blood, baked black by the spluttering fire. He tossed violently, crying out in pain and muttering of hellfire. His eyes were open now, glazed with burst veins, and his mouth was parched, his saliva all dried up.

'He cannot live, my lord,' said the surgeon.

Andrew stared back at the man. 'You're sure, sir?'

'My lord, I am personal barber to the Lord Hastings, and much experienced in all forms of surgery. But I am not a maker of miracles. This patient may live for a few days – giving time perhaps for a short pilgrimage, or a sacred oath taken on his behalf. But even then, I could not offer great hope. I have seen such wounds before, my lord. They are always fatal.'

'Then go back to the Lord Hastings,' Andrew said quietly, 'and thank him for me. I will attend him in a day or two. But I shall stay here until my friend's passing and when nothing more can be done, I will send for the priest.'

Tyballis lay alone in Andrew's bed that night, and woke early as the starlight still flickered through the unshuttered window. The hearth was dark, the fire out, and the chamber was bitterly cold. She climbed from the bed and searched for Andrew's bedrobe. Since he had not come to her, she supposed him still dressed. Then she tiptoed out to the hall.

Andrew sat on the floorboards beside the mattress and its strewn quilts and pillows. His hands loose, wrists supported by his knees, his back was bent, his head slumped forwards and there was smeared blood on his fingers. The fire still blazed and lit the great hall in leaping scarlet.

Now Davey lay undisturbed. He no longer rolled or tossed. The delirium had left him. His eyes were shut and he seemed calm. The discomfort of lying with his great wound against the pillow no longer seemed to distress him. He neither shivered nor moaned. Drew had pulled the covers up to his chin.

As Tyballis crept forward, Andrew looked up. She saw the terrible fatigue and was alarmed. His eyes, always black and unfathomable, were now moist with tears. She whispered, 'How is Davey? He seems – he looks – a little better.'

'He is dead,' murmured Andrew, looking back down. 'He died, perhaps an hour ago.'

For a moment she could think of nothing to say. Then she whispered, 'You're crying.'

Andrew smiled wearily. 'I have been. This man died for me. I knew him many years, and thought him a fool. But a gentle, kindly fool, and we are all fools, after all. Only the extent of foolishness separates us.'
She crept to Andrew's side, winding her arms around his neck. Within his bedrobe she was naked, and his hands found the way past the

277

damask, and cradled her body. 'Do you mind?' he said. 'Davey died in my arms, and I have his blood on me. Now it's on you.'

She shook her head. 'I'm so sorry. I cared for Davey, too. Everyone will miss him.'

'It is only death, after all,' Andrew murmured. 'Yet life, however temporary, is all we value, as if we hope to preserve it eternally.'

'Have you any idea who killed him?' Tyballis whispered.

'I know exactly whose sword, and whose order directed the swordsman. And I will deal with both.' He sighed, and said, 'Now I think I will go to bed.'

CHAPTER THIRTY-NINE

Sir Anthony, Earl Rivers, returned to Ludlow Castle from attendance at Parliament during the first week of March 1483, but within a few days he sent word back to the city, urgently requesting copies of certain documents. This was unusual, particularly in light of his lordship having only recently been at Westminster. A young clerk working in the offices of Mister Dymmock, Earl Rivers' London agent, noted the surprising request and promptly spoke to a gentleman who, having befriended him some weeks previously and sometimes paying him as much as a shilling for information, had asked to be kept aware of any such correspondence, however innocuous.

'Earl Rivers,' Andrew said, 'now suddenly requires proof in writing of his official appointments concerning the prince, and in particular of his personal authority to muster and arm troops in the prince's name. I have been reliably informed that in reply, copies of original letters signed by his highness have now been forwarded to Ludlow. Yet the country is at peace, the Welsh Marches show no sign of rebellion and the king is a comparatively young man in excellent health. I therefore consider the danger close and closing.'

Catesby frowned. 'The earl has every right to own copies of his letters patent, and would never be refused. But he has held his official position for many years without requesting such written confirmation. To suddenly require proof of the authority to raise armed troops must surely be seen as suspicious.'

'This has been dealt with privately,' Andrew said. 'The king will be unaware of Rivers' request.'

Catesby nodded, still frowning. 'I see. Indeed, with the weather grown mild, I understand his highness arranged to go boating next week and says he will catch a fish for his own supper before Easter interrupts all his pleasures. So, why, at such a seemingly ordinary moment, does Rivers make such an extraordinary request?'

'Indeed, it is quite clear,' Andrew said. 'I had hoped my own endeavours would have seriously delayed any attempt on the king's life. But it seems not. I now have in my possession the two last packets of arsenic ordered by Marrott, yet clearly the plot goes ahead. They have evidently discovered another supplier without my knowledge.'

'Have we failed then, my lord?'

Andrew paused, looking over Catesby's head to the long window and the spire of St Paul's cutting through the winter clouds. He sighed. 'I have recently lost a good friend who was helping me in this business. Marrott arranged his death, but the orders must have originated elsewhere. I do not forget such things. Hastings now has Throckmorton's confession. But has the king yet taken precautions?'

'I have no idea,' Catesby said, drumming his fingers on the writing table in front of him. 'My Lord Hastings has attended his highness less regularly of late, since, as you know, there were serious problems that divided them. My lord's warnings were dismissed as troublemaking and jealousy. He is now negotiating for the return of his position as Master of the Mint, but the king has refused to see him.'

'Refused?' Andrew snorted. 'Hastings is the Lord Chamberlain of England. After the king he is one of the most powerful men in the kingdom.'

'His lordship's power comes directly from the king's hand. Yet he is reduced to passing messages through the king's mistress,' Catesby smiled. 'You see, Mistress Shore also occasionally shares my Lord Hastings' bed.'

'One way of getting and supplying information.' Andrew nodded. 'But hardly discreet. Do you have similar access?'

Catesby shook his head and laughed. 'No. But they say Dorset has. Mistress Shore may be the king's favourite, but evidently she despises exclusivity. They are all generous men, I'm sure. Perhaps she'll accept your advances too, my lord, if you care to combine spying with amour.'

'Dorset?' Andrew turned suddenly and frowned. 'What nonsense is this? Lord Hastings entrusts secret information to a woman who climbs into Dorset's bed?'

'What better way to get information, my lord?'

'And what better way to make dupes of three of the most important men in the country? You had better make sure, my friend, that Mistress Shore doesn't also travel to Wales.'

The great bells of St Paul's marked three of the afternoon as Andrew left Mister Catesby's chambers, clamped his hat back on his head, adjusted his coat over the pommel of his sword, and strode up Cheapside. He then cut through the back alleys towards Bishopsgate. Turning left at Fynkes Lane, he finally approached a small doorway off the main street and, without knocking, pushed open the door and marched in.

A very large man was squatting on a stool by the hearth, his nose buried in a mug of ale as he stretched his feet to the small fire. At his side sat an elderly woman. She was mid-sentence when Andrew Cobham walked in.

Margery Blessop stopped speaking at once. She scrambled up and curtsied with a distinct creak of the knees.

'My lord. How – unexpected. If I'd known … may I offer beer, perhaps, my lord? We've no wine. Times are hard, my lord.'

'Bloody are, too,' objected Borin, peering up bleary-eyed from the chipped brim of his earthenware mug. 'Come in good time, you have, my lord. Was squealing to burst my ears, she was, and all about having no money, as if I'm to blame. Not my fault if his lordship done a runner.'

Andrew waved away the cup of beer hurriedly offered. 'Baron Throckmorton's absence must be a disadvantage, Blessop, since he was your only source of employment. So I have come to offer another.'

Borin brightened. 'Mighty obliging you were last time, my lord,' he acknowledged. 'Pay me the same again, and I'll do whatever you asks. You can surely trust me, my lord.'

Andrew smiled slowly. 'What an interesting assertion,' he said. 'I shall certainly keep it in mind.'

Margery Blessop hovered at Borin's shoulder. 'My boy is right willing and clever, my lord, and as trustworthy as they come. And now, my lord, won't you sit with us while you discuss your business? It's good beer, for it comes from the baron's own cellars.' She kicked her son's rump and hissed at him. 'Get up, you lout, and give the stool for his lordship to sit.'

'I've neither desire to drink nor to sit,' Andrew said. 'But I wish to talk with your son alone, so I require you to leave, madam. And not upstairs, since I know every word can be heard above. You will kindly leave the house. No doubt you have some errand to perform?'

Used to obeying the nobility and determined to oblige, Margery scurried to the peg and hung up her apron, and left the house, slamming the door against the bluster of winter winds outside.

Andrew turned immediately to Borin. 'Now, Mister Blessop. To business. There are several things I wish to discuss. There are two men I wish to see with some urgency, and you will find them for me. I have only a vague idea of their names, but I know their descriptions and who they work for. But first there is another matter entirely. You have recently been, let us say, deserted by your good wife. Under the circumstances, since you laid false witness leading to her arrest, I understand she will not be returning to you, and I am not interested in your complaints or self-pity. However, I should like you to tell me something about her.'

Each day the slow waning slog of winter prepared for a mild spring. The northern wastes mellowed, and the ice melted, while in the south the snowdrops pushed through the hard earth, and in their squashed barns the cattle birthed their calves and the first lambs wriggled damp from their mothers' wombs.

In a bright new gown given by Andrew from the collection at Crosby's, Tyballis went to market. Her headdress was neatly starched white, her sleeves were palest blue camelot trimmed with dark blue velvet, and her blue woollen gown, though the prettiest she had ever owned, was hidden by a new padded waistcoat striped in badger, laced in scarlet and attached to flowing skirts of deepest turquoise. She had plucked her forehead and her eyebrows, patted her cheeks to make them pink, and dabbed a little honey on her lower lip.

She took Ellen with her. Casper said, 'I'm coming, too.'

Tyballis eyed him with some severity. 'I don't think so, Mister Wallop. If you need anything in particular, I can get it for you.'

Ellen hopped up and down. She no longer froze in one of Drew's old, frayed shirts but now owned her first gown, sewed by her mother from the stained and ruined green cambric that Tyballis had recently discarded.

'We both look pretty,' Ellen observed. 'You doesn't. You ain't got no nice new clothes.'

'Pretty ain't my business,' Casper winked his only eye. 'Nor don't want no shopping neither. But 'tis Mister Cobham's orders. You ain't to go nowhere alone, missus. I gotta come, too.'

'Drew isn't here,' Tyballis pointed out with a small sigh. 'He left just after dawn and I don't expect him back until this evening.'

'Nought to do wiv it,' insisted Casper. 'You go out – I go out. No arguments.'

They left together but Casper walked a little behind, attentive and watching the crowds, shop doorways and dark openings to alleyways. Ellen danced ahead, impatient and eager. Tyballis, unperturbed, walked alone. At first she hurried through the Aldgate, avoiding a small company of liveried servants returning to The Tower from the docks. But once in the city, although a sharp wind still ruffled the rubbish in the streets and the damp chilled the air, she ambled, relieved to be away from the closed and despondent atmosphere within the house where sadness had become a habit.

Heading first for the bustle of East Cheap, she directed her companions down Fenchurch Street into Rood Lane and then Philpot Lane where she began to inspect the first of the stalls. Too early in the spring for most fresh foods, there was little for most housewives to cook but cabbage and onion pottage, perhaps flavoured with bacon rind and ham bones, but with Easter close the markets were at least well stocked with fish, cockles, eels and duck.

'Drew's hens have started to lay again, so I'll make a flan with shrimp for tomorrow,' Tyballis told Ellen. 'After that – well, we're hardly likely to invite the priest to dinner, and no one will know if we break the fast.' Casper was watching the swinging hips of a woman passing in the opposite direction, when Tyballis suddenly swirled around. 'Who was that?' she demanded.

'Who? What?' stuttered Casper, guilt ridden. 'I weren't looking at no one nor nothing.'

'That man – the red-haired creature who dodged up the lane' But no one else had noticed him. 'Come with me,' Tyballis insisted. 'I need to see – if it was – though it can't be,' and set off at some speed away from the stalls.

Philpot Lane sloped between small houses and their kitchen gardens, high walls buttressed with overhanging shadows. Grabbing Ellen's hand, Tyballis hurried after the man she'd seen. Startled, Casper puffed up behind, clutching his sword, his other hand to his belt where his knife was wedged. But Tyballis saw only occasional shoppers enjoying the glimpses of sunshine, children playing with hoops, wandering dogs baiting a lost pig and a pair of apprentices giggling at the revealed curves of her own hurrying ankles.

'I saw him,' Tyballis said, stopping abruptly. 'I know I did. Yet, how could it have been him? After all, he was so eager to get out of the country ...'

Casper caught up. 'You means Throckmorton?'

'I do indeed.' Tyballis stood mid lane, looking up towards the churchyard of St Dionis, knotting her little gloved fingers and turning around and around as if caught by the wind. 'It's not as if the wretched man is common-looking, for he's skinny and bandy, wears horrid bright clothes and has vivid red hair. The only other one alike was his brother, and he died months ago. Perhaps I'm simply going mad.'

'Nor any wonder,' said Ellen helpfully. 'What wiv Davey – and Elizabeth – and Ralph. Ma says it's turned her hair grey.'

Tyballis stared at her toes. 'Throckmorton wasn't to blame for Davey, of course – but it almost seems as though he was. And if he's somehow come back into London, it would make all that bitter loss seem for nothing.' She turned back to Casper. 'Would you stay here,' she said, 'and see if Throckmorton comes out of any of these shops or houses? I want to run up to Fenchurch Street and see if he's there – or if I can find whoever looked like him.'

'Didn't orta be alone,' muttered Casper.

'I shall take Ellen,' Tyballis offered, 'and will be back in two blinks.'

She walked quickly up to the main thoroughfare where the sun was sparkling along the little rows of windows. Fenchurch Street was busy but Tyballis could see no bobbing yellow hat, no peacock feather and no bright red hair. She peered into the shops where the vendors sat in their open doorways, abacus and weights beside them as they continued whatever craft they practised. Ellen still danced around her. 'He ain't here, nor never was,' she said, tugging at Tyballis's skirts. 'The bastard's on a ship wiv a bucket for spewing.'

Tyballis sighed. 'Your mother would be very cross to hear that sort of language, Ellen.'

'Don't care.' Ellen shook her head. 'Davey talked like that. I'm gonna talk like Davey did.'

Turning to retrace her steps to Philpot Lane, quite suddenly Tyballis stopped and stood staring ahead. Two things happened at once. She saw the flick of a tall boot below a fancy pair of hose, yellow striped in bright pink clinging tight to a thin and bandy leg. The owner had entered an apothecary's, disappearing into shadow and the pungent smell of mace, treacle and lavender. But at the moment of following, another face blocked her, a swarthy face wearing three days of dark stubble, heavy cheekbones and a wet-lipped leer.

'Elizabeth's friend, ain't you,' said the man. 'I've not forgot your face, trollop, nor what your bastard man did to me. All fancy-dressed ain't you, but a whore is a whore, however the bitch tries to cover it.'

Oliver Ingwood had a hard grip on her shoulder and the point of his knife even harder against her ribs. 'Get Casper,' she yelled and Ellen ran. Then Tyballis turned back to Elizabeth's brother and kicked his kneecap with the sharp toe of her new boots. He let her go and yowled, clutching his leg. She immediately swung her shopping basket into his face and brought her knee up into his groin. She felt the unfortunate squelch of impact as Oliver sank to his knees at her feet.

A shopkeeper emerged from his interior, scowling at the rumpus. 'What's this, then? Take your squabbles elsewhere, woman.'

Tyballis stared down at Oliver. She said, 'I thought you were supposed to be the best fighter on the streets,' and stamped hard on his foot. Oliver buckled and stumbled down again. Then Tyballis looked up to answer the irritated shopkeeper, and found herself staring into pale blue eyes, neat clipped red eyebrows, and Baron Throckmorton's startled and furious glare.

She yelled, 'Stop, thief!' at no one in particular. Every shopper in the street looked up. Throckmorton turned and raced down towards the river. Oliver Ingwood was hopping on one foot while trying to stab his knife into the slim body swaying in front of him, but Tyballis was too well wrapped. Ellen, scampering back up the street, bent, took a handful of mud and threw it into Oliver's open-mouthed snarl. He swallowed muck, spat and gagged, swore loudly and hurled his knife in the child's direction. His aim was not as good as hers had been and the knife rattled on the cobbles.

Casper had appeared at full trot. 'I can deal with this pathetic little bastard,' shouted Tyballis with unaccustomed fury. 'Get after him,' and pointed at Throckmorton's disappearing yellow-and-pink-striped hose.

Immediately a huge vibrating roll of thunder echoed from behind the blackening clouds and the sun went out as if in shock.

CHAPTER FORTY

Three men came running: a shopkeeper abandoning his leather
stitching, an elderly man hurrying from his wife's side and a
young apprentice hoping for the glory of rescuing a damsel in
distress. Tyballis did not need rescuing. She twisted, grabbed up
Oliver's fallen knife and waved it in his face. 'Nasty little pimp,' she
hissed. 'Think you can intimidate me? I've faced far bigger bastards
than you, I can tell you, and have plenty of experience in looking after
myself. Now – you move one step nearer, and I'll have this knife in
your guts, and then I'll tell the constable you ran onto it yourself.
After all, it's your knife.'

Oliver Ingwood trembled with anger. His groin throbbed and his
eyes protruded in frustration. He reached, grabbing for her wrist, and
managed to achieve exactly what Tyballis had threatened. He ran onto
his own knife. He squealed and wrenched back. 'Whore,' he seethed. A
small patch of blood oozed from his doublet below the belt. 'Fucking
Elizabeth got away, but I'll have you in her place.' And he once again
grabbed her wrist. Forced to release the knife, she let it drop. But as
Oliver bent to retrieve it, head down, she brought her knee up again,
this time hard onto his nose. She heard the sharp crack on contact.
Oliver howled. Blood poured from his face.

'You really are the most inept pimp I ever met,' said Tyballis without admitting she had never before met one.

By now they were surrounded. The continuing thunder dissuaded most, but at least eight had come over to watch. A woman reached over the apprentice and hit Oliver on the head with her parcel. Salted bacon, its strings flying as the package came undone, dealt a crushing blow. Oliver staggered, his nose still bleeding. 'Gerra doctor,' he snuffled.

'Get a constable,' shouted the woman.

Squeezing out from the centre of the squash, Tyballis looked for Casper. Then through the open door of the apothecary's from which Throckmorton had earlier emerged, someone else was quietly leaving. Unwatched by the noisy bustle around Oliver Ingwood, a slim figure slipped away and walked quickly in the opposite direction. His back was towards her and Tyballis saw only his cape. But the cape was remarkably familiar.

Casper was puffing up behind. 'Did the full circle,' he explained, 'and no bastard twitch nor a glimpse, there weren't – nor yella legs nor yella hat. But if it's him, that bugger as caused the death of our Davey, then I'll have him. He dares come back after we helped the fucker out the country, then I'll tear his head from his scrawny neck, I will. I'll gouge out his eyes and feed 'em to the crabs. I'll slice his dirty little cods from his legs and roast 'em for supper—'

'I quite understand,' interrupted Tyballis. 'I sympathise, really I do. But where on earth did he go? And why on earth did he come back?'

The constable arrived as lightning struck through the thickening clouds like swords through silk, the thunder again vibrated and it began to pour. Tyballis, Casper and Ellen ran. Tyballis looked back just once then made straight for the apothecary's.

The shop was tiny, a rich scent of spice and musk pervading. The thick window shutters had been lowered outwards and supported on portable legs, creating a counter that protruded into the street outside. But no one stood at the counter. A doorway at the back was firmly closed, and the sounds of raised voices from beyond were muffled only by the noise of the rain. Tyballis called, 'Service,' and after a few moments, a nose peeped out. Tyballis said, 'Is the shop open? I need advice – on wounds.'

The apothecary emerged, leaving the door to the back room slightly ajar. 'I have at least twenty ointments of all kinds, for wounds, for burns, for grazes and for calluses, corns, haemorrhoids, ulcers and pimples. But advice I can supply only by examining the patient, and there's no time for that today, mistress. I'm a busy man.'

'Then tell me something else,' said Tyballis quietly. 'A young gentleman has recently left your shop, wearing a red oiled cape. Do you know his name, sir?'

The apothecary sniffed and narrowed his eyes. 'Chasing your husband, are you? Well, I'll not give information on what's not my business, and besides, no customer shares his identity on such short acquaintance.'

'Then the customer before that,' said Tyballis. 'He was short and thin, dressed as a fine lord in silks and furs, and had hair as red as fire. Can you tell me his business, sir, and what he bought, if anything?'

'Certainly not.' The apothecary looked cross. 'I consider discretion an essential part of my work, and would never discuss one client with another. Indeed, madam, if you've no other business here than to poke and pry, I must ask you to leave.'

'You're most uncivil sir,' Tyballis said, and turned on her heel. But the little of the conversation she heard from the back room as she walked out, satisfied her. Out again in the rain, she pulled up her furred hood and nodded to her companions. Neither owned cloak nor hood; Casper had no more than a felt cap and Ellen had nothing at all.

'Bloody wet,' Ellen pointed out. 'And a bloody long walk home.'

'Then we'd better get going,' said Tyballis.

With great flames blazing, reflections dancing up the chimney and three huge logs spitting on the hearth, Andrew Cobham sat by the hearth. Tyballis had drawn up the cushioned settle, and with space for two to sit side-by-side, she was snuggled next to him, her head on his shoulder and his arm tight around her.

He was thoughtful. 'You know the man well enough, my love. You would not mistake him for another.'

'But Drew, how could he have got off a ship sailing east with a good wind in her sails? Surely he couldn't have jumped overboard? And why would he? It was him wanted to run away from England. He wouldn't risk drowning, just to come back and face death at home.'

'I imagine he did no such thing,' said Andrew. 'Either the ship suffered some accident and pulled in again to port. Or perhaps our dear friend was forcibly assisted to depart the ship before it sailed.'

Tyballis shook her head. 'Ralph would have seen.'

'Remember, Davey and Ralph were attacked by men who expected them and were waiting. But it was Throckmorton they wanted. And clearly there were others keeping watch by their horses – who could also have rowed over under cover of dark while everyone's attention was on the fight onshore. They'd have accosted the fool on deck before the ship got underway. Ralph was badly wounded and more concerned for Davey. Who would have noticed a rowing boat slipping back to the bank further upriver?'

'But Drew, they would have killed him at once. Wasn't that what he expected, and why he had to leave the country? But he's very much alive. Indeed, he was looking quite busy and prosperous.'

'A puzzle, my love. But one I intend solving. Certainly I doubt Throckmorton chose to leave the ship voluntarily. I imagine he made a bargain to save his skin. I have yet to find out what that bargain is.'

'And then going to an apothecary? Is it arsenic again, do you think?'

'Poison is common enough. Monkshood, dwayberry, hemlock, henbane, yew, antimony, thorn apples, cherry seeds, foxglove, laurel water, rhubarb leaves, death cap fungus ...'

Tyballis sat up in a hurry. 'Oh, please don't,' she said. 'What a lot you know about poisons – and such a horrid thought. It's bad enough losing Davey without all this talk of hideous deaths. I went to the churchyard yesterday with Felicia. It looked so sad, that little churned plot all alone in the rain.'

Andrew's fingers were gentle in her hair, smoothing behind her ears. 'Hush, my love. It's the living who concern me now. Those poisons are too well known to the medics, so home brews are little use to assassins. But arsenic is manufactured in Italy, and its effects are not commonly recognised. Being almost entirely tasteless, it is easily introduced into food, and since it is often used in tiny quantities for medicinal purposes, the poisoner can often disguise his intentions. It's also the most deadly. Throckmorton, having long ago learned of the darker market for such a substance, has often had large quantities smuggled into the country direct from Venice, bypassing the doctors' trade. But you are right, and we'll talk of other business. Indeed, I've sweeter things on my mind.'

Tyballis said, 'But what about Elizabeth's horrid brother?'

'Ah.' Andrew smiled. 'Dear Oliver. He's been taken to the Marshalsea. But he will not be there long. I intend to make sure he is quickly released.'

Tyballis sat up straight again. 'You want him let out? Why?'

'My dear,' Andrew said softly, 'must you know all my business? You'll not always like my answers. Simply, Oliver will be far harder to kill while under the jurisdiction of the Marshalsea guards. I want him free. But he will not be free for long.'

'Oh,' Tyballis said in a very small voice. She paused before adding, 'You don't really mean that, do you?'

He smiled and gathered her again into his embrace. 'Indeed, I am far more interested in saving lives than eradicating them. So, let us discuss the sweeter things I mentioned before.'

Tyballis hesitated. 'There is one more thing, Drew. Just a very little thing. In the apothecary's shop, I heard men talking behind a door. They spoke softly and I heard very little. But some words were quite distinct. They said, '... once Easter is over and the wine plentiful again.' Then one of them said, 'Is it the same recipe?' And the other said, 'The same, and more of it this time.' Then I couldn't make out anything at all, until one suddenly said, 'The man Luke has proved our saviour.' She looked up timidly at Andrew, watching his expression.

He frowned. 'You think Luke is involved in this? I doubt it, my love. There are a hundred Lukes in London, perhaps more. Luke

Parris has no interest in such matters.' He thought a moment, then said, 'When her brother attacked Elizabeth, you came running from the attic stairs. You'd been with Luke. Did he speak of anything important? I imagine he enjoyed disparaging me, and I've no need to hear of that. But did he give you doubt – cause, perhaps – to suspect him of treason?'

'Oh no, no.' She was flustered. 'And he didn't speak against you, Drew, nothing disparaging at all. He was complimentary. In fact, he said he owed you his life and freedom. I'm sure he's not involved in anything as dreadful as treason. It was just seeing that cloak, and then hearing his name. But after all, he was a monk. A man of God and the Bible.'

'A runaway monk is no monk at all,' Andrew sighed. 'And the Bible preaches bloodshed and advocates warfare as does our saintly Pope. But I consider Luke's involvement in this most unlikely, my love, and I have my reasons for thinking it. Besides, we cannot be sure of what you heard. An idle conversation perhaps, concerning some friendly celebration after Easter. So, forget suspicion and misery, my sweet. I repeat, I've a mind to other, quite different things.'

'Other business, Drew? Other troubles?'

He grinned. 'Not at all. Neither business nor troubles.' His hand slipped lower, pushing firmly past the shoulders of her gown and crawling into the small hint of her cleavage. His mouth was against her cheek and his breath was tantalising. He whispered, 'Come lie with me,' and tugged open her gown.

CHAPTER FORTY-ONE

The rain had found a tile loose in the roof over Andrew Cobham's bed and, slipping between slats and beams and the soaring chimney bricks, finally oozed a dark dampness beside the rising velvet tester. Andrew lay uncovered and at ease against his pillows, gazing up at the spread of the stain, his hands clasped behind his head. 'It will soon grow mould,' he reflected, speaking to no one in particular. 'The house is as rotten as its owner.'

Tyballis was cuddled next to him, half-asleep. Now her eyes snapped open and she wedged herself up on one elbow, staring fiercely. 'What owner? You own it.'

He smiled up into her frown. 'Indeed I do, my love. I was thinking of the owner before myself, though no doubt I'm as brutal and dissolute as he was. Are you hoping for confessions, then, and stories from my distant youth?' He shook his head slightly and looked away, as if still thinking aloud. 'No, little one,' he murmured. 'I'll permit no foolish reminiscences, allow no weak indulgent memories. That would not serve us at all.'

Tyballis lay down again with a sigh. 'I know you don't like talking about yourself,' she mumbled into his bare shoulder. 'But I'd like to know more about you, Drew. Just curiosity, I suppose, and – because I care. I don't mind telling you about myself. You've asked sometimes, and I've always answered. My life was very tedious, so it's not quite the same. But I'll tell you anything you want to know.'

'I know already.' He turned to face her again, his finger smoothing away her hair from her cheeks, tucking the curls behind her ears as he liked to do. 'I've a habit of finding whatever I want to know, my love.'

She was taken aback. 'How? Why? I'd have told you if you'd asked.'

'No one knows the whole truth about themselves. And nor does anyone else. Ask one, ask another, ask three or four. There are a hundred different answers to every question.'

'So, what was the question? And who did you ask?' She was affronted.

'You're my question.' He leaned over abruptly, kissing her eyes shut, hot breath making her blink, his mouth firm on her eyelids. 'I wanted to know exactly who I was so unaccountably in love with. So, I asked.'

'You talked to Borin?'

Her anger amused him. 'So, avenge yourself. Ask me one thing about my past, and I'll tell you the truth as I remember it. But no doubt you've already asked the others about me.'

'Well, I have,' she admitted. 'But no one seems to know anything. Besides, they're all astonishingly loyal and don't want to talk behind your back.' She sniffed, sitting up in bed and folding her arms. 'I'm quite sure you never had that problem with Borin. He'd not recognise loyalty if he bumped into it, and I'm sure he loved saying horrid things about me.'

'He did.' Andrew laughed, pulling her back down into his arms. 'Indeed, I found his complaints about you most endearing. But I'm not sufficient a fool to believe the slanders of another fool. I've long practice at translating lies into truth.'

'So how will I know you're not lying?'

'You'll believe what you want to believe, as everyone does.'

She thought a moment as she cuddled close. 'You told me once,' she murmured, 'that you'd killed a man when you were just thirteen. I don't know how long ago that was, because I don't even know how old you are now. But thirteen is so very young – to do something like that. So, who did you kill, Drew? Was it a burglar? A soldier in battle?

Defending yourself? Were you angry, or was it a mistake? Maybe just an accident?'

His hand crept over hers, playing absently with her fingers, his fingertips rubbing over her knuckles and the creases of her palm. 'My age? I'm twenty-eight now, just turned. And yes, I killed in anger. The man I killed was my father.'

Tyballis heard only the rain pelting on the roof, a thrumming, drumming rhythm that echoed over and over in her head. It beat at the same rate as her heart. She couldn't think how to reply and stared up at the spreading damp across the plaster between the old beams. Then her voice came out very small. 'Will you tell me anymore, Drew? Or mustn't I ask again?'

'Am I so interesting?' He grinned suddenly, as if shrugging off melancholy. 'But the question you have chosen, my sweet, is not at all the one I might have preferred. So, let me consider a moment, just how much I dare tell you.' Abruptly he swung his legs to the ground and marched to the garderobe. He returned almost immediately with his bedrobe over his arm and a cup of light beer in each hand. Laying the robe down, he sat on the edge of the mattress beside her, handed her one cup and drank from the other, regarding her over the brim. 'Well, my love? Still persistent? What else intrigues you?'

She sipped the beer. 'You are intriguing, Drew. So, can I ask the obvious? Why – why on earth – did you kill your own father? Was he brutal, like Borin? And you, just thirteen and him a grown man. I can't imagine how you did it. Was it terrible, your childhood? And then, afterwards? What happened then?'

'A trap of my own making, I see,' he said, still smiling. 'I promised one answer and must now give a hundred. Yet knowing my past doesn't explain me any more than your wretched husband explains you.' He shook his head. 'So, let me be brief, at least. My father was a violent man, though he had some reason. He disliked me as I disliked him. Hatred is perhaps a better word. Because of what he did, and because of my mother, I killed him. I'd turned thirteen the day before, and considered myself a man. I'd made the promise that night, to defend myself – and defend those who could do little to defend themselves. I'd not expected it to end in death, but he fought hard, and so did I.' Andrew paused, as though remembering. Then he drained his cup, saying, 'As for what happened afterwards – well, what could happen? They found no corpse but they dragged me off to gaol all the same, and I spent some weeks in Newgate. Then my mother found someone she knew with sufficient influence to arrange my release.' Andrew laughed. 'He bribed the jury. A useful tactic I've since used myself. But Newgate was a good teacher. Perhaps some of that does explain me, after all. Now,' he leaned forwards, took her cup from her grasp, and pushed her back hard against the pillows. 'That's enough of lame excuses and feeble retrospection. I'll build no memorials to my past.' His face was less than a breath from hers and she saw her own wavering reflection in his eyes. Then he pushed closer and kissed her hard on the mouth, thrusting his tongue against her tongue, lips bruising hers. Her breath caught in her throat as his breath rushed hot into her lungs. When he let her go she had forgotten her next question. She whispered, 'Oh, Drew.'

And before she could speak again, he shook his head. 'Enough for today, little one. I need to go out before midday if I'm to find Throckmorton. There are two other men I also need to question, and with all London to cross in both directions, the weather will slow me down. I can't take you with me, my sweet. Do you mind?'

'Of course I do.' She stretched, wriggling her bare toes under the dishevelled blankets. 'But with the threat of Throckmorton back in the city, I already guessed you wouldn't. So, I'll stay here, and clean your rooms.'

He laughed. 'Hiding the fingerprints, and your theft of my keys?'

'I don't, and I never did,' she sniffed. 'I dust everything because dust makes me sneeze and it looks horrid. Don't you like your windows to sparkle?'

'Do they? I hadn't noticed.' He stood, pulling his bedrobe around his shoulders. 'With a sky as wet as this, there seems little difference if the smears are outside the glass, or in. And that accumulated dust showed me, as nothing else could, whether anyone had searched my chambers. But no more. Polish whatever you like, my love, including me. I shall try not to object too much.'

'When the sun shines, the windows do sparkle prettily,' she

pointed out. She had cuddled back into the bed and now peeped at him from over the counterpane. 'But if you won't tell me anything more about yourself, Drew, will you just tell me why you do what you do? How you came to work for the king's brother?'

'A backstairs entrance to the same subject, and a transparent return to my dreary past, my love.' He grinned at her. 'Should I be so easily duped? Let us simply say I admire our noble king, and wish him long life.'

'Oh pooh. The Duke of Gloucester is young and handsome. The king is old and fat.'

'The king,' Drew laughed, 'is not yet forty years of age, and was once considered the most beautiful man in all Christendom. A king's appetite for all good things has since ruined his figure, it's true, but he still reigns with asperity. And our sweet Edward may be petulant and stubborn but he's also a cunning monarch, and a good deal better than the one before him.'

'Have you met him?' Tyballis was impressed.

Andrew opened the door, and the shadows rushed in past him. From the darkness outside, he said, 'Met the king? A few times, to bow, to kneel, to kiss his ring and finally to shuffle out again. There's no joy in meeting kings unless you covet power, and that's one thing I don't want, my love.'

Andrew had gone, closing the door softly behind him. Tyballis shut her eyes, curled down in the snug warmth his body had left behind, and smiled into the shape of his head left on the pillow. She was half-dozing when he came back.

He strode into the room as quietly as he had left it, and although a half-hour had passed, he was still wearing only his bedrobe. He had belted it only loosely, and it swung a little open. Now he sat again on the edge of the mattress, looking down calmly at her. 'They have gone,' he said.

Tyballis struggled up. 'They? Who? What?'

'Two packets of white powdered arsenic,' he said very softly. 'Two small parcels of death. Both were kept in the trunk where I also keep medicines and herbs. The trunk stands in the kitchen, as you know, and is always double locked.' He paused, as if waiting for her reaction. But shocked and suddenly frightened, she said nothing. So, he asked, 'Tell me, have you taken them, little one? For any reason? Or taken the keys? Or given the keys to someone else?'

She shook her head a little wildly. 'Oh Drew, no, none of those things, I swear it. But this is a house of thieves. Has someone picked the lock? And after what I heard – could it be Luke?'

'The trunk,' Andrew continued calmly, 'is secure against tampering. I thought it pilfer-proof. Without the two correct keys, their position known only to you, my dear, and myself, there remains a combination of levers and a fine balance of cogs to unpick. Only an expert would attempt it. I might otherwise have kept the poisons elsewhere, perhaps hidden in this bedchamber. But I had a fancy to keep them far away from the place where I sleep, and where I make love to you.' He looked intently at her, as if reading her. Then he said, 'I will question Luke. I will question the others. But first, my sweet, I beg you to tell me the truth, whatever that truth may be. Do you know anything of this, anything at all?'

Tyballis lowered her eyes to her lap. 'You don't trust me.'

'I've told you many times,' he answered her, 'that I trust no one. But you mean more to me than trust. Which is why I ask, rather than using subterfuge or threat, and why I will believe, I think, whatever you tell me.'

She looked up at him again. 'I know nothing, absolutely nothing about it, my love. I know where the keys are kept, but I've never used them, never looked in the trunk, and never given the keys to anyone else. But you've used many of those medicines in past weeks, nursing Elizabeth and then Davey and Ralph. Have you never given the keys to anyone?'

'No.' He smiled. 'I keep my secrets close, and in choosing to hide the keys in my bedchamber while storing the trunk in the pantries, I remain always conscious of security. I have explained to no other person the means of opening that trunk. It holds too many dangers, even before the arsenic was put there. Some spices can kill in large doses, and many herbs are poisonous.'

'You told me some of them.' She climbed quickly from the bed, tugging one of the blankets around her. She hurried to the garderobe and within minutes returned, her palm open. 'Look. The keys are still there where you put them, each in its separate hiding place. No one has stolen them.'

'Or if they have,' he said, 'they have also put them back.' He turned at once and left the room, barefoot and soundless.

Tyballis scrambled for her clothes. Dressing as a wealthy woman demanded a degree of manipulation she found extremely difficult on her own. At least respectably covered though dishevelled, she ran through the great dark hall and up the stairs. She heard the noise at once.

Andrew Cobham stood in the upper corridor, facing Nat. Nat was held hard back against the corridor wall, his head shoved to the plaster, the old paint flaking at the pressure. Drew's hands were on Nat's collar, gripping his shirt. 'You?' he demanded. 'You're the only one of this miserable crowd capable of breaking that lock. So, tell me now what you did, and why.'

Nat's head bobbed backwards and forwards and his neck looked pink. 'Nothing, Mister Cobham. Nothing, I swear. Honest to God.'

'I've found that those who profess their own honesty, rarely practise it,' Andrew said, loosening his grip a little. 'I also know your skills, my friend. You've a rare talent, which none of your neighbours share. So, it's you I suspect before them.'

The others were peering around their open doors. Only Ralph came out, and now stood behind his brother. 'He's done nothing, Mister Cobham,' Ralph insisted. 'I know everything he does, whether he tells me or not. And he's never broken into anything of yours, sir, nor never tried to. And to steal poisons? Why, it wouldn't enter his head, sir.'

Andrew stepped back suddenly. Nat slumped. Drew said, 'Yet the arsenic is gone. And for once I neither suspected nor expected, nor yet understand the motive. Someone has been very clever, Mister

Tame, more so than myself. Hardly unknown, but rare enough. And amongst this household, most surprising.'

Nat scratched his head, breathing fast. 'And you thought of me? Well, that's a compliment I didn't expect. Me cleverer than you, Mister Cobham? Not very likely.'

'The world is not built on the likely, Mister Tame.' Andrew smiled faintly. 'But I believe you, and apologise for the rough treatment. Now I shall go up to speak to Mister Parris. I will not be long.' He nodded to the row of creaking doors and the several heads poking nervously from their shadows. 'When I return,' he continued, 'I want to speak to everyone. Everyone. This matter is far too serious to rest unexplored. I cannot simply excuse due to friendship.'

Felicia, seeing Tyballis scrambling up the stairs, went to her and took her arm. 'But the women, sir,' she said. 'I hope you don't suspect us. And Jon is sleeping. He has been most unwell, Mister Cobham, with a winter cold and a shocking headache.'

Andrew had moved towards the attic steps, but he turned. 'I said everyone, madam.'

Felicia nodded. 'Then I shall wake Jon at once. But he will suffer for it, and the babies will surely catch the infection.'

'Infections,' Andrew shrugged, 'come in many varieties.'

CHAPTER FORTY-TWO

A ndrew left within the hour and he took Casper with him. He left Tyballis brooding. It was still raining.

He mounted one of the horses previously used to escort Throckmorton on his initial escape from the country, a horse that had come back with Davey's body across its rump. It was one of the baron's own horses that Andrew rode to Throckmorton's house in Bradstrete, dismounted outside the stables and strode into the house. The baron, vivid in scarlet and clearly dressed to travel in the rain, met him mid passage.

Andrew said, 'Your horse is a miserable bags of bones, Harold, and about as uncomfortable to ride as a lame donkey. You may have it back. But I am, of course, enchanted to find you at home. It would certainly have been far more wearisome if forced to sail to Venice just to have the pleasure of speaking with you.'

Throckmorton's face flushed the same shade as his hair and doublet. 'You! That is, I'm exceedingly pleased to have the opportunity to … explain. But Feayton, indeed, not knowing where you live – a matter you have always kept so unnecessarily secretive. But now unfortunately I am in a great hurry, sir, and must leave at once. Perhaps another time?'

'Oh, I think now will do very well,' smiled Andrew. 'I'm sure your appointment can wait. No doubt Marrott's men will manage to keep their swords in their scabbards a little longer.' He stood blocking Throckmorton's way out.

The baron snatched off his hat and flounced back to the small solar, Andrew at his heels. 'A few minutes, sir, if you must,' Throckmorton said. 'The fact is, I had every intention of escaping the country and was most obliged to you for arranging it for me. I was on board speaking to the captain, and on the point of handing over the price of my fare, when the ship was boarded. I was not pleased, as you can imagine. In fact, the captain was furious. But four armed men, very large men, took hold of me. Loudly asserting I was a criminal wanted by the king's men – terrible lies they told the captain – they dragged me off to a horrid little rowing boat they had waiting in the water below. I was taken to shore, and forced to ride back to London in their company.'

'And then?' Andrew smiled. He was standing, the closed door solid behind him.

The baron paused, eyeing the unreachable door. 'Very well, I shall tell you. They threatened me, of course. Marrott's men, as I'm sure you guessed, sir. They've instructed me to renew their – supplies – as previously required. Naturally I've promised to do so, though the next shipment will not come until after Easter. The Venetian galley – April perhaps if the weather turns fair – and then—'

'My dear Harold,' Andrew said, 'I am not at all in the mood for games. When did you deliver the arsenic, how did you get it and who took possession of it?'

Throckmorton blanched. 'No one – not yet – I have none to sell, my lord. My agent informed me weeks ago that you took the last packet yourself, and I know full well you did not deliver a single grain of it. The subsequent packet, well, you squandered it, sir, throwing it into the river. You told me so yourself. Where would I have found any other supply? You are unjust, my lord.'

'Invariably, it seems.' Andrew remained a moment looking down at the baron. Then he smiled. 'Very well, Harold. I choose to believe you. But one warning, before I go.' Throckmorton stood at once, preparing to hurry out. Andrew turned slowly and opened the door, moving aside to leave the doorway free. 'Just this,' he raised a finger. 'You should know that the poison you've been ordered to deliver to Marrott's agent is to be used for just one purpose. You may have already guessed, you may know full well or you may have no idea. Indeed, you probably do not care. But it's the king's death they plan, and although your family were once Lancastrians, will you now risk the cost of high treason? Think about it, Harold, before you persist on this course.'

Throckmorton marched past him, heading quickly for the main doors. 'I've no interest in this vain and paltry king,' he muttered, pulling his hat back over his ears. 'He's the traitor, since he usurped the crown from the true monarch more than twenty years ago. So, now let him pay with his own miserable life. It's nothing to me.'

Andrew stood within the corridor shadows, his suspicions answered as he watched the baron hurry out into daylight. Then he left the house and strode quickly in the opposite direction.

The heavy rain persisted. It also served him well. He doubled back to the corner of Bradstrete, and nodded quickly to the sodden figure waiting there. Casper hurried over. 'All done, sir?' Receiving no answer, he grinned, and proceeded to follow Mister Cobham, trotting several paces behind.

Both men walked briskly, first to the junction of Cornhill, and then into The Poultry towards the great conduit. Andrew immediately headed due west but Casper hovered at the stocks, as if waiting for someone. When a horse appeared at a slow and desultory plod, its hooves splashing through the deepening puddles, Casper followed it at a distance. The horseman did not ride west through The Poultry, but made a dejected path south past the Walbrook and into the narrow lanes around Bucklesbury and Penrith. The weather and its own disinclination kept the horse's pace slow, and Casper, slouching close to the shadowed walls, kept easily within sight.

It was at Sopars Lane that Nat took over. As Nat then trailed the horseman, Casper moved further south into Watling Street. From there he hurried into a dry but temporary seclusion within St Paul's.

The shops were shutting, for no one braved the storm-sluiced streets. As the shopkeepers raised their counters and padlocked their shutters, so the city emptied. No wind interrupted the pounding rain but sudden lightning fizzled, almost hidden behind the clouds as the thunder rolled.

Andrew meanwhile, his grand velvets soaked and his boots leaking, neared the Ludgate.

Lounging against the old wall just before the gate, a man in a well-oiled cape was waiting. And here, out of sight of the gatekeeper who was keeping his bones as warm and dry as he might, the horseman emerged from the lanes south of the cathedral. As he aimed for the way out of the city, the solitary waiting man stood forwards, as if expecting him. They were immediately joined by another man, previously hidden beneath the shadows of the gate. The two men on foot quickly converged on the horseman, but within cover of rain were as yet unnoticed. The horseman slouched in the saddle, peering around under the brim of his hat. He seemed nervous. His horse, its neck bent low, was clearly unwilling to travel any further from its warm stable.

As the two waiting men moved into position, so someone else appeared briskly from the small lanes and the deepening shadows. He was massive-shouldered and very tall, with hands like carved marble slabs. It seemed he had also been waiting, and as the other two men moved, so did he. Rivulets of water drained from his cloak into his boots. And behind him, up Bower Row, loped Nat. They came together within sight of the London wall. Disguised by rain, each figure knew his own intentions, but only one seemed immediately aware of the others.

As Andrew strode down Ave Maria Alley, he saw what he had long expected. The attack came almost at once.

The two men waiting near the Ludgate came running. Their long knives caught a sudden crack of lightning and lit silver. The horseman turned, startled, cried, 'Ambush!' And clamped his spurs hard to his horse's sides. But Nat already had the horse by its bridle, holding it firm. Confused and frightened, it reared and bucked. Its rider was hurled to the streaming cobbles but Casper quickly, helped him back to his feet. The two armed men stopped short, clutching their knives and looking around. They stared up at the giant; his enormous fists upraised, and called urgently through the muffling rain. At that same moment, Andrew strolled up Bower Row, brushing the rain from his sleeves. And close behind him on the other of Throckmorton's horses, rode Ralph.

Two other men had answered their companions' shout, racing up Bower Row towards the growing melee. One yelled, 'Grab the baron, you buggers. Leave the rest.' Four of them now, each with knife or sword drawn, pounding towards the fallen horseman. Nat pulled the riderless horse to the side of the road and held its reins firm, calming it.

Andrew looked back over his shoulder. 'Ralph, take over from Nat and hold onto both horses. We may need them.' He then turned back to Nat. 'Get to Throckmorton. Defend him if you can, but it's the other four bastards I want first.'

'And that,' Nat pointed, 'that great ox. Whose side is he on?'

Andrew smiled, squinting through the rain as he drew his sword. 'Mister Blessop,' he answered, 'at present obeys my orders.' Nat recognised the name and raised an eyebrow.

Ralph took charge of the horses and immediately Nat ran towards the fallen baron. Throckmorton, still utterly confused, was grappling with Casper. The four armed men were now onto them both. Casper, using a short sword and a long knife, kicking and cursing, counter-attacked. The baron turned desperately around and around. Of the men surrounding him he knew only Andrew and understood neither who attacked, nor who defended. He clutched his sword but was squeezed between dancing figures, flashing steel and eight swearing, fighting men, and could not summon either courage or coherence. Nat had moved beside him, boots slipping in the mud. Borin had waded in, flailing fists and club. The rain continued to pour and the thunder rattled the roof tiles.

Andrew, sword to one man's neck and his knife to his face, forced him quickly away and backwards against the wall. The man struggled, gaining one glancing cut to Andrew's cheek. Andrew did not blink. He said, 'Tell me, my friend, before you die, the name of your master. It's worth dying quick, instead of slow. I promise the difference will be worth the bargain.'

The other man stared, panting, to where his three companions were still fighting hard. They could offer no rescue, so he glared back at Andrew, and spat into the rain. 'Kill me however you want, bastard, and I'll leave the devil to make the bargains.'

Andrew's sword point pressed against the other's jugular and the first pricks of blood sprang like tiny embroidered beads. Andrew said, 'Bastard I may be, but I've some interest in mercy. I'll not let you live, for you murdered a friend of mine. But speak your master's name clearly, and I'll kill you quick.'

The man gulped, and shook his head. He had dropped his knife, but was edging sideways, aiming back towards his companions. 'Fool. I get my orders from a lord more powerful than you'd ever dream. And you'd dare kill me, just for that vile little snake?'

'The pleasure of killing you will be entirely for myself,' Andrew smiled. 'Throckmorton is of little interest to me. And I know your master's name already. Now confirm it for me, or lose your nose.'

'You can have my name, to remember as you die in the gutter. I'm Gerent Fisher, I am, and I'll have you, you bugger.' He tried to twist, sticking out one foot to trip and the other to stamp. Andrew avoided both, stepped quickly backwards and grinned. Immediately his wrist flicked to the side, spinning across Gerent's cheeks. Gerent Fisher howled. A great bloody hole appeared in the centre of his face where his nose had been, now hanging in gristle and splinters from between his eyes.

'Your master's name,' Andrew repeated patiently.

With a desperate and guttural wheeze, the man said, 'M-Marrott.' And Andrew pressed his sword home. Gerent tumbled to the puddles at his feet.

The noise of the fighting had increased. Casper was swearing, raucous and joyful. Each man's boots slipped and squeaked, the rain hurtled down upon them and the lightning again struck above. Steel swung against steel, Nat had fallen, but was up again at once, and Casper pushed between, his sword through the assailant's shoulder.

Borin glared down at the man on his knees in the gutter, reached out and put both huge hands around the man's neck, squeezing and shaking him as he had often shaken his wife. The man gulped, tongue protruding. Borin dropped him, kicked him aside, and turned to face the next. Then in front of him, Casper killed their leader. With his knife through the man's eye, the blood was glutinous and bright. It sprayed, spattering Borin's tunic.

Borin went yellow, doubled over, heaved and spewed. Then, wiping his mouth on his sleeve, he turned and ran. Back into the shadows of Ave Maria Alley, he galloped away from the smell of blood and his own rancid vomit.

Andrew looked up, and strode quickly back into the centre of the remaining confusion. Nat was clearly wounded, but so was his adversary, the only one of them still on his feet. The man Borin had strangled lay curled in the gutter, clutching his chest and barely breathing. The two others lay dead. Andrew thrust his sword through the last man's chest, and nodded to Nat. 'Ralph has the two horses there at the corner. Go to him and get your breath back. We haven't finished yet.'

Casper said, 'Best bit o' bloody exercise I've had in many a day. So, what comes next then, my lord?'

'There must be more than four men working the alleys,' Andrew nodded. 'I discovered no others coming here, but they will be on their way. We need to move north, away from this mess. Three men dead and one dying tell their own story and I've no desire to spend a night in gaol.' He looked around, frowning. 'Where's Throckmorton?' he demanded.

Casper peered into the rain-swept shadows. 'Buggered if I know. Maybe with Ralph and them horses. Or maybe hid.'

'I want him,' Andrew said. 'Find him. Bring him to me at the junction of Old Jewry and the conduit.'

'Bleedin' wet, it is,' Casper objected. 'And that there bloody big ogre, what run off? What about him? Weren't no good at nothing, he weren't. You want him, too?'

'Evidently Borin Blessop has an interesting sensitivity,' Andrew smiled. 'But he served his purpose. He identified two of the men for me – the one I killed, and the one you killed. They were the assassins who murdered Davey. They will murder no one else.'

'And this 'ere feeble bastard what he left half-strangled?' continued Casper, eyeing the silent figure on the ground. 'We finish him off?'

'I think not,' Andrew said, investigating the man with the toe of his boot. 'It serves me to have an account taken back.' He turned immediately and strode to the street corner where the two horses, still whinnied and rolled their eyes. Throckmorton was not there. 'Did no one see the wretch leave?' demanded Andrew.

Both Ralph and Nat were mounted. Ralph pointed and said, 'Your pet giant took him. Gathered him up under his arm like a sack of lentils and hurried up that other alley. I did nothing, for I thought it must be your orders. Here, take this horse, sir – or if you prefer, I'll go after them myself.'

'No.' Andrew thought a moment. 'You're still lame, my friend, and now Nat is wounded. Ride to Throckmorton's house. If he's there, one of you watch him and the other come to the conduit, where I'll be waiting. I've already sent Casper searching ahead, and I'll follow on foot.'

CHAPTER FORTY-THREE

The Marquess of Dorset was busy. A cask of sweetmeats and candied marchpanes had been presented to him as a special gift from the Castilian ambassador. Sitting alone, apart from the usual assortment of quiet servants and noisy dogs, the marquess reclined in his apartments at Westminster Palace, and was deeply involved in deciding which of the candies he liked the best. There were, however, many other equally pleasant matters on his mind.

His new appointment did not require anything much from him as yet. Indeed, the only requirement at present was to keep the whole business secret. The position did, however, promise an interesting increase in future power.

At some distance and off a different corridor from the royal apartments, Lord Marrott occupied his own solar. He was exceedingly satisfied with his friend Dorset's recent elevation, but he had other matters on his mind and more immediate activities currently in operation where his particular responsibility was paramount. Firstly, he had been entrusted with both obtaining the necessary supplies and with keeping these safe until handing them over to those specialised in their use and administration. This had been accomplished, and now he was to eliminate the supplier. There were to be no unnecessary witnesses to the business in hand, and the particular supplier was a witness too many. The fool was also entirely untrustworthy, and had already proved himself more inept than his late brother.

Meanwhile, although the new position was not yet strictly legal, Thomas Grey, Marquess of Dorset, the queen's eldest son and stepson to the monarch of the realm, was blissfully content. He decided he preferred the marchpanes flavoured with Seville orange, and began to separate these within the cask.

Dorset's uncle, the Earl Rivers, had long since been appointed Deputy Constable of The Tower of London. Although a mightily important appointment, it added little to his power or authority, for being kept permanently at Ludlow Castle on the borders of Wales, the earl could take neither command nor satisfaction in the position at The Tower. Indeed, as with many of the king's gifts of command, this constituted royal recognition without the slightest ability to profit from it. His highness's useful though devious habit of appointing those quite unable to implement the particular powers he had allotted them, was indeed long practised. Now, however, with careful instructions to his agent Mister Dymmock, the Earl Rivers had requested his authority as Deputy Constable be transferred to his nephew the Marquess of Dorset.

The gift was not his to give. It was strictly within the monarch's domain to grant or to disqualify, but since his highness would not know of it until too late, the letters patent were drawn up and official seals were affixed. The Tower was the citadel of London, and its containment would be imperative once matters had been finalised. Control of The Tower would ensure control of London's guards and armaments. There were no mistakes. Mister Dymmock was trustworthy and efficient.

Meanwhile, Lord Geoffrey Marrott was awaiting confirmation that his supplier of special merchandise had been equally efficiently eliminated. The confirmation was late arriving, but delays in such matters were common enough. Throckmorton's brother had been dispatched without the slightest problem, and no doubt the delay with this one was due simply to the weather. The weather was unusually foul for March. His lordship, however, enjoyed a large bright fire and was not incommoded by the rain.

It was another hour before he became fractious. Marrott finally began to suspect trouble and called for his page, sending the boy running to the stables. The page returned with a small, scruffy man, not dressed in a style usually seen within the palace chambers. Marrott stood abruptly and scowled.

'No word yet?' he asked curtly.

The man dropped to one knee and bowed his head. 'My lord, nothing.'

'See to it immediately,' commanded his lordship.

Tyballis sat in the firelight, watching the flames spring up the huge chimney as the logs scorched and blackened. She had been there alone for several hours when she heard the front doors open. The click was familiar and she knew someone was either leaving or entering the house. But this time it seemed too quiet, too surreptitious, and she looked up quickly. She saw only the swirl of a dark red oiled buckram cape as it flicked out through the doorway. The door closed as quietly as it had been opened. Tyballis stood just one moment, and then ran to fetch her pattens and cloak.

By the time she left the house, she had missed him. Instead, she followed the footprints, a man's boots carrying mud from the garden out onto the streets. They led to the Aldgate. The rain was pounding onto her hood, blinding and deafening, but as she hurried through the steel grey she saw the figure ahead, his cape billowing as he marched beneath the narrow arched gateway into the city. Her own footsteps were silenced by the downpour, and she kept her distance, choosing the darker side of the lanes and keeping to the overhanging shadows. The man strode on. He did not look back.

They were heading towards Little East Cheap where Tyballis had first seen him at the apothecary's. Her curiosity increased and her determination hardened, but she realised with misgivings that if required to face him and perhaps accuse him, she would know neither what to say nor what to do. Her quarry then ducked into the apothecary's shop as she had expected, but when he reappeared he changed direction, cutting up towards Bishopsgate. Soaked and hunched, Tyballis followed.

Some distance north, Andrew stood in the pounding rain and waited. He leaned against the great conduit, but it offered no shelter. His hat drooped over his ears and his thick black hair dripped ceaselessly into his collar. When he saw a solitary horseman ride towards him from Bradstrete, he strode forwards to meet him.

Ralph said, 'No one at Throckmorton House. Nat's scouring the side streets all around and Casper's run back south. But there's another possibility. Where's the Blessop household?'

Andrew said 'Come with me,' and set off east.

The gutters were washed clean and the rain ran in rivulets over the cobbles. Andrew led the way to the opening of Whistle Alley, and the horseman followed. The lightning sprang again and the thunder echoed directly above. As the rumbles faded Andrew heard faint footsteps running through the empty streets. He turned quickly. Through the curtains of rain he saw the shadow duck behind the wall. He turned again and saw a man he recognised from the Westminster stables, and knew him as Marrott's groom. He drew his sword. If there were two, there would be more. He kept walking, and Ralph still followed.

No one stopped them until they came to the Blessop house, and there Andrew stood, looking down. The great body was slumped, part-curled, part-spread, knees to the churned mud, face in puddles of blood.

Borin's eyes were open, staring glazed and blind to the slithering slush beneath his cheek. His nose was underwater where the rain pooled. His lashes sparkled, the rain draining from the flat planes of his brow and cheekbones. His mouth contorted, lips squashed into the earth, sagged, spittle-clogged, as if still breathing. His hat had fallen, his hair was soaked, but even from above the great slice through the back of his neck was visible. The rain continued to sluice, drenching the mountain of his body and clearing the blood. It washed both flesh and bone, for he had been almost decapitated.

A low voice behind Andrew said, 'More force than necessary, you think, my lord? But with such a brute, there's little point in prolonging the risk.'

Andrew turned. 'A fighter with few skills will always overcompensate,' he said softly. 'Doubtless you show more talent with your master's horses.'

The groom scowled and shook his head. Raindrops scattered from the brim of his hat. 'I've many duties, my lord, and groom is only my cover, as your lordship knows full well. Was this creature yours then, that you care about his end? I only followed orders, sir, and this man stood in my way.'

'You're after Throckmorton, I assume,' Andrew said.

'That I am, my lord. This brute carried him off, then barred the way to the house where he'd put him. His lordship is still inside.'

Andrew knew himself surrounded. He looked over his shoulder, but Ralph was no longer there. He nodded, lifted one foot and kicked in the Blessop door.

It was black inside and the darkness smelled of stale mould, dirt and urine. The heavy rain closed off the daylight and without candle or fire, only shadow entered. Andrew did not wait for his eyes to adjust, and marched directly into the gloom. He heard before he saw.

Throckmorton's voice was tremulous. 'I have the woman, Feayton. One step nearer – one smallest threat to my life – and I shall slit her throat.'

Andrew smiled. 'And I have a dozen men at my back.' Marrott's groom and two others stood close behind him; Andrew felt their breath on the back of his neck. His surcoat spilled water on the Blessop threshold, and gradually he began to see. Throckmorton stood at the foot of the tiny staircase. His face was white and terrified. He was gripping Margery Blessop so tightly that she could only squeak, but her expression was more furious than frightened. The baron's knife point was hard up under her chin and her neck was already bleeding. Throckmorton mumbled, 'Then let me go, and I'll let this ancient strumpet free, I swear. I've done nothing to you, Feayton. Why are you persecuting me?'

'Not me, Harold,' Andrew sighed. 'These are Marrott's men out for your miserable skin. Did you think your appointment with Marrott was for payment, or for friendship? Did you believe yourself finally accepted at court? I warned you that the mighty leave no witnesses. You should have left for Venice long ago.'

'I tried – I tried, my lord, you know I tried,' Throckmorton moaned. 'If I tell you everything – if I tell you the truth, sir – will you contrive my escape again?'

Andrew shook his head. 'The men at my back are Marrott's men,' he said. 'If I let you go, they'll kill you. And what is left for you to tell, Harold? I know every secret you've tried to hide for years.'

'The name,' the baron became desperate and his voice wavered, high-pitched. 'I'll tell about the poison you'd taken back – and who sold it to me a second time. Two packets. I recognised the seals. I'd bought both at the docks, then lost both to you. I got them back and sold them to Marrott's agent a week ago.'

Andrew stepped forwards. 'Who?' he demanded.

Throckmorton peered over Margery's struggling body. He had not released his grasp and her neck was bleeding heavily. 'Step back,' he warned. 'Don't threaten me, Feayton. Promise to let me go and help defend me, and I'll let the woman free, and tell the name.'

'Keep the woman,' Andrew said. 'Tell me the name now or I'll kill you both myself.'

The baron looked wildly around. Marrott's three men had entered the house but were standing back, confused. They knew Lord Feayton as a friend of their master, and had orders to kill only Throckmorton. Margery was twisting violently and Throckmorton was losing his grip. He said, now panting for breath, 'Help me, my lord, help me. I'll tell you everything. Luke was his name. I paid him well, and haven't seen him since. I took both packets to my Lord Marrott's steward that same day, and was to come back today for payment. And this – this treachery – is my thanks. I've done nothing wrong, and deserve protection.'

Andrew's expression changed. He stood very close and spoke through his teeth. 'This – Luke. What was he like? Describe him.'

'Like?' Throckmorton stuttered. 'Taller than me, clean-dressed and grey-eyed. Do you know him, my lord?'

'Perhaps.' Andrew's own eyes had gone black. He turned, moving away.

'My lord, you swore to get me out of here alive,' the baron called wildly. 'I told you what you wanted – I kept my part – you must keep yours.'

'Must?' Andrew turned back, unblinking. 'I remember no such promise, Harold. Nor should you have trusted me. I've not the slightest intention of letting you live.'

Terrified and furious, Throckmorton lunged forwards. At once Margery, his knife point glancing past her neck, turned, snarling and spitting. Unable to free herself, she grabbed her captor hard between his legs, poked his codpiece aside and squeezed. The baron howled and released her as she leapt on him, squealing and scratching. Andrew leaned over them and calmly removed Throckmorton's knife from his grasp. He nodded towards Marrott's men, still hovering in the doorway. 'Take him,' he said quietly. He left the house and stood outside, breathing deeply as the cold rain washed over him.

'Sir? Andrew, sir?' Ralph dismounted, hobbling over. 'Is everything all right? Did you find the baron? Seeing the other ruffians and then your giant lying dead there, I went back for Nat and Casper. Look, we're all here, sir. Just tell us what to do.'

Splashing through the sliding puddles and flooded gutters, Andrew walked over. He could hear the noise from the little house behind him, and ignored it. 'Get back in the saddle, my friend. I believe we have finished this part of the story. Marrott now has the arsenic in his possession and I have no conceivable method of retaking it. I intend informing the duke as soon as possible. Tomorrow I must set out for Yorkshire, though the journey will inevitably prove too slow. There is one thing I have to do first, but that I shall do alone.'

Nat leaned forwards over his horse's neck, his hands in its sodden mane. 'Let me go to Yorkshire for you, and carry the message. I've been there before and know the way well. It'll suit me, sir, and I'll prove my worth if you'll let me.'

Andrew frowned. 'That might suit me too but this business is too urgent to risk delays. You were wounded. Have you the strength? And you're sure you know the way?'

'Wounded? Why, that was just a scratch,' Nat nodded earnestly. 'And as for knowing the way, I do indeed. I had a warrant out after me once, and needed out of London fast. Stayed in York and met a girl. Came back for Ralph, but I seen the girl a few times more.'

Ralph grinned. 'The dirty bugger's got a daughter up there. My niece. Must be six year old now.'

The noise behind them stopped suddenly. Marrott's groom came to Andrew. ''Tis done with, my lord. If you've no objections, we'll get back to his lordship at Westminster and tell as how the job's finished. I can take a message, if there's one to give, sir.'

'Tell your master,' Andrew said, 'that I know his business. And you'll find four more of your companions dead or dying this side of the Ludgate.'

'That we've done already, my lord,' another of Marrott's men strode forwards. He carried an axe, and the blade was befouled. 'Captain Hetchcomb at your service, sir. And there's no need to involve the sheriff, I'm thinking?'

'No need at all,' Andrew said curtly, turning back to Nat. To either side, Marrott's men filed past, disappearing into the alleys heading west.

Nat watched them go. Then he said, 'You don't believe in trust, sir, but I am. Trustworthy, that is – and will prove it to you. Let me go to Yorkshire. I'll leave tonight if you say so.' He grinned suddenly. 'I've little to stay for as it happens, since Elizabeth's taken to sharing with Ralph, and me rudely removed to her paltry little bed. And that's not a fair bargain, sir, for 'tis a mean lumpy mattress and smells of woman without a woman in sight to cuddle nor swive.'

Andrew nodded. 'But home first, since there's nothing left here to stay for. You three go ahead before dark sets in. I'll check here, but I already know what I'll find.'

CHAPTER FORTY-FOUR

With no enclosed ceiling between roof beams and chamber below, the rain pounded, drowning out all other sound. Andrew left the door open behind him but only a grey and desultory light entered in silver shadowed puddles.

Baron Throckmorton sat on the floorboards, his back against the banisters. He appeared to be watching for who came to the door. His head was bare and his hat lay on the ground, while his pale blue eyes stared unblinking, and his mouth hung loose. Across his face the small light flitted, lingering in the eye sockets. He had been wearing scarlet, but now wore black. From his throat to his groin, he had been opened. Axed like a tree chopped for kindling, his halves lay ragged, and where the blood had soaked his clothes, the silk had hardened and become dark and stiff. Sagging a little apart but held together by his head and his spine, the baron continued to stare as though hoping for apology or explanation.

His white hollowed cheeks were scratched, but that had been done by a woman's fingers. The woman now lay at some distance, sprawled across the hearth as if set ready for the fire. Showing no obvious wound, Margery Blessop was face down in the soot, arms outstretched. Andrew immediately crossed to her side, but before bending over her he heard something behind him and turned at once;

a shuffling, a catch of breath from outside though the rain distorted sound. Having no desire to speak with frightened neighbours or the local constable, he moved silently to the door. Through the thrumming, drumming lightlessness, he watched someone crouch in the puddles beside Borin's sodden rump, her hands gently clearing his face of splattered mud and streaming water.

Andrew quickly left the doorway and stepped over to her. He knelt beside her, and put one arm firmly around her shoulders. 'I left you warm at home,' he said softly. 'What in God's name are you doing here? This is not a place for you, little one.'

'Isn't it?' Tyballis looked up, bleak-eyed. 'I never meant to come here. I wasn't disobeying you, I was following – though perhaps that doesn't matter now. Will you tell me what happened?' Her face, half-hidden within her hood, peered up. 'Did you – did you kill him, Drew?'

He hesitated. 'Will you wait for explanations until I get you home, my love?'

She shook her head and the raindrops spun arcs around her. 'He was my husband, Drew.' She was staring down at the body slumped huge by her knees. 'I don't mean I loved him. I won't grieve. I think I hated him. I ran away because I never wanted to live with him again. But to see him like this. After so many years of marriage, after sharing a bed and knowing him so well. Won't you tell me how it happened?'

Andrew sighed, taking her into his arms. 'Would it concern you, if I had killed him, my dear?'

She shook her head again. 'You would have had a reason – a good reason. Was it you?' She laid the lifeless face back into the pooled rain, staring at the blood on her fingers, then looked up again at Andrew. 'I don't think – if it was you – you'd have been so brutal. He has been killed with such violence.'

'Come away now,' Andrew said, lifting her from her knees, drawing her to the side of the road where the overhang of the houses' upper storeys offered some shelter. She laid her head against his sodden shoulder. 'Borin was working for me,' he told her, his hand to her cheek. 'He had sometimes done so in the past, before I knew you. I wanted information concerning Throckmorton, and about the men

318

who killed Davey. I sent Borin after them. That put him in danger from Marrott's hired louts. They killed him. So, perhaps the fault was mine.'

After a long pause she looked up. Her face was wet and he could not know whether she had been crying, or if it was only the rain. She said, 'And inside the house? Margery?'

Andrew kept his arms around her. The door to the Blessop house stood ajar as he had left it, and as she pulled away as if to go inside, he held her tightly. 'Better not look, my sweet. Throckmorton is there, and also your mother-in-law. He is dead. She is dead or dying.'

'Did you – was it you?' Tyballis whispered. 'And you don't even want me to go into my own house? But if Margery is alive, shouldn't I go to her?'

'I was investigating when I heard you.' He did not release her. 'But I imagine she's past help. If you'll wait here, I shall check.' He kissed her damp forehead, stood her back against the wall, and marched once more into the dark interior. The ashes drifted a little as he entered, and the shadows swung like chandeliers from roof to floor, stark across the bodies. Throckmorton stared blankly, and the silent lump of Margery's corpse had not moved. Andrew knew she was dead before he rolled her over. Her face was crushed. She had no recognisable features, not eyes nor nose nor mouth, and all her hair strung grey and limp across a bloody mess. Andrew came out again into the alley, shutting the door firmly behind him.

Tyballis was waiting just outside. He took her in his arms again. 'Both gone, my love. And now, before others come to look, I shall take you home.' He paused a moment, then said, 'No. I shall take you to Crosby's.'

'The others will be waiting,' she said in a small voice.

'I'll send one of the servants with a message,' he answered. 'I doubt a long wet trudge would help either of us, and I need no interfering constable blocking our way. Besides, for tonight I want you safe, I want you warm and well fed, and I want you to myself.'

It was only a short walk to Bishopsgate. The rain tipped unceasingly and the light was fading as they passed the row of alms houses. Across the thickened cloud cover, twilight slid dark, but neither moon nor stars were visible. The great windows of Crosby's were brilliantly lit in flickering candlelight, but from the windows of the low annexe, there was nothing. Andrew, his arm around Tyballis, hammered on the door. A servant came running, holding a torch.

The assistant valet, mounted on a sturdy horse from Crosby's stables, was entrusted with a message to deliver by word of mouth to the Cobham household, and report back within the hour.

The fire was immediately built high and hot in both the bedchamber and the parlour. Their wet clothes were bundled up and given to the servants for drying and repair, and in their place Tyballis donned only a shift, a pale gossamer thing taken from the Crosby garderobe; Andrew wore a soft linen shirt over dark grey hose. After a light supper of smoked salmon and poached bream in pepper sauce was served to Lord Feayton and his lady, they sat before the fire, curled warm and quiet, flushed with fine wine, and talked.

'Do you think me foolish,' she asked, her head nestled against the soft linen of his shirt, 'to care – just a little – about how Borin died? He was a cruel, selfish man but somehow – such silly sentiment – I remember the sweeter side. He was foolish too, you know, with no brains of his own. He just did what his mother told him. He might have been a nicer man if she'd been different.'

'Tell me,' he said softly, his fingers gentle in her hair.

'You're only comforting me. You can't really want to know.'

'Knowing has always been my business,' he smiled. 'I keep my own secrets safe, but interfere constantly with those of others. Delving into past and present, motive and into what makes a man himself, this has always been my interest. Indulge me then, my love.'

'There's so little to tell. Margery forced me to marry him, and everything changed. Though it was almost as horrid before that, with her pretending mother after my parents died, and making me her servant. I was fourteen when she told Borin to force me into bed. Of course I didn't want to do it, so he beat me and threw me down the stairs. Margery dragged me back up, tore my clothes off and pushed him on top of me. Then she sat there and watched and shouted orders at him until Borin finished. She said that meant we were married and she was the witness. I just accepted it. I'd been taught to obey her for years and it didn't occur to me to run away. Besides, Borin was so strong. He used to march around the house each night before bed, looking for rats. If he found one, and he usually did, he'd squeeze it in one hand until its eyes popped out and its back broke. The same hands he used to squeeze my breasts afterwards.'

Andrew wiped the damp sheen from her cheeks with the ball of his thumb. 'Crying, my love? For Borin? Or for yourself?'

'For lost youth.' She smiled wistfully. 'I ought to be happy he's gone. But it was a shock, you know, finding him like that. And then you coming from the house.'

'Had I been his killer,' Andrew said after a moment's pause, 'would you have accepted my hands on you – afterwards?'

'But it wasn't you. You said so.'

'No – it was not me,' he nodded. 'But I carry some responsibility, as I explained. Nor did I murder Throckmorton or Borin's mother – but I let them both die. I chose neither to risk my own life in their defence, nor raise my hand to their escape. And I have killed this day. Two men, one of Davey's murderers, and another of Marrott's henchmen. So, I also have rat's blood on my hands.'

Andrew was quiet a moment before she spoke. 'It disturbs me knowing you kill people, Drew. I wish you didn't. But you're a good man and Borin wasn't, even though he never killed anyone, at least I don't think he did. He was brutal but he wasn't courageous, and he couldn't bear blood, not ever. Even with the rats, or when he beat me, he'd look away and heave. He tried to thump me in places I wouldn't bleed. And I know you only do what you have to do, because of your work. So, I try not to mind, and I do trust you.'

He smiled. 'A great mistake.'

'I'm always making mistakes,' she murmured, 'but you're not one of them, Drew. And you haven't even asked why I was out, when you told me to stay home and wait for you.'

'I give orders either to serve my own needs or to serve another, and it would have been best if you'd kept warm indoors. But I don't always expect to be obeyed. I've no authority over you, my love, and where I may seek to dominate others, I've no desire to do so with you.'

'I went out,' she said in a hurry, 'because I wanted to follow –

someone.' She peeped up at him. 'I've been putting off telling you, but I have to explain sooner or later. I was waiting at home. I meant to be obedient. But someone tiptoed out of the house so very quietly, so carefully and unobtrusive. And I knew who it was, you see. So, I followed him.'

Andrew said softly, 'You followed Luke Parris?'

She nodded. 'You know, then. But he must have guessed he was being trailed. Or perhaps he's always wary. Anyway, he kept changing direction. Even though the weather was so horrid, he walked and walked and walked. Then eventually he left London through the Bishopsgate. I didn't want to follow him any further because I don't know my way outside London's walls, and the streets are too open. He'd have seen me. So, that's why I was walking back near my old home, and then I saw Ralph and Nat riding away, though they didn't notice me in the dark, and there were other men too, three ruffians with weapons. I thought perhaps Borin had been up to mischief. It was quite a shock when I found him.'

'I'm sorry about the shock.' Andrew's hands slid tighter. 'But tell me, did Luke stop anywhere during his wanders?'

'Briefly, at the apothecary's,' she said. 'Time enough to buy – or sell – arsenic.'

'Or other things.'

She frowned. 'Don't you believe Luke stole the poisons from your trunk, Drew? I thought you didn't trust anyone. But you dismiss any suspicion of Luke. Do you like him so much?'

'No,' Andrew said softly, his fingers again playing in her hair. 'I don't like him at all. I never have.'

Tyballis sat up a little and turned to face him, abruptly dislodging his hands. 'But you give him free lodging,' she objected. 'The best in the house, too. Luke has the entire attic to himself, with several rooms and a whole lot of furniture. And you never seem to think he's guilty of anything.'

'On the contrary.' Andrew pulled her back down against his shoulder. 'I believe Luke guilty of many things and capable of much more. But his quarters are better than others because he was the first, and has some right to them. And although I do not trust him any more than others, I will not suspect him of this particular theft until I have proof.' He smiled down at her, his fingers crawling back to her curls. 'Indeed, I've no desire to talk about Luke, nor any of this tedious business of ours. Can we turn to sweeter things, my love?'

'It's been a miserable day,' she agreed. 'I don't want to think of Luke, or Borin, or that awful baron, or anyone except us. Besides,' she smiled into his neck, 'I know exactly why you trust Luke, and why you give him preference.'

Andrew raised one eyebrow. 'You do? You surprise me, my love. But perhaps Luke has told you?' She nodded, cuddling down. So, he sighed and said, 'Then you understand. And we need speak no more of it.'

He had taken off his shirt, throwing it to the rug. Holding her against him, he lowered his hands to the hem of her shift and pulled it up over her shoulders. It joined his shirt on the floor in front of the fire. Then he sat there himself, and pulled her down beside him.

She said, 'You have a cut on your cheek, Drew. It shows up in the firelight. You didn't tell me you were wounded.'

He smiled lazily, eyes narrowed against the flames. 'Wounded? Almost to the death, my sweet. So, nurse me back to health.'

She kissed the little mark across his cheekbone, touching it gently with the tip of her tongue. Then she kissed his neck where the long narrow sinews joined his shoulder, muscle hard, tasting of musky wood smoke from the fire. She whispered, 'So – where does it hurt the most, beloved?'

It was two hours later that Andrew stood naked by the unshuttered window, staring out at the night. 'Asleep, little one?' he asked gently.

She opened her eyes. 'Mmm.'

'It has stopped raining,' he said, more to himself than to her. 'And the stars are as bright as candles.' He turned and wandered back to her, looking down. 'It's the small hours, my beloved, when the demons of memory and doubt plague the strongest of us. After a day of pain and dealing death, it's good to have company.' He knelt beside her, one fingertip tracing the sleep-soft skin of her shoulder. 'Come, little one. I'll take you to bed.' He lifted her and carried her into the bedchamber, where the fire had already guttered and sunk but the warmth lay around the room like lazy wandering fingers. He laid her beneath the covers, tucking her in, and climbed in beside her. Then he cupped her body from behind, kissed her neck and fell deeply asleep.

CHAPTER FORTY-FIVE

I t was considerably later that day when Andrew Cobham faced the Lord Hastings across his lordship's withdrawing room. He stood wide-legged, his hands behind his back, and frowned. Hastings sat, legs stretched out before him, his fingertips tapping together across the snug swell of his velveted belly.

Andrew said, 'If you choose to distrust me, my lord, then I accept your doubts as precautionary justice. But the information I bring is, as always, correct. The report I have this morning sent to the Duke of Gloucester is, in precise detail, the same as I have now related to you. But his grace of Gloucester cannot receive this information for five days at least, and by then whatever actions he decides are appropriate may be too late. It is why I have come to you, my lord. What you choose to do with this information, if anything, is not my place to question. But I ask that you accept my tale as truth.'

Lord Hastings narrowed his eyes. 'Yet you call yourself Lord Feayton, sir. I have made enquiries. That title is false. You are an impostor, and I could have you thrown into gaol.'

Mister Cobham inclined his head. 'The title is a cover. My apologies for appearing to mislead you, my lord. But his grace the duke knows my real name, and has sanctioned my use of a false one. Without a title, I would never have ensured the access I need, nor gained acquaintance with Lord Marrott and the Marquess of Dorset. My anonymity serves my work, my lord, and does not profit me in any other manner.'

'Yet to me, you come in the guise of pretence,' Hastings said, his tapping fingertips relentlessly rhythmic. 'I am asked to believe a story from the lips of a liar. And you dare pass the blame for your impersonation to the king's own brother?'

Andrew smiled. 'Never in my life have I implied that any blame lies with his grace, neither in respect of my actions nor for those of any other. But I have my orders, my lord, and will obey them.'

'Very well.' Hastings stopped tapping, and tented his fingertips, regarding Andrew Cobham over their peaks. 'Tell me your true name now, sir. Come on, out with it and let's be done with pretence.'

Andrew bowed. 'Forgive me, my lord, I do not have his grace the duke's permission to reveal my true identity.'

Hastings leaned forwards. 'Are you implying you do not trust me, sir?'

The smile persisted. 'By no means, my lord. I came here to bring information I believe imperative to the safety of our king and kingdom. Having fulfilled my responsibility, and with your permission, my lord, I will now retire. My work elsewhere is not yet over.'

Hastings sat back with a sigh. 'Off then, be off with you. You bring me neither proof nor culprit, and you come in false guise. I'll not call for the guards, but I'll not act on your tales, nor take your information to his highness. If the Duke of Gloucester believes you, he'll make his own decisions.'

Bowing low, Andrew backed until standing by the door, one hand to the handle. 'And Baron Throckmorton's written confession?' he said, looking up briefly. 'Was this not proof enough, my lord? The baron has now been murdered. Yet his confession remains in your hands, and serves no purpose.'

Hastings watched him for one moment in silence. Then, eyes narrowed again, he spoke through his teeth. 'If you dare to question my decisions, sir, I will have you arrested and beaten for insolence.

You will leave quickly, and you will not return. I shall not again permit your entrance here. Now, go.'

Casper Wallop was waiting outside the door. 'And?' he said, trotting quickly at Mister Cobham's swirling coat-tails. 'I means, what happened, my lord?'

The corridors were bright with flaring candles from a hundred sconces. The flames echoed and reflected in the long windows, rosy glass and diamond facets. Andrew said nothing until they were well distant from Lord Hastings' chambers. Then he stopped suddenly and said, 'The fool's afraid. He's frightened to pass on Throckmorton's confession. He's wasted my time.'

'Frightened of Lord Marrott?' demanded Casper, shocked.

Andrew shook his head. 'Frightened of the king.'

'But the king —'

'Precisely. But his highness won't countenance the truth. He accuses Hastings of fabricating slander simply to topple Woodville power, since they're his principal competition. Hastings has already lost considerable favour by trying to save his sovereign's life. He's now busily negotiating a peace with the king in order to get his position back, and meanwhile he'll not risk another fall in grace.'

'Bloody Woodvilles,' muttered Casper.

'But hardly the most intelligent place to ponder such opinions quite so loudly, my friend,' Andrew said. 'Now I need to see Catesby. Then I'm going home. This entire business is becoming tedious. It seems the great lords of this realm think only of their coronets, and will protect only their own skins.'

'Only just come to that conclusion, 'ave we, then?'

Andrew clipped his companion around the ear. 'Behave yourself. Or I shall send you home while I go on alone.'

'I'd follow anyway,' grinned Casper.

They collected their swords from the guard's armoury, the ostler quickly brought out the horse and Andrew remounted, not Throckmorton's sad old beast but a fine bay from Crosby's stables. Casper took the bit, and led the horse out towards Ludgate and St Paul's. It was a bright morning. The previous day's rain sparkled in every gutter, spangled windows and pooled between the sodden doorways. A faint hint of rainbow tinged the sky, the cathedral's spire cut the arc and the puddles were bathed in a wavering violet.

But Mister Catesby was out and Andrew left no written message. 'Inform your master,' he told the apprentice, 'that he is needed concerning the business he shares with Lord Feayton. And tell him that the Lord Hastings is in need of some more appropriate – direction. I shall return tomorrow.' But he did not immediately ride home. Instead he signalled to Casper to follow, and set off for Bradstrete.

Throckmorton house was, as he had expected, in turmoil. The steward Bodge opened the door, and it was Bodge whom Andrew had come to see. 'My lord,' Bodge bowed. 'His lordship is not at home. There has been an unfortunate—'

'I'm aware of the baron's death, and of its circumstances,' Andrew said quietly, and stepped inside. Servants, aprons askew, were running up and down the stairs carrying trunks, coffers and occasional items of furniture. Three liveried gentlemen stood watching, noting, itemising and murmuring. The sheriff and two assistant constables watched from the entrance to the great hall. Andrew signalled to Casper to wait, and led the steward into the small annexe. There he leaned against the window ledge and nodded. 'Mister Bodge,' he said softly, 'you have seen me here many times and you know exactly who I am. And I believe you also learned your late master's business and the nature of the merchandise he handled. Because of this you were in the process of leaving his employ.'

Bodge looked uncomfortable. 'Indeed, you are quite right, my lord. But I shall now stay until his lordship's household is satisfactorily passed into the hands of his heir.'

'The heir?' enquired Andrew, vaguely curious. 'Who is that?'

'A second cousin, I believe, my lord,' Bodge said, 'a gentleman considered of minor importance amongst Canterbury's wealthy tradesmen. Mister Esmund will now inherit the title, and is expected to take possession of this Hall within the month. But in the meantime there is the sheriff, and Assistant Constable Webb, both instructing us as to his lordship's property, regarding what should be kept in storage for Mister Esmund, and what should be handed over to the sheriff.'

Andrew nodded. 'Since we are therefore likely to be interrupted, I shall immediately get to the point. My own line of investigation comes from a higher authority, and has little to do with his lordship's death but more to do with his previous business. So, tell me who else, apart from myself, was a regular visitor here over the past two or three months?'

The steward quietly closed the door behind him. 'Four gentlemen were particular visitors in recent months, my lord,' he said. 'But I have the names of only three. The fourth, a foreign gentleman, gave his name in such an accent that I was never able to decipher the pronunciation.'

'French?' suggested Andrew.

'I believe so, my lord, or perhaps from the Italian states,' Bodge answered. 'The gentleman spoke Latin to my master, but was florid both in appearance and speech. Since I do not speak Latin myself, sir, I know nothing more. The other three, to the best of my knowledge, were respectable English gentry, and came either on normal business, or in friendship.'

'Their names?' Andrew insisted.

Bodge nodded and cleared his throat. 'A Mister Bray, a Mister Colyngbourne and a Mister Yate,' he said. 'They were frequently here both individually and together. But I was never privy to their discussions, my lord, and know nothing of their dealings with his lordship.'

Andrew frowned. 'A Mister Parris, for instance? Do you know that name?' Bodge shook his head. 'I assume,' continued Mister Cobham, 'you are prepared to confirm these identities to someone else, should I require it?'

'Oh, my lord, indeed if it will help in any way,' Bodge said. 'But I intend leaving this household at the earliest possibility and would hope to have as little to do with this regrettable business as possible.'

'I understand,' Andrew said. 'However, I expect both your discretion and your future cooperation should I ask it of you.'

Mister Cobham did not finally arrive home until mid-afternoon. It was raining again.

CHAPTER FORTY-SIX

'Luke has gone out again,' Tyballis told him. She had been cooking and came from the kitchens with flour dusting her nose.

'But this time you chose not to follow?' Andrew strode in, throwing his wet gloves and hat to a chair.

She hovered in the doorway, watching him. 'You seemed to think I shouldn't. I've been busy preparing – baking, you see, eels for the Easter Friday, and then crab soup for the Saturday – so, by the time I could even run to get my cloak, he would have been too far gone.'

'Good.' He slung off his coat and the raindrops scattered, finding their own level where the terracotta floor tiles had worn concave. 'There's little point in following phantoms. I have spent a far more interesting day, talking about you.'

She blinked. 'Me? How?'

'With your friend the assistant constable. I first met Webb while extricating you from Bread Street Gaol. Now he's investigating the deaths of three people in and around your house. I wanted to know exactly what he'd discovered, and he wanted to know how you are.'

'Did you tell him I was your – that I'm living here?' Tyballis blushed faintly.

Andrew stood over her, licked his finger and wiped away the

residue of flour decorating the tip of her nose. 'No,' he grinned. 'I didn't tell the good constable that you've become my mistress. I told him you had taken excellent lodgings in the same premises as myself, and that you were keeping well, had friends and were becoming prosperous. In fact, I told the truth, which surprises even myself.'

'But not all of the truth.'

'No one is entitled to that,' Andrew said. He had taken her into his arms and now kissed the pale curve of her forehead. Her little starched headdress was knocked askew. He straightened it. 'You realise, of course, my love,' he continued, 'the house your parents left to you lies empty, and is yours again. As a widow, you're now entitled to move back there, reside alone and do as you wish.'

She blinked up at him. 'A widow? So I am. I hadn't even thought of it.'

'A widow, owning her own property.' He nodded. 'You'll have suitors, my love.'

Tyballis stood motionless in his embrace for a moment, and then wriggled free. 'That's horrid, Drew. Don't say things like that. Or do you think I ought to rush back home and start interviewing prospective husbands?'

'I think,' he said, still grinning, 'you should do whatever suits you.'

She tossed her curls, bonnet again askew. 'What suits me,' she said rather loudly, 'is to get back to the cooking. Something smells as if it's burning, and if the eel pie is ruined, you can still damn well eat it. And I hope it scalds your tongue.' She turned with a flounce and marched back into the kitchens.

Andrew remained thoughtful, as if undecided whether to cross the hall and sit by the fire as he so often did, or go on to his own chambers. Instead he sighed, turned and followed Tyballis. He found her staring sightlessly into the great fire and the cauldron hanging there upon its chains. She held a wooden ladle, but was stirring nothing. Andrew came behind, put both arms around her and turned her to face him. Then he extricated the ladle from her grasp, popped it back into the cauldron, led her to a bench at the long kitchen table, sat and pulled her firmly onto his lap. 'You dislike being my mistress?' he asked her.

She shook her head. Escaping curls stuck to her cheeks. 'I suppose – it's just the word. It's the perception. No, I don't dislike it. Or I wouldn't – well, I wouldn't do it. But Borin always called me ... and I think Margery was one once, long ago. So, I don't like to think I'm no better. It's silly, but with you talking about suitors, as if you're trying to offload me ...' She gazed at him suddenly. 'Drew, if you do ever want to get rid of me, then say so. I have my pride, too – even if I am just a woman.'

'If you were not a woman, my sweet, you would hardly be sharing my bed.'

'Don't be annoying on purpose, Drew,' Tyballis objected, sitting up straighter. 'You know you're very rude about women sometimes, as if we're all as foolish as hens, or as scheming as your horrid Marrotts and Woodvilles. I just mean, I don't want you to keep me here out of pity.'

He sighed and his arms tightened around her. 'My beloved, do you think my feelings so capricious that I might declare my love one day, and regret it the next? I'm not so changeful, my dear. But you should know your own freedoms, and make your own choices. I offer little except my body and my heart. You have options now, and must consider them.'

She wriggled away again and stood staring down at him, flushed and increasingly angry. 'It's very considerate of you to be so blunt, Drew,' she said, a little breathless. 'But I've never asked you for anything and telling me what you won't give, isn't – nice – or even – appropriate.' Then she turned her back on him in a hurry as she continued talking. 'I never meant to become a whore, but perhaps I am now, so who cares! But you don't have to shout it at me.'

Andrew sat for a moment in startled silence. Then he stood and once again came behind her, his arms turning her forcibly, embracing her without possibility of escape. 'You will listen to me carefully,' he told her, 'before answering. But listen to my words, not to your suspicions, and then reply to what I have said, not to what you think I have implied.' She nodded into his velvets, and he said, 'A whore is a woman who sells something she has every right to barter – as does a haberdasher, a potter or a baker. But you have not sold yourself to me

– or to any man. Why take a title you think shameful, when it has no bearing on your life?'

Her words were muffled by his doublet. 'They used to call me it, Borin and Margery. But I never was. Now sometimes I think I am.'

He sat again, drawing her down with him. 'Truly, my sweet, a loving mistress is no whore. Do you also find the title of mistress demeaning? If so, you're free to leave, and I'll give whatever will make your new life comfortable. But I've no wish for you to leave, and I'll do what I can to keep you, which is why I persist now. Before knowing you, I've spoken to no woman of love, not even my mother. That may mean little to you, but to me it encompasses mountains.' He lifted her chin, tipping her face up from his velvets to look at him. 'Apart from marriage, what else do you want of me, my love?'

She blinked away the tears. 'Trust.'

'Ah.' He laughed. 'Very well. Let us say I trust you. Implicitly.'

'And stop talking about marriage. I haven't asked for it. I hated being married. It makes you sound conceited – are you such a great prize? So, stop thinking I must think this – or want that – just because I'm female. I'm me. Just me, not every other woman in the country. I'm not looking for suitors, and I don't want my house back. Perhaps I could sell it. And there certainly aren't any other men like you. So, why should I be merely one of an identical pack?'

'An impossible question. As the first woman I have ever loved, I already consider you unique, my sweet.'

She took a deep breath. 'But if you do – love me – and trust me – then why don't you tell me something about yourself?'

'To know me, you need to know my past?'

'It's about trust, and friendship,' she said. 'You know everything about me. You've never even told me what Borin said when you asked him about me, but I can guess. And now you've been talking to Rob Webb. He's known me all my life, and at least he likes me. But he still arrested me. Yet if I ask one little question about you, you act as though I'm trying to steal your purse.'

'My purse would matter less. Take it.'

'I don't want your horrid money.' She was affronted. 'And now my pies are burning. So you can just go away.'

He tightened his grip. 'My dearest, your pies are doubtless barely warm. I've been cooking in these kitchens for some years and I know exactly how long everything takes to heat. Besides, I've no intention of letting you go just yet.' He spoke softly to the wisps of hair around her ears, where the condensation was dampening her curls. 'You smell of hard work, wood smoke and baking,' he murmured, 'which is strangely alluring. So, utterly seduced as usual, I shall satisfy your curiosity if I must, and try to sooth whatever insults you think you've suffered.' He kissed her eyes as he often did, smoothing the tip of his tongue along her lashes. 'It seems you dislike being the subject of discussion during your absence,' he continued. 'But Webb simply informed me you've been mistreated all your life; how your parents were respectable people but too busy to have much time for you, how they drowned without leaving you properly protected and how your neighbours immediately took advantage. Webb claims he objected to Blessop's improper behaviour at the time but was too young to help. Indeed, it was your husband's subsequent threats which evidently inspired Webb to become a man of some property and thence a constable. You see, the wretched creature talked about himself, too, and at some length, which was shockingly tedious. I was, however, persistently polite. I wanted information, of course. But not about you, my love. About Throckmorton.'

'Oh.' Tyballis sniffed, struggling to free one hand and wipe her nose.

Andrew handed her his kerchief. 'As for the questions I asked your charming husband, they were considerably more to the point,' he added. 'And although I prefer not to go into details, his answers were precisely as you might imagine.'

She nodded, fisting the handkerchief. 'I can guess. He said I was barren, a whore, couldn't cook or darn to save my life, and – wasn't even pretty. He thought I was skinny, which of course I am. But I can cook, and my darning isn't too bad either.'

'I'm delighted to hear it,' Andrew laughed. 'That will naturally make so much difference. However, it was not what Borin said at all.'

'Really?'

'One or two highly personal remarks would hardly be appropriate to repeat,' Andrew murmured. 'Perhaps another time, though perhaps not. However, he did inform me that you were the most beautiful woman he'd ever seen. And that he couldn't believe his luck when he claimed you as his wife.'

Tyballis stared at him. 'I don't believe you. Borin despised me.'

'I first became acquainted with your Mister Blessop some years back,' Andrew told her. 'I found his lack of intelligence an irritating handicap, even though I made frequent use of his muscle power. As a messenger, he could be, let us say, alarmingly convincing, a useful tool in my line of work. Eventually, having no more patience with him, I passed him on to Throckmorton. When I discovered you, I was utterly bemused. You were not what I would have expected as Borin Blessop's wife. And it was for your sake that I began to extricate him from Newgate and prove his innocence. I knew him entirely innocent, of course, since I knew the real culprit. And I believed you might need your husband, whatever his quality.'

She was charmed, and finally smiled. 'That was kind. Though it meant me going to gaol instead. But then, you got me out, too. You're a surprising person, my love. Will you tell me more about yourself? Just a little?'

'Had you not previously thought me capable of kindness?'

'Oh, almost continuously.' She gazed hopefully at him. 'So will you?'

'That beseeching expression is quite impossible to deny.' He chuckled softly. 'So, what must I tell you, my sweet?'

She frowned. 'I want to know about you and Luke. About why you don't want to distrust him, despite what you think about everyone else. Is it only because he helped you when he was in the monastery? And most of all, I want to know why on earth you were excommunicated.'

He was momentarily silenced. 'Excommunicated?'

'Well, Luke said almost.'

'I think,' he said at last, 'we had better go into the hall. If I'm to speak of this, I prefer not to be overheard or interrupted, especially if Luke returns. Your cooking can wait, since the kitchen is open to eavesdropping.'

He led her across the corridor into the hall where the fire blazed as usual, and they sat together on the cushioned settle before the hearth. Andrew stretched his legs to the flames and said, 'I don't care to know what Luke has said of me. But I shall tell you the truth, since you ask it.'

She whispered, guilt ridden, 'Only if you want to.'

'I've surrounded myself with subterfuge for so long, for personal protection and as part of my work,' he sighed. 'But after all, it serves no purpose between us. So, let me tell you, my love, that despite my distrust of the church hierarchy, I have never been threatened with excommunication. That is a fabricated exaggeration. Luke was sent to the monastery by his father because he was an inconvenience. I went there to tell him something of some importance, and found him miserable and quite unsuited to a monastic life. So, I arranged to take him away. I was thirteen. He was ten. Eventually I brought him here.'

'You knew him already?' she said, watching him intently. 'And you were thirteen. So, you went to tell him – what you told me? That you'd killed your father?' Andrew nodded, unsmiling. Tyballis sighed. 'Drew, do you mean what I think you mean? Is Luke your brother?'

CHAPTER FORTY-SEVEN

His highness, King Edward IV of England, spent Easter Sunday on his knees in the Abbey of Westminster, head bent and hands clasped in prayer, as was customarily required of a Christian king in a Christian country. Following this he retired to his private chambers for a small fish supper and finally slept soundly, in excellent health, easy of conscience and quite alone except for the attentive but studiously hushed servants of the bedchamber.

He awoke again at dawn. It was the last day of March in the year of our Lord 1483. His highness was bare forty years old, and although admittedly somewhat corpulent, was still considered comparatively active – certainly active enough to enjoy swiving his mistresses. After a night entwined, Mistress Shore frequently served him wine and manchet, a quite informal breakfast from the hands of a quite informal attendant. The king would then attend morning Mass before enjoying a formal breakfast. But this morning it was a young man, new to the more intimate procedures of the royal household, who poured his sovereign's wine, nervously spilling a little onto the polished table. Edward frowned. 'Where's Cely?' The other attendants looked around, unaccustomed to deviations in the elaborate protocols of court.

'Forgive me, your grace,' the man stuttered, falling to his knees and almost dropping the spotless white napkin across his arm. 'Mister Cely is unwell, sire. I am honoured to take his place, but only for this morning.'

'Then hurry, and clean up the mess,' Edward said. 'Leave the wine jug. If Cely is unwell, tell him to whip egg white with cinnamon, and drink it on his knees. It helped me exceedingly when I was unwell last year. Now, off with you.'

But within the hour, his highness was doubled over, vomiting violently onto his own feather and silk counterpane.

The royal doctor was called at once. Three assistant physicians rushed to procure quantities of the same purge successfully administered the previous year when his highness had suffered a similar attack, and had recovered. However, when the cup of egg white and cinnamon appeared to worsen the situation, a more complicated purge was concocted. White hellebore roots were finely chopped and crushed, ground pomegranate seeds added with boiled rhubarb, mixed in a watery rue vinegar and offered at regular intervals. The surgeon came with the royal fleam and blooded his king immediately before the first dose was administered. Consecrated water was used to wash the royal sweat from the royal forehead, and the royal sheets were changed six times, on each occasion the royal vomit and excrement being carefully examined for diagnosis.

'His highness,' said the doctor, 'has suffered a severe fever. The hellebore purge will readjust the humours. At present his highness's urine is milky. I expect this to clear within the hour. In the meantime, the chamber must be cleansed and scented to eradicate miasmas and bad odours. I predict a complete recovery within two hours.'

But two hours later the king lay exhausted and faint, his mumblings incoherent as he pleaded for water. His tongue was greatly swollen and protruded from his gasping mouth, while his lips were cracked and dry. He continued to retch and his eyes rolled back as he began to convulse, contorting and shaking violently.

The chief doctor looked up from the bedside, and went pale. 'I cannot believe it is a serious threat to life,' he muttered. 'It is simply a disturbance of the stomach, just as it was last year.'

The assistant medic crept closer, staring down wide-eyed at the patient rolling in agony on the soiled sheets. Again he shook his head. 'A dysentery perhaps? But his highness's food is prepared with the greatest care, and tasted first by others – and no one else in the entire royal household has been taken ill this day.'

'Cely,' murmured the doctor. 'His highness's personal attendant is ill,' and hurried off to investigate.

But Cely was found to have recovered. The king did not. Every crack in door and window was sealed, the fire was built huge so that it roared and echoed up the massive chimney and the royal covers were heaped upon the royal bed. Another purge was administered, but his highness was too weak to sip it. It was dripped, drop by careful drop, into his open mouth but he choked and could not swallow. By evening the worst was feared.

While the king lay close to death on the last evening of March, a young man in apprentice's livery ran all the way from Westminster Palace to Bishopsgate and arrived so out of breath that the resident servants at the Crosby annexe could not at first understand what he was trying to say. 'Feayton,' the young man finally yelled, grasping at his collar. 'Must see Lord Feayton.'

'His lordship,' insisted the steward, 'is not at home.'

'Urgent,' gasped the man.

Casper Wallop, who had been listening on the stairs, bustled to the doorway. 'What is it?' he demanded. 'Lord Feayton ain't here, but you tell me and if I reckon it's important, I'll get word to him, quick as piss.'

The breathless apprentice stared at the one-eyed creature with singular misgivings, but he grabbed Casper's arm and began to whisper. Casper turned to the steward and other hovering servants. 'Private,' he informed them. 'Off with you.' Having heard of the circumstances of his highness's terrible illness, Casper thanked the young man, pressed a coin into his palm, grabbed his cape and set off immediately for Portsoken. Within an hour, Andrew was mounted and riding hard for the royal palace at Westminster. Here he gained admittance to the inner court of the palace despite the late hour and the blustery storm thundering over the palace roof, and requested permission to speak with his lordship the Chamberlain. The palace was in a state of confusion bordering on panic, and amid the doctors and servants of all descriptions coming and going, the gentleman calling himself Lord Feayton was immediately welcomed.

The Lord Hastings was striding his Turkey rugs, face flushed and mouth set narrow. He glared as Andrew entered, and quickly waved for the bevy of nervous servants to leave. Finally he said, 'What right have you here now, sir? Last time I informed you I would no longer grant you entrance. How dare you return to face me?'

Andrew bowed. 'My lord, I appreciate your change of mind, and thank you for seeing me. But I think you will agree that priorities have altered.'

The baron's sable sleeves swept the ground as he paced. 'So it seems, so it seems,' he said. 'And now what, sir? Do you have the effrontery to claim prior knowledge? Do you say this is Dorset's work?'

Again Andrew bowed. 'I believe it the work of Lord Marrott, my lord. Whether the Marquess of Dorset, Earl Rivers or any other man is equally culpable, I can only surmise. Once again I have no proof. But I do not believe in coincidence. I do not believe that his highness is taken ill to the point of death by purely natural means while the Lord Marrott has two packets of arsenic secreted in his chambers, and has meanwhile been plotting to kill his grace the king for almost a year.'

'It is a disaster.' Hastings collapsed into the arms of a high-backed chair, and stared into the guttering fire. 'But if I make an outcry, accusing Marrott, Dorset's closest friend … arrests would lead to an escalation of enmity, and to chaos, which would not serve at all. I will not be held to blame when I have a good notion of who truly is.'

Andrew stood, his back to the last fading flames. 'I have told you, my lord, that this attempt on his highness's life has been the inspiration of Earl Rivers, initiated from Ludlow and instigated by the servants of the Lord Marrott. Suspicion alone is insufficient, however, and I believe there are other hands in this, although the proof remains even more obscure.'

'The French,' spat Lord Hastings.

Andrew spoke quietly. 'Principally the French, my lord. Last autumn I encountered a French spy I had been tracking for some weeks. Francois Cretiene, agent of Louis of France. Before eliminating the man I questioned him at some length.'

Hastings continued to glare. 'Tortured, you mean? And you assassinated a French agent? You're a fool, sir. You should have brought him to me, or to his highness for questioning.'

Andrew smiled briefly. 'I do not indulge in torture, nor believe in its results, my lord. As for elimination – the particular circumstances did not permit the luxury of choice. It was my life or his. I chose my own.'

'So, what did this wretch tell you?'

'That King Louis pays pensions to many English lords at court.'

Hastings snorted. 'So he does. To me, for a start, which no doubt you know already. The French king pays our own sovereign in order to ensure peace. The pension isn't always paid, invariably either late or intentionally forgotten. But it's no secret. You, being who you are, sir, will surely be aware of all these facts.'

'I am, my lord.' Andrew nodded, patiently smiling. 'But the French king pays other pensions, which do not arrive late, and are never forgotten. The largest sum goes to the Earl Rivers. And there are many spies in our country, my lord; some I have questioned, while others remain elusive. One is known to me, the Italian Dominico Mancini, who reports back to the French king's doctor and counsellor. But he speaks little English and is of small consequence. Another, Jean Brassard, is a more serious threat, but I have not recently been able to trace him.'

'So, the French send their spies here, just as we send ours to France,' Hastings muttered. 'What can they say of importance?'

'That Louis XI of France wants our king dead and our country weakened and in turmoil with a child king ripe for plucking.' Andrew sighed. 'Then there is Henry Tudor.'

'That spawn of bastards?' Hastings shrunk his chin into the depths of his fur collar, glowering into the shadows of his lap. 'Calls himself Earl of Richmond, but he's just an exile and a wandering fool. He's no threat.'

'All else, yes. But he's no fool,' Andrew nodded, 'and he also has a hand in this. He has no money for bribes, but he's been sending spies, and encourages insurrection. With Edward gone, the country is expected to flounder. With a child on the throne, a puppet controlled by the powerful and greedy, England becomes vulnerable to every enemy. To France, to Henry Tudor, even perhaps to Spain.' Andrew paused, peering down at his host. Then he said suddenly, 'How is his highness, my lord? Is this already done? Or is there hope?'

'Hope, perhaps, but only a narrow vein.' Hastings looked up, grey-faced. 'I love him, you know. Edward is not just my king. He is the greatest friend I ever had; my sovereign, my brother, my son.' He looked down again, flushed. 'He has given back the honours he took before, and he has forgiven me. So, if my lord passes, without further proof I cannot even prosecute Lord Marrott. But I'll ensure the Woodvilles gain nothing from it. If his highness recovers, then I will consider – once he is strong enough – warning him again.'

'I must accept your decision, my lord.' Andrew's bow was curt. 'And I shall ride immediately for Middleham.'

'To the Duke of Gloucester? Then first wait for the final pronouncement. I expect to be called at any time now and messengers are ready to carry the news to every county.'

In the early hours of the following morning, the doctor leant over, holding the tiny mirror to his sovereign's lips. There was no condensation of breath.

Shortly after the messengers were dispatched with news of the monarch's death, his highness astounded everyone and sat up in bed. Her highness the queen fell on her knees at the bedside and sobbed with joy. A request for the young Prince Edward to be summoned from his uncle's care in Ludlow was speedily cancelled. The court was informed of the miracle, and the rush for black, morado and brunette velvets was abandoned. Other messengers were sent to the great northern cities, contradicting the original notification of death. His highness's principal doctor rejoiced, while pointing out that his diagnosis had been proved correct, and clearly his medications had saved the precious royal life.

King Edward was pale and much weakened, but he received his friends, family and Chamberlain with a slight smile and a nod, and was able to thank them for their great solicitude and many prayers. He remained in bed, and the faint smell of vomit and diarrhoea, much disguised by herbal infusions, was studiously ignored by everyone. Although presented with a bowl of milk slops and a cup of hippocras later that afternoon, his highness refused to eat, and drank only a little light beer. He also shook his head at any further administration of the purge, and emphatically refused to be blooded. He slept most of the day and all of the following night and awoke a little after dawn on Wednesday 2nd day of April. He was overheard cheerfully informing the Keeper of the Stool that he expected to make it to his forty-first birthday, after all. There were only three weeks to go.

The royal messenger set off for York with news of his highness's imminent death two hours before Andrew Cobham set off in the same direction with news of his highness's unexpected recovery.

Already mounted, hood pulled down low against the rain, Andrew spoke quietly to his servant Casper Wallop by the stables. He ordered Casper to return home at once, to inform the household and to protect Mistress Tyballis Blessop above all else. Andrew would, he said, probably return within the fortnight, but in the meantime Mistress Blessop was to stay at home, to do nothing to put her safety at risk, not to follow any of the other lodgers on their forays into London, and to be discreet in what she admitted to anyone else. Then Andrew Cobham clamped his knees to his horse's sides and rode north into the day's dimmed and desultory rising.

CHAPTER FORTY-EIGHT

I t was not empty, since she was there herself, but felt all the chill and rejection of emptiness surrounding her. She had only ever slept here in his arms, and without his arms she became strangely depressed, as though all the usual warmth now evaded her. Not Andrew's vast and crumpled bed, his vast and dust cocooned bedchamber, nor his vastly looming absence had changed, but Tyballis spent much of the remaining night hours peering dismally from beneath the swathes of counterpane, hoping he might somehow return. He did not.

He had left the previous evening after Casper had rushed panting into the hall, shouting that the king was dead. She had not seen Andrew since, though Casper had returned many hours later, quietly this time, and related his messages only to her. She was the only one still sitting up, curled half-dozing by the hearth. It was during the small hours shortly before dawn that Casper crept in the second time. She had jumped up at once, hoping it was Andrew. Casper had then whispered the news: the king was still alive, but had been so close to death that the doctor had pronounced it inevitable, and Andrew, after seeing the Lord Chamberlain, had ridden immediately for Yorkshire, and would not return for two weeks at least, it being a five-day journey or more in each direction.

Tyballis, Casper announced, was to stay at home and say nothing to anyone.

'Well,' Tyballis sniffed, 'what an exciting prospect. Hopefully I'm permitted to walk the gardens at least?' And she glared into Casper's blind eye, then turned and marched off to Andrew's empty bed.

On the morning of Wednesday, the second day of April, London was informed of his highness's illness. Twice-daily bulletins were announced at St Paul's Cross, and rumour ran quicker than the Thames. Officially the royal doctors were ensuring a rapid recovery and the king was expected to leave his sickbed within the week. Rumour said otherwise. Rumour spoke of the royal fishing trip some time previously, and how cold it had been on the river that day. Rumour also muttered of the king's more than generous appetite, and how gluttony and a surfeit of exotic foods could frequently produce a fatal flux.

Tyballis, having no intention of remaining permanently at home and seeing no logical reason to do so, went with Felicia to St Paul's and stood amongst a large crowd to hear the latest bulletins. The crowd fidgeted and men muttered to their neighbours, not only alarmed should their beloved sovereign die, but remembering the dangers of a child on the throne. Previous kings, Richard II and Henry VI for example, had inherited the crown as children, but each had sunk disregarded as the great lords battled and royal guardians fought for power. 'And who do you think we'll have ruling, if that happens again now?' they said. 'Why, an upstart Woodville queen and her upstart Woodville family, of course, that's who. They'll strip poor England's coffers bare within a month.'

Others shook their heads. 'The duke will be made Lord Protector,' they said. 'Follows precedent.'

'Gloucester? He's a long way away, and will do best to stay in Yorkshire. It'll be bloody war if he tries to oust the Woodvilles, and it'll rage through London's very streets.'

'It will be war indeed,' Tyballis whispered to Felicia, 'if Drew tells the duke that the king has been poisoned.'

'Listen,' Felicia said. 'His grace is already recovered. There'll be feasting at the palace again in a week.'

It was in the crowd that Tyballis noticed Robert Webb, and waved. He hurried over, pushing through the squash. 'It's been a long time, Mister Webb. This is my friend, Felicia. And I believe you recently met another friend of mine.'

'Since the last time – gaol – most unfortunate circumstances,' the constable apologised, blushing slightly, 'and now the shocking business of your husband, mistress, I know a good deal more about Borin Blessop, and his mother too, and will cast no blame on you for leaving them last year. But to lose a husband in such a manner must have been mighty difficult. If I can help, I would be happy to do what I can. But then there's the house. The property rightly belongs to you, and you should claim it.'

Tyballis nodded. 'I mean to sell it.'

'I was honoured to speak with Lord Feayton before Easter, when that terrible business, tragic it was, with the baron himself slaughtered just like his brother before him.'

'Baron Throckmorton,' said Tyballis with some severity, 'was a wicked man. He was lucky someone didn't kill him off months ago.'

'That's as may be,' mumbled Robert Webb, 'but I don't reckon a man can be counted as lucky when he's sawed nearly in two and left to gape like a boar on a spit. On the battlefield a sword will cleave a body in that manner, you know, without armour to slow it. But in London's streets, no! I count myself fortunate never to have fought in them terrible wars for bringing the throne back to the Yorkist's.'

'There might be another war,' Tyballis said, lowering her voice. 'If the king dies and the Woodvilles try to seize power.'

The constable frowned. 'Now, now mistress, no need to repeat them nasty rumours. With the good Lord's help, our king will live another forty years.'

'Indeed,' Tyballis mumbled, 'I pray for his highness's recovery.' For if the king died and poison was proved, she wondered how often she might ever enjoy her lover's company again.

The afternoon bulletin finished, and with little change announced regarding his highness's condition, the crowd began dispersing. The constable sighed. 'I'll put word out, if it's a sale you want on your house,' he said. 'But with the uncertainty – the king's health – well, there's not likely to be a ready market. People's frightened of what might happen, rioting and buildings torched. But I'll do what I can. Just as long as you're sure you won't sooner take possession.' He put his face down a little to hers, speaking with greater confidentiality. 'I hear – nothing improper suggested, of course, mistress – you've taken lodgings in Lord Feayton's own property. Grand, it must be.'

'Oh, it is indeed,' Felicia quickly interrupted. 'I live there too, you know. Mister – his lordship, that is, has taken in a considerable number of lodgers since the house is so large and with sweeping gardens, the grandest in the whole Portsoken Ward, and conveniently close to the Aldgate. And if you are thinking of the vicinity to the tanneries, I must tell you they are sufficiently distant for the smells hardly to bother us at all. Well, except when summer winds come from the east, of course – but that is quite another matter.'

Rob Webb smiled and turned again to Tyballis. 'Then it's no wonder you'll be selling the old house, mistress. Though being as it's where you were born, I thought maybe a sentimental attachment … but I shall put the word about and see if there's anyone buying. In the meantime, I wish you well, and if ever …' He cleared his throat, blushing. 'If you should ever feel the need of a brotherly hand – maybe even a husbandly hand – then please do think of me. It's a hard world for a young widow, I reckon, especially if the king … but that's not to be thought of.' He tipped his hat and bowed slightly. 'I hope to see you again, mistress, and not too far off in the future neither.'

On the way home Tyballis said, 'I hope you don't intend repeating that nonsense to anyone, Felicia.'

And Felicia simpered. 'My dear Tybbs, the man virtually proposed marriage. And a respectable constable too, which means he has public position, and property of some kind too. You should consider it, my dear.'

'I've not the slightest intention of ever belonging to any man ever again,' Tyballis snorted. 'Besides, being a widow is far more comfortable. It's the best way for a woman to claim her own rights and make her own decisions.'

'Well,' said Felicia, 'personally I have always found the greatest satisfaction in the blessed union of a Christian marriage. But then, dear Mister Spiers is a most exceptional man. There are not many in the world like him.'

'That's certainly true,' muttered Tyballis. 'But I'm selling my house so a cluster of horrid men don't pretend they want me, just to get their hands on the property.'

'None of my business, I'm sure.' Felicia aimed her nose skywards. 'Those who prefer the less respectable forms of partnership must doubtless make their own choices.'

'So we must. But,' Tyballis said crossly, 'I think it most unwise of you to inform anyone else of Andrew's private address. As Lord Feayton, you know, he prefers absolute secrecy.'

'Oh pooh,' Felicia said, 'I was hardly precise and never mentioned the names of the nearby streets. And no harm speaking to a constable, my dear.'

'I am fairly sure,' Tyballis pointed out, 'that Drew's secret activities are not always, shall we say, in strict accordance with the law.'

'Nonsense.' Felicia walked faster. 'Mister Cobham may be involved in espionage, but it is in the service of his highness and the Duke of Gloucester, so must surely be considered absolutely proper.'

Tyballis caught her up. 'Proper. But secret,' she said. 'Besides, Robbie Webb is just a very ordinary person despite his position, and not always as clever as he'd like to think. He can't be, if he wants to marry me. And there are so few large houses in the Portsoken near Aldgate; after your description he could certainly find me now if he wanted. Drew has always warned me about keeping silent when possible, and so please don't tell anyone else.'

'I think you have laboured the point sufficiently,' Felicia said with a sniff. 'But I assure you, dear Mister Cobham would never object to any remark of mine. Some of us are naturally respected for our wise decisions, and I flatter myself I'm one of them. Now, let us discuss matters nearer to practical necessity. What do you think we should purchase for tomorrow's dinner?'

'We?'

'Of course, Tybbs dear. Funds being a little short at present, I presumed you would buy whatever we need. But I shall help cook, I promise, and we can surely plan the meal together.'

The king's health continued to improve, and the doctors permitted a return to a solid diet. They insisted, however, that he remain permanently in the well-heated and draught-free bedchamber, and refused to consider a return to royal duties. In fact, the doctors' strictures constituted a convenient excuse, for his grace had no desire to leave his bed and had little strength for anything more strenuous than stumbling from mattress to commode and back again. His appetite remained feeble and his limbs pained him. The daily bulletins reported only the positive, but the darker truth, admitted only in private, was less reassuring.

By the eighth day of the month the weather had improved. The sun shone on the city. Alleys steamed, puddles dried and the sleek rolling surface of the Thames heaved with a golden sheen, all its filth turned to pleasant reflections. At Westminster the corridors adjoining the royal apartments had returned to order and his highness had begun to find the confinement to bed irksome. He became fractious, complaining to Mistress Shore that the continuous heating was tiring him and that tepid hippocras was all very well but he would prefer a good strong cup of red wine. He was looking forward to his first bath in a month, promised for the end of the week if there had been no relapses in the meantime. Water on naked limbs might prove dangerous, but days of vomiting and diarrhoea made the anticipation of bathing a pleasant necessity.

Tyballis and the other lodgers met together each midday for a shared dinner at the long table and again at the beginning of each dreary evening, discussing both their own daily business and what they imagined their absent host was presently up to. There had been no word from Andrew Cobham, but this was no surprise since there was no manner of communication available to him.

'Chatting with dukes and dining on roast venison and swan three times a day,' Ralph assured them. 'Our Mister Cobham is living the high life. Them lords will be falling over themselves to thank him for all he's done.'

'And ladies,' muttered Elizabeth.

Tyballis regarded her with studiously dignified silence. Ralph squeezed Elizabeth's waist and grinned. 'Not jealous, are we? Remember you're mine now, Elizabeth my love, and I reckon Mister Cobham's dreaming of our Tybbs, not dallying with them ladies of York. Besides, he'll be busy. Talking dawn to dusk, and prayers for the king every day. Up there folks is five days behind the news and will know nothing of the king getting better.'

'I cannot imagine Mister Cobham on his knees at chapel,' sighed Felicia. 'I think he would find an excuse.'

'No excuses 'mongst dukes and duchesses, not when it's the king's life needs praying for,' Ralph said.

'You must be missing Nat, too,' nodded widower Switt. 'Twinned siblings share a special understanding, they say. I understand the great sadness of loss, and I commiserate.'

'Ralph don't miss Nat when he's got me,' said Elizabeth. 'Better to share a bed with me, eh, my love?'

'Nat snored and had bony elbows,' Ralph agreed, 'but at least he never poked me awake a hundred times each night to ask if I loved him true.'

Elizabeth glared. 'Then let me back to work the streets and earn a decent wage, and I'll be out of your way.'

'You're mine.' Ralph hugged her again. 'And I love you true, so no more working with no man but me. I'll earn the wage. And with them crowds clamouring outside St Paul's, I've been earning well enough lately.'

Felicia sighed. 'My dear Jon – a little unwell today, I'm afraid, and now taking a well-earned nap – does not believe in stealing from outside churches. He believes it a sin and against God's—'

'I think,' Tyballis interrupted suddenly, 'there are some very strange noises outside. Is Drew back already? Listen – a clank and a rustle.'

'What? Where?' Casper jumped up.

'Someone from the tanneries,' Ralph stood quickly, crossing to the long windows and peering out. 'Mighty late for visitors, but they used to come sometimes, begging a scrap of food when times was bad.'

'Then why so furtive? Why don't they knock on the door?'

Although Andrew was away, they had kept up the habit of the fire. The days had warmed but the evenings were chill and gloomy, and without candles the quickening dark shortened the days. A small blaze now lit the hall, but outside the unshuttered windows, the night was pitch. 'Can't see anyone,' said Ralph. 'It'll be foxes. Wandering dogs, or ducks up from the pond.'

Tyballis was peering through another window, widower Switt beside her. 'Look, there,' he said and pointed, 'a flash in the dark. That was metal, I'd swear.'

And Tyballis said, 'We are surrounded. And they are armed.'

CHAPTER FORTY-NINE

Casper pulled his knife and snatched up the carver from the table. Ralph ran up the stairs and fetched the sword he kept in his room. Felicia raced to her chamber to protect the children, and widower Switt strode, a little bent, to the front door.

'I shall go and investigate,' he said sternly. 'An elderly man is less likely to be seen as a threat if there are thieves around.'

'Thieves?' said Tyballis. 'But that's what we are already – most of us, anyway. And indeed, Mister Switt, they might just find you an easy target.'

'In which case,' he said, 'I shall be a small loss. Indeed, there is no one to miss me. I am the perfect spearhead for any risky exploration.'

Tyballis shook her head. 'We don't need a sacrifice, Mister Switt. We need a strong united defence.'

Elizabeth was listening at the darkest window, furthest from the fire. She whispered, 'I can hear voices. Listen, two men muttering whether this is the right house. Someone else says it is ... and ... Feayton – I heard one say Lord Feayton.'

'Then it is clear they are not simply thieves,' Tyballis whispered.

'Let me at the buggers,' growled Casper. 'I'll give 'em Feayton – I'll give 'em cold steel up their arses.'

Ralph held Casper back. 'We don't know how many there are.'

'Then better not let them know we have heard them,' decided Mister Switt. 'Guard the doors, but keep out of sight.'

In the darkness each rustling murmur of branch and leaf fed suspicion, and each passing flicker of starlight suggested movement, yet proved only breeze in the trees, the patter of busy rats or the flight of an owl. Then a scratch against the doorjamb startled everyone, staring white-faced as silence hung like the wood smoke from the hearth. The first sound was a wail of thwarted indignation from upstairs and a baby's yowl. Then Casper dropped his knife, and outside footsteps suddenly retreated.

'Fool,' objected Ralph, glaring at Casper.

Elizabeth raised a finger to her lips. Upstairs the children were quiet again. Downstairs only the fire spat and hissed. Tyballis tiptoed again to the window, listened a moment, then shook her head. Now everyone was at the doors, ears to the wood. Ralph and Casper gripped their metal. Tyballis and Elizabeth grasped knives from the table, holding their breath, staring out to the front gardens.

They came quietly, and they came from behind. Creeping through the kitchens, eight men entered the great hall from beneath the staircase and the pantry corridors. Their arrival was unheard and unexpected.

The sudden shout boomed out into the great quiet emptiness. 'Drop your weapons and make no sudden moves. You are all under arrest by order of his royal highness the king. Where are the rest of you? Where is the Lord Feayton?'

Ralph whirled around. Casper leapt forwards but Ralph held him back. 'What's this?' he demanded. 'The king is sick, and you ain't in no royal livery.'

Another man pushed forwards, his sword catching the firelight as if it too were burning. 'Fools,' he sneered. 'You're outnumbered two to one and you want to argue livery? Yes, the king's sick and when he dies, you'll be in Newgate, rubbing cracked skulls against your shackles.'

Casper shrugged Ralph off and raised both hands, two knives bright. 'You ain't royal nothings, not guards nor sheriff's men. You's nothing but ruffians, same as me, you buggers. I fights good enough for two. Come try me.'

Tyballis had edged back towards the hearth but Elizabeth stepped forwards. She shouted, 'And I'll stick the first bastard to touch me.'

'I must inform you gentlemen,' Mister Switt announced, 'you are unwelcome and mistaken. Although you mention Lord Feayton, you have come to the house of Mister Andrew Cobham. Ask around the neighbourhood, and they'll tell you, for Mister Cobham is a charitable gentleman and well liked. Cobham Hall, this is, and no lord lives here nor ever has that I know of. I've heard of Lord Feayton, since his notoriety is considerable in these parts. But he lives in a secret place close to the Aldgate, and we rarely see a shadow of the man.'

'Oh, yeah?' The ruffian's leader stood brandishing his sword. 'So, who's this Andrew-fucking-Cobham then, with such a grand house to a name not never heard of? A house full of naught but a parcel of skulking fools, it seems. So, where's he, then?'

'Mister Cobham is not at home,' replied Mister Switt. 'He is a wealthy man, who often travels on business. We are his friends, guests and servants. And you have no right here. You must leave at once.'

The leader reached out and grabbed Elizabeth's arm, whirling her around, her back against his chest and his sword across her belly. 'Who's this, then?' he jeered. 'Mistress Cobham, is it, in dirty old rags torn to the tits and scars to frighten her mirror? The lady of the house, is it? Or the whore from the gutters outside?'

Elizabeth wrestled, stabbing and punching. The man squeezed her knuckles until she dropped her knife, but she twisted and scratched at his eyes. The other seven men had moved around, facing Ralph, Casper and George Switt. One laughed. 'Who's ready, then? Which fucker wants his guts spilled first?'

Tyballis jumped from the shadows by the hearth, the torch she held blazing into sudden light. A branch from the fire was the brand she hurled at the back of the ruffians' capes. One man's cap flared scarlet and the straggle of hair beneath singed a smell of scorched oil. The man screamed, dropped his sword and grabbed his head as Ralph leapt onto him. Ralph's sword went through doublet, chest and burning cape in one stroke as the squealing man whimpered into silence. Tyballis swung the torch, threatening men, clothes, cushions and tapestries. The flames roared, sweeping out like scarlet streamers through the air. Elizabeth broke free but was caught again and thrown down with a kick.

Casper launched, killing one man as he charged. Extracting his knife from one gulping throat, he waved it exultantly into the next. The man he threatened counter attacked, his sword knocking Casper's knife away. At the same time Casper swung his second knife into his assailant's kidneys, slamming the point deep home from the back. 'Stoopid bugger,' he remarked, wiping his blade on the man's shoulder as he tumbled, spitting blood. 'Ain't never learned your moves around my streets, that I wager.'

In great flaming circles, Tyballis swept her burning torch. Leaving Elizabeth moaning on the ground, the ruffian's leader strode to Tyballis, reached both hands through the swirling blaze and sliced his sword down through both torch and the hand that held it. Tyballis crumpled with a small sigh. The torch spun on alone, scattering splinters as it hurtled against the nearest window. The broken shutters caught the fire, crackled and then faded into spasmodic sparks. Casper leapt and kicked the stub of fallen torch away. Tyballis clambered to her knees, her hand badly scorched, as George Switt was knocked bleeding to the ground. Then another came thundering onto him, boots to his ribs. He groaned and collapsed. Elizabeth lay unconscious nearby. Ralph had lost his sword though Casper still clutched one blood-encrusted knife. They stood panting, faces grazed and clothes slashed, two men facing four. Three of the eight incomers were dead. One was dying. They lay where they had fallen, blood dark and sticky across floorboards. The remaining four ruffians were unhurt and well armed. The smell of scorched timbers, burnt flesh and sooty fumes filled the hall.

Ralph was yelling through the smoke. 'You'll pay for this, you bastards. Put us in Newgate, would you? When Drew marches home, he'll have your heads, every last bugger. You'll moulder in Newgate for the rest of your miserable lives.'

The leader sneered. 'Then know this, fool. In an hour the king will be dead. It's her highness will hold power in this city till Earl Rivers rides in. Then it's the whole realm they'll be leading in the name of the little prince, and Woodville enemies won't last long enough to piss out their tears. So, shut your mouths now, or I'll shut them forever.'

'Kill 'em all, Murch,' muttered another of the men. 'Get it over with.'

The leader shook his head. 'Not till that bastard Feayton shows his nose. Once we catch him you can kill the lot, but in the meantime I need hostages. When our replacements turn up with news of the king, then I'll hand over and they can decide for themselves.'

'I'll have that trollop first,' one man grinned at Tyballis, the side of his head singed, his basinet gone. 'I'll fuck her then roast the bitch.'

'Keep your stupid fancies to yourself,' growled his leader. 'This is important work, not no Southwark games. You'll obey my orders, turnip head, or answer to Lord Marrott. Now, herd these buggers. Get them into one small room somewhere, lock them in, and make sure there's no mistakes.'

'Where?' the other man stared around.

'Search,' roared the leader, and turned back towards Ralph and Casper. 'You – look after your wounded and forget any stupid heroics. We've more men expected, enough to take over this house and kill every bugger in it.'

Casper was stuttering with fury, teeth clenched, hopping from one foot to the other. 'You – you – I'll gouge out your eyeballs and stuff them up your arses. I'll split your noses from hole to chin till you suck snot. I'll – I'll—'

The ruffians' leader squinted through the smoke and shadows, turned his sword and clipped Casper over the head with the pommel. Casper bit his lip, gurgled faintly and slumped to the ground. The leader looked questioningly at Ralph. 'Your turn, beetle brain. Wot tricks you got planned, then?'

Ralph glared, looking over to where Elizabeth lay, blood trickling from her lips. Finally he said, 'Let me see to my girl. I won't fight you.'

'Mighty sensible,' nodded the man. He leaned down, taking Casper's remaining knife. 'The fight's over. You don't give me no more trouble, I'll hurt no one else till Feayton comes back.'

Ralph had already taken Elizabeth in his arms, wiping the blood from her face with his sleeve. She opened her eyes, blinked and closed them again, sinking gratefully into his embrace. Tyballis and George Switt, both silent and peering through smoke, were bewildered by pain. Ralph smiled weakly. 'It'll be all right,' he whispered to Tyballis. 'Let them tie us up. When he comes back, you know what'll happen.'

Someone kicked him in the ribs. 'Shurrup and gerrup. I've found the perfect cell. Time to follow orders, and no talking.'

CHAPTER FIFTY

Andrew Cobham's storeroom had once been the minstrel's gallery of a great hall, used for celebrations, feasting and music. Then years ago someone had enclosed and divided the space, erecting cheap plank walls and creating two separate chambers, one small, one larger. The main door carried a great iron lock, for Andrew was a man of locks and secrets and he used the larger chamber for storing many things. And here Tyballis was now dragged, the others slung in with her, some tied, some left groaning, and the door was locked behind them. There was no window, no burning fire, and no light of any kind.

Ralph, his hands roped behind his back, strode the confines, knocking blindly into straw pallets, heaped stools and other unrecognisable furniture stacked against the walls. Casper, tied by wrists and ankles, rolled on the ground cursing with loud and inventive indignation. Tyballis, appearing too weak to cause trouble, had not been tied. Now she crawled upright and lurched to Casper's side. 'Hush,' she pleaded. 'I think I can untie you, but they may be able to hear us. Stay still and keep quiet.'

Casper croaked, 'Can't use hands.'

'Your hands are fine,' Tyballis objected.

'Your'n,' Casper said, rolling into a crouched but sitting position.

'Oh. Well, they've stopped hurting so much.' Tyballis shook her head. 'My fingers are burned, but I'll be all right.'

Elizabeth, muttering under her breath as she managed to struggle from her own bindings, was trying to loosen the ropes on Ralph's wrists. George Switt remained on the ground, trembling and speechless, encrusted blood dark across his chest.

Ralph had just been freed when they heard the lock grate outside, and immediately everyone collapsed on the floor again, feigning unconsciousness. Then the door creaked open and Felicia, Jon and their four small children were shoved inside. Once again the door was locked.

Edmund and Walter, small, sleepy and confused, clung to Felicia's skirts. She carried Gyles, fast asleep in her arms. Jon stumbled, crashing into Ellen who had crouched sobbing in a corner. Ralph and Elizabeth began explaining what had happened. 'And Luke?' Felicia said. 'Is he dead? Still upstairs in the attic? Have they found him?'

Ralph shook his head. 'We've not seen Luke. Perhaps he got away. Perhaps he's run for help.'

'Or just run,' muttered Elizabeth.

Tyballis said quietly, 'It's very difficult to see, but there is everything here, if we can find it. I know this storeroom well.'

'Everything?' demanded Casper, sitting up and rubbing his head. 'Knives? Axes? Guns?'

'Cannon?' sniggered Elizabeth.

'Food?' hoped Felicia.

'If everyone would just stand very still so I can get my bearings,' Tyballis said, 'I shall be able to find some light.' She began to pace the available space, her hands outstretched, feeling for familiarity. Then she stopped suddenly, knelt, fumbled for a moment and finally straightened. She held up four fat candles and a tinderbox, gave one candle each to Ralph, Casper, Felicia and Elizabeth, then sparked the tinderbox to each wick. The little flames rose pale and tentative, lengthening into golden plumes. The smell of sweet honeycomb lingered amongst the cobwebs. 'There,' said Tyballis. 'Now let's find bedding and see to Mister Switt.'

'Drew don't use no candles,' objected Elizabeth, holding hers high so the dancing shadows fled.

Tyballis smiled. 'He only likes firelight. But there's a small stack of unused candles here in the chest, and tinderboxes, and a whole load of other things around the room. No food, of course. And no cannon, I'm afraid, but there is a sword somewhere and several knives, too. Now there's light, I can find everything. But Mister Switt first, I think.'

Scrummaging on their knees, the candlelight soaring, they discovered sufficient bedding, though some of it was damp, for a luxury of sleeping arrangements, and Felicia quickly put her three small boys to bed. Mister Switt lay sweating on the larger mattress as Elizabeth and Felicia unlaced his doublet and shirt, and wiped the blood from his wounds. 'Water?' hoped Elizabeth.

Tyballis shook her head. 'There is beer, and a small keg of wine, undrinkable I think, though it could be used for treating wounds.' She fetched rags and a jug of the wine, smelling musty. George Switt groaned and closed his eyes again. His exposed ribs arched grubby white, protruding from a concave belly. A sparse and wiry grey stubble clustered around his shrunken nipples. Partially undressed, he seemed older.

Without the possibility of counting time nor knowing whether still day, finally they slept. Ralph took Elizabeth in his arms and cuddled down against the wall. On the same mattress Casper stretched and snored, twitching in his furious dreams. On another mattress, Jon and Felicia kept their arms around their children. Jon escaped quickly into sleep, but Felicia lay awake, listening nervously for heavy footsteps and the clank of metal.

Tyballis lay beside George Switt. His wounds had seemed more serious in the light. Several ribs were broken, but a deep gash to the chest was the more troubling injury. The bleeding did not stop, even when bandaged, and she thought his lungs had perhaps been punctured. Yet he remained awake, restless and murmuring. His voice gurgled, guttural, as he swallowed blood. Tyballis whispered to him, 'Are you in pain, Mister Switt?'

'Pain? Ah, no, my dear. Not to compare with other pains I've suffered.' He blinked up at her. The remaining stub of a candle stayed lit beside them. Tyballis smiled into his eyes. She had never before noticed what a bright glassy blue they were. Not yet milky, not facing death.

She remembered how Andrew had treated her when she was ill, or hurt, or miserable. 'Tell me,' she whispered.

'Then call me George, my dear,' he murmured. 'And perhaps, for these last few minutes, we can be friends. I could only speak to a friend, you see, since one should never burden another soul with one's own troubles.'

'We are friends,' Tyballis smiled. 'Of course we are. So, tell me about your wife, George. What was her name?'

His voice was growing faint. 'My dearest Edalina. We were sweethearts as children, and I promised to marry her when I was bare six years old. When I was fifteen, we were wed at the church porch. As pretty as a little flower, she was. I was apprenticed to a joiner, and we planned a good future, but life, you know, has such different ideas. She wasn't strong, my Edalina. I stayed home to look after her, and was beaten by my master for not completing my work.'

'But you must have been very happy to be together,' Tyballis whispered.

'Indeed. Indeed. But she wanted children so badly, and each time she hoped, then it proved a disappointment. Finally, thanks be to God, we had a little daughter. Our sweet Grace. As beautiful as Edalina. Oh, for so long we were happy then, even though my dearest wife was often sick, and I earned very little.'

'But you were a family,' said Tyballis with a small sniff.

Mister Switt clutched at his chest. 'Indeed. A happy family, for seven good years. I loved music, as you know, and so did my dearest Edalina. So, I left my apprenticeship, and joined a minstrel group. That was happiness indeed. We became a great favourite at court. Sometimes little Grace came with me and danced, and Edalina sang. Money became easier, too.'

Tyballis smiled. 'I am envious, dear George. What a lovely story.'

361

'Ah, but it did not last,' he sighed. 'We travelled the country until our blessed child was just seven years on God's good earth. Then came the pestilence. That wicked plague of death that scourged the land, and caught our minstrel troop in its path.'

'Oh dear,' Tyballis whispered. 'Both of them?'

George Switt's voice had faded to little more than a breath in the night. 'I nursed my beautiful wife and my blessed daughter. But they both died, both in my arms. So disfigured, and in such pain. I stumbled blind to their funerals.' He looked up at Tyballis, his eyes blood streaked. 'It would have been easier had the pestilence taken me with them. I dream of them still, you know, though this was many, many years ago. I never had the heart to look for another wife, but sometimes, in dear Felicia's precious little Ellen, I see something of my lost child Grace. I like to sit close to Ellen, you know, and pat her soft cheek as I once did with my own daughter. But Ellen is not too willing to come beside me, and I cannot blame the child. I am too ugly and old, and she already has a good father to cling to. But watching her brings my memories flooding back.'

George Switt died in the night. Tyballis was not quite sure when, for finally, distraught and exhausted, she slept deeply. She woke to blackness, the candle gutted, and a body cold and stiff beside her.

They did not know if the night was over, but they woke, one by one, and shuffled uncomfortably at the news, for they could not bury Mister Switt. Felicia started to cry. 'The fact is,' Ralph sighed, 'the man hasn't been shriven, and isn't likely to get a place in hallowed ground, lest those buggers let us out or Drew comes back.'

'That's not likely.' Tyballis shook her head, staring down at the man who had slept beside her that night. 'It depends if it's tomorrow yet. If it is, then Drew's been gone only a week, and that's no time to get to Yorkshire and back.'

'Then we must bang on the door,' said Ralph, 'and get these ruffians to call a priest.'

'And the children are hungry,' sniffed Felicia. 'They need food.'

'Reckon we all needs a sup o' beer, and deserves it, too,' advised Casper. 'So, tell us where it's hid, and let's get the ashes out our mouths.'

Ralph and Casper laid Mister Swit at the other end of the chamber on a straw pallet, and everyone sat at the opposite end and drank stale beer. They talked a great deal, but talking solved little.

'We had better start conserving candles,' Tyballis said, lighting only one.

'And how much of all else have we, then?' asked Ralph.

Jon was drinking deeply. 'I calculate,' he said, eyeing his wife, 'we have another three days at the very least before Mister Cobham returns. And at the most? Who knows? In the past he has often been gone for months.'

Felicia had not stopped crying. 'It is all my fault,' she wept, rocking Gyles on her lap. 'Dear Tybbs warned me, but it was too late. I told the address, you know, to a constable in the city. But he was a friend and knew dear Drew as Lord Feayton.' She blushed. 'He wishes to marry our Tybbs, and seemed such a trustworthy fellow. An appointed constable of the Ward, after all, who organises the Watch. But he must have told someone, for the very same week we have these brutes imprisoning us.' She buried her face against her husband's crumpled sleeve. 'And if we die of starvation,' she snuffled, 'it will be my little ones first, for they are hungry already. And it will all be my fault.'

'Assistant constable,' Tyballis corrected her. 'But we don't know if it was him who talked. I cannot see why he would tell some stranger where Lord Feayton lives – or why anyone would think to ask him about someone he barely knows. It is very confusing.'

'My good wife,' Jon said, sitting straight, 'is not to blame. Not for anything!' Felicia smiled gratefully up at him.

Casper drained his cup and said, 'All very well. But some bugger is. Maybe them bastards at Crosby's – though I don't reckon Mister Cobham told 'em where he lives neither.' He scrambled up and plodded back to the beer keg. 'Anyone for another sup?'

'That's all we have,' Tyballis warned him.

'Won't last all of us for three days though, let alone longer,' Casper smiled cheerfully. 'So, let's be having it now, and be done with worrying.'

Ralph marched to the door and began to ram both fists upon it. 'I'll keep this up till the bastards come,' he said. 'Or break the door down instead. This wood don't feel too strong, as it happens.'

Elizabeth had been curled in a corner, nose in her cup. Only recently recovered from her brother's assault, once again she was badly bruised. Now she looked up at Tyballis. 'You said there was knives kept here? Well, get us one, then. Anyone comes to this door, I'll murder the prick.'

Ralph looked down at her. 'And get your face kicked in again? You look after yourself, girl. I'll do the slaughtering.'

'An' me.' Casper bounced over. 'Give us a knife. Give us a table leg. If there's naught but a feather, I'll ram that down their bastard throats. Let me at the buggers.'

No one came to the door, it was not unlocked and it did not break in splinters. After many minutes shouting and hammering, Ralph slumped down beside Elizabeth, and Casper began to pace the floor, avoiding Mister Switt's lonely corner. Although the three younger children grizzled continuously, everyone was used to little food, had eaten a fair supper the evening before, and no one yet suffered the sharp discomfort of genuine hunger.

Time drifted unknown, and without natural light, there was a dreary confusion and a puzzlement, a sense of endless hours passing, of days without end. They began conversations, which then faded with no conclusion and were resumed much later. As each person moved, dust billowed, caught like star spangle in the candlelight, making them sneeze. Young Walter Spiers crawled to the body of the man he had once known, and pummelled it, trying to wake George Switt. Walter's mother dragged him away.

It seemed the day was nearly over when Elizabeth ran to the door, banging and screaming. 'Unlock us, you bastards,' she yelled. 'There's a dead man here, babies what won't stop whimpering and all of us hungry. Come take out the corpse at least.'

No one came.

In the candlelight Tyballis could not see if George Switt's face had become discoloured, but there was as yet no stink of decay. The body was no longer stiff, but lay a little crooked, eyelids closed gently over their pretty blue. The heat did not enter the storeroom, so whether the day was hot or cold made little difference. It would, Tyballis hoped, be some time before the remains began to rot.

Elizabeth came eventually and sat beside her. 'Them kids,' she whispered. 'Driving me mad, they are, with that bloody noise, on and on. No wonder that bugger Spiers sleeps all day and night.'

'You might have some of your own one day,' Tyballis murmured. 'Wouldn't you like Ralph's child?'

'After ten bloody years on the streets?' Elizabeth shook her head. 'Got rid of too many and don't reckon I'll get that way again. Jumped down the stairs twice, under a horse's hooves once. Lost all the poor little bastards, thank the Lord. Olly, my brother that is, he roughed me up and I lost the last one. That were four year ago. Ain't been no more since.' She smiled, unrepentant. 'What about you, then?'

'I can't have children,' Tyballis said. 'At least, after five years married I never even got pregnant.'

'Think yourself lucky,' Elizabeth told her. 'Don't reckon Drew would want none neither.'

Tyballis lowered her eyes. 'I suppose not. So, perhaps I should be glad. But there is always that sentimental thought. His baby in my arms. Him proud, standing beside me.'

'Oh pooh,' Elizabeth said. 'All the little bastards do is whine and whimper and puke. Your belly gets flabby and you feel old enough to start praying for a way out.'

A solitary candle, placed on a stool in the centre of the room, had almost burned away and the shadows were lengthening, like mouths awaiting the gluttony of darkness. Tyballis said, 'Is it night yet, do you think? Should we sleep?'

'Night? I reckon it's only midday,' Elizabeth said. 'Though sleep, if you want. We're not doing no good anyhow.'

Tyballis had started to reply, when she was interrupted. The noise from outside their door was unmistakeable. Ralph strode to the doorway and listened. 'More arriving,' he said gloomily. 'Weapons, clanking, orders shouted. There's a whole new troop of them.'

Jon moved to stand beside Ralph and Casper. 'They're shouting that the king's dead,' he said, white-faced. 'Done at last, they say. King

Edward is gone – official – and the queen has taken over the royal council.'

'She can't do that,' whispered Felicia. 'It isn't legal.'

'Nor is poisoning your monarch,' glowered Ralph. 'But it seems that's what some filth has finally achieved.'

CHAPTER FIFTY-ONE

After many days of vomiting and the flux, his highness King Edward had finally seemed on the point of recovery, sufficient to eat a hearty dinner and inform his doctors he intended leaving his bedchamber the following day. But by three of the clock on a sunny spring afternoon, everything had changed. With a bellow of pain, the king doubled over and vomited across his sheets. Then he lurched back against his pillows and called for ale. His tongue burned, he said, his lips stung him as though swollen by bees. His servants rushed to pour him a brimming cup, but when his highness drank, he spat and moaned, saying the beer was a foul brew. The doctors were called at once. But no royal purge was needed, for the king's body was racked with pain and he could not control either the diarrhoea or the spasms.

It was a slow death. By seven of the clock, his highness finally rolled back his eyes and slumped over. His great bed was a pit of excrement and vomit, his legs convulsed, his tongue was too swollen for his mouth, and he could neither speak nor see. At a few minutes past seven on the ninth day of April, the king was pronounced dead.

Her highness had been excluded from the sickroom for fear of contagion. Apart from doctors and servants, only the Lord Hastings had been permitted entrance. King Edward died in his friend's arms, and William, Baron Hastings wept and closed his sovereign's eyes, and knew that life would never be the same again. He left the chamber far older than when he had entered it, and went immediately to inform the queen. She had taken refuge in the royal antechamber, and was clinging to her son the Marquess of Dorset for comfort. She looked up, red-eyed, as Lord Hastings entered. He nodded, face pale. Her highness screamed. The marquess embraced her, murmuring comfort. Hastings turned on his heel and left the chamber.

Far across London's shadowed alleyways and beyond the eastern confines of the city wall, Cobham Hall stood amongst its wild and tangled gardens, light blazing from every downstairs window. Smoke puffed busy and black from the highest chimney but there was no peaceful domesticity around the fireside. The upper floor was dark and empty, but in the principal hall twenty men and more discussed and argued, determining what each should do, would do and hoped to do. The four men previously occupying the hall now held no authority, stated the newly arrived captain. His was the only right to leadership, and he would give the orders and expect to be obeyed. The king was dead. They would soon follow the wishes of the Marquess of Dorset, who intended raising an army, and until Lord Feayton could be apprehended and restrained, the house and Feayton's friends and servants within it was to be guarded, its doors kept locked.

'You'll do as I say, Murch,' the captain said, hand to his sword hilt, 'or my men will round up yours and execute the bloody lot. Now, who've you gone and got locked up here? And how do you know one ain't secretly Feayton? You've never met the man. I have, but all I noticed was that bloody big broken nose.'

Murch glowered and stuck his thumbs through his belt. 'They say he's a huge ugly bugger not easy forgot, with eyes black as coals. None here like that, nor none dressed fancy like no lord neither. We got one skinny fellow, a trio o' trollops, a parcel of snivelling brats, some ancient bugger, a quiet pallid fool what fathered them kids, and a one-eyed street fighter with a foul mouth. A right barmy household for a lord, I reckon.'

'Could be in disguise,' muttered the captain.

Murch objected. 'How's a large gent going to disguise hisself as a little 'un, then?' He sniggered, looking back for approbation to his three remaining ruffians. 'This lord is unusual tall. Big as the king, I were told.'

'The late king,' the other man corrected him.

'With big shoulders, strong as an ox, they say, dark as a heathen, and a face all squashed like some wrestler from the Southwark slums. We's no one locked up in there looks even a close shave to that.'

The captain nodded. 'I'll take over now, then. You lot can bugger off. Spread the word through the city at first light. Tell how the king's dead, the Marquess of Dorset is in charge, the mighty Lord Marrott by his side, and a new rule's on its way.'

Those in the adjacent storeroom heard tramping feet as Murch and his men left the house, slamming the doors behind them. Meanwhile Captain Hetchcomb organised his troops. 'You, sweep up this mess. The place stinks of charred wood, blood and shit. I want it clean if I've to camp here for God knows how long. You, into the kitchens and sort out food and drink. There must be something stored there worth the taking. Meanwhile I'll be checking on the prisoners.'

He came with four men at his back, but he entered the storeroom alone. The men behind him held torches, a stream of light pouring like sudden liquid gold through the interior shadows. Warned by the grating of the key at the door, Ralph, Casper and the others sat quietly. They looked up as the captain strode in, and rubbed their eyes at the glare of sudden light. 'Your bastard friend killed a good man,' said Ralph. 'He's lying dead back there. He needs a Christian burial.'

Captain Hetchcomb stared down at them all. 'Get up, you scum, and address me with respect. Let me see you.'

No one moved. Then Casper grinned wide and toothless. 'We wants food and drink, and the corpse took out and treated decent. Then we'll think about a little cooperation. But forget respect. That ain't never coming your way.'

On the verge of losing his temper, the captain suddenly changed his mind. 'I'll make no deals with you treacherous rabble,' he said, 'but for the moment, I want you buggers alive.' He turned to his men. 'Fetch beer and bread, if you can find any. Not too much, mind. Alive, yes, but weak and compliant is how I want 'em. And if there's some carcass stinking the place in here, get it out. Sling the body out the back in the chicken shed where the other four dead buggers is piled.'

Ralph stood abruptly. 'We demand fair treatment,' he said. 'We're nobody's enemy and have done nothing except defend ourselves from thieves breaking into our home. If you're looking for Lord Feayton, then look elsewhere, for he's not here, nor will be. Try looking at Westminster.'

Jon Spiers stood nervously beside Ralph. 'We have small children,' he mumbled, 'needing warmth and food. Why do you keep us prisoner?'

'With the king dead,' the captain announced, 'there's a new power in the city. It's the Marquess of Dorset giving the orders, and you'll do best to remember that. Do as you're told, or suffer for it.'

George Switt's body was hauled across the dusty boards. 'We'll have the boots from that one,' one of the men muttered. 'Better than mine, they is, and more or less the same size, by the look of them.'

'Take what you likes,' the captain growled over his shoulder. 'But hurry up and get the bugger out. Now, bread and beer for this lot, and a hearty meal for the rest of us. I've missed my dinner and will need a proper breakfast afore sun-up.'

It was a little later that a small keg of beer was brought in, and an armful of black bread. Ralph immediately rationed both. The children stopped crying and munched, grouped around Felicia's legs. Tyballis waved the bread away. 'A day without food won't hurt me,' she murmured. 'I haven't the heart for eating.'

'Eat up, girl,' Elizabeth insisted. 'We've plans to make.'

'No plan turns time backwards,' sighed Ralph. 'If the king is dead indeed, then all Drew's efforts are for nothing.' He chewed the stale cheat, and gulped a mouthful of beer. 'Seems the Woodvilles took charge already. Rivers will bring the prince from Ludlow with an armed guard. Then if Drew comes back with the Duke of Gloucester, it'll be war.'

'Rivers can't leave Wales yet,' Tyballis shook her head. 'He'll need to mourn his king whether it's genuine or not. We know it's five days' ride from Yorkshire. It's maybe less from Ludlow. Perhaps they'll all arrive in London together.'

'If'n we's still alive to see,' sniffed Casper, finishing his beer.

Not knowing when they might receive more, they conserved their candles, the beer and the bread. Shuffling drearily through the shadows, they wrapped blankets around their shoulders, and sat on their spread mattresses, keeping close for warmth. They heard their captors, but saw no more of them for some time. Two chamber pots, found amongst the stored furniture, were placed at the far end of the room, but these soon overflowed and could not be emptied. The smaller children, dragging soaked nether-cloths, pissed where they sat, which included their elders' laps. Ralph, Felicia and Tyballis told stories of Sir Gawain and King Arthur. Each of the group told their own personal histories, embellished a little to add spice and flavour. They spoke of what they feared, and what they hoped. They discussed what they might do to escape from their imprisonment, and of what they imagined was happening beyond their walls. Jon and Felicia's children played, desultory and hungry, then with sudden bursts of energy as one small boy chased another and both hurtled into sobbing balls as they collided. The baby Gyles sickened and stayed in his mother's arms or clung to his sister Ellen. Hour after hour she trotted the room's length, jiggling the whining baby on her small skinny hip while his piss and vomit trickled down her skirt, her precious new dress now stinking and ragged.

News of the king's passing was sent out to every city, every great lord's castle and every township. Messengers galloped to the Welsh Marches and the uneasy borders with Scotland. All across the land unrest grew, folk dragged to their churches for the great dirge, wondering how it could have happened and fearing what might happen next. Foreign spies sent surmise and slanderous gossip back to their own sovereigns, while official letters with the royal seal of England arrived at exactly the same time, carrying news far more succinct, far less scurrilous and considerably less interesting. The Holy Roman Emperor, the Duke of Burgundy, the monarchs of Spain and the various doges of the Italian states were notified immediately. The French King Louis XI was informed, and sat back, well satisfied. In his exile in Brittany, Henry Tudor heard, and smiled. In all these places, and all across England, rumour travelled as fast as the official messengers, and while fact spoke of a lingering illness ending in the royal death from some unexplained cause, rumour spoke of strange and unnatural diseases, of portents, of sinful luxuries, of debauchery, gluttony and poison.

As his highness lay in state in a lead-lined coffin within the Abbey, so her highness the queen, her eldest son at her back, began to manoeuvre for ultimate power. It was they who summoned a meeting of the late king's council. The Marquess of Dorset, for all the late king's friendship, had never been a political advisor, simply an ally and companion in lechery. But he now entered the council chamber with his mother, claiming to represent the young king-to-be and as such was not denied. The existing council members, under mounting duress, took sides. Few dared oppose the close Woodville relatives of an imminent child-king.

Dorset and the dowager queen placed themselves at the council's head and conducted business. Principal amongst matters awaiting a decision was the date of the coronation. Once crowned, though a twelve years minor, the new king might choose his own advisors, and he was already his mother's son long controlled by his maternal uncle. Prince Edward, in his uncle's protective custody, was now officially called to the capital from his home in distant Ludlow. Her highness, as if the ultimate authority, signed the document.

'My son must come with a grand cavalcade,' the queen advised. 'There is considerable unrest in London. My dearest brother Earl Rivers is already authorised to raise armed troops in the prince's name. Now he will exercise that right. The new sovereign shall arrive safeguarded by a mighty procession.'

Lord Hastings glared. 'Madam. A king does not arrive in his capital city equipped for war against his own people. I'll not countenance any force of arms.'

Dorset banged his fist upon the table. 'You'll risk the boy's assassination? What treachery is this?'

'The people don't threaten their future king,' Hastings roared. 'It's the Woodville upstarts they hate, not their beloved king's son.'

The queen, having seated herself at the head of the table, now stood abruptly with a rustle of silk skirts. 'Speak against me, and you speak treason, my lord,' she said calmly. 'Speak against the Marquess of Dorset, and you insult the new king's stepbrother. Will you risk the new king's displeasure before he is even crowned, sir?'

'A threat I'll long remember, my lady,' Hastings said. 'And not all power is yet Woodville power. I still hold power enough to defend myself. And the Duke of Gloucester is not yet arrived.'

Dorset laughed, leaned back in his chair and stretched his long golden legs. 'Gloucester? His power lies only in the north. In the rest of England, we are so important that even without the king's uncle we can make and enforce these decisions.'

'I will reluctantly agree a royal entourage of only two thousand men,' smiled the queen, once more seating herself. 'I trust that will suffice. So small a force can surely attract no objections?' She looked around. The gentlemen of the council looked down and nodded obediently. 'Very well, then,' her highness continued, 'let us agree the date of the coronation. The fourth day of May, in two weeks' time, has been suggested. Shall we agree?'

'What of the Duke of Gloucester?' Hastings again insisted. 'He is named Lord Protector and Defender of the realm in his late highness's testament. His grace should therefore be present before any such agreement is made. He must first be consulted.'

'Gloucester again?' Dorset stared at each furrowed face around the council table. 'The Lord Protector shall have a voice but so must the king's maternal family. Let us have no more argument. Once our new sovereign is crowned, he may speak for himself and decide his own advisors.'

Hastings narrowed his eyes. 'There are many of you here who fear to antagonise our new sovereign's family. But I say the king is yet twelve years old and needs the guidance of the Lord Protector, a man long experienced in politics, who was chosen by the late king himself. I took it upon myself to inform Richard of Gloucester of the king his brother's death. And I shall inform him further, of everything that now occurs in the council chambers. Decide as you wish, but when the duke arrives, I warn you, this Woodville monopoly will shatter.'

CHAPTER FIFTY-TWO

They did not know how long it had been. Ellen had scratched marks on the wall panelling above her mattress, but no one was sure when each day began or ended. Interminable and uncountable time dragged slowly, and the guards who brought them beer and bread refused to answer questions. Most of the guards refused to speak at all.

'Five days,' Felicia said. 'Though I am hungry enough for ten.'

Ralph shook his head. 'Three, no more.'

'I reckon eight,' insisted Casper. 'Nigh ready to scream, I is. Bin expecting Mister Cobham for a bloody age.'

'I done scratched ten scratches, so's it's ten days,' said Ellen.

'You can't even count,' said Elizabeth.

'Three – four – it doesn't matter how many,' sighed Tyballis. 'Drew isn't back, the king is dead, we are being slowly starved and for all we know, war may already be raging in the streets outside. We have to do something.'

'Indeed, we must find a way or I cannot answer for the consequences,' said Felicia, holding her nose. 'This stench – the foul vapours! Is this a dungeon, or a chamber in a respectable house? Then beat a hole in the wall to clear this filth, or Gyles' death will be on your consciences.'

Tyballis had been sitting beside Ellen. With Ellen's small bare legs across her lap, she was darning the child's skirts where the dark green worsted, once part of her own gown, had badly torn. She looked up suddenly, pricking her thumb with the darning needle. 'That's it,' she said, immediately excited, and stood up in a rush. 'Knock a hole in the wall. Perhaps we really could.'

'Mistress Spiers,' said Casper with faint contempt, 'weren't talking serious. But since it's her brats what does most of the shitting, maybe she'd like to start kicking the wall down herself. I reckon I'll just sit and snigger.'

'While our friendly guards comes a running to see what all the bastard noise is about,' Elizabeth said, tossing her curls.

'No, no.' Tyballis, now standing, was staring down at them all. 'We don't bang a hole through. We cut one. I really believe we might be able to do it.'

'How long we bin here? And you only just thought of it?'

'It didn't occur to me,' explained Tyballis. 'And it still might not work. You see, this was never built as a proper room. Hasn't anyone noticed how flimsy those walls are, and how they rattle and shake every time a door is slammed outside?'

'Whole house shakes,' said Ralph gloomily. 'Wait long enough, the bloody lot will tumble.'

'It is rather ramshackle,' sighed Tyballis. 'But this chamber is the worst. There was a minstrel's gallery once. You can tell by how it's been enclosed and divided. Drew uses the next little room as a sort of study and between that room and this, the division is hardly a wall at all, just planks. An axe would be best but we have none. With the two knives I found, we could try and cut through.'

'And then what?' asked Felicia, breathless.

'Into the next chamber – and escape.' Tyballis kept her voice low. 'Drew's study leads directly down to his bedchamber with no intervening door, and from there his garderobe has access to the gardens.'

'Through the cesspit?'

'There's a back corridor,' Tyballis said. 'It goes to the kitchens and out to the pantries and sheds. Haven't any of you looked around there?'

'We have always respected Mister Cobham's private quarters,' said Felicia with dignity. 'But now – well, I do think – Jon, my dear? Do you agree?'

Jon Spiers was curled small on a mattress in the furthest shadows, peacefully asleep, one of his sons in his arms. Ralph spoke in his place. 'No matter who else agrees, I say we start right now. Which wall is it? I got one of the knives. Who's got the other?' Casper waved his steel. 'Then get your back to this wall,' Ralph said, 'and hold it steady. I'll get the knife point in, and work it.'

One knife point broke, but pushing and twisting for nearly an hour, they finally cracked the veneer and forced through to air. A tiny pulse of light glimmered beyond. 'That's it, saints be. A beautiful buggering hole, it is,' chuckled Casper. 'Well, my lovelies, we's on our way.'

'A fiddlin' pin prick, and it's taken an age. Now to cut a hole big enough to climb through?' Elizabeth sighed. 'I swear it'll take a bloody week.'

'Let's to it, then,' Casper said.

Earl Rivers, magnificent in black velvet, rode out from Ludlow Castle on a bright sunny morning, his elegant young nephew riding at his side. Behind him marched two thousand men, called to prove their duty to their monarch. It was the twenty-fourth day of April. Although his late highness was already two weeks gone, no rush had been made to lead the new king to his people. There had been the required church services, and the son given some peace in which to mourn his father. There were also other considerations. Rivers would not leave too much time between his charge arriving in London and the programmed coronation. The least possible opportunity should be left for the Lord Protector to take the reins, or to manoeuvre barriers between the king's Woodville family and the power they intended to claim. The coronation would take place on the fourth day of May. Earl Rivers planned the uncrowned sovereign's arrival in London for two days before. There would be no allowance made for the Woodvilles to be thwarted in the final hours.

Richard, Duke of Gloucester, meanwhile made his own plans. Conflicting messages had thrown Middleham Castle into turmoil. First a henchman, a secret messenger from allies at Portsoken, had brought the information the duke had been dreading. The mighty Lord Marrott was surely now in possession of the poison long kept from his grasp. The duke's spy made two matters clear. Neither the complicity of Earl Rivers, nor that of the Marquess of Dorset could be proved. It was conceivable that Lord Marrott acted alone, but act he would. So, it was with terrible sadness but no surprise that his grace soon received the news that his brother the king had died.

The great Requiem Mass had already been held at York Minster when the duke's own trusted liegeman galloped into the castle courtyard with different news, for the king lived. His highness had been dangerously ill but was now recovering. Then, some days afterwards, the dreaded message arrived, coming at great speed and with the Lord Hastings' seal. This time, without doubt, the king was dead.

There were two further messages, each written in haste, and finally two more. Amongst these was an official reckoning of the late king's Will and Testament, and of the codicils added on his highness's deathbed. This document made Richard, Duke of Gloucester, Protector and Defender of the Realm during the new king's minority. Her highness the dowager queen was no longer named as an executor, and was excluded from all specific benefit.

Some letters were quickly dispatched onwards to the mayor at York, while others, those more personal, were read and reread as the duke sat first alone in his private chamber before the great fire, then later in discussion with his quiet companion Lord Feayton, and finally together with his official advisors. The duke replied to Lord Hastings, considering his options. He sent his official condolences to the dowager queen, although she had chosen to make no contact with him, and he included a warning to the king's council. As the Protector, he trusted they would conduct business in accordance with law and tradition. One of Hastings' letters had related how they were doing no such thing. 'After endless argument, the king's entourage has been restricted to two thousand,' Hastings wrote. 'Your grace will, I trust, ride with an equal number.'

Letters were also sent to the new king, reiterating the duke's loyalty, his condolences and his intention of conducting the prince's entrance into London.

'We will assuredly meet upon the road,' Earl Rivers wrote back.

The Duke of Buckingham, behind the Duke of Gloucester the highest peer in the land but inexperienced and previously eclipsed by Woodville alliances, now came forward to announce his own intention of primary involvement. There would be a new order, new loyalties and new preferences. It was his time. He wrote to Richard of Gloucester. Messengers, their frothing mounts clattering across the castle's courtyards, arrived daily, and left again without delay.

Gloucester prepared to leave Yorkshire and ride south. But he would not, he said, lead any armed force, nor appear in aggression against either the people or his king. Only three hundred men, mounted but unarmed, were ordered to make ready. He had spent many days considering all possibilities and once decided, the duke's decisions were immovable. His decision was also based on information, uncovered by those he used for such matters, that Earl Rivers hoped to arrive in London while his grace of Gloucester was still on the road. The duke therefore planned, with a small mounted retinue, to make greater haste than Rivers would expect. They rode out on the twenty-third day of April. The sky was dull and clouded.

Clambering one by one, edging through a gap barely large enough for a dog, swallowing back excitement and keeping careful silence, each dishevelled prisoner made their escape. The children were carried, hands tight over their mouths in case of squeals. Finally, clothes snagged on splinters, everyone crawled to freedom.

Beyond their prison, the little studio chamber at Cobham Hall was unlit and the small window showed no light. After uncountable time in darkness, they had longed for light and for clarity. There was none. Tyballis tiptoed to the window, peeping out. 'We thought it was daytime, but look, it's night. There are stars, but no moon.'

'It's better,' Ralph whispered back. 'These brutes will be asleep. The dark will hide us.'

'They'll have set guards.'

Elizabeth grunted. 'Maybe not. Let's find out.'

Ralph crept to the mouth of the tiny spiral stair, testing each step. There was neither hindrance nor sound. He turned back to the others crowding behind him, and nodded. The children, warned and threatened with consequences too terrible to consider, were frightened. Felicia nursed Gyles. Jon carried Walter. Ellen took Edmund's small cold hand. Behind them the stench of their prison lingered.

Pushing Tyballis forwards as the only one who knew the way, they followed in single file. Terrified of alerting the guards, she crept down the narrow winding steps into Andrew's grand bedchamber below. Only she and Elizabeth had ever been permitted here before but there was no time for curiosity. Before their capture, Tyballis had straightened the bedclothes, and saw they had not been disturbed since. No one had explored here. There was no sign of anyone. Everyone now hesitated, listening for the sounds of alarm or of footsteps. There was nothing.

The garderobe door leading to the rear corridor and the gardens was locked but Tyballis knew where the key was kept, and lifted it soundlessly from its mat beside the privy. She took a deep breath as the door squeaked. For a moment no one moved. Then they ran.

The shadows danced. Leaf and bough swept past them, a crunch of stone, the squelch of mulched leaf fall, a tiny yelp as thorns scratched Edmund's arm, and then the gates were before them, standing wide. The alley beyond was deserted. Three men, three women and four children quickly disappeared into the night.

The Lord Hastings tirelessly fought his adversaries on the council, gradually winning the agreement of those who had backed the Woodvilles only through fear or pragmatism. Hastings was not pragmatic, nor fearful. He threatened physical attack; he threatened to leave and muster troops at Calais; and he threatened, with oblique disdain, to inform the people regarding the cause of the late king's death. Those who knew nothing stared, suspicious or confused. But Dorset flushed, leaning angry-eyed across the table. 'My Lord Hastings,' he said under his breath, 'if you have proof of some wrongdoing, then we shall – all – be pleased to know it. Proof, I repeat, would be of great interest to everyone. Speak now, or keep your peace.'

The dowager queen lifted one high arched eyebrow as Hastings watched her reactions closely. 'My lord Hastings tries to make himself important,' she said, waving her fingers in symbolic dismissal. 'He threatens, and he hints at secrets. A wretched mummery indeed. My husband died three weeks gone, and nothing has been said in all that time, yet my lord now pretends special knowledge? Enough. There is important business to resolve here.'

Hastings licked his lips. Every eye was fixed on him, waiting. 'Ah yes, the matter of proof,' he sighed. 'Proof there may be. But proof of what, I wonder? So, for now let us proceed with the business at hand.'

A buzz of uncertainty surrounded the table. The councillors appeared increasingly uncomfortable. The Duke of Gloucester had sent warning messages, had announced his intention of imminent arrival in the city, and had accepted the position of Lord Protector of the Realm in accordance with the late king's urgent desire. 'But my son's desires are now the sole consideration,' the dowager queen pointed out. 'Edward will undoubtedly decide to remain under the protection and guidance of my brother Earl Rivers, his long-time guardian, also appointed by the late king. This new Protector is simply one amongst many, and may have his seat at the council if he wishes.'

'The Duke of Gloucester,' answered Hastings, 'is specifically named as Protector of the Realm. He is not simply one amongst many. It is the duke who must govern for some years to come.'

'Prince Edward's minority will end when he is crowned,' Dorset insisted. 'There will be no further need of a Protector.'

Already the Woodvilles had begun authorising the collection of taxes and the nomination of title and entitlement. Although lacking legal imperative, Dorset had appointed Sir Edward Woodville, his uncle, as commander of the king's navy. His own improperly nominated position as Deputy Constable of The Tower gave him no such authority, but he sat himself at the head of the king's council and would not be gainsaid. Many councillors, however, were considering their own vulnerability should the Lord Protector's powers be curtailed. Finally, with some courage, they insisted the guardianship of the little king be utterly forbidden to his mother's relatives. But their sovereign-to-be was already on the road under the protection of his Woodville uncle, and was likely to remain as such by his own choice.

CHAPTER FIFTY-THREE

Andrew Cobham leaned back against the settle's cushions, stretched his long legs and put his feet up on the small trunk by the busy, blazing hearth. He then clasped his hands behind his head, sighed and closed his eyes.

Within the darkness of his own eyelids, he saw many things. He saw the great wide skies sweep serenely over a green and beautiful land. He saw the beauty ravished by an endless winding and shadowed procession of past mistake, misrule, lust and avarice. He saw the feet of armies marching across the gold-tipped hills, the sudden flash of armour in the sun and the blood-red agony of battle, pain and death.

And he saw the faces of the people who had influenced his own life. Two women. Four men. An older woman, tired and shrunken, crouching in a squalid barn amongst the hay, shielding her face with her arm and muttering madness. A man, snarling, spitting, raising his axe. Then those figures diminishing – replaced – another man, tall but elderly. Quiet, dignified, ugly, contemptuous. The old man looked away and turned his back. Then a boy approaching manhood. Frightened, crying, demanding help, beseeching, but discovering the sweet spite of treachery inspired by envy. The fourth and last man strode quickly forwards from memory's shadows, and brought with him the hopeful sun. He stood a moment, haloed by light. Not a tall man but imperious and confident, kind-eyed, decisive, loyal and determined.

Andrew sighed. Then he saw the final face; swimming in light, smiling through his thoughts. She was young and fair and beautiful, and she reached out her naked arms to him. He blinked and opened his eyes.

'My lord. You did not call. But I have come, if you wish it.' A maidservant from the castle's laundries, who had, of course, no right in his bedchamber.

Andrew regarded her for a long minute. He knew the girl well. She had come to his bed on many occasions over the years when he visited Middleham, and had always been welcomed. It was not a matter either approved or condoned in this castle of genial propriety, though an easy comfort pervaded in spite of the draughts. The duke had designed improvements to the old stone edifice, enlarging windows to let in sunshine and light. He had never been a man of shadows. Richard, Duke of Gloucester loved the light and he loved to look out on the huge wild scenery of Yorkshire, the dales and rolling green slopes. He had ordered similar improvements to windows at Crosby's, his London home. But this was not Westminster, and the lord of the castle was not his brother King Edward whose mistresses laughed openly in his wife's presence. Guests were not encouraged in sports less respectable than falconry and hunting. Yet what a man did in his bedchamber was his own business, and when the pages, the dogs and the squires were sent running from the room, they were trained to carry no gossip.

Andrew watched the girl as she started to undress, unpinning her starched cap first to let her long brown curls tumble to her waist. He had forgotten her name but she was plump and pretty and her body would be warm. He leaned forwards, his fingers to her ringlets, flicking them back. She stood a moment, naked to the hips where her shift still clung, waiting for him to take her. His palms encircled her narrow waist, holding her steady a moment. Then he gently pushed her away.

'My lord?'

'No, girl.' He shook his head. 'This is not what I want. I need to be alone.' He closed his eyes once again. The other face, the young and beautiful woman of his meandering fancies, flew back as if winged. Wide smiling eyes, sky blue, tentative, hopeful and adoring. When Andrew opened his eyes again, the little laundress had dressed and gone. He was alone as he had asked to be, but did not want to be at all.

The Portsoken streets leading down to the river were utterly deserted. There was no one ahead and there was no one following. Ralph, his arm around Elizabeth, turned to Casper and Tyballis. He whispered. 'We need to scatter – go separate ways. Hide, or run. If anyone comes after us now, we've no protection at all.'

'You have the only sword from the storeroom,' Tyballis whispered back.

'To defend all of us against a whole troop of armed guards? They'd kill us – every one of us – in minutes.'

Felicia, Gyles clutched against her chest and her other arm tight through her husband's, was white-faced in the fluttering starlight. 'But surely we need to keep together. There's safety in numbers. And I suppose we should aim for London.'

'At this time of night?' Ralph shook his head. 'Every gate is barred against us, and there's no gain in London anyway.'

'Crowds,' insisted Tyballis. 'In a crowd, we're safe. And we need to find out what's going on.'

'We know what's going on. The king's dead. Dorset has snatched power.'

'But has the new king sanctioned this? What of the Duke of Gloucester? And what of Drew?'

'If Drew was back in London,' grumbled Jon, 'he would have come home. He would have come to save us.'

'He often goes to Crosby's,' whispered Tyballis. 'He couldn't have known we'd been imprisoned. And perhaps he's with the duke, so can't come home at will.'

'There ain't no point arguing,' Casper interrupted. 'Should 'ave thought o' this afore. Too late now. Must all do what we wants. Don't need no leader giving orders, nor making no plans. I'll go where I decides.'

Tyballis looked at her toes. 'All right. Then I'll go to London alone. I'll wait till morning for the gate to be unlocked.'

'You'll wait outside the Aldgate?' exclaimed Ralph, shocked. 'That's the first place those buggers'll look for us. Wait there, and you'll be dragged back within an hour at most. And with them angry guards! I'd not like to guess what'd happen next.'

'I know the Portsoken best,' muttered Elizabeth. 'Them's my streets, my tramping ground. I'll stay this side o' the wall, and hide back in the tanneries. There's folks there who know Drew and will help me.' She looked up at Ralph's protective shoulder. 'You coming with me? Or her?'

'You,' Ralph said at once. 'I won't be risking you back in your wretched brother's clutches. Besides, we're a couple now and that's the way I want it. But Tybbs, I'll see you safe first.'

'Nonsense,' Tyballis sniffed. 'I can look after myself. I've been doing it long enough.'

Jon stepped forward. 'My responsibility is to my family,' he said, standing solid. 'My wife, my children. I have a friend lives the other side of the tanneries. A little farm he has, with pigs and cabbages. I'm taking my family there, quick as I can. Tyballis, you want to come with us – then come. I'll lead.'

She shook her head. 'No. Once Drew gets back I want to know about it. I don't want to hide where he can't find me.'

Everyone looked at each other. The night was cold. The children were shivering. 'Hurry,' Jon said, nodding to Felicia. 'I'll waste no more time talking.'

Casper turned to Tyballis. 'Reckon I'll go with you, and don't much care where. London – Jerusalem – don't matter to me neither way. So, how's about it, my Lady Feayton? You'll let yer old gaol mate look after yer again?'

Within minutes each group had separated from the others, scurrying into the darkness. Tyballis felt her eyes water and hoped it was the cold. She looked at Casper and said softly, 'Thank you. But if you'd prefer—'

Casper grinned. 'What I'd prefer,' he said, 'is to get a bastard move on. Ain't no point getting nabbed now. You want London? Then it's the river for us.' And he took hold of her elbow, steering her quickly into the narrow alley leading directly south.

Tyballis whispered, 'The river? Is that – quite – necessary?'

'Ain't no choice,' Casper said cheerfully. 'Want into the city this time o' the night? Thames is the only way. 'Sides, 'tis a proper sweet sight, the Thames. Heart of London, it is, and swells a Londoner's heart with pride. Not that I'll be wanting you to swim, mind you. I'll thieve us a boat. You just leave it to me.'

Andrew left Middleham Castle in the duke's personal entourage. Under the title of Lord Feayton, he rode a short way behind the duke, but some way ahead of the steady tramp of the attendant retainers. It was a small muster; three hundred Yorkshire men, unarmed and cheerful as the pale spring sunshine attempted to break through the cloud cover.

The Duke of Gloucester had not taken Mister Cobham fully into his confidence, but prior to leaving Middleham he had talked with him at some length.

'I have no proof,' the duke said. 'I will never forgive and I will never forget. But I cannot order Dorset's nor Rivers' executions without naming cause.'

Andrew bowed his head. 'I had proof only against Lord Marrott, your grace. But even that was lost to me. Something more yet may be found.'

The duke was leaning against the wall by the long alcoved window, his elbow to the stone. He looked out across the dales, and spoke softly to the sky. 'I know the Woodvilles. Before long they will incriminate themselves in one manner or another. Their own appetites will ensure it.'

Andrew stood by the hearth. It was empty of fire, and a great copper urn stood instead, filled with the rustle of dried flowers and wild grasses. 'Will you have me stay in London, your grace, to watch them, and all those who threaten the peace? Some of the foreign spies are still active: Mancini, Brassard, Dominguez. Lady Richmond's man Bray still keeps in regular contact with her son Henry Tudor. Colyngbourne also remains much involved.'

The duke looked back at Andrew over his shoulder. 'Between you and Brampton, you have given great service, Mister Cobham. It must certainly continue. The worst has now happened. But there will be more to come.'

'My lord.' Andrew bowed slightly. 'There have been mistakes, but I believe most were unavoidable. Edward Brampton, William Catesby and myself are always at your service. You know this.'

'You finally admit to trust, Mister Cobham?' The duke strode back, seating himself at a small table. He took up the quill, dipping the nib into the bowl of gall ink. 'You work in consort with Brampton and Catesby, and now trust their counsel?'

Andrew smiled. 'They trust mine, your grace.'

The duke laughed and handed over the small folded parchment on which he had written. 'My signed pledge of funds,' he said, 'which should cover your needs, as well as mine with regards to further service. Take this to the Chamberlain's office when we arrive in London.'

'You mean to leave at once, my lord?'

'At first light the day after tomorrow,' said the duke, 'and you will accompany me. I intend meeting up with Rivers and my nephew on the road within six days. If the earl cooperates in good faith, I may bide my time for retribution. But I would prefer he never reaches London.'

Andrew smiled again, eyes narrowed. 'I am at your service, my lord,' he repeated.

The duke shook his head. 'Not that way, my friend. You know my beliefs. This must all be legal, and if possible, seen to be legal. What is more, it must be just. His late highness entrusted me with the position of Protector and I mean to fulfil that trust to the utmost of my ability.

You know my mind and my opinions on loyalty and justice. That cannot include assassination in the dark.'

Andrew Cobham was quite prepared to do it in daylight. But he said only, 'As you wish, your grace. I shall be honoured to ride at your back.'

Both within the city walls and without, the people of London were frightened, often confused, and frequently angry. Armed ruffians strutted the streets, showing the Woodville livery and Dorset's badge. Others wearing no badge of any kind still claimed special orders and could not be refuted, robbing at knife point and at will, taking advantage of conflicting direction and mistrust. Both London sheriffs organised their voluntary constables and doubled the Watch. Despite this, fear mustered its own insecurities. No honest man willingly walked the dark alleys except in company, and no woman ventured out alone. The people feared the consequences of a child on the throne, knowing France sat large and hungry across the Narrow Sea, the French King Louis a spider waiting and watching from his throne. Even more they feared a local war. The Duke of Gloucester's appointment had been publicly announced, but the new Lord Protector lived in the north, and they had no news of him. Each day crowds gathered at St Paul's Cross, hoping for an end to confusion. Council business was not made public, but they quickly knew when Woodville agents came collecting taxes, and there was talk of a new naval commander, a Woodville lord busy arming his ships.

At the law courts, down Goldsmith's Row and through the Cheaps, in markets and shops, business continued as usual. At the docks, at the warehouses, the steelyard, wharves, wherry ranks and fishing piers, trade remained brisk. All across the land the spreading farms, villages, townships, monasteries and great estates prospered. Life bustled, ebbed and bustled again. But each man eyed his neighbour with new suspicion, kept his sword hilt close to hand as he walked the streets, and feared beginning any new commerce until the future became once again secure.

Some trust was put in Lord Hastings, for 'Surely he is a lord much experienced in political duties.' Yet the recent arrival of the Duke of Buckingham upon the scene, with his sudden show of noisy cavalcade riding London's streets from Westminster to The Tower and his proclamation of loyalty to the Lord Protector, was noticed more with nervous perplexity than hope. Indeed, when it was known that he had departed with intention of joining the Duke of Gloucester upon the road south, folk were glad to see him leave. The country's mighty lords, without a king or leader to hold them in check, were good for business but not for peaceful nights.

And the Duke of Gloucester, named Lord Protector but still absent from the city, had once brought peace to the Scottish borders, but might now bring battle to the city streets. His motto was loyalty, his proven record of discipline and trust, and his known prowess in battle meant a man who would not countenance a Woodville snatch and grab. But he had not yet arrived in the city, nor had the new young king.

An arrangement had already been agreed, messengers galloping between Middleham and Ludlow, that the Duke of Gloucester and Earl Rivers should meet and combine their forces, finally entering London together and with the Protector at the young king's side. Yet, following the great Watling Street from the Welsh Marches, the king's party did not divert, nor look to delay their progress. It was as they camped overnight at the small village of Stony Stratford that word was brought of the Duke of Gloucester's speedy and unexpected arrival at Northampton, not far distant. The earl regarded the messenger with controlled anger.

'My lord,' the messenger spoke quickly, 'his grace of Gloucester travels fast, with a small well-mounted retinue.'

Secure in the knowledge that his sister the dowager queen and his nephew the Marquess of Dorset would have begun to secure their influence as the king's declining health became obvious, and even before his death took place, Earl Rivers had good reason to believe the greater powers in London would already be Woodville adherents. He had therefore, considering it advisable for the new king to enter London in company of himself and not the Protector, planned to arrive at least a full day ahead of the Duke of Gloucester. That the Protector's smaller retinue had enabled a faster journey than Rivers had expected was unfortunate.

'You need not ride to Northampton to meet his grace,' Earl Rivers explained to his royal charge. 'We are already nearer London, and since that is our ultimate objective, there seems little gain in tiresome diversions. No doubt your highness is already tired?'

'Not entirely, uncle.' The king was cautious.

'You must sleep, my boy,' the earl said. 'I shall ride back myself and inform his grace of your intentions. Without an explanation, Gloucester is as likely to come galloping up here, troops at his back. That's something I mean to avoid. Leave everything to me. I shall ride to meet him, but will be back here with you in the morning.'

The new king, nervous, excited and inexperienced, as usual took his Uncle Rivers' advice.

CHAPTER FIFTY-FOUR

The river was not in flood and the tide was low, lying smooth between her banks. But Tyballis stood on the little swaying pier, staring down in terror at the water between the cracks. Casper, already on his knees and leaning over to unhook one of the bobbing wherry boats, looked back at her over his shoulder.

'Expecting storms, is we?'

'No – it isn't – I'm not.' Tyballis clasped her hands, keeping them still. 'But I have to admit being a little nervous of the river.'

'Bleedin' water's flat enough for them ducks to sleep on,' Casper objected. 'And so low I can see the turds at the bottom. Look,' he pointed.

Tyballis shook her head. 'There's rocks,' she whispered, 'over there. I can see them peeping up out of the waves.'

'There ain't no waves,' Casper insisted. 'What's the matter with you, lady? And them's ain't bloody rocks neither – them's just reflections. Buggering stars, they is. Now talking o' rocks – down past Southampton I seen a ship come in once, full sail with waves at her stern would put the fear of the devil into a bishop. Crushed on the rocks, it were, with bloody splinters and men screaming—'

'Please don't,' begged Tyballis. 'I have a shocking fear of water. Particularly the river. But at least it isn't high tide.'

'We got hours afore high tide,' Casper assured her. 'Don't you worry none. You'll be all right with old Casper. Promised Mister Cobham, I did. You look after her, he says. Well, maybe I ain't done too well with that so far, but I've lived close to mother Thames all my life, and she don't fright me none. As it happens, my da were a wherryman.'

Tyballis looked at him dubiously through the dark. 'You once told me your father was—'

'Don't matter none,' Casper interrupted her quickly. 'Reckon my da were a man o' many talents. Now, you just step down here.' He had brought the boat to the side of the quay, leading it by its rope to where the wooden ladder led directly down into the river. Tyballis regarded it with horrified distrust. 'I'll carry you, if you likes,' Casper offered, watching her expression. 'But don't reckon you'd like that much neither.'

She shook her head, kept her chin high and without looking down, she started to feel for each rung. It was only four steps until she hit the side of the boat. Casper held it steady, and Tyballis climbed in. She sat on the small bench, feet tight together, arms crossed around herself, and shivered. Casper hopped in beside her, took the opposite seat and began to pick the lock that held the oars horizontal to the narrow gunwales, heaved them out and began to row. Tyballis sat rigid and clutched the bench beneath her. The night breeze was cold. The stars' reflections danced alongside, keeping pace. Casper rowed fast and even. At first Tyballis closed her eyes, squeezing them shut and thinking of her sweetest memories, of childhood, of discovering Cobham Hall, sunshine over the chicken shed and the huge dishevelled bedchamber with its massive bed, and finally of Andrew's arms around her. But her thoughts cheated her, and conjured other darker memories, until she felt again the filthy water above her head and the gurgle of chugging waves filling her ears. She opened her eyes with a snap.

They had passed the soaring stone of The Tower on their right, and Casper had rowed quickly beneath the Bridge. There had been no gushing swell between the pillars, its huge shadows barely noticeable in the night's moonless black. But now, directly in front of them, a

392

lantern hung, seeming suspended in the river's width, its sudden light distorting the boat that held it. Then there was a shout. A small wherry, crossing from Southwark towards the Three Cranes Wharf, was directly in their path and a man, kneeling out from the prow, held the lantern that flickered on its pole, splashing golden circles onto the bow wave. Behind sat four men, two rowing, the others peering through the darkness. It was the man at the prow who shouted.

Tyballis stared, unblinking. 'We'll crash,' she whispered. 'It will all happen again. This time I shall drown.'

'Away with you, fool,' the man was shouting from the other boat.

'You swiving bastards,' Casper yelled back, breathless, panting, rowing hard, 'slow your pace or you'll capsize us.'

Someone in the other boat laughed. His voice rang clear in the silence of the night. 'We're on the dowager queen's business, and will slow for no one, clod. Move yourself. Get those arms bending and row faster lest we sink you.'

Someone else from the back of the boat pointed. 'It ain't just the lumpkin. There's a woman.'

'Let 'em swallow water,' chuckled the first. 'Is the female pretty? If she is, I'll fish her out. Then we'll do her a favour and strip her wet clothes off her.'

'Can't see in the dark. Probably some old crone. Hold up the lantern, Murch.' The lantern swung. The sweep of flaring flame bobbed its light on the black water below. The sooty smell of burning charcoals mingled with the rank stench of the river. Then the light settled bright and clear.

Clinging blindly to the bench, Tyballis saw, heard and gasped. She looked into the eyes of the man who had broken into Cobham Hall and imprisoned them all. She recognised him as he recognised her. Murch shouted, 'It's the same raggy trollop from that house. What's she doing here?' He nearly tumbled headfirst from the boat.

'Who's that?'

'I told you,' Murch insisted. 'She's got away somehow. And the bugger with her, bald and half-blind, that's him. They gotta be locked up again, quick. Get 'em.'

Casper stopped rowing. He raised one oar two fisted. 'Come try it, you bastards. An' won't be me what drowns.'

Wood scraped on wood. The other boat, higher-prowed and faster, crunched into the side of the smaller wherry with a splintering of planks. Water gushed through the hole. The two boats wedged, embraced, the invading keel a hand's breadth from Tyballis as she cowered back. She sprang away, clinging to the opposite gunwales. Both wherries tipped, unbalanced, shuddering and oozing filthy water. Casper thwacked his oar into Murch's face and the lantern tumbled from its pole, hurtling into the river. Black confusion descended. The stars blinked high above, a dizzying dance, the only remaining light. Shouting, cursing, creaking wood, the heaving splash of rolling water and the thump of men, heavy-booted, clambering forwards to free their craft.

The smaller wherry rocked wildly, tipping to either side as the larger boat edged out backwards and freezing water flooded in. Casper, feet slipping on rolling wet planks, raised the oar again – once more into Murch's face, and then pointed hard to the larger boat's swinging keel. Both wherries tipped and capsized in a tumbled rush, each dragging over the other. The river Thames swallowed six floundering, scrabbling, shouting bodies. Twisting, desperate arms outstretched, Tyballis screamed as she was flung into the eager sucking waves.

She opened her eyes underwater. A murky swirling blindness closed around her, a swaying obscurity of indistinguishable rubbish and the filth of the city. Her sodden skirts dragged her down. She kicked her feet but found nothing beneath. She could not breathe. Water filled her nose and mouth. For one moment through the gloom she saw legs, arms, boots and hands grabbing at each other, one heaving the other up, lunging, panic, and another pushing down. Then a face – a great bruised forehead, nose smashed, eyes shut, rocking a little as if in a dream – caught in the waves of the others' desperation but then loose, rolling gently to the bottom, and was gone. Murch would not capture her or anyone else again. But she was out of breath herself, her lungs empty, body flung first against the legs of another and then caught in the swell, lifted briefly, but finally sinking. Behind Murch, she imagined the riverbed waiting for them both.

Something tugged, she heard the terrifying roar of the hungry water and felt hands tight beneath her arms. She had no strength to fight. She let the monsters take her. The waters parted as she plunged upwards, screaming silently in terror and pain. But suddenly cold air slapped against her face, her eyes stung and she heaved a gasping thankful breath. A faraway voice croaked, 'There now. Got you safe.'

Through the night's frost she peered, still gulping air. 'Casper?'

'Course it is.' He was hunched beside her, rubbing his empty eye socket, streaming water from back and shoulders, his four thin strands of hair sleeked down over his nose. 'You all right?'

She nodded, shivering, and crouched where he had dropped her, doubled over, chin to her knees, belly and lungs wretchedly sore. 'The others?' She looked up, blinking water. Through the night's shadows, darker shadows crawled long and monstrous from the water, shaking their heads like hounds after hunting in a storm.

'Run,' Casper yelped, struggling to his feet. He reached out, grabbed her arm, and stumbled headfirst into the deeper dark away from the river. Tyballis thought she would be sick but swallowed it back, her stomach tight, head reeling, feet obedient to the need. The darkness took them. She was aware of huge shapes passing, the cranes and sheds of the wharf, then larger buildings, and the opening into an alley. Casper swung her sharp right and in, and together they ran blindly. Stubbing her toes, then squelching into the soft earth of the unpaved lane, Tyballis realised she had lost her shoes. Her clothes were drenched and the cold bit but Casper's grip on her arm dragged her on. At first, she heard the clump of chasing boots, her heartbeat as loud, but then all sound faded and soon they were running in silence. Only the faint clammy shiver of breeze froze their ears. Then Casper slowed, and Tyballis, leaning heavily against a wall, stopped. Heaving, panting, desperate for breath, she bent, staring down at her mud-caked toes. Finally, unable to stop, she was violently sick.

Casper waited. 'Best spit it out,' he approved. His voice sounded uneven and cracked. 'No river's best drunk whole. But not too long, mind, missus. I reckon we's not outta trouble yet.'

Tyballis gradually straightened, wiping her mouth with the back of her hand and pushing the dripping hair from her eyes. 'They're still behind us?'

Casper shook his head and river water flew. 'Not far's I can tell, they ain't. But won't take no risks. Still a fair bit to go afore we's safe at Crosby's.'

'I saw Murch dead,' Tyballis whispered. 'The others won't recognise us without him. But we can't go to Crosby's. In the middle of the night? Without Drew? Soaked, freezing, filthy? After all that time locked up – starved, unwashed – we must have looked like beggars before the river took us. Now I stink of vomit. No respectable house would let us in.'

'I ain't sleeping in no bloody cold streets tonight,' Casper objected. 'I's worn, and I's froze. If them snotty buggers at Crosby's won't let us in, then I'll break the bloody door in and remind them who we is.'

'I have a better idea,' Tyballis assured him. 'Not as warm and not as cosy, I'm afraid, but just as safe. It's my own house, and no one can refuse us.'

The dawn was already a fragile pink over the rooftops as they came to Whistle Alley. The door to the Blessop house was barred, but Tyballis knew how to push the back door open a crack, then lift it from its latch, rattle and force it wide. Inside, a musty smell of damp disuse and rat droppings hung heavy. The little hearth still held a smattering of ashes, and sticky black stains spread across the floor, memories of struggle and of blood.

'Right nice,' nodded Casper, collapsing onto a stool. 'An' all your'n, is it? You's a wealthy woman, mistress.'

'I have not one penny,' she smiled, sitting heavily on the little chair by the empty hearth. 'And I know you have nothing either. We've no food nor drink nor anything to sell. It will be a problem, I'm afraid.'

Casper managed a tired grin. 'Not for me it won't be, missus.'

She smiled again. The first smiles for a long time. Freedom, safety and shelter felt good, but her stomach, empty and sore from vomiting, was unlikely to be filled again any time soon. The next few days, whatever Casper's talents, would likely be desperate. 'Well, there is kindling in that tub,' she pointed. 'I am so horribly tired. With a nice fire to warm us up and dry us, I'm sure we could sleep right through the morning. Maybe right through the day.'

'But no tinderbox? Mine's soaked. It won't be lighting no fires never again, I reckon.'

'There's usually one in the tub with the kindling.' Tyballis looked vaguely around. 'It still feels like home. In a way, I wish it didn't. But it will serve us for now, and since you saved my life, Mister Wallop, I think you deserve the proper bed upstairs. I shall sleep down here. And if you're too tired to light a fire, I shall do it myself.'

'I'll be doing that,' Casper said, quickly kneeling beside the tub of sticks, 'and you'll be going upstairs to that proper bed you talks of. Me – I's happier on the floor anyways. Now get up them stairs, my girl, and get them wet clothes off. Look after you I can, but not nurse you if you catches the pneumonia.' She opened her mouth to object, but Casper shook his head.

The first tiny crackle of burning wood turned to a glare of genuine warmth. Tyballis sighed. 'My own little fire again,' she murmured. 'I never thought – I never expected – I never wanted ever to sit here again. Yet now it seems so utterly sweet. I have nearly drowned, yet come back to life. And I find life is good, after all.'

Casper looked up from the grate and scowled. 'Get going,' he ordered, busy laying more twigs. 'All that there female thinking stuff can wait for later. Bedtime, missus, so up you goes. Or likely I'll have to carry you myself.'

CHAPTER FIFTY-FIVE

'Is it you indeed, Mistress Blessop?' The face peered nervously around the partly open door.

'Good gracious,' mumbled Tyballis. 'It's only you, Mister Webb. Thank goodness. I'd thought – but never mind what I thought. There have been such unfortunate ...' Her voice faded out as Mister Webb entered the little room.

"Tis unfortunate everywhere, I'm afraid, mistress,' he said. 'There is such lawlessness throughout the city and decent citizens not safe even in their own homes. I've never known nothing like it before. First the king. Such a tragedy, and so unexpected. And now we don't know what to expect next.'

'But what don't we know?' Tyballis begged. 'I have no idea what has been happening.'

The constable blinked. 'But you could hardly have missed the troubles, since all London has started locking their doors at night. And seeing this door unbarred, well, it worried me and so I came to check. But come to think of it, you don't look well, mistress. Not well at all.'

She had been woken by the thumping on the door and had stumbled down the stairs, wrapped in the counterpane. She found

Casper already gone, a small fire spitting cheerfully on the hearth and a pale sunshine leaking in.

Now Tyballis breathed deeply and said, 'I've been – out of the city for some time. So, however little you know, Mister Webb, it is far more than I do. Has the Duke of Gloucester not arrived yet?'

'Not yet, mistress,' Robert Webb announced, 'and instead it's the Marquess of Dorset and the dowager queen have taken over.' Webb shook his head. 'With the coronation date set, there's lords and their men been arriving in the city every day, but no sign of the Duke of Gloucester. Now it's the Marquess of Dorset in the queen's name has been gathering forces and begging support, saying as how Gloucester has taken possession of the little king up north, and every nobleman must arm himself and gather forces to defend the queen and gain back her son.'

Tyballis stared in perplexity. 'You mean the Woodvilles have been trying to muster an army?'

'Exactly that, mistress.' The assistant constable looked wild-eyed. 'There's been such a hullabaloo and folks is still frightened, hearing as how the old queen means to keep the duke out and rule from behind the throne herself. But it seems them grand lords would have none of it, shouting as how Gloucester is the proper delegated Protector and so must be guardian of his little highness, it being more just that the sovereign should be with his paternal uncle than with his maternal uncles. Most are openly hostile to the Woodvilles. It's a strong leader we need, but what little respect Dorset had, it's now well-nigh lost and gone.'

'And what,' Tyballis wondered, 'is told as the cause of the king's death?'

'What should there be, mistress?' Webb frowned. 'Nothing official, anyway. Rumour, now – well, rumour has an answer for everything. But I'll not spread gossip, for there's other dangers is real enough. Perhaps I'd do best to call a doctor for you, mistress.'

'There's no need,' she assured him. 'And I'm not here alone. I have a servant – an old friend, someone I trust to look after me. Though I'd be pleased if you would come again sometime, Mister Webb, since a friendly face will seem especially welcome over the next few days.'

Constable Webb nodded fiercely. 'With the city still in chaos, well, that I will. Should the marquess raise an armed force after all, then it'll not be safe to leave the house.'

Over the following days Robert Webb continued to visit, and sometimes brought gifts: a hot pie from the Ordinary, fresh eggs from his mother's chickens, a neat white bonnet his mother now considered too frivolous for her aging dignity, and a small Seville orange, carefully wrapped. She looked apologetically towards Mister Wallop. But Casper shook his head. 'You go ahead,' he assured her. 'I don't want no nasty foreign stuff. Don't know what them things could do inside your belly.'

More important than gifts, he brought news. No armed force was in power, and peace was returning to the streets. But he continued to visit.

Tyballis, uncomfortably aware that she should not encourage Mister Webb in this tentative courtship, still accepted everything. She had no clothes and was glad of gifts. Having escaped Cobham Hall in a gown already filthy and ripped, and it had been further ruined by the river's dirty waters. She had lost her shoes and stockings, she had no headdress, and she no longer owned a cape or hood. At first she had been forced to adopt the little left of Margery Blessop's belongings, but her mother-in-law had been far shorter than she, and distinctly thick-waisted. Tyballis had made do with the shift and apron, and cutting a wide strip from her own spoiled shift, she had sewn this to the hem of Margery Blessop's old gown, at least managing to cover her ankles. Then she sat by the empty pot hanging over the fire, and cried.

Mister Wallop also brought gifts. Constable Webb would most certainly not have approved, but fortunately he did not know. Casper came home each dinnertime with enough food for at least a small meal. He brought pork skin to cook with lentils. The next day he brought a whole chicken to broil, and on the following morning half a calf's head, complete with brains and a thick cheek. A week later he brought sausages. Another time, tripe. Tyballis regarded the earthenware dish with misgivings. 'Mister Wallop,' she said reprovingly, 'you have stolen this off some poor housewife's windowsill.'

Casper ginned. 'Where d'you reckons I got all the rest, then? Ain't heard you complaining 'bout eating them great big eggs yesterday. Goose eggs, them were and a proper nice omelette they made, too. Enjoyed it meself, I did. You thought as how I'd gone and bought them eggs from a regular stall, then? Or maybe laid them meself?'

Ashamed to go out, Tyballis sat at home or curled in bed long past dawn. There seemed no point to the days, no aim, no inner sunshine, and little hope. Dreaming of past friendships made their lack now too obvious, and longing for those arms, loving protection and that particular embrace, simply resulted in tears, misery and regrets.

Her neighbours avoided her and she avoided them. Long aggrieved by the behaviour of Borin and Margery Blessop, not one of them had become a friend over past years. The house on one side, once occupied by Borin and Margery, was rented to passing lodgers, few staying long enough to give their names. Now having arrived suddenly in the night, dressed like a beggar and unchaperoned except by a man with the appearance of a Newgate bruiser or a Tom o' Bedlam, there was not a respectable soul in the street prepared to give Mistress Tyballis Blessop the time of the day. Gossip spoke of many things, and Tyballis guessed what those things were. She stayed indoors.

There was cleaning enough to keep her occupied, since the empty house had accumulated enough dust and cobwebs to fill a trunk, but housekeeping in a house she no longer loved left her feeling more bereft than ever.

Late one evening Casper came rushing in carrying a huge armful of linens, dumping them down on the floor by her feet and then sitting heavily on the stool beside her. 'Best lock the door,' he grinned. 'Might – just might – be followed.'

'Not Constable Webb?' hoped Tyballis.

'Too slow he is. T'was the Watch but reckon I gave them the slip. For all that, don't advise answering no doors if some lumpkin comes a knocking tonight.'

'Oh dear.' Tyballis eyed the interesting heap on the floor. 'Would it be safe, do you think, to have a look?'

So it was that Tyballis acquired another gown, a pink duffel that almost fitted, a pair of little black shoes with buckles (one broken), a knot of old felted stockings, an unbleached shift, two good sheets and a wheat chaff pillow without a cover. 'Well now,' Casper said, 'done rather nice, I reckon. Tomorrow I've a mind to try for them ducks down on the river.'

He sometimes also came home with news. Most was sporadic and untrustworthy, but some was unavoidable, for despite the date of the Coronation being fixed for the fourth day of May, neither the new king nor the Lord Protector had yet ridden into London. Chilly nights lightened into sun-balmy days, but unrest continued.

It was nearly the end of April when Tyballis, tucked on the chair by the last dying embers of the cooking fire, said, 'Well, Mister Wallop. Things are not too bad, after all. I expected endless disasters, you know, but instead we eat well, keep warm and dry, and feel positively cosy. Do help yourself to more ale. There is plenty still in the little keg you brought back. Indeed, life feels positively domestic. We are like an old married couple, my friend.'

Casper looked up in some alarm. 'Don't reckon Mister Cobham would be right pleased to hear that,' he said warily. 'Come to think of it, ain't rightly pleased meself. You wants a husband, missus, you go ask that there silly young constable.'

'I don't want a real husband.' Tyballis laughed. 'Don't look so caged, Mister Wallop. I'm merely grateful for how well you've provided, and I don't even miss Felicia or Ellen anymore. I feel very much at peace. In this house – before – I woke every morning sick with fear for what the day might bring. All that is utterly gone. And when I lived here, I certainly never ate so well, nor slept so soundly. That is certainly thanks to you.'

And then something very different happened.

Again Casper came puffing home with news to tell. 'Got summit for you. But you won't believe it,' he said. 'Didn't believe it myself at first. But that there pot o' stew smells good, and just as well we got leftovers, being as I weren't able to get much else this morning. Too busy I was, with other things.'

Tyballis regarded him with faint misgiving. 'You confuse me, Mister Wallop.'

'News, missus. Not common news neither. Still ain't seen no king turning up, nor mighty Protector come riding by. Them Woodvilles is still overrunning the city and shouting how they got the whole country in their clutches. No! This be our news.'

Tyballis, rather hot and pink as she stirred the steaming cauldron, glanced down impatiently at her companion. 'So what news, Mister Wallop?'

'Ah, well.' Casper stretched his legs. 'Happen you won't be as took back as I were – but it's a proper surprise, for all that. Luke it was,' he said. 'Bloody Luke Parris from the attic. I seen him scurry up Bishopsgate, and called to him. Well, we ain't seen hide nor hair of him since getting ourselves locked up, so I were pleased to see him still alive. But 'stead of turning with a wave, the bugger went running into the shadows, like t'was him caught thieving – not me! Well, course I followed. Well, where d'you think he went?'

'Gracious,' stared Tyballis. 'I have no idea. Tell me.'

'Outta London. Up to the Bethlehem Spittal where they keeps the moon loons. And there he trots, into a house just to the side o' the main building, and shut the door loud behind him.'

Tyballis paused and frowned, 'He must have escaped the house before we did. As for the hospice – I have no idea if Luke has a lot of friends.'

Casper shook his head. 'You ain't been listening right, missus. I's talking about Bethlehem Spittal – that's Bedlam as we calls it – where they locks the crazies. A separate squat, this were, but in the grounds attached, with another fence and a door covered in them prickly flowers – pink things with lots of smelly petals and nasty sharp thorns set to rip your fingers off. Just a cottage, but clean with real windows and its own chimney. And where's that swiving bugger Luke staying anyhows? How did he get away? And who's the crazy man? Him? Or another?'

Tyballis left the big wooden spoon in the pot and sat down heavily.

'I saw him going up that way once myself, and tried to follow him. But if he's simply visiting someone, then it's none of our business. I was frightened he was selling or buying poisons, but Drew said he wasn't. So, if Luke's visiting the sick, well, that's nice of him. It could be anyone.'

'His father, maybe.'

Tyballis looked at her toes. 'I don't think so. Drew told me once – Luke's father is dead. But maybe another brother. An uncle. I just don't know.'

'He were mighty secretive,' objected Casper. 'Seeing me after all this time – and the house deserted, lest them louts is all still there. But Luke Parris should've been interested to find out at the very least. You'd have thought he'd come running over to see where we all was. Yet he went scurrying off like the law was after him.'

'You didn't,' Tyballis asked tentatively, 'watch who opened the door?'

'Them walls is fast locked to keep the loonies in,' Casper told her, shaking his head. 'I were peering over the walls, but didn't see no one. Luke, he had his own key and let hisself in, he did.'

'That's a puzzle,' mused Tyballis. 'I hope Luke is all right. Clearly he has not been locked up in Bedlam himself.'

'Would be, if I had ought to do with it,' muttered Casper. 'Silly bugger.'

It was the very last day of April. London was peaceful again, and Tyballis decided she should finally leave her house, or go mad with staring at her sad little walls. She looked almost respectable now in the clothes Casper had stolen, as long as some poor housewife did not recognise her own gown and come shrieking after her. Tyballis combed her hair, pinned it neatly beneath Mistress Webb's bonnet, reknotted and tightened the garters holding up her stockings and took off her apron. She doused the cooking fire, took a deep breath and left the house. Feeling conspicuous in stolen and misfitting clothes, she did not look around but walked briskly up to Pig Street, cut across towards the London Wall, leaving the city through the Bishopsgate.

Her thoughts, when aimlessness led to the undisciplined

ponderings of past and present misery, once again fled to Andrew, his possible whereabouts and his possible return. She knew any attempt to find him might endanger herself and ruin whatever subterfuge he was now building. But the place where he lived in her head remained protected as if fur-lined, remaining warm and safe from attack. Bishopsgate Without was a long road leading north, pleasant beyond the city's stench. The sun was lying warm across her shoulders and bathing the back of her neck. Tyballis heard a blackbird sing, a song she had not heard since leaving Andrew's Portsoken gardens, and paused, thinking of him. Then she realised what she was doing. Spying on Andrew Cobham, who, being a spy himself, was particularly conscious of security and since engaged in secrecy, would certainly hate to be watched or have his life investigated. Yet somehow it brought him closer. 'It is not,' Tyballis assured the blackbird, 'that I have to know his private business. I should like to know but I would oh so much prefer if he chose to tell me himself.' She sighed, still speaking aloud. 'But it seems such a long time since I saw him, and so many horrible things have happened in that time. Somehow, if I discover something or someone close to him, it will bring me closer to him myself. I will feel part of his life again, and will dream sweeter tonight. I just pray he won't find out, and think me rude. Because really, my motives are perfectly innocent.'

She was not sure if the blackbird had believed her. So she walked on, watching carefully as the little houses crowded to her left, until finding a gap through which she could peep. Following the hospital wall, the gate she eventually found, high and locked, was of wooden planks. Tyballis could peep between the planks and she did, her eye to the crack. There was not much to see. Greenery, buildings, more walls, more houses. And there, standing in the shadow of the great hospice but with its own willow tree and roses around the fence, was a tiny house standing almost on its own. It exactly fitted Casper's description. Tyballis leaned a little closer, holding her breath. Beneath the tangle of roses, the front door of the house was opening. Tyballis saw the hand opening the door from within, wrinkled and tentative, and the protruding foot on the step, well clad in a woman's leather shoe.

Tyballis was still waiting, still holding her breath, when something tapped her so unexpectedly on the shoulder that she squeaked and whirled around with her bonnet tipped half over her eyes.

Then the deep voice said softly, 'Would you like to come in and meet her?'

CHAPTER FIFTY-SIX

Tyballis gasped, 'You're back!' and flung herself into Andrew Cobham's arms.

He was grandly dressed, as was his habit when working or visiting court. His velvets, silken wolf-grey with padded folds tight-stitched in silver thread, felt so soft against her cheeks that even his clothes embraced her. Enfolded in warmth and welcome and now muffled in velvet, she could say nothing more.

'It seems,' the voice murmured slightly above her, 'you have been missing me. But how did you know to come here, I wonder?'

She managed to look up, though saw little more than the stiff black brocade of his doublet's collar and the smooth underside of his jaw, which had lifted into a curve indicating a smile, while the rest of his face remained deep-shadowed beneath his hat. 'I've missed you terribly,' she said, small voiced. 'And I came here because – because – well, I admit it. Because I was spying. Are you awfully cross?'

His smile did not seem to diminish in the slightest. 'I should be absurd indeed if I objected to your spying, considering it is how I choose to make my living.' His arms were around her, holding her so close she could barely breathe. 'And since I have missed you quite as terribly as you seem to have missed me,' he continued, 'I cannot possibly imagine being cross with you, either awfully, or even imperceptibly. Besides, little one, cross is not a condition I am apt to experience.'

She sniffed. 'Just anger. And then you kill them.'

She heard him chuckle, and cuddled close. He said, 'But you have not answered the question, my love. I am quite sure I never gave you this address. And there is only one other person who knows it.'

'I admitted to spying,' she said, clinging to the loose silver laces of his doublet, her cheek to his heartbeat. 'Casper saw Luke here and told me. I didn't come at once because I knew it wasn't my business. Then – I just couldn't resist it. You really don't mind?'

'I said I wasn't cross,' he smiled down at her, 'not that I didn't mind. I mind – a little. The situation is not entirely simple, and I should have found it easier to explain some other way and at some other time. But since I have been rushing these last duties in order to hasten my return to you, this brings some advantage. So now you are here, you had better come in.' He reached out and unlocked the high door set into the wall, through which she had been peeping. Then, steering her gently in front of him, he brought her into the neatly crimped gardens of Bedlam. She stayed close, clutching nervously at his sleeve as he led her to the door of the cottage amongst the clambering roses. It stood open.

Tyballis whispered, 'Will you tell me first who she is?'

'My mother,' Andrew said quietly. 'She is Katerina Parris. But she will have little to tell you, since what she remembers rarely occurred. Some days are better, when at least she may remember my name.'

She remembered his name. The elderly stiff-backed woman stood on the threshold, holding to the door handle as though without support she might crumble. She was well dressed, her headdress starched, spotless and severely pinned. Her brows were unplucked, and beneath their jutting perplexity she peered. Finally she said, 'It is Andrew. But I was expecting Luke.'

'Luke may still come,' Andrew said. 'In the meantime, you must make do with me. I am back in the city only since this morning, and have come directly to pay for your lodgings.'

She lifted her chin, backing into the shadows. 'I won't trouble you for that, Andrew. His lordship will pay as always.' She pointed. 'Is that your wife, Andrew? Is it her ladyship? Or is it perhaps the queen?'

Tyballis, perplexed, followed his mother into the cottage. Andrew sat on the one long bench, Tyballis at his side. 'Her highness,' Andrew said, 'is otherwise engaged today, Maman. But I have brought a friend, and her name is Tyballis.'

'I do not always trust your friends, Andrew,' said his mother with familiar suspicion. 'But no doubt the girl is welcome enough as long as she sits still and doesn't fidget. Now, have you brought me anything interesting? Sweetmeats? Raisins? Marchpane? I have a great weakness for marchpane. Luke, you know, always brings me raisins and marchpane from the apothecary's.'

'I know,' smiled Andrew, 'since I pay for them. However, on this occasion unfortunately I have brought nothing. I did not expect to visit so abruptly, since I came simply to pay the lease on your lodgings, and then to visit perhaps tomorrow. Thanks to my friend Tyballis, however, my visit was brought forward. I shall make sure to send marchpane with Luke this afternoon.'

The woman, now sitting knees and feet tight together and hands clasped in her lap, stared unblinking at Tyballis. 'You stopped my son bringing me marchpane? Was there any particular reason for this, madam? Have you eaten it all yourself?'

Tyballis opened her mouth but had some difficulty formulating any sensible answer. Andrew interrupted her. 'My friend was unaware of your particular predilection for marchpane, Maman,' he said. 'I saw her walking outside, then, being already here, it seemed courteous to visit. The lack of marchpane will be remedied this afternoon, I assure you.' He looked aside to Tyballis. 'You may say what you like, little one. My mother is always quite content to let her mind wander a little, and will not be insulted if we talk in her presence.'

Tyballis said simply, 'I'm sorry about the marchpane.'

Andrew grinned. 'I had expected more specific curiosity, my dear.'

Tyballis clasped and reclasped her fingers. 'Well, I am curious. But I don't like to ... that is, do ... do you usually bring – the queen?'

'Tell the girl not to fidget,' said Mistress Parris from her shadows.

Tyballis stopped abruptly. Andrew chuckled. 'I tend to have as little to do with the queen – the dowager queen – as is humanly possible. My mother unfortunately suffers from delusions of grandeur, but has never been known to entertain queens, kings or princes. Nor indeed, have I.'

Mistress Parris interrupted at once. 'Don't lead the girl astray, Andrew,' she said sternly. 'You know perfectly well how frequently I invite the queen to my evening suppers, since Lord Leays encourages my every whim. I shall have to remind him regarding the marchpane, but he is usually most attentive. And we are so fond of the king as well, dear man, but Lord Leays favours the Yorkist rebels and insists we invite the Duke of York to our next Epiphany feast. I must speak to him about it. The king is an easier guest, you know, since he is rather simple and quite undemanding. But his lordship speaks critically of him, insisting he is unfit for rule. Ah, my dearest Lord Leays. And how do you find your father these days, Andrew?'

'With difficulty, Maman.' Andrew took Tyballis's small gloved hand in his, and held it firmly, offering comfort. 'And if you will forgive me one moment, madam, I should like to speak in private with my friend.'

His mother waved her fingertips. 'Go on, go on then, my boy. I have matters to attend to myself, and will be back shortly. Life is not all idle pleasure, you know. You will learn this, Andrew, when you grow a little older. For instance, the cook is waiting for direction, and I have barely had a chance to choose the midday menu. Then it has been brought to my attention that the vines need pruning, and now the vintners are due to arrive for their inspection at any hour. I must organise the gardeners. I fear discipline on the estate has grown lax. Lord Leays, dear man, is too kind with his servants. I must be off to have words with the steward.'

But she did not move, simply hung her head a little, stared a moment into her lap and then quietly closed her eyes. Andrew nodded to Tyballis. 'My mother has left the room,' he said. 'Now, child. Have you satisfied your curiosity?'

Tyballis blushed. 'It was wrong of me to come. I feel – most uncomfortable. But if you'd only told me more about yourself, and not been so persistently secretive, I would never have interfered.' She looked up at him, and then aside at the quiet uncomprehending woman opposite. 'I'm sorry,' she whispered. 'Is she really your mother?'

'Certainly,' he answered. 'This is Mistress Parris, my mother – and Luke's mother.'

'But,' said Tyballis, still whispering, 'you call yourself Cobham. Or Feayton, of course, but you always said that was made up. Are you really Andrew Parris, then?'

'Legally, yes.' He sighed, stretching his legs, long shadowed in deep grey silk hose. 'Cobham was my mother's name before she married, and I therefore claim her parentage, in preference to the man I killed.'

'I see.' Though she didn't. 'And Lord Leays, whom your mother spoke about, and Lord Feayton, the name you adopted? Do either of these men exist at all, or did they ever?' She was aware that her clutch on his hand was becoming feverish, and tried to relax. 'But I suppose I ought to explain a few things myself first. You see, rather a lot has happened since I last saw you. It has all been rather difficult.'

'Tell me,' he demanded, an eyebrow raised. 'Indeed, I was fairly sure I had never bought you a gown quite so remarkably unattractive. I can only hope you've not been reduced to selling all my gifts?'

As Mistress Parris stood and saw her visitors off at the doorway, Andrew bent and kissed her cheek. 'I shall send marchpane,' he promised. 'And I shall come to see you again quite soon.'

'Bring the king next time,' smiled his mother vaguely. 'Dear Henry. Such a nice young man. But lacks his wits, you know, and is sometimes altogether vacant.'

Tyballis curtsied. 'Goodbye, Mistress Parris,' she said. 'It was a pleasure to meet you.'

Katerina Parris straightened her back. 'Not Mistress Parris, my girl. I'll have you know I am the Lady Leays. My son will be the baron when his dear father passes on, but that will not be for a long time, I trust.' She turned to Andrew. 'You have ignorant friends, Andrew. Please educate the girl.'

'It seems I will have to, my dear,' he replied, and took Tyballis's arm. 'Look after yourself, Maman, and the estate. The vines appear sadly neglected and the verjuice will suffer. You must have a quiet word with Osbourne.'

His mother nodded, smiling. 'Osbourne. Ah, yes. I had nearly forgotten his name. I shall go and speak with him now. You go off and play, my boy. Be good now. You know your dear father worries.'

'I am always good,' said Andrew Cobham.

He went first to a drab building with a roof missing its tiles at one end. Tyballis waited outside. He reappeared almost immediately, took her arm, and left the Spittal grounds, walking together back down towards the city entrance at Bishopsgate. Finally Tyballis said, 'I'm sorry,'

Andrew looked down at her, smiling briefly. 'When you practise the art of spying, my love, you need considerably more resolution, and a stronger stomach to accept whatever surprises face you at the end. Had I been kinder, I would have steered you away from the embarrassments of Bedlam, and explained my parentage later, with greater subtlety. But my mother enjoys visitors, however brief. She will soon remember that the queen, inexplicably gowned in faded pink duffel, came to see her today. Whether her highness brought marchpane or not, I cannot be sure. But undoubtedly, they walked together in the sunshine and inspected the vines. The verjuice will inevitably prosper again from such elevated attention.'

'I see,' sighed Tyballis. 'But I'm still sorry. And now I have to tell you everything that's happened. I'm sorry about that, too.'

'I'll take you to Crosby's first,' Andrew said. 'You're presumably aware that Dorset and the queen tried to raise their own army? They were rebuffed, but there is still some upheaval in parts of the city, and you should not have been walking so far alone. I also believe you've an urgent need for food, wine, rest and certainly new clothes. You can tell me everything from the comfort of my bed, and now it seems I must also tell you whatever I will. I can postpone my duties, though not for long, since this is a time of great political change. But we will talk first, as it appears you have suffered some recent disturbance'

'Oh, much more than just disturbance. You won't go away for too long will you, my love?' she begged. 'I missed you so dreadfully. And if you'd stayed at home, none of these awful things would have happened.'

'Doubtless many things would not have occurred,' he said, leading her to the side entrance of Crosby's annexe. 'Including a somewhat pointless conversation with my mother.'

CHAPTER FIFTY-SEVEN

Andrew Cobham stood a moment outside his large and ramshackle house. He then marched indoors and looked around the remains of his hall. Tyballis had prepared him but what he saw was somewhat worse than he had expected. The smell of burning was unmistakable, one window frame scorched, the furniture strewn, chairs upturned and much broken, expensive Turkey rugs ripped, one partly burned, and straw pallets littering the boards. But the most noticeable disturbance was simple dirt. Dishes, piled with the remains of food, lay beside the straw. The food was a rotting squelch where flies had hatched, buzzing in tired exploration through the sunbeams. He sidestepped a rat, which ran squeaking beneath the table. The place stank. Having long valued, though never cherished, his home, he was faintly surprised to find himself annoyed. He was perhaps, though with a smile, feeling rather cross.

Striding quickly from the hall to his private quarters, Andrew kicked aside old bedding, thrown blankets and pillows, and unlocked the door to his bedchamber. The bed, its familiar shadows and tidied linen, still smelled sweet where Tyballis had strewn herbs across the counterpane. With the door locked and no one knowing where to search for the key, his personal chambers had not been invaded.

Andrew shut the door behind him, and took the narrow steps to the storeroom.

The brimming chamber pots and their leaking stains remained, the contents dried. Again scattered straw pallets and their hoards of piss, vomit and sweat lined the walls. The hole cut in the wall was almost woven shut with cobwebs.

The kitchens were rank and filthy. Andrew left quickly and climbed the stairs to the second floor. Every room was empty, the bedding removed to house the ruffians downstairs in the hall, each neat little home ransacked. Andrew sighed and ran up the final staircase to the attic.

Luke sat at his table, gazing vacantly through the casement window to the tops of the trees and their uneasy windswept tides. He did not turn when he heard footsteps enter. He said, 'You're back, then?'

Andrew paused before speaking. 'How do you feel, child?' he asked.

'As usual,' Luke said, turning slowly. 'Well enough. Unwell enough. Those – people – were a great inconvenience. Did you send them?'

'Even you, my dear, cannot seriously believe that,' Andrew said. 'No, they came on Lord Marrott's orders. They were sent to kill me. You remained here, all that time?'

Luke nodded. 'I hid, and locked my doors. I had a little food up here, but I soon got hungry. You should provide for such things, Andrew, and dissuade people from hunting for you. I – suffered. It wasn't fair.'

'You did not think to help your neighbours,' Andrew suggested, 'who were mistreated and imprisoned? Or, now that the ruffians have gone, attempt to clean the filth they left?'

'Why should I?' Luke said. 'I didn't do any of it. It was difficult, making no noise for so long and not being able to leave the house. And it was hard without much food or drink, and being frightened too. I missed Mother, you know. I think she missed me. The men stayed for days and days and even after they left, I couldn't be sure if they'd come back. You should have been here, Andrew. You promised to look after me.'

'I promised to look after you when I arranged for you to leave the monastery,' Andrew said, 'but not forever, my child. You are quite old enough to look after yourself, and have been doing so for years. You dislike and resent me. I understand that, and sympathise. But it means perhaps you'd be happier living elsewhere. I could buy you a cottage out by the Bethlehem Spittal. In the meantime, I have some questions.'

'Questions. Always questions. You bore me, Andrew.' Luke sighed, flinging down the book he had been holding.

Andrew smiled. 'You are not the first person to think so, little brother, but since you persist in passing your days with books and papers, aping the teachings of the monks when it is more than fourteen years since you left them, your life must be stitched with boredom, my dear.'

'How dull and uncultured you are, Drew,' Luke scowled, his fist bouncing the ink bowl. 'I like to read.'

'But you cannot read, child,' Andrew reminded him gently, 'and you cannot write, although some months ago you assured my friends you had scribed a letter to Baron Throckmorton as they had asked. Did it not occur to you that the baron, receiving a parchment of indecipherable nonsense, might suspect a trick and put those same friends in danger?'

Luke continued to scowl. 'I write better than you realise, brother. I've been teaching myself,' he muttered. 'Some of my shapes are quite clear. And I can sign my name. You taught me that yourself.'

'Very well,' Andrew sighed. 'Let us forget the past, and concentrate on the future. What are your intentions, little brother? If I buy you a home somewhere nearer Maman, will you go there?'

'Without you?'

'Certainly without me.'

Luke shook his head. 'I don't want to be alone. If you hadn't butchered Papa, he could have come with me. Maman only went mad because you killed him right on her lap.'

'You know perfectly well that isn't true.' Andrew sat, drawing the stool close to the table. 'Maman was already losing her wits, and was quite unable to cope, which is why you were sent away to the monastery. I was kept at home – even though your father loathed me

– only because I was older and could work. I killed your father in self-defence, and to protect Maman, as you know. He would have injured – perhaps killed her otherwise. A madwoman can be – let us say – irritating for a man with no control of his temper. Your father was a brutal man and did not love you. Losing him meant losing nothing. And I pay for Maman's home and her treatment, as I am prepared to pay for yours.'

'You'd buy me a cottage? A tiny hovel. While you live in a mansion.'

'My father's mansion, Luke, which is probably less comfortable than my mother's cottage. Her house is no hovel. It was the home of the head keeper, and now houses her well, keeping her safe and close to the care she needs.'

The day had begun to close in, shadows dropping thick across the garden. Luke's frown was lost in deepening green shade. 'The past again,' he said. 'You promised to talk about the future.'

'Well, let us ponder the past a little longer,' Andrew nodded. 'What can you tell me of the men who broke in here? How long did they stay? Did you hear anything they discussed, or remember any of their names?'

'No.' Luke shook his head, looking down at the scribbles carefully copied onto the papers lying over the table. 'I shut myself in and kept quiet. I didn't listen, until I heard them all march out. I don't know what day that was. Quite a long time ago, now. I've been to see Mother several times since.' He looked up suddenly. 'But if you must know, I'm glad all your wretched friends have gone too. All those vulgar women with their chests sticking out of their clothes, and the men waving swords. They were thieves and robbers and wicked people. I didn't like any of them.'

Andrew's eyes grew cold. 'Which is no doubt why you profited from their wickedness, little brother. Why you ran to the sheriff with every word you overheard, and gave information of where they might be found, and how the constable might arrest them. Did you run to Throckmorton, too, once you discovered his existence and his address from them? Did you inform Throckmorton where he might discover Mistress Tyballis? And was it you who alerted the sheriff when you heard Tyballis was heading to the market?'

417

Luke went pink, and looked away. 'I don't care. I was on the right side. I talked to the law, not the criminals. And the sheriff paid me. Baron Throckmorton paid me, too. I wish I could have told him more.'

Andrew's eyes narrowed. 'Are you in any way responsible for David Lyttle's death, child? Did your laying of information encompass that as well?' Luke stayed silent, and Andrew nodded. 'He suspected your treachery, poor Davey. Yet the fault is mine, since I also suspected and did nothing. I had hoped, despite what I guessed, that your behaviour could cause little damage. Every thief is wary of being caught, and most can look after their own backs, putting caution before trust. As I do. But Tyballis is trusting, without long practice of suspicion or care for what she says, or of watching those who watch her. Perhaps, while my thoughts were elsewhere, you achieved more damage than I knew. Perhaps I underestimated you, my dear.'

'You've always underestimated me, Drew. You think I'm stupid. But I'm not.' Luke smiled suddenly. 'I'm cleverer than you think. I'm good at pretending. I listen to how people speak, and I copy it. I copy you, too.'

'Then I should have left you in the monastery.' Andrew stood abruptly, threw a handful of coins onto the table at Luke's elbow, turned and left the room, closing the door quietly behind him. He ran downstairs and left the house entirely. The horse he had taken from Crosby's stables was waiting tethered in the garden. Andrew Cobham mounted quickly and rode away from the home he now disliked. He crossed the entire city east to west at a brisk trot, and eventually rode out through the Ludgate, which still stood open. He was aware, as he rode, of the city's unrest, of groups of armed men lounging in the shadows, of women scuttling, nervous, hands to their baskets, of fewer children playing in the gutters. But he had expected all of that. He rode on to Westminster.

It was late now, and he had little time if he wished to re-enter London before the entrances were locked against him. But at this stage he had

418

only one thing to investigate, and this was quickly made clear. It was the sanctuary at Westminster Abbey which was being utilized, just as his grace the Duke of Gloucester had predicted. In less than one hour, Andrew Cobham, answering to Lord Feayton, was fully aware of the general situation, and had begun to take note of the smaller details. He finished his exploration with a brief visit to the Lord Hastings. This time he was received with relief rather than resentment.

Baron Hastings said, 'You know then. His grace knows?'

Andrew Cobham bowed and sat. He said, 'Indeed. His grace of Gloucester expected the dowager queen to flee into immediate sanctuary as soon as the Woodville plots collapsed, and their attempts to raise armed forces against him failed.'

Hastings nodded. 'So, what I heard is correct? And you've been in Gloucester's company all this time? It's true Richard has arrested Rivers, then? You know the details? Tell me exactly how it happened.'

'Earl Rivers failed to meet his grace at Northampton as had been arranged. But to avoid confrontation, Rivers rode back to placate his grace. His excuses were lame. Naturally we had already received news from London of the king's council being subverted and the city virtually taken under Dorset's command. It needed little imagination to see that Rivers intended keeping the young king away from the designated Lord Protector. Clearly he assumed his power unassailable. His grace of Gloucester responded with considerable patience, entertaining Rivers throughout the evening, questioning and probing, allowing opportunity for explanation and time for the earl to exonerate himself. You must know, my lord, that his grace the Duke of Buckingham had joined the party at this stage, and was, with his men, also camped at Northampton. Rivers must have been conscious of the forces against him, but his conversation was persistently evasive and underlined with contempt and subterfuge. Unknown to him, word had already reached us of Dorset's attempts to take over the capital and the royal council. His grace knew that the orders originated with the earl. Naturally I was not present during the meeting, but I understand that when the earl finally retired, the Duke of Gloucester arranged for the inn to be surrounded, and had Rivers and his immediate companions arrested.'

419

'Is there nothing else?'

'Earl Rivers, Dorset's brother Sir Richard Grey and Sir Thomas Vaughn were arrested and sent north to be detained in those castles under the duke's authority. His grace, in company with the Duke of Buckingham, then advanced to meet the young king at Stony Stratford, to explain what had occurred and why. The Lord Protector and his highness are now proceeding together towards London. They will arrive in the city on the fourth day of May.'

'The day designated for the coronation?'

'Precisely,' agreed Mister Cobham. 'His grace does not intend that the coronation should take place in such a precipitous manner, nor at the instigation of the Woodvilles. It will be conducted in due time with greater dignity, and under the auspices of the Protector.'

Hastings chuckled. 'Excellent. And now the damned Woodville woman has scuttled into sanctuary, taking her whole wretched family with her. Poor Abbot Esteney will be thrown out of his comfortable home as usual, and the entire Abbey grounds will be in disarray. I'm told the queen dismantled half the palace, dragging all her precious luxuries away with her along with a parcel of servants.'

'I doubt it is my place to say,' Andrew frowned, 'but such absence of Woodville influence is likely to prove mightily convenient for the next few weeks, my lord. The Marquess of Dorset's immediate departure seems particularly comforting.'

'The court is certainly a more pleasant place without him,' Lord Hastings smiled. 'And they've declared themselves as guilty as hell, running like scared rabbits from the legal Protector's arrival, and even from the arrival of their own little Woodville king. Will they emerge for the coronation, I wonder.'

'I gather, my lord, that there are some rather more unfortunate aspects of this evasion of accountability.' Andrew Cobham was not smiling. 'The Marquess of Dorset, in his recent dubious capacity as Deputy Constable, has ordered the removal of his late highness's treasure from storage at The Tower. This has been divided between the marquess, the dowager queen and her brother Sir Edward Woodville. Sir Edward, so recently although illegally created commander of the fleet, has promptly put to sea, with the appropriated treasure in his possession. The rest accompanied her highness into sanctuary. I doubt there remains sufficient to pay for his late highness's funeral.'

Hastings leapt from his chair in fury and began to pace the room. The candles had already been lit and the flames flared and danced to the heavy thump of angry footsteps. 'The villains, how dare they!' he roared. 'They steal from the realm. They steal from the people. They steal from the new king, even though he's one of their own. Richard will struggle to raise new revenue for his Protectorate.'

'His grace has written several letters, which I delivered this morning,' Andrew nodded. 'He reminds the council to ensure the king's treasure is kept safe, and the Royal Seal secure. But in fact, both these measures have already been breached. The duke will not be pleased.'

'Pleased? He'll be biting the rugs! Good Lord, that damned Marrott and every Woodville bastard should be arrested immediately.'

'Which is no doubt why they have taken to sanctuary, my lord.'

Lord Hastings returned to his chair and collapsed heavily into its depths. 'If Edward had never – but there, the poor wretch is past regrets and I won't criticise him now he's gone. A king should be remembered for his greatness, his beneficence – not the miserable chaos he left behind him. I tell you this, sir – beware who you marry.'

CHAPTER FIFTY-EIGHT

H is fingers stroked the tucked dip between her collarbone. He had left the shutters down, and now the dawn sun bathed her neck in a soft lemon shimmer.

She mumbled, 'I was waiting. I waited ages.'

'I was here, little one. You were asleep when I came in. All night I've held you, wanting you, thinking of how you've suffered in my absence, missing you but letting you sleep.'

'Hungry?' he murmured.

She smiled back and found her voice. 'Yes. And thirsty. And excited. And I want to know everything.'

He rolled off her and sat up on the edge of the bed, squinting into the sunbeams. 'I'll call for breakfast. But as for knowing everything, my love, it's a dreary story. Marrott and the Woodvilles have already run for cover and taken everything they could steal with them.'

Tyballis curled back against the bedposts, under the sheet and the cavernous shadows of the bed's curtains. 'Then the duke will arrest them and throw them all into the dungeons. Then he can govern the country until the little king grows up, and you can go on working for him, and get richer and richer.'

Andrew shook his head, smiling as he stood and pulled his

bedrobe around his shoulders. 'They've claimed sanctuary, so there'll be no dungeons. The queen dowager chose sanctuary in Westminster Abbey once before – she knows the procedure well – and that's where she's set up court again now. She'll be impossible to move as long as the duke threatens to claim back the treasure she's taken. Dorset has scurried off with her, Marrott in his wake, and that parcel of princesses and the younger prince have been snatched up, too. The new king will arrive to find his entire family in hiding.'

'When will he arrive?'

'In three days' time. On the day previously promised for a hurried coronation – so, insuring it now cannot take place on Woodville terms. The duke is Lord Protector of the Realm, and he'll have things his way. Order will be restored.'

'Those last armed gangs will already be on the run, I expect. But I've heard the street gossip for some time now. The people are worried about a child on the throne.'

'Of course they are.' He was pouring her wine. 'A child king means a weakened country, with the greatest lords competing for power and the factions divided. There's France already watching, sniffing for blood and gold. Others are out for themselves – the Stanleys.' He paused, laughing, and passed her the wine cup. 'Stop me, my love, when I become boring. My brother reminded me yesterday how I investigate endlessly, and preach to those who have no wish to learn.'

'Your brother?' She sipped her wine, watching him over the brim. 'You didn't tell me you were going to find Luke. And you're never boring, Drew. Not to me. Not to anyone.' She shook her head, tipped up her cup and drank, saying suddenly, 'I think you're fascinating. And beautiful.'

He laughed again. 'I'd prefer not to be thought boring. But beautiful? My nose has been broken twice, and I was never an attractive brat before that. Your taste, my dear, is woeful, and your judgement awry.'

She was immediately interested. 'You must have been a very active child to break your nose twice. And you are beautiful, Drew. I like looking at you. Your jaw is so … well, forceful. And those commanding cheekbones. Your muscles are so smooth just under your skin, and I can watch them when you move, like ripples in oil. And your eyes are deep, like wells, and so black, and sometimes they speak all on their own, and sometimes they go blank, and can't be understood at all. They can go very cold, too, or burning hot, or just comfortably warm.'

Andrew gazed at her in astonishment. 'You are clearly deluded, my love. My reflection, when I cannot ignore it, shows me little but the heavy-boned fury of a wild boar.'

'Don't be ridiculous, Drew. You don't have tusks, for a start. So, you must have a very distorted mirror.' Tyballis smiled patiently. 'As for your nose, well, it's – different. Did you keep falling over, then, when you were little?'

'I was not quite so careless.' He drained his cup and refilled it, refilling hers at the same time. 'I was a careful child, finding it advisable under the circumstances. But I was careless enough to have a brutal father. Now, drink up. Another cupful and I may grow beautiful, after all.'

'Oh. So your father did it.' She set her cup aside. 'Was he that bad? And your mother said … was he really a lord?'

Andrew sighed, coming reluctantly back to sit on the bed beside her. He was well wrapped now, enclosed within the long sweeping folds of his bedrobe. Tyballis was still naked but still had pulled the sheet around her. Leaning over, he disengaged it, uncovering her to her toes, tracing the warm curves, watching her renewed arousal. 'Speaking of beautiful …'

'Drew, you're avoiding the subject. And anyway, Borin always said I was horribly plain. Barren, and plain, and skinny.'

Andrew smiled. 'And did you believe everything Borin told you?'

'Of course not. But I know I'm barren. And plain. And skinny.'

His hands now slid across the small golden swell of her belly. 'You never bore your husband a child,' he said softly. 'But the fault could have been his. Men can be barren too, you know. As for the rest, from now on you will believe me, beloved, not the fool you married. Now, come here.'

He pulled her close then, wrapping the black brocade folds of his robe around them both, he snuggled her against him like a child nestled in its mother's arms. She whispered, 'But I was pleased to be barren. I didn't want his babies. He would have been a brutal father, just as yours was. Was your mother forced to marry, too? To thrash your own son so violently that you break his nose …'

He spoke very softly as he cradled her. 'The second time he broke my nose, I killed him. I have no regrets. But in truth, I was not his son. My mother relates old stories of Lord Leays, romantic stories, which she once wished were true. But that is not how it happened. She worked on his estate, and being simple and willing and pretty, she attracted his attention. When she told him she was with child, he threw her out.'

Tyballis gulped. 'You are a lord.'

'No, my love. I am simply the bastard many men have called me.'

'And the house? His house?'

'Sad and trivial reminiscences.' He curled his fingers between her legs, stroking her thighs, speaking to the back of her neck. 'Abandoned, pregnant and alone, my mother acted without compunction, and made the mistake many women have made before. She went back to a man she'd known briefly once, who had wanted her in the past, and she made love to him. Then she told him the child she was expecting was his. He believed her, and married her.'

'But then he guessed the truth?'

'Inevitably he guessed, since we were nothing alike, and I was born a few short months after their liaison. Or perhaps she admitted it eventually. I never asked her. But her husband was a man of sudden furies and frequent drunken violence, and he beat her often. He beat me even more frequently, and once Luke was born to them, he beat the child as well. Luke resents me because his father sent him away yet kept me at home. But in fact, it was our mother who assured his safety by sending Luke to the monks. I was older, tall and strong. I was useful at home.'

'Your real father never saw you?'

'Just once.' Andrew sighed, ruffling her hair. 'You are making me remember the things I've long disdained to remember. But yes. After I killed her husband, my mother took me to see my real father. He admitted us into his home on The Strand, and we inspected each other with curiosity but little approval. I had looked in few mirrors at that age, but now I know he greatly resembled me. He must have known it, too. But he refused to acknowledge me legally, and refused to take me into his household, which is what my mother asked. He insulted her, and threw us both out. I broke the wine cup I had been holding, and threw the pieces at his feet. I never saw him again. But four years later he died without heirs. His secretary came to our door, handed my mother papers she could not read, and informed us that my father had bequeathed me a little money, and an old house in the Portsoken Ward.'

'So, he did acknowledge you. And you do remember him.'

'All I clearly remember is the great blazing fire in his hearth. A massive hearth, taking half the wall.' Andrew laughed. 'As a child I had always been cold. We could rarely afford kindling or faggots, and never logs or charcoal. I stood before that old ugly man and his haughty scowl. But all I saw were the flames and how high they sprang. Instead of loving my father, who was a stranger, and cold, I fell in love with the bliss of heat.'

Tyballis clung to him, her fingers pressed to the back of his neck and into his hair. 'So, that's why you don't care for the house he left you. You won't look after it. And you filled it with strangers and thieves.'

'Not strangers. Not entirely.' He smiled, playing absently across her breasts. 'I could not love my father's house, a place he rarely saw, the minor acquisition of a wealthy man. But Davey, Ralph – I met all of them while working for the Duke of Gloucester. The lost souls, the miserable and inane, those who chose a life without morals because morals are too expensive, or too demanding, or too heavy for a weak man to carry. I had long abandoned my own morals. A man who murders his step-father? Morals need keeping clean, a job I had no talent for. So, I felt akin, and sympathised. I gave a warm place which meant life to them, at little cost to me.'

'So, your real father was Lord Leays. And Lord Feayton? Who is he?'

'A foolish adaptation. I could not adopt his real identity, since he was known, and known to have died childless. His name was Ferant, Baron Leays. I rearranged the letters. But for myself I chose not to continue as Andrew Parris, so took my mother's name Cobham, being without pretensions.'

'What did you do – with the body?'

He paused, looking up at her a moment in silence. Then he said, 'As I still do. The river takes them.'

'Still?' Her whisper was so soft it was no more than a breath.

He answered without further pause. 'You want me, little one? And want to know me, and know my past? Then accept the truth. My mother discards the truth and lives her dreams. That's the path to madness. If you dislike my truths, you can tell me so. And make your choice to stay – or leave.'

She shivered. 'I'm not frightened of anything you've done, Drew. Once I wondered if you'd killed the other Throckmorton. When I first met you, you were carrying – something. And Throckmorton was found dead that night. I even thought you'd killed Borin.'

'I considered killing Blessop for you. But I did not.' He held her tighter, kissing her earlobe. 'The night I first met you, I came down to the river for a purpose. The tide below the bridge takes a body directly to the sea. He was a French spy, Francois Cretiene, bringing bribes from King Louis.'

'You killed him?'

'I eradicated him. He knew me and was preparing to inform Marrott – even Dorset. He attacked me, which made my decision remarkably easy.'

'Is it always easy?'

'There is nothing in life I called easy, until I met you, little one.' He paused for a moment, watching her. Tyballis sighed, 'Killing cannot be right – should not be right – even though, after everything you tried to do, the king was poisoned anyway. So much death.'

'It is not pleasant,' he smiled, 'to have one's efforts proved impotent. But I am not alone in this game, and those working against me had the greater power. Lord Marrott, Baron Throckmorton, perhaps even Earl Rivers, Dorset and others. I do not presume to rival their ambitions.'

'And the Duke of Gloucester?'

'When I was finally sure of a plot against the king, I convinced the duke, but could offer no proof. The duke warned his highness, but the king laughed. When finally I obtained it, I gave Throckmorton's written confession to Hastings. He chose, for his own safety's sake, to destroy that proof. I have not told the duke this. Should he ever discover it, he will be furious, and I pity Hastings. But I do not mourn King Edward. I never knew him as a man, and believe the Duke of Gloucester will rule England well. He will be a fine protector of the realm. And I shall continue in his service.'

They stood to watch the duke enter London, his nephew riding at his side. The boy king wore pale blue, matching his eyes, his hair a fluff of blond beneath his hat. Twelve years old and nervous, he had lost the uncle he knew well, and gained another he had rarely met before. He had been warned of his mother's hasty absence, of the circumstances and of the reason for it. But the terrible details of his father's death were too great to confide at such a moment. And now his people lined the streets and cheered him, and he was excited.

Still in mourning for his brother, the Duke of Gloucester wore black. His horse was black, his black surcoat lined in black marten, the sleeves martin-trimmed sweeping to the stirrups. His hat was black, his hose, boots and gloves all black. His grey eyes were narrowed to the wind, watching the crowds along the way. The procession was slow, and bouncing and rumbling over the cobbles some way behind his grace were the carts carrying the weapons, bearing the Woodville badge, taken from Rivers' escort. All two thousand had been dismissed, and now the duke and young king were escorted by three hundred Yorkshire men, and a small band accompanying the Duke of Buckingham, who rode to the king's left.

Andrew Cobham bowed low as the Duke of Gloucester passed. The duke saw and acknowledged him, bowing imperceptibly from the waist. He did not notice the woman close beside, but Tyballis curtsied as low as she dared while trying to keep her hems from the mud.

Once the horses had passed, she whispered up at Andrew, 'Do you think he saw me?'

Andrew's mouth twitched slightly, but he said, 'Undoubtedly, my love. There is not a man who could miss you today. You look enchanting.'

Instructed by Andrew, she had taken a new gown from the Crosby Annexe garderobe. Casper Wallop, cheerfully now back in the service he enjoyed, had brushed down the long-creased damask and Andrew had helped her dress, then stood her in front of the long mirror, showing her off. The bodice was lined satin, the colour of ripe wheat, deep-cut but trimmed for modesty in crisp white gauze. Beneath her breasts the under-gown was held tight by the stomacher in wide pleats, then swept into the stiffened saffron skirts of the over-gown, patterned in gold to her toes. The outer sleeves, cuffs to her hems, were of the same material and glimmered, the gold thread catching the sun. Tyballis had never dared be so grand before. As Andrew helped her pin the little white-and-gold headdress over her curls, she whispered, 'You know, don't you, my love, that I am shockingly improper in all this grandeur? The legislation is very strict. I am nobody, and nobodies should not be wearing satin or brocade. I am dressed well above my station.'

He grinned, clipping the last pin above her ear. 'I am Lord Feayton,' he pointed out. 'And you are my lady.'

'Am I? What a nice thought.' She whirled around, facing him, her back to the mirror. 'And you look every bit the lord, in all that wonderful silky grey velvet. But the Duke of Gloucester knows you aren't really a lord. Doesn't he mind that you break the law of the land? It's his land now.'

'Not a jot,' said Andrew, adjusting his sleeves. 'And nor does anyone else. Those laws have been ignored and broken by every citizen of England ever since the day they were laid down. I dress as I must for the work I do. By choice, I'd as soon live in wool and cambric. My clothes suit the part I play, nothing more.'

She did not mention her delight at his calling her his lady. That was a pleasure she kept to herself. But as she stood in the dappled sunshine and curtsied to the duke riding by, the young king at his side, she hoped it was exactly how everyone would see her. And she savoured the secret thrill, like a tickle inside, ready to visit again in her dreams. She was too busy inwardly hugging herself to notice the assistant constable, Mister Webb, a little further back in the crowd, his mouth open.

CHAPTER FIFTY-NINE

Having been summoned from Crosby's annexe to the main building, Andrew Cobham waited meekly before the great mahogany writing table, his hands holding his hat, clasped behind his back.

The duke continued writing. His scribing was neat, his attention absorbed as he dipped the quill's nib into the ink pot, and again to the sheet of parchment. He did not look up. It was after some considerable time that he spoke quite suddenly, voice soft. 'You knew then, Mister Cobham, that Baron Throckmorton's written confession was destroyed by the Lord Hastings before his highness's death?'

Andrew Cobham showed no sign of the surprise he felt. He said quietly, 'I did, your grace.'

Still the duke continued writing, head lowered, eyes to his papers. 'Yet you failed to inform me,' he pointed out.

'That is true, your grace,' Andrew replied.

The duke looked up abruptly, putting down his quill. 'Why?' he said. There was no evidence of anger, but his eyes had closed into expressionless hauteur and the warmth had slipped away.

'Because at first I was not sure,' Andrew replied with a slight bow. 'I was not then in immediate contact with your grace, and would not put to paper a fact so scandalous, and as yet unsure. Once I knew without doubt, it was too late.'

The duke nodded. 'So you acted on your own judgements, Mister Cobham?'

'I did. My apologies, your grace.'

'You are not paid to disguise truths, Mister Cobham,' said his grace. His gaze was direct, and he did not appear to blink. 'You are paid to bring every piece of evidence, every detail, every fact, every truth you discover – to me. You did not do so.'

Andrew bowed once again. 'I did not, my lord.'

The duke sighed suddenly and slumped back in his chair. He again took up the pen, though did not write, smoothing the feather between his fingers. When he spoke, his voice was soft again. He said, 'I have been speaking to Brampton. He told me what you did not, my friend. I am disappointed. But I have always trusted and encouraged your initiatives, and perhaps, in the end it would have been easier had I not known that Hastings, in effect, facilitated my brother's death. Had the proof of the poisoning been shown the king, he would, surely, have taken note. He need not have believed in Rivers' guilt, nor Dorset's. But Marrott would have been arrested, and his highness would have taken the precautions that could have saved his life.'

'I obtained the written confession regarding the poison,' said Andrew. 'Since you were not at Westminster, your grace, I took the proof to the Lord Hastings, as was fitting. My part was therefore done. Lord Hastings' choices from then on were not mine to question.'

'That part was well played, sir.' The Duke of Gloucester smiled at last. 'Your fault was in deciding not to inform me afterwards. Hastings has unwittingly taken a part in my brother's assassination, and must now pay for it.'

Andrew hesitated, then said, 'Forgive me, your grace, but the Lord Hastings acted in self-defence alone. We all defend ourselves as best we can.'

'As I did,' the duke said, 'by staying in the north and enjoying the peaceful pleasures of my own rule, far from the cloying scandals of the court. But you, sir, were to keep me informed of all matters of importance, and in that you failed.' He sighed again, then nodded to the wine jug. 'Pour me a cup, Cobham,' he said, 'and one for yourself. And bring a chair. Sit with me. I am not angry.'

Andrew did as he was bid, and sat, and drank. He watched the duke over the golden brim of the cup. 'When you summoned me here this afternoon, your grace,' he said slowly, 'I had rather expected to be dismissed from your service.'

The duke shook his head slightly. 'I am angry with Hastings. Not with you. You should not have denied me the truth, but in a sense, you were wise, since it was already too late, and from a distance I could not have influenced the situation, only suffered from the knowledge of it. But now I can act.'

'And I am at your service, since, by your grace, I remain in your service, my lord.'

'The coronation has been rescheduled for the twenty-second day of June,' the duke said, 'and young Edward now resides in the royal apartments at The Tower, awaiting his official crowning. Before that day, I intend resolving three other situations. First, my Lord Hastings. Then the dowager queen, and the number of those hiding in sanctuary. The young duke Richard at least must attend the coronation and be brought to The Tower to keep his brother company beforehand. Thirdly, the matter of the treasure and Sir Edward Woodville. That business is almost resolved, although not fully to my satisfaction. I have sent Brampton to reclaim the fleet, and all but two of the ships have quickly seceded and returned to us. But Woodville has misappropriated yet more treasure, claiming a good sum of money from a carrack off the south coast, while purporting to speak in the name of the king. He has fled to Brittany, and England's gold is no doubt in the hands of the exiled traitor Henry Tudor.'

'I will naturally go where you send me, your grace.' Andrew had never travelled to Brittany nor had any desire to leave England. He did not say so.

'No Protector rules unchallenged,' the duke said, quietly, as though speaking to himself. 'And no country easily conforms to a disciplined routine on finding itself under divided rule. But Dorset's recent attempt to raise an army against me before my arrival in

London was met with ridicule and rejection, even antagonism from the people, and so has confirmed my personal support, even during my absence. Yet disorder and danger have always constituted the patterns of my life since I was a child, and I am habituated to treachery and conspiracies.' He looked up again suddenly. 'You are also practised in these matters, Mister Cobham. I intend using you to full advantage, and this time I expect your cooperation in all things. Then at the end when I have organised every possible solution, and handed the reins of power on to a crowned and mature king, I will return to the north, but first I will confer on you that title which you could not yourself claim. I know your story, my friend. Forget Feayton. I will thank you for your loyalty and dub you Lord Leays.'

This time, Andrew did not hide his surprise. 'I have never coveted that name, your grace. I do not ask it.'

'I give what I believe is fitting,' the duke answered him briefly. 'I will be responding to my own sense of gratitude, rewarding loyalty as I choose, and balancing the natural order of righteousness. And in such matters I do not allow dissent, nor permit my decisions to be repudiated.'

Back in the annexe and much later, it was Casper, having been collected some days ago from Whistle Alley, who brought wine and spiced oat cakes, but he did not stay to share them. 'Not my place,' he shook his head when asked. 'You two talks about them things as don't interest me, not one little bit. You wants me – you calls.' And he puffed from the chamber.

Tyballis sipped her wine. It was a warm evening and the fire had not been laid. Ten sweet honey-scented candles stood unlit in the dim, unbreathing air. It was some time since Andrew had spoken, disclosing little of his recent conversation with the duke. Now his eyes were half-closed, as though dreaming.

Tyballis sat on the footstool at his knees, curled towards him and gazed up, her arms crossed over his lap. After a minute, she said,

'They say when a normally eloquent man stays silent, he is preparing to speak of something horribly unpleasant.'

'Ah,' Andrew smiled, 'the ubiquitous they who plague all our lives with warnings and predictions of disaster. Where are they who will promise us comfort and uninterrupted pleasure?'

'Nowhere. They don't exist.'

'Let me introduce them to you,' he said. 'Comfort? Come into my arms, little one, let me kiss you? So come into my bed, and let me love you.'

'Tell me the bad news first,' she said, watching him carefully. 'Then hold me. I'll need holding. You're going away again, aren't you? And it'll be dangerous. Where are you going? France?'

He smiled again slowly, eyes crinkling, and said, 'Brittany. But not yet.'

'Then why –?'

'First I have a man to follow,' Andrew said. 'But he knows me and knows my purpose. If I am seen, I will be attacked at once. And also a woman. She does not know me, but her lover does. So, I need a partner I can trust – at least a little. Nat has stayed with his woman in Yorkshire. The other Portsoken friends are gone or scattered.'

She felt the solid strength in the muscles of his thighs beneath her hands as she nestled against him. She nodded, and sighed, and rested her chin on her wrists. 'Dangerous, then,' she murmured. 'But not so much – not yet, anyway. And if you want someone you trust – at least a little – will I not do?'

He looked back at her, unblinking. 'No,' he said. 'You will not.'

She felt a lurch of profound disappointment. 'You don't even trust me a little? I know I've made mistakes – I've let you down—'

'Foolish beloved,' he interrupted her. 'I trust you implicitly. But it is far too dangerous. This closely involves Lord Marrott, and he would recognise you immediately.'

'Oh.' In a way, it was a relief. 'But he only saw me in the shadows of his bed curtains, and I was half-naked,' she mumbled. 'He thought I was a strumpet. If I dress up as a lady, and maybe wear a veil, he wouldn't know me at all.'

Andrew looked down at her, frowning. 'Once seen, my love, you cannot be easily forgotten. I have proved that myself.' He paused, thinking, and finally said, 'But perhaps, for one small part of the plan, you might help me. Are you sure you're prepared for the risks involved? They are considerable.'

Crosby's small annexe had become their home. With the duke now so near, Tyballis felt a sense of security even greater than before, and after the violent trespass at Cobham Hall, she adored the domestic simplicity that lit each day and warmed every hour. She could not contemplate a solitary life again after discovering the joy of companionship. 'I may not be very brave,' she admitted, 'but it would be far more frightening to sit here alone, wondering what was happening to you. Look what happened to me last time you were away! I know courage is a virtue. But perhaps being afraid of doing nothing is even more useful.'

Andrew sat in silence for some time, as if weighing one danger against another. Finally, he said softly, 'Courage is a virtue. But not all courageous men are virtuous. I do not prize courage for its own sake, nor consider fear a weakness. Yet, if you are afraid for me when I am away, then you trust me as little as I trust others.' She began to interrupt, but he laughed suddenly and said, 'Truly, if you're to stay with me and be my love, you'll learn more than courage, since danger will always be our bedfellow. This is more than my work – it is who I am. So, welcome to risk, beloved. I'll accept your offer. Tomorrow I go to Westminster. You will dress as a queen, and accompany me, where it's a queen you'll be meeting.'

CHAPTER SIXTY

This time she wore black. Her veil was stiff gauze below a neat cambric headdress, and her pale yellow curls were severely pinned back, their colour hidden. But the result had been achieved after some argument, for her brow had been heightened, and the hairline shaved upwards. Once finished, standing over her, one finger raising her chin and her gaze to his, Andrew had inspected the result.

'Not one scratch. Not one bead of blood,' he pointed out. 'Do you trust me now, little one?'

'I did. I do,' Tyballis sniffed, dislodging his grip. 'But no one has ever come at me quite like that before, not waving a knife at my face.'

'Really? Then you're lucky,' he grinned. 'It happens to me all the time.' He allowed her to sit as he stood behind, his hands on her shoulders and his mouth bent to her ear. 'Though I protest. I surely did not wave the blade at you, my love. I am, you must admit, quite practised in the business of shaving, and I believe waving the knife would have resolved very little.'

Tyballis regarded herself in the little mirror he held up to her. 'Oh well,' she conceded, 'it does look very smooth. Very fashionable. And it makes me look very ladylike and elegant. And old.'

'Therefore less like yourself,' he nodded. 'Which does not

personally please me, but will certainly suit the business at hand. Now, for the gown.'

'It is sometimes quite disconcerting,' Tyballis mumbled as she stood and obediently raised both arms for dressing, 'to discover you know a whole lot more about women's fashions than I do.'

The black silk was carefully lowered over her head and her now-smooth white brow. 'Simple expediency,' Andrew told her, suppressing his smile. 'Correct presentation is a necessary part of my job. The world is shallow. Looking the part can be more effective even than speaking the lines.'

They walked together down Bishopsgate, her hand tucked inside the crook of his elbow. Her smart new shoes clicked on the cobbles and she held the train of her skirts over her other arm. She walked straight-backed to balance the headdress, and privately decided that being a little less grand was preferable, since comfort was far more desirable than beauty. She did not say so. She said nothing at all. Andrew, however, said a great deal. He appeared to her as a resplendent shadow, a towering darkness in velvet so thick and black at her side that she was almost intimidated, and kept her lips, honey-smeared, tightly pursed.

Andrew said, 'Repeat once again, silently this time, everything I tell you, my love.' His voice was a murmur in her ear. 'It is utterly essential that you make no careless mistake. Mistakes, this time, could prove fatal. We will be regarded with some suspicion, for a man rightfully enters sanctuary only to tend to those sheltered there, or to claim shelter himself. Alone, and in the company of a lady, I will appear less threatening, but we will be challenged nonetheless. Now. You are Mary, daughter of Lord Berwick, and we are affianced. You will speak very little, since you have not long arrived in London, know nobody and are rather nervous. Naturally you are still under your father's protection, but he is indisposed at present. You will reply to any impertinent questions with a cold stare and an offended silence. This should overcome any difficulty with the gaps in our story. I am Lord Feayton, as you know. Your father recently arranged our betrothal. I assume you are an heiress of some note, but as yet we are barely acquainted, and therefore share no particular affection. We have not,

I'm sure I need not remind you, spent the past few days wrapped almost permanently together in a bed at Crosby's, quite deliciously naked and glued as one by the sweat of pleasure.'

The Abbey at Westminster backed the palace, and overlooked the Thames across the royal gardens. But the area of sanctuary, spacious, walled and secluded, was tucked between Thieving Lane and St Margaret's Church. The sun struck the great rows of the Abbey's stained-glass windows, flooding out in a kaleidoscope of haloed reflections, echoing Paradise. But the sharp spring breeze from the river did not feel sacred in the least and Tyballis shivered, trying not to cling too tightly to Andrew's luxurious sleeve.

'Cold, my love?' he murmured. 'Or a little – just a little – frightened?'

'When asked impertinent questions,' she answered, raising her chin, 'I am to stare blankly and remain silent.'

He chuckled. 'Quite right, my sweet. And when we are accosted, as we will be, you will remember that. Silence can be as valuable as any blade.'

And so Lord Feayton answered for his companion whenever they were stopped, and therefore crossed the sunny courtyard without being turned away, approaching Abbot Esteney's house where the dowager queen highness was housed.

Her highness had arranged her family's quarters with a view to a prolonged lodging. The house she occupied was grand, spacious, and now further filled with her own luxuries and servants. She did not expect an immediate pardon. Nor did she intend to facilitate the Lord Protector's future influence over her royal son by putting herself and her freedom willingly in his hands. The Duke of Gloucester inspired great loyalty within the country, but she still had many adherents. A beautiful woman can appear saintly in the eyes of the uninitiated, and although in her forties and less beautiful than she had once been, she had learned regality. She might no longer ensnare a king, but she could still sense the timorous Archbishop of York's heartbeat pounding faster whenever she approached him.

Yet sanctuary, even within the abbot's palatial dwelling, had wretched disadvantages. Neither feast nor pageant lightened the dull hours. Her personal chef prepared the dishes she favoured, and Westminster's tradesmen delivered daily, but the company remained ever unchanged. The music was limited to the ecclesiastical, and dancing, mumming and drollery were impossible to arrange. While maintaining mourning for the late king her husband, the long hours seemed even more drear.

The dowager queen was walking in the sunshine with her grown son when she noticed a possible diversion. The Marquess of Dorset noticed first, for he immediately recognised the gentleman in question. He stopped suddenly mid step, staring, one silken pink knee half-raised. His mother, a step ahead, turned and lifted her well-plucked eyebrows. 'You are acquainted, Thomas, with these persons? I doubt I have ever seen them before. What are they doing here?'

The Marquess frowned. 'I know the man well enough. Geoffrey Marrott befriended him a year or more back, but recently I discovered him to be a creature of Hastings', even of Gloucester's, and not to be trusted. In fact, I advised Marrott to eradicate the man.'

'Without evident success,' pronounced the queen. 'I intend to ignore them. Then I shall have them removed from the premises.'

But Lord Feayton could be remarkably difficult to ignore. He stood directly in the path of the illustrious company and bowed low, presenting one long and elegant black silken calf. The lady at his side, eyes hidden behind her veil's netting, curtsied deeply. The marquess did not appear to reciprocate the pleasure, and in particular did not relish being forced to introduce a man he distrusted to his mother. 'Feayton. What business have you here?'

Lord Feayton seemed unperturbed. 'An auspicious encounter, my lord. I came principally with the intention of introducing my intended bride to my old friend, but doubted to discover your lordship so promptly. Instead, in the precincts of the Abbey itself our Holy Father supplies the fortunate opportunity. May I therefore present Mary Berwick, my future wife?'

Dorset bowed stiffly. The queen, bored, nodded and walked a little apart to join her ladies.

The Marquess was trying to remember whether their friendship could ever have been classified close enough for such a contrivance, remembered only irritation and decided that Feayton was now certainly after something. Dorset pouted, making his polite acknowledgment. 'Wish you a bountiful future, Feayton. Sons, and all that. But for the moment I'm hardly in a position—'

The young lady in question lowered her eyes with maidenly modesty and curtsied again. 'Ah, sons,' Andrew smiled with faintly conspiratorial vulgarity. 'An apt blessing, my lord, from one who so well understands the importance of a fertile virility, whether within the matrimonial state or – otherwise.'

The dowager queen, overhearing this remark, again raised the exaggerated arch of high-plucked eyebrows and turned away, signalling to her cluster of ladies, a floating urgency of diaphanous satins. The marquess turned pout to scowl. 'Damned inconvenient, Feayton, as it happens,' he said. 'And if you expect some sort of official recognition from me—'

Lord Feayton at once said, 'Excellent. Your noble mother was not my quarry, Thomas. Now. A word in private?' Dorset hesitated. Feayton continued. 'Never fear, I am not courting favours, nor come with complaints. A little pointless, don't you think, under the circumstances, my lord? Your family is not exactly in a position to bestow honours just yet. No, I have come to offer help, not to beg for it.'

The Marquess of Dorset did not appear relieved. 'Help? I've no need of it, Feayton, and am master of my own destiny as always. You think me vulnerable? Handicapped? Not at all. And I'll not be discussing my personal business with you. Indeed, I am perfectly aware of your recent problematic dealings with my friend Lord Marrott. Now I'd be obliged if you'd leave me to my own affairs.'

Lord Feayton smiled and showed no intention of leaving. 'But I persist, as you see, my dear Thomas. I cannot depart without speaking – informing, I might say, having much to impart.' Andrew regarded Dorset's undisguised puzzlement, and his smile widened. 'Am I being too subtle, my friend? I fear you are unaware of one particular fact. You see, to put it bluntly, I was of the party which travelled from Middleham passing through Northampton on the last day of April just gone, and was therefore witness not only to events, but privy to the aftermath, of decisions discussed and finalised, and to, let us say, plans of a protective nature.'

Dorset jumped. 'Protective?'

'In a manner of speaking, my lord.'

Dorset was still scowling. 'How you managed to be in the party with Gloucester —' He stopped, eyeing the small silent figure of the lady at Feayton's side. 'But a word in private, you said? May I escort your charming betrothed to a place in the shade? And cooling refreshments? Hippocras and tansy cakes, perhaps?'

Tyballis sat alone in the tiny parlour and eyed the cup and two small biscuits nestled on pewter. After the breathtaking unexpectancy of actually encountering her majesty the dowager queen, Tyballis was feeling quite weak. It was therefore some few minutes before she rose, adjusted her veil and headdress, and quietly left the chamber.

She was unacquainted with the Abbey grounds, but Andrew had tutored her for some hours the night before. Stretched naked on the bed beside her, he had impressed outlines with his fingertip on the sheet, explaining each entrance, each surreptitious corner and each cobbled alley. 'She will come here,' he had told her. 'Some time immediately after the dinner hour while the sun, being at its zenith, frightens off the inquisitive meanderers and the midday services keep the priests and nobility occupied. Satisfying hunger will be the concern of all others. You will find her here – having entered, as we shall, through the Bell Tower. Try not to hover. She will be suspicious of strangers. However, I shall have Dorset safe elsewhere and your path should be unwatched.'

'And if someone else – the wrong woman – comes?'

'The one you want is small, a little taller than yourself, and considerably older. Thirty-one or two, I believe. Plump-breasted, round-faced and bright-eyed. The late king liked his mistresses beautiful, but this one, they say, is jovial with more charm of character than of appearance. Indeed, Mistress Shore is famed as unmistakable.'

'And if I still get her wrong?'

'Ask her name, my love, and if she denies it, or gives another, follow her at a distance to be sure. Your judgement must rule the situation. I shall overcome any difficulties afterwards. You need not fear mistakes.'

'Of course I do. Mistakes can be fatal. You told me so yourself.'

'No venture of espionage is without its risks, and I have spent my life overcoming them while righting the mistakes of others. Take confidence, little one. You will do very well.'

Tyballis was feeling somewhat less confident, but as she approached the Bell Tower, she saw a small bustling woman already hurrying through the archway. The woman, pretty and plump-breasted, was not ostentatiously dressed but her gown and cape were fur-trimmed and elegant. Tyballis straightened, lifted her head and walked briskly towards her. With the benefit of silken sophistication, she pretended importance.

'Mistress Shore?'

The woman pursed full pink lips. 'Forgive me, my lady. I am not authorised to speak to anyone and cannot assist you.'

Tyballis said, summoning hauteur, 'I have a message for you, Mistress Shore, but if you will not accept it, then your mission is wasted and you must return at some other time.'

Mistress Shore hesitated. 'Then may I hear the message, my lady? And ask who it is from?'

'Not standing in full daylight, you will not,' said Tyballis, turning at once. She crossed immediately to the shadows of St Margaret's Church. Dutifully, Mistress Shore kept one step behind. They entered the cool of the nave together and the sun blinked out. Tyballis kept back against the wall near the entrance. 'Now,' she said, 'I have word from a mutual friend. You know exactly who I mean. He is at present meeting with someone regarding his safe removal from this country. The suggestion is being considered at this very moment. Your own information must either wait, madam, or be entrusted to myself.'

Mistress Shore lowered her eyes. 'I would prefer to wait.'

'I understand,' Tyballis said with some impatience. 'But Thomas will be ill pleased. His discussion is now taking place with my husband, Lord Feayton, and the information you bring may be imperative to his final decision. Once my husband and I leave, we cannot return. The opportunity will be passed. But your distrust does you credit, madam. It is a shame, but caution, however inconvenient, is a virtue in situations such as these. I will not press you further.'

Mistress Shore stretched out a careful hand, touching the silken elbow of the small imperious lady. 'Perhaps, if the situation is so particularly urgent ...'

'Urgent?' Tyballis stared at the cautiously hovering fingers. 'Not to me, mistress. But to the marquess, most assuredly. You must make your choice according to your conscience. However, I imagine my credentials speak for themselves. I could hardly know of your assignation had his lordship not acquainted me with the circumstances, entrusting me with both his message and eventually – with yours.'

'I see,' whispered Mistress Shore. 'Then I need to speak with you at some length, my lady.'

It was more than an hour later when Tyballis finally scurried from the Abbey's courtyard, disappearing at once into the surrounding alleys of Westminster, her severe black gown blending into the shadows. She had hoped to find Andrew already waiting for her in the designated place, but he was not there and although she waited some minutes, he did not come. She then complied with his orders and began to make her own way back to the safety of Crosby's Place. She would not take a river carrier, so walked, dodging through the Ludgate by late afternoon and entering London alone.

It was some time before she realised she was being followed.

CHAPTER SIXTY-ONE

Well dressed and solitary, she risked the sporadic interest of any opportunistic thief, while the late hour had thinned the crowds, leaving no one to protect her, to cry, 'Stop thief,' or deter a crime by recognising the villain. It was also in deserted streets that rapists roamed. And it was in the empty darkness that assassins, like Andrew Cobham himself, did their business.

Tyballis looked around and saw no one, but when she quickened her pace, the following footsteps also quickened. She slowed. One step behind her the echo halted, then matched her speed. Remarkably patient for a thief. Knowing enough of them and understanding their tactics, she therefore doubted her pattering shadow had only robbery in mind. 'I,' she thought with some asperity, 'am supposed to be the spy. They are not supposed to be spying on me.' Then she turned abruptly, dodging from the direct route into Honey Lane. She halted at once, crushed back against the wall of St Mary's churchyard. For a moment she stopped breathing.

He peered cautiously around the corner after her, careful not to follow until sure the way was clear and empty. He could not see into the silent darkness, but Tyballis saw him. Not an old man but certainly older than she, he was elegantly dressed and she remembered seeing him earlier that day, a nameless courtier in the group around the queen's ladies, perhaps a servant of Dorset. So, this was someone sent specifically to follow her and was therefore the assassin she had imagined. Tyballis took the knife from its stitching within her sleeve where Andrew had secured it that morning. With a deep breath and a quick tug, the stitches parted. Then, as the man scurried past, she grasped the hilt and stepped out into his path.

Andrew had taught her how to imitate the posture, the appearance and the confidence of a lady. He had taught how to pluck her eyebrows to an almost invisible arch and how to shave her forehead, heightening her hairline into globe-like elegance. But he had also taught her to secrete a small knife inside the cuff of her sleeve, and finally he had taught her how to fight with it.

Tyballis, her blade already raised, sliced immediately across the man's face. There was neither time to notice his expression, nor to prepare for his retaliation. Tyballis cut again. The first slash ripped through the thin skin of his forehead and an immediate stream of blood blinded him. Astonished, he staggered back. The second cut opened his cheek. He groaned and stumbled against the wall, peering through blood, his sword drawn.

Obeying Andrew's tutorage, Tyballis then turned and ran. 'Your advantage is in surprise,' he had told her. 'You do not have the strength to stay and grapple.' Now she rushed to hide rather than attempting escape, for the pound of the man's feet was fast behind her, and as she ducked into an alcoved doorway, he had seen. He stood before her, blocking escape. It was his sword she watched, catching a beam of early moonlight within the darkling, and attentive to the menace of the steel, she was distracted. Then suddenly a large, cold hand, fingers blood slick, gripped her throat. His face was now so close that Tyballis tasted his breath. Still bleeding, mouth snarling, hat lost and hair wild, he spat at her and his fingers tightened. Her own fingers flexed on her knife hilt, and as she struggled for breath, she stabbed directly into his groin. Deflected by his codpiece, her blade lost impetus, but entered the flesh of his upper thigh. The man howled, but grabbed her tighter. Then everything changed.

Her release was so sudden that she fell. The words from the

darkness seemed to float from a great distance, spoken in cold fury and through clenched teeth.

'The name, Lacy, or I kill you here.' It was Andrew's voice.

The man spluttered, 'D-Dorset sent me, my lord.'

'Try again,' said Mister Cobham. 'Dorset was with me. Who sent you?'

'Lord Marrott sent C-Captain Het–Hetchcomb,' Lacy croaked. Andrew loosened his hold. Lacy mumbled, 'My Lord Marrott ordered Hetchcomb. Hetchcomb ordered me. J-just obeying orders, my lord. Let me go – I'll tell you everything I can.'

Tyballis watched her assailant held fast, his head forced back, as Andrew said, 'I shall not let you go just yet, Lacy. Convince me of your usefulness, and I shall consider alternatives.' He smiled at Tyballis over his prisoner's shoulder. 'All right, my love? Now Mister Lacy, as you see, is most willing to cooperate. We shall not be kept much longer.'

Mister Lacy evidently found this remark a relief. 'I b-beg you, my lord,' he said in a rush, 'if the lady needs an escort, not to wait on my behalf. And my apologies, my m-most humble apologies – simply following orders and no wish to hurt a lady. At your service, my lord.'

Andrew ignored this. 'This Hetchcomb,' he said, considering. 'Why did he not come himself? Why send a damned fool courtier too inexperienced to overcome a young woman?'

'The lady, my l-lord,' stuttered Lacy, aggrieved, 'took me by surprise. And she had a knife, my lord, which I could not have expected.' He tried to wipe the remaining trickles of blood from his eyes, but Andrew did not release his arms. 'B-besides,' he muttered, 'Hetchcomb was on his way to – told to go, that is, on other duties, my lord.'

'So, now,' smiled Andrew, 'you will tell me exactly what those other duties were. You will then tell me, in the exact words, what you were ordered to do to the future Lady Feayton, and you will then supply a list of all other information you have, including names, which I might find interesting.'

'I c-cannot be expected to know,' objected Lacy, 'what you might find interesting.'

'Oh, I think you know very well,' smiled Andrew. 'So, let us begin. First, we shall retire to a position a little more out of the way, in case of interruptions. And then you will speak quickly, remembering that I am quite capable of breaking your neck as soon as I suspect you of lying. Remembering also that you are greatly inconveniencing my lady, who is in need of a hot posset to soothe her throat, having been roughly accosted by a ruffian deserving no less than a quick death for his impudence.'

Lacy nodded as vigorously as Andrew's hold on his neck permitted, as he was hauled into the small adjacent churchyard. There Andrew sat on an overgrown gravestone while continuing to hold the other man in an uncompromising and vicelike grip. Tyballis, following closely, said, 'The horrid man tried to kill me, Drew.'

'Unforgivable,' replied Andrew with sympathy. 'Perhaps I should in all justice point out how you'd nearly killed him. But naturally the comparison is irrelevant since you, my love, were following my orders – while Mister Lacy had the disadvantage of following the damn fool orders of an idiot.' Having settled the uncomfortable young man on the gravestone, Andrew again turned to Tyballis standing before him. 'It is asking great patience of you, my love, but I fear Mister Lacy will speak less freely if you are watching him. A matter of language in front of ladies, and perhaps a reluctance to admit to ungallant acts. There is also the small matter of my being free to – persuade him. You might therefore prefer to wait within the church. Much warmer, I'm sure.'

Tyballis frowned. 'Persuade him? I'll happily stand here and kick him for you, if you like. I'm not feeling at all squeamish.' She was thoughtfully rubbing the raw marks on her neck.

Andrew shook his head. 'I shall manage better alone, my love.'

Tyballis dutifully trudged over to the church door and pushed it open. There seemed little of interest to examine inside and it was neither warm nor inviting. She was pleased when presently the squeaking door told her Andrew had come for her. He touched one finger lightly to the reddened welts around her neck, flicked aside her little starched veil and kissed her beautifully shaved brow. 'Now for home,' he said softly.

It was a good deal later that, after a concentrated half-hour of relating every detail Mistress Shore had said, Tyballis finally asked, 'So, did you let him go? Or did you kill him?'

Andrew wore only his shirt loose over his hose, and had undressed her down to her shift. He was untying the ribbons at her neck, but paused before saying, 'The marks are fading. But still painful, I imagine. Does it hurt you to swallow? There is more warmed hippocras in the jug and a salve, of sorts, in the garderobe. I'll fetch it for you.'

'You're changing the subject,' Tyballis pointed out. 'In other words, you killed him.'

'You don't seem particularly shocked,' smiled Andrew.

Tyballis shook her head. 'I expected you to,' she said briskly. 'When you told me to go away, it was obvious you didn't want me to see something. You're quite easy to read, you know. Like when you made those uncharacteristic remarks about being virile to Dorset, and with that vulgar smug grin. You never talk like that. So, I knew you just wanted to get rid of the queen. And when I ask something and you change the subject, it's because you don't want to tell me the truth.' She gazed at him with interest for a moment, then said, 'You don't like lying to me. That's nice. But you lie to other people all the time. You lied to that horrid man in the churchyard. You said you'd let him go. But you never meant to, did you?'

'No, my love. But outright slaughter once earned your disapproval, and so – a little reluctantly – I'd agreed to avoid such confrontations. Yet Lacy would have carried tales straight back to Marrott and thence to Dorset concerning the not-so-helpful Lord Feayton and his not-so-modest fiancée.'

'But won't Marrott guess anyway, when that man doesn't report back?'

'Lacy was sent by Captain Hetchcomb, not directly by Marrott. Hetchcomb will investigate first, and by then other matters will take precedence. You remember Captain Hetchcomb, no doubt, since I gather he was your captor at Portsoken. He was also your husband's murderer, I believe. With or without your approval, I intend to kill him one day. But I have risked Marrott's displeasure many times in the past, and am prepared for the consequences. In the meantime, I must report to the duke immediately after dawn. The Woodvilles are deep in plot, and a conspiracy is forming to oust Gloucester as Protector, crown the little king and reinstate Rivers as the power behind the throne.'

'Mistress Shore was careful not to speak too openly, but it wasn't difficult to see what was going on.'

'The information you discovered is invaluable, my love, and you showed great courage. I am proud of you. Now, come here. I have other uses for my beautiful bride-to-be.'

Tyballis sniffed. 'I'm not your bride-to-be-anything. Don't say that. You don't want a wife.'

He was silent a moment, watching her as his fingers traced the rise of her breasts, clearly visible through the material of the chemise. He murmured, 'The advantage of fine linen rather than the coarse fabrics you once wore, my beloved. Through this I see your neck flush. I see those secret reactions, and know when you want me – nearly as much as I want you.' His hands pressed across her and he looked up and smiled. 'Your body tells me what you need.'

She blinked and started to speak but her word ran out and she said nothing. His smile widened. 'How wise, my love. You were going to tell me how I have once again changed the subject, because I wish to avoid confrontation and will not discuss the incongruity of respectability and marriage for a man in my career.' He began very, very slowly to tease her into even tighter knots. His voice sank lower. 'But I am not changing the subject at all, little one, for the subject is still you. What I want from you. What I am prepared to do, to keep you. How much I wish to please you. How much you please me.' She could not meet his eyes, and closed her own. The heat, for the bedroom hearth blazed with fire although the day had been warm, made her dizzy. Andrew continued to murmur and his voice became part of the unreality.

He pressed his mouth to her cheek, and his voice tickled, hot and soft. 'Now I see my own hands on you, all through the pale haze of your chemise. I am spectator, removed and separate, and yet equally as aroused as the player himself.' Tyballis sighed and leaned against him. She no longer had any desire to speak. Her only desire was wrapped up in his explorations and his breath and his voice. 'Now, here, my beloved, once again I watch the secrets of your body unfold. I touch – and you quiver, and open. Your belly contracts, your body responsive.'

At last she said, 'Am I not – always –?'

He chuckled. 'Your body reacts to me. Not always your mind.'

There he made love to her – slow and languorous and playful – whispering softly to her as he examined and discovered, tracing the light and shadows of the fire across her flesh.

He laid her gently beneath the bedcovers, the pillows beneath her head, kissed the fading marks around her neck and stretched his own strength behind the tuck of her legs.

He heard when she slept. He knew the rhythmic change in her breathing and felt the slowing of her heartbeat beneath his hand. Then he carefully slipped away from her, leaving the bed and her curled within it. He bent over a moment, listening to her sleep. It was earlier than he had intended, but he considered the importance of his information warranted this, so he quickly retrieved his clothes from where he had previously discarded them. When he was ready to leave he sat a minute on the edge of the bed, and kissed her again.

'Marriage, my sweet? Would that truly please you, even with a man so clearly unsuitable, so absurdly ugly in both appearance and behaviour, sadly lacking in moral virtue, and without coin, land or prospects? Yet in my mind we are married already. And perhaps, if it would suit you, we will exchange vows once my duke is safe in his council chamber, and the risks to our country all tamed.'

CHAPTER SIXTY-TWO

Richard, Duke of Gloucester, Lord High Constable of England, Great Chamberlain, Lord High Admiral, Lieutenant General of all England's Land Forces and now Lord Protector and Defender of the Realm, had not retired to bed that night. He remained at his writing table throughout the small hours, and Andrew Cobham, crossing briskly from the annexe where he was housed, was admitted immediately, despite the early hour, to the duke's official studio at Crosby's Place. His lordship smiled. 'Not yet dawn, Mister Cobham. Only you wander the moonlit hours as sleepless as I, and have the temerity to acknowledge my habits as bad as your own.'

Andrew bowed. 'Your grace, I have passed most of the day in the Marquess of Dorset's company. I have news of specific messages smuggled into sanctuary, and of those smuggled out. I believe your grace will find my information of sufficient interest to excuse the hour.'

'You had better sit, Cobham,' nodded his grace, 'and tell me everything. Yet I invariably find the good marquess's intentions somewhat predictable.'

'Then I must begin by begging your forgiveness, my lord,' said Andrew softly. 'Much of the news I carry is, as your grace predicts, wearisomely repetitive. But some is not. Some will not please your grace, nor even, perhaps, appear immediately credible. If your grace then directs, I shall continue my investigations until I obtain verifiable proof.'

'Proof, Cobham? You obtained proof, and it was destroyed before it could do its business. Is proof this time imperative? Or simply appropriate?'

'That is for your grace to decide. As yet I have no proof, only my word and the evidence of Lord Marrott's attempts to eliminate both myself and my – assistant. I do not expect to see Lord Hastings again, unless your grace specifically orders it. But much of my information now concerns him.'

'Indeed?' queried the duke. 'Hastings is less than content with me these days. Although I have honoured Buckingham, giving him a place at my right hand, I have bestowed nothing at all on Lord Hastings since I took office as Protector. Nor will I do so until he accepts his culpability and my trust in him returns. His attempts at self-preservation facilitated my brother's death. Now, since poison cannot be incontrovertibly proved, let alone identify the hand that administered it, my own accusations remain silent. But I have spoken to his lordship. He knows my mind.'

Andrew sat before the small oak writing table, his height diminished. He chose his words carefully. 'Yet the Woodville faction widens, my lord, and Lord Hastings explores newly offered possibilities. It seems he no longer considers Dorset his enemy.'

'There is no advantage in being obscure with me, sir.' The duke leaned forwards. 'Speak clearly.'

'My lord,' Andrew continued, 'you are already aware of one Mistress Shore, a favourite companion of his late highness, and more recently of both the Lord Hastings and the Marquess of Dorset. Under pretext of delivering supplies, she freely enters sanctuary, carrying messages. She is the intermediary between both her masters.'

Andrew remained closeted for many hours past dawn. At first the chamber, shutters closed, was deep in shadow and no man took account of time's passage. The candles burned, guttered and were replaced. Wine was served, and drunk. Finally the sun rose, the shutters were taken down, light flooded the chamber, and still they talked. The duke laughed once. Andrew had said, 'I had the pleasure of confiding to Dorset your grace's intention of reinstating Earl Rivers in a position of authority. Begging your pardon, my lord, I explained how your grace considers Rivers' cooperation essential to peaceful and profitable future government, in particular due to his young highness's friendship and reliance on his Woodville uncle. I mentioned that Rivers' temporary incarceration merely serves a warning. Naturally the marquess was delighted.'

It was then that the duke had laughed. 'Dorset believed this? That even suspecting Rivers as the possible instigator of my brother's death and with full knowledge of his intended malice towards myself, I would – for expediency's sake – take him into partnership as the new king's guardian?'

Andrew nodded, the tuck at the corner of his mouth twitching. 'A self-serving pragmatist will always believe other men capable of the same, your grace.'

'As an idealist, and no pragmatist, I now consider the good marquess even more foolish than I had previously supposed,' smiled the duke. 'But are you, Mister Cobham, then considered so estimable and intimate an advisor that I make no plans, even of such a nature, without informing you?'

Andrew bowed briefly. 'Since I am the Lord Feayton, and a nobleman of unusual subtlety, secrecy and intelligence; indeed it seems so, your grace.'

The duke laughed again. 'And in consideration of this, Mister Cobham, I shall tell you that my intentions towards Earl Rivers are of a very different nature. In my capacity as Lord High Constable and Lord Protector, I have already instructed the Earl of Northumberland to instigate investigations into the plots against the realm and my person that preceded Rivers' arrest. The trial will take place within the month, and may result in his summary execution.'

'Once his suitability as the power behind the throne is seen to be entirely eliminated, your grace, there will remain only one other.'

The Duke of Gloucester continued to smile as he leaned back in his chair. 'Indeed. In order to oust me, the man the Woodvilles put forwards must be of sufficiently high office. Without Rivers, there are few remaining candidates. I doubt Stanley would consider it. Buckingham has more to gain from my life than my death and he distrusts his wife's Woodville relatives. The dowager queen naturally intends to influence her son and profit from him, but as a woman she can expect few official positions.'

'It leaves only Lord Hastings, your grace. He has not entirely repudiated the suggestion but as yet nothing has been agreed. There is only hinted subterfuge. But the bait has been taken.'

The duke spoke softly, summarising to himself. 'If Dorset and the dowager are now led to believe in Rivers' release, they will need to keep Hastings hovering until they are sure. Having first been courted, Hastings will now find himself held at a distance. His dreams of renewed prominence will be suddenly undermined. Yet Hastings knows of my own plans concerning Rivers. He will therefore fail to understand the change in Woodville focus. Hastings will probe and so become vulnerable. Meanwhile you, my fine conspirator, will get me evidence. Hastings has been a good friend in the past and I will not move against him without proof.'

Andrew paused, gazing into the sunbeams striping the table beside him. Then he said, 'I am at your service, as always.'

'You hesitated, sir.' The duke frowned. 'Yet we have already established the need for you to inform me of every detail. Do you once again hold back in accordance with your own judgements?'

Andrew nodded. 'No man speaks his mind without careful consideration, when the information is of a particularly delicate nature,' he said softly, 'and when those details are potentially dangerous, even to himself.'

'Hastings again?' The duke leaned forward once more, eyes narrowed.

'No, my lord,' Andrew answered. 'Though his knowledge of this matter is more specific and of far longer standing than my own. But in relating this information, even in accordance with your grace's instructions, I will be speaking certain treason.'

The duke's fingers tightened around the silver bowl of his cup. 'You are no traitor, Cobham. What nonsense is this?'

'I must inform your grace that this final matter greatly concerns his late highness.' Andrew sighed, and looked directly into his employer's frowning grey eyes. 'It equally concerns his highness Edward V. It further relates to your lady wife's late cousin, the Lady Eleanor Butler. You may possibly have heard rumours in past years, my lord. And undoubtedly dismissed them. But from an entirely different quarter, these rumours are about to be unearthed again, and made impossible to ignore.'

The Duke of Gloucester momentarily closed his eyes. 'Poor Clarence's story,' he said quietly to himself, 'for which he was eventually executed. I still regret my brother's ill treatment, though his own folly preceded it. It is, after all, not an easy matter to be brother to a king. Now this story surfaces again? Not only rumour but truth, then, and must be publicly accepted after all?'

It was half an hour later when the duke rose. He looked wearily across at his companion. Andrew also stood. 'Enough,' nodded the duke. 'I go to Mass. Immediately afterwards I shall have a message taken to the Bishop of Bath and Wells. Stillington need no longer wrestle with his conscience. I shall send for you if I require you again today, Cobham. In the meantime, Brittany ceases to be a priority.'

Mister Cobham bowed, left Crosby's and returned briskly to the adjacent building. He was no longer tired.

Tyballis was waiting in the small parlour. 'I have been positively demented,' she informed Andrew in on his return. 'You've been gone hours and I didn't know if you were with the duke or back at Westminster. Don't you ever sleep?'

Andrew grinned. 'I've been speaking with Gloucester. There's a great deal afoot, which you know full well, my love. And the danger escalates.'

'I didn't know it could get any worse.'

'Unfortunately, yes. So I intend teaching you something more of self-defence. Where is the knife I gave you?' Andrew, smiling, did not seem cowed by the danger he evidently expected.

Tyballis frowned at him. 'More? Didn't you think I did rather well yesterday? You said you were proud of me. I was proud of myself.'

'Yes, you did well, my love. But there can always be improvements.' He had crossed to the window but turned now, taking her hands in his. 'It seems you followed the moves I taught you, but you ran too late, giving time for him to follow. Had I not been immediately behind, he could have killed you.'

Tyballis was disappointed. 'Then I wasn't clever, after all.'

'Both clever, and brave. For a first attempt, remarkable. But now you are known, and in direct danger.' He squeezed her fingers, curling them up into fists. 'I shall teach you how to kill me,' he said.

Tyballis glared at him. 'As if I would. As if I could.'

'On the contrary.' He was laughing. 'You are probably the only person who could, my sweet, since I allow no one else close enough. You share my bed, you share my life, even my secrets. I trust you as I trust no other except the duke. You could kill me – perhaps easily. I shall teach you how.'

'I don't want to. Teach me how to kill Casper. He's back from your errand,' Tyballis said. 'An hour ago. And I know where he went, too. You told him to go and get rid of Lacy's corpse.'

Andrew smiled apologetically. 'Not the sort of thing to leave lying around,' he explained, 'especially since I prefer not to be instantly implicated in his death. I had no time last night.'

'Yes, because you wanted to get me out of the way as quickly as possible,' nodded Tyballis. 'You see, I do understand.' She paused, contemplative. 'He did deserve to die, didn't he Drew? I have been feeling a little guilty.'

'Every man and no man deserves to die, my love.' Andrew seated himself on the cushioned window seat, and pulled her abruptly down beside him. 'I have known Lacy as one of Marrott's cronies, a wood-be Woodville, always eager for self-advancement at someone else's expense and so a useful tool. He was prepared to kill. Instead he died. There is nothing more simple than dying. And now I shall teach you how to facilitate the death of anyone who threatens you.'

She leaned her head on his shoulder. 'I won't be good at it, Drew. I can't very well wear a sword, it would make me horribly conspicuous. And women are forced to be weak, aren't they?'

He sat her up straight and frowned at her. 'I don't expect you to ride fully armed into battle, but defence is important, and women learn different strengths. The dowager queen, for instance. Some believe her beauty akin to saintliness but she is also hated because her marriage to the king was unsuitable, because she plundered the wealth of the country to satisfy herself and her huge burdensome family, and because she was pitilessly ruthless and utterly self-serving. Yet all the great lords behave this way and are accepted, even admired for it. Any lord's duty is to increase his power and property. He owes it to his sons. But her highness is also hated because of her strength. Even now. She clings to sanctuary knowing the Protector blames her family for the late king's death – yet even while she hides, she conspires. She does not accept powerlessness. She promotes assassination, since while the duke lives, the Woodvilles know they can never again hold position. Elizabeth Woodville prefers plot to rest. She surrenders only in order to manipulate and rise again.'

'Well, I'm no queen. And I thought you disliked her, not admired her.'

'I both dislike and admire the woman,' Andrew said. 'And there are others, though with fewer advantages. For instance the Countess of Richmond, Henry Tudor's mother. Without beauty, instead she uses the mask of religious devotion. But in truth she's more relentless than the queen. Since suffering the callous brutality of her first husband, she has never accepted surrender.'

'Stop trying to goad me,' objected Tyballis, sitting stiffly. 'Just because I was such a puling little misery with Borin and put up with everything he did! Scared of the river, of my mother-in-law, and my own shadow, too, I suppose. But I was trying to be a good wife, and behave the way everyone said I ought to.'

Andrew grinned. 'I never suspected you of such meek compliance. Becoming my mistress must surely have shattered your ideals, my love. Have I yet corrupted you entirely, I wonder?'

Tyballis punched him in the middle of his black velvet. 'I've changed a lot – living with you. Borin made me feel like a useless baby – and you kept calling me a child when you knew me first. But you don't anymore, do you? Because I've found my courage. As for learning to kill you, there are times when it might prove very tempting. But punching you does no good at all, as if you'd bumped into a butterfly.'

'A very pretty butterfly.'

'Is my beauty akin to saintliness, then?'

He laughed. 'Since beauty seduces the honest man, so it may also come from the devil.'

'I hope you aren't comparing yourself to an honest man, Drew?'

'Honest to the cause I serve. And to you, little demon.' He pulled her back into his arms, suddenly blocking the sunlight, and kissed her. 'And I'll not risk losing you to one of Marrott's vicious dolts,' he murmured to her ear. 'So, I'll teach you how to defend yourself as best you can – a woman with a knife she knows how to use is no butterfly. Your assailant's size doesn't matter if you attack him the right way. For instance, my love, instead of punching me in the ribs where you've no chance of wounding, you should have punched me here.' And he took her hand, palm open, and tucked it hard between his legs.

Which was exactly when Casper Wallop walked in, with William Catesby right behind.

Mister Catesby stopped in the doorway and chuckled. 'Well now, my Lord Feayton,' he said. 'It seems your life is even more interesting than I had supposed.'

CHAPTER SIXTY-THREE

'Dorset is gone,' Catesby said.

'I'm surprised he waited so long.' Andrew passed the wine jug. 'Does his grace know? Has any blockade been erected? Have you informed my Lord Hastings?'

Catesby poured the wine. 'I no longer wish to be associated with my Lord Hastings' employ. I have discovered that, being out of favour with Gloucester, my lord begins to flirt with the enemy.'

'Flirtation is invariably dangerous.' Andrew smiled. 'I know your lord's temptations, Catesby, and so does the duke, for I have told him.' He fingered the silver stem of his cup, and watched the rich crimson bubbles form across the wine's surface. 'I've also informed his grace of other matters greatly concerning the security of this realm.' He looked up again at his companion. 'His late highness's unacknowledged first marriage, for instance. Naturally the duke had heard whispers since the rumours spread after their brother Clarence's arrest many years back. However, the one incontrovertible witness to that long-denied marriage had been induced, first by imprisonment and then by reward, to keep his silence. But evidently Bishop Stillington now feels it his duty to officially inform the Protector. The late king's bigamy will then be made public, and so the bastardy of his children, including that of the new king, will be openly acknowledged.'

'A disaster – a catastrophe, my lord.'

'Perhaps.' Andrew frowned into his cup. 'But it will immediately reduce the Woodville threat. There have been bastards on the throne before, of course, but by right of conquest not inheritance. This time – when it is realised that the new king is not only a child but a bastard child, and with France greedy across the Narrow Sea – I doubt the politically astute will clamour to crown him. A matter for the Protector, and the lords spiritual and temporal to consider. However, I hear that Hastings is further implicated to his detriment, since he winked at the king's second marriage in full knowledge of the first. Gloucester is not pleased.'

Catesby leaned forwards. 'He will have a great deal more to think about than old scores, and stories of Hastings' bad behaviour.' Catesby chewed his thumbnail. 'If now the young king's proven bastardy precludes him from the crown, who is next in line? Clarence's son? But to crown another child would be unfortunate – and of an attainted father?'

'I do not intend to assume,' said Andrew softly. 'I am not a member of Parliament nor of Council, and my lord duke's trust in me does not stretch to discussing such momentous matters. But I tell you this, Catesby. You might be wise to start loosening yourself from Hastings' increasingly dubious reputation. Those of his household may begin to share in his disfavour.'

For a week the weather improved as spring slithered towards summer. Showers washed the rancid effluent from the city gutters, and the sun sparkled across the puddles. The nervous unrest, armed gangs and contradictory rumours fell quiet. Peace settled tentatively across the capital. The political turmoil now bubbling beneath the placid veneer remained hidden, and the newly contented people, assuming justice and a strong leader, breathed deep and went about their usual business. The Woodvilles were quashed, the Protector now protected the realm and all seemed right with the world.

Through a series of intermediaries, the Protector had opened negotiations with her highness the dowager queen, offering promises of safekeeping should she choose to relinquish sanctuary and attend her son. The young king, now housed in the royal apartments at The

Tower, enjoyed neither the comfort of his mother nor the companionship of his younger brother. The little Duke of York remained in sanctuary, and his mother refused all pleas for either him, or herself to re-enter the world. She feared not only accusations but arrest and open condemnation. Instead she remained safe from public scrutiny, plotting the Duke of Gloucester's destruction.

The Marquess of Dorset, in company with his friend and ally Lord Marrott, had slipped away from the Abbey's sanctuary one night when the moon was shrouded and the streets were empty. Two mornings later Lord Marrott took breakfast at a small house overlooking the Cock and Pie fields outside St Giles village just beyond London's wall. Here an upstairs chamber, although cramped and less than comfortable and smelling faintly of damp thatch, was furnished with a great trestle on which seven platters and cups were set. His lordship took his place at the head. Several of the other guests were barely less illustrious. To either side sat Thomas Rotherham, Archbishop of York and John Morton, Bishop of Ely. Other less-notable gentlemen represented their more notable but cautiously absent masters. In place of the Countess of Richmond came her receiver general, Reginald Bray; in place of the dowager queen came her late husband's secretary, Oliver King; and in place of an oblivious King Edward V came his personal doctor, John Argentine. Finally Lord Hastings' legal associate John Forster pulled his chair to the table, cleared his throat and asked the first question.

'I have full knowledge of his young highness's daily routines,' promptly answered the doctor. 'And I can ensure that on whatever day is nominated, his highness the king will be accessible and fully prepared.'

'I do not believe,' stated the Archbishop of York, 'that the royal person should be removed from the royal chambers or held in any other place with even the slightest hint of force. That would be most improper, and risk his highness's antagonism. This must be done, if it is done at all, with the greatest respect.'

'It is in his highness's own interests,' said John Morton flatly.

'Quite right, my lord bishop,' smiled Oliver King. 'His highness's best interests are the only concern of his mother, the queen. And we do not have any adequate assurance that the Lord Protector holds that same degree of altruistic consideration for our new monarch – nor, it seems, for his maternal family.'

'But my lord,' John Forster said quietly, 'if his lordship Earl Rivers is reinstated to hold joint administrative powers, as you have suggested is the Protector's present intention, there will be no further need of action. My associates and I will be more than content, I assure you, and will choose to hold our peace. But my Lord Hastings has spoken to me specifically regarding this, believing adamantly that Lord Rivers will not return. He assures me that your information is entirely erroneous and perhaps maliciously advised.'

Marrott shifted a little uncomfortably in his seat. 'That remains to be seen, sir. As yet any verification is inconclusive and our plans therefore remain equivocal. But we do not have the luxury of time on our side, which is why we have approached your absent friend at this stage. Should Earl Rivers be unable to claim the position we hope for, then Lord Hastings will discover a great deal to his advantage.'

'And meanwhile risks his life,' said John Forster, unblinking.

'It will never come to that,' interrupted Lord Marrott. 'We are not men of inexperience, sir, nor casual self-seeking amateurs.'

'My mistress seeks consideration only for her noble and displaced son,' interrupted Reginald Bray with deference. 'After the coronation, with the king under the proper influence of his maternal family, then Henry Tudor, Earl of Richmond, claims the hand of one of the royal princesses in marriage. If not the eldest, the Princess Elizabeth, then the younger, Cecily. And so expects his welcome return to English soil.'

'What advantage to us in that, sir?' demanded Doctor Argentine.

'Allies, powerful allies,' sighed Reginald Bray. 'Both my lady and her son are staunch supporters of your cause, as you must surely realise, my lords.'

Oliver King doubted this, but said, 'I believe we are united in our intentions. Her highness the queen has instructed me to speak on her behalf. She wishes the king removed from the Protector's control. While the Protector holds the legal guardianship of the realm, with the king's majority not officially achieved, his highness's authority is greatly diminished. But once he is crowned, and with his mother, uncles and half-brothers behind him, he may reinstate the full power of his preferred relatives. Absolute preference will then be bestowed on all those lords who have assisted in the elimination of all present obstacles.'

Rotherham spoke carefully. 'His highness must be placed in his mother's loving embrace.'

The Bishop of Ely frowned. 'The Protector must be permanently removed.'

'Personally I cannot condone violence,' hesitated the Archbishop of York. 'A political solution must be found, and nothing attempted until his highness is able to make his own proclamations.'

'And if his highness does not agree?' said Mister Bray.

'He will,' said Doctor Argentine. 'The king is, after all, just twelve years of age. The Royal apartments in The Tower are magnificent indeed, but he feels most solitary and misses his relatives and friends. So, he will be guided by my advice, and the messages I bring from his loved ones.'

'But be sure his highness is not told too much, nor permitted to confide his knowledge to others,' said Mister Forster at once. 'If my Lord Hastings' collusion is discovered, he will not keep silent. I fear you will all be incriminated.'

'There is no risk. No risk at all,' sighed Lord Marrott. 'We have the support of the highest lords in the land, the most subtle minds and the sharpest intellects. Do you suppose we have so little control over our own security? The Marquess of Dorset and I left sanctuary as easily as a man leaves his bed each morning. We were not even seen by the city's scavengers. I doubt the Duke of Gloucester has yet discovered we are gone.'

Outside, the day was pleasant under a mild sun, and the sharp little breezes from the distant river did not impinge, nor flurry the slow white clouds above. Aimlessly crossing the cropped green of the open fields, a shepherd tapped his crook, leading his small huddle of sheep to the shade of an oak, its roots in the stream. There the shepherd sat, hitching up his smock, easing his back and dabbling his bare toes in the water. He seemed an unusually young man to so lack ambition, yet unusually tall for a farmer's boy. But although his features were deeply shadowed beneath his old straw hat, a prominent nose at least once broken, denoted a less-than-patient temper, and a remarkably firm set to the mouth suggested a man who was interested in more than his sheep.

It was some hours before Andrew returned to Bishopsgate. Late in the afternoon he entered the Crosby annexe, threw off his hat and marched into the parlour. For once no fire had been lit and the boards were streaked with sunshine. He sat beside the empty hearth, stretched his legs and called for Casper.

'Wine,' said Andrew. 'And then tell me how your mission finished.'

Casper poured wine for them both. 'Went well,' he said. 'Remarkable well, as it happens. Like yours did, I'm guessing. Set up the constabulary for a quick arrest, 'ave we, then?'

Andrew drained his cup, poured himself another and smiled. 'Not yet. Marrott and his friend are keeping interesting company, and at the moment are more useful out free than held in custody. I shall keep them under watch for a few days more. And you, my friend?'

'Me, I followed your fine Captain Hetchcomb most of the day. Never noticed me, he didn't, not for a blink.' Casper cackled and scratched his groin. ''Tis clear as the hair up me nose, the bugger's bin scouting The Tower boundaries and testing the waters as you might say.'

Andrew nodded. 'I'll report to the duke shortly. In the meantime, where is Tyballis? I had expected her here.'

Casper shook his head. 'Our Tybbs is still out on whatever tasty trail you sent her, Mister Cobham. She ain't been back since I got home.'

'Trail?' Andrew frowned suddenly. 'I sent her on none. I gave her no mission at all today, and suggested she rest. When did you get back?'

'Over an hour past.' Casper, evidently unconcerned, replenished his own cup. 'But our Mistress Blessop gets ideas of her own, she does,' he continued, mouth full. 'No doubt she's off on some daft chase. She'll be back for supper, you'll see. There ain't none as can worst our Tybbs.'

'In other words, you have no idea at all where she is gone?'

'Well, nor I have,' admitted Casper. 'Since I was out when she left, and she never said naught about leaving for nowhere last I seen of her. But she's a growed woman, and afore it's dark she'll be back.'

"Then your orders are to see to her comfort when she returns," Andrew said, frowning slightly. "Ask her to remain within the house, to rest, and to wait here for me. Sadly, I have a host of duties which cannot any longer be delayed. I shall not be back as soon as I might wish. But," and the frown turned to smile, "you may inform Mistress Blessop, that she will remain constantly safe in my thoughts."

Casper grinned. "I'll look after her, Mister Cobham. Don't you worry."

"I may find her first," Andrew nodded, "since I presume she has returned to Cobham Hall, which is where I must shortly go myself."

Andrew presented his brief report to the duke, but Tyballis was still not home when he returned to the annexe. There was rabbit stew for supper. Andrew pushed the dish away, ordered more wine and strolled to the window. It was early June, and the evening skies were light and the birds still sang. The first signs of a hazy twilight edged beyond the rooftops, but couples still strolled the streets, curfew had not rung and the city gates were still open.

Having already changed his rough undershirt for the silk-lined comfort of his bedrobe, Andrew now strode to the empty bedchamber, and began to dress again. He chose the old worn velvets that were amongst the few clothes truly his own. He then buckled on his sword, clipped his penknife into the turned leather cuff of his boot and slipped another bone-handled blade into the specially made sheath within his belt. He pulled a deep-hooded cape around his shoulders, spoke two brief words to his personal servant, and very quietly left the house.

It was finally dark as Andrew approached the Aldgate. The gatekeeper was lounging against the stone wall, enjoying a last cup of beer before the bells of St Martin's le Grand chimed for the nine o'clock curfew. Andrew walked through the high open archway, quite alone as he crossed the bridge over the great ditch, turned right from Aldgate Without and approached the Portsoken Ward.

The distant fires of the tanneries were smoking and the puffing breeze up from the sea brought the familiar stench of the Ward's main business. But without pause, Andrew kept walking until he came to the rambling and ruined gardens of his own home.

CHAPTER SIXTY-FOUR

A bleak silence absorbed the old stone, the greenery outside rambled and weeds clogged the paths. A chicken squawked, running free through the shrubbery. Andrew unlocked his front door and smelled abandonment. He strode through the great cold hall and its muffled echoes to his bedchamber. No one had slept there since he had shared the bed with Tyballis. But she was not present. Mouse droppings and a spider's web were the only additions.

He then took the main staircase to the attic door and walked directly in. The sour smell strengthened at once. Luke's scrawled papers and books were strewn across the table. Andrew went beyond and entered the bedchamber.

Luke lay in bed, naked and sweating. The bed linen stank. Andrew crossed immediately to the bedside, sat on the edge of the damp mattress and wiped back the hair from his brother's pale and uncomprehending stare. 'You are sick, child,' Andrew said. 'How long have you been like this?'

Luke blinked. 'You! Is it really you? Are you come, Drew? To take me away?'

'Damned fool,' Andrew muttered, and quickly threw back the bedcovers, abruptly exploring his brother's body. He touched Luke's neck, feeling beneath his jaw, then down under the straggles of sweat-slicked hair. He pushed his fingers beneath both armpits, searching for the signs of the Great Mortality. The young man's chest was sunken and sallow but unmarked, no rash of token haemorrhage or spreading bruises darkened the skin. Andrew looked further, pushing Luke's legs apart and feeling for buboes in the unwashed groin. Finally he sat back, sighed deeply and again pulled up the bedcovers. He said, 'You have no signs of the pestilence, child. Nor of the pox. I am not sure how to recognise the later stages of the ague, but if you have truly been ill an age, that would have killed you by now. Nor do you have the dysentery, since you have soiled your bed only with sweat.' He paused, thinking, then said, 'When did you last eat, child?'

'Eat?' croaked Luke, fractious and dry-lipped. 'And what should I eat, then? Where would I find food, with no one here to provide it, or to cook or to care for me? I am dying without a soul to notice, or even to mind. When I'm dead, perhaps you and Maman will cry, though perhaps you won't even do that. I am utterly lost.'

Andrew frowned. 'Do you tell me you have lain here, little brother, for day upon day, without the sense to find yourself food? And are simply starving?'

'Simply?' objected Luke, trying to raise himself on one elbow, but finding no strength, fell back weakly against the pillows. 'Tell me what is simple about misery? And terrible hunger? And the poverty of abandonment?'

Andrew fashioned a torch, lit it and strode out into the gardens, kicking through the tangled damp undergrowth. Eventually he returned directly to the kitchens, filled a small cauldron with water and added the herbs, salads and roots he had found, now well-scrubbed.

Back at his brother's bedside, he sat, holding the cup to Luke's mouth. 'Drink slowly,' he ordered.

'I'm not hungry anymore,' Luke whined. 'My gums hurt too much. They're all blistered with spots and bloody cracks. And the heat will burn me. I am delicate, Drew.'

'You are a damnable nuisance,' Andrew said firmly. 'And you will drink or I shall force you. Sip first, and then swallow slowly. Tomorrow I'll buy you something more appetising.'

'If I am such a nuisance,' moaned Luke, 'you had better leave me to starve.'

Andrew sighed. 'I will not leave you for now, child,' he said. 'But I had other matters to attend to, and it never occurred to me you'd fail so entirely to look after yourself. Before, when the house was full of the folk you so persistently despised, you seemed well able enough to cope.'

'You were here then.' Luke sniffed, gulping the soup. It dribbled down his chin. Andrew leaned over and wiped it off. 'You brought me nice things and gave me money and sometimes you cooked for me. Then when you went away for long times, I was stronger. I could look after myself. And there was Mistress Blessop. She brought nice platters up to my attic. Now there's no one. The food ran out when those horrid men came and locked everyone in. Then what little bits were left got full of maggots. I had no money, so I couldn't buy anything at all.'

'I left you money. Did you spend it all on Maman? And did you not think to explore outside? There are hens, eggs, fish, ducks and berries. There is a wealth of edible greenery.'

Luke coughed, spitting soup and phlegm. 'You think I know how to catch hens? Fish? And, anyway, the eggs ran out. I ate some berries but then they were gone too. The house echoed and I was alone and frightened, and I don't know what's hemlock and what's salad. You never taught me those things.'

Andrew refilled the cup from the basin he had brought up and regarded his brother. The dark bruises beneath Luke's eyes were sunken and the cheeks yellowed. 'You will take another cupful,' Andrew said. 'Then you will sleep. In the morning I'll buy food and cook you a more solid breakfast, I'll bathe you and change the bedding. But first I must go out again.' Luke started up, as Andrew pushed him back. 'Don't be frightened child. I promise to return within a few hours, and you'll be dreaming safe and warm before then. But I have my own life, and my own duties, and there is other urgent business on my mind, other matters that need my attention, and one young woman in particular who concerns me. I will not sacrifice every moment of my life to watch over you, Luke, and you must accept this.'

'Then leave me to die.'

'Don't tempt me, child.' Again Andrew held the cup to Luke's lips. 'Now drink. A little faster this time. You'll feel a great deal better tomorrow.'

As Luke slept, Andrew placed a chamber pot beside the bed, plumped up the pillows, put the basin of remaining soup on the table, closed the attic door very quietly and ran down the stairs.

Outside the stars had claimed the sky. Across the depths of chilly black, the sparkle winked a million tiny flickering torches beyond the moon's haloed aura. It was not the best time to go visiting, but Andrew again pulled his cape around his shoulders and began to trudge towards the distant tanneries. As the stink of the treated hides increased, the tannery tenements loomed. Andrew strode between the tenters and stretched leathers, barrows of stiffened skins still thick with blood, and the tubs of lime and urine ready for the scrubbing. Scraps of hide, left to putrefy, were piled for the glue-pots. Avoiding the main square, Andrew entered one of the lop-sided tenements. Quickly completing his business, he left again, walked on into the clustered village beyond and half an hour later arrived at a tiny farm beyond the tanneries, where the stench lingered but was refreshed by the smells of well-spread manure and animals still ruminating in their squashed barns. Andrew heard the children's voices before he recognised their small eager faces. Felicia Spiers turned as she heard him call, smiled widely in surprise and hurried towards him across the cabbage field.

Luke had been awake for some hours by the time Andrew returned to Cobham Hall.

'Your fever has gone,' Andrew said, his palm to his brother's forehead. 'I sympathise, but I warn you, Luke, I'll not be held hostage to your needs forever. Very soon someone else will arrive, who will help feed and care for you.' Luke sat up in a hurry and winced. 'Don't say things like that, it isn't fair. Where are you going? And who's coming?'

Andrew stopped at the doorway, looking back over his shoulder. 'Ralph is returning with Elizabeth, probably tonight. You never liked them, but they'll help care for you in return for their board. More welcome perhaps, Felicia Spiers and her family will be back here tomorrow. She'll be better able to look after you than I can.'

Luke glowered. 'I want you,' he said.

Andrew shook his head. 'Don't be petulant, Luke. I'm perfectly well aware that you dislike me as much as the others, and no doubt Felicia's kitchen skills are considerably better than my own. Certainly, she's more experienced with nursing fractious young men, and has greater patience with the sick and needy. Nor am I leaving entirely, but I've no intention of playing the trusty companion at your bedside.'

Luke pouted. 'I don't want some woman's sticky fingers on me.'

Andrew shook his head, 'I came here last evening expecting to stay only moments since I had no reason to believe you sick. I had other important reasons for coming, and someone else entirely on my mind. Indeed, it was Tyballis I'd hoped to meet up with. I assume you didn't see her yesterday?'

'Of course I didn't, or she'd have stayed and been kind,' Luke sniffed. 'So, has she run away from you, then? Were you horrid to her, just like you are to me?'

Andrew's mouth twitched slightly. 'As it happens,' he said, 'I make a habit of being particularly nice to Mistress Blessop. But she is not always – wise. And she faces dangers you cannot comprehend, child. Indeed, I believe she is perfectly safe at present, and have no reason to believe otherwise. But I like to be sure. I hope to be back here tonight, once I'm more confident of her whereabouts.'

Having crossed back into the city, he went directly to Crosby's annexe. But Tyballis had not returned and had sent no word. Andrew therefore controlled his rising doubts, and spoke at some length with Casper Wallop. Mistress Blessop, he explained, had now been absent for longer than seemed easily understandable. He further explained in some detail what was now essential both for the duke's business, being imperative for the safety of the entire country, and for the well-being of Mistress Blessop, which was paramount in his thoughts, should she be in any danger. He then changed his clothes with care, took some wine which was meant to calm his doubts, but did not, issued Casper with further orders and quickly left the building in the direction of Whistle Alley.

The old Blessop House was empty, and the door boarded. Andrew investigated briefly but clearly Tyballis was not there and had not recently been there. He strode quickly on and next visited the local sheriff's chambers, where he asked a great many questions and made several curt and specific demands. It was while he was there that Constable Webb entered.

CHAPTER SIXTY-FIVE

Tyballis glared at the man standing over her. 'I haven't the faintest idea who you are, and I haven't the faintest idea what you're talking about. You must be remarkably stupid if you think someone like me could possibly know anything at all about the Lord Protector's personal business. Now, if you'd kindly get out of my way, I wish to go home.'

'My dear lady,' frowned her interrogator. 'Deny what you will, but we have full knowledge of who you are and an even better idea of what you've been doing. And I'm afraid there's no question of permitting you to leave here until we have the answers we need. In the meantime, rest assured you will be treated with the greatest respect. But what happens eventually depends entirely on your cooperation.'

'You are clearly mad,' said Tyballis. She sat on the narrow chair, hands clasped meekly in her lap, and stared up at the nameless man who addressed her. She wore simple clothes and not the finery from the Crosby garderobe, but her insistence that she was Widow Blessop, resident of Portsoken Ward and nothing more, was clearly not believed.

Over the man's shoulder and through the window, Tyballis saw the sedge and grasses of open fields where Londoners grazed their sheep, brought their goats and ponies to feed on common land, and gathered wild herbs for the cook pot. But the day had already slouched towards a late summer evening and the fields had emptied. Tyballis sighed.

The house where she had been brought was unknown to her. She had not been able to see anything on her arrival since she had been unconscious at the time. When she had set off from Crosby's some hours previously, she had intended only to take the air. Both Andrew and Casper had left much earlier but despite their obvious urgency and the hidden difficulties of the current political situation now bubbling beneath the calm, Andrew had given her nothing whatsoever to do that morning.

'Rest,' he suggested. 'You cannot face danger every day, my love. Today at least, choose some other more peaceful pastime.'

'Sewing hems, for instance? Darning stockings, perhaps. Or plucking my eyebrows again? Because I'm a woman and therefore not capable of anything more difficult?'

Andrew had grinned, half-dressed in rough peasant costume and already more than half-concentrated on his own business. 'And our recent discussion regarding a woman's strengths? Does that confirm my masculine contempt?'

Tyballis looked scornful. 'Respect for some women. Not for the silly ones who can't even stand up to their husbands and have to be rescued and looked after all the time.' She slumped, looking away. 'Honestly, Drew, once you even told me women are useless at lying.'

He bent and kissed her cheek. 'You are good at a great many things, my love, as you know perfectly well. But bringing you into danger is hardly something I choose to do on a daily basis, and besides, what I do today cannot involve a woman at my side. Indeed, it's sheep I need. I shall take you with me tomorrow.'

So Tyballis had walked down Cheapside to look at the stalls, to hear the gossip at the market and to dream of cosy evenings with her lover in her arms again.

Both finely dressed but entirely unknown to her, they had come from the shadows but with unexpected courtesy, one either side, so that she found herself walking at their pace, tightly squeezed between them. 'My lady,' one said, 'it is a pleasure to find you enjoying the sunshine. But unexpectedly alone and far from home. And where would your future bridegroom be today, leaving you so unattended?'

'I beg you, let us escort you, my lady,' said the other, taking her elbow as though a friend of long standing.

Tyballis shook her head. 'I've no need of escort, and no desire to know you, sir,' she said, looking around a little wildly. The streets were busy, but no one took any notice of her for as yet there seemed no obvious indication of misconduct. The crowds reassured her, however, for she knew she might quickly create alarm if she wished. 'In fact,' she said rather loudly, 'if you don't leave me alone at once, I shall call for help.'

The first man smiled. 'But my dear lady, we are your help,' he said. 'We are friends of Lord Feayton, and have been sent to bring you to him.'

Tyballis stopped suddenly. 'That sounds most unlikely,' she said. 'My betrothed is – otherwise engaged today. And as for being his friends, I've never seen either of you before in my life.'

The second man smiled pleasantly. 'A quiet word in your ear, my lady, since we do not want all the world hearing those matters that are – you will understand at once – of some secrecy. You see, we work for his grace the Duke of Gloucester, our honourable Lord Protector. We have been sent by his grace, and with the full knowledge of Lord Feayton, to escort you to where your lord awaits you.'

The other continued, 'You must believe us, my lady, for otherwise how should we know you, or your relationship to his lordship? And as for his grace the duke, his word is surely law. The streets are dangerous, so if you will come with us?'

Tyballis frowned. 'There seems a great deal less danger now the Lord Protector is in charge,' she said. 'And I hardly think he has any need of me.' Unable to explain that she was not the Lord Feayton's intended bride, Tyballis hesitated. She was unsure what to believe.

'Only a few steps, my lady, and a respectable goldsmith's nearby – what could be more innocent? It is barely past midday, a bright afternoon and the city is full of shoppers. If anything displeases you,

you may call out and a dozen good citizens of London will run to your assistance.'

Just two steps, a busy, fashionable shop and no possibility of abduction. So, she had gone with them. She had been shown behind a curtain where the wares on display shone with gold, customers jostling, and no threat conceivable. Yet she had been aware of nothing more until she woke to see the glum reflection of twilight through a high window. Half-blind with headache, she managed first to sit, then stagger to her feet. She banged on the door and eventually a sad slouch of a girl had brought small-beer, though refused to speak. Another man came for her soon after.

Her interrogator remained carefully polite. Tall, plainly dressed and determined, he brought her to the empty chamber where now she sat. His threats were implied rather than spoken, but she was still a prisoner. Furious, though as much with herself as with him, Tyballis retained her dignity. Her head hurt, her heart raced and she was terrified, but she showed none of it; for life with Andrew had taught her well. 'I have no idea what you want from me,' she said. 'And anyway, why would I cooperate with ruffians who drugged and abducted me?'

'An unfortunate necessity, my lady,' bowed the man. 'But I swear I've no intention of harming you. I have promised the greatest respect. A gentleman does not mistreat his womenfolk.'

Tyballis sniffed. 'I'm not your womenfolk,' she said. 'And I'm not a lady. Nor, as far as I'm concerned, are you a gentleman. I'm Tyballis Blessop. I don't know dukes or lords and I don't know secrets. I don't know where we are either, and I should very much like to.'

'Unfortunately I cannot oblige, my lady, nor satisfy your curiosity.' The man bowed again. 'But rest assured, should you cooperate fully, afterwards I will make sure you are taken safely back to your own front door.'

'You don't know where I live,' Tyballis objected.

The man started to answer but was interrupted when the door opened abruptly and someone else strode in. Tyballis looked up in alarm. The newcomer was handsomely dressed in violet cerise with black and scarlet trimmings to both doublet and surcoat, lustrous linings of sable and rich purple hose. He slammed the door, raised a querying eyebrow to the man interrogating her and, receiving only a shake of the head, turned immediately to Tyballis.

He began, 'My lady, my apologies for—' and then stopped abruptly. He stared a moment and then growled, 'You!'

Tyballis turned pink. 'My Lord Marrott,' she said, sitting up straight and twisting her fingers in her lap. 'This is – such a surprise. I had supposed you still hiding in sanctuary to escape the impending executioner's axe.'

The Lord Marrott stood over her and glared. 'How unwise, mistress trollop, to antagonise me yet again. Your life rests in my hands, and I might easily decide not to waste any further time on you.' He turned back to his henchman, who stood somewhat startled beside him. 'This is no lady, fool. She's Feayton's whore, and I've had her in my own bed before now. Get the answers you want from her and quick about it, or I shall thrash her myself, and with the greatest pleasure.'

Tyballis stood up, trying to disguise the shaking of her knees. 'How dare you, my lord,' she said. 'So much for respect. Your servant has more manners than his master.'

Marrott stood over her, and with the flat of his hand against her face, pushed her back onto the chair. Then with slow deliberation he placed his foot on the seat between her legs so that she was trapped where she sat. He remained looming over her, his boot pinning her skirts hard to the chair, both his arms folded over his knee, his eyes hard to her eyes. 'I'll show no respect for another man's doxy,' he sneered, 'and I'll get answers out of you any way I wish. Where is Feayton?'

Tyballis remained silent. Her coarse duffle skirts stretched thinly across her lap and Marrott's humiliating pressure rubbed against the inside of her thighs. She wore her old felted stockings, which gartered only as high as her calves, so her legs had little protection as Marrott's boot pressed purposefully up towards her groin. She finally managed to say, 'If this is how you think it proper to behave, my lord, I can only be glad that the Lord Protector now rules the land.'

Marrott pressed his head down close to hers. She smelled the wine on his breath and his spittle flecked her cheek. 'Listen to me, little whore,' he said. 'This house is outside the city, it is owned by my friends, it is not watched by outsiders and your screams would not be heard. How I usually behave is not your business, nor are you capable of understanding. I have been hounded, accused, my property confiscated and my life under threat. I, one of the most powerful – most popular – am now denigrated and despised through no fault of my own. A valued friend of his highness's closest family – an ally of those rightful claimants to power – and yet I am forced to flee, to hide, to act the pauper. So, understand this, mistress whore: my patience is at an end. Annoy me further, and I will have you stripped and beaten before giving you to my men. You'll get no respect from me, and you'll get civility only if you answer my questions. Now – where is Feayton?'

She believed him. She looked down into her lap, where the dark pointed toe pressed against her. 'I have no idea, my lord. He is a busy man. I have not seen him today.'

'So, after violating sanctuary, deceiving Mistress Shore and impersonating a lady, for which you could be arrested, who was it then, who killed my man Lacy? Was it Feayton? You? Who else?'

Her expression immediately betrayed her. She knew it. So she said, 'If you mean the unpleasant young man who followed me from Westminster and then attacked me, I can tell you that a friend of mine killed him in my defence. My friend – Davey Lyttle – was simply protecting me. And I may ask, sir, why you sent your man to attack me when I had hurt no one at all?'

Marrott sneered. 'You'll answer questions, not ask them, strumpet. And you'll tell me everything you know of Feayton's dealings, Gloucester's plans, and anyone else involved. How long have you been spying for Feayton? What has he discovered?'

Tyballis shook her head. 'You go too far, sir. I do as I'm told, but I'm party to no private meetings. I've no information regarding my Lord Feayton's business, let alone his grace of Gloucester's. You insult me and call me whore. Do you also suppose me a master of espionage?'

He was silent a moment, then removed his foot from her skirts, turned and walked over to the other man. 'Keep at it, Piggot. It's obvious she knows more than she's saying. But it's true the trollop's unlikely to have access to anything important. Had she been the Lady Feayton as we thought … but a tumble in bed doesn't mean he tells her his secrets. But for the moment, she's all we've got.'

Piggot nodded. 'Insisted her name was Tyballis Blessop, my lord.'

Lord Marrott glowered, coming back to stand over her. 'But it's not your name I'm interested in now. So, let's find out how much you do know. Feayton – has he been called to Gloucester's special meeting? There's every damned lord and bishop in the land attending the council chamber tomorrow – orders of the Protector. Why? What do you know of that, wench?'

'Simply that you do not appear to have been summoned, sir, and are therefore no longer included amongst the great lords of the land,' said Tyballis, lifting her chin.

His palm slashed across her face with such force that she was thrown backwards, and the chair wobbled. Involuntarily she put her fingertips to her cheeks, shocked and stung. 'You might well cry,' Marrott spat. 'But you'll have far more to cry about if you continue to thwart me.' He turned back to Piggot. 'Forget courtesy, man, since the slut herself has no notion of manners. Get what you can out of her, and do it any way you wish.'

He slammed the door behind him, and Tyballis stared at Piggot. She had no knowledge of any great meeting at Westminster Palace, but knowing nothing might now prove more dangerous than knowing something. She clenched her teeth and her hands and waited, but this time there was no hidden knife stitched within her sleeve. 'Unfortunately,' Piggot was already saying, 'it seems you are no lady after all, mistress. In which case, the offer of eventually returning you to your own home becomes less essential. Indeed, it seems you may never see your home again. Everything, of course, depends on what you tell me now.'

Tyballis abandoned pride and wiped her eyes. 'I know nothing,' she whispered. 'I do what my lord tells me. That's all.'

At least this man kept his hands to himself. 'Whether you're a whore as his lordship informs me, or whether you're the simple widow you claim, clearly you're no fool; you act the lady well enough, you speak well and you're high spirited. Certainly you know more than you're admitting.' Piggot shook his head. 'Now, listen to me,' he said. 'You've nothing to gain in keeping silent, for, trollop or no, I'll treat you as one if you anger me. But be wise, tell me everything you know, take my orders instead of Feayton's – and I'll treat you with the respect I promised. You have everything to gain from helping us, and abandoning your Lord Feayton, a man who cannot even be bothered protecting his mistress, and simply uses her for his own ends.'

CHAPTER SIXTY-SIX

'**B**ut my lord,' stuttered the assistant constable, 'I'm well acquainted with Mistress Blessop, as you know, sir – ever since we were young. And her husband, too – before he was done down. And she's had a mighty hard time of it. But what you're telling me now, my lord, well, it doesn't make sense.'

'You'll remember your civility, Mister Webb,' interrupted the sheriff. 'If his lordship says he's affianced to Mistress Blessop, then that's how it is.'

The assistant constable hung his head. 'I'm right pleased for her, sir. And it's not that I doubt your word, not for one minute. But though I've always thought her a lady at heart, for my Tyballis to marry a lord – well, it's unexpected, and a mite hard to swallow.' He looked up suddenly and smiled. 'But she deserves no less sir, that I can promise. And it explains why I saw her a month back, dressed as grand as a duchess and watching the new little king come riding into town.'

Andrew stared down his impressively prominent nose. 'My good man, your opinions are no doubt of supreme national significance, but at the moment I believe I can dispense with them.' He looked back to the sheriff. 'I repeat, sir, my future bride appears to have disappeared. I have already investigated those places where she might have freely chosen to visit, and she has not been seen. Since lately I, and Mistress Blessop, have been unofficially involved in the removal of the Woodville faction from their usurped power, the enmity of their adherents has accelerated. I suspect foul play. You will therefore treat this matter with the utmost urgency.'

'I shall, I assure you, my lord.' The sheriff remained agitated. 'But my authority is not without barriers, sir, and if your lordship would approach one of the city dignitaries? Sadly, my means are at present limited—'

'Mine are not, sir,' Andrew interrupted him. 'And I shall ensure that those with greater authority are also informed. I intend to alert every representative of the law, up to and including his lordship the mayor. But in the meantime, I expect you to do whatever lies within your – limited – means, sir. I can be contacted at the annexe to Crosby's Place if you discover anything of interest, and I shall let you know if you can help me further.'

He promptly turned on his heel, and left a bemused Robert Webb staring at the sheriff.

'I reckon it's time to see Alderman Hopton,' the assistant constable muttered. 'And I'm pleased for her, of course, as long as it's all done right and proper. And when it comes to a choice of wedding a lord or taking a plain working man – well, there's no comparison, and that's clear. But it's a disappointment – and a lesson to those who wait too long to speak their mind.'

The sheriff reached for his quill. 'You're a gudgeon, Robert Webb, and a fool into the bargain.'

'When a grand lord like Feayton plans to wed a little widowed lass with no more to her name than a room-up-room-down in Whistle Alley,' sniffed Robert Webb, 'maybe he has improper thoughts on his mind, and it's not marriage he's offering. And if you ask me—'

'I'm not asking you, Webb, so keep your mind on your business,' said the other man. 'In the meantime at least those Frenchies will keep their swords sheathed now the Protector's got the country in hand.'

Andrew crossed the city on foot, heading west. He did not return to Crosby's to inform the Lord Protector of the situation, nor did he follow his usual habit of seeking the duke's ultimate authority to investigate as and where he wished. The sealed letter delivered to him the day before had explained, using the now-recognisable code of ambiguity, matters of the utmost urgency that would involve not only the duke himself, but all those of high office, the lords spiritual and temporal, and members of Council for many hours throughout the day. A vague and passing reference within the letter informed Mister Cobham immediately as to the cause of this urgency, and the principal subject the meeting would therefore address. Andrew would, naturally, keep this information entirely to himself. But meanwhile he was required to discover, in general terms, what was known amongst the populace, and with special reference to anyone carrying interesting information into and out of sanctuary. Yet for once these instructions, as far as Andrew was concerned, were of secondary importance. They would be fulfilled, but only while he continued his other search.

In the grand Council Chamber of Westminster Palace, the greatest dignitaries in the land were gathered, summoned by the Lord Protector for reasons unknown to most. Amongst those few fully aware of the subject in hand was the Bishop of Bath and Wells, Robert Stillington. Amongst those quite unaware of the meaning and motive but guarding an avid curiosity was William, Lord Hastings.

All curiosity was quickly satisfied as his grace the Duke of Gloucester called the meeting to order. It was then that the Bishop of Bath and Wells proceeded to explain the situation at considerable length. His fingers placed carefully and a little nervously over the golden cross about his neck, the bishop stood, gazing around at the many familiar faces seated about him. In his best ecclesiastical tones, echoes rising to the great vaulted ceiling, he began his story. He related how, during the spring of 1461, he had been the principal witness when summoned to officiate at a clandestine marriage between the young King Edward IV and the Lady Eleanor, eldest daughter of the Earl of Shrewsbury's second marriage and widow of Sir Thomas Butler. The marriage had taken place as a final result of the young king's persistent wooing of the lady, and following her insistence that both her title and character made it quite impossible for her to become his mistress. Unwilling to admit failure, his highness finally proposed a more respectable union; how honourable and seriously intended this proposal, might have been guessed but remained obscure. A secret marriage was hurriedly arranged and took place that evening. It was consummated that night and the king promptly took his lady to a secret address, where he visited her as frequently as possible over the subsequent weeks.

Others within the council chamber now stood to speak, questioning or taking up the story from where their own knowledge began or overlapped. As was already obvious, the king had not then chosen to announce his new marital state to the nation. Without any ensuing conception of the required heir, the lady was deemed probably barren. His highness, conquest now turning to boredom, ceased to visit so often. His ardour cooled. The Lady Eleanor, unhappy with her young husband's insistence on the continuing secrecy of their relationship, presented her royal groom with a carefully considered ultimatum. As a result of their subsequent agreement, the lady removed herself from her lord's bed and settled for a life of contented anonymity, affiliating herself with the religious order she had always admired. She was protected from scrutiny, presented with property and other securities, and humbly agreed to make no public announcement of her marriage. The lady knew herself the unofficial queen of the realm, but, humiliated and even a little fearful, chose to inform no one beyond her immediate family. These comprised her sister Elizabeth, Duchess of Shrewsbury, and her brother Sir Humphrey Talbot, both now willing to substantiate the facts if required.

There were others who knew and there were many rumours, but his highness had fought hard for the throne, was young, remarkably handsome and much beloved by his people. He made great use of his assets and remained ostensibly unmarried, freely wooing any beautiful woman who attracted his eye. Few denied him and, impetuous and ardent, the king did not easily accept defeat. Sometimes he used inducements, occasionally force, more often he simply used charm. But even faced with the beguiling kisses of a monarch, there were those who refused. Whether his highness entered into other clandestine marriages carefully hidden and afterwards ignored, was unknown. Certainly a scattering of unacknowledged but recognisable infants soon appeared in the king's image. But in the early summer of 1464, after an introduction by the Lord Hastings, the king was once again in love with fresh beauty, and promised anything should the Lady Grey, born Mistress Elizabeth Woodville and now widowed, willingly share his bed. As had the Lady Eleanor Butler before her, the lady would submit only if respectably married. Despite her comparative lack of title or status, a clandestine hand-fasting was quickly arranged. Such a thing had worked before, and with very little subsequent inconvenience to his highness. The nuptials then took place without any fanfare or calling of banns, and the marriage was immediately consummated.

At that time the Lady Eleanor still lived. This second marriage was undoubtedly bigamous. But the Lady Grey nee Woodville did not share the obedient, passive and religious nature of her predecessor. Her uncompromising mother threatened exposure, and the lady herself remained both delectable and enticing. Therefore, some months later that year the king, deciding marriage was in his best interests after all and choosing a moment that amused him, finally submitted and openly announced the name of his wife. This was unpopular with both lords and commoners, but once committed his highness was stubborn. There were other concerns at that time, both political and domestic, and the consequences were eventually disastrous. But she remained queen, and bore her husband many living children, amongst them two fine sons. That these children were in truth illegitimate was known to very few.

The Lady Eleanor died in 1468, and it was at this time the king informed his bride that in fact their marriage had never been legal. She agreed to make no demur, as long as the shame of bigamy was kept secret. But the secrecy of man is a matter for his conscience, whereas the laws of God are not so easily set aside. In the eyes of the Almighty, the king's bigamous second marriage could never be seen as legal, for it was conducted clandestinely, in wilful contravention of the Church's holy decrees and no papal dispensation was ever sought. Over the years this secrecy was occasionally threatened, in particular by the king's ambitious brother George, Duke of Clarence. In order to finally keep the peace, this led to Clarence's execution.

With the Lady Eleanor's demise, there seemed no further need to resurrect the past. But now, after his father's recent unfortunate death, the eldest son had become heir to the throne, as yet uncrowned but accepted as King Edward V. At present regally housed in the royal apartments within the Tower, the young king awaited his coronation. But, as a bastard, although unknown to himself, he was not his father's legal heir.

Robert Stillington, Bishop of Bath and Wells, stood once again, and confessed that he had kept his silence for many long years in obedience to his king. At first, he had been imprisoned for some months as a warning, but on accepting his sovereign's assurances had eventually been rewarded with promotion within the church. But on the late king's demise the bishop had spoken with the Protector and admitted the calamitous truth. Now, on the duke's instructions, he wished to make a full statement to all the lords of the realm. And it would be they, after long deliberation, who would finally decide what the consequences must be. They would need to come to a momentous decision and agree between them whether a bastard child should be crowned King of England – or be set aside for another, more deserving heir to inherit the throne.

The Bishop of Lincoln stood. 'My lords. Must we consecrate this bastard child as sovereign, anointing him in God's name, when in our Heavenly Lord's merciful eyes this boy's birth is the result of wickedness and sin?'

A great silence rested over the chamber. Each man, leaning forwards in agitated breathlessness, or stretching back in amazement, stared at those around him, awaiting the next astonishing development. No one spoke for some minutes. Finally the Duke of Gloucester moved his heavy chair back and stood to address the chamber. 'It is for you, my lords, to make a decision that will affect this country for many years into the future. I will not personally deliberate on this, for there are numerous experts on the laws of royal inheritance amongst you. I leave the matter in your wise and honourable hands.'

'There is time to decide at length,' frowned the bishop, 'since the coronation has already been delayed until late June in order to resolve the sensitive matter of the dowager queen's refusal to leave sanctuary, and her elder son's determination to behave as a criminal on the run.'

The Duke of Buckingham smiled. 'But this is a matter that demands conclusion, or political sensitivity will quickly become political chaos.'

It was some hours later that Andrew crossed out of London and approached a narrow house in Snore Hill south of Smithfield, overlooking the Fleet. With one hand to the hilt of his sword, he knocked loudly on the door. It was opened by a servant, bent and elderly, who appeared to recognise the visitor immediately, and announced, 'Mister Bray is not at home, my lord. Nor do I know when to expect his return. And I am not at liberty to invite your lordship within to await his return, since my master may well be travelling abroad and gone some days.'

Andrew smiled. 'To Brittany, perhaps?'

The servant attempted to close the door. 'I have no such information, my lord. My apologies, and good day to you.'

Mister Cobham began to head north towards Cow Lane, but he stopped and turned once, scanning the two upper windows of the house he had just left. There was neither light nor movement visible. Andrew sighed, dodged from Cow Lane into Chicken Lane and turned west across the fields.

CHAPTER SIXTY-SEVEN

'Turn the girl? Will she betray her lover so quickly, or will she dissemble, saying one thing to us, and another to him?'

'Begging your pardon sir,' said the other man, 'but I've spent half the night interrogating the wench. I'll grant she's clever but there's no trollop can best me. I can break a female's spirit easy enough.'

'A simple man underestimates a clever woman at his own cost, Piggot,' Reginald Bray informed him. 'As the relative and close associate of the Countess of Richmond, I can assure you there are females in this country that could out-manoeuvre the devil himself. I will not trust this Mistress Blessop without further evidence.'

Piggot nodded. 'I promise you, I've threatened and cajoled for hours, and afterwards she's slept a short miserable night locked upstairs without food or drink. She's well broke, and now she'll do what we tell her.'

'I know Lord Feayton.' Mister Bray shook his head. 'Not a handsome man certainly, but he charms the females when he wants to. If this wench thinks she's in love with him, then she'll do his bidding and try to trick us.'

'In love?' sniggered Piggot. 'A whore? In love?'

Mister Bray pursed his lips. 'As soon as Hetchcomb gets back, send him up. He's gone to scout the Tower boundaries looking for the best way to get at the little king in secret, but in the meantime, I'm telling you, the girl's deceptive – or deluded.'

'But females aren't ever in their right minds,' Piggot pointed out. 'And his lordship's furious, so something must be done.'

Andrew Cobham stood silently beneath the trees, keeping to the long shadows, and regarded the narrow house across the fields. The place was neither large nor grand enough for pretentious living. Some years ago it had been a small farmhouse but now, according to Andrew's investigations, it was rented in the name of someone who, he was quite sure, stood in place of someone else entirely, ensuring anonymity. Now, a man answering Lord Marrott's description and others of surprising importance had been seen to enter, to leave, and to return. Andrew knew that a solitary attempt at admittance would gain him no benefit. Even an aggressive arrival in the company of Casper Wallop would surely lead to a useless fight and little else. His intended bride's interrogation of Mistress Shore followed by Lacy's death had led to his own true affiliations becoming known. Quiet watchfulness was now Andrew's only option. It brought results.

Before curfew, Andrew returned to the city and on entering his own quarters in the annexe at Crosby's was informed that he was required at the main hall. After noting that Tyballis had still not returned, he crossed briskly and reported to the chief steward, was asked to wait, and was then granted entry.

His grace nodded as Andrew bowed. 'Mister Cobham, I expect information, in particular regarding the Lord Hastings. I have little time and must return directly to The Tower, but the matter of Hastings is of some urgency. Do you bring questions, or answers?'

'Both, your grace.'

The duke sighed. 'I shall answer your questions first, since I know exactly what they are. The meeting lasted much of the day, and involved, as you have certainly guessed, the disclosure of his late highness's clandestine marriage to the Lady Eleanor Butler. Discussion continued as to the validity of the king's son as heir to the throne, since Edward is now proved the child of a bigamous marriage.' Andrew, standing tall at the other side of the great table, smiled. 'Sit, sit,' the duke ordered. 'You've some right to know the outcome of these matters, Cobham, since the initial compromising information originated with you, and no doubt you can serve me better if you understand the relevant details. So, I will tell you that discussions went as I expected. Had the young Edward been a grown man of experience in warfare and politics, the result might have been different. But a twelve-years boy, long isolated from court and educated principally by his Uncle Rivers who is now held in the north on my command accused of treason, is sadly not the monarch our England surely needs. Now the child's illegitimacy is acknowledged, he is no longer his father's legal heir and will be set aside. That leaves two clear candidates. First possibility in line, my brother's child, young Warwick, Clarence's son. But the boy is younger still, and inexperienced in everything beyond reciting his prayers at bedtime. Besides, he is the child of an attainted father, which legally precludes him. I would be pleased to see Clarence's attainder absolved, but this is in the hands of parliament. Clarence's boy is not the king we need.'

Into the pause, Andrew said, 'And the second candidate, my lord?'

'You already know the answer to that, my friend,' the duke said.

Andrew, still sitting, bowed immediately. 'You have accepted this proposition, my lord. It is agreed?'

'As far as the lords have decided, this is so. But my acceptance is tentative,' the duke replied. 'Under these unusual circumstances, I will not sit a throne against the wishes of those I would rule.' He looked down at his papers spread upon the table, and to his strong, practical hands resting there. After a moment he looked up again. 'Nor will I force my conscience, or accept such a responsibility until I am utterly convinced of its right and necessity. Once this decision is made, it cannot be unmade, and I have never doubted my decisions once sealed. I have therefore demanded time to consider, yet with the country to rule, conspiracies afoot and my duty as Protector still paramount, time is not now my friend.' He sighed, tented his fingers and gazed over their peaks. 'Well, Mister Cobham? You have nothing to say?'

Andrew, his smile widening, pushed back his chair and stood, coming to the side of the table facing the Lord Protector. He quickly knelt on one knee, bowing his head. He said, 'Your highness. My life and my sword are at your service.'

The duke laughed and reached forwards, his hand to Andrew's shoulder. 'Up, man, and sit. This is not done yet.' He waited a moment before saying, 'During the lengthy discussion in the council chamber, I was interested to watch my Lord Hastings' changing expression. You have word of him, his plans, his actions, his friends? Come, Mister Cobham, I have freely answered your unasked questions. Now give me your information.'

It was some time later when Andrew left. The shadows had lengthened into night and only a pearlised glimmer behind the cloud cover denoted the shifting moon. Now the darkness was split by the golden wind-flared flame of his torch as Mister Cobham strode through the narrow streets heading directly for the river. Within a little more than half an hour, he was in the Portsoken Ward and at the battered front door of Cobham Hall. This time there was candlelight at the windows and the sounds of laughter and argument within. Andrew pushed open the door and walked into the bright warm hall. They had lit a large fire.

Some miles northwest, Tyballis sat on the chair she now loathed, and glared at the four men who faced her.

Captain Hetchcomb regarded her with furious contempt. 'I know her well. I had exceptional advice regarding the Portsoken House, which Murch and his men had overtaken and secured. We'd been informed the building belonged to Lord Feayton. But all I found was a parcel of ignorant commoners claiming not to know his lordship, and insisting the building they rented belonged to a Mister Andrew Cobham. This trollop was one of them, and a troublesome wench, too, with her arguments and defiance. I had them locked up safe, waiting the Lord Marrott's orders and hoping for their precious Feayton's return; illusive bugger. And then they got away, the whole damned ramshackle bunch of them, with me fast asleep and knowing nothing till the next morning. I'll gladly thrash the trollop for that now, if I've your permission.'

Piggot shook his head. 'Not yet, captain. Seems Mistress Blessop has considered her options. She's interested in joining our cause.'

'I expect not only reward,' Tyballis said with a sniff, 'but also civility and respect, which is more than I've been shown so far.' She paused, looking at the faces in front of her. Bray was smiling and clearly disbelieving. Piggot was stoutly convinced. Hetchcomb was livid and his fingers twitched. The fourth man was unknown to her, and she was puzzled. He was finely dressed but he stood back, as if giving precedence to the lesser men, and had so far said nothing. Tyballis took a deep breath and continued. 'It's true, of course. Lord Feayton compromised my safety, using me to speak with Mistress Shore. Now I'm known as an enemy to Lord Feayton's enemies. Yet it seems he has neither the time nor the inclination to look after me. I've been your prisoner for two long days, but my lord hasn't deigned to search for me, nor come to my rescue. Frankly I doubt he even realises I've gone. Or, thinking me compromised, he has no further use for me.' Tyballis gulped, remembering the truth which she was now forced to deny.

Reginald Bray frowned. 'Yet the Duke of Gloucester is well known for protecting his friends and employees, madam.'

Tyballis snorted. 'The Duke of Gloucester doesn't know I exist. You over-estimate me, sir.'

'Then perhaps you are of no use to us either, mistress.'

Hetchcomb stepped forwards at once. 'In which case, give the slut to me. I'll teach her a lesson she'll never forget.'

'Yes, yes, captain,' Bray said. 'Your sensitivities are dull, repetitive and interest me not in the slightest.' He looked again to Tyballis. 'And to avoid such violence and instead claim your reward, you undertake to return to your lover, discover everything he knows, and come back here to divulge each secret? And how will you convince me to trust you, mistress? Since at present, I trust you not one inch.'

'As yet I know very little, sir,' said Tyballis, 'but I can tell you something to prove my good intentions. Will you trust me then, and let me go?'

'That depends,' Reginald Bray said at once. 'Worthless information already known to us will hardly suffice.'

Tyballis took a deep breath and, praying for guidance, whispered, 'Very well, I can tell you that my Lord Feayton knows that both Lord Marrott and the Marquess of Dorset have secretly fled sanctuary, and are involved with plotting the Protector's downfall. And he knows the indirect involvement of Henry Tudor and the Lancastrian lords who befriended the exile in Brittany.' Mister Bray scowled, but said nothing. Tyballis hurried on, her voice rising. 'My Lord Feayton also suspects that Lord Hastings' support for the Lord Protector is now wavering. He says in Earl Rivers' absence, Lord Hastings sees himself as the prospective power behind the throne as soon as the new king is crowned, should the Duke of Gloucester be removed. Lord Feayton says Lord Hastings is now involved in what he calls the Woodville conspiracy.'

Four open mouths gaped at her, and four pairs of wild and furious eyes stared. Tyballis stopped speaking at once, frightened she had said too much, and awaiting the first cataclysmic response.

The unnamed gentleman smiled at last. He nodded, satisfied. Reginald Bray turned to him. 'My lord, you're convinced of the girl's honesty?'

'Honesty?' smiled the stranger. 'Certainly not. She is clearly a liar and a harlot, but that's exactly what we need. I've no use for an honest woman.'

'You're sure she's not tricking us, my lord?' insisted Bray.

The quiet man laughed. 'I knew her husband,' he said. 'Worked for both my cousins while each held the title, and gave good service. Was a bruiser and a clod, a man of some violence and no brain, but obeyed anyone who paid him.' The new Baron Throckmorton scratched in his ear and then inspected a fingernail of earwax. 'The wife presumably shows the same metal,' he continued, 'though clearly apes her betters. My cousin Harold didn't like her and told me so. Called her a whore, as most females of that class usually are. But she'll serve us well enough, I'd guess, and if she tries to play a double game, then I know how to treat her. I've too much experience of the world to be tricked by a simple whore.'

Tyballis opened her mouth in considerable surprise, and uttered, 'Throckmorton?'

Some miles due east, Felicia Spiers glowed pink with pride and Ellen turned dizzying circles, dancing with the shadows from the huge flaming fire. Ralph Tame stood silently and respectfully to one side of the hearth. At the great table beyond the scatter of scorched and ruined Turkey rugs, Elizabeth Ingwood quietly watched. And in the wide chair at the head of the table, Jon Spiers snored gently, his head tipped back and his mouth slightly open. 'Our little ones is sleeped upstairs,' Ellen informed her landlord with exhausted excitement. 'It's good – mighty good, mister, having them rooms back. We's home again at last.'

Mister Cobham looked down on the tousled curls. 'Did conditions at the farm not suit you, child?'

'Out on the scrounge didn't get nuffin out there,' Ellen admitted. 'For folks didn't have nuffin to give. On the farm there was lambkins and I had a special one. But then the farm lad slit its poor throat, right in front of me. It quivered and I seen the fright in its eyes. I wouldn't play with no animals after that. Wouldn't play with the farm lad neither.'

'My sympathies,' agreed Mister Cobham. 'Though you have seen me kill chickens before.'

The child shook her head. 'Hens is squawky things what peck each other sore. My little lambkin were gentle and never hurt no one.'

Felicia stepped in front of her daughter. 'Mister Cobham, we are exceedingly glad to be back for many reasons. And to be told that payment for our food and board is not required, well, my dear Jon echoes my gratitude, I'm sure. And we are more than ready to help, sir, and especially since it's our dear Tybbs in danger.'

Ralph said, 'Whatever's wanted, Mister Cobham, you tell us.'

Andrew stood with his back to the fire, his hands clasped behind him, legs apart and his expression lost in shadow. He regarded his tenants for some moments, then he said, 'I thank you all, and welcome you back to my home. My requirements are at present quite simple. Luke Parris may never have been a close friend to any of you in the past, but for reasons of my own, I owe him some consideration. He has been unwell. Left to his own devices he is in no longer able to feed himself, nor is his mental condition robust. Mistress Spiers, I ask you to take Luke as your particular responsibility, since he is no more than a child in many ways. A capricious child, however, and I advise no one here to impart their secrets, nor explain their business in his hearing. At present he is in bed in his usual attic chambers, and is particularly eager to accept Mistress Spier's fine cooking and maternal attentions.'

Felicia looked somewhat disappointed. 'Whatever you ask, Mister Cobham. Ellen can help me. But what of Tyballis?'

'My main concern is her evident disappearance,' Andrew continued, 'so there will be other more urgent requests to come. Tyballis may be in some danger. I shall explain exactly what I want of you before I leave again tonight.'

'You're leaving?' Elizabeth stood abruptly, and came over into the firelight. 'Already? You only just got here.'

'I've a purloined wherry tethered down at the quay, and that's my way back into London before the gates open tomorrow morning. I won't waste a night sleeping. There's a great deal to be done.'

Elizabeth sniffed. 'And no time just to have a cosy evening with your old friends? We lit the fire ready for you.'

He raised an eyebrow. 'You'd expect me to leave you, my dear, under similar circumstances? Knowing you abducted by my enemies and perhaps with a knife to your throat? Aware, what is more, that your danger was my doing? Then, instead should I enjoy a drunken romp for a few hours, followed by a hearty supper perhaps, before a good night's conscience-free sleep, while you suffered alone? Perhaps while you died?'

496

'And Casper?' frowned Elizabeth.

'Already in my service.' Andrew turned to Ralph. 'I'll take you with me,' he said, 'within the hour. But there are matters I need to explain first. So, my friends, listen while I tell you some things that very few people know.'

CHAPTER SIXTY-EIGHT

Andrew heaved the wherry's stubby prow into the shadows of the pier just beyond the Bridge, held fast to the upright pole and quickly climbed the steps to land. Immediately behind him Ralph took the oars, pushed off from the bank and rowed again out into the main swell, heading upriver towards the Ludgate. Without looking back, Andrew crossed the platform, striding from the river's chill past the Old Swan Tavern and from there directly northwards into the damp cobbles of Ebgate Street.

He had not slept for two nights but he was not conscious of exhaustion, though a troubled weariness weighed against him and a grinding ache had begun to spread from his temples across the back of his eyes. He ignored this, silently following the moonless streets to Bishopsgate and the lights of Crosby's Place.

At some considerable distance northwest, a small balding man was seated beneath a beech tree, his back to the bark and his one eye focused on a tall narrow house just across the fields. Wrapped tight in an old oiled cape, a sheep's bladder of small beer clutched in his hand, the man stared, barely blinking, at those who left the house he watched, and at those who arrived. Yawning sometimes, he scratched his groin, picked his nose to pass the time, and waited.

Some hours later as the sun's dawning bathed the cropped grass and the tree's shadows dissipated into golden light, the man heard the soft squelch of footsteps in the mud, and turned, suspicious. At once he grinned, exposing two black teeth and a wide expanse of empty brown gums. He staggered up, stretching his stiff back and legs, and trotted over towards the slim approaching figure. The two men met in the sunlit dazzle, and talked softly together for some minutes. Finally the shorter man nodded, and set off south away from the fields and the house where he had been staring at for most of the night.

The newcomer, also well wrapped in a hooded cape, trudged over to the same tree the first man had recently left, shivered, stared around him for a moment, and then began to cross the fields towards the bent and narrow house.

It was during this change of guard that someone else carefully approached the house of interest, hurrying from the opposite direction through the village of St Giles and down to the back entrance where the old shed leaned its broken walls, sharing a hidden door. This man, fast and slight of build, looked around constantly as if frightened of being followed. Then, deciding he was alone and safe, he dodged into the first of the outbuildings and peeped through the cracks in the wattle-timbered walls across the Cock and Pie fields to the front. He saw the two men, one short, one taller, speaking quietly together. Then the hiding man slipped out again from the shed, still unseen as he edged open the back door into the narrow house, squeezed inside and soundlessly closed the door behind him. Now enclosed within the black chill of the unlit stairs, he hurried immediately up to the first floor.

The Duke of Gloucester and his newly arrived duchess had removed to Baynard's Castle on the Thames, property of the duke's mother. Here, although more heavily shadowed with incessant draughts that tickled the candle flames, the vast chambers offered comfortable space for meetings and the riverside frontage facilitated travel between Westminster and the Tower. Andrew reported on demand, and was admitted after half an hour.

The duke looked up and put down his quill. He nodded, and indicated the chair drawn up to the other side of the table. 'Come in, Cobham,' he said. 'I have been expecting you.'

Andrew bowed, sat, and waited.

The duke continued, 'I'll take no risks with the safety of the city, should the plot thicken in spite of all our efforts. I am therefore in the process of summoning troops from the north. Within the hour Ratcliffe will take the letter and ride directly for York. I shall not be sending you, my friend, since I need you here. Now, tell me of Dorset, of Marrott, and of my Lord Hastings.'

'Your grace, the plot is as yet contained,' replied Andrew. 'Lord Marrott remains in the obscure farmhouse at St Giles, which I described to your grace yesterday. No one of consequence has been seen to leave as of last night, but others come and go throughout all the hours. One of their scouts has been noted speaking with Doctor Argentine, physician to young Edward.' Andrew paused, but being uninterrupted, continued. 'The same Doctor Argentine has also been seen speaking at length to one Dominico Mancini, the suspected informer to the French. Lord Hastings has not been observed entering or approaching the house in question, but has sent members of his household, and his associate John Forster has also been seen visiting there, as has Oliver King, his late highness's secretary.'

'You have access of some kind to the discussions that take place on the premises?' demanded the Lord Protector.

Andrew shook his head. 'They are cautious and I have been unable to infiltrate, nor place my own man inside. But I have already obtained the cooperation of one of the kitchen servants, who is supplying what information he overhears.' He paused, then said, 'There is another matter, my lord, which concerns this house and its occupants. My principal assistant is a young woman who is of special interest to me. She has now disappeared. I am reasonably sure she has been abducted, probably on Marrott's orders, and is quite possibly being held in the same house. Her rescue is of great importance to me. Once I have obtained her release, she will doubtless have a great deal to say of what has taken place in her hearing.'

The duke sat forward at once. 'I will give you armed men,

Cobham. Until the troops come from York, I have few at my disposal, but I have sufficient to storm one house. I will give the relevant orders to arrest Marrott and free your young woman.'

Andrew smiled faintly. 'I thank you, your grace, but forgive me – at this stage I prefer not to risk an interruption that would surely endanger my assistant further, and send the conspiracy underground with the perpetrators increasingly wary and suspicious. Any new safe house would take much time to discover, if at all, and delays could be disastrous. Above all, Lord Hastings would surely absent himself from such risk, and his involvement could no longer be verified. I understand that proof of his guilt or innocence is your grace's principal concern, and the only reason you have not yet moved to arrest the other traitors?'

'I have waited for them to implicate themselves,' murmured the duke, sitting back again in his chair. 'But Hastings' treachery moves me far more. The betrayal of a friend cuts deeper. Yet the urgency is now of another colour, for Hastings knows the situation regarding my nephews' bastardy, and the lords' discussion as to the future monarch. So, already he sees his opportunity of becoming the power behind the throne at imminent risk. He must act before the situation becomes official, or not act at all. Rotherham and Morton, whom you inform me are amongst the conspirators, also know that young Edward may no longer claim the crown by right of inheritance, and they will pass this information through to the dowager queen. So, now the conspiracy must surely encompass my death, or fail entirely. Everything will therefore be disclosed to Dorset today and the necessity for haste will increase further.'

'I therefore have very little time to complete my own plans,' Mister Cobham nodded.

'There is something else,' said the duke. 'My younger nephew, Richard of York, remains with his mother in sanctuary. She has as yet refused all pleas to reunite him with his brother. While she holds the younger boy hostage, the Woodville conspiracy gains strength. But although it is the queen who controls while Rivers is held in the north, it is Hastings who holds the key to peace. He wields considerable influence on the council, and he has the force and the power to back it. If Hastings can be dissuaded from active participation, I can eliminate this Woodville treachery without bloodshed. But with Hastings committed to taking power for himself, the crisis instantly erupts and a bloodless conclusion becomes impossible. I intend putting a final stop to this insurgence before it escalates and all the country suffers the consequences.'

Mister Cobham bent his head. 'I am at your service, my lord.'

'Then know this, Mister Cobham.' The duke leaned forwards, his voice controlled. 'The lords, already invited to a coronation that is now cancelled, must instead unite to decide the future of this land. They must gather in a city at peace, and be free to make their decisions without threat or fear. You, sir, must therefore bring me absolute proof either of Hastings' cooperation, or of his treachery.'

'It will be done, your grace.'

'Very well,' said the duke. 'And now, Mister Cobham, I shall tell you exactly what we will do next.'

Lord Marrott stood at the door of the tiny chamber. It held only dust, rudimentary furnishings and the woman standing in the shadows. Once the late king's ageing corpulence had spoiled his looks, Marrott had been considered the most handsome nobleman at court; therefore unaccustomed to being denied, thwarted or insulted. He regarded the woman who had once, for motives he could barely comprehend, chosen the great ugly hulk of Lord Feayton in preference to his own charms. But now everything was lost. He had saved his life by seeking sanctuary, and by escaping sanctuary had regained his freedom. Yet vengeance against those who had ruined him would be hard to claim. Except for the woman now standing before him.

He said, 'Now for the whore to earn her keep.'

'I have agreed to cooperate in your cause, my lord.' Tyballis took two steps back.

Marrott's rounded cheeks were pink and fresh but his eyes were cold. 'My cause? Yes, you will aid my cause, trollop, and obey me now or take a thrashing. I'm not sure which I might enjoy most.' He pushed her hard back against the wall, hoisting up her skirts. One hand forcing between her legs, his other quickly grappled with his codpiece. Tyballis managed one deep breath, and bit Marrott's ear with all her strength, hanging on until her teeth met.

As Marrott roared and Tyballis tasted his blood, the door was again hurled open and two men rushed into the room. Over his shoulder, her mouth still firmly attached to her attacker's ear, Tyballis stared in amazement at the two who entered. She recognised them both. One was the new Baron Throckmorton. The other man she knew considerably better but had expected to see even less. Marrott, bewildered and caught between pain, thwarted desire and the inexplicable intruders, whirled around. Tyballis lost her grip and was flung aside.

Throckmorton smiled faintly. 'My lord, your – you are – undone.' Marrott cursed, attempting to rehook his dangling codpiece while thrusting his partial nakedness back into its dislodged coverings. Throckmorton continued, 'Apologies for the interruption, but the usual messenger has come and brings a message of great urgency. Urgency – and disaster, sir. The Marquess awaits you downstairs at once. This house is no longer safe and must be abandoned immediately.'

Tyballis, quickly pulling down her skirts, stared in utter astonishment at the other man who had entered. As their eyes met, his own surprise was as great and he hurried back into the shadowed corridor. Marrott and Throckmorton followed, the door was locked behind them, their impatient footsteps thundered down the stairs, and Tyballis was left standing, as startled as she had ever been.

She was still wiping Marrott's blood from her mouth when Throckmorton returned. 'Come here, slut,' he ordered her. 'We're leaving this place at once. You're coming with me.'

Tyballis glowered. 'I made an agreement with the others. I'll keep my word if you let me go.'

He sneered, grabbing at her. 'Your agreement's worth nothing now. Everything's changed and there's twice the danger, so you'll do exactly as I tell you or I'll carry you off in a flour sack.'

She stared down at herself. 'But my gown is torn so I need my cloak.' Throckmorton looked her over and nodded. He was gone less than a minute but Tyballis made good use of it. She raced frantically around the grubby little room, discovered no prospective weapon, but finally snatched up an old wooden candlestick, hiding it within the folds of her skirts. When Throckmorton returned, she was meekly waiting. He wrapped an old brown cape around her shoulders, pulled the hood low over her face and thrust her out and down the stairs.

The mild spring sunshine had turned to rain and a hazy shimmering drizzle hung like gossamer over the lane. Half-pushed, half-dragged, Tyballis kept pace with her captor. Around her others were quickly leaving the house and heading in different directions, twenty men or more disappearing into the shadows. Tyballis looked for Marrott, but did not see him. She looked for the unexpected messenger whom she had been so astonished to recognise, but did not see him either. Then, as the last shadows dispersed, she saw someone else. Twisting to see better, she thought – but could not be sure – that she surely recognised him as well. With a sigh of frustration she dragged her feet as Throckmorton forced her from the house and into the rain.

He did not take her back to Throckmorton Hall, and she guessed he would not risk being seen forcing a young woman through London's streets. They headed north and east, further out into the countryside. The lanes were empty, but the sun peeped from behind the scatter of dark clouds, spangling the last raindrops into a fine golden mesh. A rainbow flickered and arched, half-formed and pale across the treetops ahead, then fragmented as the sun blinked out. Tyballis breathed in the rose and soft violet, feeling that she trudged through dissolving hope.

She thought she had seen Ralph, just a momentary glimpse as she was pushed away. But Ralph had been otherwise engaged and had not noticed her at all. His concentration was now entirely focused as he grabbed the kitchen boy while the skinny child gaped in horror at the frantic scramble around him. He was promptly hauled from the squash of running men at the front door. 'You'll come with me,' Ralph hissed, 'and quiet, now.' No one else saw. No one else cared. They were too eager to get away. The boy had been dragged halfway across the muddy slurp of the Cock and Pie Fields when the rainbow broke through. 'That,' Ralph muttered, 'is a sign of hope, they say. Well, my lad, you'd better hope his lordship takes pity on you when he sees you, or he'll have you turning on your own spit.'

'I ain't done nuffing, mister,' the boy whimpered. 'I said I'd be good, I said I'd tell as to what I seen, and I will.'

'Not that there's enough flesh on your miserable bones to be worth spit-roasting,' Ralph said. 'So, you'll speak up to his lordship and you'll keep nothing back, do you hear? He's not a merciful man, is our Lord Feayton. But the more you tell, the kinder he'll be inclined.'

'I's a spit-boy,' objected the child with a plaintive sniff. 'What went on in that draughty old place, well, it weren't naught to me. Get this, do that. Stoke the fire, grease the rod, keep turning that nasty hot handle and stop sucking them burned fingers! That's all I ever heard, mister. Not no secrets. Not no plots.'

Ralph cuffed the boy's ear. 'Stupid little bugger. I'm no country yokel. I know full well who hears the first rumours in any grand house, and where the gossip is loudest. There's not a lord's kitchen in the land doesn't know every detail of their lord's business and sometimes before he knows it himself.'

'Weren't hardly no grand lord's house,' sniffed the boy, his heels collecting mud as he was dragged along.

'Maybe. But there were lords aplenty in it,' Ralph said. 'And I'm betting you knew a fair bit of what each one said, and of what each one did. There's not a spit-boy in the land doesn't listen to gossip, with both his ears to his master's door.'

As Ralph and the boy headed southeast towards the city, so Baron Throckmorton dragged Tyballis along the northerly road beyond London. There were few who enjoyed walking in the rain. Those citizens who had been caught out, now hurried without attending to their neighbours, and those few who saw, said nothing and thought nothing. A man had every right to admonish his servant. The baron was grandly dressed, clearly a man of substance, while the girl he pushed and pulled wore ragged clothes beneath her cheap cape. His grip on her neck troubled no one. What they did not see was the point of the knife held threateningly close beneath her arm. Tyballis preserved her anger for when she might gain some benefit from it.

From High Oldbourne into Low Oldbourne, Baron Throckmorton marched his captive over the short bridge that crossed The Fleet. But avoiding the right turn towards Newgate, they turned left into Gilt Spur Street at Pie Corner, and knocked on the door of a small house. They were let in at once by an elderly woman in a greasy apron, wiping her hands on her skirts, bobbing and bowing, and bidding her lord welcome with a toothless grin. Throckmorton pushed Tyballis inside and immediately up the dark and rickety staircase. He then flung her into a dingy chamber, pulled the door shut behind him and locked it. Left alone, Tyballis caught her breath and began to look around.

Not far away, Ralph finally took a northern turn, bringing the kitchen-boy into London, following the shadows of the great Roman Wall until turning sharp left into Stinking Lane. Then he also knocked on the door of a small house, which swung open at once. There was no old crone beckoning them in, but a very tall man, broad-shouldered and imperious, dressed in the flowing grandeur of grey velvets.

'Bring him in here,' said Mister Cobham, 'and let's see what the child has to say.'

CHAPTER SIXTY-NINE

It was glum with damp. A low ceiling beam trailed cobwebs. Although without window, some light leaked in around the ramshackle doorframe, and just above the visible rafters a crack in the roof allowed entrance to both a slice of daylight and a steady trickle of rain. The bed had neither posts nor curtains, but a semblance of tattered tester hung over the headboard collecting some of the drifting debris from above. The dribbling rain missed the mattress by a whisker and collected in a puddle on the floorboards amongst the dust. Tyballis had thought the house at St Giles sadly ill-kempt but this building was far smaller, little more than a slum, yet the bed, for all its dirt and discomfort, was unusually large. Tyballis took off her cape and quickly transferred the candlestick she had previously grabbed, to a new hiding place beneath the bed's stuffed bolster. The constant weight of fear and the heartbeat of terror slunk beneath the practicalities. She was alert for any possibility of escape.

This latest claimant to the title of Throckmorton had come unexpectedly into his inheritance. The systematic deaths of his two cousins had interested him, but since they had been no friends of his, had troubled him very little. But now, having risen to such lofty status himself, he was discovering that the family business – smuggled drugs and poisons – was lost to him and the line of ultimate power had changed. He had inherited only debts and a manor in poor repair. He promptly set out to repair more than flaking plaster. It was of him, even more than dreaming of Andrew that Tyballis was thinking as, remaining fully dressed, she eventually curled on the bed with a blanket pulled resolutely up to her chin, and slept restlessly through the night.

❉

Andrew, although it was now three days since he had slept, stayed up a good deal longer. It was the early hours of the Wednesday morning when he finally agreed to rest for the remainder of the night. He intended to sleep for four or five hours, this being sufficient, he decided, to restore his energies. In case of bodily disobedience, he instructed Ralph to awaken him at the appropriate time later that morning.

While Tyballis slept fitfully, constantly awakened by fear and distrust, her dreams interrupted by night terrors, Andrew immediately entered a state reminiscent of coma and remained deeply unconscious, uninterrupted by any of the careful noises around him. When he finally opened his eyes, he saw Ralph's face gazing earnestly down upon him. Andrew blinked away the last shreds of sleep. He smiled faintly and said, 'Is it that time already, my friend?'

Ralph cleared his throat, and shook his head with apologetic sympathy. 'Well, Mister Cobham, in a manner of speaking it is. The time being whatever it is, or whenever it is, as you might say.'

Andrew wedged himself up on both elbows. 'Instead I might say you're being purposefully obscure. Where's the boy?' he demanded. 'You haven't let him go?'

Ralph shook his head again. 'No, nor the brat hasn't got nowhere to go. Lived under the kitchen bench at that other house, and has neither parents nor guardian to take him in. Harry, he's called. Harry Ringer. Begging your pardon, he's having his supper in your kitchens.'

'Supper?' queried Andrew, one eyebrow raised. 'Have I not slept at all, then?'

Ralph looked contrite. 'Indeed, you slept long and deep, sir, and I hadn't the heart to wake you. I did try to call at the hour you asked, give or take, that is, since I'd no clock. But you never roused nor even blinked, sir, and so I let you be.'

Andrew sat up in a hurry. 'Damnation, Ralph. It was important. What time is it now by your reckoning?'

'Nine of the clock, Mister Cobham, for I heard the curfew bell not a minute past.' Ralph had moved back to the doorway, as if expecting retaliation.

'Nine at night?' demanded Andrew.

Ralph nodded sorrowfully. 'It is. You slept all day, but I've not wasted those hours. The boy talked a great deal, is full of gossip and ready to admit to everything. Feed the brat, and he'll chatter on till you clout him to shut up. And he's promised to talk to the duke, too, sir, if that's where you intend taking him now.'

Andrew abruptly swung his legs from the bed and began to dress. 'Yes, I shall go immediately to Crosby's. But what of Tyballis, Mister Tate? What if I've slept while she suffered?'

'Tybbs is alive, sir.' Ralph helped Andrew with his doublet and coat. 'The boy knows she was there, and saw her, too. And he says she's in no danger, for she promised to turncoat, and spy for Dorset. She's to be set free and come back to you, sir, collecting information to relate back to them.'

Andrew paused. 'A great relief, I admit, should it be true,' he said eventually. 'So, we act now. I must be off to Baynard's, and I'll take the boy with me.'

Tyballis was still slumped miserably on the bed when the old woman entered, bringing a bowl of gruel and a cup of ale which she placed on the floor beside her. 'Well then,' she said, wrinkling her whiskered nose. 'Ain't got no thanks? No common manners? This is good food, it is, miss, and all I got in the house. Be grateful, or you'll get naught tomorrow.'

'I am starving,' Tyballis frowned, 'and half-dead of thirst.'

The woman indicated the bowl with a well-knuckled finger. 'Lucky, you are, to get it. His lordship says as how you're no more than a dirty whore and so to let you starve. My Christian good nature has took pity on you, that's all.'

Tyballis drank the ale before speaking. 'Who are you?' she asked, spooning the gruel.

The woman shook her head. Grey hair streaked in white escaped from her cap. 'I'm to answer no questions, his lordship said,' she mumbled, backing hurriedly. 'Don't talk to the whore, he says. So, I won't. Nor can you make me, for I'm a loyal servant, and always have been. I was little Esmund's nurse, and looked after him afore he was neither man nor baron, after his mamma died young, and his papa went off fighting for the king.'

Tyballis finished the gruel. 'It was an excellent meal,' she lied, 'and thank you indeed. You are most kind. And although you must not answer my questions, perhaps you could tell me where the baron is now?'

'Can't tell,' the woman shook her head and further dislodged her cap. 'Won't tell. Nor won't tell when his lordship is due back, nor that he's likely gone home to his own grand house, I reckon, coming back here maybe tomorrow. There's happenings to sort at the Tower for the new little king, and orders from the mighty Marquess of Dorset. For he's an important gentleman, is my little Esmund, and will surely see to all them things first afore he comes back to deal with you.'

'An important man indeed,' gulped Tyballis. 'And, being such a beautiful house and such a nice bed, I imagine perhaps – is this your house, mistress?'

'That it is,' said the woman, snatching up the empty cup and bowl. 'Bought it for me hisself, my dear lord did, out of kindness and noble righteousness. And it's my bed you're in, while I sleeps on the pallet downstairs, for his lordship wants you locked up safe. Keep the wench hungry, and say naught to her, my Esmund says. Which is what I'll be doing, just like he told me. So, I'll answer no questions, and will not tattle neither. You get to sleep now, and cause no trouble.'

Tyballis smiled, which was an effort. 'May I at least know your name, mistress? And anything the Lord Esmund mentioned of his intentions towards me?'

The woman looked suspicious and sniffed. 'Manners, it is, to give my name, I reckon. So, it's Mary – Mary Notrin, and a respectable spinster I am. As for his lordship, I'm not to tell. But you'll not be leaving here in a hurry, that's for sure. And he'll be teaching you a lesson, his lordship will, and punish you good and proper for your wicked ways.'

Andrew crossed southwards through the city's darkened lanes and approached the evening lights of Baynard's Castle. Harry marched at his side, Andrew's hand heavy on his shoulder. Once inside, Andrew reported to the steward, requesting a private audience with the Lord Protector, using the word of code with which he was already familiar. He remained in brisk discussion with the duke for only minutes, then again crossed the city, still firmly leading Harry north to the annexe at Crosby's where Ralph was waiting. Drew passed the young spit-boy into Ralph's care with instructions to return to the rented property in Stinking Lane for the night, then to check again on the St Giles house once the city gates were opened on the following morning before finally returning home to Portsoken. Once Ralph and the boy had left, Andrew set out directly for the river.

With the Bridge closed for the night, he crossed the river by boat and took the Long Southwark Road to the apartment above the tavern where William Colyngbourne lodged. The tavern was closed, and the upper chamber deserted, so after hammering on the door over the stables, Mister Cobham extracted the information he required from the ostler, who had staggered out in his undershirt and rubbing his eyes.

'He's secretive, is Mister Colyngbourne,' the ostler shook his head. 'Takes a riverboat regular, he does, and goes to the city, or further west up to St Giles. Has a few grand friends, as I reckon you knows, being a lord yourself, sir, like as not.'

'Names, man,' Andrew demanded.

'There's a Mister Yate and a Mister Perryvall, though I heard tell as how Perryvall were drowned some months back. Then the mighty Baron Throckmorton – and a Lord Feayton what's been a few times. I can't remember no more, sir.'

But Andrew had already left and was marching through the long shadows back to the stolen wherry he had left tethered at the Southwark steps. It was already a fine Thursday morning when he arrived at the London residence of the Baron of Throckmorton, and hammered on the front door.

It took some time for the steward to answer the summons, and when he did, he appeared to be in a state of dishevelled confusion as he informed Mister Cobham that the baron was not at home. "Where has he gone and when will he return?" Andrew demanded.

After obtaining the information he needed, he left abruptly and strode towards Gilt Spur Street to Pie Corner. It was now well past midday, but the thought of a missed dinner did not enter Andrew Cobham's head.

At Cobham Hall in the Portsoken Ward, Ralph finally sank down beside the faithfully permanent fire, and thrust the young spit-boy Harry into Elizabeth Ingwood's wary embrace. 'What,' demanded Elizabeth, 'am I supposed to do with this?'

Harry wriggled free. 'Don't trouble yerself, lady. I don't need nuffing.'

'He needs a good dinner and a good wash, little bugger,' said Ralph. 'And a smile, since the lad's done his duty by Mister Cobham and talked his guts out. But now there's another task he must do. There's a house right over at St Giles. I'll escort both of you there and explain what's afoot in more detail, but it's you have to take the brat inside, Elizabeth. I'm known there now, so can't go in. Harry'll say you're his sister, bringing him back to work. There'll be just a bunch of servants inside, like as not, though with a risk of someone more important poking around. But there's a hiding place under the floorboards upstairs. That's what the lad's going to show you. And the papers inside that hiding place are valuable as gold. Mister Cobham needs them. Grab the lot and stuff them down your shift. I'll be waiting in the fields outside and will take you both straight to the annexe at Crosby's. Mister Cobham will meet us all there this evening.'

CHAPTER SEVENTY

Tyballis heard the baron's arrival downstairs with the slam of the door, shouts of insult and demand, and finally peace as the perfumes of roast beef spiralled up to her bedchamber. The meat smelled more burned than succulent, but Tyballis had not eaten that day and only cabbage gruel the day before. She would have welcomed any food, burned or otherwise.

Sometime later the baron's footsteps resounded on the stairs. The door was unlocked and Throckmorton marched in. He kicked the door shut behind him though did not bother to lock it again. There were stains of wine and meat juices on his shirt and half open doublet, his mouth was greasy and his eyes shifted with a lack of focus that suggested advanced intoxication. Tyballis scrambled back as far as the headboard permitted. She edged her fingers beneath the bolster, feeling for the hidden candlestick.

'Well?' Throckmorton said, voice slurred. 'Has a few days without food taught you anything? Are you ready for the rest of your punishment?'

One thing that Tyballis had learned from her husband was that men were more dangerous drunk than sober. She said quietly, 'Punishment for what, my lord? I don't even know you, and never crossed you. I offered to help Lord Marrott and collect information for him. Why should I be punished?'

The baron looked momentarily confused. Then he brightened, remembering. 'You were involved in my cousin's death. Your house it was, you murdering trollop. What do you say to that?'

'I was not living there at the time, my lord.' She shook her head. 'The previous baron was visiting my late husband, who often worked for him. They were both killed by an unknown hand. The constable investigated and someone in the Lord Marrott's employ was suspected. Captain Hetchcomb would be my guess.'

'Marrott's my – friend,' spat the baron. His breath smelled and there was chewed meat between his teeth. 'It's Marrott told me to take you away. Told me to do what I like with you. She's a liar, he told me. Pretends she'll spy for us against Feayton. But more likely she'll spy for Feayton against us. And she knows too much now. Finish her off. So, your troublemaking ends here.'

'F-Feayton will find out what you've done,' Tyballis stuttered. Her fingers closed around the stem of the hidden candlestick behind her. 'You'll be arrested. Executed. Marrott, too.'

Throckmorton shook his head. His legs straddled hers, and his hair flicked against her face and stung her eyes. 'Lord Marrott's on the high seas as we speak, and I'm a lord now. Lords can do what they like. They get away with murder all the time. Lock up their wives, rape the milkmaids, beat their servants. Common practice, it is, they all say so. And now, I'm a lord too. So, please me and I might let you live a few days. Come on, whore, do your job. You know how to please a man.'

Tyballis tightened her grip on the candlestick. 'If you kill me you'll have to face the law – the Protector.'

'Gloucester? He's finished. He'll be dead before the week's out. Hastings, Morton – they know how to deal with the likes of him. The little king's ours, and will be back with his mother tomorrow, doing what the queen tells him – issuing orders, arrests, executions. Feayton's the fool. Dorset and Hastings will rule the land in the king's name and my friend Marrott will be welcomed back.' As he spoke, he leaned over her, grabbing at her neck. She felt his nails scratch along her flesh.

'You!' Tyballis yelled. 'You're worse than your filthy cousin.' But other words were floating at the back of her mind. Insistent reminders. Andrew's voice in her head. Don't wait for anything, don't stop to think, don't talk or plead. Don't give a man time to prepare – to retaliate – or strike. Attack before he sees what you're doing. And make it hard. Strike to kill. The first blow must finish him. Let him back at you and you may not have the strength to defend yourself. She struck.

Drunk and indecisive, unsure whether hungry for blood or rape, the baron was head down and aiming for the opening of her gown and the visible rise of her breasts. The candlestick was solid oak, large, ornate and heavy. Using all the strength she had, she smashed it over his head, her hand tingling and the vibration shuddering through her wrist. The second blow must be immediate, her memory's echoes reminded her. You can never be sure the first attack has succeeded, so assume the worst. Do not give him time to recover. Strike again, hard and fast. She brought up both knees, slamming straight up into his groin as she brought the candlestick down a second time on the back of his skull. His full weight slumped, crushing Tyballis beneath him. Grasping the baron's hair, she flung him off her, then stared at her hands, warm with blood. Wriggling free, she clambered from the bed but looked back, wondering if she had killed him. The blood still spread where he lay on his back, head lolling, mouth open. She grabbed the candlestick once more, quietly opened the unlocked door and began to tiptoe downstairs.

The woman was standing, hands on her hips, glaring up through the shadows. She screeched, 'What?' and reached out, hands clawing. Tyballis tried to duck and fell backwards onto the stairs, her heels missing the tread and scrabbling for the next step. As she tumbled, the woman was already on top of her. Tyballis screamed, 'Wait!' and swung the candlestick. It caught the woman's forehead, glancing off. Mary blinked and shook her head as though irritated by a wasp. She fisted one hand. Tyballis shrank back as the fist smashed into her face, the shock and pain intense. She wondered if her nose had been broken, which made her think of Andrew. Again, she wielded the candlestick. The woman grabbed her wrist, bent it backwards, snatched her weapon from her and with a snarl, flung Tyballis down and sat on top of her. Her haunches squelched down, her pelvis grinding, Mary grunted, 'There's blood on you, hussy, and your tits is all hanging out. So, what you done to my little Esmund, then? How's you got away?'

'He let me,' Tyballis spluttered. 'He sent me off. Go up – go look.'

'If you hurt my baby,' Mary threatened, 'then I'll finish you, I will. And here was me giving what little food I had, you greedy trollop. I fed you from my own poor pot, I did. And there's the thanks.'

'Your precious baron's a rich man,' Tyballis wheezed. 'Why doesn't he buy you food? Because he's a mean bastard. He doesn't deserve loyalty.'

'You speak ill o' my baby,' Mary warned, 'and I'll rip your lying tongue out your throat.'

Tyballis sank back. Mary's breath smelled of cow dung, the sweat beneath her armpits was rancid stale and her huge weight made Tyballis dizzy. She closed her eyes, feeling faint as she whispered, 'Your Esmund needs you. He wants you – upstairs. He's all right, but he's – bleeding. Only a nose-bleed. But he needs his dearest nurse.'

Mary sat in silence, considering this information with some care. No sound came from upstairs. The dust beams hung motionless in the day's warmth, waiting for developments. Eventually Mary began to move, upending first from the buttocks to the knees, and then slowly upright. The dust swirled again. Remaining flat, Tyballis lay squashed and gasping. Mary looked down on her with a snort. Her grubby hems brushed over Tyballis's face as the woman stalked to the stairs and began to thump upwards.

Tyballis rolled over and crawled to the door. Standing in the corner, bright in its tasselled scabbard, Throckmorton's sword leaned against the wall where he had unbuckled and left it. Tyballis looked from the door to the sword, and back again. She tested the door handle. The door opened. Snatching up the sword, she hurtled outside, and ran. She was halfway up the road when she remembered telling Andrew, 'A woman can't wear a sword, can she? How ludicrous. How ridiculously conspicuous.' Now she refastened her belt around it, buckled it tight though fumble fingered, and looked around for a dark place to rest, catch her breath and readjust her clothing. Gilt Spur Street was not so far from the dangers of London, and if seen so dishevelled by some ruffian lounging nearby, she risked rape and the same fate she had just escaped. She also risked arrest for she was covered in blood, and the blood was not her own, nor did she have a cloak to disguise it. She could only hide.

A tiny alley ran off to the right and Tyballis hurried into its darkness. She huddled there, calming her breathing and clearing her head. She could smell Throckmorton's blood on her, and Mary Notrin's sweat smeared over her skirts. Then she leaned over and vomited bile. Muck splashed on her shoes, its stench as nauseating as the others. Then staggering on a little, she found her legs would no longer obey her, so she sank to the damp ground where shadows striped the mud and leaned back against the wall behind her. Her breath sounded shallow in her own ears. At least she wasn't hungry, for the thought of food made her belly churn. Other thoughts disgusted her even more. She hoped she had killed Throckmorton, but she also hoped she had not. Killing a man – even such a man – was a black weight, settling like a brick in her stomach. She remembered his head hanging loose on its scrawny neck, then soaking the sheets in slime. Tyballis started to cry.

Just a short distance south, Andrew strode briskly up Gilt Spur Street and rounded the bend into Pie Corner. He marched directly to the tiny house at the end and, without knocking, immediately opened the door and entered the darkness within. The house was unlit. Noise of considerable disturbance echoed from upstairs, sounds of sobbing, choking and swearing. He took the steps several at a stride and entered the only upper chamber.

It was sometime later when he left, and at once began to search every cranny and every inch of the surrounding area.

Now cold, Tyballis had curled within the deepest shadows, her back to the open alleyway, warming her body with her arms. She heard footsteps once, and shivered, cringing closer into her hiding place, her fingers hovering over the hilt of the sword at her hip. But the footsteps passed her by, and eventually she slept a little, although her dreams soon turned to demons. She woke to pain. The blood on her clothes had dried, but the stains were thick and hard. Entering London, even if it was not yet curfew, would expose her to the many folk leaving and entering. Past curfew, and the gates would be locked. Should she find her way into the city, and even in the dark, she did not think she could make it all the way to Crosby's annexe without being stopped either by the law or by some new assailant. There was a more obvious path, where she was less likely to be seen and could rest often along the way. But it would take all night and she was not sure of the right roads. It meant avoiding London and following the shadow of the wall across to the north of Portsoken. Then she would more easily recognise the streets and find her way home. She expected no one living there anymore except perhaps Luke, and he would be incapable of looking after her but she could look after herself until one day Andrew would surely come. Even without knowing what had happened to her, or of the house in Gilt Spur Street, nor even of Throckmorton's involvement, he would surely search for her when he had time, and eventually return to the Portsoken Ward and Cobham Hall.

Just minutes before curfew, Andrew re-entered London and briskly crossed the city's breadth towards Bishopsgate, where Ralph, Elizabeth and the child Harry waited for him at the Crosby annexe. Casper had ensured a large fire, but it was a warm evening and the previous day's rain puddles had all dried. The Crosby servants had been instructed to retire early and it was Casper who let his master in.

They sat around the blazing hearth, Harry cross-legged on the floor. Ralph and Elizabeth, greatly impressed by their surroundings, squeezed together on the settle. Andrew stood, one elbow to the great wooden slab supporting the fireplace. He read quickly through the papers they had brought from the house in St Giles. He looked up and nodded. 'This is sufficient to cost Hastings his head,' he said quietly. 'I shall take these documents to the duke immediately. He will see Hastings at the meeting tomorrow, so he must have these first. But Tyballis is still out there somewhere. I'd hoped she'd come directly here after escaping Throckmorton. She might still arrive tonight if she got through the gates before curfew, though I doubt it. It's too late now. But I won't leave her out there alone in the cold. After speaking to the duke, unless she's arrived back here in the meantime, then I'm off again. If I've not returned by morning, Casper, you stay here with the boy. Gloucester may ask to question him again before the council meeting. Ralph, Elizabeth – you go back to Portsoken. She might go there if I don't find her first.'

Harry sniffed and chewed his thumbnail. He had been served with a sumptuous supper and was now sleepy. Casper looked at him with vague dislike. 'Me? Looking after this cruddy little brat? You reckons me for a babysitter, then?'

'And should Tyballis arrive here while I'm gone,' continued Andrew without any indication of sympathy, 'you will upend one of the pageboys from his pallet and send him immediately to Portsoken to inform me. You'll then ensure Tyballis is given whatever she requires, be it food, bath, rest or a physician. While lodging here, I'm authorised to call on Gloucester's personal physician at any time should I think it necessary. You will do so in my name if needed.'

'Mistress Blessop turns up, ain't no need to tell me what to do,' objected Casper. 'Looking after that maggoty little turd – that's one thing. Looking after our Tybbs, well, that's quite another.'

'But it's strange,' mumbled Ralph, 'considering what you said, Mister Cobham. You found that bastard Throckmorton dead as a squashed flea and some beggar woman claiming as how our Tybbs clubbed the bugger and done him in, and then run off not an hour previous. So, why didn't she come straight here?'

Elizabeth sniffed into Ralph's sleeve, which she was clutching.

'You're all bloody stupid,' she proclaimed. 'Gone to the big house, hasn't she! That's where she calls home – not here.'

Andrew frowned. 'But Crosby's is far closer, and this is where she'd expect to find me.'

'You could be anywhere.' Elizabeth shook her head. 'Here – there – gone tomorrow – back yesterday. You've never been a predictable bugger, after all. And being scared, and maybe hurt – killed a man, which ain't nice, 'specially the first time – and maybe got his blood on her – so, she'd make for the place she feels safest. Not here amongst all them fancy lords and you maybe gone out. At Portsoken, she's herself. We women have sensibilities.'

Andrew was silent a moment. 'I've a long walk to Baynard's and must deliver these papers to the duke before he takes to his bed,' he said, turning thoughtfully towards the door. 'But you may be right, Elizabeth. Afterwards I'll go straight to the old house. Casper, I've changed my mind. Once the sun's up, head for Portsoken with Ralph.'

'And this snotty little worm, too?' demanded Casper. 'Or does I chuck him in the river? Go fishin' maybe, and use the bugger as bait?'

Harry looked down at his knees, sniffed and patiently picked his nose. 'He can't be left here,' Andrew nodded. 'Take him with you.'

'Come back and sleep first,' Ralph advised. 'Tybbs'll be safe with Felicia if she's gone there.'

'But if she is not there,' Andrew said, 'then she is lost somewhere, and possibly in danger. I will not sleep until I have her safe.'

CHAPTER SEVENTY-ONE

The Duke of Gloucester, Lord Protector and Defender of the Realm, was not in bed. The incriminating papers were spread out on the writing table in front of him, one heavily be-ringed hand holding them flat. His grace looked up. 'Well, Mister Cobham,' he said, his voice unusually harsh, 'it seems the man I once called friend has indeed plotted my overthrow and death. First to kidnap my nephew from the Tower, then to settle himself as the power behind the throne with Woodville cooperation, to the inevitable ruination of the realm. The proof you have brought me this time is beyond value.'

'Incontrovertible proof for once,' Andrew nodded. 'It is rare to find a traitor who dares openly put his seal to his intentions.'

'Dorset no doubt insisted on something more tangible than simple word of mouth,' said the duke. 'Every man on this list is risking his life, and would demand reassurance that each of his companions shared the same risk. Traitors always most fear the treachery of their allies.'

'And I still hold the witness, your grace, should you wish to question him again,' Andrew said.

The duke frowned. 'Keep the child safe in case he is needed in the future.' He was silent for some time, his eyes lowered once again to the papers spread on his writing table. Andrew did not interrupt.

Finally Gloucester spoke again, this time softly, as though to himself. 'And so we have it,' he murmured. 'My brother's death may never be avenged and justice never done, for how he died remains unknown. The wretch Throckmorton bought arsenic into the country and sold it to Marrott, who may have used it but for what purpose I cannot now be sure. I suspect Earl Rivers of planning to increase Woodville power through conspiracy and murder, but I cannot prove it. I suspect Dorset's compliance, but cannot prove that either. Although I doubt it, it is conceivable, Cobham, that you have been misled and misdirected. I will not accuse without surety nor act without conviction.' He paused, sighing. 'But this Hastings' betrayal can be proved, and I hold that proof now. That it is him of all those I thought friends, saddens me. But ambition does not make friends, it seems. I thank you, Mister Cobham. You have done remarkably well though I do not enjoy your gifts.'

Andrew bowed. 'And the new Baron Throckmorton lies dead, by an unknown hand.'

The duke said, 'You know my insistence on law and justice by now I hope, Mister Cobham.'

Andrew smiled. 'I can assure your grace I did not kill the man. And there is no further heir to the Throckmorton title, I believe, but there will soon be others who buy smuggled poisons from La Serenissima. Yet the business that now concerns me, your grace, is that of my companion. I have discovered the manner of her abduction, and eventually she will be another witness to the matter in hand. But she is no longer where she was taken. I continue to search for her.'

'Then I will not keep you any longer this night,' said the duke. 'If you need assistance, Cobham, you shall have it.'

Andrew sighed. 'I thank you, your grace, but I believe I am close to finding her. Indeed, it seems she may have rescued herself.'

'A strong woman then, Mister Cobham.'

'Most assuredly, my lord. And yet I thought her weak, when I first met her.' Andrew looked up and smiled. 'I have discovered it is sometimes remarkably pleasant to be proved wrong.'

'I have never found it so,' the duke replied. 'The character of the

Lord Hastings is a case in point. May I know your companion's name, sir?'

Andrew bowed again. 'Mistress Tyballis Blessop, your grace.'

'Not Mistress Cobham yet?' The duke smiled. 'In the meantime, you have my authority to call on troopers, constables or my physician should you have need. In the meantime, the conspiracy ends here. On the morrow I shall have the traitors arrested, and Hastings must pay with his life before this treachery causes the death of many more. The ecclesiastics cannot be so summarily dealt with, and unfortunately Dorset remains free. He will run, of course, as Marrott already has. But there will be no uprising, no captured prince from the Tower, and no disruption within the city. I believe I have some small reputation for resolving insurrections with the minimum of bloodshed and suffering. This will be no exception. I trust you find your friend quickly, sir, and then I shall count this matter finally closed.'

Andrew stepped back, about to take his leave. He said only, 'And may I inquire, your grace, as to the other relevant business, not yet resolved?'

'Are you asking me whether I intend accepting England's crown?' The duke nodded. 'An impetuous question, my friend, but under the circumstances, not unacceptable. First the validity of Bishop Stillington's testimony must be verified. There are others in that lady's family to be approached and the lords must take their time with such a momentous decision. And in the end, should the choice finally rest with me, well Mister Cobham, I believe I shall accept.'

Persistently wary and increasingly tired, Tyballis headed east, keeping to the shadows, the walls and the back lanes. She scurried across the gardens of St Bartholomew's Priory, unseen amongst the shrubbery. The moon, little more than a sickle, was shrouded and the darkness hid her. Fore Street, following the outskirts of the great city wall, was wide and open but no one walked that late, and this was outside the jurisdiction of the Watch. Tyballis hurried across the turgid gurgle of the Walbrook and stared ahead at the grounds of the Bethlehem

Hospital stretching before her. Unpaved lanes led over fields and long strips of well-tended allotment. She could hear the Bedlam dogs barking continuously from their kennels and hoped they were safely locked. Then, clutching Throckmorton's sword to her side, she crossed the green as a sharp frosty wind whistled down from the moors. With a sudden stab of longing, Tyballis wondered if Andrew's mother, just a short walk beyond the main courtyard, was curled snug in her cottage, dreaming of entertaining the queen on the morrow. Tyballis could almost smell the marchpane and shook her head, without the heart to laugh at herself.

Just before crossing Bishopsgate Without, she turned and peered down. The London ditch was too deep and too noisome to crawl into, used as an open sewer for the houses just within the wall. Instead across the main road, she searched for another hidden place in which to sleep. Eventually it was only a tree, an old oak with arms spreading a green canopy over the worn earth below. Pigs had been scrubbing there for acorns and no grass grew, but sitting with her back to the thick trunk, Tyballis felt sheltered. The sword hilt poked into her ribs, but she kept it close. She did not mean to sleep too long. The stars sprang like tiny church candles from the cold black above. From somewhere, perhaps from Bedlam, a dog was barking at the moon. Tyballis closed her eyes. She hoped to dream of Andrew.

Andrew went directly from Baynard's to Portsoken. With the city gates locked fast for the night, once again he approached the river, unroped one of the wherries from the steps, picked the lock that held the oars, and rowed swiftly downstream. The stars reflected like minute beacons on the water's surface. He rowed through silver dancing spangles.

CHAPTER SEVENTY-TWO

The young man stared down at the body on the bed, grunted and scratched his chin. He looked back at the seething and furious woman waiting impatiently behind him. 'He's dead,' said the captain.

'You think I need you stupid bugger to tell me that?' screeched Mary Notrin. 'Clear as piss, it is. What I want to know is – what are you going to do about it?'

Hetchcomb shook his head. 'Bury the poor bastard, I suppose,' he pondered, one finger gingerly poking at Baron Throckmorton's motionless ribs. 'Perhaps send for the priest. Throckmorton got any family left, has he?'

'His lordship,' Mary sniffed, still furious, 'ain't got no one 'cept me. So, I'll go for the priest, but I'll go for the constable, too. This was bloody murder, it was, and must be answered for.'

'Difficult.' Hetchcomb again scratched his chin. 'Best not involve the constable. Unusual circumstances, I'm afraid. You say the girl did it? Well, there's others implicated as wouldn't want the situation investigated too closely, with lords far more important than Throckmorton. And the sly hussy will only say it was self-defence.'

'I fed her,' wailed Mary with bitter regret. 'He said to leave the bitch starving, but I give her my best gruel. And then she slaughters my baby, and runs off without a sorry nor a thank you.'

Mary was clinging to the corner of the bed, wild-eyed and quivering. Her huge breasts shuddered and swung as she spoke, bursting from her apron and the gown beneath. Dark sweat stains streaked black beneath her arms and across the bulges of her waist. Hetchcomb eyed the woman with dislike. 'Quiet, fool. You want the neighbours coming to gawp? This must be kept secret.'

The corpse was spread-eagled over the mattress. His codpiece was awry, his doublet unlaced, and around his neck were the assorted stains of food wine, and copious amounts of blood. His head was tilted back at an unusual angle, and his mouth was full of greenish vomit, the thick slime now dried and cracked around his lips. His eyes, still open, glared up at the bed's cobwebbed tester with milky surprise while beneath his skull the blood was a blackened mess. Hetchcomb said, 'Choked on his own spew by the looks of things.'

'The trollop hit my baby over the head with a nasty big candlestick,' objected Mary. 'I took it off her. I'd have broked her miserable face with it if I'd knowed what she did afore she ran.' Mary sidled up to the bedhead, patting the baron's ruined shoulder. 'Look at his poor dear life's blood all spilled and spoiled,' she said. 'I'll get the bitch, I will. And that other interfering bugger. I told him I would, and so I shall.'

Hetchcomb looked up with a frown. 'Him? Who?'

'The fancy man as come to look and poke around,' Mary explained. 'Said his name were Feayton. I told him it were that murdering little hussy as did my poor Esmund in. Asked a hundred questions he did, and went rummaging all through the house. He done told me not to call the constable, too, but I reckon I shall – and then go watch that trollop swing at Tyburn.'

Hetchcomb walked immediately to the door, but turned back with a snarl. 'You'll not go near the law, madam, do you hear? Or I shall send you to the same grave as your wretched master. But Feayton is known to me. And now I shall certainly avenge your foolish Esmund for you, and I shall do it with the greatest of pleasure.'

Mister Cobham reached his old house shortly before dawn, with the stars still bright in a clear night sky. The little cold wind carried the stench of the tanneries, but the sweet damp smell of growth in the surrounding gardens cleansed the air. Andrew pushed the front door open and walked directly into the hall. The fire had sunk low across the massive hearth with a smattering of wood ash and a drift of soot. He kicked the last smouldering remains and a faint spark sizzled. Once within his own private quarters, he saw no sign that Tyballis had returned. Nothing had been disturbed. He stopped, shoulders slumped, and took one deep breath of utter disappointment.

Back in the hall, he heard footsteps and turned. A small figure had scampered down the stairs and stopped abruptly in front of the fire's last flicker. Andrew gazed down at her. 'Ellen. Where's your mother?'

Ellen curtsied. 'Sleep, sir. And my pa. I bin up with them babies grizzling.'

Andrew nodded. 'And have you seen Mistress Tyballis in the past hours? Yesterday, or tonight?'

The child shook her curls. 'No, mister. I ain't seen our Tybbs for ever so long. I only seen Mister Luke, and my ma and pa, and them babies, and Hob the baker's boy. He brung fresh bread for the feeding of Mister Luke. We et some, too.'

'Very well.' Andrew strode towards the front doors. 'Tell your mother I'll be back, hopefully within a few hours.' He stopped a moment, untied his purse and emptied several coins into Ellen's small grubby palm. 'If I return with Tyballis as I intend to, she'll need hot food. It'll likely be dinnertime by then.'

Ellen brightened. 'Real meat and such, mister? For all of us?'

First light was creeping over the rooftops as Andrew strode out again, heading north. He held a small torch, tapers lit from the fire, but the flame swept and flared in the wind, shuddering into sudden scattered sparks that stung his hand. The roads up from Portsoken towards the High Street and beyond were cut across by alleyways, churchyards and small walled gardens. There were a thousand places to search. With the torch held high, Andrew called her name, though softly, for folk were rising and he wanted neither witness nor interruption. On reaching open ground where the houses were sparse, he called louder. No one answered.

The torch blew out in the wind's sharp whine and he dropped the remaining stubs, stamping out the cinders. Walking on, he peered carefully into each dark corner. Slowly, since he scoured every lane and retraced his steps a dozen times, he came through Hounds Ditch and almost to Bishopsgate Without. He had traced a hundred traitors and foreign spies over the years, discovering those who, for many reasons, did not wish to be found. It did not occur to him that he might fail this time. He was aware only of the risk of reaching her too late.

It was finally the daylight shrinking the shadows which helped him find what he was looking for. At first, now mortally tired himself, he almost passed her by. She was deeply asleep, and had curled so tight beneath the tree that she seemed part of the undergrowth; a shapeless pile of fallen leaves where pigs had scavenged. Then the leaves moved and he saw her foot twitch. Quickly Andrew bent over the small body, his face to hers, listening for her breath. He put his hand very softly to her cheek and called her name.

Tyballis bounced up in wild terror and swung the sword. From her lap where it had lain ready and unsheathed, she sliced it hard left and stabbed upwards. The metal caught the sunbeams through the branches.

Considerably surprised, Andrew lurched back, parrying with one upraised arm. He felt the blade cut through layers of velvet, shirt and flesh within, and knocked it forcibly away. With his other arm he reached out and steadied Tyballis, catching her as she stumbled. She grunted, disengaging hand from hilt, and gazed unbelieving into Andrew's amused smile. 'It is,' he said softly, nursing his wounded arm, 'an unusual greeting. Are you not pleased to see me, little one? I must warn you, once castrated I shall be far less use to you.'

Then, finally believing and with a small squeak of delight, Tyballis tumbled into his arms. He grasped her, one palm clasping her uncovered curls, holding her head firmly against his shoulder. Her voice was muffled by his velvets. She whispered, 'My love. You are a miracle.'

'Unlikely.' He smiled and sat with her beneath the tree, cradling her on his lap. 'I have often wondered what I am,' he said. 'But that was never one of my guesses. Now tell me, my love, are you well? Are you hurt?'

'No.' She managed to shake her head. 'I have a very sore throat and I feel sick. But I slept well. I never thought I'd like sleeping outside, but the fresh air was nice, and the stars were pretty and there was the smell of warm tree bark instead of gutters. But I think the ants have found me, and now I ache.'

'I have come to take you home, little one. Back to Cobham Hall.'

'That's where I was going. It seemed an awfully long way.'

'Unfortunately, it is still a long way,' Andrew told her. 'Too far for me to carry you without stopping many times. Can you walk a little?'

'Of course I can.' She nestled against him. 'I'm happy now, I'm extremely hungry – and I'm longing to get home.'

He nodded. 'You have a great deal to tell me, and I have some things to tell you. But before any of that, I shall wrap you warm in my bed, feed you a hearty dinner with hippocras, and then kiss you for a very long time.' It was as he was speaking that Andrew realised beneath his encircling arm, she was stained with blood. He looked down bemused, and said, 'My love, are you sure you're not injured?'

'No. It's that horrid man's blood. That's why I had to hide.'

Andrew helped her stand, steadied her and looked her over with careful scrutiny. 'Very well,' he said at last, shrugging off his coat and wrapping it around her shoulders, fastening the frayed and hanging laces tight across her body. 'I can avoid the main roads, but at this hour there'll be crowds approaching the Aldgate.'

Tyballis had discovered something else. 'But you're bleeding, too. Did I do that? Have I hurt you?'

'Almost decapitated,' he informed her. 'You have a fine hand with a sword, my love. But now we must start to walk, for I want you home.'

When Tyballis saw the Cobham Hall walls rise up against the sun, she was too tired to run, but smiled and leaned her head against Andrew's shoulder. They walked through the gardens together, kicking aside the weed-matted shrubbery and avoiding the sudden squawk of a chicken. At the end of the overgrown path, the doors were open and Felicia was waiting on the doorstep, Ellen peeping from behind her skirts.

'The fire is lit,' Felicia said, beaming wide, 'and dinner is ready.'

Andrew took Tyballis immediately to his quarters, telling Felicia to bring strong wine, hippocras and food. 'There's a great deal to discuss in private,' he told Tyballis, 'and although you claim to be unhurt, I'm not yet convinced.' He then pointed to the bed. 'In,' he commanded. 'Or shall I undress you first?'

'I'm almost undressed already.' She returned his coat, flung the stolen sword and baldric to the rug, then clambered quickly onto the bed and snuggled there, half-propped back against the pillows and the huge oak headboard. The fire blazed, crackling and busy, the room was bright and hot, and the sunbeams through the smeared windowpanes reflected dewdrop shadows across the floorboards.

Andrew sat on the edge of the mattress facing her, sipping his wine as he watched her eat the pottage Felicia had brought. Eventually, when she had nearly finished, he said, 'Now, my love, I know about Throckmorton, but there is a great deal I cannot know. So, will you tell me precisely what happened?'

She was amazed. 'You know about Throckmorton? How?'

'I've had most of the conspirators under surveillance for some time,' he told her briefly. 'I finally discovered the house in Gilt Spur Street, and went there yesterday. Unfortunately I arrived shortly after you left. I expected to find you nearby, but instead you were remarkably elusive.'

'I was hiding. I was frightened.'

He took the empty bowl from her, and pressed a cup of steaming spiced wine into her hands. 'Now, let us be practical, my sweet. You are safe now and I have no intention of leaving you. So, without fear or embarrassment, will you tell me exactly what occurred, and if any of this blood is your own?'

'None of it.' She shook her head, nose buried in aromatic steam. 'So, is Throckmorton ... is he – all right?'

Andrew paused a moment, frowning. 'He is dead, my love. Were you unaware you'd killed him?'

Tyballis drained the cup. 'I was hoping I hadn't.'

He took the cup from her and refilled it. 'On the contrary, I consider it an excellent result. And there'll be no repercussion. I assume it was self-defence.'

'Yes, it was. But how do you know everything, Drew, when this only happened a few hours ago?'

'I am far more interested in your story, my love.' With a finger beneath her chin, he lifted her face to his, gazing directly into her eyes. 'Will you tell me without subterfuge, little one? Did he rape you?'

She shook her head. 'I hit him with a candlestick.'

'A wise decision.'

'He was already drunk, so he was easier to hit. But I couldn't be sure he was dead. He bled a lot, but he was still twitching when I ran away. I very much wanted to kill him but now I don't like thinking I really did. It makes me feel sick.'

Andrew moved beside her, leaning back against the piled pillows and taking her in his arms, her head against his cheek. 'I understand, my love,' he murmured. 'But the man deserved to die for many reasons. He was a traitor, and would soon have died by the axe. No doubt your candlestick provided a quicker end.'

'Before I thought – but now I'm confused. Does it get easier?'

He chuckled softly. 'Perhaps. Though I must point out that slaughtering innocent passers-by has never been my habit. Now, let us begin at the beginning. Who took you and where? It is six days since I last held you in my arms, and I have been wretched without you. I have missed you desperately, little one.'

'You really missed me?' She was momentarily delighted.

Andrew sighed. 'My love, can you doubt it? I have slept very little in that time, and eaten less.' He smoothed the tangled curls from her forehead and tucked them behind her ears, one of his many familiar habits which she had been missing so desperately. 'Do you need such reassurance? Then let me tell you it is a new experience for me to miss a woman, but for the past few days I have considered little else.' She was silent, and he grinned down at her. 'Do you believe me so callous

I could lose you for so long and not miss every inch of you? While reporting to the duke, it's the image of your smile I see in my mind.' He sighed. 'I should be holding you now, but if I do, it will inevitably end one way and until you are recovered, I must wait. But I can promise you this, my own, these threats and abductions will cease. By tomorrow there will be peace in the country, and I doubt I shall risk letting you out of my sight again.'

'Those are lovely things to say,' Tyballis whispered.

Andrew said, 'But forgive me, I must know everything, my sweet. Both for your sake, and for the information you can give—'

Ralph's voice interrupted, calling, 'We are back, Mister Cobham. Are you here? Is Tybbs safe?'

At the same moment Casper roared, 'Come quick, afore I kick this little shit into the kitchens where he belongs.'

Then as Andrew swung his legs from the bed, somebody squealed, a thump of feet resounded on the stairs and Felicia shouted, 'What? What?' as the child Harry began to yell.

'What's that nasty bugger doing here?' Harry shouted in aggrieved surprise. 'That ain't proper – no, nor decent neither. You says how you brung me here to tell on them. Now who's gonna tell on who?'

CHAPTER SEVENTY-THREE

The council chamber at the Tower was cold. Since the window openings were small, the daylight was obscured, allowing only a pale gloom to enter. Huge wax candles were lit in the sconces and their shadows flared like leaping demons across the ancient stone walls. A charcoal brazier stood in one corner and oil lamps were set upon the tables.

Eight members of the council had been called to attend, and as Protector of the Realm, the Duke of Gloucester greeted each man as they assembled. Finally he signalled for them to sit as he slumped within the deep-armed chair, one hand resting on the table to his left, a pile of folded papers held flat beneath his palm. The scratching back of chairs and shuffling of position was brisk. He remained quite still until every man had settled. Buckingham took the place to the duke's right, the Lord Hastings to his left. Behind each chair a small group of the lords' aids and secretaries jockeyed for space.

Then, slowly pushing back his chair, the duke stood. He looked down over the company of men before him, and paused. Then he gathered up the papers he had brought, and addressed the council. 'My lords, I bid you welcome. Today I have called you here, for we have many pressing matters to discuss. I am forced to speak to you both as Lord Protector and as High Constable of England in dealing with a grave threat to this realm and its government.' He spoke quietly, forcing the company's silent and concentrated attention. 'I intend to uncover a conspiracy,' he said, 'which has for some weeks threatened the peace of our country. There are plans to abduct his grace the king from his royal lodgings here in the Tower, to cause my downfall – and ultimately my death.'

Amongst the gathering were faces more surprised, those more alarmed and those more frightened than others, but every man, for different reasons, was shocked from his lassitude as the great doors opened and a small troop of armed men entered and stood against the walls to surround the chamber, barring the way out.

The duke turned first to Hastings, who now appeared white-lipped in the lamplight. 'You, Lord Hastings,' the duke said, 'who have always spoken against insurrection, injustice and treachery, what would you advise, sir, as the penalty for conspirators such as these?'

Hastings rose to his feet. He looked defiant, gazing directly into Gloucester's eyes. He spoke loudly and did not flinch. 'I would, your grace, be impelled to recommend execution as the rightful punishment for such treachery.'

Gloucester bowed. 'So be it, Hastings,' he said, pausing to look around the chamber before speaking again. His voice remained quiet and controlled. 'In my capacity as High Constable of England, I now proclaim this council chamber my Constable's Court. By right of legal precedent and royal prerogative, this court is hereby empowered to try, pass judgement and sentence without appeal. Lord Hastings, I am satisfied the evidence against you is conclusive, and amongst these rebels your powers of array constitute the greatest threat to peaceful government. These papers I now present in evidence include treasonous documents bearing the signatures of those I hereby accuse, together with written depositions given under oath by witnesses presently held in custody.' A great intake of breath shattered the utter silence, and the candles across the chamber flickered, as though caught by the breeze. The duke waited a moment, and then continued. 'I herewith order the immediate arrest of the barons Hastings and Stanley, his lordship the Bishop of Ely and his grace the Archbishop of York.' This time the Protector raised his voice, and turned directly to face Hastings. 'The others shall be taken into custody forthwith. Arrests of other persons involved but not here present are taking place at this moment across London. I have this morning before dinner signed the necessary warrants. You, my lord, may speak now if you have anything to say in your defence.'

The armed guards moved suddenly, laying hands on those under arrest. Men stood quickly, their chairs tipping behind them. Lord Stanley roared, 'This is a mistake, your grace,' and pounded his fist on the small table before him.

The Lord Protector frowned, holding up the sheath of papers. 'Those rash enough to put their names to this agreement have incriminated themselves. One of these signatures is that of Reginald Bray, receiver-general in your lady's household, sir.'

'Damnation,' spluttered Stanley. 'Every man here knows I am not the governor of my lady's household. Damn it, I haven't even seen the woman in two months.' As he was led to the doors, a muted and carefully muffled chorus of sniggers echoed around the chamber.

'Your protest is noted, my lord,' said the duke. 'But amongst the culprits named here are those whose whereabouts are unknown.' The duke continued speaking as the papers to which he referred were passed for scrutiny amongst those lords remaining. 'The Marquess of Dorset, the principal example, has already escaped. The ports are being watched, but I do not expect his immediate arrest, nor do I consider him the principal danger. Lord Marrott, his friend, has also signed here. But although I believe Marrott's actions have been devious and destructive, I consider him little more than a dupe. His escape is unfortunate, but he is no leader of men.' Once again the duke turned to the Lord Hastings, still standing ashen-faced in the lamplight, his arms now pinned to his sides. 'My lord,' the duke said, 'without your involvement, your power and status, this plot would soon have wavered, crumbled and failed. I hold you responsible for giving prominence to a gathering of arrogant fools and blunderers. Your own arrogance led you to dream of becoming the power controlling a puppet king, a child in thrall to his mother. Deceived by urgency, you overlooked how haste breeds error. Having lost my favour for reasons you well know, you chose not to wait and work for the return of that favour, but instead to jeopardise the peace of our country in order to satisfy your own ambition.' He paused a moment, looking around at the other shocked and avid faces. Finally his gaze returned to Lord Hastings. 'Will you speak now, and address your peers in this chamber, or have you no defence, my lord?'

Hastings raised his head, his eyes cold with unexpressed anger, but his voice remained low. 'The evidence against me is beyond denial. I made my choice, and will now accept the consequences. I have nothing more to say.'

Within the subsequent shuddering silence, the rustle of papers unfolding seemed like secret breathing. The great candles dipped their flames as outside the wind whined across the battlements. Buckingham passed the pages to his neighbour, John, Baron de Howard, who nodded. 'And those whose names are not set down here? Those too menial to sign, those who have considered but not yet decided whether to join this travesty? What message do we send them? How do we stop this, before it escalates?'

'With the arrest of the principal culprit. It will finish now.'

The duke now spoke slowly. 'Very well,' he said. 'Baron Hastings, in my capacity as Lord Protector of the realm and High Constable of England, I hereby authorise your immediate arrest for high treason and by the law of this land I sentence you to immediate execution. There is neither doubt nor justification and your death will save much bloodshed. I cannot therefore countenance pleas for clemency.' His voice softened. 'I undertake to discharge your debts and safeguard your property for the Lady Katherine your wife, and for your heirs, taking them into my protection. May God have mercy on your soul.'

Andrew Cobham strolled wearily out into the main hall, bootless and his doublet unlaced. He regarded the newcomers with faint amusement. 'When I requested your return here today,' he said softly, 'I do not remember suggesting you disrupt the entire household. Yes, Tyballis is safe, and is resting, and is grateful for your concern. No doubt she'll want to speak to you all. But not yet.' He looked down on the scarlet-faced child who was glaring across the firelight towards the foot of the stairs. 'As for you, brat,' he continued, 'what the devil are you shouting about?'

Harry pointed one quivering finger, arm outstretched. 'Him,' he said with dramatic emphasis.

Andrew looked. On the lower step, Felicia stood, one arm cradling Ellen, the other arm around her husband. Behind and three steps higher into the long shadows, stood Luke. Andrew frowned and took a step towards them.

Ralph grabbed Harry's collar, pulling the child from Casper's grasp. 'What are you talking about, you little bugger?' he demanded. 'Explain yourself.'

'He's wiv them,' Harry announced, voice shrill. 'He ain't wiv us at all.'

Andrew took two further steps forwards, but stopped abruptly. Smashing through the adjacent window with a crash of splintering glass, a small rock hurtled, rebounded and landed at Andrew's feet. A slight rustling outside turned to noises of scrambling boots amongst the undergrowth. Immediately a voice roared, 'Come out, Feayton, come out and face us, you bastard. Come answer to the king for your treachery. And bring your murdering whore with you.'

Within the hall, everybody stopped. Andrew looked quickly from the stairs to the window, then shook his head and strode to the hearth. Elizabeth, already there, was gazing wide-eyed at the broken glass and the rock on the floor. Andrew beckoned to the others. 'Here,' he ordered, 'come here and keep close together. Those watching outside cannot see you by the hearth, nor the movement of your shadows through the window. No missile can reach you, and you can use the fire as defence if required.'

Felicia and her family scurried across, Felicia whispering, 'But my babies, Mister Cobham, they are still asleep in our bedchamber.'

Andrew said, 'As long as they sleep, they are safer upstairs,' He turned to Luke. 'Stay quiet and stay here, child.'

His brother, bewildered and insulted, came to huddle by the fire as ordered, but glowered and poked at the spit-boy. 'What did he mean, Drew, that horrid boy? Who is he, anyway? There's enough noisy

538

children already in this house. And what's happening? Who threw that stone?'

'For the moment,' Andrew said, 'it seems we are under attack, and I'm interested in nothing else. Wait here while I fetch Tyballis. We must keep together.'

She came barefoot, pattering in from the bedchamber and clutching Andrew's heavy bedrobe around her. She had again buckled Throckmorton's baldric across her shoulder, and the sword hung in its place at her side. Andrew brought her close to the fire, dragging another chair into the reflections of the flames. She sat there beside Elizabeth, staring in amazement at the broken window. Harry crouched at her knee and whispered, 'You don't know me, missus, but I knows you. You was in that house where I worked, and I seen you. I were the spit-boy. If you et my roast beef – then it were me as cooked it.'

Tyballis smiled wanly. 'I was never given roast beef in that house,' she said. 'I had very little to eat at all.'

'Hush,' Felicia begged. 'Tybbs, dear, it is exceedingly good to see you after all this time – but those men must still be outside. The door is not barricaded, and they may burst in at any moment.'

'It would be easier for us if they did,' Andrew said quietly. 'Besieged, we know neither how many there are, nor how they might strike next. If they dared face us, unless badly outnumbered, I've no doubt of the result.'

'Outnumbered?' squeaked Felicia. 'We have only four men present, since poor Luke is a young man of peace and has no experience of weapons.'

Tyballis stood up in a hurry. 'Four men?' she objected. 'What about Elizabeth and me? And you can butcher a chicken, Felicia, so you can stab a ruffian, too. As for Luke—'

'You have a sword,' Felicia objected.

Andrew held up one finger. 'Quiet now. Casper, collect all serviceable knives from the kitchen, and there's a wood axe by the back door. Ralph, you are already armed. Keep your metal ready.'

'There's Father's old sword upstairs,' Luke muttered. 'It's under my bed. Must I go and fetch it?'

'Let it stay there,' Andrew told him. 'It's bent and rusted, and you've no idea how to use it. Casper will give you a knife.' He turned to the others. 'We're under siege, but this is no military exercise. It seems they have no gunpowder, only stones, so their principal weapon will be fire. Keep close and alert, away from windows and doors.'

'They'll burn us out?' Felicia moaned.

'Gyles is asleep,' Jon interrupted, reaching for the sleeping baby in his wife's arms. 'I'll carry my poor son back up to bed. The children must be protected. There may be hundreds of soldiers outside.'

Andrew raised an eyebrow. 'Soldiers? What makes you say that?'

Jon looked at his boots. 'That voice spoke of – treachery – to the king.'

'As yet there is no king, and no monarch has sent soldiers to this house.' Andrew frowned as he strode to the broken window and, keeping within the shadows, looked out. There was no movement, and no sound outside. He returned at once to the hearth and the people grouped around it. 'There are a handful of ruffians at the most. Jon, you will stay down here. I will ensure your children's protection.'

Casper had returned from the kitchen bristling with weapons and began to parcel them out, handing a carving knife to Jon and another to Elizabeth. He kept the axe for himself, and piled the other knives on the rug before the fire. Ellen darted forwards and grabbed one. She hissed, 'I'll protect them babies.'

Outside, the silence seemed more furtive, a hint of movement that might have been no more than a squirrel, a hunting ferret or the chickens scurrying back to their shed. With the afternoon sun shining brightly, it was difficult to believe in threats. At last Andrew said, 'They hope I'll lose patience, and go out to them.'

Tyballis shook her head a little wildly. 'Oh, don't. They'd kill you at once.'

He smiled. 'I'm not so easily eliminated, I promise, and I've no intention of leaving the house. We have the advantage here, and I'll preserve that as long as it suits me. These are clearly Throckmorton's henchmen, since they named my woman a murderer. No one else has reason to call you that.'

'They called you a murdering whore,' sniggered Elizabeth. She fingered the knife now lying across her lap. 'Makes a change. There was folks used to call me that.'

Casper marched the few steps from hearth to window, and back. 'Ain't easy, cooped up just waiting,' he muttered. 'Why let them buggers call the tune? I want at 'em. I'll take the lot of 'em, I will, no trouble. I'll rip their arms off and break their maggoty little noses. Reckon there'll be ten out there at the most.'

'I doubt their force is that strong,' Andrew said. He was very still, standing before the fire and staring down into the flames. 'But you will stay here and follow orders. You will all follow orders.'

Ellen tugged at his doublet. 'Please, mister. What's that nasty boy doing here? I don't like him.' Harry still sat cross-legged on the rug, fidgeting with a small hole in the knee of his hose.

Andrew replied quietly, 'Harry is here at my invitation, Ellen, and as a guest, he must be made welcome. After this nonsense is over, it seems he has something to tell me. But I have understood already, and will deal with it when the time is right.'

Luke said loudly, 'The brat was trying to accuse me of something.' He glared at the child, then at Andrew. 'But whatever it was, I didn't do it.'

Ellen marched to Harry and poked her tongue out at him. 'You leave our Luke alone,' she said in a gruff whisper. 'He belongs to us cos he's the gent in our attic. You ain't got no right to say nuffing.'

Harry pulled a face. With one small hand fisted and a stare of determined belligerence, Ellen walloped Harry on the nose. Harry swore, and grabbed both her arms, dragging her down on top of him. Felicia squealed, dragging the children apart and crushing Ellen's objections to her bosom. Casper grabbed Harry and clipped him around the ear. 'Bloody little scruff,' Casper roared. 'You was told to keep quiet.'

Andrew remained unmoving, his eyes still on the dance of the flames. 'So much for circumspection,' he sighed. 'Let us see if this will encourage our assailants to show themselves, after all.'

'Probably out there manoeuvring,' Ralph decided. 'Surrounding the house. Watching all ways out. Taking up positions.'

'There are not enough of them for that,' Andrew said, nodding towards the unbarred front doors. 'More than twenty, they would have rushed us. More than ten, they would be shouting abuse or throwing missiles, attempting to goad us outside. No, I doubt there are more than five. And I shall wait. Anyone leaving this house could be picked off by an archer hiding in the bushes.'

Quiet settled once again, only broken by the spit and crackle of the fire sending soft echoes up the chimney.

Then three windows smashed at once in an explosion of shattered glass.

CHAPTER SEVENTY-FOUR

The windows of The Tower's great council chamber did not look down on the small flat green where a makeshift block had been set up with sawdust packed around its base, but the ravens roosting on the battlements watched, already attentive. The executioner had been waiting for some time, silently leaning on the well-worn handle of his axe. Then there was a bustle, muttering and shouting as the guards and the accompanying lords approached. The warm sunshine reflected from the blade of the axe, momentarily blinding the small crowd. Lord Hastings looked down at his feet, his bare toes in the sawdust. Quietly he removed his surcoat and hat, handing them to one of the guards. Then he unlaced the collar of his doublet, and that of his shirt beneath, leaving his neck exposed. At his elbow, a priest was muttering from a prayer book. Hastings turned to the small gathering. Some of the men, although it was warm, were shivering. The shock had not yet passed.

Lord Hastings spoke loudly. Across the open ground and resounding against the ancient mossy stone all around, his voice rang clear. 'Beware ambition, my lords,' he said. 'I commend you all to loyalty in the service of his grace the king.' He laughed. 'Whoever that might yet be.' He looked briefly up to the masked executioner. 'I come unprepared. I've no coin on me to pay you, my good man, since the occasion is, let us say, unexpected. Take my coat and boots as recompense, if you will.' Then he bent his head to the block.

Richard of Gloucester and Henry Stafford, Duke of Buckingham, stood together in the council chamber. One guard stood outside the doorway. No one else was present. The noise from outside could not be heard. Buckingham tucked his hands inside his sleeves. 'This news will speed faster than the tide. By nightfall, fear and rumour will rattle every city door, and any other miserable conspirators will scatter. With one stroke, the insurrection is over, your grace.'

Gloucester spoke softly, though more to himself than to his companion. 'I regret this. With all my heart, I regret it.'

'Not as much as he will,' Buckingham said.

Richard looked up. 'But it is a sad waste. I have known the man all my life and thought him an ally. He was my brother's closest friend. I will arrange for his burial next to Edward, in the chapel at Windsor.'

'A great honour, for a miserable traitor. You'll not attaint him?'

'No, I gave my word I'd see his wife and heirs protected. But there will be many titles and positions to disperse, and you shall gain from that, Harry. We are entering difficult times, with the throne unsettled. France watches, and Louis licks his lips. I've sent to York for armed guards, but it will be weeks before they can arrive. So, I chose to crush this uprising before it gains greater force. Now Hastings' death must be a lesson to all those considering treachery. His head may save a fountain of bloodshed.'

'You're decided, then?' Buckingham demanded. 'You'll accept the throne? Without you, Richard, the country is lost. We might as well surrender to France and be done with it. In God's name, what other decision can you make?'

'It has not yet been offered,' Gloucester reminded him. 'The lords and the church continue to deliberate, and I shall accept the crown only if it is the combined will of the people, who know little of this yet.'

'And if the throne is offered, as it surely must?'

'Then an explanation of the circumstances will be announced at St. Paul's Cross, the city dignitaries must be involved, and from my mother's castle, I shall await the outcome. She has already pressed me to accept, as does my lady. I am prepared.' He paused, crossing to the narrow window. The sky was almost cloudless and a raven was sitting on the far battlements, watching the bustle below. The raven stretched its wings, letting the warm breeze ruffle its feathers. The duke turned again, and nodded to Buckingham. 'There are few alternatives. I know this. But destiny's wheel rarely runs smooth, and already conspirators gather, smelling opportunity. Bickering for advancement. Old jealousies, plotting for whatever rule will gain them most.'

'And the Woodville bitch?' Buckingham swept to a tall chair and sat, stretching out a plump leg. 'Don't tell me she wasn't behind the Hastings plot. Not Dorset – he's less brains than a scullion. It was that damned matriarch, crouching in sanctuary like a spider in her web. She was the instigator, I'll warrant, and hatched the plot to lure Hastings in.'

Gloucester leaned back against the wall. 'Perhaps. Without Earl Rivers, her power is much diminished and she needed a new ally. But it is more to me that she holds the younger prince hostage. He must be released, and sent to his brother.'

'Those negotiations have already been dragging on for weeks. The wretched woman is too stubborn.'

'So can I be, my friend.' Gloucester smiled. 'My two nephews must be united before the change of rule is announced. They will be a target for every ambitious man with treachery on his mind. The French will want the boys dead. So will the exile Tudor. His mother still plots and schemes. She was also involved in the Hastings debacle, as you heard. I accused her husband, but Stanley is too careful to ever put his name to such a risk. I shall let him seethe a day, and then order his release.'

'And the bastard princes,' Buckingham demanded. 'What of them at the end of it all? Yes, there's those who'll want them dead. But there's others will use them against you. Your enemies will proclaim young Edward the rightful king, bastard or no. Every damned traitor under the sun will rally either to kill the brat, or to crown him.'

Gloucester sighed. 'Indeed, but the country is not entirely peopled with traitors, Harry. Most men dream of quiet prosperity under a strong leader. The Tower is the safest stronghold in all England and I shall keep the boys here. In time, when sweet peace returns, I'll arrange to send them north where my other nephews are lodged at Sheriff Hutton, and Edward's children can join them there in comfort. But if the risk grows? Well, then I'll arrange for both boys to be sent to a place of greater safety and in secret. But there is time for that, and first I have other considerations.'

'So, you'll execute no one else?' Buckingham pouted. 'Though it seems this conspiracy was widespread and you've had others arrested.'

'Beyond the Woodvilles, hardly widespread. Meddlers. Small men aiming higher. For those who resent their lack of power, there are only two ways up. The lazy and the stupid choose treachery.'

Buckingham frowned. 'And that Shore woman? I believe you arrested your brother's whore.'

'A king's mistress misses both power and indulgence when her lover dies. So, Mistress Shore jumped from bed to bed, unwisely choosing those of both Dorset and Hastings, the two most powerful she could find, since I was not available myself.' He laughed softly. 'So, she carries messages and dabbles in dangerous mischief.'

'And the other villains?' Buckingham persisted.

'They'll remain in custody for the time being.' Gloucester was again watching the raven, now preening her breast feathers in the sunshine. His back to Buckingham, he said, 'What say you, Harry – will you keep Morton safe for me?'

'The Bishop of Ely? Not a man I admire.'

'Nor should you, my friend. He's a creature of dark hatreds, and he hates me amongst others. But I can't take his life without causing uproar from Canterbury to Rome, though his affiliation to the church is hypocritical at best. So, I shall keep him out of the way for as long as possible. He's too clever to leave free. I'll entrust him to your safekeeping, Harry, but don't try making friends with him or turning him to our ideas. He's wily. Lock him up at Brecon, and forget the wretch.'

'I shall. And throw away the key.'

The duke leaned on the stone window ledge, still gazing out. He could see nothing, but knew without doubt that his orders had been obeyed, his instructions carried out, and that it was over. The raven had flown.

The three windows at Cobham Hall shattered simultaneously in a bright splintering of sunlit glass. Shards scattered across the boards. Three boulders hurtled high to the beams, then crashed to the ground, rolling and spinning. At the same moment long shadows appeared at each of the windows. Three arrows arched through the broken panes. One embedded in the far wall, its shaft quivering. The other two fell useless, for there had been no one at which to aim.

Everyone stood in startled silence, waiting for the next onslaught. It did not come. Eventually Andrew stepped forwards and picked up one of the fallen arrows. He brought it back to the fireside, holding it up in the light. It was fletched in goose and tipped in copper. 'It is well made,' he said, turning it over between his fingers. 'An expensive toy to waste. They are becoming desperate.'

'Desperate?' Felicia shrank back. 'But they have bows, and we do not. They have the advantage.'

'We have the advantage,' Andrew repeated. 'Unless they smoke us out, we can stay here until they're forced to give up and leave.'

'Fire?'

'Doubtful,' Andrew said. 'The house is surrounded by greenery. Any fire would become immediately uncontrollable. The houses nearby are built of wood and thatch. Burn us, they burn Portsoken and beyond.'

Elizabeth looked up. 'Would they care about that?'

Andrew shrugged. 'Perhaps not. But they'd care about catching fire themselves. They could run off before the flames take hold, but could not then pick us off as we're forced outside.'

'But why, Drew?' Tyballis said. 'What are they after? Because of Throckmorton? But what good will this do?'

He looked down at her, then to the others standing behind. 'They called my lady a murderess, therefore whoever they are, they knew Throckmorton, know he had taken you captive, and now know of his

547

death. But he had no trained archers in his employ, nor could afford a private army. And how did they know to come here? Throckmorton's retainers can have no idea where I live. But this house was attacked before, when Marrott tried to have me killed. So, I'd guess Marrott is after revenge.'

'Hetchcomb,' whispered Tyballis.

'It seems likely,' Andrew nodded. 'But on the first occasion, Dorset and the queen dowager had taken control of the entire capital. They held power. Marrott suspected me and sent his people to kill me off. How many men were there under Hetchcomb? Twenty? More? Well, times have changed. And as I've said, I doubt there are more than five men out there now.'

'You always think you know everything, Drew. But you can't be sure,' Luke was muttering from his corner in the shadows.

'No. I can't be sure. But I make a habit of being right. It is my job.' Andrew looked down with a sudden smile and handed the arrow to Harry. 'Keep it,' he said. 'You want to be a spit-boy all your life? Or train at the butts, and be an archer in the new king's service?'

Harry grabbed the arrow and grinned. 'I will. I reckon I'd be a good archer. And the little king's much the same age as me. Reckon I could look after him.'

'As it happens,' smiled Andrew, 'I believe a great deal is about to change, Harry, but any king will welcome those ready to fight for him. Perhaps I shall find you a suitable place in the royal household, once trained.'

Harry remained open-mouthed and Ralph said, 'You can arrange that, Mister Cobham? We know nothing of this.'

Andrew leaned his elbow back against the lintel, one foot to the grate. 'It is like this, my friends. We are under attack from a parcel of fools hoping to entice us outside for immediate slaughter, and will risk their own small numbers while believing they will soon be reinforced. They have made one important mistake, however. Clearly, they know of the conspiracy I have been investigating for the past weeks, and were presumably a part of it. But whereas I know the Woodville plot has utterly failed, they still believe in its success. They are unaware that today the Duke of Gloucester called a meeting at

The Tower, and disclosed this treachery. I had already presented his grace with proof of the Lord Hastings' guilt, which Harry here had obtained for me.' Turning to Tyballis, he added, 'Casper and Ralph have also been assisting me.'

'And me,' muttered Elizabeth.

'It is probable the meeting ended with Lord Hastings' arrest. That was the Protector's intention. So, it is not the Duke of Gloucester who lies defeated, leaving me without support. It is Hastings who is finished, Rotherham and Morton in custody, Marrott on the run and the Woodvilles scattered. The men outside cannot yet know this, nor yet realise that the reinforcements they hope for will never come.'

'Tell them, then,' said Tyballis, bouncing up and snatching at her sword. 'Go and shout out of the window. Tell them it's useless and they must surrender. If it's that vile creature Hetchcomb out there, I'd like to kill him myself.'

Andrew grinned. 'Your new-found success at assassination appears to have gone to your head, my love. But never fear, I'm sure one of us will finish him off, unless he runs first. But telling him the truth would serve no purpose. He would simply not believe me.'

Harry, still gripping the arrow, said, 'I'll sneak out, then. Take a message. Find the duke. Call the constable. Bring back guards.'

'Horrid little spit-boy,' objected Ellen. 'Them men'd spit you on that silly arrow.'

'Wot don't sound like a bad idea to me,' interrupted Casper.

Felicia had long finished feeding Gyles, who once again slept in her arms. She said, 'Well, we need help from somewhere. Does the boy know where to go?'

Andrew looked down at the boy and shook his head. 'No, Harry, I'll not risk your life. You're too valuable as a witness to the conspiracy, should further proof be needed.'

The boy sniggered. 'Valuable as a witness. Not fer meself, then?'

'I'll go,' said Ralph, striding forwards. 'I've more chance of defending myself if caught, and more chance of convincing the duke's men, too.'

Elizabeth stood beside him. 'No – me! The buggers dare catch me?

Well, I'm just a whore passing by, and will offer a quick kiss on my way out.'

Casper said, 'Hold off, hold off. It's me the best street fighter in London, and best at slipping the constables, too. So, I'm the best bugger to send.'

Andrew turned abruptly to Luke. 'Well, child, what about you? With all this courageous self-sacrifice from the others, you offer nothing? Yet you well understand the meaning of treachery, and you know exactly where to find the sheriff.'

'That – that's mean, Drew.' Luke looked at his brother with tearful resentment. 'You know I wouldn't dare. It's not fair to say that.'

'You then, my friend?' Abruptly Andrew turned to Jon, his smile suddenly cold and his eyes black and expressionless. 'Would you undertake to risk and save us all?' he asked. 'You could leave here, no questions asked – and there would be no knowing what became of you.'

Jon stood in the shadows, his arm around Felicia. He did not move at first, but blushed a little. He said, 'I'm not sure what you're implying, Mister Cobham. No one can accuse me of cowardice, I'm sure, and I've helped you before in this espionage business, as I hope you remember. I must protect my wife and children.' Then, removing his arm from Felicia's shoulders, he took a step forwards. 'But of course,' he decided, 'if I can serve you best by fetching a constable, well, I am more than willing, sir. I can slip out by the kitchen door. I'm not afraid.'

Felicia squeaked and clung tighter to her husband's arm, but Andrew's smile widened, and his black eyes lit with sudden amusement. 'How astute of you, Mister Spiers,' he said. 'But I'm sending nobody. I have a far better idea.'

CHAPTER SEVENTY-FIVE

A ndrew led his party of assorted lodgers to the great staircase and began, one by one, to usher them up. They carried no light and he warned them to silence, but silence was difficult when the balustrade groaned, swinging on its wobbling banisters, and the broken treads squeaked with each tentative step. Everyone clutched armfuls of what they had been told to bring. Knife blades rang, metal on metal. The cauldron from the kitchen clanked, and water splashed. Ellen felt cobwebs brush against her face, dropped the stones she clutched, and gasped, apologetic. But no violent intrusion interrupted them, and it seemed no one from outside had heard. They gathered in Ralph's chamber, which he had once shared with Nat but now in comfort with Elizabeth. The window, the largest in all the bedchambers, opened freely with shutters unbroken.

Each deposited their burden as Ralph bent to light the fire. Andrew and Casper hung the great cauldron of water there, shuddering on its chains. Water slopped with a hiss, but the flames blazed anew. Elizabeth opened the shutters just sufficient to peep out, yet hiding the flare of light from the hearth behind her. 'I can see two ugly bastards sitting under the big beech tree. One's got his bow across his knees. Reckon the other's asleep.'

Tyballis was at her shoulder. 'I can see another. Down there, look, close to the house. I think it's Hetchcomb.' Andrew came across to her, keeping his back to the shutters. She whispered to him, 'That vile man thinks he'll take us over like he did last time. But this time you're here. He's going to get a shock.'

'Perhaps,' Andrew said softly, 'but remember, my love, this is not our last chance. If this fails, we can still wait out the night. But if we try this plan at all, it must be soon, before the light fails.'

'Not long to twilight,' Ralph nodded.

Felicia had put Gyles to bed in her own chamber. She crept back quietly and went to stoke up the fire. Jon sat by the hearth, his chin in his hands. Luke was sitting on the bed. He stared at the cauldron, muttering, 'Boiling and hissing. The devil's wicked work.'

'This water's near hot already,' Casper squinted one-eyed into the steam.

'As soon as it boils, bring it here to the window,' Andrew ordered.

Ellen was piling her stones while Harry explored, collecting anything heavy enough to serve as a missile. 'That's my chamber pot,' said Ralph. 'Put it back.'

'We survive this, you can crap outside under a bush like every other bastard in London,' objected Casper, still gripping his axe.

Andrew and Ralph held their swords unsheathed, the others wielded knives. Luke was using his to clean his fingernails. Felicia stared at her blade with dislike. 'You've carved meat with it before now,' Tyballis told her.

Felicia frowned. 'Not off a man.'

'Hush,' Andrew put a finger to his lips. 'They are moving.'

Down amongst the garden's shadowy greens, four men had gathered. Three carried bows. All seemed furtive, glancing to the house and then to the long path leading back towards the main road. Their captain quickly joined their muster, his hands to their shoulders. He kept his voice low. From above it was impossible to hear what he said, but each of his men nodded in response.

'It is Hetchcomb,' whispered Tyballis.

'Mister Cobham, they're planning something,' Ralph whispered. 'If they dare come closer up to the house, well, now we're ready for them.'

They came. Creeping under cover of bush and tree, they followed Hetchcomb. Abruptly he pointed towards the double doors and at once two of his men swerved, heading for the hall's main entrance. Hetchcomb and the other two, keeping tightly together, approached the central window. One of the archers raised his bow and slotted an arrow to the nock.

Andrew's voice was little more than a breath. 'The cauldron now – boiling or not – bring it. We ignore those at the doorway. Concentrate on these three below us. Just one step nearer.'

He signalled immediately. The shutters suddenly came crashing down and the window was thrown open as Casper and Andrew tipped the great cauldron of water directly down. The screams were instantaneous. Hetchcomb and one of his archers were drenched in scalding liquid, leaping and howling as they rushed back. The third man swore and darted out of range.

Casper laughed. Ralph, peering over his head, said, 'First shot to us.'

'Two of them are running,' Tyballis called from her place on the other side of the window, her face, damp and pink, emerging from the steam. 'But one is still there – look – staring up at us. His face is horribly scorched.'

'Hetchcomb,' Ralph said, peering down. 'He starved us when he was here before. Let the worm burn.'

The captain stood as though pinned to the ground, a blasted tree struck and broken by lightning. His upturned face, shining in the sinking sunlight, was a glistening slither of ruined flesh. His eyes were bloody, and his lips fell away as though melting from his mouth. The other man howled and screamed as he ran. But Hetchcomb remained silent. Felicia came and stood beside Tyballis, looking over her shoulder. 'The pain has sent him mad,' she whispered. 'But that hideous villain nearly killed my poor babies. Let him suffer.'

The solitary standing figure wavered at the knees and slowly sank, drowning in the waves of foliage around him until he lay curled amongst the bushes, his knees drawn up to the ruin of his chin. His bleeding eyes were open but he did not move.

'I believe he is dead,' Andrew said softly. 'His heart, perhaps – or enough water down his gullet to boil him from within.' He turned, looking suddenly around the room. Then he frowned, pausing a moment as though looking for something he did not see. Everyone except Luke was now clustered together, peering through the window, pushing for the chance to see a little more. Luke continued to sit alone on the bed. He was crying.

'And the others down there,' Elizabeth said, 'what of them buggers as pushed indoors?'

'I intend finding out.' Andrew crossed quickly to the open door, speaking over his shoulder. 'Casper, come with me. The rest of you stay here. Felicia, will you see to Luke? Tyballis and Ralph, keep watch by the window. Elizabeth, you're a good-enough shot. One stone, and aim for Hetchcomb. I want to know if he's dead before I get down there. If he moves, call me.' There was no longer need for silence. This time Andrew's running footsteps resounded down the stairs.

The two who had breached the doors, now stood inside, uncertain in the hall's shadows. One held his bow high, the arrow to the nock and aimed at Andrew's chest. 'Stop there, you shit,' the man growled. 'You've gutted my mates, but you'll not get me so easy. Say your prayers, for they're the last ones you make.' The archer drew back his bowstring.

Andrew had stopped three steps up. He said, 'Casper, get the other one,' and at the same moment his sword point entered the bowman's eye. The blade arched smooth and slid directly through the eyeball with a black squelch. The arrow clattered to his feet as the man died. Andrew pressed his metal deep, then stepped back and wiped his sword on the dead archer's fallen body. 'I never understand,' he murmured to himself, 'why men choose to speak before attacking. Such delay is most unwise. Who do they seek to impress?' He turned to Casper who was swinging his axe. Already his assailant was on his knees as the axe sliced through the man's neck. The head toppled, chin to chest, held to the body only by gristle and a shattered splinter of spine.

Casper nodded at Andrew. 'Ain't so easy beheading a fellow, after all,' he remarked. 'I sees why them executioners generally make such a muck of it. Usually takes them two or three hacks, they says, and I heard of six or more. Well, now I gets it. Necks is tougher than you'd think.'

'Nevertheless, my friend,' said Andrew softly, 'I believe you have made an adequate attempt. The man is quite definitely dead.'

'Well,' admitted Casper with some pride, 'reckon would take a mighty big bandage to stick that skull back on again. But the bugger's made a right mess of your floor.'

'At the moment,' Andrew said, 'that is not my principal concern. Outside now, my friend. There is someone else I'm looking for.'

'Right,' agreed Casper, 'there's two more little turds out there, though one burned rotten. And there's that lousy captain of your'n.'

'None of those bother me in the least.' Andrew strode through the open doors and looked around his garden's twilit gloom. Hetchcomb's corpse was a pale grey bundle in the damp, his eyes, now milky, still gazing upwards. But the shadows were merging as the last of the sunshine disappeared behind the treetops. 'It is someone else entirely I want now,' Andrew said.

Casper was immediately behind him, his boots silent in the soft earth. 'Ain't no one else here,' he objected. 'What you want now?'

'I was sadly unobservant,' Andrew smiled, 'but as we tipped the cauldron, so the result below became sufficient distraction. But now I realise how someone slipped away.'

'From up there? From down here? Who?' Casper demanded.

'Who? Jon Spiers, of course. The one who betrayed us all some time ago, yet was entirely overlooked by me,' Andrew said. 'Now Mister Spiers has left the house. I'd guess the men by the doors recognised him and let him go. But he cannot have gone very far.' Casper stood, mouth open and one foot raised, momentarily speechless. 'You are not a heron, Mister Wallop,' said Andrew curtly, walking abruptly away down the main path. 'Move, or we will lose him. Get round to the stables, check the sheds and the chicken coop. Listen for anyone crawling amongst the bushes.'

The sun sank and the clouds turned pink. Beyond the roof of the old house, the crimson tinge strengthened. One of the smaller chimneys puffed dark from Ralph's guttering fire. Behind the smoke, the sky gleamed. The weathervane, the wind motionless in its iron sails, was a black silhouette against vivid cerise as Andrew approached the broken gates at the end of the path. He had already heard voices, and he knew what he would find.

One of Hetchcomb's men barred the way out, and before him, grappling and cursing, was Jon Spiers. 'You fool,' Jon spat. 'I'm a friend. Your master knows me.'

The other man had been burned. One side of his face shone more virulent than the sky. Both his hands were scarred and shedding skin, but in spite of the pain, he held fast to his captive. 'My captain's dead, you bastard. And so will you be now.'

Jon twisted free. He still grasped the knife given to him inside the house. He slashed out, but the other man dodged, coming back with his own sword. Jon hissed, 'I'm a friend, I tell you. Your men at the doors knew me. How else would I be free?'

'Know you? I know you for murdering scum. My hands – my face – you've ruined me. And you'll pay.'

Again, Jon twisted free. He was not a large or a strong man, but he was quick. 'Dorset will have you whipped for this,' he spat. 'I've important information for the marquess. Let me pass.'

Andrew stepped from the shadows. He said softly. 'Dorset has no further need of your information, my friend. I imagine he is halfway across the sea to Brittany. The trouble you now face is your own.' Hetchcomb's man had stopped and now shrank back against the stone wall, nursing his wounded hands. Jon turned at once and raced for the gates. The other man stuck out his foot. Jon yelped and tripped, dropping his knife and sprawling in the dirt. Andrew kicked the fallen knife away and took Jon by both his hair and the neck of his shirt, hauling him up. He smiled at Throckmorton's burned henchman. 'Get away now, if you value your life,' he told him. 'Your comrades are gone, and your leaders arrested.' As the man slunk immediately through the gateway and disappeared, Andrew looked down at Jon. 'Before I kill you, I would know one thing,' he said. 'The itch of curiosity, no more. Was it hatred of me? Envy? Resentment? Some strange passion for the Woodville cause? Or simply for the money?'

Jon squirmed in Andrew's grip, hanging like a chicken ready for plucking. 'Forgive me,' Jon gasped. 'I'll never – not again. I swear it.

Don't kill me, Mister Cobham. Think of my children – of my wife. I am not a well man.'

'Indeed?' queried Andrew. 'Is your health so poor? A sad reflection on my generosity over the years, perhaps. Did the food and board I supplied free of charge not bring sufficient comfort? Yet you sleep deep and often, signs of a clear conscience, they say.'

'Little Ellen,' Jon spluttered. 'Think of my babies.'

'I try not to,' Andrew said. 'But if I must, I should no doubt decide they were better off without a murdering traitor for a father. You stole poison and put it in Marrott's hands. You knew why I had it locked safely away. And you knew what use it would be put to, if taken by others.' His eyes, cold and black, were just inches from the other man's. Jon's feet were lifted from the ground and kicking wildly, his hands pummelling helplessly at Andrew's tightening fingers at his throat. In desperation Jon's old, scratched boots, heavy wooden soled, connected over and over against Andrew's shins. Andrew neither winced nor moved. He continued speaking, his voice soft with latent menace. 'You are a murderer, Mister Spiers,' he said. 'You killed your king. Now, do I hand you over to be drawn, hanged and quartered, or do I break your neck myself?'

'I never meant—'

'You are a dealer in regicide, the most heinous of crimes. And you betrayed me. You betrayed every friend you have, and you betrayed your family. Or does your wife collude in your treachery?'

'She knows nothing. I couldn't tell her.' Jon was now scarlet. Andrew's grip on his collar was strangling him. He wriggled weakly and now his legs dangled limp. He pleaded, 'I will make amends, sir. Forgive me, I beg you.'

'I never forgive,' Andrew said. 'But you have not answered my question, Mister Spiers. Did you love the Woodville cause, then?'

Jon was dizzy and growing faint. 'I wanted – just the comfort – a little of the riches other men have. You're a rich man, Mister Cobham. You pretend not to be, but with a house like this – clothes – the duke as your friend. I wanted – some of the same.'

Andrew paused a moment. Then he said, 'That was the wrong answer, Mister Spiers. Passion, I might understand. An earnest belief in the wrong cause, I might overlook. But to murder for gain is a vile business. Have you any idea of the suffering caused in death by poison? Do you know the agony of arsenic? Do you care?'

Jon's voice was barely discernible. His child's blue eyes popped, bursting from their skull. He whispered, 'I never thought—'

Andrew nodded. 'Your own death,' he said, 'will not be as terrible, my friend. I shall make it quick.'

The sunset raged in swirls of rushing vermillion as Andrew broke Jon Spiers' pale neck. Above them each cloud was lined in saffron, and streaks of cobalt sprang like swords across the horizon. The small snap was barely audible. Andrew laid the lifeless body flat on the damp grass and turned at the crunch of footsteps. Casper stood in silence behind him.

Andrew said, 'You see, the hand is far quicker than the axe.'

Casper nodded, almost timid. 'You've a mighty strong hand, then, Mister Cobham, to break a man so easy.'

'It was only a little neck.' Andrew stood slowly, looking up at the house at the end of the pathway and the last rays of the burnished sunset sinking behind. All the windows had turned to scarlet. 'And I am – sadly – much practised,' he said. 'Now let us go home.'

It was some days later and the great city lay peaceful beneath the summer sky. Rumour abounded but no further conspiracies marred the law of the land and under the continued rule of the Protector, all seemed right in the world.

The Portsoken Ward basked beneath the stars and the chimneys at Cobham Hall smoked long into the night. Tyballis lay quiet and naked in Andrew's arms. His fingertips brushed across her shoulder and his breath, leaning over her, was hot. Where their bodies touched, the sweat of their previous lovemaking clung. Yet although the great fire raged over the hearth at the far end of the chamber, its mighty flames had sunk. They no longer roared high, but the burnished heat glowed like a rising sun at the end of the bed.

They had made love, then slept for some hours, and finally awoke together with the rattle of the broken shutters and the first threat of a storm. The rain came suddenly, thrumming on the roof tiles and hurtling against the window. Snapping into immediate awareness, Andrew grinned, his face flushed by the fire's last reflections. Tyballis was still sleepy, and his breath was in her eyes. She whispered, 'Is it morning already then, my love?'

He shook his head. 'I doubt it's more than two of the clock, and still night. You must sleep longer.'

She wriggled up against the pillows, looking back earnestly at him. 'There's been something on my mind for some days. If I say it now, then I can dream sweet again. It's about Jon. So I have to say I'm sorry.'

Andrew smiled, slow to decipher her words. 'There are only two of us to blame,' he said. 'Jon Spiers, and myself.'

Outside, the thunder rolled like the echoes of cannon fire. Inside, the warmth contained them in a cavern of silent shadows. The bed curtains, half-closed, became a secret chamber within the chamber. The high bedposts and their carved intricacies marked the boundaries. The hanging silks were the containing walls. Above them the tester's fraying raggedness ballooned, embroidered in dust. Engulfed by pillows all in disarray from their previous lovemaking, Tyballis wiped away sleep's stickiness from the corners of her eyes. 'But you see,' she explained, 'when I was Marrott's prisoner, I saw Jon at that house. Marrott called him the "usual messenger" but I just thought you'd sent him there – that it was all one of your tricks, that Jon was helping you, spying and taking false messages. But I should have warned you, just in case. So, I was to blame – just a little. And don't say you're to blame, when you're not at all.'

'What spy worth his salt,' Andrew smiled, 'does not recognise the traitor in his own household?'

Tyballis smoothed her hand against his cheek. 'You didn't trust me when you first knew me. Now I understand why.'

'Trust creates vulnerability. It is not a gift I am usually capable of giving.'

'I trust people before I think about it. Silly perhaps, when you remember who I was married to.'

'And yet,' Andrew smiled, leaning over to trace her arm from shoulder to wrist, 'neither of us suspected Jon Spiers.'

'He was always asleep. That's another way of hiding, isn't it? Perhaps that's why he did what he did. To feel more important.'

Andrew leaned back beside her, staring over the bed's footboard at the dying ashes. 'Why Spiers did what he did does not interest me. I am more concerned as to why I failed to discover it. He used Luke's name when selling poison and trading information. I was told this, and it distracted me. But I should have guessed. Jon's child Ellen was the only one who saw how I opened the chest containing the arsenic. A better lockpick perhaps, than I realised, and being keen to prove her pride, no doubt later showed her father. Tomorrow his wife will take her children back to the farm. She refused my invitation to remain here. I am not surprised.'

Tyballis snuggled to his side and slipped her arm around his waist where his body was smooth and strong and flat. 'It was always pride, wasn't it, Felicia sticking up for Jon and pretending he was grand when we all knew he wasn't. Back on the farm she'll say Jon died a hero – helping you fight off the attack. She'll tell her boys that when they grow up. Ellen may remember, but she probably doesn't understand what really happened. They'll all grow up admiring their father's memory.'

'Does lying ever prove sweeter than the truth?' Andrew's words were muffled against her neck. 'Perhaps it is, since truth is all such nonsense. My memories of my father – of both of those who claimed fatherhood over me – are not so sweet. But in the end the hero and the traitor are the same man. It depends who judges, and the side on which that judge sits.'

CHAPTER SEVENTY-SIX

Across the thousand crowded roofs of London, the sunshine blazed. It sparkled on crooked chimney pots and glistened on the wet yellow slime of the cobbles below. The passing clouds reflected across a myriad of mullioned panes. The duke stood against the same clouds, and although he was not a tall man, he appeared as a giant, with his head in the sky. Though considerably taller, Andrew spoke to him as to that giant. They walked together along the battlements of Baynard's Castle, the busy river way below and the city stretched out beyond.

'I do not consider it a failure.' The duke's voice, blown by the wind, seemed unusually gentle.

'Yet Geoffrey Marrott's escape troubles me,' replied his companion. 'I cannot even know if his late highness died by Marrott's hand – or not. The lack of proof, the unknown intentions – these must usually exonerate any suspect. But there is no doubt that Marrott pedalled poisons, wherever those poisons may have finished. Yet he has escaped to Brittany and will never be accused of his crimes.'

'He will die when his time comes,' nodded the duke, 'as shall we all. In the meantime, he has lost everything – power, riches, ambition, hope. Vengeance belongs to the Lord, and should not be our concern.'

'Not vengeance, but justice, your grace. In that I accept failure.'

The duke continued. 'He will be attainted and lose his title when parliament sits. Meanwhile Throckmorton has no heirs. Take his house if you want it.'

Andrew bowed slightly but shook his head, the feather in his cap flattened by the wind. 'If it pleases you, your grace, I prefer not. It retains an atmosphere of petty wretchedness and memories of threat.'

'Something in the Strand, then. Near enough to the city, yet just a stone's throw from Westminster and the court, should I need you.'

'Apologies, your grace.' Andrew smiled. 'But the palaces of The Strand slope down to the river. Sadly, my intended bride does not care for the Thames.'

The duke's sables ruffled, but the sun was in his eyes, turning his sudden smile golden. 'You are difficult to please, Mister Cobham. So, where shall I house you, then?'

'Indeed, I have no idea, your grace.'

The duke laughed. 'No doubt you will make up your mind at some time, and then I shall be happy to oblige you. In the meantime, you will oblige me by choosing some property, not too modest if you please, and within my reach. I shall continue to need you, my friend. By tradition a crown increases one's enemies, rather than diminishing them.'

'You will be a great king, your grace. Of that I have no doubt.'

The duke frowned. 'A strong leader, sir, that I can promise you.' He glanced up as a flock of swallows twisted, looping against the bright sky, briefly darkening the sunshine. He appeared to be talking to the sun. 'The council has now drawn up the official request for parliament to approve. I shall accept the crown in memory of my father,' he said softly, 'who would have made a greater king, had God permitted. And for the sake of my son and his sons, and for the absolute exclusion of all those who – perhaps – schemed to murder my brother.' He turned back to Andrew, smiling suddenly. 'And principally for the weal of the people, who need the security of the leadership I can bring. I am not loath, nor reluctant, now I have made my decision. All my life has passed in training, and now I see the reason. I enjoy leadership. My birthright. My pleasure.'

'I believe England will share in that pleasure, your grace.'

'And your pleasure, Andrew? What is that to be?' The duke drew his great sable-lined coat around him as the wind sharpened. His black embroidered sleeves, fur-cuffed, trailed a little across the cold stone. 'You speak of your intended bride. So, you turn respectable at last.'

Andrew Cobham wore his old grey velvets, seams gaping. He did not seem to notice. He said, 'I will marry Tyballis Blessop, if she accepts me, your grace, once the final banns are called.'

'No clandestine marriage then, my friend?'

'A lesson learned from my betters,' Andrew smiled. 'I shall therefore stand at the church porch, and cheerfully take my oath before the priest.'

'In which case most men procure a ring for the priest to bless. You have already obtained a ring for your bride?' The duke began to walk from the battlements towards the open doorway leading to the winding stair and the chambers below. 'Very well. I shall supply it. You must not expect to be an impoverished lord of my realm, my friend. Nor continue to dress in the clothes I doubt your steward would choose to wear, once you employ one.'

Andrew looked down at himself in some surprise, then strode into the sudden black of the stairwell behind the duke. The draught followed them as their footsteps echoed down the steps. 'I have never been much interested in such matters, my lord, unless they serve my work.'

The duke's amusement floated back, his voice hollow in the chill. 'Then no doubt your wife will advise you, sir. A nobleman must remember his appearance as a statement of his wealth and position. And I intend arranging your business accordingly.'

It was late when Andrew returned to Cobham Hall, but he was elated rather than tired. He poured wine, and took his woman to bed. Tyballis kissed his ear. 'So, after tomorrow when Felicia and the children leave, there's just Ralph and Elizabeth and Casper living here with us. And Luke?' she whispered. 'Will he stay?'

'No.' Andrew's voice was lazy as his hands wandered. 'The attack on the house further weakened his wits. He can no longer cope alone. I shall find him a comfortable home with my mother. A larger cottage where they can play at independence, but within the Bedlam compound. And I shall leave this place in Ralph's care. No doubt Nat will return at some time, and together they can run a boarding house on the premises. They'll still be useful to me sometimes, in my work.'

'Casper, and that little boy, too?'

'I shall find places for them both in my own household.'

'And me?' She blinked up into his half-closed eyes.

'I'm taking you away, beloved,' he murmured. 'If you'll come.'

She was just a little disappointed. 'Oh. Back to Crosby's, then? My old house has never sold, you know, so we could go there if you like. It's only small, and not terribly comfortable – well, not like here – but I can build big fires for you every day.'

He waited for her to finish, watching her carefully. Then he spoke softly, as though hesitant. 'I must tell you, little one, although I think you know already, I am not what you might call a good man.' She began to remonstrate but he did not let her interrupt. 'My work over many years has led me into dark places. My contempt for mankind has made that easy. I've never taken pleasure in killing, but nor have I ever regretted it. Yet too much association with the dark can leave a man discovering the same shadows within himself. I have killed too often, and those shadows are part of me now.'

This time she interrupted. 'For a man who hates to answer questions, this is different. Why are you saying such things?'

'Truth can prove an uncomfortable foundation. But I use lies as a tool, not as a cloak, and I have never chosen to lie to myself. So, I would tell you the truth.'

He frowned and suddenly Tyballis thought she knew. Her skin prickled and all the sleepy warmth fled. The sounds of the rain beat heavier, and a whistle of wind blew down the chimney, belching out smoke. The fire's warmth no longer reached her, and her body became suddenly ice. She whispered, 'So, you're warning me. That's why you're sending me away from this house. And telling me you're not a good person, as if I won't be losing anything worth having. Because you're leaving me.'

He stared at her in surprise, then answered slowly, 'No, my love. I am asking you to marry me.'

The pause stretched. His words made no sense to her. Very small-voiced, she said, 'Marry? You don't ... do you think you have to? That you owe me?'

Andrew shifted uneasily back, moving a little further from her against the heaped pillows. He said, as if the truth of his explanation concerned him, 'Perhaps, in part. But in fact, I rarely feel obliged, or hold myself to duty. Do you believe duty has a place between us? My life has always been urgent with secrets. Personal needs have rarely absorbed me, not through virtue but through focus. That same narrow vision also enabled me to ignore the needs of others. Except with you.'

'The duke,' she murmured.

'When I met him,' Andrew said, 'my life was all empty space. The duke filled a void I had no other way of filling. With you, it is entirely different.'

Tyballis scrambled abruptly to face him, sitting with her back to the guttering fire, the great embroidered eiderdown wrapped around her knees. The palliasse beneath the mattress creaked. 'I'm not different,' she said, frowning at him. 'I'm just the woman you lie with. Before me there was Elizabeth. And before her – I expect there was always someone. You say you never thought about your own personal needs, but this is filling your needs, isn't it? And that's all I am to you.'

'I've fulfilled those desires when convenient. But I never before thought of using the word love.'

'I'm struggling to understand you.' She was trying to read his face, but his eyes were cold black through the dissipating swirls of smoke. 'I'm struggling to understand why you ask me to marry you,' she said, 'when a wife is surely the very, very last thing you want.'

Andrew sighed. 'Desire. Love.'

'Desire doesn't matter,' she said. 'I'll sleep with you anyway, if you want me to. But I can't marry you, love. I couldn't – not to do – that – to you.'

Her words seemed swallowed by thickening smoke, tasting sooty as the rain pelted down outside. Andrew barely moved, though his fingers snapped to his palms and his knuckles tightened. This time the pause was imperceptible. He said, 'How wise, my love. No doubt I should make as bad a husband as I do a man of trust. One day you will find better. You would certainly be safer with your Constable Webb.'

Tyballis blinked. 'How do you know about that?'

'I am who I am, my sweet.' Andrew closed his eyes. 'Which is why I have brought you too often into danger. And why you will be better off without me.'

Her belly seemed full of stones, and she swallowed back tears. Again, she tried to read his expression. It occurred to her that his voice had changed, and his face had changed, and now he was speaking to her as he spoke to others, devoid of warmth. Something – some hope, the comfort of trusting intimacy – had left him. Then she realised something else she had not expected. In sudden panic her words tumbled over each other. 'You understand – why I said – and you know what I mean, don't you? Please tell me you understand. Even if I'm not sure I do. That is, you always understand me and see through me and know best. So, you know you don't want to marry me, and you know that I know. Say you know.'

His large-boned face, the heavy twist of his nose and hooded eyes all seemed to soften and he watched her with a gentle sympathy. 'At the moment, my love, I seem to understand very little. But I know you'd be most unwise to accept me. You have made your choice, but I must also make mine. So, even without the commitment of marriage, will you stay with me, little one – for at least as long as it brings you comfort?'

He was leaning back now against the headboard and the pillows, one leg bent and his knee supporting his wrist. His naked body was patterned in a flickering flush of rosy reflections. His shins were badly marked, great black swirls of bruising from Jon's wooden-soled boots. Earlier that evening, as Tyballis had lain in Andrew's arms before making love. Now she sat and glared at him. 'You're refusing to understand me,' she accused him.

For a moment he said nothing. Then, very slowly, he began to smile. The smile started in the little tuck at the corners of his mouth, then stretched outwards, and flicked up into his eyes. Where they had been cold and black, expression suddenly danced again. He gazed at her a moment in clearing perplexity and said, 'Am I to believe, little one, that you turned me down for my sake?'

'Of course,' she said crossly. 'Why else would I? Like you said, the duke fills up your life. You don't have time for anything else except tumbling into bed when you – well, with those desires you talked about. And I keep getting into trouble and you keep having to rescue me, which must get very irritating.' She drew a deep breath before rushing on. 'I love you so very much and I want you so very much, but after Borin I'd so very much like a husband who sat beside me in the evenings, and just held my hand, and kissed my cheek and said sweet things. To walk in the sun together sometimes, just for idle pleasure, and talk about what to make for dinner, and what's fresh in the market. So, I'd always want what you wouldn't want, and I'd get in your way.'

Andrew's amusement settled into a contented patience across his face. 'As it happens, despite my concerns for your safety, I thoroughly enjoy rescuing you, my love, and would miss it if life became too tame.' He relaxed and regarded her fondly. 'But I have not the faintest idea what may be fresh in the market,' he told her. 'And as for what to make for dinner, perhaps we should leave such matters to the cook.'

'What cook?'

'The one I intend to employ in the new house.'

Confusion made her cross. 'What house, Drew?'

His smile had deepened. 'The house of Lord Leays, my love.'

'You're not making any sense,' she told him. 'That's where we live now.'

Andrew shook his head. 'No, little one, not this house. This dilapidated ruin once belonged to my father, but he is not the Lord Leays I refer to.'

Increasingly puzzled, Tyballis insisted, 'I don't know which lord you're talking about, Drew. And I love this horrid old house and all its strange rambling passages, and the bits that fall down, and the places all full of holes. I even love the dust. It's where I found myself, and then friends, and then you, and fell in love. Crosby's is so much more beautiful, but it's intimidating and it's not ours. Here, I'm at home. I belong.'

He let her talk, smiling patiently. Then suddenly he sat forward and, both hands to her shoulders, pulled her against him. 'Yet you do know the new Lord Leays very well, my sweet. I am speaking of myself, once the Duke of Gloucester is crowned king. He insists I should wear a title of some sort, and he is not a man to accept arguments.'

'King? King Richard?'

'I admit,' Andrew informed her, 'it is the middle of the night. You are assuredly tired, and our lovemaking was, let us say, energetic – and now I have amazed you with unexpected pleas for marriage. But you are rarely so slow to grasp the point, beloved, and are usually considerably more intelligent than this.'

She wriggled, trying to emerge from his embrace. 'Honestly, Drew,' she complained, 'if you'd just make sense for a change.'

Andrew released her so abruptly that she squeaked. He regarded her for one breath, then slowly swung his legs from the bed and walked naked to the cushioned seat by the window. Lifting its lid, he took something, and walked across to the hearth. He held two tall beeswax tapers, pressed them into their silver sticks, and lit them from the fire's ashes. The flames sprang tiny, then leapt huge. He set them both on the small table, came back to the bed and sat looking at her. For the very first time since she had known him, Tyballis had watched Andrew light candles. The light danced golden, as though with newborn pleasure.

'First of all,' he told her placidly, 'let me inform you that due to the late king's sons' proven bastardy, Gloucester is now heir to the throne. He chooses to accept the crown only in accordance with the will of the people, which will surely be settled after public explanations at St. Paul's Cross and elsewhere. But the council has already drawn up the official request for parliament to approve, and our new king's coronation will probably take place sometime next month. Yes, he will be King Richard III, and I believe he will be a great leader. The Woodvilles and the Lancastrian traitors will creep off to hide in their Breton cellars, France will sniff and curse with whispers of merde and turn its back, and England will thrive and grow strong in the sunshine.'

Tyballis sat straight against her pillows, her face limpid in the candlelight. But it was not kings she was interested in. She said, 'You've never done that before.'

Andrew paused for a moment before he said, 'Speak of politics?'

She shook her head. 'Light candles.'

'Ah,' and Andrew took her back into his embrace, cradling her face against the warmth of his chest. 'I have been a man too long in the shadows, my love, too fond of my secrets, hiding perhaps even from myself. I will no longer deny the light of disclosure. I follow a man who will be a wise king, and he chooses to offer me a title.' He smiled down into her wide-eyed astonishment. 'So, will you marry me, little one?'

She mumbled into the warm hollow of his collarbone, 'You think I'll say yes just because you'll be a lord and I'll want to be a lady?'

'No.' He pulled her tightly against him, one hand firm across her breasts. 'You'll accept me because I desire you with every inch of my body. Because missing you is like losing my arms, and I can neither eat nor sleep. And because when I do sleep, I wish for a bed where your body nestles tight to mine; when I do eat, I wish to do so in your company; and when I drink, I wish to fill your cup before my own. And I intend to protect you, little one, even though in many ways I consider you my protection. It must therefore be, I presume, what the minstrels call love. And to that I choose to surrender entirely. So, will you surrender to me, my beloved, and marry me, for pity, for the title, or for any other reason you please?'

Tyballis no longer pulled away. Her toes curled as she tugged him down into the bed and stretched against him, though his height was much greater, and her head remained at his shoulder while her toes prickled his ankles. She wrapped her legs around his. Her toes curled again, and she whispered several things, with her face quite squashed by the muscles of his chest and her breath tickling his chest. Outside there was sudden thunder and the broken window shutters rattled noisily again in the wind. Andrew could not actually hear a word she said, but it no longer seemed to matter.

CHAPTER SEVENTY-SEVEN

I t was, eventually, a different bed and a different chamber.
No dust trails drifted from the ceiling beams, no frayed threads hung from the silken bed curtains and no tapestry had faded in the sunbeams. The pillows were feather-soft, and the counterpane was silver damask, lined and trimmed in squirrel. The shutters did not rattle, and no slats were missing. The floorboards were polished, the Turkey rugs were thick, and the walls were heavy with embroidered arras. But there was no fire built across the great hearth, for a blazing summer warmed each corner, and two tall candles graced their sconces. It was a grand chamber in a grand house, and it had recently been refurbished to its owners' design.

The new king was travelling far away. He journeyed slow, introducing himself to all England's citizens and to those distant towns which relied on rumour since official messages were rare, and therefore had barely understood the events of previous months. The king's progress wound through England's gentle countryside, but his grace's royal entourage did not include all of his most trusted servants. Appointed to positions of official dignity within the capital city, these men continued their secret business undercover. London bustled, but there would always be the discontented, the conspirators and those who expected personal benefit under a different reign. So,

King Richard ordered his spies to pay careful attention to the safety of the young bastard princes still comfortably housed in the Tower but vulnerable to plots and treachery. There were orders left to smuggle both boys in great secrecy across the sea to Flanders should danger come too close. But for now, the summer was ablaze in vibrant pageantry, and few believed in misery to come.

Lord Leays was making love to his wife.

When he paused, she opened her eyes and gazed up at him, mesmerised. 'Too heavy?' He smiled, teasing.

'A lady never feels crushed.' Her fingers crept around his back, finding the familiar valleys beneath his shoulder blades, she knew her touch made him shiver, enjoying her power.

He held her afterwards as he reached behind and tugged up the bedcover, tucking it around her, again enclosing them both in caverns of shadow. He began to smooth back her hair, and the strands of pale curls from her eyes and mouth. Then he bent and kissed her briefly. His lips brushed her forehead and his tongue moistened and warmed each eyelid, like a cat waking her newborn. He murmured, 'If you do not pause, little one, and throw me off, and tell me how tired you feel, I shall be impelled to take you again.'

She opened her eyes, the lashes glistening wet. 'It should be you feeling too tired,' she whispered.

He shook his head slightly so that all the thick black length of his hair tumbled forwards as he wedged himself up on his elbows, removing the full force of his weight from her body. 'Bedding you exhilarates me.'

She mumbled, 'You never seem tired. Everything about you is so – different. Some men – they have different reasons for making love to their wives, and they want different things.' She held her breath a moment, waiting for him to understand but he frowned and seemed not to understand at all. Finally she said, 'You remember, don't you, my love, that I'm barren? Now you're a lord, you will want an heir.'

He gazed down at her, bemused. 'I thought it was me who liked to talk nonsense while I bed you.'

'I've caught the habit.'

He kissed her deep once more. 'I've small experience of good fatherhood,' he said. 'Let what happens, happen. What we lack matters not one jot in comparison to what we've gained. We have a good king again, my love, and great hopes for a safe future. This is your home now, and where we both belong. There'll be neither war nor famine nor pestilence, just peace and prosperity. We face a golden age. The man I admire sits England's throne, and the woman I adore lies in my arms. There's no one will spoil that for many a long year, you'll see, my love.'

She was losing her voice and her breath. 'No need for spying? You'll be bored and restless.'

'I shall discover contentment.'

'Unless the king sends you to Brittany, after all.'

'To spy on Henry Tudor?' Andrew smiled. 'I doubt it,' he murmured. 'That miserable wretch has neither rightful claim, nor good reputation. All he has in his favour is a determined mother. His highness considers that threat insignificant.' Andrew paused, savouring the familiar cushion of her body. 'Life,' he said finally, his voice no more than a little warm breeze against her cheek, 'is about to prove itself sweet as marchpane, little one.'

The End

AUTHOR'S NOTE – HISTORY OR HUMBUG?

In the late 15th century at the time during which this book is set, events in England were moving fast. This is one of the most explosive periods in history, but sadly much contemporary documentation is lacking. There are verified facts – often overlooked even by historians – especially those with their own bias to promote – but much of the turmoil can be understood only via assumption and rumour.

Naturally this book is fictional. Most of my characters are fictional, and so is the plot. However, where real historical characters have been introduced, I have endeavoured to replicate those actions which would seem most probable under the circumstances, fitting what we know of their real aims and personalities. I must therefore point out that the theory concerning the death of King Edward IV by poison does not follow general historical opinion. There is no proof of this whatsoever. On the other hand, the puzzles and anomalies surrounding the king's surprising death are there for all to study, and in particular Earl Rivers' curious behaviour shortly prior to the king's death is all absolutely accurate. This means there are some serious questions which have never yet been even remotely explained, and therefore the idea that King Edward IV might have been poisoned is not my own. The theory has existed for centuries.

The king's death in 1483 was entirely unexpected. He was a fairly young man, dying just days before his forty-first birthday, and although there are definite indications that he was no longer a fit and active man, being possibly obese, he suffered from no specific known complaint. Nor was any medical diagnosis publicly acknowledged at the time. Those contemporaries who documented the situation came to varying conclusions, such as 'a surfeit of ---', a 'chill caught during inclement weather', and 'general gluttony'. It appears there were rumours of poison at the time but in the medieval era the rumour of poison accompanied the sudden and unexpected death of many powerful figures. However, it is strange that the king himself, the man most watched and cosseted in the entire country, should have died so unexpectedly and from causes unexplained. Medieval medicinal practice is generally supposed to have been ignorant and sometimes even dangerous, but doctors were not all as stupid as we sometimes now imagine, and the diagnosis (if not the treatment) for tumours, stroke, pneumonia, TB and many other fatal illnesses was thoroughly understood.

The suggestion that arsenic could well have been the cause has since been explored by Richard E. Collins, and presented in the book The Death of Edward IV Part II by J. Dening and R. E. Collins , published in 1996.

For introducing me to this interesting theory, along with a huge amount of other insights and documented information on Richard III and his era, I would particularly like to thank Annette Carson for her fascinating and informative book RICHARD III: THE MALIGNED KING which is based on exemplary research principally using primary sources.

The other important scene in my book which differs fundamentally from traditional assumption, is the accusation and speedy execution of William, Lord Hastings. In a somewhat bizarre and unfinished story, later entitled 'The History of King Richard III', Sir Thomas More wrote in the second/third decade of the 16th century that Baron Hastings was arrested and arbitrarily beheaded within minutes of accusation without trial or justice of any kind. No document at the time of the event has corroborated the details of More's story. The only reports remaining to us from that time simply state that Lord Hastings was accused of treason, (some claim his innocence, others saying nothing either way) and was executed accordingly. It does appear that the execution took place on the same day as the arrest, therefore leaving no time for a normal common-law trial by jury. The execution 'within minutes' claimed much later by Thomas More, however, is not only unsubstantiated but highly unlikely since the arrest took place during a full council meeting in the presence of some of the most powerful lords of the land. Because Richard III in his more mundane dealings with his subjects (both before and after becoming king) was particularly punctilious concerning matters of justice and law, this act of sudden execution has surprised many and led traditional thinkers to suppose it was an act of sudden fury, both illegal and unjust, proving Richard to be the ambitious villain they assume he was.

At the time Richard was not yet king. It is, however, probable that in his capacity as 'Protector and Defender of the Realm against enemies both external and internal', he could sanction indictment and trial where treason was concerned. And contemporary accounts definitely state that treason was the accusation. No details of what the treason entailed have survived, although a public proclamation was made within hours of the event. One report stated that Hastings was charged with laying an ambush for the Protector, bringing concealed arms into the council chamber so that he could attack him unawares. There was, of course, no lack of witnesses. Indeed, contemporary accounts profess no surprise nor outrage at the Protector taking justice into his own hands, indicating their acceptance of his right to do so. The law concerning treason at that time was not so clear cut.

Concurrently with his protectorship Richard also held the office of High Constable of England, conferred on him for life. This was a military office with its own Constable's Court which tried cases of treason under the Law of Arms (as opposed to the common law). It was a court with authority to act summarily, without normal process of indictment, without trial by jury, and without appeal against the sentence of the Constable whose authority in such matters was second only to that of the king. We cannot know whether Richard conducted an ad hoc trial by empanelling persons and officers already present at the Tower – it is possible, but the Constable's Court followed no strict procedure and was not required to keep records, although witnesses could be called. Certainly we cannot assume there was no trial – although this appears to be the assumption most people have adopted these days – based on the Thomas More stories.

If the powerful magnate Hastings had hatched a treasonous conspiracy (which certainly appears to be the case and was quoted at the time even by those hostile to Richard himself) a quick solution to a highly dangerous situation might have seemed the best deterrent. Other influential council members were present and would have both stood witness and discussed the necessary solution to the situation. Certainly this was not a vendetta against Hastings since several others were arrested at the same time – both within the council chamber and elsewhere. Indeed, arrests were carefully timed to coincide, even those taking place at some distance across London. Clearly the action was planned to minimise danger, and put a quick stop to whatever had been plotted and then discovered.

Therefore the picture I present in this book is certainly a possibility. Once again there exists no particular evidence that such an event occurred but certainly, the Constable held the power to order a summary trial without jury in whatever place he wished, and without warning. He himself could be the judge. Whether he used it or not we cannot know, but since Richard held such power, I see no reason for him NOT to have used it... As usual with this controversial king, on the basis of present evidence the truth remains hidden. The myth has superseded the few actual facts we know for sure – and most of the contemporary documentation concerning his later life was quickly destroyed or wildly misrepresented by the victorious Tudor regime which followed.

All the other historical situations described in my novel are accurate according to what is known from historical records. The actions of the Woodville family, the difficulties following King Edward's death, the circumstances of his death (though not the cause), and the election of Richard III as king following the declaration of King Edward's marriage as bigamous, are all absolutely accurate according to contemporary accounts and the remaining official documentation.

I am much indebted to many historical experts and books for my research on this era – both those Tudor sources clearly antagonistic towards Richard III's reign and those contemporary and less politically biased accounts, then also to those more modern and muted studies which attempt to cut through the old propaganda, presenting a more open-minded summary of whatever can be discovered concerning this eventful and puzzling time in history.

PRINCIPAL HISTORICAL CHARACTERS

KING EDWARD IV

Edward was king of England from 1461 to 1470 and again from 1471 to 1483. His reign was interrupted by one of the swings of fortune and bloody battle during the so-called Wars of the Roses. Edward, son of the Duke of York, successfully claimed the throne on behalf of his dynasty after the reign of Henry VI of the Lancastrian dynasty was challenged. This was not only because King Henry was the grandson of a usurper (King Henry IV) but also because of his incompetence and the corruption and numerous injustices he presided over. Edward IV ruled over England for many long though rarely peaceful years. His death at age 40 and from unknown cause was most unexpected.

KING EDWARD V

Edward IV's eldest son who was expected to inherit the crown after his father's death in April 1483. However, following the disclosure of his father's bigamous marriage which rendered him illegitimate, he was barred from the throne and replaced by Richard, Duke of Gloucester as Richard III in June 1483. The twelve year old remained housed in apartments in the Tower with his younger brother until sometime probably during September 1483 when both the boys seemingly disappeared. Their fate still remains unknown.

GEORGE, DUKE OF CLARENCE

Younger brother to King Edward IV and elder brother to Richard, Duke of Gloucester, George was rarely satisfied with his secondary role in life. He rebelled against the king and joined the armies, backed by the French, which were attempting to claim the throne back for Henry VI. Then he changed sides again. This rebellion was eventually routed and Clarence was pardoned by his brother. The uneasy relationship continued however, and Clarence was finally arrested for treason and executed in 1478.

RICHARD, DUKE OF GLOUCESTER, LATER KING RICHARD III

King Edward IV's youngest brother and the only one still alive at the time of Edward's death. He was already the second most powerful man in the country, but his power base was principally in the north of England and he resided mostly in Yorkshire with his wife and young son. After receiving news of the king's death and accepting that he had been named Protector and Defender of the Realm in his brother's Will, Richard journeyed to London to take on this constitutional role, an office which placed him in charge of the safety of the country during the boy-king's childhood. There were, however, challenges to his authority generated by desire for control on the part of the heir's maternal family, who then mount a rebellion. This was unsuccessful and within two months the Royal Council, being informed of the late king's bigamy which thus barred the young prince from the throne, called a parliamentary assembly which decided to offer Richard the crown as next in line. He accepted and was crowned King Richard III.

WILLIAM, BARON HASTINGS

An extremely powerful magnate and good friend to Edward IV, from whom he profited until the king's death in 1483. At first Hastings appeared to welcome the Protectorship of Richard, Duke of Gloucester, and showed considerable suspicion towards the

Woodville/Grey family who made up young Edward V's maternal family. However, in June of the same year Hastings unexpectedly changed his mind and became involved in a plot against Richard, at that time still Protector of the Realm. He was arrested with others during a meeting of the Royal Council at the Tower. Although the chroniclers agree that Hastings was executed for treason, there is no surviving record of any evidence or trial.

ELIZABETH SHORE (NOW OFTEN KNOWN AS JANE SHORE)

The much favoured mistress of King Edward IV. After his death, she became mistress both to the Lord Hastings, and to the Marquess of Dorset, both of whom were said to have vied for her attentions. She appears to have been implicated in the accusation of treason made against the Lord Hastings, and was among those arrested. She was released into the custody of Richard III's Solicitor General, Thomas Lynom, who then married her.

ELIZABETH, EDWARD IV'S QUEEN

A character of considerable interest who caused much scandal during her lifetime. An unexpected bride, the lady's large family benefited considerably from her sudden elevation to royalty. She was a few years older than the king and was already a widow with two sons. After her husband's death, she became involved in attempts to position herself and her family as the 'power behind the throne' and oust Richard of Gloucester from his position as Protector of the Realm. When these attempts gained little public support and finally failed, the dowager queen ran into sanctuary before Richard arrived in the capital. There she and her daughters stayed for some considerable time but when her marriage to the king was declared bigamous, she made no public demur, asked for no church ruling on the subject nor appealed for Papal intervention. After the failed rebellion generated by her family she remained unharmed and eventually made her peace with Richard, requesting that her absent son also do so.

THOMAS GREY, MARQUESS OF DORSET

Queen Elizabeth's elder son by her first marriage, hence Edward IV's step-son. The king and Thomas Grey eventually became close and were known as partners in 'excess'. After the king's death, Dorset and his mother were among the principal movers in attempting to over-ride the authority of the new Protector, and take power for themselves as the family of the new king during his minority.

ANTHONY WOODVILLE, EARL RIVERS

Queen Elizabeth's brother, who abandoned the Lancastrian cause when his sister married Edward IV, choosing to support the new Yorkist regime instead. Known as an educated man with a love of literature, he was the principal member of a group appointed to the governorship of the king's eldest son. After the king's death, Rivers escorted the heir from Ludlow to London, but during the journey events became both complex and suspect, and Richard, Duke of Gloucester, arrested the earl. Later, with his family stirring up opposition to the Protectorate, Rivers was tried by the Duke of Northumberland and subsequently executed. No contemporary explanation of his treason or the nature of some of his unusual behaviour at that time has since come to light.

SIR EDWARD WOODVILLE

Also Queen Elizabeth's brother, Sir Edward was of a tempestuous and rebellious nature intent on a military career. Along with his family he refused to recognise the Protectorship after King Edward IV's death. He put to sea with a fleet funded by a large portion of the royal treasure which disappeared at that time. Ordered to return by the Royal Council, he rebelled and instead sailed for Brittany to join Henry Tudor.

WILLIAM CATESBY

A lawyer of good reputation who worked for many including Lord Hastings; and after Hastings's execution he became a loyal servant and trusted adviser of King Richard III.

DOMINICO MANCINI

An Italian cleric in the pay of the French, who visited England between late 1482 and July 1483. On his return to France he wrote a summary of what he had seen, concentrating on information his masters wanted to hear. Some of what he wrote about only happened before his arrival or after his departure. His account is valuable for being contemporaneous, but is heavily slanted with his own opinions and numerous inaccuracies.

ACKNOWLEDGMENTS

I have the greatest pleasure in acknowledging the enormous help and encouragement which has been given to me throughout the months I spent writing this book by my family and friends, in particular my daughter Gill and my granddaughter Emma without whom I could not have reached this stage. I also wish to thank the two much admired experts on the historical era that serves as a background to my fictional story.

The first of these, Annette Carson who has recently been a major part of the Looking For Richard project, backing Philippa Langley and John Ashdown Hill in discovering the exact place of Richard III's long lost grave in Leicester, England, in August 2012 and so, with the negotiated co-operation of the archaeological team at Leicester University, finding his certified remains. She is also the author of three excellent non-fiction books on the life of this medieval king and the mysteries and controversies surrounding him. Her remarkable first book, Richard III: The Maligned King, has now been followed by outstanding others. The second historical expert is Brian Wainwright, author of the brilliant books Within the Fetterloch, The Adventures of Alianore Audley and more.

I am immensely grateful to both for their immense generosity and expertise, for although I write fiction, I am extremely serious about the absolute accuracy of my backgrounds and the authenticity of all historical facts included in my stories. But naturally, should any mistakes have crept in unannounced, the fault is mine.

Barbara Gaskell Denvil

ABOUT THE AUTHOR

My passion is for late English medieval history and this forms the background for my historical fiction. I also have a love of fantasy and the wild freedom of the imagination, with its haunting threads of sadness and the exploration of evil. Although all my books have romantic undertones, I would not class them purely as romances. We all wish to enjoy some romance in our lives, there is also a yearning for adventure, mystery, suspense, friendship and spontaneous experience. My books include all of this and more, but my greatest loves are the beauty of the written word, and the utter fascination of good characterisation. Bringing my characters to life is my principal aim.

Made in the USA
Las Vegas, NV
09 January 2024

84134970R00347